Praise for *The Lay of the Land*

The Lay
of the Land

RICHARD FORD

BLOOMSBURY

First published in Great Britain 2006
This paperback edition published 2007

Copyright © 2006 by Richard Ford

Bloomsbury Publishing Plc
36 Soho Square
London W1D 3QY

www.bloomsbury.com/richardford

A CIP catalogue record for this book
is available from the British Library

ISBN 9780747585992

10 9 8 7 6 5 4 3 2 1

Printed in Great Britain by Clays Ltd, St Ives plc

The paper this book is printed on is 100% post-consumer waste recycled.

KRISTINA

The Lay of the Land

Are You Ready to Meet Your Maker?

Last week, I read in the *Asbury Press* a story that has come to sting me like a nettle. In one sense, it was the usual kind of news item we read every a.m., feel a deep, if not a wide, needle of shock, then horror about, stare off to the heavens for a long moment, until the eye shifts back to different matters—celebrity birthdays, sports briefs, obits, new realty offerings—which tug us on to other concerns, and by mid-morning we've forgotten.

But, under the stunted headline TEX NURSING DEATHS, the story detailed an otherwise-normal day in the nursing department at San Ysidro State Teachers College (Paloma Playa campus) in south Texas. A disgruntled nursing student (these people are always men) entered a building through the front door, proceeded to the classroom where he was supposed to be in attendance and where a test he was supposed to be taking was in progress—rows of student heads all bent to their business. The teacher, Professor Sandra McCurdy, was staring out the window, thinking about who knows what—a pedicure, a fishing trip she would be taking with her husband of twenty-one years, her health. The course, as flat-footed, unsubtle fate would have it, was called "Dying and Death: Ethics, Aesthetics, Proleptics"—something nurses need to know about.

Don-Houston Clevinger, the disgruntled student—a Navy vet and father of two—had already done poorly on the midterm and was probably headed for a bad grade and a ticket home to McAllen. This Clevinger entered the quiet, reverent classroom of test takers, walked among the desks and toward the front to where Ms. McCurdy stood, arms folded, musing out the window, possibly smiling. And he said to her, raising a Glock 9-mm to within six inches of the space just above the mid-point between her eyes, he said, "Are you ready to meet your Maker?" To which Ms. McCurdy, who was forty-six and a better than average teacher and canasta player, and who'd been a flight nurse in Desert Storm, replied, blinking her periwinkle eyes in curiosity only twice, "Yes. Yes, I think I am." Whereupon this Clevinger shot her, turned around slowly to address the astonished nurses-to-be and shot himself in approximately the same place.

I was sitting down when I began to read this—in my glassed-in living room overlooking the grassy dune, the beach and the Atlantic's somnolent shingle. I was actually feeling pretty good about things. It was seven o'clock on a Thursday morning, the week before Thanksgiving. I had a "happy client" closing at ten at the realty office here in Sea-Clift, after which the seller and I were going for a celebratory lunch at Bump's Eat-It-Raw. My recent health concerns—sixty radioactive iodine seeds encased in titanium BBs and smart-bombed into my prostate at the Mayo Clinic—all seemed to be going well (systems up and running, locked and loaded). My Thanksgiving plans for a semi-family at-home occasion hadn't yet started to make me fitful (stress is bad for the iodine seeds' half-life). And I hadn't heard from my wife in six months, which, under the circumstances of her new life and my old one, seemed unsurprising if not ideal. In other words, all the ways that life feels like life at age fifty-five were strewn around me like poppies.

My daughter, Clarissa Bascombe, was still asleep, the house quiet, empty but for the usual coffee aromas and the agreeable weft of dampness. But when I read Ms. McCurdy's reply to her assassin's question (I'm sure he had never contemplated an answer himself), I just stood right up out of my chair, my heart suddenly whonking, my hands, fingers, cold and atingle, my scalp tightened down against my cranium the way it does when a train goes by too close. And I said out loud, with no one to hear me, I said, "Holy shit! How in the world did she ever know that?"

All up and down this middle section of seaboard (the *Press* is the Jersey Shore's paper of record), there must've been hundreds of similar rumblings and inaudible alarms ringing household to household upon Ms. McCurdy's last words being taken in—like distant explosions, registering as wonder and then anxiety in the sensitive. Elephants feel the fatal footfalls of poachers a hundred miles off. Cats exit the room in a hurry when oysters are opened. On and on, and *on* and on. The unseen exists and has properties.

Would I ever say that? was, of course, what my question meant in realspeak, and the question everybody from Highlands to Little Egg would've been darkly pondering. It's not a question, let's face it, that suburban life regularly poses to us. Suburban life, in fact, pretty much does the opposite.

And yet, it might.

Faced with Mr. Clevinger's question and a little pushed for time, I'm sure I would've begun soundlessly inventorying all the things I hadn't done yet—fucked a movie star, adopted Viet-

namese orphan twins and sent them to Williams, hiked the
Appalachian Trail, brought help to a benighted, drought-ravaged
African nation, learned German, been appointed ambassador to
a country nobody else wanted but I did. Voted Republican. I
would've thought about whether my organ-donor card was
signed, whether my list of pallbearers was updated, whether my
obituary had the important new details added—whether, in other
words, I'd gotten my message out properly. So in all likelihood,
what I would've said to Mr. Clevinger as the autumn breezes
twirled in through the windows off bright Paloma Playa and the
nursing girls held their sweet bubble-gum breaths waiting to
hear, would've been: "You know, not really. I guess not. Not
quite yet." Whereupon he would've shot me anyway, though
conceivably not himself.

When I'd thought only this far through the sad and dreary
conundrum, I realized I no longer had my usual interest in the
routinesof my morning—fifty sit-ups, forty push-ups, some neck
stretches, a bowl of cereal and fruit, a manumitting interlude in
the men's room—and that what this story of Ms. McCurdy's
unhappy end had caused in me was a need for a harsh, invigorating, mind-clearing plunge in the briny. It was the sixteenth of
November, a precise week before Thanksgiving, and the Atlantic
was as nickel-polished, clean-surfaced and stilly cold as old
Neptune's heart. (When you first buy by the ocean, you're positive
you'll take a morning dip every single day, and that life will be
commensurately happier, last longer, you'll be jollier—the old
pump getting a fresh prime at about the hour many are noticing
the first symptoms of their myocardial infarct. Only you don't.)

Yet we can all be moved, if we're lucky. And I was—by Ms. McCurdy. So that some contact with the sudden and the actual seemed demanded. And not, as I found my bathing suit in the drawer, got in it and headed barefoot out the side door and down the sandy steps into the brisk beach airishness—not that I was really frightened by the little saga. Death and its low-lying ambuscade don't scare me much. Not anymore. This summer, in clean-lawned, regulation-size, by-the-numbers Rochester, Minnesota, I got over Big-D death in a swift, once-and-for-all and official way. Gave up on the Forever Concept. As things now stand, I won't outlive my mortgage, my twenty-five-year roof, possibly not even my car. My mother's so-so genes—breast-cancer genes giving percolating rise to prostate-cancer genes, giving rise to it's anybody's guess what next—had finally gained a lap on me. Thus the refugees' sad plight in Gaza, the float on the Euro, the hole in the polar ice cap, the big one rumbling in on the Bay Area like a fleet of Harleys, the presence of heavy metals in mothers' milk—all that *seemed* dire, it's true, but was frankly tolerable from my end of the telescope.

It was simply that, moved as I was, and with the coming week full of surprises and the usual holiday morbidities, I wanted reminding in the most sensate of ways that I was alive. In the waning weeks of this millennial year, in which I promised myself as a New Year's/New Century's resolution to simplify some things (but haven't quite yet), I needed to get right, to get to where Ms. McCurdy was at her ending song, or at least close enough to it that if I was faced with something like the question she was faced with, I would give something like the answer she gave.

So, in my bare feet, with a cold breeze pricking my exposed back, chest, legs, I tender-footed it up and across the gritty berm, through the beach grass and off onto the surprisingly cold sand. A white lifeguard stand stood nobly but vacated on the beach. The tide was out, revealing a glistening, black, damp and sloping sand plain. Someone had broken off for firewood the beach sign, so that only OWN RISK was left in red block letters on its standard. Sea-Clift, midline-Jersey Shore, midline-November, can be the best of locales and days. Any one of the 2,300 of us who live here year-round will tell you. The feeling of people nearby enjoying life, whiling it away, out for a ramble, taking it in, is everywhere about. Only the people themselves are gone. Gone back to Williamsport and Sparta and Demopolis. Only the solitary-seeming winter residents, the slow joggers, the single-dog walkers, the skinny men with metal detectors—their wives in the van waiting, reading John Grisham—these are who's here. And not even them at 7:00 a.m.

Up the beach and down was mostly empty. A container ship many miles offshore inched along the horizon's flat line. A rain squall that would never reach land hung against the lightening eastern sky. I took a sampling glance back at my house—all mirrored windows, little belvederes, copper copings, a weather vane on the top-most gable. I didn't want Clarissa to get up from her bed, have a stretch and a scratch, cast a welcoming eye toward the sea and suddenly believe that her dad was taking the deep-six plunge alone. Happily, though, I saw no one watching me—only the first sun warming the windows and turning them crimson and hot gold.

Of course, you'd know what I wondered. Who wouldn't? You can't go for a November morning's rejuvenating, self-actualizing dip, craving a taste of the irrefutable, the un-nuanced, of nature's necessity, and not be curious to know if you're on a secret mission. Secret from yourself. Can you? Certainly *some*, I thought, as the languid and surprisingly frigid Atlantic inched up my thighs, the sand creamy and flat under my toes, my dangle parts beginning to retract in alarm, surely *some* slip peacefully over the transom of pleasure craft (as the poet supposedly did), or swim out far too far of an evening, until the land falls dreamily away. But they probably don't say, "Ooops, uh-oh, damn, look-it here. I'm in a real mess now, am I truly not?" Frankly, I'd like to know what the hell they do say while they wait in death's anteroom, the lights of the departing boat growing dim, the water colder, choppier than anticipated. Maybe they *are* a little surprised by themselves, by how *final* events can suddenly seem. Though by then, there's not a whole hell of a lot they can do with the info.

But they're not surprised *qua* surprised. And as I waded up to my waist and began vigorously shivering, a taste of salt on my lips, I recognized I was *not* here, just off the continent's edge, to stage a hasty leave of it. No sir. I was here for the simple reason that I knew I would never have answered Don-Houston Clevinger's fatal question the way Sandra McCurdy did, because there was still something I needed to know and didn't, something which the shock of the ocean's burly heft and draw made me feel was still there to be found out and that could make me happy. Academics will say that answering *yes* to death's dire question is the same as answering *no*, and that all things that seem distinct are really identical—that only our need separates the wheat from the chaff. Though it's, of course, their living death that makes them think that way.

But, feeling the ocean climb and lick my chest and my breath go short and shallow—my two arms beginning to resist the float away to nowhere—I knew that death was different, and that I needed to say *no* to it now. And with this certainty, and the shore behind me, the sun bringing glories to the world's slow wakening, I took my plunge and swam a ways to feel my life, before turning back to land and whatever lay waiting for me there.

Part 1

1

Toms River, across the Barnegat Bay, teems out ahead of me in the blustery winds and under the high autumnal sun of an American Thanksgiving Tuesday. From the bridge over from Sea-Clift, sunlight diamonds the water below the girdering grid. The white-capped bay surface reveals, at a distance, only a single wet-suited jet-skier plowing and bucking along, clinging to his devil machine as it plunges, wave into steely wave. "Wet and chilly, bad for the willy," we sang in Sigma Chi, "Dry and warm, big as a baby's arm." I take a backward look to see if the NEW JERSEY'S BEST KEPT SECRET sign has survived the tourist season—now over. Each summer, the barrier island on which Sea-Clift sits at almost the southern tip hosts six thousand visitors per linear mile, many geared up for sun 'n fun vandalism and pranksterish grand theft. The sign, which our Realty Roundtable paid for when I was chairman, has regularly ended up over the main entrance of the Rutgers University library, up in New Brunswick. Today, I'm happy to see it's where it belongs.

New rows of three-storey white-and-pink condos line the mainland shore north and south. Farther up toward Silver Bay and the state wetlands, where bald eagles perch, the low pale-green cinder-block human-cell laboratory owned by a supermarket chain sits alongside a white condom factory owned by Saudis. At this distance, each looks as benign as Sears. Each, in fact, is a good-neighbor clean-industry-partner whose employees and executives send their kids to the local schools and houses of worship, while management puts a stern financial foot down on drugs and pedophiles. Their campuses are well landscaped and policed. Both stabilize the tax base and provide locals a few good yuks.

From the bridge span I can make out the Toms River yacht basin, a forest of empty masts wagging in the breezes, and to the north, a smooth green water tower risen behind the husk of an old nuclear plant currently for sale and scheduled for shutdown in 2002. This is our westward land view across from the Boro of Sea-Clift, and frankly it is a positivist's version of what landscape-seascape has mostly become in a multi-use society.

This morning, I'm driving from Sea-Clift, where I've lived the last eight years, across the sixty-five-mile inland passage over to Haddam, New Jersey, where I once lived for twenty, for a day of diverse duties—some sobering, some fearsome, one purely hopeful. At 12:30, I'm paying a funeral-home visitation to my friend Ernie McAuliffe, who died on Saturday. Later, at four, my former wife, Ann Dykstra, has asked to "meet" me at the school where she works, the prospect of which has ignited piano-wire anxiety as to the possible subjects—my health, her health, our two grown and worrisome children, the surprise announcement of a new cavalier in her life (an event ex-wives feel the need to share). I also mean to make a quick stop by my dentist's for an on-the-fly adjustment to my night guard (which I've brought). And I have a Sponsor appointment at two—which is the hopeful part.

Sponsors is a network of mostly central New Jersey citizens—men and women—whose goal is nothing more than to help people (female Sponsors claim to come at everything from a more humanistic/nurturing angle, but I haven't noticed that in my own life). The idea of Sponsoring is that many people with problems need nothing more than a little sound advice from time to time. These are not problems you'd visit a shrink for, or take drugs to cure, or that require a program Blue Cross would co-pay, but just something you can't quite figure out by yourself, and that won't exactly go away, but that if you could just have a common-sense conversation about, you'd feel a helluva lot better. A good example would be that you own a sailboat but aren't sure how to sail it very well. And after a while you realize you're reluctant even to get in the damn thing for fear of sailing it into some rocks, endangering your life, losing your investment and embittering yourself with embarrassment. Meantime it's sitting in gaspingly expensive dry dock at Brad's Marina in Shark River, suffering subtle structural damage from being out of the water too long, and you're becoming the butt of whispered dumb-ass-novice cracks and slurs by the boatyard staff. You end up never driving down there even when you want to, and instead find yourself trying to avoid ever thinking about your sailboat, like a murder you committed decades ago and have escaped prosecution for by moving to another state and adopting a new identity, but that makes you feel ghastly every morning at four o'clock when you wake up covered with sweat.

Sponsor conversations address just such problems, often focusing on the debilitating effects of ill-advised impulse purchases or bad decisions regarding property or personal services. As a realtor, I know a lot about these things. Another example would be how do you approach your Dutch housekeeper, Bettina, who's stopped cleaning altogether and begun sitting in the kitchen all day drinking coffee, smoking, watching TV and talking on the telephone long-distance, but you can't figure out how to get her on track, or worst case, send her packing. Sponsor advice would be what a friend would say: Get rid of the boat, or else take some private lessons at the yacht club next spring; probably nothing's all that wrong with it for the time being—these things are built to last. Or I'll write out a brief speech for the Sponsoree to deliver to Bettina or leave in the kitchen, which, along with a healthy check, will send her on her way without fuss. She's probably illegal and unhappy herself.

Anybody with a feet-on-the-ground idea of what makes sense in the world can offer advice like this. Yet it's surprising the number of people who have no friends they can ask sound advice from, and no capacity to trust themselves. Things go on driving them crazy even though the solution's usually as easy as tightening a lug nut.

The Sponsor theory is: We offer other humans the chance to be human; to seek and also to find. No donations (or questions) asked.

A drive across the coastal incline back to Haddam is not at all unusual for me. Despite my last near decade spent happily on the Shore, despite a new wife, new house, a new professional address—Realty-Wise Associates—despite a wholly reframed life, I've kept my Haddam affiliations alive and relatively thriving. A town you used to live in signifies something—possibly interesting—about you: what you were once. And what you *were* always has its private allures and comforts. I still, for instance, keep my Haddam Realty license current and do some referrals and appraisals for United Jersey, where I know most of the officers. For a time, I owned (and expensively maintained) two rental houses, though I sold them in the late-nineties gentrification boom. And for several years, I sat on the Governor's Board of the Theological Institute—that is, until fanatical Fresh Light Koreans bought the whole damn school, changed the name to the Fresh Light Seminary (salvation through studied acts of discipline) and I was invited to retire. I've also kept my human infrastructure (medical-dental) centered in Haddam, where professional standards are indexed to the tax base. And quite frankly, I often just find solace along the leaf-shaded streets, making note of this change or that improvement, what's been turned into condos, what's on the market at what astronomical price, where historical streets have been revectored, buildings torn down, dressed up, revisaged, as well as silently viewing (mostly from my car window) the familiar pale faces of neighbors I've known since the seventies, grown softened now and re-charactered by time's passage.

Of course, at some unpredictable but certain moment, I can also experience a heavy curtain-closing sensation all around me; the air grows thin and dense at once, the ground hardens under my feet, the streets yawn wide, the houses all seem too new, and I get the williwaws. At which instant I turn tail, switch on my warning blinkers and beat it back to Sea-Clift, the ocean, the continent's end and my chosen new life—happy not to think about Haddam for another six months.

What is home then, you might wonder? The place you first

see daylight, or the place you choose for yourself? Or is it the someplace you just can't keep from going back to, though the air there's grown less breathable, the future's over, where they really don't want you back, and where you once left on a breeze without a rearward glance? Home? Home's a musable concept if you're born to one place, as I was (the syrup-aired southern coast), educated to another (the glaciated mid-continent), come full stop in a third—then spend years finding suitable "homes" for others. Home may only be where you've memorized the grid pattern, where you can pay with a check, where someone you've already met takes your blood pressure, palpates your liver, slips a digit here and there, measures the angstroms gone off your molars bit by bit—in other words, where your primary care-givers await, their pale gloves already pulled on and snugged.

*M*y other duty for the morning is to act as ad hoc business adviser and confidant to my realty associate Mike Mahoney, about whom some personal data is noteworthy.

Mike hails from faraway Gyangze, Tibet (the real Tibet, not the one in Ohio), and is a five-foot-three-inch, forty-three-year-old realty dynamo with the standard Tibetan's flat, bony-cheeked, beamy Chinaman's face, gun-slit eyes, abbreviated arm length and, in his case, skint black hair through which his beige scalp glistens. "Mike Mahoney" was the "American" name hung on him by coworkers at his first U.S. job at an industrial-linen company in Carteret—his native name, Lobsang Dhargey, being thought by them to be too much of a word sandwich. I've told him that one or the other—Mike Lobsang or Mike Dhargey—could be an interesting fillip for business. But Mike's view is that after fifteen years in this country he's adjusted to Mike Mahoney and likes being "Irish." He has, in fact, become a full-blooded, naturalized American—at the courthouse in Newark with four hundred others. Yet, it's easy to picture him in a magenta robe and sandals, sporting a yellow horn hat and blowing a ceremonial trumpet off the craggy side of Mount Qomolangma—which is often how I think of him, though he never did it. You'd be right to say I never in a hundred years expected to have a Tibetan as my realty associate, and that New Jersey homebuyers might turn skittish at the idea. But at least about the second of these, what might be true is not. In the year and a half he's worked for me, since walking through my Realty-Wise door and asking for a job, Mike has turned out to be a virtual lion of revenue generation and business savvy: unceasingly farming listings, showing properties, exhibiting cold-call tenacity while proving artful at coaxing balky offers, wheedling acceptances, schmoozing with buyers, keeping negotiating parties in the dark, fast-tracking loan applications and getting money into our bank account where it belongs.

Which isn't to say he's a usual person to sell real estate along-side of, even though he's not so different from the real estate seller I've become over the years and for some of the same reasons—neither of us minds being around strangers dawn to dusk, and nothing else seems very suitable. Still, I'm aware some of my competitors smirk behind both our backs when they see Mike out planting Realty-Wise signs in front yards. And though occasionally potential buyers may experience a perplexed moment when a voice inside them shouts, "Wait. I'm being shown a beach bungalow by a fucking Tibetan!"—most clients come around soon enough to think of Mike as someone special who's theirs, and get over his unexpected Asian-ness as I have, to the point they can treat him like any other biped.

Looked at from a satellite circling the earth, Mike is not very different from most real estate agents, who often turn out to be exotics in their own right: ex-Concorde pilots, ex-NFL linebackers, ex-Jack Kerouac scholars, ex-wives whose husbands ran off with Vietnamese au pairs, then wish to God they could come back, but aren't allowed to. The real estate seller's role is, after all, never one you fully *occupy*, no matter how long you do it. You somehow always think of yourself as "really" something else. Mike started his strange life's odyssey in the mid-eighties as a telemarketer for a U.S. company in Calcutta, where he learned to talk American by taking orders for digital thermocators and moleskin pants from housewives in Pompton Plaines and Bridgeton. And yet with his short gesturing arms, smiley demeanor and aggressively cheerful outlook, he can seem and act just like a bespectacled little Adam's-appled math professor at Iowa State. And indeed, in his duties as a residential specialist, he's comprehended his role as being a "metaphor" for the assimilating, stateless immigrant who'll always be what he is (particularly if he's from Tibet) yet who develops into a useful, purposeful citizen who helps strangers like himself find safe haven under a roof (he told me he's read around in Camus).

Over the last year and a half, Mike has embraced his new calling with gusto by turning himself into a strangely sharp dresser, by fine-tuning a flat, accentless news-anchor delivery (his voice sometimes seems to come from offstage and not out of him), by sending his two kids to a pricey private school in Rumson, by mortgaging himself to the gizzard, by separating from his nice Tibetan wife, driving a fancy silver Infiniti, never speaking Tibetan (easy enough) and by frequenting—and probably supporting—a girlfriend he hasn't told me about. All of which is fine. My only real complaint with him is that he's a Republican. (Officially, he's a registered Libertarian—fiscal conservative, social moderate, which makes you nothing at all.) But he voted for numbskull Bush and, like many prosperous newcomers, stakes his pennant on the plutocrat's principle that what's good for him is probably good for all others—which as a world-view and in spite of his infectious enthusiasm, seems to rob him of a measure of inner animation, a human deficit I usually associate with citizens of the Bay Area, but that he would say is because he's a Buddhist.

But as for my role as his business adviser, Mike's name has gotten around some in our mid-Shore real estate circles—it's no longer possible for any single human act to stay long out of the public notice—and as of last week he was contacted by a sub-division developer up in Montmorency County, close to Haddam, with a proposition to enter a partnership. The developer has obtained a purchase option on 150 acres currently planted in Jersey yellow corn, but that lies slap in the middle of the New Jersey wealth belt (bordering the Delaware, bordering Haddam, two hours to Gotham, one from Philly). Houses there—giant mansionettes meant to look like Versailles—go for prices in the troposphere, even with current market wobbles, and anybody with a backhoe, a cell phone and who isn't already doing hard time can get rich without even getting up in the morning.

What Mike brings to the table is that he's a Tibetan *and* an American and therefore qualifies as a bona fide and highly prized minority. Any housing outfit that makes him its president automatically qualifies for big federal subsidy dollars, after which he and his partner can become jillionaires just by filling out a few government documents and letting a bunch of Mexicans do the work.

I've explained to him that in any regular business situation, a typical American entrepreneurial type *might* let him act as substitute towel boy at his racket club—but probably not. Mike, however, believes the business climate's not typical now. Many arrivees to central Jersey, he's told me, are monied subcontinentals with luxury fever—gastroenterologists, hospital administrators and hedge-fund managers—who're sick of their kids not getting into Dalton and Spence and are ready to buy the first day they drive down. The thinking is that these beige-skinned purchasers will look favorably on a development fronted by a well-dressed little guy who sorta looks like them. He and I have also discussed the fact that house sales are already leveling and could pancake by New Year's. Corporate debt's too high. Mortgage rates are at 8.25 but a year ago were at six. The NASDAQ's spongy. The election's going in the toilet (though he doesn't think so). Plus, it's the Millennium, and nobody knows what's happening next, only that something will. I've told him now might be a better time to spend his ethnic capital on a touchless car wash on Route 35, or possibly a U-Store-It or a Kinko's.

These businesses are cash cows if you keep an eye on your employees and don't invest much of your own dough. Mike, of course, reads his tea leaves differently.

This morning, Mike has offered to drive and at this moment has his hands cautiously at ten and two, his eyes hawking the Toms River traffic. He's told me he never got enough driving time in Tibet—for obvious reasons—so he enjoys piloting my big Suburban. It may make him feel more American, since many vehicles in the thick holiday traffic on Route 37 are also Suburbans—only most are newer.

Since we rolled out of Sea-Clift and over the bridge toward the Garden State Parkway, he has spoken little. I've noticed in the office that he's recently exhibited broody, deep-ponder states during which he bites his lower lip, sighs and runs his hand back across his bristly skull, frowning apparently at nothing. These gestures, I assume, are standard ones having to do with being an immigrant or being a Buddhist, or with his new business prospects, or with everything at once. I've paid them little attention and am happy to be silently chauffeured today and to take in the scenery while shifting serious thoughts to the outer reaches of my brain— a trick I've gotten good at since Sally's departure last June, and since finding out during the Olympics in August that I'd become host to a slow-growing tumor in my prostate gland. (It *is* a gland, by the way, unlike your dick, which is often said to be, but isn't.)

Route 37, the Toms River Miracle Mile, is already jammed at 9:30 with shopper vehicles moving into and out of every conceivable second-tier factory outlet lot, franchise and big-box store, until we're mostly stalled in intersection tie-ups under screaming signage and horn cacophony. Black Friday, the day after Thanksgiving, when merchants hope to inch into the black, is traditionally the retail year's hallowed day, with squadrons of housewives in housecoats and grannies on walkers shouldering past security personnel at Macy's and Bradlees to get their hands on discounted electric carving knives and water-filled orthopedic pillows for that special arthritic with the chronically sore C6 and C7. Only this year—due to the mists of economic unease—merchants and their allies, the customers, have designated "gigantic" Black Tuesday and Black Wednesday Sales Days and are flying the banner of EVERYTHING MUST GO!—in case, I guess, the whole country's gone by Friday.

Cars are everywhere, heading in every direction. A giant yellow-and-red MasterCard dirigible floats above the buzzing landscape like a deity. Movie complexes are already opened with queues forming for *Gladiator* and *The Little Vampire*. Crowds press into Target and International Furniture Liquidator ("If we don't have it, you don't want it"). Christmas music's blaring, though it's not clear from where, and the traffic's barely inching. Firemen in asbestos suits and Pilgrim hats are out collecting money in buckets at the mall entrances and stoplights. Ragged groups of people who don't look like Americans skitter across the wide avenue in groups, as though escaping something, while solitary men in gleaming pickups sit smoking, watching, waiting to have their vehicles detailed at the Pow-R-Brush. At the big Hooper Avenue intersection, a TV crew has set up a command post, with a hard-body, shiny-legged Latina, her stiff little butt turned to the gridlock, shouting out to the 6:00 p.m. viewers up the seaboard what all the fuss is about down here.

Yet frankly it all thrills me and sets my stomach tingling. Unbridled commerce isn't generally pretty, but it's always forward-thinking. And since nowadays with my life out of sync and most things in the culture not affecting me much—politics, news, sports, everything but the weather—it feels good that at least commerce keeps me interested like a scientist. Commerce, after all, is basic to my belief system, even though it's true, as modern merchandising theory teaches, that when we shop, we no longer really shop *for* anything. If you're really looking for that liquid stain remover you once saw in your uncle Beckmer's basement that could take the spots off a hyena, or you're seeking a turned brass drawer pull you only need *one of* to finish refurbishing the armoire you inherited from Aunt Grony, you'll never find either one. No one who works anyplace knows anything, and everyone's happy to lie to you. "They don't make those anymore." "Those've been back-ordered two years." "That ballpoint company went out of business, moved to Myanmar and now makes sump pumps . . . All we have are these." You have to take what they've got even if you don't want it or never heard of it. It's hard to call this brand of zero-sum merchandising true commerce. But in its apparent aimlessness, it's not so different from the real estate business, where often at the end of the day, someone goes away happy.

We've now made it as far as the Toms River western outskirts. Motels are all full here. Used-car lots are Givin' 'em Away. A bonsai nursery has already moved its tortured little shrubs to the back, and employees are stacking in Christmas trees and wreaths. Flapping flags in many parking lots stand at half-staff—for what reason, I don't know. Other signs shout Y2K MEMORABILIA SCULPTURE! INVEST IN REAL ESTATE NOT STOCKS! TIGHT BUTTS MAKE ME NUTS! WELCOME SUICIDE SURVIVORS. Yellow traffic cones and a giant blinking yellow arrow are making us merge right into one lane, alongside a deep gash in the freshly opened asphalt, beside which large hard-hatted white men stand staring at other men already down in the hole—putting our tax dollars to work.

"I really don't understand that," Mike says, his chin up alertly, the seat run way forward so his toes can reach the pedals and his hands control the wheel. He eyes me as he navigates through the holiday tumult.

I, of course, know what's bothering him. He's seen the WELCOME SUICIDE SURVIVORS sign on the Quality Court marquee. My having cancer makes him possibly worry about me in this regard, which then makes him fret about his own future. When I was at Mayo last August, I left him in charge of Realty-Wise, and he carried on without a hitch. But on his desk last week I saw a *New York Times* article he'd downloaded, explaining how half of all bankruptcies are health-related and that from a purely financial perspective, doing away with oneself's probably a good investment. I've explained to him that one in ten Americans is a cancer survivor, and that my prospects are good (possibly true). But I'm fairly sure that my health is on his mind and has probably brought about today's sudden test-the-waters probing into suburban land-development. Plus, in exactly a week from today I'm flying to Rochester for my first post-procedure follow-up at

Mayo, and he may sense I'm feeling anxious—I may be—and is merely feeling the same himself.

Buddhists are naturally unbending on the subject of suicide. They're against it. And even though he's a free-market, deregulating, *Wall Street Journal*-reading flat-taxer, Mike has also remained a devotee of His Holiness the Dalai Lama. His screen saver at the office actually shows a beaming color photograph of himself beside the diminutive reincarnate, taken at the Meadowlands last year. He's also displayed three red-white-and-blue prayer flags on the wall behind his desk, with a small painting of the thousand-armed Chenrezig and beside these a signed glossy of Ronald Reagan—all for our clients to puzzle over as they write out their earnest money checks. In the DL's view, utilizing a correct, peaceful-compassionate frame of mind will dissolve all impediments, so that karmically speaking we get exactly what we should get because we're all fathers of ourselves and the world's the result of our doing, etc., etc., etc. Killing yourself, in other words, shouldn't be necessary—about which I'm in complete agreement. Apparently, the smiling-though-exiled precious protector and the great communicating Gipper line up well on this, as on many issues. (I knew nothing about Tibet *or* Buddhists and have had to read up on it at night.)

It's also true that Mike knows something about my Sponsoring work, which has made him decide I'm spiritual, which I'm not, and prompted him to address all sorts of provocative moral questions to me and then purposefully fail to understand my answers, thereby proving his superiority—which makes him happy. One of his recent discussion topics has been the Columbine massacre, which he believes was caused by falsely pursuing lives of luxury, instead of by the obstinance of pure evil—my view. In the otherwise-pointless Elián González controversy, he sided with the American relatives in a show of immigrant solidarity, while I went with the Cuban Cubans, which just seemed to make sense.

Mike's moral principles, it should be said, have had to learn to operate in happy tandem with the self-interested consumer-mercantile ones of the real estate business. Working for me he gets one-third of 6 percent on all home sales he makes himself (I take two-thirds because I pay the bills), a bonus on all big-ticket sales *I* make, plus 20 percent on the first month of all summer rentals, which is nothing to bark at. There's another bonus at Christmas if I feel generous. And against that, I pay no benefits, no retirement, no mileage, no nothing—a good arrangement for me. But it's also an arrangement that allows him to live good and buy swanky sporting-business attire from a Filipino small-man shop in Edison. Today he's shown up for his meeting in fawn-colored flared trousers that look like they're made of rubber and cover up his growing little belly, a sleeveless cashmere sweater in a pink ice-cream hue, mirror-glass Brancusi tassel-loafers, yellow silk socks, tinted aviators, and a mustard-colored camel hair blazer currently in the backseat— none of which really makes sense on a Tibetan, but that he thinks makes him credible as an agent. I don't mention it.

And yet there's much about America that baffles him still, in spite of fifteen years' residence and patient study. As a Buddhist, he fails to understand the place of religion in our political doings. He has never been to California or even to Chicago or Ohio, and so lacks the natives' intrinsic appreciation of history as a function of landmass. And even though he's a real estate salesman, he doesn't finally see why Americans move so much, and isn't interested in my answer: because they can. However, during the time he's been here, he's taken a new name, bought a house, cast three presidential ballots and made some money. He's also memorized the complete *New Jersey Historical Atlas* and can tell you where the spring-loaded window and the paper clip were invented—Millrun and Englewood; where the first manure spreader was field-trialed—in Moretown; and which American city was the first nuclear-free zone—Hoboken. Such readout, he believes, makes him persuasive to home buyers. And in this, he's like many of our citizens, including the ones who go back to the Pilgrims: He's armed himself with just enough information, even if it's wrong, to make him believe that what he wants he deserves, that bafflement is a form of curiosity and that these two together form an inner strength that should let him pick all the low-hanging fruit. And who's to say he's wrong? He may already be as assimilated as he'll ever need to be.

*M*ore interesting landscape for the citizen scientist now passes my window. A Benjamin Moore paint "test farm," with holiday browsers strolling the grassy aisles, pointing to this or that pastel or maroon tile as if they were for sale. More significant signage: SUCCESS IS ADDICTIVE (a bank); HEALTHY MATE DATING SERVICE; DOLLAR UNIVERSITY INSTITUTE FOR HIGHER EARNING. Then the cement-bunker Ocean County Library, where holiday offerings are advertised out front—a poetry reading on Wednesday, a CPR workshop on Thanksgiving Day, two Philadelphia Phillies players driving over Saturday for an inspirational seminar about infidelity, "the Achilles' heel of big-league sports."

"I just don't understand it," Mike says again, because I haven't answered him the first time he said it. His pointed chin is still elevated, as if he's seeing out the bottom of his expensive yellow glasses. He looks at me, inclining his head toward his shoulder. He's wearing a silver imitation Rolex as thick as a car bumper and looks—behind the wheel—like a pint-sized mafioso on his way to a golf outing. He is a strange vision to be seen from other Suburbans.

"You don't understand 'Tight butts make me nuts'?" I say. "That's pretty basic."

"I don't understand suicide survivors." He keeps careful eyes on the Parkway entrance, a hundred yards ahead of us.

"It just wouldn't work as well if it said 'Welcome Suicide Failures,' " I say. The names Charles Boyer, Socrates, Meriwether Lewis and Virginia Woolf tour my mind. Exemplary suicide success stories.

"Natural death is very dignified," he says. This is the kind of "spiritual" conversation he likes, in which he can further prove his superiority over me. "Avoiding death invites suffering and fear. We shouldn't mock."

"They're not avoiding it and they're not mocking it," I say. "They like getting together in a multipurpose room and having some snacks. Haven't you ever thought about suicide? I thought about it last week."

"Would you attend a suicide survivors meeting?" Mike roams his tongue around the interior of his plump cheek.

"I might if I had time on my hands. I could make up a good story. That's all they want. It's like AA. It's all a process."

Mike's bespectacled face assumes a brows-down ancient look. He doesn't officially approve of self-determination, which he considers to be non-virtuous action and basically pointless. He believes, for instance, that Sally's sudden leaving last June put me in a state of vulnerable anxiety, which resulted from the specific, non-virtuous activity of divisive speech, which was why I got cancer and have titanium BBs percolating inside my prostate, a body part I'm not sure he even believes in. He believes I should meditate myself free of the stressful idea of love-based attachments—which wouldn't be that hard.

A state police blue flasher's now in sight where the on-ramp angles up to enter the Parkway. Cars are backed up all the way down to 37. An ambulance is somewhere behind us, *whoop-whooping*, but we can't pull over due to the road construction. A police copter hovers above the southbound lanes toward Atlantic City. Traffic's halted there in both lanes. Some of the ramp cars are trying to turn around and are getting stuck. People are honking. Smoke rises from somewhere beyond.

"Did you seriously think about suicide?" Mike says.

"You never know if you're serious. You just find out. I've survived to be in Toms River this morning."

A wide, swaying orange-and-white Ocean County EMS meat wagon, bristling with silver strobes, shushes past us on the shoulder, rollicking and roaring. Lights are on inside the swaying box, figures moving about behind the windows, making ready for something.

"Don't go up there," I say, meaning the Parkway. "Take the surface road."

"Shit!" Mike says, and cranes around at the traffic behind us so he's not forced up onto the ramp. "A pain in the ass." Buddhists have no swear words, though cursing in English pleases him because it's meaningless and funny and not non-virtuous. He looks at me in the sly, secret way by which we've come to communicate. He has no real interest in suicide. A significant portion of the essential Mike may now have gone beyond the selfless Buddhist to be the solid New Jersey citizen-realtor. "In your lifetime, you'll spend six and a half years in your car," he says, merging us into the left lane that goes under the Parkway overpass. All the traffic's going there now. "Half the U.S. population lives within fifty miles of the ocean."

"Most of them are right here with us today, I'd say."

"It's good for business," he says. And that is nothing but the truth.

Surface roads are never a pain in the ass, no matter where we roam. And I'm always interested in what's new, what's abandoned, what's in the offing, what will never be.

Route 37 (after we make a wrong turn onto 530, then correct to 539 and head straight as a bullet up to Cream Ridge) offers rare sights to the conscientious observer. The previous two drought years have rendered the sand-scrubby New Jersey pine flats we're passing a harsh blow, having already been deserted by the subdivision builders in search of better pickings. Vestigial one-strip

strip commercials go by now and then, usually with only one store running. Travelers have dumped piles of 24-pack Bud empties in many of the turn-outs, as well as porcelain sinks, washer-dryers, microwaves, serious amounts of crumpled Kleenexes and a clutter of defunct car batteries. Several red-stenciled posters are nailed to roadside oaks, announcing long-forgotten paint-ball battles in the pines. (We're near the perimeter of Fort Dix.) At the turn-off for Collier's Mills Wildlife Management Area, a billboard proclaims a WILD WEST CITY—MASTODON EXHIBIT AND WATER SLIDE. A few cars, dust-caked green Plymouths and a rusted-out Chevy Nova with white shoe-polish 4-$ales on their windshields, sit on the dry shoulder at the woods' edge. One lonely-guy sex shop lurks back in the trees with a blinking red-and-yellow roof sign, awaiting whoever's out here to abandon his pet but finds himself in the mood for some nasty. The White Citizen's Action Alliance has "adopted" the highway. The only car we pass is an Army Humvee driven by a soldier in a helmet and a camo suit.

And though all seems forsaken, back in the pines are occasional tracts of weathered pastel ranch-looking homes on curved streets with fireplugs, curbs and power poles in place. Most of these residences have windows and front doors ply-boarded and spray-painted KEEP OUT, their siding gone gray as a battleship, foundations sunk in grass that's died. It's not clear if these were once lived in or were abandoned brand-new. Although on one of the winding streets that opens onto the highway, Paramour Drive, I make out as we flash by, two boys—twelve-year-olds—side-by-side together on the empty asphalt. One sits on a dirt bike, one's on foot. They're talking while a mopish fluffy dog sits and watches them. The pink house they're in front of has a fallen-in wheelchair ramp to the front door. All its windows are out. No cars are in evidence, no garbage cans, no recycle tubs, no amenities.

In sum, this part of Route 37's the right place to go through a gross of rubbers, shoot .22s, drink two hundred beers, drive fast, toss out an old engine or a load of snow tires or a body. Or, of course, to become a suicide statistic—which I don't mention to Mike, who's sitting forward, paying zero attention to the landscape. It might as well be time travel to him, though he clicks on the radio once for the ten o'clock news. He's, I know, worried that Gore might push through in the Florida Supreme Court, but there's no rumor of that, so that he goes back to silently dry-running his meeting in Montmorency County, and fidgeting over trading in his minority innocence for the chance to wade into the heavy chips—something any natural-born American wouldn't think twice about.

*T*he morning's plan is that once we make contact with Mike's land developer—at the proposed cornfield site—I'm to take an expert read on the character. Then he and Mike will hie off for a shirtsleeve, elbows-on-the-table, brass-tacks business lunch and afternoon plat-map confab, where Mike'll hear the pitch, look him in the eye and attempt his own cosmic assessment. He and I'll then hook up at 6:45 at the August Inn in Haddam and drive back to Sea-Clift, during which time I'll offer my "gut," take the gloves off, connect some dots, do the math and every-thing'll come clear. Mike believes I have a "knack for people," a matter in dispute among the actual people who've loved me. Our scheme, of course, is the sort of simple one that makes perfect sense to everybody, and then goes bust no matter how good everyone's intentions were. For that reason, I'm going in with earnest good feeling but little or no expectation of success.

I've said nothing so far about my own Thanksgiving plans, now just two days away and counting, and that involve my two children. My reticence in this matter may owe to the fact that I've organized events to be purposefully unspectacular—consistent with my unspectacular physical state—and to accommodate as much as possible everyone's personal agendas, biological clocks, comfort zones and need for wiggle room, while offering a pleasantly neutral setting (my house in Sea-Clift) for nonconfrontational familial good cheer. My thought is that by my plan's being unambitious, the holiday won't deteriorate into apprehension, dismay and rage, rocketing people out the doors and back to the Turnpike long before sundown. Thanksgiving *ought* to be the versatile, easy-to-like holiday, suitable to the secular and religious, adaptable to weddings, christenings, funerals, first-date anniversaries, early-season ski trips and new romantic interludes. It often just doesn't work out that way.

As everyone knows, the Thanksgiving "concept" was originally strong-armed onto poor war-worn President Lincoln by an early-prototype forceful-woman editor of a nineteenth-century equivalent of the *Ladies' Home Journal*, with a view to upping subscriptions. And while you can argue that the holiday commemorates ancient rites of fecundity and the Great-Mother-Who-Is-in-the-Earth, it's in fact always honored storewide clearances and stacking 'em deep 'n selling 'em cheap—unless you're a Wampanoag Indian, in which case it celebrates deceit, genocide and man's indifference to who owns what.

Thanksgiving also, of course, signals the beginning of the gloomy Christmas season, vale of aching hearts and unreal hopes, when more suicide successes, abandonments, spousal thumpings, car thefts, firearm discharges and emergency surgeries take place per twenty-four-hour period than any other time of year except the day after the Super Bowl. Days grow ephemeral. No one's adjusted to the light's absence. Many souls buy a ticket to anyplace far off just to be in motion. Worry and unwelcome self-awareness thicken the air. Though strangely enough, it's also a great time to sell houses. The need to make amends for marital bad behavior, or to keep a wary eye on the tax calendar or to deliver on the long-postponed family ski outing to Mount Pisgah—all make people itchy to buy. There's no longer a real off-season for house sales. Houses sell whether you want them to or not.

In my current state of mind, I'd, in fact, be just as happy to lose Christmas and its weak sister New Year's, and ring out the old year quietly with a cocktail by the Sony. One of divorce's undervalued dividends, I should say, is that all the usual dismal holiday festivities can now be avoided, since no one who didn't have to would ever think about seeing the people they used to say they wanted to see but almost certainly never did.

And yet, Thanksgiving won't be ignored. Americans are hard-wired for something to be thankful for. Our national spirit thrives on invented gratitude. Even if Aunt Bella's flat-lined and in custodial care down in Ruckusville, Alabama, we still "need" her to have some white meat and gravy and be thankful, thankful, thankful. After all, *we* are—if only because we're not in her bedroom slippers.

And it *is* churlish not to let the spirit swell—if it can—since little enough's at stake. Contrive, invent, engage—take the chance to be cheerful. Though in the process, one needs to skirt the spiritual dark alleys and emotional cul-de-sacs, subdue all temper flarings and sob sessions with loved ones. Get plenty of sleep. Keep the TV on (the Lions and Pats are playing at noon). Take B vitamins and multiple walks on the beach. Make no decisions more serious than lunch. Get as much sun as possible. In other words, treat Thanksgiving like jet lag.

Once I'd moved from Haddam, married Sally Caldwell and set up life on a steadier footing in Sea-Clift (where, of course, there is no actual clift), the two of us would spend our Thanks-givings together in a cabin in New Hampshire, near where the first Thanksgiving occurred. Sally's former in-laws—parents of her former (AWOL) husband, Wally, and salt-of-the-earth Chicago-North-Shore old New Dealers—owned a summer cottage on Lake Laconic, facing the mountains. Fireplaces were all the heat there was. These were the last bearable days before the pipes were drained, phones turned off, windows shuttered and china locked in the attic. The Caldwells—Warner and Constance, then in their seventies—thought of Sally as a beloved but star-crossed family member, and for that reason anything they could do for her couldn't be enough, even with me in atten-dance, as the ambiguous new presence.

Sally and I would drive up from New Jersey on Wednesday night, sleep like corpses, stay in bed under a big tick comforter until we were brave enough to face the morning chill, then scramble around for sweaters, wool pants and boots, making coffee, eating bagels we'd brought from home, reading old *Holidays* and *Psychology Todays* before embarking on a moderately strenuous hike to the French-Canadian massacre site halfway up Mount Deception, after which we took a nap till cocktail hour.

We watched moose in the shallows, eagles in the tree tops, made comical efforts to fish for trout, watched the outfitter's seaplane slide onto the lake, considered getting the outboard going for a trip out to the island where a famous painter had lived. Once, I actually took a dip, but never again. At night we listened to the CBC on the big Stromberg-Carlson. I read. Sally read. The house had plenty of books by Nelson DeMille and Frederick Forsyth. We made love. We drank gin drinks. We found pizzas in the basement freezer. The one rustic restaurant that stayed open offered a Thanksgiving spread on Thursday *and* Friday—for hunters. We each felt this vacation strategy was the best solution, with so many worse solutions available. In other words, we loved it. By Saturday noon, we were bored as hammers (who wouldn't be in New Hampshire?) and antsy to get back to New Jersey. Happy to arrive; happy to leave—the traveler's mantra.

This past Labor Day, when I was far from chipper from my Mayo siege, it occurred to me that the smart plan for the millennial Thanksgiving, with the Caldwells' cottage no longer mine, was to lead a family party back to Lake Laconic, be tourists, take over a B&B, go on walks, wade in cold shallows, paddle canoes, skip rocks, watch for eagles and drink wine (not gin) in the late-autumn splendor. A low-impact holiday for a low moment in life, with my family convened around me.

Except, my son Paul Bascombe, now twenty-seven and leading a fully-embedded, mainstreamed life in Kansas City, where he writes laughable captions for the great megalithic Hallmark greeting-card entity ("an American icon"), said he wouldn't come if he had to drive all the way to "piss-boot New Hampshire." He had to be at work on Monday, and in any case wanted to see his mother, my former wife, now living in Haddam.

My daughter, Clarissa, twenty-five, agreed a soft-landing Lake Laconic holiday might be "restorative" for me and help me get over "a pretty intense summer." She and her girlfriend, the heart-stoppingly beautiful Cookie Lippincott, her former Harvard roommate, took charge when I flew back from Mayo in a diaper and in no mood for laughs. (Lesbians make great nurses, just like you'd think they would: serious but mirthful, generous but consistent, competent but understanding—even if yours happens to be your daughter.) During my early recovery days, I took her and Cookie to the Red Man Club, my sportsman's hideout on the Pequest, where we shot clay pigeons, played gin rummy, fished for browns till midnight and slept out on the long screen porch on fragrant canvas army cots. We took day trips to the Vet for the last days of the Phillies' season. We visited Atlantic City and lost our shirts. We hiked Ramapo Mountain—the easy part. We went on self-guided tours to every passive park, vernal pond and bird refuge in the guidebook. We read novels together and talked about them over meals. We managed to assemble a family unit—not your ordinary one, but what is?—one that got me back on my feet and pissing straight, took my mind off things and made me realize I didn't need to worry much about my daughter (which doesn't go for my son).

But then in the midst of all, Clarissa decided she should take a sudden, divergent "new" path, and parted with Cookie to "try men" again before it was too late—whatever that might mean. Though what it meant at the moment was that with her brother not attending, my New Hampshire Thanksgiving idyll fell through in an afternoon, with my house in Sea-Clift elected by default.

For this Thursday, then, I've ordered a "Big Bird et Tout à Fait" Thanksgiving package from Eat No Evil Organic in Mantoloking, where they promise everything's "so yummy you won't know it's not poisoning you." It comes with bone china, English cutlery, leaded crystal, Irish napkins as big as Rhode Island, a case of Sonoma red, all finished with "not-to-die-for carob pumpkin pie"—no sugar, no flour, lard or anything good. Two thousand dollars cheap.

I've devised a modest guest list: Clarissa, with possibly a new boyfriend; Paul with his significant other, driving in from K.C.; a refound friend from years gone by, widower Wade Arsenault, who's eighty-something and a strange father-in-law figure to me (being father to an old flame). I've also invited two of my men friends from Haddam, Larry Hopper and Hugh Wekkum, good fellows of my own vintage, former charter members of the Divorced Men's Club and comrades from the bad old days, when we were all freshly singled and at wits' end to know how to tie our shoes. Unlike me— and maybe wiser—neither Hugh nor Larry has married again. At some point they both realized they never would—just couldn't find the low-gear pulling power to mount another love affair, couldn't even imagine kissing women. "I felt like a homeless man groping at a sandwich," Larry has confided with dismay. So with no patience or interest in the old dating metronome, he and Hugh figured out they were seeing more of each other than they were of anybody else. And after Hugh had a by-pass, Larry moved him into his big white Stedman House with attached slave quarters on South Comstock. They've ended up playing golf every day, and Hugh hasn't had any more heart flare-ups. There's no hanky-panky, they assure me, since both are on blood thinners and couldn't hanky the first panky even if the spirit was in them.

I've also thought about inviting my former wife, Ann Dykstra, now a well-provided widow living, as mentioned (of all places), in Haddam, having purchased back her own former house from me at 116 Cleveland (no commission), a house she'd lived in previously, then abandoned and sold to *me* when she married her second husband, Charley O'Dell, and moved to Connecticut, following which I lived there for seven years, then moved to the Shore for my own second try at happiness. Aldous Huxley said— after reading Einstein—that the world is not only stranger than we know but a lot stranger than we *can* know. I don't know if Huxley was divorced, but I'm betting he had to be.

Since Sally's departure in June, and my life-modifying trip to Mayo in August, I've spoken with Ann a few times. Nothing more than business. She conducted the house re-resale using the same vicious little lawyer she'd used to divorce me back in '83, and didn't come to the closing, to which I'd grinningly brought a bouquet of nasturtiums to commemorate (in a good way) life's imperial strangeness. But then, one warm evening in September, just as I'd constructed a forbidden martini and was sitting down in the sunroom to watch the campaign coverage on CNN, Ann called up and just said, "So, how are you?" It was as if she was holding a policy on my life and was checking on her investment. We've always kept our contacts restricted to kid subjects. She didn't understand what Paul was doing in K.C., and wouldn't discuss the concept that her daughter was a lesbian (which I assume she blames me for). Once before, she'd inquired about my health, I lied, and then we didn't know what else to say. And to her more recent question about how I was, I lied again that I was "fine." Then she told me about her mother's Christmas letter describing trouble with her dental implants, and about her once giving holy hell to Ann's since-deceased father, for failing to leave Detroit with her in '72 (when she divorced him) and come enjoy the sunsets in Mission Viejo.

We hung up when that was over.

But. But. Something had been opened. A thought.

Since September, we've had coffee once at the Alchemist & Barrister, exchanged calls about the children's trajectories and plights, gone over house eccentricities only I, as former owner, would know about—furnace warranty, water-pressure worries, inaccurate wiring diagrams. We have not gone into my medical situation, though obviously she's wise to plenty. I don't know if she thinks I'm impotent or have continence issues (not that I know of, and no). But she's exhibited a form of interest. In her husband Charley's last grueling days on earth—he had colon cancer but had forgotten about it because he also had Alzheimer's—I agreed to sit with him and did, since none of his Yale friends were brave enough to. (Life never throws you the straight fastball.) And since then, two years ago, some sort of low ceiling of masking clouds that had for years hung over me where Ann was concerned has slowly opened, and it's almost as if she can now see me as a human being.

Not that either of us wants a "relationship." What's between us is almost entirely clerical-informative in nature and lacking the grit of possibility. Yet there are simply no further grievances needing to be grieved, no final words needing to be spoken, then spoken again. We are what we are—divorced, widowed, abandoned, parents of two adults and one dead son, with just so much of life left to live. It is another facet in the shining gem of the Permanent Period of life that we try to *be* what we *are* in the present—good or not so good—this, so that accepting final credit for ourselves won't be such a shock later on. The world *is* strange, as old Huxley noticed. Though in my view, my and Ann's conduct is also what you might reasonably hope of two people who've known each other over thirty years, never gotten completely outside the other's orbit and now find the other still around and able to make sense.

But the final word: Ann would say no to my invitation if I extended it. She's recently gone to work—just to keep busy—as an admissions high-up at De Tocqueville Academy, where I'm meeting her today, and where she has, Clarissa says, made some new friends among the gentle, introverted, over-diploma'd folk there. She's also, Clarissa reports, been appointed coach of the

De Tocqueville Lady Linksters (she captained at Michigan in '69), and, I'm sure, feels life has taken a good turn. None of this, of course, specifically explains why she wants to see me.

*P*olitical placards sprout along Route 206 when we detour around Haddam toward the north. Local contests— assessor, sheriff, tax collector—were settled weeks back, though a feeling of unfinality hangs in the suburban air. Here, now it's fat yellow Colonial two-of-a-kinds and austere gray saltboxes with the odd redwood deck house peeping through leafless poplars, ash and bushy mountain laurels. Some recidivist Bush sentiment is alive on a few lawns, but mostly it's solid-for-Gore in this moderate, woodsy, newer section of the township (when Ann and I were young newcomers down from Gotham in 1970, it was woods, not woodsy). The placards all insist that we the voters who voted (I went for Gore) really meant it this time and still mean it and won't stand for foolishness. Though of course we will. And indeed, cruising past the uncrowded, familiar roads late in my favorite season, these bosky, privileged precincts feel punky and lank, swooning and ready for a doze. As we used to say, yukking it up in the USMC about recruits who weren't going to make it, "You'll have to wake him up just to kill him." In these parts, it's a good time for an insurrection.

No real commerce flourishes on this stretch of 206. Haddam, in fact, doesn't thrive on regular commerce. Decades of Republican councilmen, building moratoriums, millage turn-downs, adverse zoning reviews, traffic studies, greenbelt referendums and just plain shit-in-your-hat high-handedness have been disincentives for anything more on this end of town than a Forestview Methodist, the odd grandfathered dentist's plaza, a marooned Foremost Farms and one mediocre Italian restaurant the former Boro president's father owns. Housing is Haddam's commerce. Whereas the real business—Kia dealerships, muffler shops, twenty-screen movie palaces, Mr. Goodwrench and the Pep Boys—all that happy horseshit's flourishing across County Line Road, where Haddamites jam in on Saturday mornings before scurrying back home, where it's quiet.

I never minded any of that when I sold houses here. I voted for every moratorium, against every millage to extend services to the boondocks, supported every not-in-my-neighborhood ordinance. In-fill and gentrification are what keep prices fat and are what's kept Haddam a nice place to live. If it becomes the New Jersey chapter of Colonial Williamsburg, with surrounding farmlands morphed into tract-house prairies, carpet outlets and bonsai nurseries, then I can take (and did take) the short view, since the long view was forgone and since that's how people wanted it.

What exactly happened to the short view and that drove me to the Shore like a man in the Kalahari who sees a vision of palm trees and sniffs water in the quavery distance—that's another story.

Since we've crossed into Haddam Township, Mike's fallen to sighing again, raking his hand back through his buzzed-off hair, squinting and looking fretful behind his glasses as we head out toward the Montmorency County line. His driving has devolved into fits and spurts in the lighter township traffic. Two times we've been honked at and once given the finger by a pretty black woman in a Jaguar, so that his piloting's begun to get on my nerves.

I again know what he's on about. Mike's belief, and I subscribe to it myself, is that at the exact moment any decision *seems* to be being made, it's usually long after the real decision was actually made—like light we see emitted from stars. Which means we usually make up our minds about important things far too soon and usually with poor information. But we then convince ourselves we *haven't* done that because (a) we know it's bone-headed, and no one wants to be accused of boneheaded-ness; (b) we've ignored our vital needs and don't like to think about them; (c) deciding but believing we haven't decided gives us a secret from ourselves that's too delicious not to keep. In other words, it makes us happy to bullshit ourselves.

What Mike does to avoid this bad practice—and I know he's fretful about his up-coming meeting—is empty his mind of impure motives so he can communicate with his instincts. He often performs this head-rubbing, frowning ritual right in the realty office before presenting an offer or heading off to a closing. He does this because he knows he frequently holds the power to tip a sale one way or the other and wants things to work out right. I'm sure if you're a Buddhist, you do this all the time about everything. And I'm also sure it doesn't do any good. They teach this brand of soggy crappolio in the "realty psychology" courses that Mike took to get his license. I just came along years too early—back when you only sold houses because you wanted to and it was easy and you liked money.

The other scruple I'm sure is thrumming in Mike's brain is that during his fifteen years in our country he's swung rung to rung up the success ladder, departing one cramped circumstance for a slightly less cramped next one. He arrived from India to his Newark host family, segued on to Carteret and the industrial-linen industry, then to a less nice section of South Amboy, where he worked for an Indian apartment finder. From there to Neptune, Neptune to Lavallette—both times as a realty associate. And from there to me—an impressive climb most Americans would think was great and that would get them started filling up their garages with Harleys and flame-sided Camaros and snow machines and straw deer targets, their front yards sprouting Bush-Cheney placards, their bumpers plastered with stickers that say: I TAKE MY ORDERS FROM THE BIG GUY UPSTAIRS.

But to Mike, the assumption that Lavallette, New Jersey, ought to seem like Nirvana to a smiling little brown man born in a wattle hut in the Himalayas is both true and not true. Deep in his hectic night's sleep, with his estranged wife in her estranged home in the Amboys, his teenagers up late noodling on their laptops with SAT reviews, his Infiniti safely "clubbed" in the driveway, Mike (I would bet) wonders if this is really *it* for him. Or, might there not be just a smidgen more to be clutched at? Real estate, the profession of possibility, can keep such dreams fervid and winy for decades.

Haddam, therefore, makes him as nervous as a debutante. It makes plenty of people feel that way. All that serenely settled, arborial, inward-gazing good life, never confiding about what it knows (property values), so near and yet so far off. All that pretty possibility set apart from the regular social frown and growl. Haddam's rare rich scent is sweetly breathable to him—as we drive past out here on 206—there behind its revetment of Revolutionary oaks and survivor elms, from its lanes and cul-de-sacs, its wood ricks, its leaf rakage, its musing, insider mutter-mutter conversations passed across hedges between like-minded neighbors who barely know one another and wouldn't otherwise speak. Haddam rises in Mike's mind, a citadel he could inhabit and defend.

It's just not likely to happen. Which is fine as long as he doesn't venture too close—which he's almost done—so that his immigrant life flashes up in grainy black and white and not quite good enough. This, of course, happens to all of us; it's just easier to accept when the whole country's already your own.

"You know, when Ann and I moved to Haddam thirty years ago, none of this was out here," I say to be encouraging as we pass a wood-lot soon to be engulfed beside Montmorency Mall. COMMERCIAL SPACE FOR SALE is advertised. "Not even a deer-crossing sign." I smile at him, but he frowns out ahead, his seat pressed close-up to the wheel, his mind in another place, across a gulf from me. "If you lived here then, you wouldn't be home now."

"Ummm," Mike grunts. "I can see that, yes." My attempt doesn't work, and we are for a time sunk in reverential silence.

A mile into Montmorency County, 206 drops into a pleasant jungly sweet-gum and red-clay creek bottom no one's quite figured how to bulldoze yet, and the old road briefly takes on a memorial, country-highway feel. Though we quickly rise again into the village of Belle Fleur, old-style Jersey, with a tall white Presbyterian steeple beside a sovereign little fenced cemetery, and just beyond that, a seventies-vintage strip development, with two pizza shops, a laundrette, a closed Squire Tux and an H&R Block— and across on the facing side of the road two deserted, dusty-screened redbrick Depression houses (homes to humans once) from when 206 was a scenic rural pike as innocent and pristine as any back road in Kentucky. Another double-size wooden sign with big red lettering spells an end to the houses: OWNER WILL SELL, REMOVE OR TRADE. It's a perfect site for a Jiffy Lube.

Mike takes a left past the church and commences west. And right away the atmosphere changes, and for the better. Somewhere out ahead of us lies the Delaware, and all can feel the relief. Though Mike's now consulting his watch and a scribbled-on pink Post-it while the road (Mullica Road) leaves the strip development for the peaceable town 'n country housing pattern New Jersey is famous for: deep two-acre lots with curbless frontage, on which are sited large but not ominous builder-design Capes, prairie contemporaries and Dutch-door ranches, with now and then an original eighteenth-century stone farmhouse spruced up with copper gutters and an attached greenhouse to look new. Yews, bantam cedars and mountain laurels that were scrubby in the seventies are still young-appearing. The earth is flat out here, poorly drained and clayey. Plus, it's dry as Khartoum. Still, a few maples and red oaks have matured, and paint jobs look fresh. Kids' plastic gym sets and chain-link dog runs clutter many back lawns. Subarus and Horizons stand in new asphalt side drives (the garages jammed with out-of-date junk). Everything's exactly as they pictured it when it was all a dream.

Passing on the left now, opposite the houses, lies a perfect, well-tended cut cornfield extending prettily down to Mullica Creek, remnant of uses that predate memory but a plus to home buyers prizing atmosphere. Though you can be sure its pristine prettiness is giving current owners across the road restless nights for fear some enterpriser (such as the one driving my car) will one day happen along, stop for a look-see, make a cell-phone call and in six months throw up a hundred minimansions that'll kick shit out of everybody's tax bills, fill the roads, jam the schools with new students who score eight million on their math and verbal, who steal the old residents' kids' places at Brown, and whose families won't speak to anybody because for religious reasons they don't have to. Town 'n country takes a hike.

Every morning, these original settlers who bought in at 85K— on what was Mullica Farm Road—frown down at their mutual-fund numbers, retotal their taxes against retirement investitures and wonder if now might be the time to roll over their 401s, move to the Lehigh Valley and try consulting before beating it to Phoenix at age sixty-two. Median house prices out here are at 450K, the fastest market in the land—last year. Only, that's not holding. One or two neighbors already have BY OWNER signs up, which is worrisome. Though to me it's all as natural as pond succession, and no one should regret it. I like the view of landscape in use.

Small, dark-skinned yard personnel with backpack blower units that make them look like spacemen are busy in many yards here, whooshing oceans of late-autumn leaves and heaping them in piles beside great black plastic bags, before hauling them away in their beater trucks. The cold sky has gone cerulean and untroubled (weather being what passes for drama in the suburbs). I don't miss Haddam, but I miss this—the triggering sense of emanation that a drive in what was once the country ratchets up in me. And today especially, since I'm not risking or pitching anything, am off duty and only along for moral support.

"Is Michigan in Lansing or Ann Arbor?" Mike says, blinking expectantly, hands again in the prescribed steering positions. We are nearing our rendezvous and he's on the alert.

He knows I bleed Michigan blue but doesn't really know what that means. "Why?"

"I guess there're some pretty interesting things going on at Michigan State right now." He is speaking officially. Practicing at being authentic.

"Did they discover a featherless turkey in time for Thanksgiving?" I say. "That's what they're good at over there."

A man stands alone on the wide grassy lawn of a bright yellow bay-windowed Dutch contemporary where Halloween pumpkins still line the front walk. He's barefoot, wearing a white tae kwon do suit and is performing stylized Oriental exercises—one leg rising like a mantis while his arms work in an overhand swimming motion. Possibly it's a form of pre-Thanksgiving stress maintenance he's read about in an airline magazine. But something about my Suburban, its rumbling, radiant alien-ness, has made him stop, put palm to brow to shade the sun and follow us as we go past.

"In my new-product seminar last week"—Mike nods as if he's quoting Heraclitus (I, of course, pay for this)—"I saw some interesting figures about the lag between the top of the housing market and the first downturn in askings." His narrow eyes are fixed stonily ahead. I used to eat that kind of computer spurtage for breakfast, and made a bundle doing it. But since I arrived at the Shore, I'm happy to list 'em 'n twist 'em. When man stops wanting ocean-front, it'll be because they've paved the ocean. "I guess they've got a pretty good real estate institute over there," Mike blathers on about Moo-U. "Using some pretty sophisticated costing models. We might plug into their newsletter." Mike can occasionally drone like a grad student, relying on the ritual-reflexive "I guess" to get his most significant points set in concrete. ("I guess Maine's pretty far from San Diego." "I guess a hurricane really whips the wind up." "I guess it gets dark around here once the sun sets.")

"Did you read any reports from Kalamazoo College?"

Mike frowns over at me. He doesn't know what Kalamazoo means, or why it would be side-splittingly hilarious. His round, bespectacled, over-serious face forms a suspicious tight-lipped question mark. Sense of humor can become excess baggage for immigrants, and in any case, Mike's not always great company for extended periods.

Ahead on the left rises an ancient white concrete silo standing in the cornfield, backed by third-growth hardwood through which midday light is flashing. A weathered roadside vegetable stand, years abandoned, sits at the road shoulder, and alongside it a pale blue Cadillac Coupe de Ville. When Ann and I arrived to Haddam blows ago, it was our standard Saturday outing to drive these very county roads, taking in the then-untouched countryside up to Hunterdon County and the river towns, stopping at a country store where they cooked a ham and eggs breakfast in the back, buying a set of andirons or a wicker chair, then pulling over for squash and turnips and slab-sided tomatoes in a place just like this, taking it all home in brown paper sacks. It was long before this became a wealth belt.

I'm thinking this old roadside stall may actually have been one of our regulars. MacDonald's Farm or some such place. Though it wasn't run by a real farmer, but a computer whiz from Bell Labs, who'd taken an early buyout to spend his happy days yakking with customers about the weather and the difference between rutabagas and turnips.

This dilapidated vegetable stand is also clearly our rendezvous point. Mike, pink Post-it in his fist, swerves us inexpertly straight across the oncoming lane and rumbles into the little dirt turn-out. The Caddy's driver-door immediately swings open, and a large man begins climbing out. He is a square-jawed, thick-armed, tanned and taut Mediterranean, wearing clean and pressed khakis, a white oxford shirt (sleeves rolled Paul Bunyan-style), sturdy work boots and a braided belt with a silver tape measure cube riding his hip like a snub-nose. He looks like he just stepped out of the Sears catalog and is already smiling like the best, most handsome guy in the world to go into the sprawl business with. His Caddy has a volunteer fire department tag on its bumper.

My gut, however, instantly says this is a man to be cautious of— the too neatly rolled sleeves are the giveaway—a man who is more or less, but decidedly not, what he seems. My gut also tells me Mike will fall in love with him in two seconds due to his large, upright, manly American-ness. If I don't watch out, the deal'll be done.

"What's this guy's name again?" I've heard it but don't remember. We're climbing out. The big Caddy guy's already standing out in the dusty breeze, laving his big hands as if he'd just washed them in the car. Outside here, the wind's colder than at the Shore. The barometer's falling. Clouds are fattening to the west. I have on only my tan barracuda jacket, which isn't warm enough. Money says this guy's Italian, though he's all spruced up and could be Greek, which wouldn't be better.

"Tom Benivalle." Mike frowns, grabbing his blazer from the backseat.

I rest my case.

"Mr. Mahoney?" the big guy announces in a loud voice. "Tom Benivalle, gladda meetcha." Gruff, let's-cut-the-bullshit Texas Hill Country drawl resonates in his voice. He's seemingly not disturbed that a tiny forty-three-year-old Tibetan dressed like a Mafia golfer and with an Irish name might be his new partner.

Though it's all an act. Benivalle is a storied central New Jersey name with much colorful Haddam history in tow. A certain Eugene (Gino) Benivalle, doubtless an uncle, was for a time Haddam police chief before opting for early retirement to Siesta Key, just ahead of a trip to Trenton on a statutory rape charge brought by his fourteen-year-old niece. Tommy, clean-cut, helmet-haired, big schnoz, tiny-dark-eyed good groomer, looks like nothing as much as a cop, up to and including a gold-stud earring. This could be a sting operation. But to catch who?

Mike thrusts himself forward, his face flushed, and gives Benivalle a squinch-eyed, teeth-bared, apologetic grin, along with a double-hander handshake I've counseled him against, since Jerseyites typically grow wary at free-floating goodwill, especially from foreigners who might be Japanese. Though Mike isn't having it. He reluctantly introduces me as his "friend" while buttoning his blazer buttons. We've agreed to keep my part in this hazy, though I already sense he wishes I'd leave. Tom Benivalle enfolds my hand in his big hairy-backed one. His palm's as soft as a puppy's belly, and he transmits an amiable sweet minty smell I recognize as spearmint. He's applied something lacquerish to his forehead-bordering hair that makes it practically sparkle. The prospect that Benivalle might represent shadowy upstate connections isn't unthinkable. But face-to-face with him, my guess is not. My guess is Montclair State, marketing B.A., a tour with Uncle Sam, then home to work for the old man in the wholesale nursery bidnus in West Amwell. Married, then kids, then out on his own, tearing up turf and looking around for new business opportunities. He's probably forty, drives his Caddy to mass, drinks a little Amarone and a little schnapps, plays racquetball, pumps minor iron, puts out the odd chimney fire and voted for Bush but wouldn't actually hurt a centipede. Which is no reason to go into business with him.

Benivalle turns from our handshake and strides off as a gust of November breeze raises grit off Mullica Road and peppers my neck. He's cutting to the chase, heading to the edge of the cornfield to showcase the acreage, demonstrate he's done his homework, before sketching out the business plan. Put the small talk on hold. It's how I'd do it.

Mike and I follow like goslings—Mike flashing me a deviled look meant to stifle early judgment. He's *already* in love with the guy and doesn't want the deal queered. I round my eyes at him in phony surprise, which devils him more.

"Okay. Now our parcel runs straight south to Mullica Creek," Benivalle's saying in a deeper but less LBJish voice, raising a long arm and pointing out toward the silo and the pretty band of trees that follows the water's course (when there's water there). "Which *is* in the floodplain." He glances at me, heavy brows gathering over his black eyes. He knows I know he knows I know. Still, full disclosure, numbers crunched, regulations read and digested: My presence has been registered. It's possible we've met somewhere. Benivalle bites his bottom lip with his top teeth—familiar to me as the stagecraft of our current President. Sharp wind is gusting but fails to disturb a follicle of Benivalle's dense black do. "So," he goes on, "we establish our south lot lines a hundred feet back from the mean high-water mark—the previous hundred-year flood. The creek runs chiefly west to east. So we have about a hundred twenty-five available acres if we clear the woods and grade it off."

Mike is smiling wondrously.

"How many units do you get on a hundred and twenty-five?" I say this because Mike isn't going to.

Benivalle nods. Great question. "Average six thousand with a footprint of about sixty-two per." This means a living room the size of a fifties tract home. Benivalle tucks his big thumb in under his braided belt, rears back delicately on his boot heels and continues staring toward Mullica Creek as if only in that way can he say what needs saying next. "The state's got its setback laws— you prob'ly know all that—for homes this size. You got some wiggle room on your street widths, but there's not that much you can fudge. So. I'm expecting a density of forty on three-acre lots, leaving some double lots for presale or all-cash offers. Maybe if you got a friend who's interested in building a ten-thousand-footer." A smile at the prospect of such a Taj Mahal. He is now addressing me more than Mike, whom he seems to want to treat benevolently, instead of as just some little foreign team-mascot type who can probably do a good somersault.

"How much do they cost?" Mike finally says.

"High-end, a buck-twenty per," Benivalle answers quick. He, I see, has old, smoothed-over acne craters in both cheeks. It gives him a Neville Brand stolidness, suggesting old humiliations suffered. It also gives him a Neville Brand aura of untrustworthiness that's oddly touching but isn't helped by the earring. No doubt Mrs. B. talks about his face to her girlfriends. He also has extremely regular, straight white teeth, which make him look dull.

"That's seven hundred twenty thousand," I say.

"A-bout." Benivalle laps his bottom lip over his top one and nods. "We don't see much high-end fluctuation out here, Mr. Baxter." Why not Mr. Bastard? "They see it, they buy it, or else they don't. They've all got the dough. Down in Haddam last year, they got a double-digit spike in million-dollar deals. Our problem's the same as theirs."

"What's that?"

Benivalle unaccountably smiles at the luck of it. "Inventory. Used to be it was location in this business, Frank. If I can call you that."

"You bet." I make my cheeks smile.

"Now go over to Hunterdon County and Warren, it's way different. Prices rose twenty-three, twenty-four percent here this year. Median price is four-fifty." Benivalle brusquely scratches his rucked neck like Neville Brand would, and in a way that makes him look older.

"You don't own the land, do you?" Mike suddenly says, forgetting that he's supposed to help buy it. He's been in a swoon since his two-hander was reciprocated. The thought that this out-of-date farmland, this comely but useless woods, this silted, dry creek could be transformed into a flat-as-a-griddle housing tract, on which behemoth-size dwellings in promiscuous architectural permutations might sprout like a glorious city of yore and that it could all be done to his bidding and profit is almost too much for him.

"I've got an option." Benivalle nods again, as though this was news not to be bruited. "The old guy who used to operate this vegetable stand"—his big mitt motions toward the tumbledown gray-plank produce shack—"his family owns it."

"MacDonald," I suddenly realize—and say.

"Okay," Benivalle says, like a cop. "You know him? He's dead."

"I used to buy tomatoes from him twenty-five years ago."

"I used to pick those freakin' tomatoes," Benivalle says matter-of-factly. "I worked for him. Like—"

"I probably bought tomatoes from you." I can't keep from grinning. Here is a human being from my certifiable past—not all that common if you're me—who may actually have laid his honest human eyes on my dead son, Ralph Bascombe.

"Yeah, maybe," Benivalle says.

"What happened to ole MacDonald?" I'm forgetting the option, the floodplain, inventory, footprint, usable floor space.

Memory rockets to that other gilded time—red mums, orange pumpkins, fat dusty tomatoes, leathery gourds, sunlight streaming through the roof cracks in the warm, rich-aired produce stand. Ralph, age five or six, would march up to the counter and somebody—Tommy Benivalle, acned, furiously masturbating high schooler and reserve on the JV wrestling squad—would look gravely down, then slip my son a root beer rock candy on condition he tell no one, since Farmer MacDonald got a "pretty penny" for them. It became Ralph's first joke. Every penny a pretty penny.

"He passed." Meaning ole MacDonald. "Like I said. A few years ago." Tom Benivalle's not at ease sharing the past with me. He brushes a speck of phantom road grit off his oxford cloth shirtsleeve. On his breast pocket there's stitched a tiny colorful pheasant bursting into flight. He buys his shirts from the same catalog I buy mine—minus the pheasant.

Silence momentarily becalms us while Benivalle refinds the skein of business talk. He is not the bad guy I thought. I could mention my son. He could say he remembered him. "He's got a daughter up in Freylinghuysen," he says about the now dead owner. "I approached her about this. She was okay."

"You must've known her when you were kids."

Mike's still staring at the acreage in his mustard blazer, dreaming conquest dreams. A whole new *it* has bumped up onto his horizon. Lavallette no longer the final *it*. He and Mrs. Mahoney might see eye-to-eye again.

"Yeah, I sorta did," Benivalle says scratchily. "He worked at Bell Labs, the old man. My dad had a decorative-pottery place up in Frenchtown. They did some business." How do I know these natives? I should've been an FBI profiler. Sometimes no surprise can be a blessing. I, however, am not the business partner here. My job is to be the spiritual Geiger counter, and see to it Benivalle understands Mr. Mahoney has serious (non-Asian) backers who know a thing or two. I'm sure I've done that by now. Thoughts of my son go sparkling away.

"I'm going to take off," I say, turning toward Mike, who's still staring away, dazzled. "I've gotta see a man about a horse."

Benivalle blinks. "So, then, are you in the horse business?" It's his first spontaneous utterance to me—besides my name—and it causes him to ravel his brow, turn the corners of his mouth up in a non-smile, touch a finger to the stud in his earlobe and let his eyes examine me.

I smile back. "It's just an expression." Mike unexpectedly turns and looks to me as if I'd spoken his name.

"I get it," Benivalle says. He's ready for me to get going, for it to be just the two of them, so he can start making his spiel to Mike about having himself certified for all that government moolah so they can start moving Urdu speakers down from Gotham and Teaneck. He may think Mike's a Pakistani. My work here is done, and fast.

Mike and I begin our walk back across the gusty turn-out toward my Suburban. Sweet pungence of leaf-burn swims in the air from the linked back yards across Mullica Road, where a homeowner's daydreaming against his rake, garden hose at the ready, peering into the cool flames and curling smoke, indifferent to the good-neighbor ordinances he's breaching, wool-gathering over how *things* should most properly *be*, and how they once *had been* when something he can't exactly remember was the rule of the day and he was young. It could all be put back into working order, he knows, if the Democrats could be kept from boosting the goddamned fucking election that he, because he was on a business trip to Dayton and had jury duty in Pennington the second he got home, somehow forgot to vote in. "Whatever It Takes" should be the battle hymn of the republic.

"So, I'll see you later," Mike says, nose in the breeze as we come to my parked vehicle. He's feeling tip-top about everything now, even though seeming eager is incautious.

"I'll be at the August," I say. Benivalle has already headed toward his Caddy. He has no inclination for good-byes with strangers. "Gladda meetcha," I shout to him in the stiff wind, but he's already mashing a little cell phone to his ear and can't hear me. "Yeah. I'm out here at the parcel," I hear him say. "It's all great."

"What do you think?" Mike says barely under his breath. His flat freckled nose has gone pale in the cold, his small pupils shining with hope for a thumbs-up. His spiffy business outfit—expensive shoes and blazer—makes him seem helpless. His lapel, I see, sports a tiny American flag in the buttonhole. A new addition.

"You just better be careful." My fingers are on the cold door handle.

Mike hands me the keys he's removed. "No choices are ever absolutely right," he says and frowns, trying to be confident.

"Plenty are absolutely crazy, though. This isn't Buddhism, it's business."

"Oh, yes! I know!" He consults the sky again. A front, maybe cold New Jersey rain, true harbinger of winter, is coming in now. I'm colder already, my hands frozen. My barracuda jacket is water-resistant, not waterproof. "Just don't let him talk you into signing anything." I'm climbing stiffly into the driver's side, where the seat's too far forward. "If you don't sign, they can't put you in prison."

Prison scares the crap out of him. Our bold, new-concept American lockups are the stuff of his nightmares, having seen too many documentaries on the Discovery Channel and knowing what happens on the inside to gentle souls like him.

"We'll talk about it tonight," I say out my window, which I'd like to close.

"You think belief's a luxury, I know." Breeze flaps his trouser legs. He's fidgeting with his gold pinkie ring without seeking my eye. Benivalle starts up his Coupe de Ville with a noisy screech of fan-belt slippage.

"I guess if you think it is, it is," I say, getting the seat resituated and not entirely sure what I mean by that.

"You talk like a Buddhist." He actually giggles, then narrows his little lightless eyes and hugs his blazered shoulders in the cold.

Anyone, of course, can talk *like* a Buddhist. You just turn every cornpone Will Rogers cliché on its ear and pretend it's Spinoza. It wouldn't be hard to be a Buddhist. What's hard is to be a realist. "Buddhism-schmuddhism," I say.

Mike enjoys coarse American talk for the same reason he enjoys random cursing—because it's meaningless. You can't insult the Buddha, only yourself for trying. "So, we can talk later?" He looks down at his big fake Rolex, as if time was what mattered now.

"We'll talk later, yep." My window's going up. He's retreating. Possibly the wind's chasing him, because he begins half-skipping, half-running/shuffling, everything but a cartwheel toward the waiting blue Cadillac. For a man of his size, race, age, religion and manner of fussy dress, he is a funny spectacle—though spirited, which can take you a far distance.

As I pull away, I take a departing look at the cornfield stretching down to Mullica Creek, its gentle fall and charming hardwood copse, soon to be overwhelmed by grumbling, chuffing, knife-bladed Komatsus and Kubotas, cluttered with corrugated culverts, rebar and pre-cut king posts, ready-mixers lined up to 206, every inch flattened and staked with little red flags prophesying megahouses waiting on the drawing boards. The neighbor across the road, watching his dreams go up in smoke, has his point: Someone should draw the line somewhere.

I say silent adieu to the ground my son trod and will no more. The old lay of the land. E-eye, E-eye, OOOOOOO.

2

Driving the scenic route back to Haddam—Preventorium Road to the rock quarry (where certified mafiosos once dumped their evidence), past the SPCA and the curvy maple-lined lane along the mossy old Delaware Canal, past the estate where retired priests snooze away days in tranquilized serenity and hopeful non-reflection—I'm for an instant struck: What would real scientists, decades on, say about us here on our own patch of suburban real estate?

I knew a boy back at Michigan, Tom Laboutalliere, who dedicated his whole life to "reading" little birds-feet scratch marks on ossified clods of ancient tan-colored mud and possibly turds. From such evidence, he conjured what the ancient Garbonzians were doing back in 1000 B.C. in *their* little square of earth. By studying cubic tons of dirt—his field data—what he got his hands on and sifted through screens were the Garbonzians' precious laundry receipts. The little birds-feet tracks were actually their writings, which made it unassailable, using infrared spectroscopy and carbon dating, that a mighty lot of army uniforms had needed repair and entrail despotting and caustic herbal soaks between about 1006 and 1005. So that he concluded (everyone was amazed) that a considerable amount of nonstop pulverizing, disemboweling and tearing limb from limb had gone on during that period, and—his great, tenurable discovery—that's why we now think of those long-ago, far-distant folk as "warlike."

None of us should suppose that this type of years-on digging won't winkle out our own naked truths. Because it will. Which merits some consideration.

Most evidence, of course, will just be the stuff Mike and I cruised past on Route 37 this morning, strewn along the road shoulder, in the pine duff and dusty turn-outs. This civilization, future thinkers will conclude, liked beer. They favored wood-paper products as receptacles for semen and other bodily excretions. They suffered hemorrhoids, occasional incontinence and erectile dysfunctions not known to subsequent generations. They thought much about their bowel movements. Sex was an activity they isolated as much as possible from daily life. They disliked extraneous metal things. They were faltering in their resolve about permanence vis-à-vis possibility and change, as evidenced by their shelters being in good condition but frequently abandoned, with others seemingly meant to last only five years or less. I'm not certain what the signs about paint-ball wars will teach them, or, for that matter, Toms River itself, should it last another year. Fort Dix they'll understand perfectly.

But future delvers will also think—and Mike's and Tom Benivalle's plans lie in my brain like a piece of heavy driftwood—how much we all lived with, banked and thrived on, got made happy or sad by what was *already there*! And how little we ourselves *invented*! And by how little we *had* to invent, since you could get anything you wanted—from old records to young boys—just by giving a number and an expiration date to an electronic voice, then sitting back and waiting for the friendly brown truck. Our inventions, it'll be clear, were only to say yes or no, like flipping off a light switch or flipping it on. Future scholars might also conclude that if we ever did think of trying something different—living in the Allagash and eating only tubers; becoming a mystic, taking a vow of poverty and begging on the roadside in Taliganga; if we considered having six wives, never cutting our hair or bathing and holing up in an armed compound in Utah; in other words, if we ever gave a thought to worming our way outside the box to see what was out there—we must've realized that we risked desolation and the world looking at us with menace, knew we couldn't stand that for long, and so declined.

Possibly I tend toward this glum future perspective because, like millions of other journeying souls, I've lately received *the* call—from my Haddam urologist, possibly phoning from the golf course or his Beemer, casually commenting that my PSA "values" were "still higher than *we* like to see . . . so *we'd* better get you in for a closer looky-look." That can change your view, let me tell you. Or maybe it's because I've graduated to the spiritual concision of the Permanent Period, the time of life when very little you say comes in quotes, when few contrarian voices mutter doubts in your head, when the past seems more generic than specific, when life's a destination more than a journey and when who you feel yourself to be is pretty much how people will remember you once you've croaked—in other words, when personal integration (what Dr. Erikson talked about but secretly didn't believe in) is finally achieved.

Or possibly I take the view I do just because I've been a

real estate agent for fifteen years, and can see that real estate's a profession both spawned by and grown cozy with our present and very odd state of human development. In other words, I'm implicated: You have a wish? Wait. I'll make it come true (or at least show you my inventory). If you're a Bengali ophthalmologist with your degree from Upstate and have no desire to return to Calcutta to "give back," and prefer instead to expand life, open doors, let the sun in—well, all you have to do is travel down Mullica Road, let your wishes be known to a big strapping guinea home builder and his smiling, nodding, truth-dispensing, dusky-skinned sidekick, and you and civilization will be on the same page in no time. They'll even name your street after your daughter—which those same scientists can later puzzle over.

Up to now I've thought this basic formula was a good thing. But lately I'm less sure I'm right—at least as right as I used to be. I can take the matter up with Mike in the car later, when home's in sight.

M ike's handoff to Benivalle has taken less time than expected, and it's only noon when I merge onto westbound Brunswick Pike, the corner where once stood a big ShopRite when I lived nearby but which now contains a great silver and glass Lexus palace with wall-to-wall vehicles and a helipad X for buyers on the go, and across from it a giant Natur-Food pavilion where formerly stood a Magyar Bank. If I shake a leg and don't attract a speeding ticket, I can make the funeral home before they begin shooing mourners out to ready Ernie McAuliffe's casket for its last ride.

The Haddam cemetery—which I intend to avoid—lies directly behind where I once resided at 19 Hoving Road, and is the resting place of my aforementioned son Ralph, who died of Reye's at age nine and would be almost thirty now. He "rests" there behind the wrought-iron fence among the damp oaks and ginkgoes, alongside three signers of the Declaration, two innovators of manned flight and innumerable New Jersey governors. I don't go there anymore, as the saying has it. I've learned by trial and much error to accept that Ralph is not coming back to his mother and me. Though every time I venture near the cemetery, I dreamily imagine he still might—which I deem to be a not-good thought pattern, and to violate the Permanent Period's rule of the road about the past. Mike has told me the Dalai Lama contends that young people who die are our masters who teach us impermanence, and I've tried to think of things this way.

In truth, it's no longer even physically possible to cruise past my old Hoving Road house—a sweet, sagging, old Tudor half-timber on a well-treed lot, which I sold to the Theological Institute in the eighties, and who then transformed it into an ecumenical victims' rights center. (Land-mine victims, children-soldier victims, African-circumcision victims, families of strangled cheerleaders, all became regular sights on the sidewalkless street.) However, due to fierce nineties property-value wars, my former residence was demo'd the instant the Korean Fresh Lighters took over, and the ground sold for a fortune. Efforts were made to recycle the old pile using chain saws and flatbed trucks. Some ecumenicists wanted it hauled to Hightstown and rechartered as a hospice, whereas others wanted it moved to Washington's Crossing and turned into an organic restaurant. For a week, the neighborhood association, fearing the worst, stood a vigil and actually erected a human chain against the recycling people. But without notice, one night the Koreans dispatched a jumpsuited wrecking crew, trucked in dismantling equipment, trained two big klieg lights on the house, lighting up the neighborhood like an invasion from space. And by seven in the morning all four walls—within which I'd started a family, experienced joy, suffered great sadness, became lost to dreaminess, but through it all slept many nights as peaceful as a saint under the sheltering beeches and basswoods—were gone.

Legal remedies were sought—to enjoin something, punish someone. The neighborhood has many lawyers. But the Koreans instantly cashed in the lot for two million to a thoroughbred breeder from Kentucky with big GOP connections. In a year, he'd put up a lot-line to lot-line three-quarter-size replica of his white plantation-style mansion in Lexington, complete with fluted acacia-leaf columns, mature live oaks from Florida, an electric fence, mean guard dogs, a rebel flag on the flagpole and two Negro jockey statues painted his stable colors, green and black. "Not Furlong" is what he called the place, though the neighbors have found other names for it. All problems were deemed my fault for selling out originally back in '85. So mine is not a popular face around there now, though many of my old neighbors have also moved on.

*B*runswick Pike glides me in through Rocky Ridge, back into Haddam Township, and becomes Seminary Street along the banks of the widened stream referred to by locals as Lake Bimble, for the German farmer who owned the river bank and, as a Tory in the Revolution, gave aid and comfort to Colonel Mawhood's troops, and who for his trouble got bound to a sack of ballast rocks and tossed in the stream—Quaker Creek—by General Washington's men, there to stay.

Since I lived here for twenty years, I know what to expect farther in on Seminary two days before Thanksgiving. A melee. People stocking up and leaving for Vermont and Maine, the cozy Thanksgiving states; others arriving for family at-homes, students back from Boulder and Reed, divorcées visiting children, children visiting divorcées—the customary midday automotive hector brought about by a town become a kind of love-it/hate-it paragon of suburban amplitude gone beyond self-congratulation to the point of entropy. (Greenwich minus the beach, times three.)

Plus, there's the further complication of the town fathers' decision to mount a Battle of Haddam re-enactment right in town. I read this in the Haddam *Packet*, which I still receive in Sea-Clift. Uniformed Redcoats and tattered Continentals in homespun, carrying period musketry, eating homemade hardtack and wearing tricorn hats, jerkins and knee pants, their hair in pigtails, will be setting up drill fields, redoubts and headquarters all around the Boro, staging assaults and retreats, bivouacs and drumhead courts-martial, digging latrines and erecting tenting at the sites where these occurrences actually occurred back in 1780—though the current sites may now be Frenchy's Gulf, Benetton or Hulbert's Classic Shoes. This was done once before, for the bicentennial, and it's all happening again for the Millennium in an effort to rev up sidewalk appeal. Though some merchants—I heard this at the bank last week—are already sensing retail disaster, and have retained counsel and are computing lost revenue as damages. This includes the bank itself.

The other distraction making movement into the Square near-impossible is that the Historical Society, in a fit of Thanksgiving spirit and under the rubric of "Sharing Our Village Past," has converted the entire Square in front of the August Inn and the Post Office into a Pilgrim Village Interpretive Center. Two Am. Civ. professors from Trenton State with time on their hands have constructed a replica Pilgrim town with three windowless, dirt-floor Pilgrim houses, trucked-in period barnyard animals, and lots of authentic but unhandy Pilgrim implements, built a hand-adzed paled fence, laid in a subsistence garden and produced old-timey clothes and authentically inadequate footwear for the Pilgrims themselves. Inside the village they've installed a collection of young Pilgrims—a Negro Pilgrim, a Jewish female Pilgrim, a wheelchair-bound Pilgrim, a Japanese Pilgrim with a learning disability, plus two or three ordinary white kids—all of whom spend their days doing toilsome Pilgrim chores in drab, ill-fitting garments, chattering to themselves about rock videos while they hew logs, boil clothes, rip up sod, make soap in iron caldrons and spin more coarse cloth, but now and then pausing to step forth, just like soap-opera characters on Christmas Day, to deliver loud declarations about "the first hard days of 1620" and how it's impossible to imagine the character and dedication of the first people and how our American stock was cured by tough times, blab, blab, blab, blab—all this to whoever might be idle enough to stop on the way to the liquor store to listen. Every night the young Pilgrims disappear to a motel out on Route 1, fill their bellies with pizza and smoke dope till their heads explode, and who'd blame them?

Merchants on the Square—the Old Irishman's Kilt, Rizzutto's Spirits, Sherm's Tobacconist—have taken a more tolerant view of the Pilgrim shenanigans than they have of the battle re-enactors, who whoop and carry weapons, and stay out at the actual battlefield in Winnebagos and bring their own food and beer and never buy anything in town. The Pilgrims, on the other hand—which is probably how they were always viewed—are seen as a kind of peculiar but potentially attractive business nuisance. It's hoped that passing citizens who pause to hear the overweight paraplegic girl give her canned speech about piss-poor medical facilities in seventeenth-century New Jersey, and how someone in her state of body wouldn't have lasted a weekend, will then be moved by an urge to buy a Donegal plaid vest or a box of toffees or Macanudos or half a case of Johnnie Walker Red.

There's even talk that a group representing the Lenape Band— New Jersey's own redskins, who believe *they* own Haddam and always have—is setting up to picket the Pilgrims on Thursday, wearing their own period outfits and carrying placards that say THANKS FOR NOTHING and THE TERRIBLE LIE OF THANKSGIVING and stirring up a bad-for-business backlash. There's likewise a rumor that a group of re-enactors will go AWOL, march to the Pilgrims' defense and re-enact a tidy massacre on the front steps of the Post Office. This is all probably skywriting by the boys at United Jersey and represents less truth than their wish that something out of the ordinary could happen so they can quit boring themselves to death approving mortgage after mortgage.

What it all comes down to, though, as with so many vital life issues and blood-boiling causes, is traffic and more traffic. An ambulance carrying our President and Pope John Paul couldn't make it the two blocks from the Recovery Room Bar to Caviar 'n Cashmere in less than three-quarters of an hour, by which time both these tarnished exemplars would be out on the street walking.

*L*ong manorial lawns sweep down to the north side of Brunswick Pike, facing the lake, with heavy hemlock growth and rhododendron splurge giving the white, set-back, old-money mansions their modesty protection. In my years selling houses here, I sold three of these goliaths, two twice, once to a famous novelist. Still, I take my first chance to turn off, to avoid the town traffic, and pass along onto bosky, stable, compromise-with-dignity Gulick Road—winding streets, mature plantings, above-ground electric, architect-design "family rooms" retrofitted onto older reasonable-sized Capes and ranches a year beyond their paint jobs. (I sold twenty of these.) Yukons and Grand Cherokees sit in driveways. Older tree houses perch in many oaks and maples. New mullions have been added to old seventies picture windows and underground sprinklers laid in. It's the suburban sixties *grown out*, with many original owner-pioneers holding fast to the land and happy to be, their "new development" now become solidly *in-town*, with all the old rawness ironed out. It's now a "neighborhood," where your old Chesapeake, Tex, can take his nap in the street without being rumbled over by the bottled-water truck, where once-young families have become older but don't give a shit, and where fiscal year to fiscal year everybody's equity squeezes up as their political musings drift to the right (though it feels like the middle). It's the height of what's possible from modest beginnings, and as near to perfection as random settlement patterns and anxiety for permanence can hope for. It's where I'd buy in if I moved back—which I won't.

Though passing down these quiet, reserved streets—not splashy but good—I sometimes think I might've left for the Shore and Sea-Clift a bit too soon in 1992, since I missed the really big paydays (I still made a pot full). But by then I had an unusual son in my care, clinging precariously to his hold on Haddam High. (He actually graduated and left for college at Ball State— his odd choice.) I had a girlfriend, Sally Caldwell, who was giving me the old "now or never." I was forty-seven. And I was experiencing the early, uneasy symptoms—it pretty quickly got better—of the Permanent Period of life. I couldn't have told you what that was, only that after Paul left for Muncie, I began to feel a sort of clanking, mechanistic, solemn sameness about flogging these very houses, whereas earlier in my realty life I'd felt involved in, even morally committed to, getting people into the homes they (and the economy) wanted themselves to be in (at least for a while). Though what had always accompanied my long state of real estate boosterism was a sensation I've described in differing ways using differing tropes, but which all speak to the dulling complexity of the human organism. One such sensation was of constantly feeling *offshore*, a low-level, slightly removed-from-events, wooing-wind agitation that doing for others, in the frank, plain-talk way I was able to as a house seller, generally assuaged but never completely stilled. *Experiencing the need for an extra beat* was another of my figures. This I'd felt since military school in Mississippi—as if life and its directives were never quite all they should be, and, in fact, should've meant more. Regular life always felt like an unfinished flamenco needing, either from me or a source outside me, a completing beat, after which tranquillity could reign. Women almost always did the trick pretty neatly—at least till the whole thing started up again.

There were other such expressions—some warriorlike, some sports-related, some hilarious, some fairly embarrassing. But they pointed to the same wearying instinct for *becoming*, of which realty is an obvious standard-bearer profession. I really did fantasize that if Clinton could just win the White House in '92, then a renaissance spirit would open like a new sun, whereby through a mysterious but ineluctable wisdom I would be named ambassador to France—or at least the Ivory Coast. That and a lot more didn't happen.

Only, neuron by neuron, over a period of months (this was nearing the middle of the doomed and clownish Bush presidency) I realized I was feeling different about things. I remember sitting at my desk at my former employer, the Haddam realty firm of

Lauren-Schwindell, tracking down some computerized post-sale notes I'd made on a house on King George Road that had come back on the market six months later, sporting a 30 percent increase in asking, and overhearing a colleague three cubicles away saying, just loud enough for me to take an interest, "Oh, that was Mr. Bascombe. I'm sure he would never do or say that." I never found out what she was talking about or to whom. She normally didn't speak to me. But I went off to sleep that night thinking of those words—"Mr. Bascombe would never . . ."— and woke up the next morning thinking them some more. Because it occurred to me that even though my colleague (a former history professor who'd reached the end of her patience with the Compromise of 1850) could say what Mr. Bascombe would never do, say, drive, eat, wear, laugh about, marry or think was sad, Mr. Bascombe himself wasn't sure *he* could. She could've said damn near anything about me and I would've had to give the possibility some thought—which is why I'd never take a lie-detector test; not because I lie, but because I concede too much to be possible.

But very little about me, I realized—except what I'd *already* done, said, eaten, etc.—seemed written in stone, and all of that meant almost nothing about what I *might* do. I had my history, okay, but not really much of a regular character, at least not an inner essence I or anyone could use as a predictor. And something, I felt, needed to be done about that. I needed to go out and find myself a recognizable and persuasive semblance of a character. I mean, isn't that the most cherished pre-posthumous dream of all? The news of our premature demise catching everyone so unprepared that beautiful women have to leave fancy dinner parties to be alone for a while, their poor husbands looking around confused; grown men find they can't finish their after-lunch remarks at the Founders Club because they're so moved. Children wake up sobbing. Dogs howl, hounds begin to bark. All because something essential and ineffable has been erased, and the world knows it and can't be consoled.

But given how I was conducting life—staying offshore, waiting for the extra beat—I realized I could die and no one would remember me for anything. "Oh, that guy. Frank, uh. Yeah. Hmm . . ." That was me.

And not that I wanted to blaze my initials forever into history's oak. I just wanted that when I was no more, someone could say my name (my children? my ex-wife?) and someone else could then say, "Right. That Bascombe, he was always damn *blank*." Or "Ole Frank, he really liked to *blank*." Or, worst case, "Jesus Christ, that Bascombe, I'm glad to see the end of his sorry *blank*." These blanks would all be human traits I knew about and others did too, and that I got credit for, even if they weren't heroic or particularly essential.

Another way of saying this (and there're too many ways to say everything) is that some force in my life was bringing me hard up against what felt like my *self* (after a lengthy absence), presenting me, if I chose to accept it, with an imperative that all my choices in recent memory—volitions, discretions, extra beats, time spent offshore—hadn't presented me, though I might've said they had and argued you to the dirt about it. Here, for a man with no calculable character, was a hunger for *necessity*, for something solid, the thing "character" stands in for. This hunger could, of course, just as easily result from a recognition that you'd never done one damn substantial thing in your life, good or otherwise, and never would, and if you did, it wouldn't matter a mouse fart—a recognition that could leave you in the doldrums' own doldrum, i.e., despair that knows it's despair.

Except, I'll tell you, this period—1990–92—was the most exhilarating of my life, the likes of which I'd felt once, possibly twice, but not more and was reconciled perhaps never to feel again, just glad to have had it when I did, but whose cause I couldn't really tell you.

What it portended—and this is the truest signature of the Permanent Period, which comes, by the way, when it comes and not at any signifying age, and not as a climacteric, not when you expect it, not when your ducks are in a row (as mine back in 1990 were not)—it portended an end to perpetual becoming, to thinking that life schemed wonderful changes for me, even if it didn't. It portended a blunt break with the past and provided a license to think of the past only indistinctly (who wouldn't pay plenty for that?). It portended that younger citizens might come up to me in wonderment and say, "How in the world do you live? How do you do it in this uncharted time of life?" It portended that I say to myself and mean it, even if I thought I said it every day and already really meant it: "This is how in the shit I *am*! My life is *this* way"—recognizing, as I did, what an embarrassment and a disaster it would be if, once you were dust, the world and yourself were in basic disagreement on this subject.

Following which I set about deciding how I should put the

next five to ten years to better use than the last five—progress being the ancients' benchmark for character. I'd by then started to worry that Haddam might be *it* for me—just like Mike sweats it about Lavallette—which frankly scared the wits out of me. As a result, I immediately resigned my job at Lauren-Schwindell. I put my house on Cleveland Street on the rental market. I proposed marriage to Sally Caldwell, who couldn't have been more surprised, though she didn't say no (at least not till recently). I cashed in the Baby Bells I'd been adding to since the breakup. I made inquiries about possibilities for real estate at the Shore and was able to buy Realty-Wise from its owner, who was retiring to managed care. I made an unrejectable offer on a big tall-windowed redwood house facing the ocean in Sea-Clift (the second-home boom hadn't arrived there yet). Sally sold her Stick Style beach house in East Mantoloking. And on June 1, 1992, with Clinton nearing the White House and the world seeming more possible than ever, I drove Sally to Atlantic City and in a comical ceremony in the Best Little Marriage Chapel in New Jersey, a pink, white, and blue Heidi chalet on Baltic Avenue, we tied the knot—acted on necessity, opted for the substantial in one simple act. We ended up saying good-bye to the day, my second wedding day and Sally's, too, and the first full day of the Permanent Period, eating fried clams and sipping Rusty Nails at a seaside fish joint, giggling and planning the extraordinary future we were going to enjoy.

Which we did. Until I came down with a case of cancer shortly after Sally's first husband came back from the dead, where he'd been in safekeeping for decades. Following which everything got all fucked up shit, as my daughter, Clarissa, used to say, and the Permanent Period was put to its sternest test by different necessities, though up to now it's proved durable.

Mangum & Gayden Funeral Home, on one-block, oak-lined Willow Street, is a big yellow-and-brown-shingled Victorian, with a full-gingerbread porch above a bank of vociferous yews, with dense pachysandra encircling a large, appropriately-weeping front-yard willow and a thick St. Augustine carpet out to the sidewalk. For all the world, M&G looks like a big congenial welcoming-family abode where people live and play and are contented, instead of a funeral parlor where the inhabitants are dead as mallets and you feel a chill the instant you walk in the front door. What distinguishes it as a mortuarial establishment and not somebody's domicile is the discreet, dim-lit MANGUM & GAYDEN—PARKING IN REAR lawn sign, a side porte-cochère that wasn't in the original house design and two or three polished black Cadillacs around back with apparently nothing to do. A recent Haddam sign ordinance forbids any use of the word *funeral*, though Lloyd Mangum got his grandfathered. But nobody flying over at ten thousand feet would ever look down and say, "There's a funeral home," since it's nestled into a row of similar-vintage living-human residences that list for a fortune. Lloyd says his Haddam neighbors seem not to mind residing beside the newly dead, and proximity has never seemed to put the brakes on resale. Most new buyers must feel a funeral home is better than a house full of attention-deficit teens learning the snare drum. And Lloyd, who's a descendant of the original Mangum, tells me that mourners routinely stop by for a visitation with Aunt Gracie, then throw down a huge cash as-is offer for building and grounds before they're out the door. Lloyd and family, in fact, live upstairs.

I park a ways down Willow and walk up. The new weather announced in the skies over Mullica Road is quickly arriving. Metallic rain smell permeates the air, and clouds back over Pennsylvania have bruised up green and gray for a season-changing blow. In an hour it could be snowing—a sorry day for a funeral, though when's a good day?

Outside on the bottom front step, having a smoke, are Lloyd and another man known to me, both friends of the deceased and possibly the only other mourners. Ernie McAuliffe, to be honest, took his good sweet time departing this earth. Everybody who cared about him got to say they did three times over, then say it again. His wife, Deb, had long ago moved back to Indiana, and his only son, Bruno, a merchant mariner, came, said his brief strangled good-bye, then beat it. Ernie himself took charge of all funerary issues, including terminal care out at Delaware-Vue Acres in Titusville, and set out notarized instructions about who, what and when to do this, that and the other—no flowers, no graveside folderol, no funeral, really, just boxed up and buried, the way we'd all probably like it. He even made arrangements with an unnamed care-giver to ease him out when it all got pointless.

I am, I realize, violating Ernie's wishes by being here. But his obit was in the *Packet* on Saturday, and I was coming over with Mike anyway. Why do we do things? For ourselves, mostly. Ernie, though, was a grand fellow, and I'm sorry he's no more. *Memento mori* in a sere season.

Ernie was, in fact, the best of fellows, someone anybody'd be happy to sit beside at a bar, a wounded Viet vet who still wore his dog tags but didn't let any of that bring him low or fill him with self-importance. He'd seen some ugly stuff and maybe did a bit of it himself. Though you wouldn't know it. He talked about his exploits, about that war and his fellow troopers and the politicians who ran it, the way you'd describe how things had gone when your high school football squad went 11–0 but lost the state championship to a scrappy but inferior team of small-fry opponents.

Ernie was brought up on a dairy farm near La Porte, Indiana, and went to a state school out there. When he left the Army minus his left leg, he went straight into the prosthetic-limb business as a super-salesman and ended up "opening" New Jersey to modern prosthetic techniques, then managing some big accounts and finally owning the whole damn company. Something about the savagery of war and all the squandered youth, he said to me, had made him feel prosthetics, rather than dairy herding, was his calling in this life, his way of leaving a mark.

Ernie, even with a space-age leg, was a great tall drink of water who walked up on the ball of his one good foot, which was barge material, wore his brown hair long and pomaded, with a prodigious side part that made him resemble a forties Hollywood glamour boy. He also was said to possess the biggest dick anybody'd ever seen (he would sometimes show it around, though I never got to see it) and on certain occasions was given the nickname "Dillinger." He had a superlative sense of humor, could do all kinds of howling European accents and wacky loose-jointed walks and was never happier than when he was on the golf course or sitting with a towel draped over his unit, with his fake leg leaned against the wall, playing pinochle in the nineteenth hole at the Haddam Country Club. Deb was said to have gone back to Terre Haute for sexual reasons—probably so she could sleep with a normal man. Ernie, however, only spoke of her with resolute affection, as though to say, You can't know what goes on between a man and a woman unless you write the novel yourself. He never, for obvious reasons, lacked for female companionship.

Of my two fellow mourners on Mangum's front steps, the other is Bud Sloat, known behind his back as "Slippery Sloat." Both are in regulation black London Fogs, in tune to the weather. Lloyd is tall, bare-headed and solemn, though Bud's wearing a stupid Irish tweed knock-about hat and saddle oxfords that make him look sporting and only coincidentally in mourning.

Both Lloyd and Bud are members of the men's group that "stepped up" when Ernie found out he had lymphoma and started going down fast. They organized outings to the Pine Barrens and Island Beach (close to where I live) and down to the Tundra swan sanctuary on Delaware Bay, where they trekked the beach (as long as Ernie was up to it), then sat around in a circle on the sand or on the rocks and told stories about Ernie, sang folk songs, discussed politics and literature, recited heroic poems, said secularist prayers, told raunchy jokes and sometimes cried like babies, all the while marveling at life's transience and at the strange *beyond* that all of us will someday face. I went along once in late October, before Ernie needed transfusions to keep himself going. It was an autumn morning of pale water-color skies and clear dense air—we were just down the beach from my house— five of us late middle-agers in Bermudas and sweaters and tee-shirts that said *Harrah's* and *Planned Parenthood*, plus ever-paler one-legged "Whatcha" McAuliffe (his other nickname), looking green and limping along without much stamina or joie de vivre. I thought it would just be a manly hike down the beach, skimming sand dollars, letting the cold surf prickle our toes, watching the terns and kestrels wheel and dip on the shore breezes, and in that fashion we would re-certify life for those able to live it.

Only at a certain point, the four others, including Lloyd and Bud, circled round poor Ernie—stumping along on his space-age prosthesis but still game in spite of being nearly dead—and rapturously told him they all loved him and there was no one in hell who was a bit like him, that life was here and now and needed to be felt, that death was as natural as sneezing. Then to my shock, like a band of natives toting a canoe, they actually picked Ernie up and walked with him—peg leg and all—up on their shoulders right into the goddamn ocean and, while cradling him in their interlaced arms, totally immersed him while murmuring, "Ernie, Ernie, Ernie" and chanting, "We're with you, my brother," as if *they* had lymphoma, too, and in six weeks would be dead as he'd be.

Once such bizarre activities get going, you can't stop them without making everybody feel like an asshole. And maybe calling a halt would've made Ernie feel lousier and even more foolish for being the object of this nuttiness. One of the immersion team was an ex-Unitarian minister who'd studied anthropology at Santa Cruz, and the whole horrible rigamarole was his idea. He'd e-mailed instructions to everyone, only I don't have e-mail (or I wouldn't have been within a hundred miles of the whole business). Ernie, however, because nobody had warned him, either, struggled to get the hell out of his captors' grip. He may have thought they were going to drown him to save him from a drearier fate. But the defrocked minister, whose name is Thor, started saying, "It's good, Ernie, let it happen, just let it happen."

Ernie's depleted blue eyes—his whites as yellow as cheap mustard—found me standing back on shore. For an instant, he gaped at me, his bony visage tricked and sad and too well loved. "What the fuck's this, Frank? What's going on?" He said this to me, but to everyone else, too. "What the fuck're you assholes doing to me?" It was at this point that they immersed him in the cold water, cradling him like a man already dead. He howled, "Ooooooowwoooo. Goddamn it's cold!"

"It's good, Ernie," Thor droned in his ear. "Just let it happen to you. Go down into it. It's *g-o-o-d*." Ernie's mouth turned down like a cartoon character's. His shoulders went limp, his head lolled, his dismayed gaze found the sky. Once they had him immersed, they touched his face, his chest, his head, his hands, his legs, I guess his ass.

"I'm dying of goddamn cancer," Ernie suddenly cried out, as if his dignity had suddenly been refound. "Cut this shit out!"

I didn't take part. Though there was a moment just as they lowered poor Ernie into the Atlantic's damp grasp (nobody

stopped to think he might catch pneumonia) when he looked back
at me again on the beach, his eyes helpless and resigned but also
full of feeling, a moment when I realized they were doing for
Ernie all the living can do, and that it was stranger that I was on
the sideline and, worse yet, that Ernie knew it. You usually don't
think about these things until it's too late. Even so, I'd never let
anything like that happen to me, no matter how far gone I was
or how beneficial it might be for somebody else.

I mean, who let who down, for crap sake?" Bud Sloat says. "If
you can't win your own goddamn home state, and the Dow's
at ten forty-two, and your state's as dumb-ass as Tennessee, I'd
quit. I'd just fuckin' quit."

Bud's not talking in the hushed tones appropriate to the
dead-lying-inside-the-big-frosted-double-doors, but just jabbering
on noisily about whatever pops into his head. The election. The
economy. Bud's a trained attorney—Princeton and Harvard
Law—but owns a lamp company in Haddam, Sloat's Decors,
and has personally placed pricey one-of-a-kind designer lighting
creations in every CEO's house in town and made a ton of
money doing it. He's sixty, small, fattish and yellow-toothed, a
dandruffy, burnt-faced little pirate who wears drugstore half
glasses strung around his neck on a string. If he wasn't wearing
his Irish knock-about hat, you could see his strawberry-blond
toupé, which looks about as real on his cranium as a Rhode
Island Red. Bud is a hard-core Haddam townie and would
ordinarily be wearing regulation Haddam summer dress: khakis,

nubble-weave blue blazer, white Izod or else a pink Brooks' button-down with a stained regimental tie, canvas belt, deck shoes and a little gold lapel pin bearing the enigmatic letters YCDBSOYA, which Bud wants everybody to ask him about. But the day's chill and solemnity have driven him back to baggy green cords, the dumbbell saddle oxfords and an orange wool turtleneck under his London Fog, so he looks like he's headed to a late-season Princeton game. He only lacks a pennant.

Bud's a blue-dog Democrat (i.e., a Republican) even though he's yammering, trying to act betrayed by fellow Harvard-bore Gore, as if he voted for him. Bud, though, absolutely voted for Bush, and if I wasn't here, he'd admit right now that he feels damn good about it—"Oh, yaas, made the practical businessman's choice." Most of my Haddam acquaintances are Republicans, including Lloyd, even if they started out on the other side years back. None of them wants to talk about that with me.

"How's old Mr. Prostate, Franklin?" Bud's worked up an unserious glum-mouth frown, as if everybody knows prostate cancer's a big rib tickler and we need to lighten up about it. My Mayo procedure came to light (regrettably) during our men's "sharing session" on the cold beach with Ernie in October, just before he got dunked in the ocean for his own good. We all agreed to tell a candid story, and that was the only one I had, not wanting to share the one about my wife hitting the road with her dead husband. I know Bud wants to ask me how it feels to walk down the street with hot BBs in your gearbox, but doesn't have the nerve. (For the most part it's unnoticeable—except, of course, you never don't know it.)

"I'm all locked and loaded, Bud." I stand beside them at the bottom of the steps and give Bud a mirthless line-mouth smile of no tolerance, which re-informs him I don't like him. Haddam used to be full of schmoes like Bud Sloat, yipping little Princetonians who never missed New Year's Eve at the Princeton Club, showed up for every P-rade, smoker, ball game and fund-raiser, and wore their orange-and-black porkpie hats and tiger pajamas to bed. These guys are all into genealogy and Civil War history, and like to sit around quoting Mark Twain and General Patton, and arguing that a first-rate education as prelude to a life in retail was exactly what old Witherspoon had in mind back in 17-whatever. Bud's business card, in collegiate Old Gothic embossed with the Princeton crest and colors (I admit to admiring it), reads, *There's the Examined Life. And Then There's the Lamp Business.*

"Nothing's really happening inside now, Frank," Lloyd murmurs in his seasoned mourner's voice, cupping a smoke down by his coat pocket and letting a drag leak out his big nose. From where I stand, I can see right inside Lloyd's nostrils, where it's as dark as bituminous coal. Lloyd buried my son Ralph from out of this same house nineteen years ago, and we've always shared a sadness (something he's probably done with eight thousand people, many of whom he's also by now been called on to bury). Every time he sees me, Lloyd lays a great heavy mitt on my shoulder, lowers his bluish face near mine and in a Hollywood baritone says, "How're those kids, Frank?" As if Clarissa and Paul, my surviving children, had stayed eternally five and seven in the same way Ralph *is* eternally nine. Lloyd's as big, tall, sweet and bulky as Bud is fat, weasly and lewd—a great, potatoschnozzed, coat hanger–shouldered galoot who years ago played defensive end for the Scarlet Knights, has soulful mahogany eyes deep-set in bony blue-shaded sockets and always smells like a cigarette. It's as if Lloyd became an undertaker because one day he gazed in a mirror and noticed he looked like one. I'd be happy to be buried by Lloyd if I felt okay about being buried—which I don't. "We put Ernie in a viewing room for an hour, Frank, just in case, but we need to get him along now. You know. Not that he'd care." Lloyd nods professionally and looks down at his wide black shoe toes. A burning Old Spice cloud mingled with tobacco aroma issues from somewhere in the middle of Lloyd. I didn't intend to *view* Ernie, or even the box he's going out in.

From the side of the building, the headlights of a long black Ford Expedition glow out through the weather's gloom, ready to transfer Ernie to the boneyard, where a grave's probably already opened. Lloyd always uses SUVs for unattended interments. Without pageantry or a hushed ruffle, life's last performance becomes as matter-of-fact as returning books to the library.

"Do you know what the death woman said?" Bud Sloat's round pink face is tipped to the side, as though he's hearing music, his shrewd retailer's eyes hooded to convey self-importance.

"What woman? What's a death woman?" I say.

Lloyd exhales a disapproving grunt, shifts back in his under-taker brogans. Squeaky, squeaky.

"Well, you know, Ernie agreed to let this psychologist woman from someplace out in Oregon be present when he died. *Actually* died." Bud keeps his face cocked, as if he's telling an off-color joke. "She wanted to ask him things right up to the last second, okay? And then say his name for ten minutes to see if she could detect any efforts of Ernie wanting to come back to life." Bud frowns, then grins—his thin, purple and extremely un-kissable lips parted in distaste, indicating Ernie was indisputably not our sort (Old Nassau, etc.) and here's final proof. "Great idea, huh? Wouldn't you say?" Bud blinks, as if it's too astonishing for words.

"I guess I'd have to think about that," I say. Though not for long. This is news I don't need to hear. Though, of course, it's exactly what people who stand outside funeral homes while the body's inside cooling always yak about. Now it can be told: Who he fucked, aren't we glad we're smarter, where'd the money go, isn't it a credit to us he's in there and we're out here.

Bud wheezes a little laughlike noise down in his throat. "You need to hear what she said, though. This Professor Novadradski. Naturally it'd be a Ruskie."

I think a moment about Ernie mugging his "Rooshan" accent and pounding the table at the Manasquan Bar years and years behind us now, when Russian meant something. "*Nyet, nyet, nyet,*" he'd growled and shouted that night about some crazy thing, took off one of his loafers and pounded it like Khrushchev, sweated and drank vodka like a Cossack. We all laughed till we cried.

"What she said was—and I got this from Thor Blainer" (the defrocked Unitarian minister). "He said the male nurse out at Delaware-Vue came in and gave Ernie the big shot because he'd been having a pretty rough time there for a day or so. Just walked in and did the deed. And in about three minutes, Ernie quit breathing, without ever saying anything. Then this Russian woman—right down in his face—starts saying his name over and over. 'Er-nie, Er-nie. Vat're you tinking? How dus you feel? Dus you see some colors? Vich vunz? Are you colt? Dus you hear dis voice?' She said it, of course, in a soothing way, so she wouldn't scare him out of coming back if he wanted to."

Lloyd's heard enough and heads off around the side of the building to check on the Expedition, its headlights still shining into the mist. Some sound audible only to undertakers has reached his ears, alerting him that a new matter needs his expertise. He ambles away, hands down in his topcoat pockets, leaning forward like he's curious about something. Lloyd's heard these stories a jillion times: corpses suddenly sitting up on the draining table; fingers clutching out for a last touch before the fluid gurgles in; bodies inexplicably rearranged in the casket, as if the occupant had been capering about when the lights were out. The human species isn't supposed to go down willingly. Lloyd knows this better than Kierkegaard.

"Okay, Lawrence," I hear Lloyd say from around the side. "Let's get 'er going now."

A tall young black man dressed in a shiny black suit, white shirt and skinny tie, and bundled into a bulky green-and-silver Eagles parka with a screaming eagle over the left breast, emerges from the porte-cochère beside the building. He's flashing a big knowing grin, as if something supposed to be serious—but not really—has gone on inside. He stops and shares whatever it is with Lloyd, who's facing down, listening, but who then just shakes his head in small-scale amazement. I know this young man. He is Lawrence "Scooter" Lewis, surviving son of the deceased Everick Lewis, and nephew of the now also deceased Wardell, enterprising brothers who made buckets of dough in the early nineties gentrifying beaten-up Negro housing in the Wallace Hill section of town and selling it to newcomer white Yuppies. I sold them two houses on Clio Street myself. Lawrence, I happen to know, went to Bucknell on a track scholarship but didn't last, then entered the Army Airborne and came home to find his niche in town. It's not an unusual narrative, even in Haddam. Scooter, who's younger-looking than his years, gives me a sweet smile and a small wave of unexpected recognition across the lawn, then turns and walks back toward his waiting Expedition before he's seen that I've waved back.

"Now hear me out, Frank." Bud's short upper lip begins to curl into a sneer. I'm not going to be glad to have heard this story, whatever it is. I hope Ernie has had the good grace in death to be still and not make a fool of himself. "The second this Ruskie gal quits saying 'Er-nie, Er-nie,' she puts her ear down close to him, where she can hear the slightest sound. And when the room's quiet, she hears—she swears—what sounds like a voice. But it's coming from Ernie's *stomach*!" Bud flashes another astonished smile, which wipes away his sneer. "I swear to God, Frank. *She* swears the voice was saying 'I'm here. I'm still here.' Out of his *goddamn* stomach." Bud looks exactly like the old-time actor Percy Helton, round, raspy-voiced, craven and mean, his fishy eyes saucered in mock horror that is actually gleeful. "Doesn't that beat the shit out of everything you ever heard?"

Bud, for some reason, opens his mouth as if a sound was meant to emerge, but none does, so that (having already looked in Lloyd's nose) I now have to see his short, thick, mealy, café au lait–colored tongue, broad across as Maryland, and, I'm sure, exuding vapors I don't want to get close to. Men. Sometimes the world is way too full of them. What I'd give this second for a woman's ministering smell and touch. Men can be the worst companions in the world. Dogs are better.

"She also said he was alive in a sexual sense. What do you think about that?" Bud blinks his sulfurous little peepers while fingering his half-glasses-on-a-string outside his black overcoat.

"Death's like turning off the TV, Bud. Sometimes a little light stays on in the middle. It's not worth wondering about. It's like where does the Internet live? Or can hermits have guests?"

"That's bullshit," Bud snarls.

"You probably hear more bullshit than I do, Bud." I smile another mirthless, unwelcoming smile.

Snow of the thin, stinging variety has begun to skitter before the burly November wind, turning the St. Augustine greener and crunchy. Sharp bits nick my ears, catch in my eyelids, sprinkle the jaunty-angled top of Bud's tweed hat. Contrary to expectation, I wish I was inside, standing vigil beside Ernie in his box, and not out here. I remember a night years past when a young, lean but no less an asshole Buddy Sloat—still practicing divorce law and before the unexamined life of lamps caught his fancy—started a row over, of all things, whether a deaf man who rapes a deaf woman deserves a deaf jury. Bud's view was he didn't. The other guy, an otolaryngologist named Pete McConnicky, a member of the Divorced Men's Club, thought the whole thing was a joke and kept looking around the bar for someone to agree with him and ease the pressure Bud felt about needing to be right about everything. Finally, McConnicky just smacked Bud in the mouth and left, which made everybody applaud. For a while, we all referred to Bud as "Slugger Sloat," and laughed behind his back. It'd be satisfying now to hit Bud in the mouth and send him back to the lamp store crying.

Bud, however, doesn't want to talk to me anymore. He watches the Black-Mariah Expedition creep out from the porte-cochère, wipers flapping crusts of new snow, big headlight globes cutting the flurry, gray exhaust thickening in the cold. Ernie McAuliffe's dark casket is in the windowed, curtained luggage-compartment, as lonely and uncelebrated as death itself—just the way Ernie wanted it, no matter how his belly ached to disagree. Scooter Lewis sits high in the driver's seat, shining face solemn in self-conscious caution. Lloyd watches from the grass beside the driveway. He probably has another of these occasions in half an hour. The funeral business is not so different from running a restaurant.

Unexpectedly, though, before Scooter can navigate the big Expedition out onto the street and turn up toward Constitution and the cemetery, a squad of Battle of Haddam re-enactors (Continentals) comes higgledy-piggledy, hot-footing it around the corner at the bottom end of Willow Street. These "patriots" are running, muskets in hand, heavy-gaited, their homespun socks ragged down to the ankles, shirttails flapping, beating a hasty retreat, or so it seems, from a smaller but crisply organized company of red-coated British Grenadiers hurrying around the same corner in a stiff little formation, their muskets at order arms, bayonets glinting, black regimental belts and boots, crimson tunics and high furry hats catching what muted light there is. They present an impressive aspect. The Continentals have been whooping and shouting warnings and orders on the run. "Get to the cemetery and deploy." One's waving an arm. "Don't fire till you see the whites of your eyes." From the funeral home lawn, I see this man is an Asian and small and rounded in his homespuns, though his command voice has real authority.

The Redcoats, once onto the corner, very smartly form two lines of five, crosswise of the street, five kneeling, five standing behind. A tall, skeletal officer hurries up beside them and without any buildup barks an Englishy-sounding command, raises a bulky cutlass into the New Jersey air. The Grenadiers shoulder their weapons, cock their hammers, aim down their barrels and—right in the middle of Willow Street, in the cold misting snow, as it must've been back in 1780—cut loose up the street at the Americans, who're just in front of Mangum & Gayden's (in time to be shot) and blocking Scooter Lewis's path in his Expedition.

The English musketry produces a loud, unserious cracking sound and gives out a preposterous amount of white smoke from barrel and breech. The Continentals, swarming past the funeral home, turn as the volley goes off, and from various positions—kneeling, standing, crouching, lying on the yellow-striped asphalt—fire back with similar unserious cracks and smoke expenditures. And right away, two Brits go right over as stiff as duckpins. Three Continentals also get it—one who's taken cover behind the hearse's fender, with Ernie in the back. The Americans make a much more anguished spectacle out of dying than the English, who seem to know better how to expire. (It's a strange sight, I'll admit.) The remaining Grenadiers calmly begin to reload, using ramrods and flinting devices, while the Continentals—forefathers to guerrillas and terrorists the world over—just turn and begin hightailing it again, whooping and hoo-hawing up to Constitution, where they clamber around the corner and are gone. It hasn't taken two minutes to fight the Battle of Willow Street.

Lloyd Mangum, Bud Sloat and I, with Scooter behind the wheel of his hearse, have simply stood in the wet grass and borne silent witness. No humans have emerged from neighbor houses to inquire what's what. Musket smoke drifts sideways in the snowy, foggy Willow Street atmosphere and engulfs for an instant my Suburban, parked on the other side. The sound of the Continentals, shouting orders and yahooing, echoes through the yards and silent sycamores. Other muskets discharge streets away, other manly shouts are audible above the muffled sound of campaign snares and a bugle. It is almost stirring, though I'm not in the mood. Ernie, once a combatant himself, would've gotten a charge out of it. He'd have wondered, as I do, if any of the soldiers were girls.

The British—minus two—have now re-formed as a moving square and begun marching back around the corner onto Green Street. The three "dead" Continentals have recovered life and begun strolling back down Willow, muskets on their shoulders, barrel ends forward, looking to join up with their enemies, who're now waiting, dusting off their jodhpurs. A clattering blue New

Jersey Waste truck lumbers around the corner. Two teenage black boys cling outside to the hold-on bars, making wagon-master noises to signal the stops. It's "pickup Tuesday." Oversized green plastic cans sit at the end of each driveway, beside red recycling tubs. Details I haven't noticed.

The black kids on the garbage truck say something sassy to the Continentals that makes the boys crack up and swing outward on their handgrips like amazing acrobats. Neither of them is fazed when one irregular points a musket at them and simulates a volley, though it makes the soldiers laugh as they disappear around the corner.

"You know what Ernie's putting on his gravestone?" Lloyd's come to stand beside me, Old Spice gunk a halo around him. He has a wheeze deep down in his chest, and the coarse black follicles around the helix of his left ear are the same as in his nose. Lloyd is a man not much made in America now, though once there were plenty: men without preconditions or sharp angles the world has to contend with, men who go to work, entertain important, unsensational duties, get home on time, mix a hefty brown drink after six, enjoy the company of the Mrs. till ten, catch the early news, then trudge off to bed and blissful sleep. I don't usually like being around men my age—since they always make me feel old—but Lloyd's the exception. I like him immensely, with his somber, pensive, throwback visage of times and shaving lotions of yore. He is good value—earnest, sympa-thetic, solid to the bone and not overcomplicated—just the way you'd hope your undertaker would be. Tom Benivalle, in his secret best sense of himself, is Lloyd, which is what I found likable about him. He's aware of who he pretends to be. Though Benivalle's the modern version, with angles and twitchy cell-phone impatience that things might not turn out right. All of it in an Italian pasta box.

"What's that?" I say to Lloyd about Ernie's gravestone. Bud has wandered up the funeral home steps and is just entering the front door. Snow's falling harder now, though it won't last. My Philadelphia early-bird news channel didn't even mention snow when I woke at six.

"He's putting *He suffered fools cheerfully.*" Lloyd's pale blue lantern-jaw face rearranges itself from somber to happy.

I look at Lloyd again but, due to the difference in our heights, am forced—again—to look right up his hairy spelunkle of a left nostril. "That's great."

Scooter Lewis, in the Expedition, has let the New Jersey Waste truck rumble past and begins negotiating a respectful turn onto Willow. He has another serious game face on. No winks or smiles or eye rolls. The garbage truck boys stare back at the hearse mistrustfully.

"Ernie'd have liked having a battle in the middle of his funeral, don't you think, Frank? An un-funeral." Ernie liked to put *un* in front of words to make fun of them. Un-drunk. Un-vacation. Un-rich. "It was at a time when I was still un-rich." When he said it, we all said it. Un-fuck. Un-Jersey.

"I'm surprised everyone doesn't ask for a battle," I say. "Or at least a skirmish." I've never discussed "arrangements" with Lloyd, but perhaps I should, since I have a deadly disease.

"I wouldn't stay in business long if they did." Lloyd exhales a breath he seems to have been holding in for some time. Lloyd has seen Ernie in the last hour, dead as a posthole digger, but seems to be none the worse for it.

"What business would you be in, Lloyd, if you weren't in the dead-person business?"

"Oh, lord." He's watching the Expedition bearing our friend come to a stop at Constitution, red blinker flashing a left turn. Scooter, in the driver's seat, cranes his neck both directions, then eases out and silently disappears toward the cemetery. Lloyd is satisfied. "I've sure thought about it, Frank. Hazeltine"—Lloyd's well-upholstered wife, named for God only knows what tribe of abject Pennsylvania Kallikaks—"would like me to sell it out. To some chain. Quit livin' in a funeral home. Her family are all potato farmers in PA. They don't get this here. Kids're in Nevada."

One of Lloyd's three is my son Paul's age—twenty-seven—and, unlike my son, who has a career in the greeting-card industry, is a computer wizard who started his own mail-order business selling office furniture made from recycled organic food products and now owns six vintage Porsches and an airplane.

Lloyd frowns at the thought of Pennsylvania potatoes and retirement. "But I don't know."

"Is it the smell of the embalming fluid or the sob of the crowd, you think, Lloyd?" Lloyd doesn't answer, though he has a good sense of humor and I know is letting these words silently amuse him. It is his gift. There's no use having a somber day cloud everything.

"So what's the plan for Thanksgiving, Frank? The family?

The works?" Lloyd's oblivious to what my "family" entails, except "those two kids." I've, after all, been gone eight years. Lloyd's likely picturing his own brood: Hazeltine, Hedrick, Lloyd, Jr., and Kitty—the funeral-directing Mangums of Haddam. "You're living where right now?" (As if I was a Bedouin.)

"Sea-Clift, Lloyd." I smile to let him know it's a positive change and he's asked me about it before. "Over on the Shore."

"Yep, I get it. That's nice. Real nice, over there."

We both turn to a storm door closing, a cough, a footfall. Bud's coming down the steps, walking a little gimpy, as if he's worried about slipping. The snow's sticking but no longer falling.

"Looks like you got some more business in there, Lloyd. The Van Tuyll girl. And who's that *old* party?" Bud resettles his dick under his London Fog, which is why he was walking bowlegged. He went in for a piss, which is what I'd like to do, but not in there.

"Harvey Effing's mother," Lloyd says reluctantly. "She was ninety-four."

"Oh my God," Bud says. He's been nosing around the other viewing rooms after his leak and without even taking off his Irish hat, having a whiff of different deaths. It's made him giddy. " 'Paging Mr. Effing. Call for Mr. Effing. Effing party of two.' We used to play that on Harvey up at the Princeton Club." Bud the clubman is pleased by this memory. He's done with the matter of noises from Ernie's innards and their possible cosmic significance. We're just three men out on the snowy front walk again, waiting for permission to disengage. To remain longer threatens divulgences, confidences, the connection of dots in no need of connecting. The job description for *mourner* is simply to stay on message.

I'm, however, hungry as a leopard and realize I'm standing with my mouth partway open in anticipation of food, just the way a leopard would. Having to piss a lot makes me not drink much, which makes me forget to eat. Though it's also because I have no more words I want to speak.

"How's the realty business, Frank?" Bud says insincerely.

"It's great, Bud. How's lamps?" I close my yap and try to smile.

"Couldn't be brighter. But let me ask you something, Frank." Bud pushes his little cold hands officiously down in his coat pockets and spaces his saddle oxfords wider apart and sways back like a racetrack tout.

The grassy ground is already turning bare again as the snow vanishes. It could easily begin to rain. I'm not sure I don't detect the pre-auditory rumble of thunder. "I hope it's simple, Bud." I'm not in the mood for complexity. Or candor. Or honesty. Or anything, including jokes.

"It's something I started asking people when I'm selling them a lamp, you know?" Bud beetles his brow in a look appropriate to philosophical inquiry.

I cast a wary eye Lloyd's way. He's looking at his brogans again, jeweled with dampness. I'm sure he's already taken this quiz.

"What've you learned in the realty business, Frank? In how many years now?"

"I don't remember."

"Pretty long, though. Twenty years?"

"No. Or yes. I don't remember."

Bud sniffs back through his little ruby-veined nose, then wags his shoulders like a boxer. "A while, though."

"I thought you liked the unexamined life, Bud."

"For selling lamps," Bud snaps. "I was at Princeton, Frank, with Poindexter and that crowd. Empirical all the way. I had a scholarship over to Oxford but went on and attended Harvard Law. It was the sixties."

"I never believe people, Bud."

"Well, you can sure as shit believe that."

Bud's translucent eyelids snap like a crow's. He's misunderstood me. He thinks I've deprecated his academic accomplishment, about which I couldn't care less.

"That's my answer to your question, Bud. How could I not know you went to Princeton? You probably haven't told me more than four hundred times. I'm sure Harvey Effing's mother knows you went to Princeton. You probably reminded her when you were in there."

"Your answer is *what*?" Bud says.

"My answer is, I tend not to believe people."

"About what?"

Lloyd groans down in his tussive chest. All day, death, and now questions.

"About anything. It lets people act freely. I realized it one day. A guy told me he was driving back to his motel for his checkbook then coming right back to where we'd been looking at a condo over in Seaside Park. He was going to write me a check for twenty-five thousand on the spot. I knew he exactly intended to. And I was going to stand there and wait till he came back. But I realized, though, that I didn't believe a fucking thing he said. I just pretended to, to make him feel good. That's what I've learned. It's a big relief."

"Did the guy come back," Lloyd asks.

"He did, and I sold him the condo."

Bud's livery lips wrinkle in distaste meant to signify concern. "You've gotten deep since your prostate flare-up."

"My prostate didn't *flare up*, you asshole. It had cancer. I believe that, though. If you trust people unnecessarily, it incurs an obligation on everybody. Suspending judgment's a lot easier. Maybe you can do that with lamps."

"Makes sense," Lloyd says quietly. "I probably feel the same way." He lowers his big funereal brow at Bud as a warning.

"Whatever." Bud makes a display of looking around the empty yard, as if Harvey Effing's mother was calling him. The driveway's empty. Water's puddling from the melted snow. The postman, in his blue government sweater and blue twill pants, is just traversing the lawn from next door in some wiggly black galoshes he hasn't bothered to snap. He radiates a wide, welcoming postal-carrier got-something-for-you smile and hands Lloyd a stack of letters bound with a red rubber band.

"That's great," Lloyd grunts, and smiles but doesn't peek at his letters. Surely some are heart-warming thank-yous for all the above-and-beyond kindness by the M&G staff when Uncle Beppo was "taken," and for the extra time needed so a long-estranged brother could arrive from Quito, especially since Uncle B. wasn't discovered in his apartment until some time had passed. I wonder what Lloyd's answer was to the what-have-you-learned question.

"*Whatever*'s about it," I say to Bud, who's still gooning around the yard at nothing. I believe I detect a ghostly Parkinson's tremor in Bud's chin, something he may not know about himself. His pudding chin is slightly oscillating, though it may be because I yelled at him and made him nervous. "I want you to understand, Bud. When I didn't believe the guy'd come back, it wasn't that I *dis*believed him. I just decline to make people have to bear extra responsibility for their own insecure intentions. Having to be believed is too big a burden. I thought you studied philosophy. It isn't so hard."

"Okay, that's fine." Bud smiles faintly and pats me softly on the front of my barracuda jacket, as if I was about to start throwing punches and needed calming.

"Fuck you, Bud."

"Yeah, yeah. Okay. That's great. Fuck me." Bud fattens his bunchy cheeks and smirks. The funeral contingent has now lost its funerary decorum. I'm, of course, largely to blame.

"Better get going." Lloyd's stuffing his mail into his overcoat pocket.

"Time to," Bud says. He's staring straight at Lloyd's chest, so as not to have to face me. "Hope you feel better, Frank."

"I feel great, Bud. I hope *you* feel better. You don't look so good."

"Chasing a cold," Bud says, and commences walking in his gimpy gait across the damp lawn, heading down Willow, back toward Seminary and the unreflective lamp business. It's why I hate men my age. We all emanate a sense of youth lost and tragedy-on-the-horizon. It's impossible not to feel sorry for our every little setback.

"Those kids coming to visit, are they?" Lloyd's happy to be upbeat.

"They sure are, Lloyd." We're watching Bud cross Willow, stamping grass and snow-melt off his oxfords, clutching his coat collar up around his neck. He doesn't look back, though he thinks we're talking about him.

"You can't enter the same stream twice, can you, Frank?" Lloyd says.

I look squarely at Lloyd, as if by gazing on him I'll come to know what he means, since I don't have the vaguest idea, though I'm certain it has something to do with the life lessons we both know: takes all kinds; for every day, turn, turn, turn; life'd be dull if we were all the same. "Small blessings," I say solemnly.

"Thanks for showing up. We needed some bodies." This is not a pun to Lloyd. He is a born literalist and couldn't survive otherwise.

"It was a good thing," I lie, and think a thought about Ernie's epitaph and how smart a cookie he was to know what to say at the end. We should all be that smart, all heed the lesson.

Surprisingly—though probably *not* that surprisingly—the inside of my Suburban when I climb in is gaseous with stinging, whanging anti-Permanent Period ethers that make me have to run the windows down to get a usable breath. Conceivably it's low blood sugar from being starved, which makes me clench my jaw. When you have cancer in your nether part, *plus* a bolus of radiant heavy metal—most of which has spent its payload by now, though it's my keepsake forever—your systems don't run on autopilot like they used to. Everything begs for suspicious notice— a headache, loose bowels, erectile virtuosity or its opposite, blood-shot eyes, extra fingernail growth. Dr. Psimos, my Mayo surgeon, explained all this. Though once my procedure was over, he said, nothing on a daily basis would be caused *per se* by my condition, unless I went prospecting for uranium, in which case my needle would point out the mother lode up my butt.

"It'll be in your mind, Frank, but that's about it," Psimos said, leaning back, self-satisfied in his doctor chair, like a forty-year-old labcoated Walter Slezak. His tiny Mayo seventh-floor pale-green office walls were full of diplomas—Yale, the Sorbonne, Heidelberg, Cornell, plus one designating him a graduate of the Suzuki Method of pianism. Those hirsute sausagey digits, capable of injecting hot needles into tender zones, also contained "The Flight of the Bumblebee" in their muscle memory.

It was our presurgical chat, the entire duration of which he sat teasing a bad backlash out of a tiny silver fly reel, using those same meaty fingers, assisted by a surgical clamp and some magnifying spectacles. Out his little window, the entire Mayo skyline— the bland tan hospital edifices, smokestacks, helipads, radar dishes, antennae, winking red beacons, everything but anti-aircraft batteries and ack-acks—projected the reassuring solidity of a health-care Pentagon to wayward pilgrim patients like me and the King of Jordan.

I didn't know what to say back. I hadn't had "a procedure" since once in the Marine Corps on my ailing pancreas, which got me out of Vietnam. I knew what was going to happen—the BBs, etc.—and figured the biopsy had already been worse. I wasn't scared till I found out I shouldn't be. "Most things that happen to me anymore happen in my mind," I said pathetically. My knees were shaking. I had on red madras Bermudas and a *Travel Is a Fool's Paradise* tee-shirt to try to look casual. I'm sure he knew what was happening.

It was a sunny, humid Minnesota Friday, last August. I'd watched the Olympic 4x100 relay that morning at the Travelodge. "Procedures," it seems, only take place on Mondays. But terrifying doctor chats are all slated for Fridays, to ensure that the maximum stomach-churning, molar-crunching jimjams will fill up your weekend.

"I'm just an ole surgeon around here, Frank." Psimos held his antique reel away from his jowly, mustachioed Walterish face and frowned at it through his magnifiers. "They don't pay me millions to think, just cut 'n paste stuff. I'll fix you up Monday so you're back firing. But I can't help what goes on in the brain department. That's over on West Eleven, across the street." He gave his heavy Greek brows a couple of insolent flicks.

"I'm looking forward to it," I said idiotically, my asshole as hard as a peach pit.

"I bet you are." He smiled. "I bet you really are."

And that was that.

*A*ll this woolly, stinging, air-sucking breathlessness inhabiting my Suburban is about nothing but death, of course—big-D *and* little-d. The Permanent Period is specifically commissioned to make you quit worrying about your own existence and how everything devolves on your *self* (most things aren't about "you" anyway, but about other people) and get you busy doin' and bein'—the Greek ideal. Psimos, I bet, practices it to perfection, on the links, at the streamside, in the operating theater, at the Suzuki and over lamb patties on the Weber. Surgeons are past masters at achieving connectedness with *the great other* by making themselves less visible *to* themselves. Mike Mahoney would love them.

Still, too much death can happen to you before you know it, and has to be staved off like a bad genie and stuffed back in its bottle.

*I*motor slowly past the trudging, bescroffled, pre-Parkinsonian Bud Sloat, just crossing Willow in the mist, head down in his Irish topper and sad toupé, heading toward the back lot of the CVS and Seminary Street, where his lamporium sits next door to the Coldwell Banker. I have a thought to shove open the passenger door and haul him in out of the rain, put a better end to things between us. He's possibly as death-daunted as I am (even assholes get the willies). A moment of unfelt fellowship might be just the ticket to save us from a bad afternoon. But Bud's intent on missing the puddles and saving his saddle oxfords, his hands down in his topcoat pockets, and in any case he's the sort of jerk who thinks every unrecognized vehicle contains someone inferior and worthy of disdain. I couldn't stand the look on his face. In any case, I have nothing I could even lie about to make him feel better.

Though Bud's question about the real estate business has set off belated silent alarms, and I feel a sudden cringe up near my diaphragm, brought on by the thought that real estate *might be my niche* the way undertaking's Lloyd's and Bud's is lamps. A strangled voice within me croaks, Nooo, nooo-no-no, no. I should know that voice, since I've heard it before—and recently.

Tell a dream, lose a reader, the master said (I do my best to forget mine). But you can't un-know what you know, as attractive as that might be.

In two consecutive weeks now, I've twice dreamed that I wake up in the middle of my prostate procedure just as the BBs—which in the dream are actually hot—go rolling down a lighted slot into my butt, a slot that looks like a pinball-machine gutter that Psimos, dressed in tails, has moved into the OR. In another one, I'm shooting baskets in a smelly old wire-windowed gym and I simply can't miss—except the score on the big black-and-white scoreboard doesn't change from 0–0. In a third, I somehow know jujitsu and am boisterously throwing little brown men around in a room full of mattresses. In another, I keep walking into a CVS like the one on Seminary, asking the pharmacist for a refill of my placebos. And in still another, I wake up and realize

I'm forty-five, and wonder how I managed to fritter so much of my life away. And there are others.

Life-lived-over-again dreams, these are—no question; and the little *no, no, no* anti-Permanent Period voice, an alarm bespeaking a sharp downturn in outlook, for which I have God's own plenty of excuses these days. When you start looking for reasons for why you feel bad, you need to stand back from the closet door.

However, one of the pure benefits of the Permanent Period— when you're as nose-down and invisible to yourself as an actualized unchangeable non-becomer, as snugged into life as a planning-board member—is that you realize you can't completely fuck everything up anymore, since so much of your life is on the books already. You've survived it. Cancer itself doesn't really make you fear the future and what might happen, it actually makes you (at least it's made me) not as worried as you were before you had it. It might make you concerned about lousing up an individual day or wasting an afternoon (like this one), but not your whole life. I try to impart this hopeful view to oldsters who wander down to the Shore in their blue Chrysler New Yorkers to "look at houses," but then get squirrely about making a mistake, and end up scampering home to Ogdensburg and Lake Compounce, thinking that what I've told them is nothing but a sales pitch and I won't be around when the shit train pulls in and the house market bottoms out just as their adjustable mortgage starts to steeple (I certainly won't). But once I've explained that it's seashore property I'm showing them and God isn't making any more of it, and you can get your money out any day of the week, I just want to say: Hey! Look! Take the plunge. Live once. You're on the short end of this stick. He isn't making any more of *you*, either.

What I usually see, though, is nervous, smirking, irritable superiority (like Bud Sloat's) that's convinced there's something out there that *I* could never know about—or else I wouldn't be a know-nothing real estate agent—but that *they* goddamn well know all about. Most humankind doesn't want to give up thinking they can fuck up the whole works by taking the wrong step, by shoving the black checker over onto that wrong red square. It makes them feel powerful to believe they own something to be cautious about. These people make terrible clients and can waste weeks of your time. I've developed a radar for them. But in fairness to these reluctant home-seekers—their chins on their chests the way Bud's is today—and who're thinking more positively about having that aluminum siding installed instead of paying for a whole new place, or about buying that new pop-up camper or checking fares on Carnival Lines (however they can throw some money away, but not too much): There *are* legitimate downsides to the Permanent Period. Permanence can be scary. Even though it solves the problem of tiresome becoming, it can also erode optimism, render possibility small and remote, and make any of us feel that while we can't fuck up much of anything anymore, there really isn't much to fuck up because nothing matters a gnat's nuts; and that down deep inside we've finally become just an organism that for some reason can still make noise, but not much more than that.

This you need to save yourself from, or else the slide off the transom of life's pleasure boat becomes irresistible and probably a good idea.

3

Stopped at the red light at Franklin and Pleasant Valley, my Suburban interior musty-damp and my feet warming with the defroster on high, the outside day has turned gloomy. Wind gusts against the hanging traffic light, making it yaw and twist and sway. Rain sheets the street. My car thermometer says the outside temp's dropped to thirty-six, and lights have prickled on inside houses. Haddamites are getting indoors, holding hats to heads. Pilgrims in the Square are packing it in. It's 1:00 p.m.

Something to eat and somewhere to piss are now high priorities, and I turn down Pleasant Valley toward Haddam Doctors Hospital, which has become my best-choice solo-luncheon venue since I moved away—in spite of its being the sad setting of my son's final hours so long ago. It's odd, I'll admit, to eat lunch in a hospital. But it's no stranger than paying your light bill at the Grand Union, or buying your new septic tank from the burial-vault dealer. Form needn't always follow function. Plus, it's not strange at all if you can get a decent meal in the process.

Decades ago, when I arrived in Haddam, you could grab a first-rate cheese steak in a little chrome and glass, plastic-booth diner lined with framed sports glossies and presided over by muttering old townies who wouldn't speak to you because you were an outsider. And there was still a below-street-level, red-walled Italian joint serving manicotti and fresh bluefish, where they'd let you read your paper, fill you up, then get you out for cheap. Cops ate there, as did seminary profs, ancient librarians and the storied old HHS baseball coach who'd had a cup of coffee with the Red Sox once, and who'd sneak over in his blue-and-white uniform for a double vodka and a smoke before afternoon practice.

I loved it here then. The town had the ambling, impersonal, middling pleasantness of an old commercial traveler in no real hurry to get anywhere. All of which has gone. Now either you're forced into mega-expensive "dining" or to standing in a line behind hostile moms in designer sweats pushing strollers into the Garden of Eatin' Health Depot and who're fidgeting over whether the Roman ceviche contains fish on the endangered list or if the coffee's from a country on the Global Oppression Hot 100. By the time you get your food, you're pretty much ready to start a fistfight—plus, you're not hungry anymore.

At Haddam Doctors, by contrast, strangers are always welcome, parking's easy in the visitors lot and it's cafeteria-style, so no waiting. There's no soul-less plastic ware. Everything's spotless, tables cleaned antibacterially in record time. The long apple-green dining hall has an attractive commissary busy-ness bespeaking serious people with serious things in mind. And the food's cooked and served by big, smiling, no-nonsense, pillowy black women in pink rayon dresses, who can make a meat loaf so it's better cold than hot, and who always slip a little ham bone into the limas so you get back to your car with a feeling you've just had a human, not an institutional, experience. The cooks' husbands all eat there—always the sure sign.

At lunch, you often share your table with some elderly gentleman with a wife in for tests, or a worried young couple whose child's there for back straightening, or just some ordinary citizen like me grabbing a plate lunch before hitting it again. Restrained but understanding smiles are all that's ever shared. ("We've all got our woes, why blab 'em?") Nobody opens up or vents (you might complain to some poor soul worse off than you). White-smocked M.D.'s and crisp-capped nurses sit together by the windows, chatting while patient families eye them hopefully, wondering if *he*'s the one and if they could interrupt for just one question about Grampa Basil's EKG. Only they don't. Stately decorum reigns. Occasionally, there's an outburst of strange laughter, followed by a few Turkish words from the blue-trousered floor orderlies that break through the tinkle and plink of eating and surviving. Otherwise, all is as you'd want it. (Oddly, there's no such positive ambience at Mayo—only an earth-tone, ergonomically-designed food court where patients stare wanly at other patients and pick at their green Jell-O.)

Plus, in Haddam Doctors, if anyone gets his Swiss steak down the wrong pipe or swallows an ice cube or suffers a grand mal, there's plenty of help—Heimlich masters, wall-mounted defibrillators and Thorazine injections in all the nurses' pockets. Beginning with when Ralph was a patient and his mother and I lived in the hospital days and nights, the most untoward thing I've witnessed was a streaker, a banker I knew who'd suffered reversals in the S&L crisis and ended up in the psycho ward, from which he made a brief but spectacular break (eventually, he got on at another bank).

However, when I wheel in toward Visitor Lot A, just after one, I see that something not at all regular's afoot at the hospital. The big, usually glassed-in front windows of the cafeteria—inside which the doctors and nurses usually sit—are at this moment being ply-boarded over, with yellow crime-scene tape stretched across. Several uniformed Haddam police and detectives wearing badges on cords around their necks are standing out in the sorry weather, writing notes on pads, taking pictures and generally reconnoitering the scene. Glass from the empty windows is strewn out on the damp grass, and tan wall bricks and aluminum splinters and cottony insulation have been spewed as far as the visitors lot. Police and fire department vehicles with flashers flashing are nosed at all angles around the doctors' parking lot and the ER entrance, along with two panel trucks from network affiliates. A man and a woman with ATF stenciled on the backs of their windbreakers are conferring with a large man in a fireman's white hard hat and fireman's coat. Yellow-slickered police are carefully outlining bits of debris with spray paint, while others use surgical gloves and what look like forceps to tweeze evidence into plastic bags they drop into larger black garbage bags that other cops are holding.

Up the four storeys of the hospital, faces are at all the windows, peering down. Two policemen in black commando outfits and holding automatic weapons stand at the lip of the roof like prison guards, watching the proceedings below.

What's happened here, I don't know. It can't be good. That I do know.

Suddenly, a *clack-clack* on my passenger-side window scares me out of my pants. A round, inquisitive woman's face, with a blue plastic-covered cop hat pulled down to her eyebrows, hangs outside the glass, staring in at me. An oversized black flashlight barrel shows above the window frame, its hard metal rim touching the glass, its beam shining over my head. The face's mouth moves, says something I can't make out, then a hand with pudgy fingers makes a little circular roll-'er-down motion, which I instantly perform from my side, letting in a gust of cold.

"Hi," the woman says from outside. She smiles so as not to seem officially menacing. "How're we doing, sir?" Her question intends that I need to be doing fine and be eager to say so. Rain mist has dampened her shiny black hat bill and made her cheeks shiny.

"I'm great," I say. "What's happened here?"

"Can you state your business here for me today, sir?" She blinks. She's a thick, pie-faced woman who looks forty but is probably twenty-five. Her teeth are small and white, and her lips thin and unhabituated to smiling except in official ways. She's undoubtedly been a law enforcement major somewhere and had plenty of practice looking in car windows, though her aspect isn't alarming, only definite. I'm not doing anything illegal— seeking lunch. Though also wanting pretty seriously to take a leak.

"I just came for lunch." I smile as if I'd divulged a secret.

The policewoman's smooth face doesn't alter, just processes info. "This is a hospital, sir." She glances up at Haddam Doctors four-storey tan-brick facade as if to make sure she's right. On her yellow slicker a black name tag says *Bohmer* over a stamped-on black police badge. A microphone is Velcro'd to her left shoulder so she can talk and still hold a gun on you.

I know it's a hospital, ma'am, I'm tempted to say; my son died in it. Instead, I chirp, "I know it's a hospital, but the cafeteria's a super place for lunch."

Officer Bohmer's smile renounces a little of its definiteness and becomes amused and patronizing. She sees now that I'm one of *those* people, the ones who eat their lunch in the fucking hospital, who sit in libraries all day leafing through *Popular Mechanics*, World War II picture books and topless-native layouts in *National Geographic*s. The ones who don't fit. She's rousted my type. We're harmless when kept on a short leash.

"What happened inside there?" I ask again, and look toward the police goings-on, then back to Officer Bohmer, whose heifer eyes have fixed me again. Outside air is making my hands and cheeks cold. Her shoulder microphone crackles, but she doesn't attend to it.

"Tell me again, sir, what your business here is," she says in a buttoned-up way. She takes a peek through at the backseat, where I've got two Realty-Wise signs I'm taking to the office.

"I came for lunch. I've done it for years. The lunch is good. You should eat there."

"Where do you live, sir?" Staring at my signs.

"Sea-Clift. I used to live here, though."

Her eyes drift back to me. "You lived here in Haddam?"

"I sold real estate. I own my own company on the Shore. Realty-Wise."

"And how long have you lived over there?"

"Eight years. About."

"And you lived here before?"

"On Cleveland Street. And before that on Hoving Road."

"And could I just have a look at your driver's license?" Officer Bohmer is the picture of female resolve and patience. She glances up and over the hood of my Suburban, checking to see how quick her backup could arrive in case I produce a German Luger and not a billfold. "And your registration and proof of insurance."

I get about retrieving these documents—first from my wallet, then, under Officer Bohmer's interested eye, from the glove compartment, where a pistol would be if I had one.

She takes my documents in her pink digits, pinching the papers and getting them wet, looking up once to match my face to my picture. Then she hands them all back. More static crackles in her mike, a male voice says something that includes a number, and Officer Bohmer turns her chin to the little speaker and in a different, harder-edged voice snaps, "Negative on that. I'll maintain a twenty." The man's voice replies something unintelligible but also authoritative, and the transmission is over. "Thanks, that's great, Mr. Bascombe. Now I need you to turn 'er around and head on out again. Okay?"

"Can you tell me what happened over there?" I ask for the third time.

"Sir. A device detonated outside the cafeteria this morning."

A *device*. "What kind of device? Anybody hurt?" I say this to Officer Bohmer's raincoat belly.

"We're trying to find out what happened, sir."

In the blast area, I see police are huddling around something on the ground, and another uniformed officer is taking a photograph of it, the little digital camera held clumsily out in front of him.

Officer Bohmer's slick yellow raincoat front and imposing black flashlight barrel are all I can see from inside as she steps back from my window and with the flash makes a tiny sweeping movement to indicate what she'd like to see my car do. "Just turn 'er around right here," her police academy voice says again, "and take 'er right out the way you came."

A gas leak is what I'm thinking. Some pressurized container for hospital use only, that got too close to a pilot light. Yet something that requires the ATF?

My tires squeeze and scrape as I make the tight turn-around in the hospital drive—a Suburban doesn't change course easily. I take a look at the boarded cafeteria windows and the squads of police and firemen and hospital officials milling in the drizzle and the lights of their idling vehicles, the black-suited commandos standing roof guard just in case. The faces at the windows are all taking note of my car. "What's he doing?" "Read the license number." "Why are they letting him go?" "Who's to blame? Who's to blame? Who's to blame?"

Officer Bohmer is now gone from sight as I "take 'er right out." But another policeman in a yellow rain slicker and black cop's hat is up ahead, stopping cars as they turn in and dispatching them elsewhere.

"Any idea who did this?" I say to this new man as I idle past. He is an older officer I know, or once did, a big Polack with heavy brows, a pale, smooth face and mirthful eyes—Sgt. Klemak, a Gotham PD veteran, escaped to the suburbs. He once gave me an unjustified yellow-light summons that set me back seventy bucks, but wouldn't remember me now, which is just as well.

"We're doing our best out here, *sir*!" Sgt. Klemak shouts over the traffic and rain hiss. He seems to be having fun doing his job.

"Are you sure something exploded?" I'm speaking upward, rain needles pelting my nose and chin.

"You can go ahead and turn right, sir!" Officer Klemak says with a big smile.

"I hope you guys take care of yourselves."

"Oh, sure. Piece a cake. Just take 'er right around and have a splendid day. Get 'er home safely."

"That'd be nice," I say, then ease back out onto Pleasant Valley and put the hospital behind me.

I now have a fierce need to piss. Plus, violent crime, instead of dousing my appetite, has inflamed it to queasiness. I drive straight out 206 to the remodeled Foremost Farms Mike and I passed earlier. I park in front, hustle in for my leak (which I now do more than seems humanly possible), then find the cold case, pick out a cellophane-sealed beef 'n bean burrito, radiate it in the microwave, draw a diet Pepsi, pay the Pakistani girl in the purple sari, then hustle back to my car and consume all in three minutes with paper napkins spread over my lap and jacket front. The burrito's been *hecho a mano* by the Borden Company down

in Camden and is as hard as a cedar shingle, the interior as cold
and pale as mucilage, and of course tastes wonderful. Although
it's 180 degrees off my prostate-recovery, tumor-suppressing
Mayo diet of 20 percent animal product, 80 percent whole grains,
tofu and green tea, which only monks can survive on.

When I'm finished, I stuff my garbage in the can provided,
then climb back in and turn on the local FM station, in case
there's some news about the hospital incident. And indeed a
metallic backyard-radio-station sound opens up—WHAD, the
"Voice of Haddam," where I once recorded novels for the blind.
Static, static, static—the rain's a problem. ". . . in Trenton have
been dispatched . . ." *Static, static, static.* ". . . an average of ten
threatening . . . a month . . . been . . . no name pending . . ."
Crackle, snap, poppety-pop. ". . . all critical-care patients . . .
mercy . . . a search is under way . . . Chief Carnevale stated. . . .
credible . . ." *Static, static, static.* ". . . more on our regular . . ."
Ker-clunk . . . "Stran-gers-in-the-night,   dee-dah-dee-daaah-
dah . . ."

Little help. But still. Hard to contemplate—a medium-anxiety,
good-neighbor suburban care facility like Haddam Doctors,
where the whole staff's from Hopkins and Harvard (no one tops
in his class), all sporting eight handicaps, all divorced a time or
two, kids at Choate and Hotchkiss, everyone as risk-averse as
concert cellists (no one does serious surgery)—hard to contemplate
here being the target of a "device." Unless somebody wanted his
vasectomy reversed and couldn't, or somebody's tonsils grew back,
or a set of twins got handed off to the wrong parents. Though
these wrongs have tamer remedies than renting a U-Store-It,

stockpiling chemicals and brewing up mayhem. You'd just sue, like the rest of humanity, and let the insurance companies take the hit. That's what they're there for.

When I start up and defrost the windshield, it's suddenly 1:40. I'm due for my Sponsor visit on the affluent Haddam West Side at two.

Though as I wheel back out onto busy, rain-smacked 206 and head west, I recognize that while the willies I experienced after my funeral home visit certainly were due to a too-close brush with the Reaper (normal in all instances), they might also have been nothing more than the usual yellow caution flag, which signals that being marooned in your car on a dreary day in a cold town you once lived in, but don't now, can be chancy. Especially if the town is this one, and especially if you're in my state of repair. Activities may need to be curtailed.

I actually began experiencing adverse intimations about Haddam during my last years here, close to ten years ago (I always thought I loved it). And not that a realtor's view would ever be the standard one, since realtors both live life in a town yet also huckster that place's very spirit essence for whopper profits. We're always likely to be half-distracted from regular life—like a supreme court justice who resides in a place as anonymously as a postal employee but constantly processes everybody else's life in his teeming brain so he can know how to judge it. My life in Haddam always lacked the true resident's naïve, relief-seeking socked-in-ed-ness that makes everyday existence feel like a warm bath you relax into and never want to leave. Surveying property lines, memorizing setback restrictions, stepping off footprint limits and counting curb-cuts all work a stern warp into what might otherwise be limitless, shapeless, referenceless—and happily thoughtless—municipal life. Realtors share a basic industry with novelists, who make up importance from life-run-rampant just by choosing, changing and telling. Realtors make importance by selling, which is better-paying than the novelist's deal and probably not as hard to do well.

By 1991, the year before I left and the year my son Paul Bascombe graduated from HHS and headed off to Indiana to begin studies in Puppet Arts Management (he'd mastered ventriloquism, did a hundred zany voices, told jokes and had already staged several bizarre but sophisticated puppet shows for his classmates), by then Haddam—a town where I'd felt genuine residence and that'd been the *mise-en-scène* for my life's most solemn adult experiences—had entered a new, strange and discordant phase in its town annals.

In the first place, real estate went nuts, and realtors even nuttier. Expectations left all breathable atmosphere behind. Over-pricing, under-bidding, sticker shock, good-faith negotiation, price reduction, high-end flux were all banished from the vocab-ulary. Topping-price wars, cutthroat bidding, forced compliance, broken lease and realty shenanigans took their place. The grimmest, barely habitable shotgun houses in the previously marginal Negro neighborhoods became prime, then untouchable in an afternoon. Wallace Hill, where I sold my rental houses to Everick Lewis, was designated a Heritage Neighborhood, which guaranteed all the black folks had to leave because of taxes (many fled down south, though they'd been born in Haddam). Agents sold their own homes out from under their own families and moved spouses, dogs and kids to condos in Hightstown and Millstone. New college graduates passed up med and divinity school and buyers bought million-dollar houses from twenty-one-year-olds straight out of Princeton and Columbia with degrees in history and physics and who barely had their driver's licenses.

In '93, after I'd left, yearly price increases had hit 45 percent, there was no affordable housing anywhere and buyers were paying full boat for tear-downs and recyclables and in some instances were burning houses to the ground. Some Haddam companies (not Lauren-Schwindell) required out-of-town clients to submit their AmEx number and authorize thousand-dollar debits just to be shown a house. Though by Christmas, there was nothing to show anyway, not even a vacant lot.

The end came personally for me at the convergence of three completely different (and unusual) events. One Saturday afternoon I was at my desk, typing an offer sheet on a property situated on the rear grounds of the former seminary director's residence, down the street from where I myself once lived on Hoving. The building was nothing but a rotting, ruined beaverboard shack that had once been the Basque gardener's storage shed for toxic herbicides, caustic drain openers, banned termite and Asian beetle eradicators, and would've alerted the state's environmental police except in Haddam, no inspection's required. As I filled out the green blanks on my computer, occasionally staring longingly out the front window at traffic-choked Seminary

Street, I began—because of the property I was selling and the preposterous price it was commanding—to muse that a malign force seemed to be in full control of every bit of real property on the seaboard, and possibly farther away. Possibly everywhere.

This force, I began to understand, was holding property hostage and away from the very people who wanted and often badly needed it and, in any case, had a right to expect to own it. And this force, I realized, was the economy. And the practical effect of this force—on me, Frank Bascombe, age forty-five, of ordinary, unexalted and, up to then, realizable aspirations—was to render everything too goddamn expensive. So much so that selling even one more house in Haddam—and especially the gardener's toxic hovel, on whose site was planned a big-windowed, one-man live-in studio for a sculptor who mostly lived in Gotham and was willing to pay 500K—was going to be demoralizing as hell.

What I was thinking, of course, as cars edged thickly past the Lauren-Schwindell window and passengers stared warily in at me at my desk, knowing I was totaling figures that would give them a heart attack—what I was thinking was real estate heresy. I would get burned at the real estate stake by my agent colleagues (especially the twenty-one-year-olds) if they knew about it. What we were supposed to do if we had qualms—and surely some did—was douse them. On the spot. Take a deep breath, go wash your face, lease a new Z-car, buy a condo in Snowmass, learn to fly your own Beech Bonanza, maybe take instruction in violin making. But ship as much fresh money as possible to the Caymans, then spend the rest of the time putting your feet up on your desk and chortling about how work's for the other ranks.

Except everyone's entitled to some glimmering *sense of right* in his (or her) own heart. And part of that sense of right—for real estate agents anyway—involves not just what something *ought* to cost (here we're always wrong) but what something *can* cost in a world still usable by human beings. Every time I heard myself pronounce the asking price of anything on the market in Haddam, I'd begun to feel first a sick, emptied-out, semi-nauseated feeling, and then an impulse to break into maniac laughter right in a client's startled face as he sat across my desk in his pressed jeans, Tony Lamas and fitted polo shirt. And that growing sense of spiritual clamor meant to me that right was being violated, and that my sense of usefulness at being what I'd been being was exhausted. It was a surprise, but it was also a big relief. It was like the experience of the sportsman who's shot ducks in the marsh all his life but one day, standing up to his ass in freezing water, with the sky silvered and dark specks on the horizon beginning to take avian shape, realizes he's killed enough ducks for one lifetime.

The second way I knew I'd reached the end of my rope in Haddam was simpler, though more garish and immediately life-diverting.

During the summer of 1991—when the daffy elder Bush was still ruffling his own duck feathers in the aftermath of Desert Storm—a home sale, on tiny Quarry Street, opposite St. Leo the Great Catholic Church, culminated in a SWAT-team extraction when the owner-occupant refused to vacate the house he'd signed papers and already closed on. The man ran right out of the lawyer's office, back across neighbors' front lawns to his erstwhile family home, where he took a position in an attic dormer window and, using a varmint rifle, held off Haddam police, two hostage-negotiators and a priest from St. Leo's for thirty-six hours before giving in, being led defiantly out the door in front of the same neighbors and the new owners, then riding off in chains to the state hospital in Trenton.

No one was hurt. But the reason for the behavior was the seller's discovery that his house had appreciated 18 percent between offer-acceptance and the lawyers' closing, which made the thought of all that lost money and the smirking ridicule from the neighbors, who were holding on for another season, just too much to bear. For weeks afterward, tension and threat hung over the town. Two new police officers were added. Threat sensitivity courses were made mandatory in our office, and a "conflict resolution half point" was added to closing costs when a bank approved super balloon notes to first-time buyers purchasing from sellers with greater than ten years' longevity.

Nothing, however, prepared anyone for the outlandish worst. A trucking magnate of Lebanese extraction made a full-price offer on a rambling, walled monstrosity far out on Quaker Road, owned by the reclusive grandson of a south Jersey frozen-potpie magnate, who'd turned up his nose at the family business to become a competitive stamp collector. The house was a great weed-clogged Second Empire mishmash with a rotted roof, sagging floor joists, scaling paint, disintegrating masonry and cellar dampness due to being in the floodplain. It wasn't even a candidate to be torn down, since regulations prohibited replacement. When I took the realtors' cavalcade tour, I couldn't find one timber or sill that wasn't corrupted by something. Everybody who showed it presented it as uninhabitable. The land, we felt, was a write-off to some rich tree-hugger conservationist who'd turn it into "wetlands" and make himself feel virtuous.

The trucking magnate, however, wanted to come in with a big improvement budget, rebuild everything up to code, restore the house to mint condition, plus add a lot of exotic fantasy landscaping and even let tame animals roam the grounds for the grandkids.

But when he submitted his full-price bid, saw it accepted, put three-quarters down as earnest money, the hermetic owner, Mr. Windbourne, decided to take the house off the market for a rethink, then a week later listed it again with a 20 percent increase in asking and had five new full-price offers by noon of the first day—two of which he accepted. The trucking guy, Mr. Habbibi, who was known in the Paterson area as a patient man who didn't mind using muscle when it was needed, naturally protested all this double-dealing, though none of it was illegal. He drove out to the Windbourne house in an agitated state but still in hopes of bettering the new offers and resuscitating his deal. Windbourne—wan, gaunt and blinking from long hours in the dark staring at stamps—came to the front door and said that the fantasy landscaping and tame animals sounded to him more suited to towns like Dallas or Birmingham, not Haddam. He laughed at Habbibi and closed the door in his face. Habbibi then drove to a marine supply in Sayreville (this is the strangest part, because Habbibi didn't own a boat), bought two marine flare pistols and two flares, drove back to Quaker Road, confronted Windbourne at his door and offered him the deal they'd already agreed to, plus 20 percent. When Windbourne again laughed at him, informed him this was America and that Habbibi had "loser's remorse," Habbibi went back out to his car, got his flare pistols, stood out in the yard of what he'd hoped would be his dream oasis, shouted Windbourne's name and shot him when he answered the door a third time. After which, Habbibi got back in his car, turned on the radio and waited for the police to show up.

Haddam house prices dropped 8 percent in one day (though that lasted less than a week). Habbibi was also trucked off to the loony bin. Windbourne's relatives drove up from Vineland and completed the sale to one of the other buyers. Realtors started carrying concealed weapons and hiring bodyguards, and the realty board passed an advisory to raise commissions from 6 to 7 percent.

At about this time, I was experiencing the first airy intimations of the Permanent Period filtering through my nostrils like a sweet bouquet of new life promised. Things had also gotten to a put-up-or-leave stage with Sally Caldwell. Selling houses in Haddam had evolved to a point at which I couldn't recognize my personal motives for even doing it. And on the waft of that bouquet and by the simple force of puzzlement, I decided it was time to get out of town.

But before I left (it took me to the sultry days of that election summer to get my affairs untangled), I noticed something about Haddam. It was similar to how the stolid but studious Schmeling saw *something* about the mute, indefatigable, but reachable Louis—in my case, something maybe only a realtor could see. The town felt different to me—as a place. A place where, after all, I'd dwelled, whose sundry homes and mansions I'd visited, wandered through, admired, marveled at and sold, whose inhabitants I'd stood long beside, listened to and observed with interest and sympathy, whose streets I'd driven, taxes paid, elections heeded, rules followed, whose story I'd told and burnished for nearly half my life. All these engraved acts of residence I'd dutifully committed, with staying-on as my theme. Only I didn't like it anymore.

The devil is in the details, of course, even the details of our affections. We'd, by then, earned a new area code—cold, unmemorable 908 supplanting likable time-softened old 609. New blue laws had been set up to keep pleasure in check. Traffic was deranging—spending thirty minutes to go less than a mile made everyone reappraise the entire concept of mobility and of how important it could ever be to get anywhere. Seminary Street had become the preferred home-office address for every species of organization whose mission was to help groups who didn't know they comprised a group become one: the black twins consortium; support entities for people who'd lost all their body hair; the families of victims of school-yard bullying; the Life After Kappa Kappa Gamma Association. Boro government had turned all-female and become mean as vipers. Regulations and ordinances spewed out of the council chamber, and litigation was on everyone's lips. A new sign ordinance forbade FOR SALE signs on lawns, since they sowed seeds of anxiety and a fear of impermanence in citizens not yet moving out—this was rescinded. Empty storefronts were outlawed *per se* so that owners forced to sell had to *seem* to stay in business. An ordinance even required that Halloween be "positive"—no more ghosts or Satans, no more flaming bags of feces left on porches. Instead, kids went out dressed as EMS drivers, priests and librarians.

Meanwhile, new human waves were coming, commuting *into* Haddam instead of *out to* Gotham and Philly. A small homeless population sprouted up. Dental appointments averaged thirteen months' advance booking. And residents I'd meet on the street, citizens I'd known for a generation and sold homes to, now refused to meet my eyes, just set their gaze at my hairline and kept trudging, as if we'd all become the quirky, invisible "older" town fixtures we'd encountered when we ouselves had arrived decades ago.

Haddam, in these devil's details, stopped being a quiet and happy suburb, stopped being subordinate to any other place and became a *place to itself*, only without having a fixed municipal substance. It became a town of others, for others. You could say it lacked a soul, which would explain why somebody thinks it needs an interpretive center and why it seems like a good idea to celebrate a village past. The present is here, but you can't feel its weight in your hand.

Back in the days when I got into the realty business, we used to laugh about homogeneity: buying it, selling it, promoting it, eating it for breakfast, lunch and dinner. It seemed good—in the way that everyone in the state having the same color license plate was good (though now that's different, too). And since the benefits of fitting in were manifest and densely woven through,

homogenizing seemed like a sort of inverse pioneering. But by
1992, even homogeneity had gotten homogenized. Something
had hardened in Haddam, so that having a decent house on a
safe street, with like-minded neighbors and can't-miss equity
growth—a home as a natural extension of what was wanted from
life, a sort of minor-league Manifest Destiny—all that now
seemed to piss people off, instead of making them ecstatic (which
is how I expected people to feel when I sold them a house:
happy). The redemptive theme in the civic drama had been lost.
And realty itself—stage manager to that drama—had stopped
signaling our faith in the future, our determination not to give
in to dread, our blitheness in the face of life's epochal slowdown.

In short, as I stood out on Cleveland Street watching green-
suited Bekins men tote my blanketed belongings up the ramp
under matching green-leaf, sun-shot oaks and chestnuts just
showing the pastel stains of autumn 1992, I felt Haddam had
entered its period of era-lessness. It had become the emperor's
new suburb, a place where maybe someone might set a bomb
off just to attract its attention. The mystics would say it had lost
its crucial sense of East. Though east, to the very edge, was the
direction I was then taking.

The circumstances of my Sponsor visit this afternoon—in
Haddam, of all places—are not entirely the standard ones.
Normally, my Sponsoring activity is centered on the seaside
communities up Barnegat Neck, where I know practically no
one and typically can swing by someone's house or office, or

maybe make a meeting in a mall or a sub shop, not use up a whole afternoon and be back at my desk in an hour and change. But yesterday, due to other volunteers wanting off for Thanksgiving, I received a call wondering if I might be going to Haddam today, and if so, could I make a Sponsor stop. I've kept my name on the Haddam list since I'm regularly in and out of town, know relatively few people anymore, and because—as I've said—I know the town can leave people feeling dismal and friendless, even though every civic nook, cranny and nail hole is charming, well-rounded and defended, and as seemingly caring, congenial and immune to misery as a fairy-tale village in Switzerland.

Sally actually prompted my first Sponsor visits four years back. She'd grown depressed by her own work—a company that mini-bused terminally ill Jerseyites to see Broadway plays, provided dinner at Mama Leone's and a tee-shirt that said *Still Kickin' in NJ*, then bused them home. Constant company with the dying, staying upbeat all the time, sitting through *Fiddler on the Roof* and *Les Misérables*, then having to talk about it all for hours, finally proved a draw-down on her spirits after more than a decade. Plus, the dying complained ceaselessly about the service, the theater seats, the food, the acting, the weather, the suspension system on the bus—which caused employee turnover and inspired the ones who stayed to steal from the oldsters and treat them sarcastically, so that lawsuits seemed just around the corner.

In 1996, she sold the business and was at home in Sea-Clift for a summer with not enough to do. She read a story in the *Shore Plain Dealer*, our local weekly, that declared the average American to have 9.5 friends. Republicans, it said, typically had more than Democrats. This was easy to believe, since Republicans are genetically willing to trust the surface nature of *everything*, which is where most friendships thrive, whereas Democrats are forever getting mired in the meaning of every goddamn thing, suffering doubts, regretting their actions and growing angry, resentful and insistent, which is where friendships languish. The *Plain Dealer* said that though 9.5 might seem like plenty of friends, statistics lied, and that many functioning, genial, not terminally ill, incapacitated or drug-addicted people, in fact, had *no* friends. And quite a few of these friendless souls—which was the local hook—lived in Ocean County and were people you saw every day. This, the writer editorialized, was a helluva note in a boun-teous state like ours, and represented, in his view, an "epidemic" of friendlessness (which sounded extreme to me).

Some people over in Ocean County Human Services, in Toms River, apparently read the *Plain Dealer* story and decided to take the problem of friendlessness into their own hands, and in no time at all got an 877 "Sponsor Line" authorized that would get a person visited by another tolerant and feeling human not of their acquaintance within twenty-four hours of a call. This Sponsor-visitor would be somebody who'd been certified not to be a pedophile, a fetishist, a voyeur or a recent divorcée, and also not simply someone as lonely as the caller. The cost of a visit would be zilch, though there was a charities list on a Web site someplace, and contributions were anonymous.

Sally got wind of the Sponsor Line and called to inquire that very afternoon—it was in September—and went over for a screening interview and, probably because of her work with the dying, got right onto the Sponsors list. The Human Services people had figured out a digitized elimination system to ensure that the same Sponsor wouldn't visit the same caller more than once, *ever*. Callers themselves were screened by psych grad students and a profile was worked up using a series of five innocuous questions that ferreted out lurkers, stalkers, weenie wavers, bondage aficionados, self-published poets, etc.

The idea worked well right from the start and, in fact, still works great. Sally started going on one but sometimes three Sponsor visits a week, as far away as Long Branch and as close in as Seaside Heights. The idea pretty quickly caught on in other counties, including Delaware County, where Haddam is. A cross-referenced list of people like me who operate in a wider than ordinary geographical compass was compiled. And after signing up, I made Sponsor visits as far away as Cape May and Burlington—where I do some bank appraisals—or, as here in Haddam today, when I just happen to be in the neighborhood and have some time to kill. I originally thought I might snag a listing or two, or even a sale, since people often need a friend to give them advice about selling their house, and will sometimes make a decision based on feeling momentarily euphoric. Though that's never happened, and in any case, it's against all the guidelines.

Nothing technical's required to be a Sponsor: a willingness to listen (which you need in liberal quantities as a realtor), a slice of common sense, an underdeveloped sense of irony, a liking for strangers and a capacity to be disengaged while staying sincerely focused on whatever question greets you when you walk in the door. There have been concerns that despite the grad student screening, innocent callers would be vulnerable if a bad-seed Sponsor made it through the net. But it's been generally felt that the gain is more important than the modest statistical risk—and like I said, so far, so good.

It turns out that the hardest thing to find in the modern world is sound, generalized, disinterested advice—of the kind that instructs you, say, not to get on the Tilt-A-Whirl at the county fair once you've seen the guys who're running it; or to always check to see that your spare's inflated before you start out overland in your '55 roadster from Barstow to Banning. You can always get plenty of highly specialized technical advice—about whether your tweeter is putting out the prescribed number of amps to get the best sound out of your vintage Jo Stafford monaurals, or whether this epoxy is right for mending the sea kayak you rammed into Porpoise Rock on your vacation to Maine. And you can always, of course, get very bad and wrong advice about most anything: "This extra virgin olive oil'll work as good as STP on that outboard of yours"; "Next time that asshole parks across your driveway, I'd go after him with a ball-peen hammer." Plus, nobody any longer wants to help you more than they minimally have to: "If you want shirts, go to the shirt department, this floor's all pants"; "We had those Molotov avocados last year, but I don't know how I'd go about reordering them"; "I'm going on my break now or I'd dig up that rest room key for you."

But plain, low-impact good counsel and assistance is at an all-time low.

I stress low-impact because the usual scope of Sponsor transactions is broad but rarely deep—just like a real friendship.

"When you sharpen that hunting knife, do you run the stone *with* the cutting edge or *against* it?" For better or worse, I'm a man people are willing to tell the most remarkable things to— their earliest sexual encounters, their bankruptcy status, their previously unacknowledged criminal past. Though Sponsorees are not encouraged to spill their guts or say a lot of embarrassing crap they'll later regret and hate themselves (and you) for the minute you're gone. Most of my visits are, in fact, surprisingly brief—less than twenty minutes—with an hour being the limit. After an hour, the disinterested character of things can shift and problems sprout. Our guidelines specify every attempt be made to make visits as close to natural as can be, stressing informality, the spontaneous and the presumption that both parties need to be someplace else pretty soon anyway.

In my own case, my demeanor's never grim or solemn or clergical, or, for that matter, not even especially happy. I steer clear of the religious, of sexual topics, politics, financial observations and relationship lingo. (On these topics, even priests', shrinks' and money analysts' advice is rarely any good, since who has much in common with these people?) My Sponsor visits are more like a friendly stop-by from the bland State Farm guy, who you've run into at the tire store, asked over to the house to tweak your coverage, but who you then enlist to help get the lawn sprinkler to work. So far, my Sponsorees have done nothing to take extra advantage, and neither have I gone away once thinking a "really interesting" relationship has been unearthed. And yet if you impulsively blab to me that you stabbed your Aunt Carlotta down in Vicksburg back in 1951, or went AWOL from Camp Lejeune during Tet, or fathered a Bahamian baby who's now fighting for life and is in need of a kidney transplant for which you are the only match, you can expect me to go straight to the authorities.

With all these provisos and safety nets and firewalls, you might expect most callers to be elderly shut-ins or toxic cranks who've savaged all their friends and now need a new audience. Or else cancer victims who've gotten sick of their families (it happens) and just need somebody new to stare intensely into the face of. And some are. But mostly they're just average souls who need you to go out to their garage to see if their grandfather's hand-carved cherry partners' desk has been stolen by their nephew, the way it was foretold in a nightmare. Or who want you to write a dunning letter to the water department about the three-hour stoppage in June—while the main line was being repaired—demanding an adjustment in the next month's bill.

There are also prosperous, affluent, young-middle-aged, 24/7 type A's. These people are often the least at ease and typically want something completely banal and easy—to tell you a joke they think is hilarious but can't remember to tell anybody they know because they're too busy. Or women who want to yak about their kids for thirty minutes but can't because it's incorrect—in their set—to do that to their friends. Or men who ask me what color Escalade looks good against the exterior paint scheme of their new beach house in Brielle. But on three separate occasions—one woman and two men—the question I answered was (based on just two minutes' acquaintance) did I think she or he was an asshole. In each case, I said I definitely didn't think so. I've begun to wonder, since then, if this isn't the underlying theme of most all my Sponsorees' questions (especially the rich ones), since it's the thing we all want to know, that causes most of our deflected worries and that we fear may be true but find impossible to get a frank opinion about from the world at large. Am I good? Am I bad? Or am I somewhere lost in the foggy middle?

I wouldn't ordinarily have thought that I'd get within two football fields of anything like Sponsoring, since I'm not a natural joiner, inquirer or divulger. Yet I know the difficulty of making new friends—which isn't that the world's not full of interesting, available new people. It's that the past gets so congested with lived life that anyone in their third quartile—which includes me—is already far enough along the road that making a friend like you could when you were twenty-five involves so much brain-rending and boring catching up that it simply isn't worth the effort. You see and hear people vainly doing it every day—yakkedy, yakkedy, yakkedy: "That reminds me of our family's trips to Pensacola in 1955." "That reminds me of what my first wife used to complain about." "That reminds me of my son getting smacked in the eye with a baseball." "That reminds me of a dog we had that got run over in front of the house." Yakkedy, yakkedy and more goddamn yakkedy, until the ground quakes beneath us all.

So—unless sex or sports is the topic, or it's your own children—when you meet someone who might be a legitimate friend candidate, the natural impulse is to start fading back to avoid all the yakkedy-yak, so that you fade and fade, until you can't see him or her anymore, and couldn't bear to anyway. With the result that attraction quickly becomes avoidance. In this way, the leading edge of your life—what you did this morning after breakfast, who called you on the phone and woke you up from your nap, what the roofing guy said about your ice-dam flashings—*that becomes all your life is*: whatever you're doing, saying, thinking, planning *right then*. Which leaves whatever you're recollecting, brooding about, whoever it is you've loved for years but still need to get your head screwed on straight about—in other words, the important things in life—all of *that*'s left unattended and in need of expression.

The Permanent Period tries to reconcile these irreconcilables in your favor by making the congested, entangling past fade to beige, and the present brighten with its present-ness. This is the very deep water my daughter, Clarissa, is at present wading through and knows it: how to keep afloat in the populous hazardous mainstream (the yakkedy-yak and worse) without drowning; versus being pleasantly safe in your own little eddy. It's what my more affluent Sponsorees want to know when they make me listen to their unfunny jokes or crave to know if they're good people or not: Am I doing reasonably well under testing circumstances? (Thinking you're good can give you courage.) It also happens to be precisely the dilemma my son Paul has settled in his own favor in the embedded, miniaturized mainstream life of Kanzcity and Hallmark. He may be much smarter than I know.

Depth may be all that Sponsoring really lacks—with sincerity as its mainstay. Most people already feel in-deep-and-dense enough with life involvement, which may be their very problem: The voice is strangled by too much woolly experience ever to make it out and be heard. I know I've felt that way more in this fateful year than ever before, so that sometimes I think I could use a Sponsor visit myself. (This very fact may make me a natural Sponsor, since just like being a decent realtor, you have to at least harbor the suspicion that you have a lot in common with *everybody*, even if you don't want to be their friend.)

My other reason for getting involved in Sponsoring is that Sponsoring carries with it a rare optimism that says some things can actually work out and puts a premium on inching beyond your limits, while rendering Sponsorees less risk-averse on a regular daily basis and less like those oldsters in their blue New Yorkers who won't make a mistake for fear of bad results that're coming anyway.

And of course the final reason I'm a Sponsor is that I have cancer. Contrary to the TV ads showing cancer victims staring dolefully out though lacy-curtained windows at empty play-grounds, or sitting alone on the sidelines while the rest of the non-cancerous family stages a barbecue or a boating adventure on Lake Wapanooki or gets into clog dancing or Whiffle ball, cancer (little-d death, after all), in fact, makes you a lot more interested in other people's woes, with a view to helping with improvements. Getting out on the short end of the branch leaves you (has me, anyway) *more* interested in life—any life—not less. Since it makes the life you're precariously living, and that may be headed for the precipice, feel fuller, dearer, more worthy of living—just the way you always hoped would happen when you thought you were well.

Other people, in fact—if you keep the numbers small—are not always hell.

The last thing I'll say, as I pull up in front at #24 Bondurant

Court, residence of a certain Mrs. Purcell, where I'm soon to be inside Sponsoring a better outcome to things, is that even though other people are worth helping and life can be fuller, etc., etc., Sponsoring has never actually produced a greater sense of connectedness in me, and probably not in others—the storied lashing-together-of-boats we're all supposed to crave and weep salty tears at night for the lack of. It could happen. But the truth is, I feel connected enough already. And Sponsoring is not about connectedness anyway. It's about being consoled by connection's opposite. A little connectedness, in fact, goes a long way, no matter what the professional lonelies of the world say. We might all do with a little less of it.

Number 24, where lights are on inside, is built in the solid, monied, happy family-home-as-refuge style, houses Haddam boasts in fulsome supply, owing to its staunch Dutch-Quaker beginnings and to a brief nineteenth-century craving for ornamental English-German prettiness. Vernacular, this is sometimes called—neat, symmetrical, gray-stucco, red-doored Georgians with slate roofs, four shuttered front windows upstairs and down, a small but fancy wedding-cake entry, curved fanlight with formal sidelights, dentil trim and squared-off (expensive) privet hedges bolstering the front. Intimations of heterodoxy, but nothing truly eye-catching. Thirty-five hundred square feet, not counting the basement and four baths. A million-two, if you bought it this very afternoon—complete with the platinum BMW M3 sitting in the side drive—though with the risk that a surveilling neighbor will come along before you sign the papers and snake it away for a million-two-five so he can sell it to his former law partner's ex-wife.

Bondurant Court is actually a cul-de-sac off Rosedale Road. Three other residences, two of them certifiable Georgian stately homes, lurk deep within bosky, heavily treed lawns on which many original willows and elms remain. The third home-like structure is a pale-gray flat-roofed, windowless concrete oddity with a Roman-bath floor plan built by a Princeton architect for a twenty-five-year-old dot-com celebrity who no one speaks to for architectural reasons. Children aren't allowed to go there on Halloween or caroling at Christmas. Rumors are out that the owner's moved back to Malibu. I'm surprised not to see a Lauren-Schwindell sign out front, since one of my former colleagues sold him the lot.

Number 24—the great neighbor-houses' little sister—would be a great buy for a new divorcée with dough, or for a newly-wed lawyer couple or a discreet gay M.D. with a Gotham practice who needs a getaway. If I could've sold easy houses like this, instead of overpriced mop closets you couldn't fart in without the whole block smelling it, I might've stayed.

And like clockwork, as I stride up the flagstones toward the brass-knockered red door—two shiny brass carriage lamps turning on in unison—I experience the anti-Permanent Period williwaws lifting off of me and the exhilaration of whatever's about to open up here streaming into my limbs and veins like a physic. One could easily wonder, of course, about a Mr. Definitely Wrong being set to spring out from the other side of the heavy door—John Wayne Gacy in clown gear, waiting to eat me with sauerkraut. What would the termite guy or the Culligan Man do, faced as they are with the same imponderables on a daily basis? Just use the old noodle. Stay alert for the obviously weird, attend your senses, drink and eat nothing, identify exits. I've, in fact, never really feared anything worse than being bored to bits. Plus, if they're gonna, they're gonna—like the little town in Georgia the tornado ripped a hole through when everybody was at church on Sunday, believing such things didn't happen there.

Everything happens everywhere. Look at the fucking election. *Ding-dong. Ding-dong. Ding-dong.*

A melodious belling. I turn and re-survey the cul-de-sac— wet, cold, bestilled, its other ponderous residences all bearing lawn signs: WARNING. THIS HOUSE IS PATROLLED. The big Georgians' many leaded windows glow through the trees with antique light, as though lit by torches. No humans or animals are in view. A police car or ambulance *wee-up, wee-ups* in the distance. Cold air hisses with the rain's departure. A crow calls from a spruce, then a second, but nothing's in sight.

Noises become audible within. A female throat is cleared, a chain lock slid down its track. The brass peephole darkens with an interior eye. A dead bolt's conclusively thrown. I rise a quarter inch onto my toes.

"Just a moment, pu-lease." A rilling, pleasant voice in which, do I detect, the undertones of Dixie? I hope not.

The heavy door opens back. A smiling woman stands in its space. This is the best part of Sponsoring—the relief of finally arriving to someone's rescue.

But I sense: Here is not a complete stranger. Though from out on the bristly welcome mat, the back of my head feeling a breeze flood past into the homey-feeling house, I can't instantly supply coordinates. My brow feels thick. My mouth is half-open, beginning to smile. I peer through the angled door opening at Mrs. Purcell.

It couldn't be a worse opening gambit, of course, for a Sponsor to stare simian-like at the Sponsoree, who may already be fearful the visitor will be a snorting crotch-clutcher escapee from a private hospital, who'll leave her trussed up in the maid's closet while he makes off with her underthings. The risk for doing Sponsor work in Haddam is always, of course, that I might know my Sponsoree: a face, a history, a colorful story that defeats disinterest and ruins everything. I should've been more prudent.

Except maybe not. Some days, I see whole crowds of people who look exactly like other people I know but who're, in fact, total strangers. It's my age and age's great infirmity: overaccumulation—the same reason I don't make friends anymore. Sally always said this was a grave sign, that I was spiritually afraid of the unknown—unlike herself, who left me for her dead husband. Though I thought—and still do—that it was actually a positive sign. By thinking I recognized strangers I, in fact, *didn't* recognize, I was actually reaching out to the unknown, making the world my familiar. No doubt this is why I've sold many, many houses that no one else wanted.

"Are you Mr. Fruank?" Dixie's definitely alight in the voice: bright, sweet and rising at the end to make everything a happy question; vowels that make *you* sound like *yew*, *handle* like *handull*. Central Virginia's my guess.

"Hi. Yeah. I'm Frank." I extend an affirming hand with a friendlier smile. I'm not a leering crotch-clutcher or a dampened-panty faddist. Sponsors omit last names—which is simpler when you leave.

"Well, Ah'm Marguerite Purcell, Mr. Fruank. Why don't you come in out of this *b-r-r-r* we're havin'." Marguerite Purcell, who's dressed in a two-piece suit that must be raw silk of the rarest French-rose hue, with matching Gucci flats, steps back in welcome—the most cordial-confident of graceful hostesses, clearly accustomed to all kinds, high to low, entering her private home on every imaginable occasion. Haddam has always absorbed a small population of dispirited, old-monied southerners who can't stand the South yet can only bear the company of one another in deracinated enclaves like Haddam, Newport and Northeast Harbor. You catch glimpses of their murmuring Town Cars swaying processionally out gated driveways, headed to the Homestead for golf-and-bridge weekends with other white-shoed W&L grads, or turning north to Naskeag to spend August with Grandma Ni-Ni on Eggemoggin Reach—all of them iron-kneed Republicans who want us out of the UN, nigras off the curbs and back in the fields, the Suez mined, and who think the country missed its chance by not choosing ole Strom back in '48. Hostesses like Marguerite Purcell never have problems money can't solve. So what am I doing here?

"Ahm just astonissshed by this weathuh." Marguerite's leading me through the parquet foyer into a living room "done" like no living room I've seen (and I've seen a few) and that the staid Quaker exterior gives no hint of. The two big front windows have been sheathed with shiny white lacquered paneling. The walls are also lacquered white. The green-vaulted ceiling firmament has tiny recessed pin lights shining every which way, making the room bright as an operating theater. The floors are bare wood and waxed to a fierce sheen. There are no plants. The only furnishings are two immense, hard-as-granite rectilinear love seats, covered in some sort of dyed-red animal skin, situated on a square of blue carpet, facing each other across a thick slab-of-glass coffee table that actually has fish swimming inside it (a dozen lurid, fat, motionless white goldfish), the whole *objet* supported by an enormous hunk of curved, polished chrome, which I recognize as the bumper off a '54 Buick. The air is odorless, as if the room had been chemically scrubbed to leave no evidence of prior human habitation. Nothing recalls a day when regular people sat in regular chairs and watched TV, read books, got into arguments or made love on an old braided rug while logs burned cheerily in a fireplace. The only animate sign is a white CO_2 detector mid-ceiling with its tiny blinking red beacon. Though on the wall above where a fireplace ought to be, there's a gilt-framed, essentially life-size oil portrait of an elderly, handsome, mustachioed, silver-haired, capitalist-looking gentleman in safari attire, a floppy white-hunter fedora and holding a Mannlicher .50 in front of a stuffed rhino head (the very skin used to make the couch). This fellow stares from the wall with piercing, dark robber-baron eyes, a cruel sensuous mouth, uplifted nose and bruising brow, but with a mysterious, corners-up smirk on his lips, as if once a great, diminishing joke has been told and he was the first one to get it.

"This wuss my husbund's favorite room," Marguerite says dreamily, still primly smiling. She establishes herself on the front edge of one of the red love seats, facing me across the aquarium table, squeezing together, then shifting to the side her shiny stockinged knees. She possesses thin, delicately veined ankles, one of which wears a nearly invisible gold chain flattened beneath the nylon. She is all Old Dominion comeliness, the last breathing female you'd think could stomach a room as weird as this. Obviously, she married it, but now that the Mister's retreated to his place on the wall, she doesn't know what in the fuck to do with it. This may be what she wants me to tell her. Anyone—but me— couldn't resist asking her a hundred juicy, prying, none-of-your-business questions. But, as with all Sponsor visits, I heed the presence of an invisible privacy screen between Sponsoree and self. That works out best for everybody.

From where I sit, Marguerite seems to have the lens softened all around her—a trick of the pin lights in the celestial green ceiling. She's maybe mid-fifties but has a plush, young-appearing face she's applied a faint rouging to, a worry-free forehead, welcoming blue eyes, with an obviously sizable bustage under her rose suit jacket, and an amorous full-lipped mouth, through which her voice makes a soft whistling sound ("ssurely," "hussbund's"), as if her teeth were in the way. My guess is she's the hoped-for result of a high-end makeover—a length somebody might gladly go to for the chance of an enduring (and rich) second marriage. Her hair, however, is the standard bottle-brown southern *do* with a wide, pale, scalp-revealing middle part going halfway back, with the rest cemented into a flip that only elderly hairdressers in Richmond know how to properly mold. Southern socialites—my schoolmates' mothers at Gulf Pines Academy, who'd drive down from Montgomery and Lookout to speak briefly to their villainous sons through lowered windows of their Olds Ninety Eights—wore exactly this hair construction back in 1959. I actually find it sexy as hell, since it reminds me of my young and (I felt) clearly lust-driven fourth-grade teacher, Miss Hapthorn, back in Biloxi.

When she led me into the lifeless and over-heated living room, I noticed Marguerite stealing two spying looks my way as if I, too, might've reminded her of somebody and wasn't the only one searching time's vault.

And she's now examining me again. And not like the beguiling Virginia hostess who sparkles at the guest, hoping to find something she can adore so she can decide to change her mind about it later, but with the same submerged acknowledging I detected before. These magnolia blossoms, of course, can be scrotum-cracking, trust-fund bullies who secretly smoke Luckies, drink gin by the gallon, screw the golf pro and don't give an inch once money's on the table. Only they never act that way when you first make their acquaintance. I'm wondering if I sold her a house back in the mists.

Though all at once my heart, out ahead of my brain, exerts a boulderish, possibly audible *whump-whoomp-de-whomp*. I know Marguerite Purcell. Or I did.

The knees. The good ankles. The ghosty anklet. The bustage. The plump lips. The way the peepers fasten on me, slowly close, then stay closed too long, revealing an underlying authority making decisions for the composed face. (The lisp is new.) She may remember me, too. Except if I admit it, Sponsorship loses all purchase and I'll have to beat it, just when I got here.

Marguerite reopens her small pale blue eyes, looks self-consciously down, arranges her pretty hands on her rose skirt hem, flattens the fabric across her knee-tops, smiles again and recrosses her ankles. No one's spoken since we sat down. Maybe she's also having a day when everybody looks like somebody else and thinks nothing of this moment of faulty recognition. And maybe she's *not* the woman I "slept" with how many years back (sleep did eventually come), when her name was Betty Barksdale —"Dusty" to her friends—then the beleaguered, abandoned wife of Fincher Barksdale, change-jingling local M.D. and turd. He left her to join some foreign-doctors outfit in deepest Africa, where he reportedly went native, learned the local patois, took a fat African bride with tribal scarrings, began doctoring to the insurgents (the wrong insurgents) and ended up in a fetid, lightless, tin-sided back-country prison from which he eventually found his way to a public square in a regional market town, where he was roped to a metal no-parking post and hacked at for a while by boy soldiers hepped up on the amphetamines he'd been feeding them.

But even if Marguerite *is* the metamorphosed Dusty from '88, I may not be that easy to recollect. Most high jinks aren't worth remembering anyway. Behind her warm, self-conscious smile, she might be silently saying, What is it now? This guy? Frank . . . um . . . something? Something about when my first husband, something, I guess, didn't come back or some goddamn thing. Who cares?

I'd lobby for that. We don't have to revisit a tepid boinking we boozily committed upstairs in her green-shingled Victorian on Westerly Road that Fincher stuck her with. Though if it *is* her, I'd like (silently) to compliment the impressive metamorphosis to magnolia blossom, since the Dusty I knew was a smirky, blond, slightly hard-edged, cigarette-smoking former Goucher girl who made fun of her husband's blabbermouth east Memphis relatives and about what he'd think if he ever knew she was rogering the realtor. He never got to think anything.

Though the wellspring of transformation is almost always money. It works miracles. First Fincher's big life-insurance policies, then the lavishments of old Clyde Beatty Purcell all worked their changes. Ex-friends who knew her as sorrowing, needful Dusty could all go fuck themselves. (I'd like to know if I look as old as she does. Possibly yes. I've had cancer, I'm internally radiated, in recovery. It happens.)

Marguerite's warm society smile has faded to a querulous pert, designating confusion. I've become quiet and may have alarmed her. Her eyes elevate above my head to gaze toward the blocked-off front windows, as if she could see through them to the dying day. She wags her soft chin slowly, as though confirming something. "I don't want to talk about our politics, Mr. Frank, it's too depresssin'." Politics is strictly verboten in Sponsoring anyway. Hard to think we could be on the same side. "In the *New Yawk Times* today, Mr. Bush said if Florida goes to the Dem-uh-crats, it could be ahrmed insurrection. Or worse. That rascal Clinton. It'ss shocking." She frowns with disdain, then she sniffs, her nose darting upward as if she'd just sniffed the whole disreputable business out of the air forever.

But with this gesture, the Marguerite-Dusty-Betty deal is sealed. In our night of brief abandon, after I'd shown her a gigantic Santa Barbara hacienda on Fackler Road (she wanted to squander all Fincher's money so he *couldn't* come home), we two wound up on bar stools at the Ramada on Route 1, with one thing following fumblingly the next. I had a well-motivated prohibition against casual client boinking, but it got lost in the shuffle.

As the night spirited on and the Manhattans kept arriving, Dusty, who'd begun referring to herself as "the Dream Weaver," gradually gave in to a strange schedule of abrupt smirks, fidgets, tics, brow-clenchings, lip-squeezings, cheek-puffings, teeth-barings and fearsome eye-rollings—as if life itself had ignited a swarm of nervous weirdness, attesting to the great strain of it all. It rendered our subsequent lovemaking a challenge and, as I remember it, unsuccessful, except for me, of course. Though the next morning when I was skulking out through the kitchen door (I thought before she could wake up), I encountered Dream Weaver Dusty, already at the sink in a faded red kimono, staring wanly out the window, hair askew and barefoot, but with an unaccountably graceful, empathetic welcome and a weak smile, wondering if I wanted an English muffin or maybe a poached egg before I disappeared. She was hollow-eyed and certainly didn't want me to stay (I didn't). But the night's stress-plus-booze-inspired tangle of tics, warps and winces had also vanished, leaving her exhausted but calm. Vanished, that is, except for one—the one I just saw, the tiny heavenward flickage of nose tip toward ceiling, punctuating a subject needing to be put to rest. Its effect on me now is to inspire not what you'd think, but even franker admiration for her reincarnation and the proficient adaptation to the times. How many of us, faced with a bad part to play, wouldn't like to slip offstage in act one, then reappear in act three as an entirely different personage? It's a wonder it doesn't happen more. My wife, Sally, did the exact opposite when, far along in the play, she went back to being the wife from act one who never got the ovation she deserved.

I look out the arched doorway to the parquet foyer and to closed doors leading farther into the house. Is anyone else in here with us? A loyal servant, a Cairn terrier, possibly old Purcell himself, hooked to tubes and breathing devices, up the back stairs, watching game shows.

"I don't want to talk about politics, either." I smile back like a kindly old GP with a pretty patient presenting with nonspecific symptoms that don't really bother her all that much. Possibly there are indistinct rumblings happening inside her brain—an English-muffin moment without a place in time.

"I have a strange question to ask you, Frank." Marguerite's delicate shoulders go square, her back straightens, fingers unlace and re-lace atop her shiny knees. Perfect posture, as always, ignites the low venereal flicker. You never know about these things.

"Strange questions are our stock-in-trade," I offer back genially.

"I don't suppose you're an expert in this." Eyelids down and holding. I nod, expressing competence. Marguerite has worked a little free of her plantation accent. She's more downtown *Balmur*. Her limpid blues rise again and seek the absent window behind me and blink in an inspiration-seeking way. "I have a very strange urge to confess something." Her eyes stay aloft.

I am as noncommittal as Dr. Freud. "I see."

The room's glistening white walls, firmamental ceiling and aquarium table holding motionless, creepily mottled goldfish all radiate in silent stillness. I hear a heat source *tick-tick-ticking*. One of the crows outside issues a softened caw. It's a *Playhouse 90* moment, one interminable soundless shot. How do you get a room to smell this way, I wonder. Why would you want it to?

Marguerite's slender left hand, on which there's a ring supporting an emerald as big as a Cheerios box, wanders to above her left breast, fingertips just touching a pin made of two tiny finely joined golden apples, then returns to her knee. "But I really have nothing to confess. Nothing at all." Her gaze falls to me plaintively. It is the look of someone who's spent twenty-five years in customer service at the White Plains Saks, feels okay about it, but now realizes something more challenging might've been possible. It's disheartening to encounter this look in a woman you like. "It's a little unnerving," she says softly. "What do you think, Frank?" Her full lips push tantalizingly outward to signify candor.

"How long have you been feeling this way?" I am still all doctorish-Sponsorish concern.

"Oh. Sixss months."

"Did anything seem to cause it?"

Marguerite inhales a deep chest-swelling breath and lets it out. "No." Two blue eye blinks. "I keep thinking whatever it is will just come to me while I'm boiling a putatuh. Somebody'd abused me as a child, or my mother'd been a woman of mixed blood." Or you once fucked your realtor when you had a whole nuther identity. This trunk lid we won't open. "I certainly don't want something terrible to be true. If I've forgotten something terrible, I'm happy for it to stay that way."

"I can't blame you there." My eyes fasten on her for the benefit of verisimilitude.

"I call it a need to confess. But it's maybe something else."

"What else could you maybe call it?"

Marguerite suddenly sits up even more erectly, her softened features alert. "I haven't really thought about that."

"You might just have to make it up, then."

Her mouth now transforms into a mirthless almost-smile. I believe she may have quickly crossed her eyes and instantly uncrossed them—another of the eighties-era tics. "I don't know, Frank. Maybe it's an urge to clear sssomething up."

My face, by practice, expresses nothing. Ann and I used to ask each other—when one of us would register a complaint the other couldn't properly address: "What's your neurosis allowing you to do that you couldn't do otherwise?" Mostly the answer was to complain and enjoy it. This might be the urge that Marguerite's experiencing. "Would you really like to know what to confess, no matter what?" I ask. "Or would you be happy to just quit feeling this way and never confess anything?"

"I guess the latter, Frank. Iss that horrible?"

"Maybe if you murdered somebody," I say. Put arsenic in their smoothie at the health club. "Did you murder anybody?" Fincher wouldn't count.

"No." She clasps her hands and looks distressed, as if she sort of wished she could say she *had* murdered somebody, make me believe it, then take it all back, leaving behind a zesty fragrance of doubt. "I don't think I have the right character for that," she says wondrously.

My bet, though, is she's never done anything wrong. Married a shit, been treated shabbily, forgettably rogered the realtor, but then reconstituted herself, married a better sod who left her well-off and didn't stick around for *forever*. It's not all that different from the story behind many doors I knock on, though it doesn't make much of a climax and I'm not usually a ghost presence. But—the guy with the sailboat that's driving him nuts; Bettina, the fractious Dutch housekeeper—there *is* the need to tell, which is its own virtue and complaint. That's why I'm here—it could be the modern dilemma. But like many modern dilemmas, it's susceptible to a cure.

"I'm not sure we have characters, Marguerite. Are you? I've thought a lot about it." I press my lips together to signal this is my judgment *in re* her problem. Any suspicion that I might *be* the problem is entirely nugatory.

"No." A quarter smile of recognition emerges onto her whole face. I wonder if I already said this to her sixteen years ago in some post-coital posturings. I hope not. "No, I'm not. I'm Epissscopalian, Frank, but I'm not religious."

I give a wink of "me, neither" assurance. "We may think we have a character because it makes everything simpler."

"Yes."

"But what we do have for sure," I say supremely, "is memories, presents, futures, desires, hatreds, et cetera. And it's our job to govern those as much as we can. How we do that may be the only character we have, if you know what I mean."

"Yes." She is possibly stumped.

"*Your* job, I think, is to control your memory so it doesn't bother you. Since from what you say, it shouldn't bother you. Right? There isn't even a bad memory there."

"No." She clears her throat, lets her eyes drop. I may be veering near privileged subjects, where I don't want to veer, but the truth is the truth. "And how do I do that, Frank?" she says. "That's the problem, isn't it?"

"No. I don't think that's the problem at all." I'm beaming. I certainly *should* have been able to explain this decades back, in the kitchen, over our muffin. Isn't that where we want our casual couplings to lead us? To someone we can tell something to? Even if there isn't anything to tell. Maybe it's me who's reincarnated. "I don't think there *is* a problem," I say enthusiastically. "You just have to believe this feeling of wanting to confess something is a natural feeling. And probably a good omen for the future." My eyes roam up and catch the knowing gimlet eye of old Purcell, bearing down on me in his white-hunter outfit. I am your surrogate here, I think, not your adversary. It is the genius soul of Sponsoring.

"The future?" Marguerite clears her throat again, stagily. We've moved onto the bright future, where we belong.

"Sometimes we think that before we can go on with life we have to get the past all settled." I am as soulful as a St. Bernard. "But that's not true. We'd never get anyplace if it was."

"Probably not." She's nodding.

Then neither of us says anything. Silences are almost always affirming. I cast a wary eye down into the aquarium, glass as thick as a bank window and beveled smooth all around its rhomboid to guard against gashed shins, snagged hems, toddlers and pets poking their eyes out. My face is mirrored back in the Buick bumper—as rubbery as the Elephant Man. I see one of the huge, glaucal goldfish looking at me. How would one feed them? Probably there's a way. Possibly they're not real—

"Ah yew plannin' on a big Thanks-givin'?" I hear Marguerite say, Dixie, again, the music in her voice.

I smile stupidly across the table. When I first had my titanium BBs downloaded, I experienced all sorts of strange enervated zonings out and in, often at extremely unhandy moments—across the desk from a client who'd just signed an offer sheet obligating him to pay $75,000 if the deal fell through; or listening to a man tell me how the death of his wife made an instant sale a matter of highest priority. Then, ZAP, I'd be lost in a reverie about a Charlie Chan movie I saw, circa age ten, and whether it was Sidney Toler or Warner Oland in the title role. Again, Psimos says these "episodes" are not relatable to treatment. But I say baloney. I wouldn't have them if I didn't have what I *do have*. Either it was the BBs or the *thought* of BBs—a distinction that's not a difference.

"Do you have childrun?" I'm sure she's wondering what the hell's wrong with me.

"Yeah. Absolutely." I'm fuzzy-woozy. "They're coming. For Thanksgiving. Two of 'em." Sponsors aren't supposed to tell *our* stories. Expanded human contexts lead to random personal assessments. We're here to do a job, like the State Farm guy. Plus, now that we've gotten past it, I don't want to risk a needless *revisitus* of who was who, when *when* was when. It's not the key to Marguerite's mystery. There is no key. There is no mystery. We all live with that revelation.

I abruptly stand right up, straight as a sentry as if on command, but am woozy still. Satisfactory visit. Needs to be over. Done and done well. If I had a clipboard, it'd now be under my arm. If I had a hat, I'd be turning it by its brim.

"Are you leavin'?" Marguerite looks up at me, surprised, but automatically rises (a little stiffly) to let me know it's okay and not rude if I have to go. She looks hopefully across the strange aquarium table, then takes a hesitant turning step toward the foyer, her two feet going balky, as though they'd gone to sleep in their Guccis. "I 'magine you have other ssstops to make." (Do I walk like that?)

I'm eager to go, though still light-headed. Sponsor visits are more demanding than they seem and adieus can be unwieldy. People of both genders sometimes need to lavish hugs on you. I'm nervous Marguerite's going to spin round when we hit the parquet, take both my hands in her two warm ones, bull her way inside the invisible screen, peer into my bleary orbs, smile a smile of lost laughter and past regret and say something outrageous. Like: "We don't have to pretend anymore." Though we do! ". . . fate didn't intend us . . . it's true and it's sssad . . . but you've counseled me so well . . . couldn't you hold me for just a moment? . . ." I'll have a heart attack. You think you'll always be open to these impromptu clenches and whatever good mischief they lead to. But after a while you're not.

However, Marguerite says, "This election's made a mess out of everybody's Thanksssgiving, hasn't it, Fruank?" She turns to me in the entryway (I'm fearful) but is smiling ruefully, her veined hands folded at her rose pink waist like a schoolmarm. The little joined apples are glowing cheerfully. She clicks on the soft overhead globe, suffusing us in a deathly glow that guarantees, I trust, no smoochy-smoochy.

"I guess so." My eyes find the brass umbrella stand beside the door, as if one of the umbrellas is mine and I want it back. I must be going, yes, I must be going.

"You know, when I called to assk for a visit today—and I have these vissits quite often—I intended to ask for help in drafting a letter to President Clinton explaining all we have to be thankful for in this country. And then this other funny old business just popped up."

"Why'd you change your mind?" Why ask *that*! I've Sponsored so well up to now! I flinch and move my toes nearer the door. Cold breeze purrs beneath it, chilling my ankles and giving me a shiver. *Heat does not reach front foyer.* A prospective buyer wouldn't notice this till it's too late. I grasp the cold brass knob and twist-test it. Left, right.

"I'm really not sssure now." Marguerite's eyes cast down, as though the answer was on the floor.

I give the knob a quarter right twist, staring at the dark roots of Marguerite's hairline, up the regimental center part to nowhere. She looks up at me brazenly, eyes shining not with stayed tears but with resolve and optimism. "Do you think life's ssstrange, Frank?" At her waist, her fingers touch tips-to-tips. She's smiling a wonderful, positivistic Margaret Chase Smith smile.

"Depends on what you compare it to." If it's death, then no.

"Oh my." One eye narrows at me in tolerant ridicule. "That's really not a very good ansswer. Not for a ssmart boy like yew."

"You're right. Sorry."

"Let's just ssay it *isss* strange. That's the thought to ssay good-bye on, isn't it?"

"Okay." I give the ponderous door a ponderous tug. Cold damp instantly falls in on us like a tree.

"Thank you ssso much for coming." Marguerite cocks her pretty head like a sparrow, her nose flicking up. In no way does she mean "Thanks for coming back *finally*." She extends a soft, bonily mature hand for me to grasp. I take it like a Japanese businessman, give her a firm double-hand up-down up-down, the kind I counsel Mike never to do, then turn loose quick. She looks in my eyes, then down to regard her empty hand, then smiles, shaking her head at life's weirdness. Women are stronger (and smarter) than men. Whoever doubted it? I attempt my manliest affirming smile, say *good* and *bye* between my lips and teeth, step out onto the bristly mat, into the frigid afternoon that looks like evening. Surprisingly, the red door closes hard behind me. I hear a lock go click, footsteps receding. Miraculously, and not a moment too soon, I'm history (again).

Back in the car, my heart—for reasons best known to Dr. DeBakey—*again* goes cavorting. *Whumpetty, whump-de-whumps* like a stallion in a stall when smoke's in the air. My scalp seizes. My skin prickles. Metallic ozone tang's in my mouth, as if something foreign had been in the car while I was inside. I sit and try to picture stillness, hold my cheek to the cold-fugged

window glass, make myself simmer down so as not to lapse into
"a state." Possibly I should put in my night guard.

Everyone's wondered: Will I *know* if I'm having a heart attack?
The people who've had them—Hugh Wekkum, for one—say
you can't *not* know. Only goofballs mistake it for acid reflux or
over-excitement when you open the IRS letter. Unless, of course,
you *want* to be in the dark—in which case everything's possible.
EMS technicians testify—I read this in the Mayo newsletter I'm
now sent whether I want it or not—that when they ask their
patients, stretched out on sidewalks turning magenta, or doubled
over in the expensive box seats at Shea, or being wheeled off a
Northwest flight in Detroit, "What seems to be the trouble, sir?"
the answer's usually "I think I'm having a fucking heart attack,
you dickhead. What d'you think's wrong?" They're almost always
right.

I am *not* having a heart attack, although having a Sea Biscuit
heartbeat may mean something's not perfect, following on my
partial fadeout inside Marguerite's. (The beef 'n bean burrito on
an empty stomach is a suspect.) I take a peek through the hazy
glass out at #24, cast in shapeless shadows. Lights downstairs are
off, though the carriage lamps still burn. But Marguerite is now
standing at an upstairs window, looking down at my car, wherein
I'm trying to stop my galloping heart. I believe she's smiling.
Enigmatic. Knowing. I'm willing to bet she has no friends, lives
isolated in the world of her inventions—helpfully underwritten
by gobs of dough. I could go back inside and be her friend. We
could speak of matters differently. But instead, I turn the key,
set the wipers flopping, the defrost whooshing, the wheels to

rolling—the bass *gur-murmur-murmur* of my Suburban's V-8 fortifying me just like the commercials promise. I am on my way to De Tocqueville and to Ann.

But. Let no man say here was not a successful Sponsoring— even if our present selves were under pressure from our past, which is what the past is good at. It's not so different from thinking you know people when you don't. Life *is* strange. What can we do about it? Which is why Sponsors are never concerned with underlying causes. My counsel was good counsel. Significant hurdles were cleared. One talked, one listened. Human character (or a lack thereof) was brought into play. A good future was projected. I'm actually now wondering if Marguerite could've been an older sister to Dusty and known nothing of me, only shared certain sibling nervous disorders. People, after all, have sisters. Whoever she was, she had legitimate issues I had a peculiarly good grasp on, and not just about reigniting the pilot light or reading the small print on the dehumidifier warranty. Something real (albeit invented) was bothering someone real (albeit invented). There are few enough chances to do the simple right thing anymore. A hundred years ago this week—in our grateful and unlitigious village past—this kind of good deed happened every day and all involved took it for granted. Looked at this way, Thanksgiving's not really a mess but more than anything else, commemorates a time we'll never see again.

4

I should say something about having cancer, since my health's on my mind now like a man being followed by an assassin. I'd like not to make a big to-do over it, since my view is that rather than *good* things coming to those who wait, *all* things—good, bad, indifferent—come to *all* of us if we simply hang around long enough. The poet wasn't wrong when he wrote, "Great nature has another thing to do to you and me . . . What falls away is always. And is near."

The telescoped version of the whole cancer rigamarole is that exactly four weeks after my wife, Sally Caldwell, announced she and her posthumous husband, Wally (a recent, honored guest in our house), were reconvening life on new footings and blah, blah, blah, blah, in earnest hope of gaining blah, blah, blah, blah, and better blah, blah, blah, blah, *I* happened to notice some dried brown blood driblets at about pecker height on my bedsheets, and went straight off to Haddam Medical Arts out Harrison Road to find out what might be going on with what.

I was in robustest of health (so I thought) in spite of Sally's unhappy departure—which I assumed wouldn't last long. I did my sit-ups and stretches, took healthful treks down the Sea-Clift beach every other day. I didn't drink much. I kept my weight at 178—where it's been since my last year at Michigan. I didn't smoke, didn't take drugs, consumed fistfuls of daily vitamins, including saw palmetto and selenium, ate fish more than twice a week, conscientiously divided each calendar year into test results to test results. Nothing had come up amiss—colonoscopy, chest X ray, PSA, blood pressure, good cholesterol and bad, body mass, fat percentage, pulse rate, all moles declared harmless. Going for a checkup seemed purely a confirming experience: good-to-go another twelve, as though each visit was diagnostic, preventative and curative all at once. I'd never had a surgery. Illness was what others endured and newspapers wrote about.

"Probably nothing," Bernie Blumberg said, giving me a wiseacre, pooch-mouthed Jewish butcher's wink, stripping his pale work gloves into a HAZARD can. "Prostatitis. Your gland feels a little smooshy. Slightly enlarged. Not unusual for your age. Nothing some good gherkina jerkina wouldn't clear up." He snorted, smacked his lips and dilated his nostrils as he washed his hands for the eightieth time that day (these guys earn their keep). "Your PSA's up because of the inflammation. I'll put you on some atomic-mycin and in four weeks do another PSA, after which you'll be free to resume front-line duties. How's that wife of yours?" Sally and I both went to Bernie. It's not unusual.

"She's in Mull with her dead husband," I said viciously. "We might be getting divorced." Though I didn't believe that.

"How 'bout that," Bernie said, and in an instant was gone—vanished out the door, or through the wall, or up the A/C vent or into thin air, his labcoat tails fluttering in a nonexistent breeze. "Well, look here now, how's that husband of yours?" I heard his voice sing out from somewhere, another examining room down a hall, while I cinched my belt, re-zipped, found my shoes and felt the odd queasiness up my butt. I heard his muffled laughter through cold walls. "Oh, he certainly should. Of course he should," he said. I couldn't hear the question.

Only in four weeks, my PSA showed another less-than-perfect 5.3, and Bernie said, "Well, let's give the pills another chance to work their magic." Bernie is a small, scrappy, squash-playing, wide-eyed, salt 'n pepper brush-cut Michigan Med grad from Wyandotte (which is why I go to him), an ex-Navy corpsman who practices a robust battlefield triage mentality that says only a sucking chest wound is worth getting jazzed up about. These guys aren't good when it comes to bedside etiquette and dispensing balming info. He's seen too much of life, and dreams of living in Bozeman and taking up decoy-carving. I, on the other hand, haven't seen enough yet.

"What happens if that doesn't work?" I said. Bernie was scanning the computerized pages of my blood work. We were in his little cubicle office. (Why don't these guys have nice offices? They're all rich.) His Michigan and Kenyon diplomas hung above his Navy discharge, next to a mahogany-framed display of his battle ribbons, including a Purple Heart. Outside on summer-steamy Harrison Road, jackhammers racketed away, making the office and the chair I occupied vibrate.

"Well"—not yet looking all the way over his glasses—"if that happens, I'll send you around the corner to my good friend Dr. Peplum over at Urology Partners, and he'll get you in for a sonogram and maybe a little biopsy."

"Do they do little ones?" My lower parts gripped their side walls. Biopsy!

"Yep. Uh-huh," Bernie said, nodding his head. "Nothin' to it. They put you to sleep."

"A biopsy. For cancer?" My heart was stilled. I was fully dressed, the office was freezing in spite of the warping New Jersey heat, and silent in spite of the outside bangety-bangety. Cobwebby green light sifted through the high windows, over which hung a green cotton curtain printed with faded Irish setter heads. Out in the hallway, I could hear happy female voices—nurses gossiping and giggling in hushed tones. One said, "Now that's Tony. You don't have to say any more." Another, "What a *rascal*." More giggling, their crepe soles gliding over scrubbed antiseptic tiles. This near-silent, for-all-the-world unremarkable moment, I knew, was the *fabled* moment. Things new and different and interesting possibly were afoot. Changes could ensue. Certain things taken for granted maybe couldn't be anymore.

I wasn't exactly afraid (nobody'd told me anything bad yet). I just wanted to take it in properly ahead of time so I'd know how to accommodate other possible surprises. If this shows a propensity to duck before I'm hit, to withhold commitment and not do *every goddamn thing* whole hog—then sue me. All boats, the saying goes, are looking for a place to sink. I was looking for a place to stay afloat. I must've known I had it. Women know "it's taken" two seconds after the guilty emission. Maybe you always know.

"I wouldn't get worked up over it yet." Bernie looked up distract-edly, glancing across his metal desk, where my records lay.

My face was as open as a spring window to any news. I might

as well have been a patient waiting to have a seed wart frozen off. "Okay, I won't," I said. And with that good advice in hand, I got up and left.

I won't blubber on: the freezing shock of *real* unwelcome news, the "interesting" sonogram, the sorry but somehow upbeat biopsy particulars, the perfidious prostate lingo—Gleason, Partin, oxidative damage, transrectal ultrasound, twelve-tissue sample (a lu-lu there), conscious sedation, watchful waiting, life-quality issues. There're bookstores full of this nasty business: *Prostate Cancer for Dummies, A Walking Tour Through Your Prostate* (in which the prostate has a happy face), treatment options, color diagrams, interactive prostate CD-ROMs, alternative routes for the proactive—all intended for the endlessly prostate-curious. Which I'm not. As though knowing a lot would keep you from getting it. It wouldn't—I already had it. Words can kill as well as save.

And yet. From the grim, unwanted and unexpected may arise the light-strewn and good. My daughter—tall, imperturbable, amused (by me) and nobody's patsy—re-arrived to my life.

Clarissa is twenty-five, a pretty, stroppy-limbed, long-muscled, slightly sorrowful-seeming girl with hooded gray eyes who'd remind you of a woman's basketball coach at a small college in the Middlewest. She has a square, inquisitive face (like her mother's), is pleasant around men without being much interested in them. She is sometimes profane, will mutter sarcastically under her breath, likes to read but doesn't finally say much (this, I'm sure, she got taught at Harvard). She wears strong contact lenses and frequently stares at you (me) chin down and for too long when you're talking, as if what you're saying doesn't make much sense, then silently shakes her head and turns away. She maintains a great abstract sympathy for the world but, in my mind, seems in constant training to be older, like children of divorce often are, and to have abandoned her girlishness too soon. She's said to have the ability to give memorable off-the-cuff wedding toasts and to remember old song lyrics, and can beat me at arm wrestling—especially now.

Though truth to tell, Clarissa was never a "great kid," like the bumper stickers say all kids have to be now. She was secretive, verbally ahead of herself—which made her obnoxious—sexually adventurous (with boys) and too good at school. The fault, of course, is her mother's and mine. She was loved silly by both of us, but our love was too finely diced and served, leaving her with a distrustful temper and pervasive uncertainties about her worth in the world. What can we do about these things after they're over?

Clarissa's and my relationship has been what anyone would expect, given divorce, given a brother she barely remembers but who died, given another brother she doesn't much trust or like, given a pompous stepfather she detested until he grew sick (then unexpectedly loved), given parents who seemed earnest but not ardent and given strong intelligence nurtured by years away at Miss Trustworthy's School in West Hartford. She and I together are fitful, loving, occasionally over-complicating, occasionally heated and rivalrous and often lonely around each other. "We're normal enough," Clarissa says, "if you back away a few feet"—this being her young person's faultless insight, wisdom not given to me.

I am, however, completely smitten by her. I do not believe she is permanently a lover of women, though I signed off on her orientation long ago and regret the dazzling Cookie's no longer around, since Cookie and I hit it off better than I do with most women. Clarissa's and my cohabitation during my convalescence has allowed her to think of me as a sympathetic, semi-complex-if-often-draining, not particularly paternal "older person" who happens to be her father, on whom she can hone her underused nurturing skills. And at the same time I've put into gear my underused fatherhood skills and tried to offer her what she needs—for now: shelter, a respite from love, a chance to exhale, have serious talks and set her shoulders straight before charging toward her future. It is her last chance to have a father experiencing his last chance to have the daughter he loves.

Three weeks ago, the day after Halloween, Clarissa and I were taking my prescribed therapy walk together up the beach at Sea-Clift, me in my Bean's canvas nomad's pants and faded blue anorak (it was cold), Clarissa in a pair of somebody else's baggy khakis and an old pink Connemara sweater of mine. Dr. Psimos says these walks are tonic for the recovering prostate, good for soreness, good for swelling, and the sunlight's a proven cancer fighter. Walking around every day with cancer lurking definitely commits one's thoughts more to death. But the surprise, as I already said, is that you fear it *less*, not more. It's a privilege, of an admittedly peculiar kind, to get to think about death in an almost peaceful frame of mind. After all, you share your condition—a kind of modern American condition—with 200,000 other Americans, which is comforting. And this stage of life— well past the middle—seems in fact to be the ideal time to have cancer, since among its other selling points, the Permanent Period helps to cancel out even the most recent past and focuses you onto what else there might be to feel positive about. Not having cancer, of course, would still be better.

On our beach walk, Clarissa began declaiming lengthily about the presidential election (which hadn't happened yet). She detests Bush and adores our current shiftless President, wishes he could stay President forever and believes he exhibited "courage" in acting like a grinning, slavering hound, since, she said, his conduct "revealed his human-ness" (I was willing to take his human-ness on faith, along with mine, which we need not exhibit to people who don't want us to). It's clear she identifies him with me and would make unflattering high-horse excuses for me the way she makes them for him. These same-sex years of her life have left her not exactly a feminist, which she was in spades at Miss Trustworthy's, but strangely tolerant toward men—which we all hoped would be the good bounty of feminism, though so far have little to show for it. Looked at another way, I'm satisfied to have a daughter who has sympathy to excess, since she'll need it in a long life.

One of her current career thoughts for life after Sea-Clift and her life without Cookie, is to find employment with a liberal congressman, something Harvard graduates can apparently do the way the rest of us catch taxis. Only, she loathes Democrats for being prissy and isn't truly sure what party she fits in with. My secret fear is that she's pissed away her vote on sad-sack, know-it-all Nader, who's responsible for this smirking Texas frat boy stealing a march into the power vacuum.

When her declaimings were over, we walked along the damp sand without saying much. We've taken many of these jaunts and I like them for their freedom to seem everyday-normal and not just the discipline of disaster. Clarissa was carrying her black cross-trainers, letting her long toes grip the caked sand where the ocean had recently withdrawn. Tire tracks from the police patrols had dented the beach surface in curvy parallels stretching out of sight toward Seaside Park, where a smattering of autumn beach habitués were sailing bright Frisbees for Border Collies, building sand skyscrapers, flying box kites and model planes or just leisurely walking the strand in twos and threes in the breeze and glittering light. It was two o'clock, normally a characterless hour in the days after the time change. Evening rushes toward you, although I've come to like these days, when the Shore's masked with white disappearing winterish light yet nothing's nailed down by winter's sternness. I'm grateful to be alive to see it.

"What's it like to be fifty-six?" Clarissa said breezily, sandy shoes adangle, her strides long and slew-footed.

"I'm fifty-five. Ask me next April."

She adapted her steps to mine to stress a stricter precision for dates. I'm aware that she purposefully chooses subjects that are not just about her. She has always been a careful conversationalist and knows, in her Wodehousian manner, how to be a capital egg—though she's much on her own mind lately. "I'm wrong a lot more," I said. "That's one thing. I walk slower, though I don't much care. It probably makes you think I deal well with a challenging world. I don't. I just walk slower." She kept her stride with mine, which made me feel like an oldster. She's as tall as I am. "I don't worry very much about being wrong. Isn't that good?"

"What else?" she said, concertedly upbeat.

"Fifty-five doesn't really have all that much. It's kind of open. I like it." We have never discussed the Permanent Period. It would bore or embarrass her or force her to patronize me, which she doesn't want to do.

Clarissa crossed her arms, clutched her shoes, toes askew in a dancer's stride she used to practice when she was a teen. My own size tens, I noticed, were slightly pigeoned-in, in a way they never were when I was young. Was this another product of prostate cancer? *Toes turn in. . . .*

"Who do you think's turned out better, me or Paul?" she said.

I had no answer for this. Though as with so many things people say to other people, you just dream up an answer—like I told Marguerite. "I don't really think about you and Paul turning out, *per se*," I said. I'm sure she didn't believe me. She's mightily concerned with the final results of things these days, which is what her furlough with me at the beach is all about in a personal-thematic sense: how to make her outcome not be bad, in the presence of mine seeming not so positive. A part of her measures herself against me, which I've told her is not advisable and encourages her to be even older than she can be.

Between my two offspring, she is the "interesting," gravely beautiful star with the gold-plated education, the rare gentle touch, the flash temper and plenty of wry self-ironies that make her irresistible, yet who seems strangely dislocated. Paul is the would-be-uxorious, unfriendly non-starter who pinballed through college but landed in the mainstream, sending nutty greeting-card messages into the world and feeling great about life. These things are never logical.

But when it comes to "turning out," nothing's clear. Clarissa's become distant and sometimes resentful with her mother since declaring herself to "be with" Cookie her sophomore year in college, and now seems caught in a stall, is melancholy about love and loss, and exhibits little interest in earning a living, pursuing prospects or making a new start—something I want her to do but am afraid to mention. Yet at the same time she's become an even more engaging, self-possessed, if occasionally impulsive, emerging adult, someone I couldn't exactly have predicted when she was a conventional, girlish twelve, living with her mother and stepfather in Connecticut, but am now happy to know. (I've loaned her Sally's beater LeBaron convertible as transportation, and since Halloween have put her to work with Mike making cold calls at Realty-Wise, which she halfway enjoys.)

Paul, on the other hand, has rigorously fitted himself in—at least in his own view. He's purchased a substantial two-storey redbrick house (with his mother's and my help) in the Hyde Park district of K.C., drives a Saab, has gotten fat, endured early hair loss, raised a silly mustache-goatee, and—his mother's told me—asks every girl he meets to marry him (one may now have said yes).

But by striving hard to "turn out," Paul has rejected much, and for that reason replicated in early adulthood precisely who he was when he was a sly-and-moody, unreachable teenager, rather than doing what his sister did. And by finding a "home" institution that cultivates harmlessly eccentric fuzzballs like himself and lets them "thrive and create" while offering a good wage and benefits package, Paul has witnessed independence, success-in-his-chosen-environment and conceivably flat-out happiness. All things I apparently failed to provide him when he was a boy.

Paul now lives snugly in the very town where he finally, by a circuitous routing, graduated college—UMKC—(a certain kind of American male fantasy is to live within walking distance of your old dorm). He now attends three university film series a week, has all of Kurosawa and Capra committed to memory, admits to no particular political affinities, enrolls in extension courses at the U, sits on a citizen watchdog committee for crimes against animals and wears bizarre clothes to work (plaid Bermudas, dark nylon socks, black brogues, occasionally a beret—the greeting-card company couldn't care less). He has few friends (though three who're Negroes); he takes vacations to the Chiefs' training camp in Wisconsin, eats too much and listens to public radio *all day long*. He disdains wine tastings, book and dance clubs, opera, Chinese art, dating services and fly-tying groups, preferring ventriloquism workshops, jazz haunts downtown and hopeless snarfling after women, which he calls "moonlighting as a gynecologist." All he shares with his sister is a temper and a wish somehow to be older. In Paul's case, this means a life lived far from his parents—a fact that his mother finds to be a shame but to me seems bearable.

When I visited Paul in K.C. last spring—this was before my cancer happened and before Sally departed—we sat at a little bookshop/pastry/coffee place near his new house, which he wouldn't let me visit due to phantom construction work going on. (I never got inside, only drove past.) While we were sitting and both having a chestnut *éminence* and I was feeling okay about the visit (I'd stopped by on a trip to my old military school reunion), I imprudently asked how long he intended to "hold out here in the Midwest." Whereupon he viciously turned on me as if I'd suggested that dreaming up hilarious captions for drug-store card-rack cards wasn't a life's work with the same *gravitas* as discovering a vaccine for leukemia. Paul's right eye orbit isn't the exact shape as his left one, due to a baseball beaning injury years ago. His sclera is slightly but permanently blood-mottled, and the tender flesh encircling the damaged eye glows red when he gets angry. In this instant, his slate-gray right eye widened—significantly more than the left—as he glared, and his mustache-goatee, imperfect teeth and doofus get-up (madras Bermudas, thin brown socks, etc.) made him look ferocious.

"I've sure as fuck done what you haven't done," he snarled, catching me totally off guard. I thought I'd asked a newsy, innocent question. I tried to go on eating my *éminence*, but somehow it slid off its plate right down into my lap.

"What do you mean?" I grabbed a paper napkin out of the dispenser and clutched at the *éminence*, heavy in my lap.

"Accepted life, for one fucking thing." He'd become suffused in anger. I had no idea why. "I reflect society," he growled. "I understand myself as a comic figure. I'm fucking normal. You oughta try it." He actually bared his teeth and lowered his chin in a stare that made him look like Teddy Roosevelt. I felt I'd been misunderstood.

"What do you think *I* do?" I was leveraging the sagging pastry back up onto its lacy paper plate, having deposited a big black stain on my trousers. Outside the bookshop, a place called the Book Hog, shiny Buicks and Oldses full of Kansas City Republicans cruised by, all the occupants giving us and the bookstore looks of hard-eyed disapproval. I wished I was leagues away from there, from my son, who had somehow become an asshole.

"You're all about *development*." He snorted lustily, as if development meant something like sex slavery or incest. I knew he didn't mean real estate development. "You're stupid. It's a myth. You oughta get a life."

"I *do* believe in development." I said, and geezered around to see who was moving away from us in the shop, sure some would be. Some were.

"If the key fits, wear it." Paul burned his merciless gap-toothed Teddy Roosevelt smile into me. His short, nail-gnawed fingers began twiddling. This conversation could never have happened between me and my father.

"What's your favorite barrier?" he said, fingers twiddling, twiddling.

"I don't know what you're talking about."

"The language barrier. What's your favorite process?" He smirked.

"I give up," I said, my crushed *éminence* pathetic and inedible back up on its greasy paper plate.

Paul's eyes gleamed, especially the injured one. "I know

you do. It's the process of elimination. That's how you do everything."

I was back in my rental car, needless to say, and headed to the airport in less than an hour. I will be a great age before I try my luck with a visit there again.

Clarissa's state of precarious maturation couldn't be more different. Since college, she's started a master's at Columbia Teachers, intending to do work with severely disabled teens (her brother's mental age), volunteered in a teen-moms shelter in Brooklyn, trained for the marathon, taken some acting lessons, campaigned for local liberals in Gotham and generally lived the rich, well-appointed girl-life with Cookie—who's a foreign-currency trader for Rector-Speed in the World Trade Center and owns a power co-op on Riverside Drive, looking out at New Jersey. All seemed in place for a good long run.

Only, during this Gotham time—four years plus since college—Clarissa has told me, her life seemed to grow more and more *undifferentiated*, "both vertically and horizontally." Everything, she noticed, began to seem a part of everything else, the world become very fluid and seamless and not too fast-paced, though all "really good." Except, she wasn't, she felt, "exactly facing all of life all the time," but was instead living "in linked worlds inside a big world." (People talk this way now.) There was school. There was her group of female friends. There was the shelter. There were the favorite little Provençal restaurants nobody else knew about. There was Cookie's many-porched

Craftsman-style house on Pretty Marsh in Maine (Cookie, whose actual name is Cooper, comes from the deepest of unhappy New England pockets). There was Cookie, whom she adored (I could see why). There was Wilbur, Cookie's Weimaraner. There were the Manx cats. Plus some inevitable unattached men nobody took seriously. There were other "things," lots of them—all fine as long as you stayed in the little "boxed, linked" world you found yourself in on any given day. *Not* fine, if you felt you needed to live more "out in the all-of-it, in the big swim." Getting outside, moving around the boxes, or over them, or some goddamn thing like that, was, I guess, hard. Except being outside the boxes had begun to seem the only way it made sense to live, the only "life strategy" by which the results would ever be clear and mean anything. She had already begun thinking all this before I got sick.

My coming down with cancer amounted to nothing less than a great opportunity. She could take a break from her little boxed-linked Gotham world, claim some "shore leave," dedicate herself to me—a good cause that didn't require complete upheaval or even a big commitment, but which made her feel virtuous and me less bamboozled by death—while she lived at the beach and did some power thinking about where things were headed. "Pre-visioning," she calls this brand of self-involved thinking, something apparently hard to do in a boxed-linked world where you're having a helluva good time and anybody'd happily trade you out of it, since one interesting box connects so fluidly to another you hardly notice it's happening because you're so happy—except you're not. It's a means of training your sights on things (pre-visioning) that are really happening to you the instant they happen, and observing where they might lead, instead of missing all the connections. Possibly you had to go to Harvard to understand this. I went to Michigan.

Clarissa seems to think I live completely in the very complex, highly differentiated larger world she's interested in, and that I "deal with things" very well all at once. She only believes this because I have cancer and my wife left me both in the same year and I apparently haven't gone crazy yet—which amazes her. Her view is the view young people typically take of older citizens, assuming they don't loathe us: That we've all seen a lot of stuff and need to be intensely (if briefly) studied. Though surviving difficulties isn't the same as surviving them well. I don't, in fact, think I'm doing that so successfully, though the Permanent Period is a help.

But there have been days during this rather pleasant, recuperative autumn when I've looked at my daughter—in the kitchen, on the beach, in the realty office on the phone—and realized she's at that very moment pre-visioning me, wondering about my life, reifying me, forecasting my eventualities as presentiments of her own. Which I suppose is what parents are for. After a while it may be *all* we're for. But there have also been gloomy days when rain sheeted the flat Atlantic off New Jersey, turning the ocean surface deep mottled green, and mist clogged the beach so you couldn't see waves yet could view the horizon perfectly, and Clarissa and I were both in slack, sorry-sack spirits—when I've thought she might fancifully envy me being "ill," for the way illness focuses life and clarifies it, brings all down to one good issue you can't quibble with. You could call it the one big box, outside which there isn't another box.

Once, while we were watching the World Series on TV, she suddenly asked if she might've had a twin sister who'd died at birth. I told her no but reminded her she'd had an older brother who died when she was little. And of course there was Paul. It was just a self-importanc-ing question she already knew the answer to. She was trying to make sure that what was true of herself was what she knew about, and wanted to hear it from me before it was too late. It's similar to what Marguerite asked in our Sponsor visit. In a woman Clarissa's age, you could say it was a respectable form of past-settlement, though again I'm not sure a settled past makes any difference, no matter how old you get to be.

And of course I know what Clarissa does not permit herself to be fearful of, and is by training hard-wired to confront: *making the big mistake*. Harvard teaches resilience and self-forgiveness and to regret as little as possible. Yet what she *does* fear and can't say, and why she's here with me and sometimes stares at me as if I were a rare, endangered and suffering creature, is unbearable pain. Something in Clarissa's life has softened her to great pain, made her diffident and dodgy about it. She knows such fear's a weakness, that pain's unavoidable, wants to get beyond fearing it and out of those smooth boxes. But in some corner of her heart she's still scared silly that pain will bring her down and leave nothing behind. Who could blame her?

Is it from me, you might reasonably ask, that she's contracted this instinct for crucial avoidance? Probably, given my history.

Looking after me, though, may be a good means to pre-vision pain—mine, hers, hers about me—and make her ready, toughen her up for the inevitable, the one that comes ready or not, and that only your own death can save you from. It's true I love her indefatigably and would help her with her "issues" if I could, but probably I can't. Who am I to her? Only her father.

*C*larissa and I reached our usual turn-around point on our beach walk—the paint-chipped, dented-roof Surfcaster Bar, built on stilts behind the beach berm and, due to the past summer's tourist fall-off, still open after Halloween. Is it the Millennium Malaise, the election, the stock market or everything altogether that's caused everybody in the country to want to wait and see? Knowing the answer to that would make you rich.

The shadowy, wide-windowed bar had its lights burning inside at a quarter to three. A few silhouetted Sea-Clift bibbers could be seen within. A forceful pepperoni and onion aroma drifted down to the beach, making me hungry.

Clarissa stood on one foot, putting her shoe on, a trick she performed with perfect balance, slipping it on behind her, mouth intent, lip bit, as if she was a splendid-spirited racehorse able to tend to herself.

We'd talked enough about how she and Paul had "turned out," about me, about what I thought about marriage now that my second one seemed in limbo. We'd talked about how we both felt estranged from world events on the nightly news. It bothered her that a story was important one week, then forgotten the next, how that had to mean something about disengagement, loss of vital anchorage, the republic becoming ungovernable and irrelevant. There wasn't much we disagreed on.

A colder midafternoon breeze plowed in off the ocean, elevating the kites and Frisbees to brighter heights. We were starting back. Clarissa put her arm on my shoulder and looked beyond me, up to the ghostly drinkers behind the Surfcaster's picture window. "Einstein said a man doesn't feel his own weight in free fall," she said, and looked away toward the pretty, clouded coastal heavens, then gave her head a shake as if to jog loose a less pretentious thought. "Does that go for women, do you think?"

I said, "Einstein wasn't that smart." I just felt good about the beach, the breeze, the scruffy little bar above us behind the dune, where men I'd sold houses to were spying down on Clarissa with admiration and desire for the great beauty I'd somehow scored. "He sounds serious but isn't. You're not in free fall anyway."

"I don't like binary ways of thinking. I know *you* don't."

"*And* and *but* always seem the same to me. I like it."

The long southerly coastline stretched toward my house and now seemed entirely new, observed from a changed direction. Where we were walking was almost on the spot where the team of German sappers came ashore in 1943 with hopes of blowing up something emblematic but were captured by a single off-duty Sea-Clift policeman out for a night-time stroll with his dog, Perky. The sappers claimed to be escaping the Nazis but went to Leavenworth anyway and were sent home when the war was over. Local citizens of German descent wanted a plaque to commemorate those who resisted Hitler, but Jewish groups opposed and the initiative failed, as did an initiative for the policeman's statue. He was later murdered by shady elements who, it was said, got the right man.

From the south I breathed the pungent, sweet resinous scent from the National Shoreline Park, closed by then for the approaching winter. On the beach, discreetly back against the grassy berm, a family unit of Filipinos, one of our new subpopulations, was holding a picnic. These newcomers arrive in increasing numbers from elsewhere in the Garden State, take jobs as domestics, gardeners and driveway repairmen. One has opened a Chicago-style pizzeria beside my office. Another has a coin laundry. A third, a dirty-movie theater in Ortley Beach. Everyone likes them. Our VFW chapter officially "remembers" their brave support of our boys after the terrible march on Bataan. A Filipino flag flies on the 4th of July.

These beach lovers had established an illegal campfire and were laughing and toasting weenies, seated around on the cold sand, enjoying life. The men were small and compact and wore what looked like old golfer's shirts and new jeans and sported wavy, lacquered coifs. The women were small and substantial and peered across the sands at Clarissa and me with lowered, guilty eyes. *We're entitled*, their dark looks said, *we live here*. One man cheerfully waved his long fork at us, a blackened furter hanging from its prongs. A boom box played, though not loud, whatever Filipino music sounds like. We both gave a wave back and plodded toward home.

"As much as you think your life is just another life, it is, I guess," Clarissa said, her long legs carrying her ahead of me. A flat, nasal New England curtness had long ago entered her inflection, as if words were chosen for how she could say them more than for what they meant. She's young, and can still show it. She was now bored with me and was no doubt thinking about getting back to the house and on the phone to the new "friend" she'd tentatively invited for Thanksgiving but who didn't have a name yet—and still doesn't.

"Do you ever think that you were born in New Jersey and thanked your lucky stars, since you could've been born in south Mississippi like me and had to spend years getting it out of your system?" There was not much for us to talk about. I was vamping.

Something about the Filipinos had turned her disheartened. Possibly their small prospects had begun to seem like hers.

"I guess I don't think about that enough." She smiled at me, hands deep in her khaki pockets, her cross-trainers toeing through the tide-dry sand, eyes bent down. This was suddenly a female persona younger than she was and attractive to boys, who were now on the agenda. And then it vanished. "So, what're the big persuasive questions, Frank?" *Persuasive* was another favorite word, along with *vertical* and *horizontal*. It was serious-sounding and made her seem like a smart no-bullshitter. Not a kid. You're persuasive, you're not persuasive. She was trying to pre-vision me again.

"The *really big* ones. Let's see," I said. "Can I remember my shoes are in the shoe shop before thirty days go by and they get donated to the Goodwill? What's my PIN number? Which're the big scallops? Which Everly Brother's Don? Have I actually seen *Touch of Evil* or just dreamed I did? Like that." I turned my attention to an acute and perfect V of geese winging low a quarter mile offshore, headed, it seemed, in the wrong direction for the season. The eyesight's good, I thought, better than my daughter's, who didn't see them.

"Should I become like you, then?" Tall, handsome, unwieldy girl that she is, sharp-witted, loyal and as attentive to goodness as Diogenes, she almost seemed to want me to say, *Yep. And let me keep you forever; let nothing change any more than it has. Be me and be mine. I won't be me forever.*

"Nope, one of me's enough," is what I did say, and with a thud in the heart, watching the geese fade up the flyway until they were gone into a bracket of sun far out in the autumn haze.

"I don't think it'd be so bad to be you," she said. Outlandishly, then, she took my right hand in her left one and held it like she did when she was a schoolgirl and was briefly in love with me. "I think being you would be all right. I could be you and be happy. I could learn some things."

"It's too late for that," I said, but just barely.

"Too late for me, you mean." My hand in hers.

"No. I don't mean that," I said. Then I didn't say much more, and we walked home together.

What Clarissa *actually* did for me was take a firm grasp on the suddenly slack leash of my cancer-stunned life, which I'd begun to let slip almost the instant I got the unfavorable biopsy news.

You think you know what you'll do in a dire moment: pound blood out of your temples with your fists; scream monkey noises; buy a yellow Porsche with your Visa card and take a one-way drive down the Pan-American Highway. Or just climb into bed, not crawl out for weeks, sit in the dark with bottles of Tanqueray, watching ESPN.

What I did was transcribe onto a United Jersey notepad a shorthand version of what the doctor read off: my new diagnosis. "Pros Ca! Gleas 3, low aggr, confined to gland, treatment ops to disc, cure rate + with radical prostetec, call Thurs." This note I stuck on my electric pencil sharpener, then I drove up to Ortley Beach and showed a small sandy-floored, back-from-the-beach prefab to a couple who'd lost their son in Desert Storm and who'd lived under a cloud ever since, but one day snapped out of it and decided a house near the ocean was the best way to celebrate mourning's closure. The Trilbys, these staunch citizens were. They felt good about life on that day, whereas they'd been miserable for a decade. I knew they didn't want to go home empty-handed and had more to be happy about than I did to be morose. So, for a few hours I forgot all about my prostate, and before the hot August afternoon was concluded, I'd sold them the house for four twenty-five.

That night, I slept perfectly—though I did wake up twice with no thought that I had cancer, then remembered it. The next day, I called Clarissa in Gotham to leave a message for Cookie about some tech stocks she'd advised me to unload, and almost as an afterthought mentioned I might have to put up with "a little surgery" because the sawbones over at Urology Partners seemed to think I had minor . . . prostate cancer! My heart, exactly the way it did sitting out front of Marguerite's house, lurched *bangety-bang-bang* like a cat trapped in a garbage pail. My hands went sweaty on the desktop in my at-home office. I got light-headed, tight-brained, seemed unable to keep the receiver pressed to my ear, though of course it was mushed so close it hurt for a week.

"What kind of surgery?" Clarissa spoke with her competent, efficient cadence, like a veteran court clerk.

"Well, probably they just take it out. I—"

"Take it out! Why? Is it that bad? Do you have a second opinion?" I knew her dark eyebrows were colliding and her gold-flecked gray irises snapping with new importance. Her voice was more serious than I hoped mine sounded, which made me want to cry. (I didn't.)

I said, "I don't know." The receiver wobbled in my hand and pinched the helix of my ear.

"When're you seeing this doctor again?" She was terrifyingly businesslike. "This doctor" indicated she thought I'd gone to a cut-rate, drive-thru cancer clinic in Hackensack.

"Friday. I guess maybe Friday." It was Monday.

"I'll come down tonight. You've got insurance, I hope."

"It's not that urgent. Prostate cancer's not like bamboo. I'll survive tonight." I'd already looked at my Blue Cross papers, contemplated not surviving the night.

"Have you told Mom?"

I jabbingly imagined telling Ann—a "by the way" during one of our coffee rendezvous. She'd be not too interested, maybe change the subject: *Yeah, well that's too bad, ummm.* Divorced spouses—long divorced, like Ann and me—don't get over-interested in each other's ailments.

"Have you told Sally?" I sensed Clarissa to be writing things down: *Dad . . . cancer . . . serious.* She favored canary yellow Post-its.

"I don't have her number." A lie. I had a 44 emergency-only number but had never used it.

"Let's don't tell Paul yet, okay? He'll be strange." We didn't need to say he was already strange. "I can get a ride to Neptune with a girl in my theory class. You'll have to pick me up."

"I can drive to Neptune."

"I'll call when I leave."

"That's great." Great was not what I meant to say. Oh-no-oh-no-oh-no is what I meant to say—but naturally wouldn't. "What are we going to do?"

"Do some checking around."

I heard paper tearing on her end, then the other line go *click-click, click-click, click-click.* Someone else was needing her attention. "What about school?"

She paused. *Click-click.* "Do you want me not to come?"

I hadn't felt desperate, but all at once I felt as desperate as a condemned man. My way—the easy way—had seemed like the good way. Her way, the court clerk's way, was full of woe, after which nothing would be better. What do twenty-five-year-old girls know about prostate cancer? Do they teach you about it at Harvard? Can you Google up a cure? "No. I'm happy for you to come."

"Good."

"Thanks." My heart had gone back to, for my age, normal. "I'm actually relieved." I was smiling, as though she was standing right in front of me.

"Just don't forget to pick me up. Think Neptune."

"I can remember Neptune. Jack Nicholson's from Neptune. I've got cancer, but my brain still works."

*C*larissa moved herself in that night and in two days drove Sally's LeBaron to Gotham and brought back ten blue milk crates of clothes, books, a pair of in-line skates, a box of CDs, a Bose and a few framed pictures—Cookie and Wilbur and her, me and Cookie in front of a Moroccan restaurant I didn't remember, her brother Paul in younger days on her mother's husband's Hinckley in Deep River, a group of tall, laughing rowing-team girls from college. These she installed in the guest suite overlooking the beach. Cookie drove down on Thursday in her diamond-polished forest green Rover and stood around the living room smoking oval cigarettes, fidgeting and trying to act congenial. She knew something was happening to her, but wanted not to go to extremes.

When Cookie was leaving, I walked out to her car with her. She and Clarissa had stated their good-byes upstairs. Clarissa hadn't come down. The story was that this was just until I got back on my feet. Though I was on my feet.

As I've said, Cookie is teeth-gnashingly beautiful—small and a tiny bit stout, but with a long, dense shock of black hair tinted auburn, black eyes, arms and legs the color of walnuts, silky-skinned, a round Levantine-looking face (in spite of her Down East Yankee DNA), with curvaceous plum-color lips, a major butt and thick eyebrows she didn't fuss over. Not your standard lesbian, in my experience. Somewhere in the past, she'd incurred a tiny, featherish swimming-pool scar at the left corner of her lip that always attracted my attention like a beauty mark. She wore a pinpoint diamond stud in her right ear, and had a discreet tattoo of a heart with *Clarissa* inside on the back of her left hand. She spoke in a hard-jaw, trading-floor voice trained to utter non-negotiable words with ease. She's Log Cabin Republican if she's an inch tall.

Cookie took my arm as we stood on the pea-gravel drive with nothing to say. Terns cried in the August breeze, which had brought the sound of the sea and an oceany paleness of light around to the landward side of the house. A sweet minty aroma inhabited her blue silk shirt and white linen trousers. I felt the heft of her breast against my elbow. She was happy to give me a little jolt. I was surely happy to have a little jolt, under the circumstances. I was seeing the doctors again the next day.

"I feel pretty good, considering," Cookie said in her hard-as-nails voice. "How do you feel, Mr. Bascombe?" She never called me Frank.

I didn't want to ponder how I felt. "Fine," I said.

"Well, that's not bad, then. My girlfriend's taking a furlough. You've got cancer. But we both feel okay." This was, of course, the manner by which every man, woman, child and domestic animal in Cookie's Maine family accounted for and assessed each significant life's turning: dry, chrome-plated, chipper talk that accepted the world was a pile of shit and always would be, but hey.

I wondered if Clarissa was at an upstairs window, watching us having our brisk little talk.

"I'm hopeful," I said, with no conviction.

"I think I'll go have a swim at the River Club," she said. "Then I think I'll get drunk. What're you going to do?" She squeezed my arm to her side like I was her old uncle. We were beside her Rover. Her name was worked into the driver's door, probably with rubies. My faded red Suburban sat humped beside the house like a cartoon jalopy. I admired the deep, complex tread of her Michelins—my way to sustain a moment with an arm wedged to her not inconsiderable breast. If Cookie'd made the slightest gesture of invitation, I'd have piled in the car with her, headed to the River Club and possibly never been heard from again. Lesbian or no lesbian. Girlfriend's father or no girlfriend's father. The world's full of stranger couples.

"I've got a good novel to read," I said, though I couldn't think of its author or its title or what it was about or why I'd said that, since it wasn't true. I was just thinking she was a stand-up girl, touching and unforgettable. I couldn't conceive why Clarissa would let her go. I'd have lived with her forever. At least I thought so that morning.

"Did you get rid of Pylon Semiconductor?"

"I'll do it tomorrow," I said, and nodded. Squeeze, squeeze, squeeze—my arm, arm, arm.

"Don't forget. Their quarterlies're out way below projected. There'll be a change at CFO. Better get busy."

"No. Yes." Wilbur, the mournful yellow-eyed Weimaraner, stood in the backseat, looking at me. Windows were left open for his benefit.

"You know I love Clarissa, don't you?" she said. I was learning to like her hacksaw delivery.

"I do." She was pulling away. This was all I was getting.

"Nothing good comes easy or simple. Right?"

"That's been my experience." I smiled at her. Can you love someone for three minutes?

"She just needs some context now. It's good for her to be here with you."

Context was another of their frictionless Harvard words. Like *persuasive*. It meant something different to my demographic group. To my quartile, context was the first thing you lost when the battle began. I didn't much like being a *context*—even if I was one.

"Where's *your* father," I asked. Her father was rich as a sheikh, I'd been told, had done things murky and effortless for the CIA sometime, somewhere. Cookie disapproved of him but was devoted. Another impossible parent in a long line.

Mention of the *pater* made her brain go spangly, and she smiled at me glamorously. "He's in Maine. He's a painter. He and my mom split."

"Are you *his* context?"

"Peter raises Airedales, builds sailboats and has a young Jewish girlfriend." (The venerable trifecta.) "So probably not." She shook her fragrant hair, then pressed a button on her key chain, snapping the Rover's locks to attention, taillights flashing *hello*. Wilbur wagged his nubby tail inside. "I hope you feel better," she said, climbing in. I saw the ghost outline of her thong through her white pants, the heartbreaking bight of her saddle-hard butt. She smiled back at me from the leather driver's capsule—I was gooning at her, of course—then let her gaze elevate to the house, as if a face *was* framed in a window, mouthing words she could take heart from: *Come back, come back*. She didn't know Clarissa very well.

"I'm hopeful, remember," I said, more to Wilbur than to her.

She fitted on her heavy black sunglasses, pulled her seat belt across and kicked off her sandals to grip the pedals of her rich-man's sporting vehicle meant for the Serengeti, not the Parkway. "Why does this feel so goddamned strange?" she said, and looked sorrowful, even behind her mirroring shades. "Isn't it strange? Does this feel strange to you?" Reflected in her Italian lenses I was a small faraway man, pale and frail and curved—insignificant in lurid-pink plaid Bermudas and a red tee-shirt that had *Realty-Wise* on it in white block letters. She switched on the ignition, shook out her hair.

"It's a little strange," I admitted.

"Thank you." She smiled, her elbows on the steering wheel. Frowning and smiling were not far apart in her repertoire and went with the voice. "Why is that?" Wilbur nuzzled her ear from the backseat. A plaid blanket had been installed—also for his benefit. She closed the door, laid her arm on the window ledge so I could see the heart with my daughter's name scored on her plump little dorsum.

"Uncharted territory." I smiled.

A single limpid tear wobbled free from beneath her glasses' frame. "Ahhh." She might've noticed the tattoo.

"But it's all right. Uncharted territory can be good. Take it from me." I'd happily have adopted her if she wouldn't let me sleep with her at the River Club.

"Too bad you weren't my father."

Too bad you're not my wife, flashed in my mind. It would've been an inappropriate thing to say, even if true. She should've been with Clarissa, like I should've been with Sally. There were a hundred places I should've been in my life when I wasn't.

She must've thought it was a good thing to have said, though, because when I was silent, standing staring at her, what she said was, "Yep." She patted Wilbur's head on her shoulder, clamped the big Rover into gear—its muffling system tuned like a Brahms organ toccata—and began easing out my driveway. "Don't forget to sell your Pylon," she said out the window, wiping her tear with her thumb as she rolled over the gravel and onto Poincinet Road and disappeared.

What Clarissa did—while I drove off to the Realty-Wise office on Tuesday, indomitably showed two houses, performed an appraisal, scrounged a listing, attended a closing and generally acted as if I didn't have prostate cancer, just a touch of indigestion—was to attack "my situation" like a general whose sleeping forces have suffered a rear-guard sneak attack and who needs to reply with energetic force or face a long and

uncertain campaign, whose outcome, due to attrition and insub-
ordination and bad morale among the troops, is foregone to be
failure.

Dressed in baggy gym shorts and a faded Beethoven tee-shirt,
she brought her laptop to the breakfast room and set up on the
glass-topped table that overlooks the ocean through floor-to-
ceiling windows and simply ran down everything in creation that
had to do with what I "had." She spent all week, till Friday,
researching, clicking on this, printing that, chatting with cancer
victims in Hawaii and Oslo, talking to friends whose fathers had
been in my spot, waiting on hold for hot lines in Atlanta, Houston,
Baltimore, Boston, Rochester, even Paris. She wanted, she said,
to get as much into her "frame" as she could in these crucial
early days so that a clear, confident and anxiety-allaying battle
plan could be drafted and put in place, and all I (we) had to do
was make the first step and the rest would take care of itself just
the way we'd all like everything to—marriage, buying a used car,
parenting, career choices, funeral arrangements, lawn care. I'd
show up from the realty office in rambling but wafer-thin good
spirits at 12:45, armed with a container of crab bisque or a Caesar
salad or a bulldog grinder from Luchesi's on 98th Ave. We'd sit
amidst her papers and beside her computer, drink bottled water,
eat lunch and sort through what she'd learned since I'd escaped—
on the run, you can believe it—five hours before.

I was far too young for "watchful waiting," she'd determined,
whereby the patient enters a Kafkaesque bargain with fate that
maybe the disease will progress slowly (or not progress), that
normal life will fantastically reconvene, many years march

triumphantly by, until another *whatever* picks you off like a sniper (hit by a tour bus; a gangrenous big toe) before the first one can finish you. It's great for seventy-five-year-olds in Boynton Beach, but not so hot for us fifty-fives, whose very vigor is the enemy within, and who disease tends to feast on like hyenas.

"You've got to do *something*," Clarissa said over her picked-at sausage and pepper muffaletta. She looked to me—her father in a faltering spirit—like a glamorous movie star playing the part of a fractious, normally remote but frightened movie daughter, performing just this once her daughterly duty for a dad who's not been around for decades but now finds himself in Dutch, and is played by a young Rudy Vallee in a rare serious role.

A second opinion was nondiscretionary—you just do it, she said, licking her fingertips. Though, she added (Beethoven glaring at me, leonine), that a nutritional history that's included "lots of dairy" and plenty of these rollicking sausage torpedoes was definitely one of many "contributing toxic elements," along with too little tofu, green tea, bulgur and flax. "The literature," she said matter-of-factly, stated that getting cancer at my age was a "function" (another of the banned words) of the unwholesome Western lifestyle and was "a kind of compass needle" for modern life and the raging nineties tuned to the stock market, CNN, traffic congestion and too much testosterone in the national bloodstream. Blah, blah, blah, blah. Chinese, she said, never get prostate cancer until they come to the U.S., when they join the happy cavalcade. Mike, in fact, was now as much at risk as I was, having lived—and eaten— in New Jersey for more than a decade. He wouldn't believe a word of this, I told her, and would burst out yipping at the thought.

I looked wistfully out at the sparkling summer ocean, where yet another container ship was plying the horizon, possibly loaded with testosterone, seeming not to move at all, just sit. Then I imagined it filled with all the ordained foods I'd never eaten: yogurt, flaxseed, wheat berries, milk thistle—but unable to get to shore because of the American embargo. Come to port, come to port, I silently called. I'll be good now.

"Do you want to know how it all works?" Clarissa said like a brake mechanic.

"Not all that much."

"It's a chain reaction," she said. "Poorly differentiated cells, cells without good boundaries, run together in a kind of sprawl."

"Doesn't sound unfamiliar."

"I'm speaking metaphorically." She lowered her chin in her signature way to bespeak seriousness, gray eyes on me accusingly. "Your prostate is actually the size of a Tootsie Roll segment, and where *your* bad cells are, the biopsy says—down in the middle—is good." She sniffed. "Would you like to know exactly how an erection works? That's pretty amazing. Physically, it seems sort of implausible. In the books it's referred to as a 'vascular event.' Isn't that amusing?"

I stared across the table and did not know how to say "no more," other than to scream it, which wouldn't have sounded as grateful as I wanted to seem.

"It's interesting," she said, looking down at her papers as if she wanted to dig one out and show me. "You probably never had problems, did you, with your vascular events?"

"Not that often." I don't know why I picked that to say,

except it was true. What we were talking about now was all strangely true.

"Did you know you can have an orgasm without an erection?"

"I don't want one of those."

"Women do it, sort of," she said, "not that you'd be interested. Men are all about hardness, and women are all about how things feel." *All about*: yet another item on the outlawed list. "Not too difficult to choose, really."

"This isn't funny to me," I said, utterly daunted.

"No, none of it is. It's just my homework. It's my lab report in my filial-responsibility class." Clarissa smiled at me indulgently, after which I went back to the office in a daze.

N ext day, we met again over lunch and Clarissa, now dressed in a faded River Club polo and khaki trousers that made her look jaunty and businesslike, told me she basically had it all figured now. We could put a plan in force so that when I went back to Urology Partners in Haddam on Friday to review my treatment options, I'd be "holding all the cards."

Hopkins and Sloan Kettering were first-rate, but the real brain-trust treasure trove was Mayo in Rochester. This came from computer rankings, from a book she'd read overnight and from a Harvard friend whose father was at Hopkins but liked Mayo and could probably get us in in a jiffy.

The options, she felt, were pretty much straightforward. My Gleason score was relatively low, general health good, my tumor positioned such that radioactive iodine-seed implants, with a titanium BB delivery system, could be the "way to go" if the Mayo doctors agreed. Having "the whole thing yanked," she said (here her eyes fell to the toasted eggplant napoleon I'd bitten the bullet and brought back), was better in the philosophical sense that having no transmission is better than keeping an old beat-up one that might explode. But the side effects of "a radical" involved "lifestyle adjustments and a chance of impairment" (adult diapers, possibly a flat-line on my vascular events). The procedure itself was tolerable, though drastic, and in the end you might not live any longer, while "quality-of-life issues" could be "problematic."

"It's a trade-off," she said, and bit her lower lip. She looked across at me and seemed not to like this conversation. It was no longer a lab report, but words that shed shadowy light on another's future in, as it's said, real time. "Why not take the easier route if you can?" she said. "I would." As always, the best way out is not through.

"They put seeds in?" I said, baffled and contrary.

"They put seeds in," Clarissa said. She was reading from a sheet of paper she'd printed out. "Which are the size of sesame seeds, and you get anywhere up to ninety, under general anesthetic, using stainless-steel needles. Minimal trauma. You're asleep less than an hour and can go home or wherever you want to go the same day. They basically bombard the shit out of the tumor cells and leave the other tissue alone. The seeds stay in forever and become inert in about three months. Once they're in, there's some minor side effects. You might pee more for a while, and it might hurt some. You can't let babies sit in your lap, at first, and you have to try not to cough or sneeze real hard, because you can launch one of these seeds out through your penis—which I guess isn't cool. But you won't set off airport security, and the risk to pets is low. You won't infect anybody you *have sex*"—on the restricted list—"with. And you probably won't be incontinent or impotent. Most important"—she squinted at the paper as if her eyes were blurring, and scratched a finger into the thick hair above her forehead—"you won't be letting this take over the core of your manhood, and the chances are in ten years you'll be cancer-free." She looked up and turned her lips inward to form a line, as if this hadn't necessarily been so pleasant, but now she'd done it. "If you want me to," she said, picking up a scrap of eggplant and bringing it purposefully toward her mouth, "I'll go out to Mayo with you. We can have a father-daughter thing, with you having your radioactive seeds sown into your prostate."

"I don't think that's the job for the daughter," I said. I'd already decided to do whatever she said. Talking to your father about his dysfunctions and impairments wasn't a job for the daughter, either. But there we were. Who else would I want to help me? And who would?

"Okay," Clarissa said amiably. "I don't mind, though. I don't know what the daughter's job really is." She chewed her eggplant while staring at me, leaning on her knobby elbows. She looked like a teen eating a limp French fry. She quietly burped and looked surprised. "It'd be nice if the wife was around. That's a different screenplay, I guess. Marriage is a strange way to express love, isn't it? Maybe I won't try it."

I, at that instant, thought of "the wife," just like people do in movies but almost never in actual life. We usually think about

absolutely nothing in these becalmed moments, or else about
having our tires rotated or buying a new roll of stamps. Writers,
though, like to juice these moments to get at you while you're
vulnerable. What I actually *did* think of, however, was Sally—
sitting down to this very glass-topped breakfast table last June,
with the hot sun on the water and bathers standing in the surf,
contemplating immersion. A tiny biplane had buzzed down the
beachfront, pulling a fluttering sign that said NUDE REVIEW—NJ
35 METEDECONK. I had the *New York Times* flattened out to the
sports page and was skimming a story about a Lakers win, before
heading to the obits. It was the morning Sally told me she was
leaving for Scotland with her long-presumed-dead former
husband, Wally, who'd strangely visited us the week before. She
loved me, she said, always would, but it seemed to her "important"
(there are so many of these slippery words now) to finish "a
thing" she'd started—her ossified marriage, which I'd thought
was kaflooey. It seemed, she said, that I didn't "all that much
need" her, and that "under the circumstances" (always treacherous) it was worse to be with someone who didn't need you
than to let someone who maybe did be alone—i.e., Wally, a boy
I'd actually gone to military school with but never knew before
he showed up in my house. In other words (I supplied this part),
she loved Wally more than me.

I sat there while Sally said some other things, wondering how
in hell she could conclude I didn't need her, and what in hell
"need" meant when another person's "need" was in question.

Then I cried. But she left anyway.

And that was that—right at the table where Clarissa said she'd go to Mayo with me to have my prostate radiated and (as the world says) "hopefully" my life saved.

"I understand the drive south of Red Wing along the Mississippi is gorgeous in the summer." Clarissa was standing, stacking my lunch plate onto hers.

"What's that?" My interior head, for many plausible reasons, felt restless—my grip on the moment, her offer, Sally's departure, the setting overlooking the Sea-Clift beach, the idea of Red Wing, my newly defined physical condition and survival possibilities all scrabbling for attention.

"I was thinking about what I could do while you were in the hospital. I looked Minnesota up on the Web." She smiled the beautiful smile I knew would sink a thousand ships, but was now saving mine. "Minnesota's okay. In the summer anyway."

"I'm sorry, sweetheart. I wasn't paying attention." I smiled up at her.

"I don't blame you," Clarissa said, moving her long bones and having a stretch in the sunlight that fell in on us out of the August sky. Oddly enough, and for an instant, I felt glad about everything. "If I'd heard what you heard," she said, "I wouldn't pay much attention, either." And that was finally the way the whole matter was decided.

5

The drive out to De Tocqueville minds the woodsy curves of King George Road away from Haddam *centre ville*, along the walled grounds of the Fresh Light Seminary, now (in the view of local alarmists) under the control of South Korean army factions. The tall, gaunt, flat-roofed old buildings the Presbyterians built loom beyond the darkening, oak-clustered Great Lawn like a New England insane asylum, though within, all souls are saved instead of lost. Single yellowed windows glow high up the building fronts. Fall classes are ended. Foreign students far from Singapore and Gabon, with no chance of travel home, are locked in their dorm rooms front-loading Scripture into their teeming brains, fine-tuning their homiletic techniques in front of the closet mirror, experiencing, no doubt, the first intimation that most believers aren't *real* believers and don't care what you say if you just take their minds off their woes. Some motivated seminarians, I see, have stretched a brash white-red-and-blue banner between two sentinel oaks, proclaiming BUSH IS GOD'S PRESIDENT AND CHARLTON HESTON IS MY HERO.

Traffic out King George has slackened to a trickle, as though a get-out-of-town-now whistle had sounded, whereas normally it's bumper-to-bumper down to Trenton, three to seven. But the nearing holiday and worsening weather have returned

Haddam to its later-after-hours, nothing-happening somnolence, which all would love to legislate, with day workers, secretaries and substitute teachers broomed out back to their studio apartments and double-wides in Ewingville and Wilburtha.

Possibly it's a side effect of the Millennium (which doesn't seem to have other effects), or else it's my recent indisposed passage in life, but often these days I'm thunderstruck by the simplest, most commonplace events—or nonevents—as if the regular known world had suddenly illuminated itself with a likable freshness, rendering me pleased. Geniuses must experience this every day, with great inventions and discoveries the happy results. ("Isn't it neat how birds fly. Too bad we can't. . . ." "If you just rounded off the sides of this granite block, you could maybe move it a mite easier. . . ." etc., etc.) My recent fresh realizations were on the order of being amazed that someone thought to put a yellow light in between the green and the red ones, or that everybody takes the road from Haddam to Trenton for granted but nobody thinks what a stroke of brilliance it was to build the first road. None of these has made me feel I could invent anything myself, and I don't share my perceptions with others, for fear of arousing suspicions that I've gone crazy due to my treatment. And of course I don't have anybody to share perceptions with anyway. (Clarissa would be bored to concrete.) And to be truthful, my feeling of low-wattage wonder is usually tinged with willowy sadness, since these alertings and sudden re-recognitions carry with them the sensation of seeing all things for the final time— which of course could be true, though I hope not.

Not long ago, I was in my Realty-Wise office, at my desk

with my sock feet up, reading the National Realty Roundtable Agents' Bulletin—a tedious article from their research department about *locked, float-down* mortgage rates being the wave of the future—when my eye slipped down to a squib at the end that said, "When asked what practical value there is in knowing if neutrinos possess mass, Dr. Dieter von Reichstag of the Mains Institute, Heidelberg, admitted he didn't have the foggiest idea, but what really amazed him was that on a minor planet that circles an average-size star (earth), a species has developed that can even ask that question."

I'm sure this had some interesting connections to *locked, float-downs* and to what amazing product enhancements they are in the residential mortgage market (I didn't read to the end). But the amazement Dr. von Reichstag admitted to is more or less what I feel with frequency these days, albeit about less weighty matters. Dr. von Reichstag may also feel the same sensation of last-go-round somberness that I feel, since all new sensations carry in their DNA intimations of their ending. Viewing the new in this way almost certainly relates to having cancer, and with being an older fast-fading star myself.

But driving out King George, on the road to meet my ex-wife—a meeting I have trepidations about—I experience in this late-day gloom another of my illuminations, one that interests me, even though it strikes me as tiresome. Simply stated: What an odd thing it is to *have* an ex-wife you have to have a *meeting* with! Millions, needless to say, do it day in and day out for legions of good reasons. Chinamen do it. Swahilis do it. Inuits do it. Anytime you see a man and woman sitting having coffee in a food court at the mall, or having a drink together in the Johnny Appleseed Bar, or walking side-by-side out of the Foremost Farms into a glaring summer sun holding Slurpees, and you instinctively force onto them your own understanding of what they could be up to (adulterers, lawyer-client, old high school chums), it's much more likely you're seeing an ex-wife and ex-husband engaged in contact that all the acrimony in the world, all the hostility, all the late payments, the betrayals, the loneliness and sleepless nights spent concocting cruel and crueler punishments still can't prevent or not make inevitable.

What *is* it about marriage that it won't just end? I've now had two go on the fritz, and I still don't get it. Sally Caldwell may be asking this question wherever she is with the shape-shifting Wally. I hope it's true.

But is this how life is supposed to be—loving someone, but knowing with certainty you'll never, never, never (because neither of you remotely wants it) have that person except in this sorry ersatz way that requires a "meeting" to discuss who the hell knows what? Clarissa doesn't agree and believes all things can be adjusted and made better, and that Ann and I can finally blubbety, blub, blub. But we can't. And, in fact, if we could, doing so would represent the very linked boxes Clarissa herself claims to hate. Only they'd be mine and Ann's boxes. A lot of life is just plain wrong. And the older I get, the more clearly and often wrong it seems. And all you can do about it—which is what Clarissa is trying to pre-vision—is just start getting used to it, start selecting amazement over bewilderment. This whole subject, you might say, is just another version of fear of dying.

But my bet is 80 percent of divorced people feel this way—bewildered yet possibly also amazed by life—and go on feeling it until the heavy draperies close. The Permanent Period is, of course, the antidote.

The turn-off to De Tocqueville Academy is like the entrance to a storied baronial game preserve—a lichenous, arched stone gate carved with standing stags holding plaques with Latin mottoes on them. The gate alone would cause any parent driving little Seth or little Sabrina, in the backseat of the Lexus reading Li Po and Sartre three levels above their age group, to feel justly served and satisfied by life. "Seth's at De Tocqueville. It's rilly competitive, but worth every sou. His fifth-grade teacher's got a Ph.D. in philosophy from Uppsala and did his post-doc at the Sorbonne—"

Inside the gate, the road, murky in early-dark and drizzle, narrows and passes into first-growth hardwood, dense and primordial. Yellow speed moguls proliferate. Roadside signs let the uninitiated know what sort of place he or she's entering: We're Liberal! GORE FOR PRESIDENT placards just like out on Route 206 clutter the grassy verge as my headlights pass, while others demand that someone GET US OUT!, that PEACE IS WORTH VIOLENCE, that we all should STOP THE CARNAGE! I'm not sure which carnage they have in mind. There's one lonely Bush sign, which I'm sure has been put up to preserve the endowment, since no one here would vote for Bush any more than they'd vote for a chimp.

A pair of whitetails suddenly appears in my headlights, and I have to idle up close and beep-beep before they snort, flag their tails and saunter onto the road edge and begin nibbling grass, unfazed. De Tocqueville, back in the twenties, was in fact a vaunted hunting woods for rich Gotham investment bigwigs (part of the carnage) and was then called Muirgris, which is embossed on the gate in Latin. Packard-loads of happy fat men in tweeds rumbled down on weekends, disported like pashas, drank like Frenchmen, consorted with ladies imported from Philly and occasionally stepped outside to blow the local fauna to smithereens, before packing up on Sundays and happily motoring home.

Muirgris is now De Tocqueville—and a bane of the old roisterers—a "sanctuary" overrun with deer, turkeys, skunks, possum, squirrels, raccoons, porcupines, some say a catamount and a bear or two, all of which enjoy refuge. Disgruntled Haddam home owners living outside the Muirgris boundaries have voiced complaints about predation issues (deer and bunnies eating their winged euonymus) and made dark threats about hiring professional hunter-trappers to "thin the herd" using controversial net-and-bolt devices, all of which has the gentle De Tocqueville staffers up in arms. There have been property-line confrontations, township-council shouting scenes, police called at late hours. Lawsuits have been filed as the animals have crowded inside, seeking protection, and new worries about Lyme disease, bird flu and rabies are now rumored. A relative of one of the original old sports, an interior design consultant from Gotham, gave a speech at commencement, saying his forebear would want Muirgris to stay up with the new century's values and be as "green" today as he was "bloody-minded" in his own time. So far, the issue is far from decided.

I wind a cautious way down to campus—speed bump to speed bump. The school's buildings are all sited around the old rogues' hunting lodge, a regal log and sandstone Adirondack-style dacha now converted into an "Admin Mansion," with earth-friendly faculty and classroom modules built down into the woods, as if prep school was a dreamy summer camp on Lake Memphremagog, instead of a hot petri dish where the future of the fortunate gets on track, while the less lucky schlump off to Colgate and Minnesota-Duluth. My son Paul didn't rate a sniff here ten years ago.

Ann's styleless brown Honda Accord sits alone in the shadowy, sodium-lit faculty lot, the rest of the De Tocqueville staff long gone for Turkey Day festivities. It's possible Ann wants to discuss the children today: Clarissa's revised gender agenda and lack of life direction; Paul's arrival tomorrow with a companion; how to apportion visiting hours, etc. She may, in fact, be afraid of Paul, as I slightly am, though he claims she's his "favorite parent." Having children can sometimes feel like a long, not very intense depression, since after a while neither party has much left to give the other (except love, which isn't always simple). You're each, after all, taken up with your own business—staying alive, in my case. And for reasons they have no control over, the children are always aware they're waiting for you to croak. Paul has expressed this very view as a "generic fact" of parent-child relations, point-blank to his mother, which is probably why she fears him. Clarissa's current gift-of-life to me is the rarest exception, though one partly entered on by her—and why not—because it allows her to think of herself as equally rare and exceptional.

In any case, conversations with one's ex-wife always exist in a breed-unto-themselves/zero-gravity atmosphere that's attractive for its old familiarities, but finally less interesting than communication with an alien. Whenever I'm around Ann, no matter how civil or chatty or congenial we manage it, no matter what the advertised subject matter (it was worse when the kids were younger), her silent thoughts always turn to the old go-nowhere ifs and what-ifs, all the ways "certain people" (who else?) *should be*, but mysteriously are *not*. Try, try, try to be better. Award good-citizenship medals, wait patiently at bedsides, shell out my last dime for kids' therapy— still Ann can't ignore the one fatally blown circuit from long ago, the one that doused the lights and put karmic unity forever out of reach. The Permanent Period again stands me in good stead here by allowing me to take for granted exactly who I am—good, or awful—not who I should be, and along the way blurs the past to haze. But Ann is finally a life-long essentialist and thinks there's a way all things *should* be, no matter how the land lies around her feet. Whereas I am a lifelong practitioner of choices and always see things as possibly different from how they look.

But even with these asymmetries being in continuous effect, I constantly carry around a sometimes heart-wrenching, hand-sweating fear that Ann will manage to die before I do (the odds there have clearly shifted to my favor). Each time I'm about to see her—the few times since she moved back to Haddam last year—I've sunk myself into a deep fret that she's about to release a truckload of bad news. A mysterious lesion, a "shadow," a changed mole, blood where you don't want blood, all requiring ominous tests, the clock ticking—all things I know about now. Following which, I won't know what the hell to do! If loving somebody you'll never really know again and only rarely see can be difficult—though I don't really mind it—think about having to *grieve* for that person long after any shared life is over, life that could've made grieving worthwhile. You think grief like that, grief once removed, can't be experienced? It can kill you dead as a mackerel. I, in fact, wouldn't last a minute and would head straight to the Raritan bridge at Perth Amboy and leave my car a derelict on the Parkway. Think about that the next time you see such a vehicle and wonder where the driver went.

De Tocqueville Academy is a day school only. Even the Arab and Sri Lankan kids have well-heeled host families and good places to go—the Vineyard, the Eastern Shore—for holidays. A couple of dim fluorescent lights are left burning in the Admin Mansion, just like at the seminary, and down toward the classroom modules, past the postmodern ecumenical chapel, toward the glass-exterior athletic installation, a scattering of yellow lights prickles through the oaks and copper beeches as the day is ending. I'm confident I'm being observed on a bank of TV screens from some warm security bunker close by, the watchful crew standing around with coffee mugs, studying me, a "person of interest, doing what, we don't know," my name already jittering through the FBI computer at Quantico. *Am I wanted? Was I wanted? Should I be?* I'm surprised Ann can stand it here, that the practical-bone, non-joiner Michigan girl in her can put up with all this supervised, pseudo-communal, faux-humanistic, all-pull-together atmosphere that infests these private school faculties like mustard gas—everyone burnishing his eccentricities smooth so as to offend no one, yet remaining coiled like rattlers, ready to "become difficult" and "have problems" with colleagues whose eccentricities aren't burnished the same way. You think it's the psychotic parents and the hostile, under-medicated kids who drive you crazy. But no. It's always your colleagues—I know this from a year's teaching at a small New England college back in the day. It's the Marcis and the Jasons, the exotic Ber-nards and the brawny Ludmillas, over for the Fulbright year from Latvia, who send you screaming off into the trees to join the endangered species hiding there. In-depth communication with smaller and smaller like-minded groups is the disease of the suburbs. And De Tocqueville's where it thrives.

Ann has given me directions to the indoor driving range where we're to meet. Footlights lead around the old plutocrats' hunting lodge, down a paved, winding trail under dripping trees, past brown-shingled, clerestoried class buildings, each with a low rustic sign out front: SCIENCE. MATH. SOCIAL STUDIES. FILM. LITERATURE. GENDER. Ahead, at a point farther into the woods—I see my breath in the cedar-scented air—I can make out a high lighted window. Below is a glass double door kept open just for me with a fat swatch of weather carpet. This I head for, my jaw tightening like a spring, my neck sweating, my hands fidgety. I don't feel at all vigorous, and vigorous is how I always want to feel when I present myself to Ann. I also don't feel at ease in my clothes. I've always been a dedicated solid-South, chinos, cotton shirt, cotton socks 'n loafers wearer—the same suiting I packed in my steamer trunk when I came up from Mississippi to Ann Arbor in '63, and that's done the job well enough through all life's permutations. It's not, in fact, unusual attire for Haddam, which again has its claque of similarly suited crypto-southerners—old remittance men who trace back to rich Virginia second sons of the nineteenth century and who arrived to seminary study bringing along their colored servants (which is why there was once a stable Negro population in the Wallace Hill section—now gentrified to smithereens). To this day, a seersucker suit, a zesty bow tie, white bucks and pastel hosiery are considered acceptable dress-up (post–Memorial Day) at all Haddam lawn parties.

Nowadays, though, and for no reason I understand, what I find myself wearing seems to matter less than it used to. Since August, I no longer look in mirrors or glance into storefront windows, for fear, I guess, I'll glimpse a worrisome shoulder slump that wasn't there before, or an unexplained limp, or my chin hung at a haggard angle on my neck stem. We're best on our guard against becoming the strange people we used to contrast ourselves favorably to: those who've lost the life force, lost the essential core vigor to keep up appearances, suffered the slippage you don't know has slipped until it's all over. I definitely don't want to find myself turning up at a closing wearing copper-colored Sansabelts, a purple-and-green-striped Ban-Lon, huaraches with black socks and sporting a yawing, slack-jaw look of "whatever." Lost, in other words, and not remembering why or when.

In the present moment, it's my tan barracuda jacket I'm uneasy about. I bought it at a summer's-end sale from the New Hampshire catalog outfit I usually buy from, thinking it'd be nice to own something I'd never owned before—a wrong-headed impulse, since I now feel like some rube showing up to take flying lessons. Plus, there're the green-and-blue argyles and fake suede, Hush Puppy-like crepe-soled tie-ups I bought in Flint, Michigan, on a one-day trip in October. They were on sale in a shoe-store clearance where odd shoes in odd sizes were lined up on the sidewalk, and I felt like a fool not to find *something*, even if I never wore it. Which I now have. I don't know what Ann will think, having gotten used to seeing me the old way during years of divorced life. If I could, I'd ditch the jacket out here in the yew shrubs, except I'd freeze and catch cold—the BBs having done a job on my immune department. So, uneasiness or not, I'm consigned to present myself to Ann just as I am.

At the end of the winding asphalt path (it's only 4:00 p.m. but as good as dark), the Athletic Module is a state-of-the-art facility with lots of gigantic windows facing the woods, floating stairways and miles of corridors with exposed brightly-painted pipes and ductwork to give the impression the place had once been a power plant or a steel mill. It was designed by a Japanese architect from Australia, and according to the *Packet*, the Tocquies all refer to it as "Down Under," though the actual name is the Chip and Twinkle Halloran Athletic and Holistic Health Conference Center, since Chip and Twinkle paid for it.

Dim ceiling lights reflect off the long, echoing, buffed corridor floor when I step in where it's warm. Dank swimming pool water, sour towels, new athletic gear and sweat make the hot air stifling. I hear the consoling sound of a lone basketball being casually dribbled on a gym floor that's out of sight. No one's in the dark glassed-in events office. The turnstile is disengaged to let anyone pass. The indoor driving range is supposedly down the corridor, then right, then right again. I can't, though, resist a peek at the "Announcements" case by the events window. I regularly check all such notice boards in Sea-Clift—by the shopping carts at Angelico's, above the bait tank at Ocean-Gold Marina—standing arms folded, studying the cards for kittens lost, dinette sets to sell, collections of Ezio Pinza '78s, boats with trailers, boats without, descriptions of oldsters wandered off, the regular appeal for the young motorcycle victim in the ICU. Even Purple Hearts are for sale. You can eavesdrop on the spirit of a place from these messages, sense its inner shifts and seismic fidgets—important in my line of work, and more accurate than what the Chamber of Commerce will tell you. Real life writ small is here, etched with our wishes, losses and dismays. I occasionally pluck off a "For Sale by Owner" note and leave it on Mike's desk for follow-up—which usually comes to nothing. Though it might. I once saw the name of an old Sigma Chi brother on a notice board on Bourbon Street in New Orleans, where I'd gone to a realtors' meeting. Seems my onetime bro Rod Cabrero had been last seen there, and family members in Bad Axe were worried and wanted him to know he was loved—no residual bad feelings about the missing checks and stock options. Another time up in Rumson, right here in the Garden State, I saw a notice for a "large Airedale" found wandering the beach, wearing a tag that said "Angus," and instantly recognized it as the lost, lamented family treasure of the Bensfields on Merlot Court in Sea-Clift—a house I'd sold them less than a year before. I was able to effect the rescue and will get the listing again when they're ready to sell. Just like the home-for-sale snapshots we put in our office window, these message boards all say "there's a chance, there's hope," even if that chance and that hope are a thousand-to-one against.

Here, the *"Noticias del Escuela"* board is none too upbeat. "Have you been raped, fondled, harassed, or believe yourself to be, by a De Tocqueville faculty member, staff or security person? THERE'S HELP. Call [a phone number's supplied]." Another insists, "You don't have to be a minority to suffer a hate crime." (Another number offered.) A third simply says, "You can grieve." (No number is given, but a name, Megan, is in quotes.) There's also a schedule for blood testing (hepatitis C, AIDS, thyroid deficiency). A typed note is posted here from Ann about the Lady Linkster tryouts and team meeting. Another one says, "Fuck Bush," with the inflaming verb x-ed over. And one, in red, simply says, "Don't keep it to yourself, whatever it is. Culturally, we are all orphans." De Tocqueville seems not only funless but careworn and fatigued, where any time you're not studying, you'd better be worrying or dodging unwanted experiences. I'm glad Paul didn't get in, which isn't to say I'm thrilled with how things have gone.

Ann Dykstra is visible, alone and practicing, when I peer through the tiny door window into the blazing-lit inner sanctum of the indoor driving range (formerly a squash court). She doesn't know I'm here watching but is aware I *might* be, and so is going extra scrupulously through her ball placement, club-face address, feet alignment, shoulder set, weight distribution and outbound stare toward a nonexistent green. A white catch-net with golf balls scattered around has been established at the squash court's front wall, and behind it an enlarged color photograph of a distant links course on some coast of Scotland. All this is in preparation for her perfectly grooved, utterly fluid, head-down, knees-bent, murderous swing, the lethal metal-headed driver striking the nubbly ball so violently as to crush it into space dust. "This is how the fucker's done and always will be. No matter what asshole's watching or isn't"— is what I read this daunting display to say in so many words.

She doesn't glance toward the door, which I'm safe behind in the corridor darkness, but begins placing a second ball onto a pink rubber tee fixed into a carpet of artificial grass, and re-commences the fateful protocol of striking.

I don't want to go in. To enter will only ruin something that *is* and is perfect, by intruding a clamorous, troublesome, infuriating, chaotic *something else*. I'd forgotten, watching Ann through the peephole like a witness viewing a suspect, how much a perfect golf swing is an airtight defense against all bothersome "others." Once I knew that, long ago when I wrote sports: That for all athletes—and Ann's a good one—a perfect stroke protects against things getting over-complicated. I would actually slink away now if I could.

But just as I take an opportunistic look down the corridor with a thought to escape, Ann, I find, is staring at me—my partial, reluctant face obviously visible through the double-thick window. Her lips inside move in speech I can't hear. I again have an urge to run, become an optical illusion, down the hall, around a corner, be no more. But it's too late. Way too late for escape.

I push in the heavy, air-sucking door and Ann's words come into my ears. ". . . thought you were the security guy, Ramon," she says, and smiles cheerlessly at my presence. She has her driver in hand like a walking stick and goes back to addressing the new ball as if I *were* Ramon. "I don't like to be watched when I'm in here. And he watches me."

"You looked pretty solid." I'm guessing this is the appropriate compliment.

"How are you?" Ann calmly lays her club face to the ball's surface without touching it. I'm holding the heavy door open, barely inside. The brightly lit room smells like heated wood products.

"I'm great." I mean to act vigorous even if I'm not. Ann and I haven't seen each other in months. A chummy, hygienic phone chat would've been as good or better than this. The dense air is already thickening with ifs and what-ifs. "Nice place in here," I say, and look up and around. A black video camera's on a tripod to the left, a wooden team bench sits against the white squash court wall. The Scottish links course has been holographed right onto the plaster behind the catch-net. It could just as well be a chamber for a lethal injection.

"It's okay. They rigged this place up for me." Ann lightly taps her white ball off its tee, bends to retrieve it. She is turned out just as I've seen her all our life, married and apart—golf shorts (pink), white shoes (Reeboks with pink ankleless socks), a white polo with some kind of gold crest (De Tocqueville no doubt), white golf glove, and a pair of red sunglasses stuck in her hair like a country-club divorcée. She now exudes—unlike thirty years ago, when I couldn't get enough of her—a more muscular, broader-backed, stronger-armed, fuller-breasted, wider-hipped aura of athleticized sexlessness, which is still bluntly carnal but isn't helped by her blonded hair being cut in a tail-less ducktail a prison matron might wear, and her pale Dutch-heritage skin looking sweat-shiny and paper-thin. The fly of her shorts has inched down from the top button due to ungoverned belly force. I'm sorry to say there's nothing very appealing about her except that she's herself and I'm unexpectedly glad to see her. (Clenching has now made my third molar, left side, lower, begin to ache in a way that makes my jaw tighten. I should put in my night guard, which is in my pocket.)

Ann walks in a long, slightly up-on-toes gait over to the pine bench and leans her driver into a rack where other clubs stand. She sits on the pine and begins untying her golf shoes. I'm stationed in the doorway, feeling both reluctance and enthusiasm, longing and uxorious remorse. I don't know why I'm here. I wish I knew a hilarious golf joke but can only think of one that involves a priapic priest, a genie in a bottle and a punch line she wouldn't like.

"Somebody blew out the lunch room windows at the hospital," I say. Not a great conversation starter. Though why did no one at the funeral home mention it? News in Haddam must travel more slowly than ever. Everyone in his own space. Even Lloyd Mangum.

"Why?" Ann looks up from her shoelaces, bent over her thick, shiny knees. Pushing through her polo-shirt back is the wide, no-nonsense imprint of a brawny sports bra.

"I don't know. The election. People get pissed off. Doctors are all Republicans."

"How's real estate?"

"Always a good investment. They aren't making any more of it." I smile and round my eyes as a gesture of geniality.

Ann sets her Reeboks, toes out, under the bench atop the miserable green turf. She disapproves of my selling houses (Sally loved it, loved it that I think of real estate as related to Keatsian negative capability, with the outcome being not poetry but generalized social good with a profit motive). Ann fell in love with me when I was an aspiring (and failing) novelist, but since then has lived in Connecticut, grown rich and may have no use for negative capability. She may consider selling real estate to be like selling hubcaps on Route 1. She could be a Republican herself, though when I married her, she was a Soapy Williams Democrat.

I step all the way inside the warmed, dazzling, wood-scented room and let the door suck closed behind me. I don't know where to go or what to do. I need a golf club to hold. Though it's not so bad in here—unexpectedly satisfying, strangely intimate. We're at least alone for once.

"I have something I want to say to you, Frank." Ann leans back against the white wall, which has been recently repainted. She looks straight at me, her pale cheeks tightened and the downward tug at the corners of her mouth signifying importance of an ominous kind. Using my name always means "serious." I feel my hands and lips spontaneously (I hope invisibly) tremble. I do not need bad news now.

Ann wiggles her sock feet on the phony turf and looks down.

"Great"—my smile my only defense. Maybe it *is* great news.

Maybe Ann's marrying Teddy Fuchs, the gentle-giant math teacher who everybody thought was a queer but was just shy and had to wait (till age sixty) for his camps-survivor mother to pass on. Or maybe Ann's decided to cash in Charley's annuity and live on the Costa del Sol. Or maybe she's figured out a meaningful new way to explain to me what an asshole I am. I'm all ears for any of that. Just nothing medical. I've had it with medical.

"Can I tell you a story?" She's still looking down at her pink socklets as if she drew assurance from them.

"Sure," I say. "I like stories. You know me." Her gray eyes dart up, warning against familiarity.

"I went into Van Tuyll's Cleaners the other day to check on a damage claim about a pair of pants they'd stained and hadn't paid me for. I was mad, and you can't really sue your dry cleaners over a pair of pants, but I thought of going in the shop and doing something disruptive to punish them. They really aren't very nice people."

Bring in some deer urine or maybe set a skunk loose behind the counter. I've thought of doing that. Just not a "device." I haven't moved an inch from where I've been under the too-warm lights.

"Anyway," Ann says. "When I got to the shop, down that little Grimes Street alley"—fine address for a dry cleaners—"a typed card was taped inside the door that said, 'We're closed due to the tragic death of our daughter Jenny Van Tuyll, who lost her life last Saturday in a traffic accident in Belle Fleur. She was eighteen. Our life will never be the same. The Van Tuyll family.' I actually had to sit down on the edge of the shop window to keep myself from fainting. It just overtook me. That poor Jenny Van Tuyll. I'd talked to her fifty times. She was as sweet as she could be. And that poor family. And there I was, mad about my goddamned Armani pants. It seemed so stupid." Ann squints at her feet, then raises her eyes to me.

Sad news. But not as bad as "I've got a fast-growing enceph-aloblasty and probably only about a month to keep breathing." "It's bad," I say gravely. Though I think: But you really can't feel worse about it just because of your Armani pants. They *are* a dry-cleaners. You wouldn't even know about this if you weren't already mad at them.

Ann lowers her ocean-gray eyes, then lifts them to me signifi-cantly, and all the remembered shock and grief and impatience with me are absent from her gaze. An indoor driving range is an odd place to have this conversation. We have had a child to die, of course—in the very hospital where someone exploded a bomb today. Surely there's no need to talk about that now. For a while after Ralph's death, Ann and I met at the grave on his birthday. This being after our divorce. But eventually we just quit.

"Do you wonder, Frank, if when you feel something really forcefully—so forcefully you know it's true—do you ever wonder if how you feel is just how you feel that particular day and tomorrow it won't matter as much?"

"No doubt about it," I say. "It's a good thing. We need to question our strong feelings, though we still need to be available to feel them. It's like buyer's remorse. One day you think if you don't have a particular house, your whole life's ruined. Then the next day you can't imagine why the hell you ever considered it.

Though plenty of times people see a house, fall in love with it, buy it, move in and never leave till they get taken out in a box." For some reason, I'm grinning. I wonder if the video camera that's pointed at me is operating, since something's making me uneasy, so that I'm racketing on like Norman Vincent Peale.

Ann has taken her red sunglasses out of her matron-athlete's hair and carefully folded them while I'm blabbering, as if whatever I'm saying must be endured.

"It's just hard to know," I say, and inch back against the door through which I spied Ann a while ago teaching a stern lesson to an innocent Titleist.

"I know I've told you this, Frank," she says, carefully laying her Ray-Bans on the pine seat beside her as a means of shutting me up about buyer's remorse. "But when Charley was so bad off, and you drove up those times to sit with him in Yale-New Haven, when his real friends got preoccupied elsewhere, that was a very, very excellent thing to have done. For him. And for me."

It only lasted six weeks; then off he went to heaven. Through his haze, Charlie thought I was someone named Mert he'd known at St. Paul's. A few times he talked to me about his first wife and about important twelve-meter races he'd attended, and once or twice about his current wife's former husband, whom he said was "rather sweet at times" but "ineffectual." "A Big-Ten graduate," he said, smirking, though he was nutty as a coon. "You couldn't imagine her ever marrying that guy," he said dreamily. I told Charley the fellow probably had some good qualities, to which Charley, from his hospital bed, handsome face drained of animation and interest, said, "Oh, sure, sure. You're right. I'm too tough. Always have been." Then he said the whole thing over again, and in a few days he died.

Why would I do such a thing? Sit with my ex-wife's dying husband? Because it didn't bother me. That's why. I could imagine someone having to do it to me—a total stranger—and how nice it would be to have someone there you didn't have to "relate" to. I don't want to visit the subject again, however, and fold my arms across my chest and look down like a priest who's just heard an insensitive joke.

"It made me see something about you, Frank."

"Oh." Noncommittal. No question mark. I don't intend asking what it might be, because I don't care.

"It's something I think you would've said was always true about you."

"Maybe."

"I don't think I've always thought so. I might've when we were kids. But I quit about 1982." She picks up her white golf glove and folds it into a small package.

"Oh."

"You're a kind man," Ann says from the team bench.

I blink at her. "I *am* a kind man. I was a kind man in 1982."

"I didn't think so," she says stoically, "but maybe I was wrong."

I, of course, resent being declared something I've always been and should've been known to be by someone who supposedly loved me, but who wasn't smart or patient or interested enough to know it when it mattered and so divorced me, but now finds herself alone and it's Thanksgiving and I conveniently have cancer. If this is leading to some sort of apology, I'll accept, though not with gratitude. It could also still be a clear-the-decks declaration before announcing her engagement to oversized Fuchs. Our bond is nothing if not a strange one.

"You can't live life over again," Ann says penitently. She smiles up and across at me, as if telling me that I'm kind has gotten something oppressive off her chest. All dark clouds now are parting. For her anyway.

"Yeah. I know." A pearl of sweat has slid out of my hairline. It's hot as hell in here. What I'd like to do is leave.

"I didn't know if you really did know that." Ann nods, still smiling, her eyes sparkling.

"I understand conventional wisdom," I say. "I'm a salesman. Placebos work on me."

Ann's smile broadens, so that she looks absolutely merry. "Okay," she says.

"Okay," I say. "Okay what?" I glance at the tri-podded Sony, useful for showing Lady Linksters hitches in their backswings. "Is that goddamn thing turned on?"

Ann looks up at the black box and actually grins. Many years have elapsed since I've seen her so happy. "No. Would you like me to turn it on?"

"What's going on?" I'm feeling dazed in this fucking oven. It must be what a hot flash feels like. First you get hot; then you get mad.

"I have something to say." She is solemn again.

"You told me. I'm kind. What else? I accept your apology." Ungiven.

"I wanted to tell you that I love you." Both her hands are

flat down beside her on the bench, as if she or the bench were exerting an upward force. Her gray eyes have trapped me with a look so intent I may never have seen it before. "You don't have to do anything about it." Two small tears wobble out of her eyes, although she's smiling like June Allyson. Sweat, tears, what next? Ann sniffles and wipes her nose with the side of her hand. "I don't know if it's again, or still. Or if it's something new. I don't guess it matters." She turns her head to the side and dabs at her eyes with the heel of her hand. She breathes in big, breathes out big. "I realized," she says mournfully, "it's why I came back to Haddam last year. I didn't really know it, but then I did. And I was actually prepared to do nothing about it. Ever. Maybe just be your friend in proximity. But then Sally left. And then you got sick."

"Why are you telling me this now?" My mouth's been ajar. These are not the words I want to say. But the words I want to say aren't available.

"Because I went to Van Tuyll's cleaners, and their pretty daughter was dead. And that seemed so unchangeable—dying just blotting things out. And I thought I'd invented ways to be toward you that let me pretend that being mad at you wasn't changeable, either—or whatever it is. But those ways can be blotted out, too. I guess there are degrees of unchangeableness. *Love*'s a terrible word. I'm sorry. You seem upset. I decided I'd just tell you. I'm sorry if you're upset." Ann hiccups, but catches her hiccup in her throat as a little burp, just like Clarissa. "Sorry," she says.

"Are you just telling me this because you're afraid I'm going to die, and you'll feel terrible?"

"I don't know. You don't have to do anything about it." She picks up her sunglasses and puts them back up in her hair. She reaches beneath the bench, produces a pair of brown penny loafers she puts on over her pink socks. She looks around where she's sitting for something she might be leaving, then stands in the blaring lights, facing me. "My coat's behind you." She's fast receding into the old protocols that she, for one moment, had gotten beyond and out into the open air, where she caught a good whiff and held it in her lungs. The poet promised, "What is perfect love? Not knowing it is not love, some kind of interchange with wanting, there when all else is wanting, something by which we make do." I'm not making do well at all. Not achieving interchange. I am the thing that is wanting. After so long of wanting.

I turn clumsily, and there is Ann's jacket on a coat-rack I hadn't seen, a thin brown rayon-looking short topcoat with a shiny black lining—catastrophically expensive but made to look cheap. I take it off the old-fashioned coat tree and hand it over. Heavy keys swag inside a pocket. Its smell is the sweet powdery scent of womanly use.

"I'll let you walk me out to my car." She smiles, putting her brown coat on over her golfing uniform. She moves by, but I am not ready with a touch. She pulls open the air-sucking squash-court door. A breath of cool floods in from the corridor, where it'd seemed warm before. She turns, assesses the room, then reaches beyond me and snaps off the light, throwing us into complete, studdering darkness, closer together than we have been in donkey's years. My fingers begin to twitch. She moves past me into the shadowy hall. I almost touch the blousy back of her coat. I hear a boy's voice down the long hall. "You asshole," the voice says, then laughs—"hee, hee, hee, hee." A basketball again bounces echoingly on hardwood. *Splat, splat, splat.* A *kerchunk* of a gym door opening, then closing. A girl's voice—lighter, sweeter, happier—says, "You give love a bad name." And then our moment is, alas, lost.

*I*t's only 5:30, but already dead-end nighttime in New Jersey. Nothing good's left of the day. Heading across the cold, peach-lit parking lot, Ann at first walks slowly, but then picks it up, going briskly along toward her Accord. The sulfur globes atop the curved aluminum stanchions light the damp asphalt but do not warm. All here seems deserted except for our two vehicles side-by-side, though of course we're still being watched. Nothing goes unobserved on this portion of the planet.

We have said nothing more, though we understand that saying nothing's the wrong choice. It is for me to declare something remarkable and remarkably important. To add to the sum of our available reality, be the ax for the frozen sea within us, yik, yik, yik, yik. Though I'm for the moment unable to fit my thoughts together plausibly or to know the message I need to get out. Ann and I are on a new and different footing, but I don't know what that footing might be. The Permanent Period and its indemnifying sureties are in scattered retreat out here in the post-rain De Tocqueville lot. They have sustained too many direct hits for one day and have lost some potency.

"I've lived here almost a whole year now." Ann walks resolutely beside me. "I can't say I love Haddam. Not anymore. It's odd."

"No," I say. "Me, either. Or, me, too."

"But . . ?"

"But what?" We're back to our old intractable, defensible selves. Asking "What?" means nothing.

"But nothing." She fishes the clump of jingly keys out of her top-coat pocket and fingers through them beside her car. It was this way when we visited Ralph's grave on his birthday in the spring: a negotiated peace of little substance or duration, pleasing no one, not even a little. Then she says, "I suppose I should say one more thing." It's cold. Clouds are working against the moon's disk. I'm tempted to put a hand on her shoulder, ostensibly for warmth's sake. She is wearing golfing clothes, after all, in falling temps.

"Okay." I do not put a hand on her shoulder.

"All those things I said in there." She quietly, self-consciously clears her throat. I smell her hair, which still hints of the warm wood inside and something slightly acidic. "I meant all that. And what's more, I'd live with you again—where you live, if you wanted me to. Or not." She sighs a businesslike little sigh. No more tears. "You know, parents who've lost a child are more likely to die early. And people who live alone are, too. It's a toxic combination. For both of us, maybe."

"I already knew that." Everybody reads the same studies, takes the same newspapers, exhibits the same fears, conceives the same obsessive, impractical solutions. Our intelligence doesn't account for much that's new anymore. Only, I don't find that discouraging.

It's like reading cancer statistics once you've been diagnosed—they become a source of misplaced encouragement, like reading last night's box scores. Misery may not love company. But discouragement definitely does. "Would-you-like-to-come-over-on-Thursday-and-have-Thanksgiving-with-me? I-mean-with-us-with-the-children?" With blinding swiftness these ill-conceived words leave my mouth, taking their rightful place among all the other ill-conceived things I've said in life and taking the place of something better I should've said but couldn't say because I was paralyzed by the thought of living with Ann and that she's now concluded I'm alone.

She clicks her car unlocked and swings the door out. Clean, new-car bouquet floods our cold atmosphere. The dimly lit cockpit begins pinging.

Ann turns her back to me as if to put something inside the car—though she's carrying nothing—then turns back, chin down, eyes trained on my chest, not my (shocked) face. "That's nice of you." She's smiling weakly, June Allyson-style again. *Ping, ping, ping.* It's other than the invitation she wanted and a poor substitute—but still. "I think I'd like that," she says, her smile become proprietary. A smile I haven't seen trained on me in a hundred years. *Ping, ping, ping.*

And just then, as when we are children sick at home with a fever in bed late at night, suddenly everything moves a great distance away from me and grows small. Softened voices speak from a padded tube. Ann, only two feet away, appears leagues away, her pinging Accord all but invisible behind her. The *pinging, ping, ping* comes as if from fresh uncovered stars high in the cold sky.

"That's great," her distant voice says.

Ann looks at my face and smiles. We are now not merely on different footings but on different planets, communicating like robots. "You'll have to give me directions, I guess."

"I will," I say robotically, cheeks and lips smiling a robot smile. "But not now. I'm cold."

"It *is* cold," she says, ignition key in hand. "When's Paul arriving?"

"Paul who?"

"Paul, our son." *Ping, ping.*

"Oh." Everything's smashing back into close quarters, the night hitting me on the nose. Real sound. Real invitation. Real disaster looming. "Tomorrow, I guess. He's en route." For some reason I say *route* to rhyme with *gout*, a way I never say it.

"Is that a new jacket," she asks. "I like it."

"Yeah. It is." I'm stumped.

She looks at me hard. "Do you feel all right, Frank?"

"I do," I say. "I'm just cold."

"There are a lot of things we haven't talked about."

"Yeah."

"But maybe we will." And instead of crossing the gulf of years to give my cold cheek a buss with cold lips, Ann gives me three pats on my barracuda jacket shoulder—pat, pat, pat—like a girl in a riding habit patting the shoulder of an old saddle nag she's just had a pleasant but not especially eventful ride on. "Paul's coming to my house for dinner tomorrow. I asked Clary, but she declined, of course." Same proprietary equitational smile and voice. Time for your rubdown and a nose bag. *Ping, ping, ping.* "I guess I'll see you for dinner Thursday."

"Okay."

"Call me. Tell me how to get there."

"Yes. I will. I'll call you." *Ping, ping.*

She looks at me as if to say, I know you might die right here and now, but we're going to pretend you won't and everything'll be fine, old fella. And it is in this manner we manage our good-bye.

*A*s if someone, someone *else*, someone in a panic, someone like me but not me, was piloting my dark capsule, I am down the drizzly midnight De Tocqueville entrance lane like a NASCAR driver, my tires barely registering the speed moguls, skidding on each curve, sending deer, possum and catamount leaping into the sheltering woods, until I'm out past the signage, out the gate and *out*, back onto 27, headed into town. I of course have to piss.

And, no surprise, I am locked in a fury of regret, self-reproach and bafflement. Why, why, why, why, why did I *have* to ask? Why can't I be trusted *not* to ask? What hysteria chip in my personal hard drive impels me to self-evident disaster? Does anything teach us anything? Do seventeen years of perfectly acceptable divorced life, following clear-cut evidence of incompatibility, *not* dictate steering wide of Ann Dykstra, no matter how much I love her? *Does* cancer make you stupid as well as sick? If there was a Sponsor, a palmist, a shrink open late, dispensing mercy and wisdom to drop-ins, I'd beg, write a big check, dedicate quality hours. As stated, our intelligence doesn't account for much.

I wish, for the very first time, for a cell phone. I'd call Ann from the car and leave a cringing message: "Oh, I'm a terrible, terrible man. Mistake after mistake after mistake. You were always right about me. Just please don't come for Thanksgiving. We'd have an appalling time. I've booked you an A-list banquette at the Four Seasons, selected the right Dom Pérignon, arranged for Paul Newman and Kate Hepburn to be on your either side (where they'll definitely want to talk to you), ordered the baked Alaska in advance. Keep the limo, take a friend. . . . Just keep away on Thanksgiving. Even though you love me. Even if I'm dying. Even if you're lonely. Take my word for it."

If we'd only had our just-finished conversation on the phone—from home, without the tears, the sock feet, the lonely, converted, over-heated squash court—none of this would be happening. When I was at Mayo I met a hog farmer from Nebraska up on the urology floor, same as me, but who'd had a stroke and could barely speak to anyone. His happy, fat, grinning, scrubbed-face farm wife did the talking while he worked his eyebrows and nodded and smiled at me furiously but in total silence. Except on the phone, the wife told me, old Elmer'd yak and laugh and philosophize hours on end and never miss a beat or a connection, could even tell dirty jokes. Something's to be said for disembodied communication. Too much credit's given to the desultory *intime*. It's why the governor's never at the prison when the deed's being done.

I stop on the darkened roadside in front of a big, well-treed, hedge-banked, wide-lawned Norman Tudor that was actually moved to its present site twenty years ago from the Seminary grounds. There are few cars on this stretch of 27, so I can shuffle unnoticed up against the dark, dripping cedar hedge, in the damp leaf duff, and piss out the two cups I've accumulated since I can't remember when but which have suddenly begun to make me panicky. A diaper would be a fail-safe, but I'm holding the line there.

Then I'm back in the car and headed into Haddam, relieved, vaguely exhilarated, as only a blessed leak can bestow, though with my jaw screwed down even tighter, a faint flicker-rill in my lower abdomen more or less where I calculate my aggrieved prostate to be, my blood pressure for sure spiked, my life shortened by another thirty seconds—all this because I have now traitorously returned myself to the everyday, detail-shot, worry-misery-gnawing mind-set that I *hate*: how to un-invite the unwisely invited dinner guest who'll torpedo the otherwise-nice-enough family meal. This is what Clarissa experiences as linked boxes, the slippy-sliding world within worlds of everyone's *feelings* being on the line *all the time*, of perfect evenings with perfect overachiever dinner partners, the world of keeping calendars straight, of not forgetting to call back, always sending a note, the world of ducks-in-a-row, *i*'s dotted, *t*'s crossed and recrossed, of making sure the wrong person is *never* invited, or else everything's fucked up horrible and you're to blame and no one gets one ounce of closure. It's the world she's fled, the social Pleistocene tar pit that the Permanent Period is dedicated to saving you from by canceling unwanted self-consciousness, dimming fear-of-the-future in favor of the permanent, cutting edge of the present. By this measure, I shouldn't care if Ann comes to Thanksgiving dressed as Consuelo the Clown, squirts everybody with seltzer, honks her horn and sings arias till we're ready to strangle her. Because, in a little while it'll be over, no one will be any different and the day will end as it would've anyway: me half-asleep in front of the TV, watching the second game on Fox. It'd be a thousand times better—for my prostate, for my diastole and systole, for my life span, mandibular jaw muscles, embattled molars—for me just to rear back, har off a big guffaw, throw open the doors, push out the food, crack open my own big bottle of DP and turn ringmaster to the whole joyless tent-full.

Except that's not how I fucking well feel about it.

And how I *do* feel is not good. My Easter-egg-with-the-down-sized-family-inside's been cracked. The usual Permanent Period protocols aren't restoring order. My brain's buzzing with unwanted *concerns* it wasn't buzzing with an hour ago.

When I first got my bad prostate news in August, and in the hours before Clarissa became my partisan-advocate, I stood out on the deck, stared at the crowded beach and silvered Atlantic and thought how just one day before this day I didn't know what I then knew. I tried to drift back to the bliss that didn't know enough to count itself bliss, have a moment of reprieve, stuff the genie back in. Several times I even said out loud to the warm wind and the aroma of sunblock and salt and seaweed, as transistors buzzed the top-40 countdown and no one noticed me watching from above—I'd say, "Well. At least nobody's told me I have cancer." But of course before fresh well-being could swell in my chest and return me inside with a precious moment captured, I was reduced to gulping, squeezing, straining tears and feeling worse than if I'd never kidded myself. Don't try this.

And what's zooming around my brain now is the certainty that Ann Dykstra knows next to nothing about me anymore— except what the kids tell her privately—nothing about Sally or about the particulars of my condition, and hasn't bothered to ask. That may be what she meant by "more to talk about," which puts it mildly. But for starters, I'm married and holding out hope I can stay that way. My medical condition is "subtly nuanced," though that may not mean much to her, since she buried one husband only two years ago. Women have things wrong with them just like men, and, as far as I can tell, don't act as bothered by it. Ann probably assumes I'm adrift and ought to be grateful for any life raft heaved my way. I'm not.

Plus, why would *she* be attracted to *me*? And now? I must be much paler from my ordeal. I'm definitely thinner. Am I stooped, too? (I said I never look.) Are my cheekbones knobby? My clothes grown roomy? I'm sure this is how old age and bad health dawn on you—gradually and unannounced. Just all at once people are trying to persuade against things you want to do and always have done: *Don't* climb that ladder. *Don't* drive after dark. *Don't* postpone buying that term life. The Permanent Period, *again*, is set against this type of graduated obsolescence. But its strengths again seem in retreat.

Ann, of course, has also crudely played the "Ralph card" by referring to parents who lost children and the connecting path to early death—which is close to a cheap shot and offers no reason for us to get back together. I mean, if having my son die condemns me to an early exit, can that mean there are interesting new choices open that weren't before? Becoming a synchronized sky diver? Sailing alone around the world in a handmade boat? Learning Bantu and ministering to lepers? No. It's information that releases me to do nothing different and, in fact, almost challenges me to do nothing at all. It's like dull heredity, whereby you learn you have the gene that causes liver cancer, only you're too old for the transplant. Better not to know.

Though the truest, deep-background reason Ann is courting me (I know her as only an ex-husband can) is for a private whiff of the unknown, to provide the extra beat in her own life by associating it with a greater exigence than the Lady Linksters can offer: *me*, in other words, my life, my decline, my death and memory. Her daughter's on a similar search. If you think this kind of mischief is unthinkable, then think again. As I used to preach to my poor lost students at Berkshire College back in '83, when I wanted them to write something that wasn't about their roommate's acne or how it felt to be alone in the dorm after lights were out and the owls were hooting: If you can say it, it can happen.

6

I motor past the brick-and-glass-facaded village hall, lit up inside like a suburban Baptist church. Thick-chested policemen stand inside, talking casually while a poor soul—a thin, shirtless Negro—waits beside them in handcuffs. Does this bear on the Haddam Doctors Hospital "event" today? A known troublemaker, one of the usual suspects in for a round of grilling? Since there are no TV cameras or uplink trucks out front, no flak jackets, no FBI windbreakers, no leg irons, my guess is not. Just someone who's had too much pre-holiday fun and now must pay the price.

Seminary Street, when I cruise in just past six, appears reduced to its village self. The streets crews have strung up red and green twinkly Christmas lights and plastic pine-needle bunting over the three intersections. (The "no neon" ordinance is a good thing.) A modest team of rain-geared believers is setting up a lighted crèche on the lawn at the First Prez, where in days gone by I occasionally snuck in for a restorative, chest-swelling sing. Two women and two men are kneeling in the wet grass, training and retraining misty floods and revolving colored lights into the manger's little interior, while others cart in ceramic wise men and ceramic animals and real hay bales to set the scene. All is to be up and going for the first holiday returnees.

Across the street—below the United Jersey Bank sign, its

bleary news crawl streaming out-of-town events—a gaggle of local kids, all boys, stands slouched in the pissy weather, wearing baggy jeans cut off at the calves, long white athletic jerseys and combat boots. This is the Haddam gang element, children of single moms back-in-the-dating-scene, and dads working late, who arrive home too tired to wonder where young Thad or Chad or Eli might be, and head straight for the blue Sapphire in the freezer. These kids merely long for attention, possibly even a little tough-love discipline, and so are willing to provide it for each other, their mode of communication being bad posture, bad complexion, piercings, self-mortifications, smirky graffiti from Sartre, Kierkegàard and martyred Russian poets. In his day, Paul Bascombe was one of them. He once spray-painted "Next time you can't pretend there'll be anything else" on the wall of the high school gym, for which he was suspended, though he said he didn't know what it meant.

These idle kids—six of them, under the bright galloping news banner—are taunting the Presbyterian crèche assemblers, who occasionally look across Seminary and shake their heads sadly. Gamely, one ball-capped man comes out to the curb, where I stop at the light, and shouts something about lending a hand. The kids all smile. One shouts back, "Eat me," and the man— probably he's the preacher—fakes a laugh and goes back.

And yet, as it always could, the town works its meliorating blessing on me and my mood. There's nothing like a night-time suburban town at holiday season to anesthetize woe out of the feelable existence. I cruise down past the Square, where the Pilgrim Village Interpretive Center is now closed and padlocked against pranksters, the Pilgrims all hied off to their motel rooms, period animals stabled and safe in host back yards, the re-enactors disappeared into their Winnebagos, their uniforms drying, tomorrow's skirmishes vivid in their minds. At the I Scream Ice Cream, customers are crowded in under the lights, while others wait outside against the damp building, having a smoke. A thin queue has formed at the shadowy Garden Theater—a Lina Wertmüller offering I saw a hundred years ago, reprised for the holiday, the ship's-prow marquee proclaiming *Love and Anarchy*. It's the holiday. Not much is shaking.

My rendevous with Mike at the August is not until 6:45. I have time to slide by my dentist's, on the chance he'll be in late doing a pre-holiday bridge repair and can make a quick adjustment to my night guard before I head out to Mayo next Tuesday. I turn around in the Lauren-Schwindell lot—my old realty firm. All's dark within, Real-Trons sleeping, desks clean, alarms armed, not open until Tuesday no matter who wants what. A big cheery orange banner in the window proclaims GOBBLE, GOBBLE, GOBBLE, which I understand means "Thanks."

I drive back up to Witherspoon, which goes direct to 206 and Calderon's office. The gang-posse hangs out under the bank sign, eyeing me pseudo-menacingly, though this time my notice is captured by the crawl, a miniature, bulb-lit Times Square above them, to which they're oblivious. *Quarterlysdown29.3 . . . ATTdown 62% . . . Dowclose10.462 . . . HappyThanksgiving2000 . . . LLBean Chinamadeslippers recalledduetodrawstringdefectabletochoketoddlerusers . . . PierreSalinger testifiesreLockerbiecrashsez "Iknowwhodidit" . . . Airlineblanketsandheadrestssaidnotsanitized . . . Buffalostymiedunder15" lakeeffectsnow . . . HorrorstorieswithFlaballots: "Whatinthenameof Godisgoingonhere?"workersez . . . NJenclavesuffersmysteriousbomb detonlinktoelectionsuspec'd . . . TropicaldepresWaynenotlikelytomake land . . . BigpileupontheGarden State . . . HappyThanksgiving . . .*

These things are never easy to read.

I turn and pass down Witherspoon, the old part of Haddam, from when it was a real town—the old hardware, the old stale-but-good Greek place, the pole-less barbershop, the old Manusco photography gallery where everyone got his and her graduation portraits done until Manusco went to prison for lewdness. A new realtor's moved in here—Gold Standard Homes—beside the Banzai Sushi Den, where few customers are visible through the window. The tanning salon's in full swing for those heading to the islands. *Bombdeton . . . linktoelectionsuspec'd*—I "speak" these quasi-words in a mental voice that sounds portentous, though I don't think it could be true. Such a thought doesn't want to stay in mind and drifts away on the rainy evening's odd movie-street limbo, overtaken quickly by a thought that I can get my night guard fixed before heading home. I wonder, driving again along untrafficked Pleasant Valley Road past the cemetery fence, if I mentioned to Ann about the bomb, or if I told Marguerite during my Sponsor visit, or did she mention it to me, and did I go past Haddam Doctors before or after my funeral home stop? I can spend hours of a perfectly sleepable night wondering if I've kept such things straight, getting it all settled, then starting the process over, then wondering if I've contracted chemically induced Alzheimer's and pretty soon won't know much of anything.

Here again is the hospital, its upper storeys lit up like a

Radisson, its middle ones blacked out, its broken ground floor exterior turned incandescent by spotlights on metal scaffolds, shining alarmingly onto the distressed earth, turning the air pale metallic through the rain and dark. Humans—I see the FBI and ATF in blue rain jackets and white hard hats, and plenty of yellow-coated HPD—are in motion around the scene, so many hours after, their movement stylized and ominous. Yellow police tape cordons most of the grounds, and plenty of official vehicles, including an ambulance, a fire truck, more cruisers and two black panel trucks are parked helter-skelter inside the perimeter, as if something else is anticipated. No faces appear at the high hospital windows. The upper floors, the burn unit, the oncology ward, the ICU and maternity wings—the alpha and omega services— are in full swing, nobody with time for a crime scene outside. Officers, the same as earlier, their blue-flashing police cars parked up on the curb, wave me and the few other drivers on through. Red fusees sputter on the pavement.

Naturally, I'd love to shake loose some info, a name, a theory, a motive, a clue, but no one would spill any beans. "You'll know as soon as we know." "Everybody's doing their best out here." I stare up at the babyish rain-slick face of the young traffic cop, cold under his cop hat. He's rosy-cheeked, accustomed to smiling, but for the moment is as stern as a prosecutor. He peers inside my car with another practiced gaze. Anything suspicious here? Any tingle that says, "Maybe?" Any sign this could be Mr. Nutcase? A BUSH? WHY? sticker. A REALTOR sticker. Faded red Suburban with an Ocean County transfer station windshield sticker. *Haven't I seen you pass by here already today? Maybe you'd better pull over. . . .* I glide through, glancing in the rearview. He watches me as the red of my taillights fades into the dark, reads my license numbers, registers nothing, turns to the next car.

I turn onto Laurel Road, and immediately ahead is Calderon's office, on the back side of an older blond-brick sixties dental plaza that fronts on 206 and where I've always used this rear entrance. As I cruise up Laurel, toward the little three-storey cube down a flight of steps below a grassy embankment, I see two sets of lights are, in fact, glowing within. One suite, I know, is the *endo* guy, finishing off an after-hours root canal on some friend's impecunious sister. Another is the dental psychologist who works, evenings-only, on secretaries and dress-shop clerks who don't have the moolah for implants but still want to feel better about their smiles.

But no lights issue from Suite 308—Calderon's office. All's dark and buttoned up. Although up ahead, out at the curb as if awaiting a bus, is someone who actually looks like Calderon— topcoat, beret, a big-featured face distinguishable by black horn-rims and a black mustache I'm used to seeing sprouted behind his dental mask while he scrutinizes my bicuspids through a plastic AIDS shield. Here is my dentist—an odd vision to encounter after dark. Calderon's probably my age, the doted-on only son of Argentine renaissance scholar-diplomats who couldn't go home. He attended Dartmouth in the sixties and settled in New Jersey after dental school. He's a tall, handsome, wry-mouthed, dyed-hair pussy hound, married to the fourth Mrs. Calderon, a young, tragically widowed, crimson-haired Haddam tax lawyer who makes poor Calderon dye his mustache, too, and work out like a decathalete at Abs-R-Us Spa in Kendall Park to keep him looking younger than she is. In his dental practice, Calderon affects bright tangerine clinical smocks, shows Gilbert Roland oldies on the patients' TV instead of tapes about what's wrong with your teeth and only hires blond knockout assistants who make the trip over worthwhile. He was briefly a member of our Divorced Men's Club in the eighties and still is known to specialize in married female patients who require their cavities be filled at home. I'm always cheered up by my visits, since not only do I leave with shiny teeth, soft tissue checked, fillings tucked in tight and a feeling of well-being, but I'm also happy to pass an hour with another consenting adult who understands the lure of the Permanent Period but who hasn't had to dream it up the way I did. I, in fact, sometimes go right to sleep in the chair, with my mouth propped open and the drill whirring.

It makes me feel good now just to see Calderon waiting for who-knows-what out on the curb, though it's a long shot he'll take me back inside and knock off an adjustment.

I shoot down my driver's side window and angle over, satisfied if we only share a word. Calderon immediately smiles conspiratorially—with no idea who I am. Rain drizzle whooshes past on 206, thirty yards away.

"*Hola, Erno. ¿Dónde está el baño?*" I say this out my window—our usual palaver.

"*El Cid es famoso, ¿verdad?*" Ernesto beams a big scoundrel's smile, still not recognizing me, but putting his big veneers on display. His are white as pearls and made for him by a dental colleague at his wife's insistence. In his beret, he looks more like an old-timey film star than a philandering gum plumber. "Monet didn't have a dentist, I guess." This bears upon some lusty joke he told me the last time and has treated all his patients to for months. I don't remember it exactly, since I haven't been in since April. He doesn't know I've had/have cancer—which is a relief, since it makes me forget it. "What're you do-ing out here, *a-mi-go*, looking for houses to sell?"

Ernesto pretends to be more Latin than he is after thirty years. I've heard him on the phone with his denture lab in Bayonne. He could *be* from Bayonne. He does know who I am, though. Another small benison.

"I was hoping for a little after-hours dental attention." He'll think I'm kidding, but I'm not. Though having a night guard in my pocket feels ridiculous.

"No! *Hombre!* Don't tell me. Look at myself." He gaps back his topcoat to display a tuxedo with flaming red piping. His shoes are the shiny patent-leather species, and he's wearing a red bow tie and a red-and-green-striped cummerbund that does everything but blink and play music. Calderon's headed somewhere fancy, while I'm adrift on the back streets with a sore mandible. Who could expect a dentist to be late for a dinner party just because a patient's in need?

"So where's your big shindig?" I'm happy to get into the party spirit if I can't get my night guard fixed.

"Bet-sy went to see her old daddy in Chevy Chase. So . . . I am left alone once again *con* my thoughts. *¿Entiendes?* I'm going to New Jork to my club." Ernesto's donkey eyes brim with the promise of extramarital holiday high jinks. He's regaled me in the dentist's chair with winking accounts of his upper-Seventies "gentleman's club," where it's understood he'd be happy to take me and where I'd have the time of my life. Everything top-drawer. The best clientele—former Mets players, local news anchors, younger-set mafiosi. Black tie required, high-quality champagne on ice, the "ladies," naturally, all Barnard students with great personalities, making money for med-school tuition. I've pictured the "gentlemen" rumpus-ing round the plush-carpeted, damask-wallpapered rooms with their tuxedo pants off, in just their patent-leather pumps, dark socks and dinner jackets, comparing each other's equipment, of which it's my guess Ernesto probably has a prize specimen.

"Sounds like a blast," I say.

"Yeees. We have loads of fun. They send me down the leemo. Sometimes you should come with me." Ernesto nods to certify I wouldn't be sorry.

I have, just then, the recurrent aching memory of the long walk Clarissa and I took last August through the sun-warmed, healthy-elm-shaded streets of Rochester, a town noted for its prideful *thereness* and for looking like a small Lutheran college town instead of medical ground zero. It was the Friday before my procedure on Monday, and we'd decided to walk ourselves to sweaty exhaustion, eat an early dinner at Applebee's and watch the Twins play the Tigers on TV at the Travelodge. We hiked out State Highway 14 to the eastern edge of town—on our feet where others were driving—beyond the winding streets of white-painted, well-tended, green-roof neighborhoods, past the Arab-donated Little League stadium and the federal medical facility and the Olmsted County truck-marshaling yard, beyond the newer rail-fenced ranch homes with snow machines, bass boats and fifth-wheelers For Sale on their lawns, past where a sand and gravel operation had cracked open the marly earth, and farther on to where dense-smelling alfalfa fields took up and a small, treed river bottom appeared, and the glaciated earth began to devolve and roll and slide greenly toward the Mississippi, fifty miles away. NO HUNTING signs were on all the fence posts. The summer landscape was as dry as a razor strop, the corn as high as an elephant's gazoo, the far, hot sky as one-color gray as a cataract. There was, of course, a lake.

On a little asphalt hillcrest beside where the highway ribboned off to the east, Clarissa and I stopped to take the view back to town—the great, many-buildinged Mayo colossus dominating the pleasant, forested townscape like a kremlin. Impressive. These buildings, I thought, could take good care of anybody.

Sweat had beaded on Clarissa's forehead, her tee-shirt sweated through. She passed a hand across her flushed cheek. A green truck with slatted sides rumbled past, kicking up hot breeze and sand grit, leaving behind a loud, sweetish aroma of pigs-to-market. "This is where America's decided to receive its bad news, I guess, isn't it?" She suddenly didn't like being out here. Everything was far too specific.

"It's not so terrible. I like it." I did. And do. "Given the alternatives."

"You would."

"Wait'll you're my age. You'll be happy there're places like this to receive you. Things look different."

"Maybe you should just move out here. Buy one of those

nice, horrible houses with the green roofs and the green shutters and mullioned windows. Buy a Ski-Doo."

I'd already given that some thought. "I think I'd do fine out here," I said. We were both pretending I'd be dead on Monday, just to see how it felt.

"Great," she said, then turned dramatically on her heel to gaze down the highway eastward. We were traveling no farther that day. "You think you'd do fine anywhere."

"What's the matter with that? Is it a mark of something to be unhappy?"

"No," she said sourly. "You're very admirable. Sorry. I shouldn't pick on you. I don't know why I bother."

I started to say, Because I'm your father, I'm all that's left— but I didn't. I said, "I understand perfectly. You have my best interests at heart. It's fine." We started back walking to town and to the things town had in store for me.

*E*rnesto stares down at me off the curb the way he would if he was waiting for my mouth to numb up. It dawns on me he has no real idea who I am. I am real estate-related but possess no name, only a set of full-mouth X rays clamped to a cold white screen. Or maybe I'm the carpet-cleaning guy from Skillman. Or I own the Chico's on Route 1, a place I know he skulks off to with his Lebanese hygienist, Magda.

Up in my darkened rearview, I see what may be Ernesto's leemo, its pumpkin-tinted headlights rounding onto Laurel and commencing slowly toward us.

"What's up for Thanksgiving in *su casa*, Ernesto?" I have somehow become pointlessly cheery. Ernesto eyes the white stretch, then glances back at me warily, as if I might just be the wrong person to witness this. He flicks a secret hand signal to the driver, and in so doing makes himself look effeminate instead of *mal hombre machismo*. Maybe one of the nice-personality Barnard girls with her gold-plated health report is waiting in the backseat, already popping the Veuve Clicquot.

"What's going on what?" he says, his horn-rims and beret getting misted, his smile not quite earnest.

"Thanksgiving," I say. "*¿Qué pasa a su casa?*" I'm deviling him, but I don't care, since he won't fix my night guard.

"Oh, we go to Atlantic City. Always. My wife likes to gamble at Caesars." He's departing now, inching crabwise toward the limo, which has halted a discreet distance down Laurel. In my side mirror I see the driver's door swing open. A tall chorus-girl-looking female in silver satin shorty-shorts, high heels and a white Pilgrim collar with a tall red Pilgrim hat just like on the Pennsylvania highway signs gets out and pulls open the rear door. "I have to go now." Ernesto looks back at me a little frantically, as if he might get left. "*Hasta la vista*," he adds idiotically.

"Hugo de Naranja to you, too."

"Okay. Yes. Thanks." In the mirror I see him hustle down the street, giving the chorus-girl driver a quick peck and scampering in the limo door. The Pilgrim chauffeur looks my way, smiles at me scoping her out, then climbs back in the driver's seat and slowly pulls around me and up Laurel Road.

It wouldn't be bad to be in there with ole Ernesto is what I think. Not so bad to have his agenda, his particular species of ducks lined up. Though my guess is, none of it would work out for me. Not now. Not in the state I'm currently in.

The Johnny Appleseed Bar, downstairs at the August Inn, where I'm meeting Mike Mahoney, is a fair replica of a Revolutionary War roadhouse tavern. Wide, worn pine floors, low ceilings, a burnished mahogany bar, plenty of antique copper lanterns and period "tack"—battle flags with snakes and mottoes, encrusted sabers, drumheads, homespun uniforms encased in glass, framed musket-balls, framed tricorn headgear—with (the *pièce de résistance*) a wall-sized spotlit mural in alarmingly vivid colors of a loony-looking J. Appleseed seated backward astride a gray mule, saucepan on head, a Klem Kadiddlehopper grin on his lascivious lips, mindlessly distributing apple seeds off the mule's bony south end. Which apparently was how the West was won. For years, Haddam bar-stool historians debated whether Norman Rockwell or Thomas Hart Benton had "executed" the Appleseed mural. Old-timers swore to have watched both of them do it at several different times, though this was disproved when Rockwell stayed at the inn in the sixties and said not even Benton could paint anything that bad.

I'm always happy in here any time of day or night, its clubby, bogus, small-town imperviousness making me sense a safe haven. And tonight especially, following today, with only a smattering of holiday tipplers nursing quiet cocktails along the bar, plus an anonymous him 'n her tucked into a dark red leather banquette in the corner, conceivably doing the deed right there—not that anyone would care. A wall TV's on without sound, a miniature plastic Yule tree's set up on the bottle shelf, a strand of silver (flammable) bunting's swagged across the mirrored backbar. The old sack-a-bones bartender's watching the hockey game. It's the perfect place to end up on a going-nowhere Tuesday before Thanksgiving, when much of your personal news hasn't been so festive. It's one thing to marvel at what a bodacious planet we occupy, the way Dr. von Reichstag did, where humans ruminate about neutrinos. But it's beyond marveling that those humans can invent a concept as balming to the ailing spirit as the "cozy local watering hole," where you're always expected, no questions asked, where you can choose from a full list of life-restoring cocktails, stare silently at a silent TV, speak non sequiturs to a nonjudgmental bartender, listen (or not) to what's said around you—in other words, savor the "in but not all in," "out but not all out" zeitgeist mankind would package and sell like hoola-hoops if it could and thus bring peace to a troubled planet.

After my sad divorce seventeen years ago, and before I was summoned to the bar of residential realty, I found myself on a stool here many a night, enjoying a *croque monsieur* from the upstairs kitchen, plus seventy or eighty highballs, sometimes with a "date" I could smooch up in the shadows, then later slithering (alone or à deux) up the steps out onto Hulfish Street and into a warm Jersey eventide with not a single clue about where my car might be. I frequently ended up lurching home to Hoving Road (avoiding busier streets, and cops), and diving straight into bed and towering sleep. I may have experienced my fullest sensation of belonging in Haddam on those nights, circa 1983. By which I mean, if you saw a fortyish gentleman stepping unsteadily out of a bar into a dark suburban evening, staring around mystified, looking hopefully to the heavens for guidance, then careening off down a silent, tree-bonneted street of nice houses where lights are lit and life athrum, one of which houses he enters, tramps upstairs and falls into bed with all his clothes on—wouldn't you think, Here's a man who belongs, a man with native roots and memory, his plow deep in the local earth? You would. What's belonging all about, what's its quiddity, if not that drunk men "belong" where you find them?

It's 6:25 and Mike is not yet in evidence. Hard to imagine what a diminutive Tibetan and a macaroni land developer could do *together* for an entire afternoon of rotten weather. How many plat maps, zoning ordinances, traffic projections, air-quality regulations, floodplain variances and EEOC regs can you pore over without needing sedation, and on the first day you ever laid eyes on each other?

From the elderly bartender, I order a Boodles, eighty proof, straight up, take a tentative lick off the martini-glass rim and feel exactly the way I want to feel: better—able to face the world as though it was my friend, to strike up conversations with total strangers, to see others' points of view, to think most everything will turn out all right. Even my jaw relaxes. My eyes attain good focus. The bothersome belly sensation that I probably erroneously associate with my prostate has ceased its flickering. For the first time since I woke at six in Sea-Clift and knew I could sleep another hour, I breathe a sigh of relief. A day has passed intact. It's nothing I take for granted.

My fellow patrons are all Haddam citizens I've seen before, may even have done business with, but who, because of my decade's absence, pretend never to have laid eyes on me. Ditto the bean-pole, white-shirted, green-plastic-bow-tied bartender, Lester, who's stood the bar here thirty years. He's a Haddam townie, a slope-shouldered, high-waisted Ichabod in his late sixties, a balding bachelor with acrid breath no woman would get near. He's given me the standard, noncommittal "Whatch-ouhavin," even though years ago I listed his mother's brick duplex on Cleveland Street, next door to my own former house, where Ann now lives, presented him two full-price offers in a week, only to have him back out (which he had every right to do) and turn the place into a rental—a major financial misreading in 1989, which I pointed out to him, so that he never forgave me. Often it's the case that no matter how successful or pain-free a transaction turns out—and in Haddam there was never a bad one—once it's over, clients often begin to treat the residential agent like a person who's only half-real, someone they've maybe only dreamed about. When they pass you in a restaurant or mailing Christmas cards at the PO, they'll instantly turn furtive and evade your eyes, as if they'd seen you on a sexual-predators list, give a hasty, mumbled, noncommittal "Howzitgoin?" and are gone. And I might've made them a quick two mil or ended a bad run of vein-clogging hassles or saved them from pissing away all in a divorce or a Chapter 11. At some level—and in Haddam this level is routinely reached—people are embarrassed not to have sold their own houses themselves and resentful about paying the commission, since all it seems to involve is putting up a sign and waiting till the dump truck full of money stops out front. Which sometimes happens and sometimes doesn't. Looked at from this angle, we realtors are just the support group for the chronically risk-averse.

Lester's begun using the remote to click channels away from the hockey game, staring up turkey-necked, gob open at the Sanyo bracketed above the flavored schnapps. He's carrying on separate dialogues with the different regulars, desultory give-and-takes that go on night to night, year to year, never missing a beat, just picked up again using the all-purpose Jersey conjunction, *So*. "So, if you put in an invisible fence, doesn't the fuckin' dog get some kinda complex?" "So, if you ask me, you miss all the fuckin' nuance using sign language." "So, to me, see, flight attendants are just part of the plane's fuckin' equipment—like oxygen masks or armrests. Not that I wouldn't schtup one of them. Right?" Lester nibbles his lip as he flips past sumo wrestling, cliff divers in Acapulco, two people who've won a game-show contest and are hugging, then on past several channels with different people dressed in suits and nice dresses, sitting behind desks, talking earnestly into the camera, then past a black man in an ice-cream suit healing a fat black woman in a red choir robe by making her fall over backward on a big stage—more things than I can focus on in my relaxed, not-all-in, not-all-out state of mind.

Then all at once, the President, my president—big, white-haired, smiling, puffy-faced and guileless—*his* face and figure fill the color screen. President Clinton strolls casually, long-strided, across a green lawn, suppressing an embarrassed smile. He's in blue cords, a plain white shirt, a leather bomber jacket and Hush Puppies like mine. He's doing his best to look shy and undeserving, guilty of something, but nothing very important— stealing watermelons, driving without a learner's permit, taking a peek through a hole in the wall of the girls' locker room. He's got his Labrador, Buddy, on a leash and is talking and flirting with people off-camera. Behind him sits a big Navy copter with a white-hatted Marine at attention by the gangway. The President has just saluted him—incorrectly.

"Where's the fuckin' Mafia when you need them bastards?" Lester's growling up at the tube. He makes a pistol out of his thumb and index finger and assassinates the man I voted for with a soft pop of his lizard lips. "Ain't he havin' the time of his fuckin' life with this election bullshit. He loves it." Lester swivels around to his patrons, his mouth sour and mean. "Country on its fuckin' knees."

"Easier to give blow jobs," one of the regulars says, and thumbs his glass for a fill-up.

"And you'd know about that," Lester says, and grins evilly.

The couple in the back booth, who've been doing whatever away from everybody's notice, unexpectedly stands up, moving their banquette table noisily out of the way, as if they thought a fight was about to erupt or their sexual shenanigans required more leg room. All five of us, plus an older woman at the bar, have a gander at these two getting their coats on and shuffling out through the tables. Happily, I don't know them. The woman's young and thin and watery-blond and pretty in a sharp-featured way. He's a short-armed, gangsterish meatpie with dark curly hair, stuffed into a three-piece suit. His trousers are unzipped and part of his shirttail's poked guiltily through the fly.

"What's your hurry there, folks?" Lester yaps, and leers as the couple heads for the red EXIT lozenge and up to the street.

The noisy drinker down the bar leans forward and smirks at me. "So whadda *you* think?" He is Bob Butts, owner (once) of Butts Floral on Spring Street, since replaced by the Virtual Profusion and going great guns. Bob is red-skinned, fattish and embittered. His mother, Lana, ran the shop after Bob's dad died in Korea. This was prehistoric Haddam, when it was a sleepy-eyed, undiscovered jewel. When Lana moved to Coral Gables and remarried, Bob took over the shop and ran it in the ground, gambling his brains out in Tropworld, which was new in Atlantic City: Bob's a first-rate dickhead.

The two men beyond him, I don't know, but are shady, small-time Haddam cheezers I've seen six hundred times—in Cox's News or in the now-departed Pietroinferno's. I have an idea they're involved with delivering the *Trenton Times* and possibly less obvious merchandise. The hatchet-faced, thin-haired woman, wearing a blowsy black dress suitable for a funeral, I've never seen, though she's apparently Bob's companion. It would be easy to say these four are members of a Haddam demimonde, but in fact they're only regular citizens holding out in defiance, rather than making the move to Bordentown or East Windsor.

"What do I think about what?". I lean forward and look straight at Bob Butts, raising my warming martini to my lips.

President Clinton has disappeared off the screen. Though I wonder what he's doing in real time—having a stiff belt himself, possibly. His last two years haven't been much to brag about. Like Clarissa, I wish he was running again. He'd do better than these current two monkeys.

"All this election bullshit." Bob Butts cranes forward, then back, to get a better look at me. Lester's pouring him another 7&7. Bob's haggard lady friend gives me an unfocused, boozy stare, as if she knows all about me. The two *Trenton Times* guys muse at their shot glasses (root beer schnapps, my bet). "Some guy got blown up over at the hospital today. Bunch of pink confetti. This shit's gone too far. The Democrats are stealin' it." Bob's wet, bloodshot eyes clamp onto me, signaling he knows who I am now—a nigger-lovin', tax-and-spend, pro-health-care, abortion-rights, gay-rights, consumer-rights, tree-hugging liberal (all true). Plus, I sold my house and left the door open to a bunch of shit Koreans, and probably even had something to do with him losing the flower shop (also true).

Bob Butts is wearing a disreputably dirty brown shawl-collar car coat made of a polymer-based material worn by Michigan frosh in the early sixties but not since, and looks like hell warmed over. He has on chinos like mine and white Keds with no socks. He's been in need of a shave for several days. His thin, lank hair is long and dirty and he could do with a bath. Obviously, Bob's experiencing a downward loop, having once been handsome, clever, gaunt to the point of febrile Laurence Harvey effeminance. Like Calderon, he cut a wide swath through the female population, who he used to woogle in his back room, right on the stem-strewn metal arranging table. That's maybe all you can hope for if you're a florist.

"I don't really see what the Democrats have to do with whoever got blown up at the hospital," I say. I half-turn and take a casual, calculated look back at the Appleseed mural, brightly lit by a row of tiny silver spotlights attached to the low ceiling. By looking at goofball Johnny, I'm essentially addressing nut-case Bob. This is the message I want subliminally delivered. I also don't want Bob to think I give half a shit about anything he says, since I don't. I'm ready right now for Mike to show up. But then I can't resist adding, "And I don't see where the Democrats are stealing anything, unless getting more votes could be said to be a form of theft. Maybe *you* do. Maybe it's why you're not in the flower business anymore."

"Could be said." Bob Butts grins idiotically. "Could be said you're an asshole. That could be said."

"It's already been said," I say. I don't want to fan this disagreement beyond the boundary of impolite bar argument. I'm not sure what would wait out past that frontier at my age and state of health and with a big drink already under my belt. And yet the same irresistible urge makes me unable not to add, still facing the Appleseed mural, "It's actually been said by even bigger shit-heels than you are, Bob. So don't worry too much about surprising me." I shift around on my bar stool and entertain the rich thought of a second chilled Boodles. Only, I hear scuffling and wood being scraped. The hatchet-faced woman says, "Oh, Jesus Christ, Bob!" Then a bar stool like the one I'm sitting on hits the floor. And suddenly there's a fishy odor in my nostrils and mouth, and

Bob Butts' small, rough hands go right around my neck, his whiskery chin jamming into my ear, his throat making a gurgling noise both mechanical, like a car with a bad starter, and also simian—*grrrrr*—into my ear canal—*"Grrrrr, grrrrr, grrrrr"*—so that I tip over off my bar stool, which tumbles sideways, and Bob and I go sprawling toward the pine floor. I'm trying to grab a fistful of his reeking car coat and haul it in the direction I'm falling so he'll hit the floor first and me on top—which bluntly happens. Though the bar stool next to mine—heavy as an anvil—topples down onto me with a clunk in my rear rib cage that doesn't knock the breath out of me but hurts like shit and makes me expel a not-voluntary "oooof."

"Cocksucker, you cocksucker." Bob Butts is gurgling in my ear and stinking. *"Grrrr, errrr, grrrr."* These are noises (I for some reason find myself *thinking*) Bob probably learned as a child, and that were funny once, but now come into play in a serious effort to murder me. Bob's grip isn't exactly around my windpipe, only my neck, but he's squeezing the crap out of me and digging his grimed fingernails into my skin. My flesh is stinging, but I don't feel shocked or in any jeopardy, except possibly from the fall.

No one else in the bar does anything to help. Not Lester, not the two *Trenton Times* palookas, not the witchy, balding woman in widow's weeds who's invoked Jesus Christ. They simply ignore Bob and me wrestling on the floor, as if a new bar customer, in for a Fuzzy Navel, might think it was great to see two middle-aged guys muggling around on the damp boards, trying to accomplish nobody's too sure what-in-the-fuck.

All of this begins to seem like an annoyance more than a fight, like having someone's pet monkey hanging on your neck, though we're down on the floor and the stool's on top of me and Bob's going "*Grrrr, errrr, grrrr*" and squeezing my neck, his breath and hair reeking like week-old haddock. Suddenly, I lose all my wind and have to buck the bar stool off my back to breathe, and in doing so I get my knee in between Bob's own squirming, jimmering knees and my right elbow into his sternum, just below where I could interrupt *his* windpipe. I lean on Bob's hard breast bone, stare down into his bulging, blood-splurged eyes, which register that this event may be almost over. "Bob," I half-shout at him. His eyes widen, he bares his long yellow teeth, refastens a fisted grip on my neck tendons and croaks, "Cocksucker." And with no further prelude, I go ahead and jackhammer my kneecap straight up into Bob's nuttal pouch pretty much as hard as I can—given my weakened state, given my lack of inclination and the fact that I've had a martini and had hoped the evening would turn out to be pleasant, since so much of the day hadn't.

Bob Butts erupts instantly in a bulbous-eyed, Gildersleevian "*Oooomph,*" his cheek and lips exploding. His eyes squeeze melo-dramatically shut. He lets go of my neck and goes as flaccid as a lifesaving dummy. Instead of more "*Grrrr, errr, grrr,*" he groans a deep, agonizing and, I'll admit, satisfying "*Eeeeeuh-uh-oh.*"

"You fuckin' scrogged 'im, you cheap-ass son of a bitch," the hatchet-faced woman shouts from up on her bar stool above us, frowning down at Bob and me as if we were insects she'd been interested in. "Fight fair, fucker." She decides to toss her drink at me and does. The glass, which has gin in it, hits my shoulder, but most of its contents hit Bob, who's grimacing, with my elbow point—excruciatingly, I hope—nailed into his sternum.

"All right, all right, all right," Lester says behind the bar, as if he couldn't really give a shit what the hell's going on but is bored by it, his spoiled, impassive shoe-salesman's mug and his green plastic bow tie—relic of some desolate Saint Paddy's day—just visible to me beyond the bar rail.

"All right *what*?" I'm holding Bob at elbow point. "Are you going to keep this shit bucket from strangling me, or am I going to have to rough him up?" Bob makes another gratifying "*Eeeeeuh-uh-oh*," whose exhalation is foul enough that I have to get away from him, my heart finally beginning to whump.

"Let 'im get up," Lester says, as though Bob was his problem now.

Bob's blond accomplice hauls a big shiny-black purse off the floor beside her. "I'll get 'im home, the dipshit," she says. The two other bar-stool occupants look at me and Bob as if we were a show on TV. On the real TV, Bush's grinning, smirking, depth-less face is visible, talking soundlessly, arms held away from his sides as if he was hiding tennis balls in his armpits. Other humans are visible around him, well-dressed, smooth-coifed, shiny-faced young men holding paper plates and eating barbecue, laughing and being amused to death by whatever their candidate's saying.

Using the bar stool, I raise myself from where I've straddled Bob Butts, and feel instantly light-headed, weak-armed, heavy-legged, in peril of falling back over on top of Bob and expiring. I gawk at Lester, who's taking away my martini glass and scowling at me while Bob's lady friend pulls him, wallowing, off the floor.

She squats beside me, her scrawny knees bowed out, her skirt opened, so that I unmercifully see her thighs encased in black panty hose, and the bright white crotch patch of her undies. I avert my eyes to the floor, and see that my night guard has fallen out of my pocket in the tussle and been crunched in three pieces under the bar rail. It makes me feel helpless, then I scrape the pieces away with my heel. Gone.

Bob is up but bent at the waist, clutching his injured testicles. He's missing one of his Keds, and his ugly yellow toenails are gripping the floor. His hair's mussed, his fatty face blotched red and white, his eyes hollowed and mean and full of defeated despisal. He glares at me, though he's had enough. I'm sure he'd love to spit out one more vicious "Cocksucker," except he knows I'd kick his cogs again and enjoy doing it. In fact, I'd be glad to. We stand a moment loathing each other, all my parts—hands, thighs, shoulders, scratched neck, ankles, everything but my own nuts— aching as if I'd fallen out a window. Nothing occurs to me as worth saying. Bob Butts was better as a lowlife, floral failure and former back-room lady-killer than as a vanquished enemy, since enemy-hood confers on him a teaspoon of undeserved dignity. It was also better when this was a homey town and a bar I used to dream sweet dreams in. Both also gone. Kaput. On some human plain that doesn't exist anymore, now would be a perfect moment and place from which to start an unusual friendship of opposites. But all prospects for that are missing.

I turn to Lester, who I hate for no other reason than that I can, and because he takes responsibility for no part of life's tragedy. "What do I owe you?"

"Five," he snaps.

I have the bat-hide already in hand, my fingers scuffed and sticky from my busted knuckles. My knees are shimmying, though fortunately no one can see. I give a thought to collecting up my shattered night guard pieces, then forget it.

"Did you used to live here?" Lester says distastefully.

This, atop all else, does shock me. More than that, it disgusts me. Possibly I don't look exactly as I looked when I busted my ass to flog Lester's old mama's duplex in a can't-miss '89 seller's market—a sale that could've sprung Lester all the way to Sun City, and into a cute pastel cinder-block, red-awninged match box with a mountain view, plus plenty left over for an Airstream and a decent wardrobe in which to pitch sleazy woo to heat-baked widows. A better life. But I *am* the same, and fuck-face Lester needs to be reminded.

"Yeah, I lived here," I growl. "I sold your mother's house. Except you were too much of a mamma's-boy asshole to part with it. Guess you couldn't bear leaving your leprechaun tie."

Lester looks at me in an interested way, as if he'd muted me but my lips are still moving. He rests his cadaver hands on the glass rail, where there's a moist red rubber drying mat. Lester doesn't actually look much different from Johnny Appleseed, which may be why the August Inn people (a hospitality consortium based in Cleveland) keep him on. He still wears, I see, his big gold knuckle-buster Haddam HS ring. (My son refused his.) "Whatever," Lester says, then turns down the pasty corners of his mouth in disdain.

I'd like to utter something toxic enough to get through

even Lester's soul-deep nullity. The least spark of anger might earn me the pleasure of kicking his ass, too. Only I don't know what to say. The two *Trenton Times* delivery goons are frowning at me with small, curious menace. Possibly I have morphed into something not so good in their view, someone different from who they thought I was. No longer the invisible, ignorable, pathetic drip, but a rude intruder threatening to take too much attention away from their interests and crap on their evening. They might have to "deal" with me just for convenience sake.

Bob Butts and his harridan lady friend are exiting the bar by way of the stairs up to Hulfish Street. "*Naaaa*, leave off, you asshole," I hear the old blondie growl.

"This fuckin' stinks," Bob growls back.

"*You* stink is what," she says, continuing with difficulty, one leaning on the other, up toward the cold outdoors, the heavy door going *click* shut behind them.

I stare a moment, transfixed by the bright apple-tinted Disneyish mural of clodhopper Johnny, straddling his plug bass-ackwards, saucepan on top, dribbling his seed across Ohio. These bars are probably a chain, the mural computer-generated. Another one just like this one may exist in Dayton.

I unexpectedly feel a gravity-less melancholy in the bar, in spite of victory over Bob Butts. In the ponderous quiet, with the Sanyo showing leather-fleshed Floridians at long tables, examining punch-card ballots as if they were chest X rays, Lester looks like a pallid old ex-contract killer considering a comeback. His two customers may be associates—silent down-staters handy with chain saws, butcher's utensils and Sakrete. It's still New Jersey here. These people call it home. It might be time to wait for Mike outside.

"Ain't you Bascombe somethin'?" One of the toughs frowns down the bar at me. It's the farther away one, seated next to the shot-glass rack, a round, barrel-chested, ham-armed smudge pot with a smaller than standard hat size. His face has a close-clipped beard, but his cranium is shaved shiny. He looks Russian and is therefore almost certainly Italian. He produces a short unfiltered cigarette (which Boro regulations profoundly forbid the smoking of), lights it with a little yellow Bic and exhales smoke in the direction of Lester, who's rummaging through the cash drawer. I would willingly forswear all knowledge of any Bascombe; be instead Parker B. Farnsworth, retired out of the Bureau—Organized Crime Division—but still on call for undercover duties where an operative needs to look like a real estate agent. However, I've blown my cover over Lester's mother's house. I feel endangered, but see no way free except to fake going insane and run up the stairs screaming.

So what I reluctantly say is, "Yeah." I expect the smudge pot to snort a cruel laugh and say something low and accusing—a widowed relative or orphan nephew I gave the mid-winter heave-ho to so I could peddle their house to some noisy Jews from Bedminster. I've never done that, but it doesn't stop people from thinking I have. Someone in my old realty firm for sure did it, which makes me a party.

"My kid went to school with your kid." The bald guy taps his smoke with his finger, inserts it in the left corner of his small mouth and blows more smoke out the front in little squirts. He lets his eyes wander away from me.

"My son Paul?" I am unexpectedly smiling.

"I don't know. Maybe. Yeah."

"And what was your son's name? I mean, what's his name?"

"Teddy." He is wearing a tight black nylon windbreaker open onto what looks like an aqua tee-shirt that exhibits his hard basketball-size belly. His clothes are skimpy for this weather, but it's part of his look.

"And where's *he* now?" Likely the Marines or a good trade school, or plying Lake Superior as an able seaman gaining grainy life experience on an ore boat before coming home to settle into life as a plumber. Possibilities are plentiful and good. He's probably *not* authoring wiseacre greeting cards and throwing shit fits because he feels underappreciated.

"He ain't." The big guy elevates his rounded chin to let cigarette smoke go past his eyes. His drinking buddy, a bony, curly-headed weight-lifter type with a giant flared nose and dusky skin—also wearing a nylon windbreaker—produces a Vicks inhaler, gives it a stiff snort and points his nose at the ceiling as if the experience was transporting.

I get a noseful clear over here. It makes the room suddenly wintry and momentarily happy again. "You mean he stayed home?"

"No, no, no," Teddy's father says, facing the backbar.

"So, where is he?" This is, of course, 100 percent none of my business, and I already detect the answer won't be good. Prison. Disappeared. Disavowed. The standard things that happen to your children.

"He ain't on the earth," the big guy says. "Now, I mean." He removes his cigarette and appraises its red tip.

No way I'm heading down *this* bad old road. Not after having had my own dead son flashed like a muleta by my wife I'm no longer married to. Since Ralph Bascombe's been absent from the planet, I haven't gone around yakking about it in bars with strangers.

I stand up straight in my now-soiled barracuda—sore kneed, neck burning, knuckles aching—and look expressionlessly at this short, cylindrical fireplug of a man who's suffered (I know exactly, or close enough) and has had to get used to it. Alone.

The big guy swivels to peer past his friend's face at me. His dark, flat eyes don't glow or burn or teem, but are imploring and not the eyes of an assassin, but of a pilgrim seeking small progress. "Where's *your* kid?" he says, cigarette backward in his fingers, French-style.

"He's in Kansas City."

"What's he do? He a lawyer? Accountant?"

"No," I say. "He's a kind of writer, I guess. I'm not really sure."

"Okay."

"What happened to your son?"

Why? Why can't I just do what I say I will? Is it so hard? Is it age? Illness? Bad character? Fear I'll miss something? What this man's about to say fairly fills the bar with dread, bounces off the period trappings, taps the drumheads, jingles the harnesses, swirls around Johnny Appleseed like a Halloween ghost.

"He took his own life," the palooka says without a blink.

"Do you know why?" I ask, full-in-now, with nothing to offer back, nothing to make a man feel better in this season when all seek it.

"Look at those fucks," Lester snarls. Candidate Gore and his undernourished running mate have commandeered the TV screen in their shirt sleeves, walled in behind stalks of microphones in front of an enormous oak tree, looking grave and silly at once. Gore, the stiff, is spieling on soundlessly, as if he's admonishing a seventh grader, his body doughy, perplexing, crying out to put on more weight and be old. "Haw!" Lester brays at them. "Whadda country. Jeez-o fuck." If I had a pistol I'd gladly shoot Lester with it.

"No. I don't." The big Trentonian bolts his drink and has a last drag on his smoke. He doesn't like this now, is sorry he started it. Just an idle question that led the old familiar wrong way. "What I owe you?" he says to Lester, who's still gawking at Gore and Lieberman gabbling like geese.

"A blow job," Lester says without looking around. "It's happy hour. Make me happy."

The skint-headed guy stubs his smoke in his shot glass, lays two bills on the bar but doesn't rise to the bait. I get another hot whiff of Vicks as the two men shift around to depart. Off the stool, the big guy's actually small and compact, and moves with a nice, comfortable, swivel-shouldered Fiorello La Guardia rolling gait, like a credible middleweight.

"Good talking to ya," he says. His taller, more threatening friend looks straight at me as he steps past, but then seems embarrassed and diverts his eyes.

"Remember what we talked about," Lester shouts as they head toward the stairs. ·

"You're already on the list," the bald guy's stairwell voice says as the metal door clanks open and their footfalls and muttering voices grow soft, leaving me alone with Lester.

Mike hasn't arrived. I stare at Lester's satchel-ass behind the bar as if it foretold a mystery. He glances around at me (I'm still queasy after my Bob Butts set-to). He has put on tortoiseshell-framed glasses and his practically chinless face is hostile, as if he's just before invoking his right to refuse to serve anyone. I could use the pisser. Once it was by the exit, but the old smoothed brass MEN plaque is gone and the wall's been bricked up. The gents must be upstairs in the inn.

"Who'dju waste your vote on?" Lester says. I transfer my stare from trousers seat to the plastic Christmas tree on the backbar. I'm unwilling to leave till Mike gets here.

"I voted for Gore." The sound of these four words makes me almost want to burst out laughing. Except I feel so shitty.

Lester bellies up to the bar in front of me. His frayed gray-white shirt bears tiny dark specks of tomato juice on its front. His black bartender trousers could use fumigating. He lays his big left hand, the one with the Haddam HS ring on it, palm-down on the eurathaned compass of the bar. The ring's *H* crest is bracketed by two tiny rearing stallions on either side, with the numeral 19 below one stallion, and 48 the other. I peer at Lester's fingers, which promise prophesy. He uses his other index finger to point toward his long left thumb. "Let me show you some-thing," he says, sinister, matter-of-fact, staring down at his own fingers. "This is your Russian. This next one's your spic. This one's your African. This last one's your Arab or your sand nigger—whichever. You got your choice." Lester raises his eyes to me coldly, smiling as if he was passing a terrible sentence.

"My choice for what?"

"For what language you want to learn when you vote for fuckin' Gore. He's givin' the country away, like the other guy, except his dick got in his zipper." Lester, as he did earlier, nibbles his lip—but as though he might punch me. "You probably respect my opinion, don't you? That's what you guys do. You respect everybody's fuckin' opinion. Except you can't respect *everybody's* opinion." Lester has made a brawler's fist out of his prophetic hand and leans on it to draw closer to me over the bar. Vile, minty fixative smell—something he's been told to use when he meets the public—has been adulterated by an acrid steam of hate. It would make me nauseated if I didn't think Lester was about to assault me.

"No," I say. "I don't respect your opinion." My voice, even to me, lacks determination. I stand back a step. "I don't respect your opinion at all."

"Oh. Okay." Lester smiles more broadly but keeps on staring hate at me. "I thought you thought everybody was just like everybody else, everybody equal. All of us peas in a fuckin' pod."

It *is* what I think, but I won't be able to explain that now. Precisely at this flash point—and surprisingly—Mike walks out of the stairwell and through the door of the Johnny Appleseed, looking like a happy little middle-manager, in his mustard blazer and Italian tassel-loafers, though he has the spontaneous good sense to halt under the red EXIT as if something was about to combust. It may.

"It *is* what I think," I say, and feel stupid. Lester's eye shifts contemptuously to Mike, who looks disheartened but is, of course, smiling. "And I think you're full of shit!" I say this too harshly and somehow begin to lose my balance on the tumbled-over bar stool I haven't had a chance to put back upright. I am falling yet again.

"Is the midget a friend of yours now?" Lester sneers, but his eyes stay nastily on Mike, object of all he holds loathsome, treacherous and wrong. The element. The thing to be extirpated.

I feel hands on my shoulder and lumbar region. I am now *not* falling (thank God). Mike has moved quickly forward and kept me mostly upright. "He *is* my friend," I say, and accidentally kick the bar stool against the brass foot rail with a loud clanging.

Lester just grimly watches the two of us teetering around the floor like marionettes. "Get out," he snarls, "and take your coolie with you." Lester is an old man, possibly seventy. But meanness and bile have made him feel good, able to take an honest pleasure in the world. Old Huxley was right: stranger than we *can* know.

"I will." I'm pushing against Mike with my left arm, urging him toward the exit. He has yet to make a noise. What a surprise all this must be. "And I'll never come in this shithole again," I say. "I used to like this place. You'd have been a lot better off if you'd sold your mother's house and moved to Arizona." Why I say these things—other than that they're true—I can't tell you. You rarely get the exit line you deserve.

"Blow it out your ass, you fag," Lester says. "I hope you get

AIDS." He scowls, as if these weren't exactly the words he wanted to say, either. Though he's said them now and ruined his good mood. He turns sideways and looks back up at the TV as we meet the cold air awaiting us in the stairwell. A hockey game is on again, men skating in circles on white ice. The sound comes on, an organ playing a lively carnival air. Lester glances our way to make sure we're beating it, then turns the volume up louder for a little peace.

U p on the damp sidewalk bordering the Square, white HPD sawhorses have been established along the Pilgrim Interpretive Center's wattle fence so that during Pilgrim business hours pedestrians can stand and observe what Pilgrim life was once all about and hear Pilgrims deliver soliloquies. A youngish boy-girl couple in identical clear plastic jackets and rain pants stands peering over into the impoundment, shining a jumbo flashlight across the ghostly farm yard. The young husband's pointing things out to the young wife in a plummy English voice that knows everything about everything. They've let their white Shihtzu, in its little red sweater, go spiriting around inside the mucked-up yard, rooting the ground and pissing on things. "Sergei?" the husband says, using his most obliging voice. "Look at him, darling, he thinks this is all brilliant." "Isn't he funny? He's *so* funny," his young wife says. "Those hungry buggers would probably eat him," the young man observes. "Probab-lee," the wife says. "Come along, Ser-gei, it's 2000, old man, time to go home, time to go home."

Mike and I cross the shadowed Square to my car, parked in front of Rizutto's. Mike still has said nothing, acknowledging that I don't want to talk either. A Buddhist can nose out disharmony like a beagle scenting a bunny. I assume he's micro-managing his private force fields, better to interface with mine on the ride home.

All the Square's pricey shops are closed at seven o'clock except for the liquor store, where a welcoming yellow warmth shines out, and the Hindu proprietor, Mr. Adile, stands at his white-mullioned front window, hands to the glass, staring across at the August, where few guest rooms are lit. In steel indifference to the holiday retail frenzy elsewhere, nothing stays open late in Haddam except the liquor store. "Let 'em go to the mall if they need hemorrhoidal cream so bad." Shopkeepers trundle home to cocktails and shepherd's pie once the sun goes past the tree line (4:15 since October), leaving the streets with a bad-for-business five o'clock shadow.

Up on Seminary, where I cruised barely an hour ago, the news crawl at United Jersey flows crisply along. The stoplight has switched to blinking yellow. The Haddam gang element has skittered home to their science projects and math homework, greasing the ways for Dartmouth and Penn. The crèche is up and operating on the First Prez lawn—rotating three-color lights, red to green to yellow, brightening the ceramic wise men, who, I see, are dressed as up-to-date white men, wearing casual clothes you'd wear to the library, and not as Arabs in burnooses and beards. Work, I suspect, continues apace at the hospital—where someone got blottoed today. Ann Dykstra's home, musing on things. Marguerite's feeling better about what's not worth confessing. And Ernie McAuliffe's in the ground. Altogether, it's been an eventful though not fulfilling day to kick off a hopeful season. The Permanent Period needs to resurge, take charge, put today behind me, where it belongs.

In a moment that alarms me, I realize I haven't pissed and that I have to—so bad, my eyes water and my front teeth hurt. I should've gone upstairs in the Appleseed, though it would've meant beseeching Lester and letting him savor the spectacle of human suffering. "Hold it!" I say. Mike halts and looks startled, his little monk's face absorbing the streetlamp light. Good news? Bad news? More unvirtuous thoughts.

My car would make for good cover and has many times since the summer—on dark side streets and alleys, in garbage-y roadside turn-outs, behind 7-Elevens, Wawas, Food Giants and Holiday Inn, Jrs. But the Square's too exposed, and I have to step hurriedly into the darkened Colonial entryway of the Antiquarian Book Nook—ghostly shelving within, out-of-print, never-read Daphne du Mauriers and John O'Haras in vellum. Here I press in close to the molded white door flutings, unzip and unfurl, casting a pained look back up the side street toward the Pilgrim farm, hoping no one will notice. Mike is plainly shocked, and has turned away, pretending to scrutinize books in the Book Nook window. He knows I do this but has never witnessed it.

I let go (at the last survivable moment) with as much containment as I can manage, straight onto the bookshop door and down to its corners onto the pavement—vast, warm tidal relief engulfing me, all fear I might drain into my pants exchanged in an instant for full, florid confidence that all problems can really be addressed and solved, tomorrow's another day, I'm alive and vibrant, it's clear sailing from here on out. All purchased at the small cost of peeing in a doorway like a bum, in the town I used to call home and with the cringing knowledge that I could get arrested for doing it.

Mike coughs a loud stage cough, clears his throat in a way he never does. "Car coming, car coming," he says, soft-but-agitated. I hear girdering tires, a throaty V-8 murmur, the two-way crackle in the night, the familiar female voice directing, "Twenty-six. See the man at 248 Monroe. Possible 103-19. Two adults."

"Coming," Mike says in a stifled voice.

There's never very much and I've almost done it, though my unit's out and not easily crammed back in tight quarters. I crouch, knees-in to the door frame, piss circling my shoes. I cup my two hands, nose to the door glass the way Mr. Adile peered out from the liquor store window, and stare fiercely *in* with all my might— dick out, unattended and drafty. I'm hoping my posture and the unlikelihood that I'm actually doing what I'm doing will suppress all prowl-car attention, and that I won't be forced by someone shining a hot seal beam to turn around full-flag and set in motion all I'd set in motion, which would be more than I could put up with. Warm urine aroma wafts upward. My poor flesh has recoiled, my heart slowed by the cold pane against my forehead and hands. The Book Nook interior is silent, dark. My breathing shallows. I wait. Count seconds . . . 5, 8, 11, 13, 16, 20. I hear, but don't see, the cruiser surge and speed up, feel the motor-thrill and the radio-crackle pulse into my hams. And then it's past. Mike, my Tibetan lookout, says, "They're gone. Okay. No worries." I tuck away, zip up quick, take a step back, feel cold on my sweated, battered neck, cheek and ears. I might be okay now. Might be okay. No worries. Clear sailing. All set.

Mike sits in motionless, ecclesiastical silence while I drive us home—Route 1 to 295 to NJ 33, skirt the Trenton mall tie-ups, then around to bee-line 195, to the Garden State toward Toms River. Cold rain has started again, then stopped, then started. The temperature's at 31, the road surface possibly coated with invisible ice. My suede shoes, I regret, smell hotly of urine.

Mike would've understood little of events at the Appleseed, only the last part, which seemed (mysteriously) concerned with him. And like any good Buddhist, he's decided the less made of negativity, the better. For all I know, he could be meditating. Anger is just attachment to the cycle of birth and death, while we live in thick darkness that teaches that all phenomena (such as myself) have inherent existence, and we must therefore distinguish between a rope and a snake or else be a dirty vase turned upside down and unable to gain knowledge. This was all in the book Mike left on my desk after my Mayo procedure. *The Road to the Open Heart.* Giving it to me represents his belief that I basically appreciate such malarkey, and that one of the reasons we get along so well and that he's become a fireball real estate agent is, again, that—due to my being "pretty spiritual" in a

secular, pedestrian, all-American sort of way—we see many things
the same. Namely, that few outcomes are completely satisfactory,
it's better to make people happy—even if you have to lie—rather
than to harm them and make them sad, and we should all be
trying to make a contribution.

The Road to the Open Heart is a big, showy coffee-table slab
chocked full of idealized, consciousness-expanding color photographs of Tibet and snowy mountains and temples and shiny-
headed teenage monks in yellow-and-red outfits, plus plenty of
informal snapshots of the Dalai Lama grinning like a happy
politician while meeting world leaders and generally having the
time of his life. Supposedly, the little man-god wrote the whole
book himself, though Mike's admitted he probably didn't have
time to "write" write it—one of the lies that make you feel better.
Though it doesn't matter since the book is full of his most
important teachings boiled down to bite-size paragraphs with
easy-to-digest chapter headings even somebody with cancer could
memorize, which was what the monks were doing: "The Path
to Wisdom." "The Question We Should All Ask Ourselves."
"The Sweet Taste of Bodhicitta." "The Middle Way." Mike left
a bookmark at page 157, where the diminutive holiness talks
ominously about "death and clear light," followed by some more
upbeat formulations about the "earth constituent, the water
constituent, the fire constituent, and the wind constituent,"
followed by another photograph of the very view you've just
been promised—if you're spiritual enough: an immaculate dawn
sky in autumn. At this moment, the book's in a stack on my
bedside table, and on one of these last balmy autumn days I

intend to take it down to the ocean and send it off, since in my view the Lama's teachings all have the ring of the un-new, over-parsed and vaguely corporate about them—which, of course, is thought to be good, and a famous tenet of the Middle Way. What I needed, though, post-Mayo, was the New and Completely Unfamiliar Way. To me, the DL's wisdom also seemed only truly practicable if your intention was to become a monk and live in Tibet, where these things apparently come easy, whereas I just wanted to go on being a real estate agent on the Jersey Shore and figure out how to get around a case of prostate cancer.

Mike and I did talk about *The Road to the Open Heart* in the office one day while combing through some damage-deposit receipt forms to identify skippers—although our talk mainly concerned my son Ralph and was to the point that there are many mysteries and phenomena that can't be apprehended through sense or reason, and that Ralph might have a current existence as a mystery. It was then that he told me about young people who die young becoming masters who teach us about impermanence—which, as I said, I can buy, the Permanent Period not entirely withstanding.

Still, you can take the Middle Way only so far. Asserting yourself may indeed lead to angry disappointment—the DL's view—and anger only harms the angry and karma produces bad vibes in this life and worse ones in the next, where you could end up as a chicken or a professor in a small New England college. But the Middle Way can just as easily be the coward's way out. And based on what Mike probably heard back in the Johnny Appleseed, I'd feel better about him if he'd get in a lather about being called a coolie, insist we turn around, drive back to Haddam and kick some Lester ass, then head home laughing about it— instead of just sitting there in the reflected green dashboard glow composed as a little monkey under a Bodhi tree. East meets West.

I'm still feeling a little drunk, in addition to being roughed up, and may not be driving my best. My hands are cold and achy. My knees stiff. I'm gripping the wheel like a ship's helm in a gale. Twice I've caught myself broxing the be-jesus out of my unprotected molars. And twice when I took my eyes off the red taillight smear and the shoe-polish black highway, I found I was going ninety-five—which explains Mike's leaden silence. He's been scared shitless since Imlaystown, and is in a frozen fugue state, from which he's picturing the radiant black near-attainment as I send us skidding off into a cedar bog. I dial it back to seventy.

Today has gone not at all how I intended, although I've done nothing much more than what I planned—with the obvious exceptions of the hospital being detonated, having Ann ask me to marry her and getting into a moronic fight with Bob Butts. It's loony, of course, to think that by lowering expectations and keeping ambitions to a minimum we can ever avert the surprising and unwanted. Though the worst part, as I said, is that I've cluttered my immediate future with new-blooming dilemmas exactly like young people do when they're feckless and thirty-three and too inexperienced to know better. I wouldn't have admitted it, but I may still possess a remnant of the old feeling I had when *I* was thirty-three: that a tiny director with a megaphone, a beret and jodhpurs is suddenly going to announce "Cut!" and I'll get to play it all again—from right about where I crossed the bridge at Toms River this morning. This is the most pernicious of anti-Permanent Period denial and life sentimentalizing, which only lead you down the road to more florid self-deceptions, then dump you out harder than ever when the accounts come due, which they always do. It also suggests that I may not be up for controversy the way I used to be, and may have lapsed into personal default mode.

We're nearing the 195 junction with the Garden State, where millions (or at least hundreds of thousands) are now streaming south toward Atlantic City—not a bad choice for Turkey Day. It's the stretch of highway we detoured around this morning due to police activity. I shoot through the interchange as new lighted town signage slips past: Belmar, South Belmar, pie-in-the-sky Spring Lake, all sprawling inland from the ocean into the pine scrub and lowlands west of the Parkway. HUNGRY FOR CAPITAL. REGULAR BAPTIST CHURCH—MEET TRIUMPH AND DISASTER HEAD-ON. HOCKEY ALL NIGHT LONG. NJ IS HOSPITAL COUNTRY. Any right-thinking suburbanite would like to feel confident about these things.

I'm aware Mike's been cutting his eyes at me and frowning. He can possibly smell my soaked shoes. Mike occasionally broadcasts condescending, hanging-back watchfulness, which I take to mean I'm acting too American and not enough the velvet-handed secular-humanist-spiritualist I'm supposed to be. (This always pisses me off.) And perched on his seat in his fawn trousers, pink sweater, his ersatz Rolex and little Italian shoes with gold lounge-lizard socks, he's pissing me off again. I'm like chesty old Wallace Beery ready to rip up furniture in the barroom and toss some drunks around like scarecrows.

"What the fuck?" I say, as menacing as I can manage. All around us are mostly tour buses, Windstars and church-group vans headed down to see Engelbert Humperdinck at Bellagio. Mike ignores me and peers ahead into the taillit traffic, little hands gripping the armrests like he's in a hurtling missile. "Are you going into the land-developing business and start throwing up trophy mansions for Pakistani proctologists and make yourself rich, or what? Aren't I supposed to hear the pitch and give you the benefit of my years of non-experience?" The aroma I've been sniffing since we left Haddam is not just urine but also, I think, garlic—not usual from Mike. Benivalle has given him the full gizmo—some gloomy *il forno* out on 514, where ziti, lasagne and cannoli hang off the trees like Christmas candy.

Mike turns a serious and judicious look my way, then returns to the taillight stream, as if he has to pay attention in case I don't.

"So? What?" I say, less Wallace Beery-ish, more mentorish Henry Fonda-like. The car in front of us is a wide red Mercedes 650 with louvered back windows and some kind of delta-wing radar antenna on the trunk. A big caduceus is bolted to the license plate holder and below it a bumper sticker says ALL LIFE IS POST-OP. GET BUSY LIVING IT. Back-lit human heads are visible inside, wagging and nodding and, I guess, living it.

"Not sure." Mike is barely audible, as if speaking only to himself.

"About what? Is Benivalle a cutie pie?" *Cutie pie* is our office lingo for shit-heel walk-ins who waste your time looking at twenty listings, then go behind your back and try to buy from the seller. *Cutie pie* sounds to us like mobster talk. We always say we're "putting out a contract" on some "cutie pie," then laugh about it. Most cutie pies come from far east Bergen County and never buy anything.

"No, he's not," Mike says morosely. "He's a good guy. He took me to his home. I met his wife and kids—in Sergeantsville. She fixed a big lunch for us." The ziti. "We drove out to his Christmas tree farm in Rosemont. I guess he owns three or four. That's just one business." Mike's laced his fingers, pinkie ring and all, and begun rotating his thumbs like a granny.

"What else does he do?" I'm only performing my agreed-to duty here.

"A mobile-home park that's got a driving range attached, and he owns four laundromats with Internet access with his brother Bobby over in Milford." Mike compresses his lips to a stern little line, all the while thumbs gyrating. These are rare signs of stress, the inner journey turning bumpy. Entrepreneurship clearly unsettles him.

"Why the hell does he need you to go into business with him? He's got a plate-full. Has he ever developed anything except Christmas trees and laundromats?"

"Not so far." Mike is brooding.

In Benivalle's behalf, he is, of course, the model of the go-it-alone, self-starter that's made New Jersey the world-class American small-potatoes profit leader it is. Before he's forty, he'll own a chain of Churchill's Chickens, a flush advertising business, hold an insurance license and be ready to go back to school and study for the ministry. Up from the roadside vegetable stand, he's exactly what this country's all about: works like a dray horse, tithes at St. Melchior's, has never personally killed anyone, stays in shape for the fire department, loves his wife and can't wait for the sun to come up so he can get crackin'.

Which doesn't mean Mike should risk his hairless little Tibetan ass in the housing business with the guy, back-loaded as that business is with cost over-runs, venal subcontractors slipping kickbacks to vendors, subpar re-bar work, off-the-books payouts to inspectors, insurers, surveyors, bankers, girlfriends, the EPA and shady guys from upstate—anybody who can get a dipper in your well and sink you into Chapter 11. Guys like Benivalle almost never know when to stay small, when a laundromat in the hand is worth two McMansions in the cornfield. This deal smells of ruin, and neither one of them needs a new ruin when 30-years are at 7.8, the Dow's at 10.4, and crude's iffy at 35.16.

"He's also got an eighteen-year-old who's mentally challenged," Mike says, and aims a reproving glower to indicate I'm, again, more American than he's comfortable with—though he's just as American as I am, only from farther east.

"So what? He's raking it in." A mind's picture of my son Paul Bascombe's angry face—not a bit challenged—predictably enters my thinking with predictable misgiving.

"His wife's not really well, either," he says. "She can't work because she has to drive little Carlo everywhere. They'll have to put him in a care facility next year. That's expensive." Mike, of course, has a seventeen and a thirteen-year-old with his wife, now in the Amboys—little Tucker and little Andrea Mahoney. Plus, because he's a Buddhist, he's crippled by seeing the other guy's point of view about everything—a fatal weakness in business. I'm crippled by it, too, just not when it comes to giving advice.

"Yeah," I say, "but it's not *your* kid."

"No." Mike stops gyrating his digits and settles himself on the passenger's seat. He's thinking what I'm thinking. Who wouldn't?

We're suddenly five hundred yards from Exit 82 and Route 37. Our turn-off. I have no memory of the last 15.6 miles—earth traversed, traffic negotiated, crashes avoided. We're simply here, ready to get off. The red Mercedes with the caduceus dematerializes into the traffic speeding south—a Victorian manse on the beach at Cape May in its future, a high-roller suite at Bally's.

I slide us off to the right. And then instantly, even in the dark, the crumpled remains of a tour bus come into view. Undoubtedly it's the *bigpileupontheGardenState* that made the news crawl and stoppered the Parkway this morning when we tried to get on. The big Vista Cruiser's down over the corrugated metal barriers into the pine and hardwoods, flipped on its side like a wounded green-and-yellow pachyderm, left-side tires and undercarriage exposed to the night air, a gash opened in the graded berm, as if lightning had ripped through.

All passengers would be long gone now—medi-vac'd to local ERs or just limped away, dazed, into the timber. There's no sign of fire, though the big tinted vista windows have been popped out and the bus skin ripped open through the lettering that says

PETER PAN TOURS (no doubt the Jaws of Life were used). Men in white jumpsuits are at this moment maneuvering a giant wrecker down the embankment from the Route 37 side, preparing to winch the bus upright and tow it away. No one who isn't getting off at Toms River would see anything, though an Ocean County deputy's at the ramp bottom, directing traffic with a red flare.

Neither Mike nor I speak as we slow and get directed by the deputy toward the left, in the direction of the bay bridge. Something about the accident requires a reining in on our conversation about Benivalle's family sorrows. Tragedies, like apples and oranges, don't compare.

Route 37 back through Toms River is changed from the Route 37 we traveled this morning. Road construction's shut down and the sky's low, mustard-colored and muffled, the long skein of traffic signals popping green, yellow, red through a salty seaside haze. Only it's not a bit less crowded—due to the Ocean County mall staying open 24/7, and all other stores, chains, carpet outlets, shoe boutiques, language schools, fancy frame shops, Saturn dealerships and computer stores the same. Traffic actually moves more slowly, as if everyone we passed this morning is still out here, wandering parking lot to parking lot, ready to buy if they just knew what, yet are finally wearing down, but have no impulse to go home. The old curving neon marquee at the Quality Court has had its WELCOME amended. No longer SUICIDE SURVIVORS, but JERSEY CLOGGERS and the BLIND GOLFERS' ASSOC are welcomed. The blind golfers have earned a CONGRATS, though they're unlikely to know about it.

My neck, arms, jaw and knuckles have gone on throbbing

and burning where miscreant Bob Butts throttled me. Bob should be thinking life over in the Haddam lockup, awaiting my decision to bring charges. I've been able to let the unhappy prospect of Ann coming to Thanksgiving sink out of mind. But the slow-motion consumer daze on the Miracle Mile has revived it. It's the time of day in the time of year when things go wrong if they're going to.

In Ann's case, she simply didn't have any attractive Thanks-giving plans (not my fault), wished she did and exerted her will (strong-woman-getting-to-the-bottom-of-things) on *me*, in a depleted state. She's ignored Sally like temporary house help, played the sensitive dead-son card, the kind-man card, plus the *L* word, then stood back to watch how it all filters out. For years, I dreamed, shivered and thrilled at the idea of remarrying Ann. I pictured the whole event in Technicolor—though I could never (I wouldn't admit it) work the whole thing through to its fantas-tical end. There was always a *difficulty*—a door I couldn't find, words I got wrong—like in the dream in which you sing the national anthem at the World Series, except a lump of tar's for some reason stuck to your molars and your mouth won't open.

But this visit and all attached to it seem like the wrongest of wrong ideas even if I'm wrong as to motivation (I've had it with tonight). I don't even know Ann's politics anymore (Charley's I knew: Yale). I could also be impotent—though no trial runs have been attempted. She and the children have grinding life issues I don't want to share. And I have to piss too much to be perpet-ually amusing at dinner parties. Given Ann's power-point certainty about *everything*, I'd end up a will-less sheep at De

Tocqueville faculty do's, a partial man who sees life from a couch in the corner. Plus, I have this sleeping-panther cancer that could roar back on me.

We all need to take charge of who we spend our last years, months, weeks, days, hours, minutes, seconds, final fidgeting eye-blinks with, who we see last and who sees us. Like the wise man said, What you think's going to happen to you after you die is what's going to happen. So you need to be thinking the right things in the run-up.

"They bundle up those Christmas trees so they look like torpedoes," Mike says out of the blue, taking his glasses off and rubbing them on his blazer cuff, blinking eyes attentively. We're passing the bonsai nursery, transformed now into a bulb-strung Christmas tree lot. "There's a big machine that does it. Then they're trucked out to vendors in Kansas. All Tommy's customers're in Kansas." He's thinking about commerce in general—if it's a good idea or if it could possibly be his punishment for cheating someone out of his wattle ten centuries back. Belief, in Mike's view, is not a luxury, but still needs to keep pace with known facts and established authority—in his case, the economy. It's the theory-versus-practice rub that all religions fail to smooth over.

We've passed beyond the mall-traffic chaos and are headed toward the bay bridge, along the strip of elderly clam shacks, red-lit gravel-lot taverns, Swedish massage parlors, boat-propeller repairs and boss & secretary tourist cabins from the fifties, when it was a hoot to come to the Shore and didn't cost a year's pay. Out ahead spreads Barnegat Bay and across it the low sparse necklace lights of Sea-Clift, visible like a winter town on a benighted prairie seen from a jetliner. It's as beckoning as heaven. New Jersey's best-kept secret, where I'll soon be diving into bed.

Mike goes reaching under his pink sweater as if reaching for a package of smokes, his gaze cast over the dark frigid waters toward the bull-semen lab. And from his inside blazer pocket he produces, in fact, *a pack of smokes*! Marlboro menthols, in the distinctive green-and-white crushproof box—my parents' favorites and my own fag of choice during my military school days of experimentation eons ago. I could never hack it, though I perfected the French inhale, learned to finger a fleck off my tongue tip à la Richard Widmark and to hold one clenched between my teeth without smoke getting in my eyes.

But Mike? Mike doesn't smoke cigarooties! Buddhists don't smoke. Virtuous thinking can't possibly permit that. Does he know about his already-increased cancer susceptibility that comes with the oath of citizenship? To see him expertly strip open the pack like a fugitive is shocking. And revelatory—as if he'd started whistling "Stardust" out his butt.

I look over to be sure I'm not hallucinating, and for an instant veer into the other bridge lane and nearly wham us into a septic-service truck on its holiday way home. The truck's horn blares into the background, leaving me strangely excited.

"You mind if I smoke?" Mike looks preoccupied and vaguely ridiculous in his little dandy's threads. He even has his own matches.

"Not a bit." My surprise is really just the surprise of waking up to the moment in life I'm currently in: I'm in my car, driving over the Barnegat bridge with a forty-three-year-old Tibetan real estate salesman who's my employee and looking to me for advice about his business future and who's now smoking a cigarette! An act I've never known him to perform in eighteen months. We're a long way from Tibet out here. "I didn't know you were a Marlboro man."

He's already fired up, cracked the window and blown a good lung-full into the slipstream. "I smoked when I worked in Calcutta." He's referring to his telemarketer days of selling Iowa beef and electronic gadgets to New Jersey matrons from bullpens in the subcontinent. What a life is his. "I quit. Then I started again when I got separated." He takes another hungry suck. He already has it half-burned down, rich, stinging gray smoke hissing through the window crack. With one simple, indelible act he's no longer strictly a Tibetan, but has become the classic American little-guy, struggling under a wagonload of tough choices and plagued by uncertainties he has no experience with—in his case, about whether to become a sleazy land developer. It's our profoundest national conundrum: Are things getting better, or much worse? Poor devil. Welcome to the Republic.

"I was thinking when we were driving through Toms River." Mike actually plucks a fleck of tobacco off his tongue tip Dick Widmark-style. "All that mess back there, those people driving around aimlessly."

"They weren't aimless," I say. "They were looking for bargains." I'm still thinking about the septic truck that almost flattened us. Some guy heading home to Seaside Park, kids at the front windows, hearing the truck rumble in, happy wife, supper steaming on the table, brewsky already cracked, TV tuned to the Sixers.

"So much of life's made up of choosing things created by other people, people even less qualified than ourselves. Do you ever think about that, Frank?" He is graver than grave now, fag in mouth, its red tip a beacon as we reach the Sea-Clift end of the bridge. The illuminated NEW JERSEY'S BEST KEPT SECRET sign flashes past Mike's face and glasses. Once again, his snappy apparel and anchorman voice don't go together, as if someone else was talking for him. I'm about to be treated to some Buddhist ex cathedra homiletics in which I'm a hollow, echoing vessel needing filling with someone else's better intelligence—all because I'm patient and forbearing.

"We don't originate very much," Mike adds. "We just take what's already there."

"Yeah, I've thought about that." This very morning. Possibly he and I even talked about it and he's appropriated it and made it the Buddha's. I'm tempted to call him Lobsang. Or Dhargey—whichever one comes first—just to piss him off. "I'm fifty-five years old, Mike. I'm in the real estate business. I make a good living selling people houses they didn't *originate* and I didn't, either. So I've thought about a lot of these things over the years. Are you just a numbnuts?"

Lighted houses, wimmering up on the bay side as we circle off the bridge, are mostly ranches with remodeled camelbacks, and a few larger, modern, all-angles board-and-battens that solidify the tax base. I've sold a bunch of them and expect to sell more.

Mike further narrows his old-looking little eyes. This isn't what he expected to hear. Or what I expected to say.

"I mean, what about mindfulness being a glass of yak milk sitting on your head?" This is straight out of the Dalai Lama book, which I've read part of—mostly on the crapper. "I mean, you aren't acting very fucking mindful." I'm speeding again, off the bridge and onto Route 35, Ocean Avenue, the Sea-Clift main drag, also the main drag for Seaside Heights, Ortley Beach (with a different boulevard name), Lavallette, Normandy Beach, Mantoloking—concatenated seaside proliferance all the way to Asbury Park. Mike's Infiniti is parked at the office. I've so far given him little good advice about becoming a housing mogul. Possibly I have very little good advice to give. In any case, I'll be glad to have him out of the car.

Northbound Ocean Avenue is a wide, empty one-way separated from southbound Ocean Avenue by two city blocks of motels, surfer shops, bait shops, sea-glass jewelers, tattoo parlors, taffy stores (all closed for the season), plus a few genuine lighted-and-lived-in houses. In summer, our beach towns up 35 swell to twenty times their winter habitation. But at nine at night on November 21st, the mostly empty strip makes for an eerie, foggy fifties-noir incognito I like. No holiday decorations are up. Few cars sit at curbs. The ocean, in frothy winter tumult, is glimpsable down the side streets and the air smells briny. Parking meters have been removed for the convenience of year-rounders. Two traditional tomato-pie stands are open but doing little biz. The Mexicatessen is going and has customers. Farther on, the yellow LIQUOR sign and the ruby glow of the Wiggle Room (a summer titty bar that becomes just a bar in the winter) are signaling they're open for customers. A lone Sea-Clift town cop in his black-and-white Plymouth waits in the shadows beside the fire department in case some wild-ass boogies from East Orange show up to give us timid white people something to think about. A yellow Toms River Region school bus moves slowly ahead of us. We have now traveled as far east as the continent lasts. There's much to be said for reaching a genuine end mark in a world of indeterminacy and doubt. The feeling of arrival is hopeful, and I feel it even on a night when nothing much is going good.

Mike's clammed up since I scolded him about being mindful. We have yet to develop a fully operational language for conflict in the months he's been with me. And by being scolded, he's possibly been tossed back onto painful life lessons—the telemarketers' bullpen with its cynical Bengali middle-management bullies; ancient, happy-little-brown-man stereotypes; muscular-McCain-war-hero imagery and plucky Horatio Algerish immigrant models—all roles he's contemplated in his odyssey to here but that don't really cohere to make a rational world.

Though I don't mind if Mike's being pushed out of his comfort zone. He's like every other Republican: nervous about commitment; fearful of future regret; never saw a risk he wouldn't like somebody else to take. Benivalle may have done his dreams brusque disservice by putting his own little domestic Easter egg on display. Since what he's done is make Mike stop, think and worry—bad strategy if your customer's a Buddhist. Mike's now being forced to consider his own Big Fear—the blockade that has to be broken through sometime in life or you go no further. (I used to think mine was death. Then cancer taught me it wasn't.)

Mike now has to figure out if his big fear is the terror of

going on ahead (into the mansioning business) or the terror of *not*; if he's ready to buy into the proposition most Americans buy into and that says "You do this shit until either you're rich or you're dead"; or if he's more devoted to his old conviction that dying a millionaire is dying like a wild animal, attachment leads to disappointment and pain, etc. In other words, is he really a Republican, or is this dilemma the greening of Mike? Flattening pretty cornfields for seven-figure mega-mansions isn't, after all, really *helping* people in the way that assisting them to find a modest home they want—and that's already there—helps them. Benivalle's idea, of course, is more the standard "we build it, they come," which Mike uncomfortably sniffed back in Toms River: If we build Saturns, they will want to drive them; if we build mini-crepe grills, they will want to eat mini-crepes; if we invent Thanksgiving, they will try to be thankful (or die in the process).

My Realty-Wise office sits tucked between a Chicago-Style Pizza that previously occupied my space, and the Sea-Clift Own-Make Candies, that's only open summers and whose owners live in Marathon. The pizza place is lighted inside. The tricolor flag still leans out from its window peg over the sidewalk (Italy is the official kingdom-in-exile on the Shore). Bennie, the Filipino owner, is alone inside, putting white dough mounds back in the cold box and closing down the oven until Saturday, when everybody will crave a slice of "Kitchen Sink." Some days, when the humidity's high, my office smells like rich puttanesca sauce. I can't tell if this inclines clients more, or less, to buy beach property, though when they aren't serious enough to get in the car and go have a look at something up their alley, I often later see them next door, staring out Bennie's front window, a slice on a piece of wax paper, happy as clams for having exercised self-control.

Mike's silver Infiniti, with a REALTORS ARE PEOPLE TOO sticker on the back bumper and a Barnegat Lighthouse license plate, sits in front of my white, summery-looking, cubed building, which announces REALTY-WISE in frank gold-block lettering on its front window like an old-time shirtsleeve lawyer's office. Home-for-sale snapshots are pinned to a corkboard that's visible inside the door. In general, my whole two-desk set-up is decidedly no-frills when compared to the Lauren-Schwindell architect's showplace on Seminary, which shouted Money! Money! Money! Nothing along this stretch of the Shore compares to Haddam, which is good, in my estimation. Here at this southern end of Barnegat Neck, life is experienced less pridefully, more like an undiscovered seacoast town in Maine, and no less pleasantly—except in summer, when crowds rumble and surge. When I came over with my broker's license in '92, seeking a place to set up shop, all my competitors gave me to understand that everyone was collegial down here, there was plenty of business (and money) to go around for someone who wanted not to work too hard but keep on his toes (handle summer rentals, own a few apartments, do the odd appraisal, share listings, back up a competitor if things got tight). I purchased old man Barber Featherstone's business when Barber opted for managed care near his daughter's in

Teaneck, and everybody came by and said they were glad I was
here—happy to have a realty veteran instead of a young cutthroat land shark. I took over Barber's basic colors—red and
white (no motto or phony Ivy League crest)—substituted Realty-
Wise for Featherstone's Beach Exclusives, and got to work.
Anything fancier wouldn't have helped and eventually would've
made everyone hate my guts and be happy to cut me off at the
knees whenever they had the chance—and there are always
chances. As a result, in eight years I've made a bundle, missed
the stock market boom—and the correction—and hardly worked
a lick.

The WE'RE OPEN sign's been left hanging inside the glass door
since yesterday, and in the shadowy interior, where Mike and I
sit at two secondhand metal desks I got at St. Vincent de Paul
to make us not look like sharpsters but doers, the red pin light's
blinking on the ceiling smoke alarm. Of course I have to piss
again, though not frantically. Later in the day the urge is worse.
Mornings and early afternoons, I often don't even notice. I can
use the office facilities rather than wait for home (which could
get tricky).

Mike is still aswarm with thoughts. He's stuffed another cigarette out the window and breathed a deep sigh of anti-Buddhist
dismalness. His Marlboro and garlic, and my pissed-on shoes,
have left my car smelling terrible.

There's no good reason to resume our conversation about
mindfulness, glasses of yak milk, what we originate and what we
don't. I have no investment in it and was only performing my
role as devil's advocate. In my view, Mike is *made* for real estate

the way some people are *made* to be veterinarians and others tree surgeons. He may have found his niche in life but hates to admit it for reasons I've already expressed. I would hate to lose him as my associate—no matter how unusual an associate he is. I might arrange to have a Sponsor visit him, some stranger who could tell him what I'd tell him.

Still, old Emerson says, power resides in shooting the gulf, in darting to an aim. The soul becomes. My soul, though, has become tired of this day.

"You're not under any big time constraint in all this, are you?" I say this to the steering wheel without looking at him. The interior instruments glow green. The heat's on, the car's at idle. "I'd be suspicious if there was some kind of rush. You know?"

"House prices went up forty percent last year. Money's cheap. That won't last very long." He is morose. "When Bush gets in, the minority program'll dry up. Clinton would keep it. So would Gore." He sighs again deeply. He dislikes Clinton for uncoupling China trade from human rights, but of course would fare better with the Democrats—like the rest of us.

"Does Benivalle like Bush?"

"He likes Nader. His father was a lefty." Mike absently pulls on his undersized earlobe. A gesture of resignation.

"Benivalle's green? I thought they were all cops. Or crooks."

"You can't generalize."

Though generalization's my stock-and-trade. And I like Benivalle less for getting in bed with the back-stabbing *Nadir*. "Isn't it odd that you like Bush, and he's killing off your minority whozzits. And you're thinking of going into business with a liberal."

"I don't *like* Bush. I voted for him." Mike impatiently unsnaps his seat belt. He has ventured valiantly forth as a brave citizen and come back an immigrant vanquished by uncertainty. Too bad. "I feel regret," he says solemnly.

"You haven't done anything bad," I say, and attempt a smile denoting confidence.

"It doesn't attach to doing." And he's suddenly smiling, himself, though I'm sure he's not happy.

"You just got out beyond your stated ideological limits," I say. "You can always come back. *Devil's advocate*'s just a figure of speech. My belief system hasn't defeated your belief system."

"No. I'm sure it hasn't." Mike frames his words as a verdict.

"There you go." Ours is a rare conversation for two men as different as we are to have in a car, though I wish it could be over so I could grab a piss.

"I understand you think this is not a good thing to do," he says.

"I don't want to keep you from anything but harm," I say. "You'll just have to understand what you understand."

*B*ennie, the pizzeria owner, has taken his Italian flag inside and is letting himself out his front door, locking up using a ring of keys as big as a bell clapper. He has his white apron draped over his arm for at-home laundering. He's a small, crinkly-haired, mustachioed man and looks more Greek than Filipino.

He's wearing flip-flops, a red shirt and black Bermudas that reveal white ham-hock thighs. He glances at Mike and me, shadowy male presences in an idling Suburban, gives us a momentary stare, possibly puts us down for queers—though he should recognize me—then finishes his lock-up and walks away toward his white delivery van farther down the block.

Mike says he feels regret, but what he feels is lonely—though it's logical to confuse the two. He'll probably never feel true regret, which is outside his belief system. When he gets back to his empty house in Lavallette, he'll turn up the heat, call his pining wife in the Amboys, speak lovingly of reconciling, talk sweetly to his kids, meditate for an hour, connect some significant dots and pretty soon start to feel better about things. As an immigrant, he knows loneliness can be dealt with symptomatically. I could ask him over for Thanksgiving. But I've made a big-enough mess with Ann, and don't trust my instincts. Anything can be made worse.

In our silence, my mind strays to Paul again, already on his soldiering way over from the Midwest, his new "other" manning the map under the dim interior lights so there's no need to stop. (Why do so many things happen in cars? Are they the only interior life left?) I wonder where exactly they are at this moment. Possibly just passing Three Mile Island in his old, shimmying Saab? I already sense his commotional presence via consubstantive telemetry across the dwindling miles.

Mike's small, lined, smiling face waits outside my car door. Cold ocean fog swirls behind him, giving me a shudder. I've briefly zoned again. Oh my, oh me.

"Suffering, I think, doesn't happen without a cause." He nods consolingly in at me, as if I was the one in the pickle.

"I don't necessarily look at things that way," I say. "I think a lot of shit just happens to you. If I were you, I wouldn't think so much about causes. I'd think more about results. You know? It's my advice."

His smile vanishes. "They're always the same," he says.

"Whatever. You're a good real estate agent. I'd be sorry to lose you. This is the fastest-growing county in the East. Household income's up twenty-three percent. There's money to be made. Selling houses is pretty easy." I could also tell him there'd be virtually zero Buddhists in Haddam to be buddies with—just Republicans by the limo-full, who wouldn't associate with him, not even the Hindus, once they found out he's a developer. He'd end up feeling sad about life and moving away. Whereas here, he wouldn't. I don't say that, though, because I'm out of advice. "I'll be in in the morning," I say, all business. "Why don't you take the day and think about things. I'll steer the ship."

"Sure. Good. Okay." He goes reaching in his trousers for his keys. "Have a happy Thanksgiving." He puts the accent on the *giving*, not on the *thanks* as we longer-term Americans do.

"Okay." I sound and feel vapid.

"Do you explode fireworks?" His car lights flash on by themselves.

"Different holiday," I say. "This is just eating and football."

"I can't always keep things straight." He looks at me inside my cold cockpit and seems delighted. A minor holiday miscue lets him feel momentarily less American (in spite of his lapel-pin flag) and makes his other errors, failures and uncertainties feel more forgivable, just parts of those things that can't be helped. It's not a wrong way to feel—less responsible for everything. Mike closes the door, taps the glass with his pinkie ring and gives me a silly, grinning half bow with a thumbs-up, to which I involuntarily (and ridiculously) give him a half bow back, which delights him even more and into another thumbs-up but no bow. I am the hollow, echoing vessel between the two of us now. I have my patience and forbearance for my ride home, but as this long day of events comes to its close, I have little more to show.

Part 2

7

At 3:00 a.m., I'm suddenly awake, which is not unusual these days. A late-night call to the toilet, or else something from the day ahead or the day past, abruptly breaking through the tent of sleep to invade my brain and set my heart to beating fast. Sleep's a gossamer thing for over-fifties, even women. Normally, I can breathe deep and slow, adjust my hearing to the hiss of the sea, project my mind into the oceany dark and am asleep without realizing I'm not awake. Though when that doesn't avail—and sometimes it doesn't—I seek repose by editing my list of prospective pallbearers, noting a crucial addition or deletion, depending on my mood, followed by a review of who I intend to leave what to when the day comes, then reviewing all the cars I've owned, restaurants I've eaten in and hotels I've slept in during my fifty-five years of ordinary life. And if none of these performs, I inventory all the acceptable ways of committing suicide (without scaring the shit out of myself—all cancer patients do this). And if nothing else works—sometimes that happens, too—I file through the names of every woman I ever made love to in my entire life (surprisingly more than I'd have thought), at which point sleep comes in half a minute, since I'm not really very interested, whereas with the others, I sort of am. Clarissa has told me that when sleep eludes her, she recites a South-Sea

Fijian mantra, which goes: "The shark is not your demon, but the final resting place of your soul." This I'd find disturbing, so that if it ever did put me to sleep, it would give me a bad dream, which would then wake me up and I'd be stuck till morning.

My room now is cold and nearly lightless but for the red numerals on the clock, the ocean sighing toward daylight, still hours on. I've been dreaming I rescued a stranger from the sea outside my house and have been declared a hero (a sure sign of *needing* rescue). I awoke to hear the sound of my own name whispered in the night air.

"Frank-ee," I hear, "Frank-ee." My heart's racing like Daytona, my fingers and arms up to my shoulder webby and immobilized with slowed blood flow and dormancy. Normally, I maintain the recommended Dead Crusader position—flat on my back, feet together, wrists crossed on my chest as though a sword is in hand. But I'm surprisingly on my stomach and may possibly have been swimming in the sheets. My neck aches from my Bob Butts tussle. I've popped a sweat like an athlete on a jog. "Frank-ee." Then I hear boisterous laughing. "Haw, haw, haw." A door slamming. *Splat.*

When I arrived home last night from Haddam, a sports car, a shiny, pale blue, underslung Austin-Healey 1000, sat beside Sally's LeBaron convertible in the driveway, its motor warm (I checked). Green-numeral LIVE FREE OR DIE license plates. A red Gore sticker was half torn off its back bumper. Later, I climbed the stairs to my bedroom and heard Clarissa's radio, low and soft, tuned to the all-night jazz station in Philadelphia—Arthur Lyman playing "Jungle Flute" on a piano. A bottle lip clinked against a glass rim, a hushed man's (not a very young man's) voice was saying, humorously, "Not so bad. I wouldn't say. Not so bad." Silence opened as the two took in my footfalls and my door squeaking and a cough I felt required to cough, if only to say, Yes, things're fine. Fine, fine. Things're all fine. Then another tinkle-clink, Clarissa's languorous laugh, the word *father* casually spoken in a low but not too low voice, and then silence.

But now the door splat outside the house. My name whispered, then "Haw, haw, haw." Clearly, it's my neighbors.

Next door on Poincinet Road, eighteen feet from my south wall, my immediate neighbors are the Feensters, Nick and Drilla. I sold them their house in '97. Nick is a former Bridgeport fire-fighter who became a millionaire recycling old cathode-ray tubes, and then to his shock won the Connecticut lottery. Not the big one. But the big-enough one. He and Drilla had been weekenders in Sea-Clift, plus two set-aside weeks in August, consigning to me their pink, white-trimmed Florida-style bungalow on Bimini Street to rent for a fortune, May to October, which is our season. But when the big money rolled in, they sold the pink bungalow, Nick quit work, they pulled up stakes in Bridgeport and let me put them into #5 Poincinet Road—a modern, white-painted, many-faceted, architect's dream/nightmare with metal-banistered miradors, copper roof, decks for every station of the sun, lofty, mirrored triple-panes open on the sea, imported blue Spanish tile flooring (heated), intercoms and TVs in the water closets, in-wall vacuums and sound system, solar panels, a burglar system that rings in Langley, built-in pecky cypress everythings, even a vintage belted Excalibur that the prior owners, a gay banking couple with an adopted child who couldn't stand the damp, just threw in for the million eight, full-boat, as a housewarming present. (Nick sold it for a mint.)

The Feensters moved down, eager beavers, on New Year's Day, '98, ready to take up their fine new life. Only, their sojourn in Sea-Clift has turned out to be far from a happy one. I frankly believe if they'd stayed in Bridgeport, if Nick had stayed connected to the cathode-ray business, if Drilla had stayed working in the parts department at Housatonic Ford (where they loved her), if maybe they'd bought a transitional house in Noank and kept their rental here, practiced gradualism, not moved the whole gestalt in one swoop to Sea-Clift, where they didn't know anyone, had nothing to do, weren't adept at making new connections and, in fact, openly suspected everyone of hating them because of their ridiculous luck, then they might've been happier than a typical couple in the Witness Protection Program—which is how they seem.

Their Sea-Clift life seemed to go careening off the rails the instant they arrived. Our beach road, which contains only five houses, once contained twenty and stretched for a mile north along the beach, each large footprint facing the sea from behind a sandy, oat-grass hillock nature had placed in the ocean's way. We Poincinet home owners—three other residents, plus me (excluding the Feensters)—all understand that we hold our ground on the continent's fragile margin at nature's sufferance. Indeed, the reason there are now only five of us is that the previous fifteen "cottages"—grandiloquent old gabled and turreted Queen Annes, rococo Stick Styles, rounded Romanesque

Revivals—were blown to shit and smithereens by Poseidon's wrath and are now gone without a trace. Hurricane Gloria, as recently as 1985, finished the last one. Beach erosion, shoreline scouring, tectonic shifts, global warming, ozone deterioration and normal w&t have rendered all us "survivors" nothing more than solemn, clear-headed custodians to the splendid, transitory essence of everything. The town fathers prudently codified this view by passing a no-exceptions-ever restriction against new construction down our road, grandfathering our newer, better-anchored residences, and requiring repairs and even normal upkeep be both non-expansive and subject to stern permit regulation. In other words, none of this, like none of us, is going to last here. We made our deal with the elements when we closed our deal with the bank.

Except the Feensters didn't, and don't, see things that way. They tried, their first summer, to change the road's name to Bridgeport Road, have it age-restricted and gated from the south end, where we all drive in. When that failed—at a tense planning-board meeting with me and other residents opposing—they tried to close access to the beach farther up, where the old cottages once sat in a regal row. Public use, they argued, deprived them of full enjoyment and drove values down (hilarious, since Adolf Eichmann could own a beach house down here and prices would still soar). This was all hooted down by the surfer community, the surf-casting community, the bait-shop owners and the metal-detector people. (We all again opposed.) Nick Feenster grew infuriated, hired a lawyer from Trenton to test the town's right to regulate, arguing on constitutional grounds. And when this failed, he stopped speaking to the neighbors and specifically to me and put up signs on his road frontage that said DON'T EVEN THINK OF TURNING AROUND IN THIS DRIVEWAY. KEEP OUT! WE TOW! BELIEVE IT! PRIVATE PROPERTY!!! BEACH CLOSED DUE TO DANGEROUS RIPTIDE. BEWARE OF PIT BULL! They also erected an expensive picket-topped wooden fence between their house and mine and installed motion-sensitive crime lights, both of which the town made them take down. Generally, the Feensters came to seem to us neighbors like the famous family that can't be made happy by great good luck. Not your worst-nightmare neighbor (a techno-reggae band or an evangelical Baptist church would be worse), but a bad real estate outcome, given that signs were positive at first. And especially for me was it a bad outcome, because while not wanting recipe swapping, drill-bit borrowing or cross-property-line chin-music razz-ma-tazz, I would still enjoy the occasional shared cocktail at sundown, a frank but cordial six-sentence exchange of political views as the paper's collected at dawn or a noncommittal deck-to-deck wave as the sun turns the sea to sequined fires, filling the heart with the assurance that we're not experiencing life's wonders *entirely* solo.

Instead, zilch.

My misdelivered mail (Mayo bills and DMV documents) all gets tossed in the trash. Only scowls are offered. No apologies are extended when their car alarm whangs off at 2:00 p.m. and ruins my post-procedure nap. There's no heads-up when a roof tile blows loose and causes a behind-the-wall leak while I'm out in Rochester. Not even a "Howzitgoin?" on my return last August, when I wasn't feeling so hot. Twice, Nick actually set up a skeet thrower on his deck and shot clay pigeons that flew (I thought) dangerously close to my bedroom window. (I called the cops.)

At one point a year ago, I asked one of my competitors, in strict confidence, to make a cold call to the Feensters, representing a nonexistent, high-roller, all-cash client, to find out if Nick might take the money and go the hell back to Bridgeport, where he belongs. The colleague—a nice, elderly ex-Carmelite nun who's hard to shock—said Nick stormed at her, "Did that asshole Bascombe put you up to this? Why don't you go fuck yourself," then bammed the phone down.

A couple of us up the road have discussed the mystery of what we think of as the "Toxic Feensters," standing out on sand-swept Poincinet on warm afternoons through the fall. My neighbors are a discredited presidential historian retired from Rutgers, who admitted fudging insignificant quotes in his book about Millard Fillmore and the Know-Nothing Party of 1856, but who sued and won enough to live out his years in style. (College lawyers are never any good.) There's also a strapping, bulgy-armed, khaki-suited petroleum engineer of about my age, from Oklahoma, Terry Farlow, a bachelor who works in Kazakhstan in "oil exploration," comes home every twenty-eight days, then returns to Aktumsyk, where he lives in an air-conditioned geodesic dome, eats three-star meals flown in from France and sees all the latest movies courtesy of our government. (I guarantee you're never neighbors with people like this in Haddam.) Our third neighbor is Mr. Oshi, a middle-aged Japanese banker I've actually never talked to, who works at Sumitomo in Gotham, departs every morning at three in a black limousine and never otherwise leaves his house once he's in it.

We're an unlikely mix of genetic materials, life modalities and history. Though all of us understand we've tumbled down onto this slice of New Jersey's pretty part like dice cast with eyes shut. Our sense of belonging and fitting in, of making a claim and settling down is at best ephemeral. Though being ephemeral gives us pleasure, relieves us of stodgy house-holder officialdom and renders us free to be our own most current selves. No one would be shocked, for instance, to see a big blue-and-white United Van Lines truck back down the road and for any or all of us to pack it in without explanation. We'd think briefly on life's transience, but then we'd be glad. Someone new and possibly different and possibly even interesting could be heading our way.

None of us can say we understand the unhappy Feensters. And as we've stood evenings out on the sandy road, we've stared uncomprehending down Poincinet at their showy white house marred by warning signs about towing and pit bulls and dangerous but fallacious riptides, their twin aqua-and-white '56 Corvettes in the driveway, where they can be admired by people the Feensters don't want to let drive past. Everything that's theirs is always locked up tight as a bank. Nick and Drilla go on beach power walks every day at three, rain, cold or whatever, yellow Walkmen clamped on their hard heads, contrasting Lycra outer garments catching the sun's glow, fists churning like boot-camp trainees, eyes fixed straight up the beach. Never a word, kind or otherwise, to anyone.

Arthur Glück, the defamed, stoop-shouldered ex-Rutgers prof, believes it's a Connecticut thing (he's a Wesleyan grad). Everyone up there, he says, is accustomed to bad community behavior (he cites Greenwich), plus the Feensters aren't educated.

Terry Farlow, the big Irishman from Oklahoma, said his petroleum-industry experience taught him that conspicuous new wealth unaccompanied by any sense of personal accomplishment (salvaging cathode-ray tubes not qualifying as accomplishment) often unhinges even good people, wrecks their value system, leaves them miserable and turns them into assholes. The one thing it never seems to do, he said, is make them generous, compassionate and forgiving.

It seemed to me—and I feel implicated, since I sold them their house and made a fat 108K doing it—that the Feensters got rich, got restless and adventuresome (like anybody else), bought ocean-front but somehow got detached from their sense of useful longing, though they couldn't have described it. They only know they paid enough to expect to feel right, but for some reason don't feel right, and so get mad as hell when they can't bring all into line. A Sponsor visit, or a freshman course on Kierkegaard at a decent community college, would help.

With the clairvoyance of hindsight, it might also have worked that if the Feensters were dead set on Sea-Clift, they would've been smarter to stay away from ocean-front and put their new fecklessly gotten gains into something that would keep longing alive. Longing can be a sign of vigor, as well as heart-stopping stress. They might've done better down here by diversifying, maybe moving into their own Bimini Street bungalow, adding a second storey or a greenhouse or an in-ground pool, then buying a bigger fixer-upper and fitting themselves into the Sea-Clift community by trading at the hardware store, subbing out their drywall needs to local tradesmen, applying for permits at the town clerk's, eating at the Hello Deli and gradually matriculating (instead of bulling in), the way people have from time's first knell. They could've invested their lottery winnings in boutique stocks or a miracle-cure IPO or a Broadway revival of *Streetcar* and felt they were in the thick of things. Later, they could've turned their cathode-ray-tube business into a non-profit to help young victims of something—whatever old cathode-ray tubes do that kills you—and made everyone love them instead of loathing them and wishing they'd go the hell away. In fact, if one or the other of them would get cancer, it would probably have a salubrious effect on their spirits. Though I don't want to wish that on them yet.

The bottom line is: Living the dream can be a lot more complicated than it seems, even for lottery winners, who we all watch shrewdly, waiting to see how they'll fuck it up, never give any loot away to AIDS hospices or battered children's shelters or the Red Cross, the good causes they'd have sworn on their Aunt Tillie's grave they'd bankroll the instant their number came up. This is, in fact, one reason I keep on selling houses—though I've had a snootful of it, don't need the money and occasionally encounter bad-apple clients like the Feensters: because it gives me something to feel a productive longing about at day's end, which is a way to register I'm still alive.

F rank-ee." A heavy pause. "Frank-ee." My name's being called from the chilled oceany night, beyond the windows I've left open to invigorate my sleep. There are no sounds from Clarissa's room, where she's entertaining Mr. Lucky Duck, and where they may even be asleep now—she in bed, he on the floor like a Labrador (there's so little you can do to make things come out right).

I climb stiffly out, blue-pajama-clad, and go to the window that gives down upon the sand and weedy strip of no-man's-land between me and the Feensters, the ground where the fence used to be. No light shines from the three window squares on the three stacked levels of white wall facing my house. We're bunched together too close in here despite the choker prices. Lots were platted by a local developer in cahoots with the planning board and who saw restrictions coming from years away and wanted to retire to Sicily.

Faint fog drifts from sea to land, but I can see a shadowy triangular portion of the Feensters' front yard, where the gay bankers planted animal topiary the Feensters have let go to hell in favor of aggressive signage. A grown-out boxwood rhino and part of a boxwood monkey are ghostly shapes in the mist. Seaward I can see the pallet of shadowed beach, with a crust of white surf disappearing into the sand. In the night sky, there's the icebox glow of Gotham and, in the middle distance, the white lights and rigging lines of a commercial fisher alone at its toils. In these times of lean catches, local captains occasionally dispose of private garbage on their overnight flounder trips. A fellow in Manasquan even advertises burials at sea (ashes only) beyond the three-mile limit, where permits aren't required. Many things seem thinkable that once weren't.

From between the houses, the Glücks' big tomcat, William Graymont, strolls toward the beach to scavenge what the shore-birds have left, or perhaps snare a plover for his midnight meal.

When I tap the glass, he stops, looks around but not at me, flicks his tail, then continues his leisurely trek.

No one's said my name again, so I'm wondering if I dreamed it. But all at once a light snaps on in the Feensters' third-floor bathroom, the Grecian marble ablution sanctum off the spacious master suite. Television volume blaring yesterday's news headlines goes on, then instantly goes silent. Drilla Feenster's head and naked torso pass the window, then pass again, her bottle-blond hair in a red plastic shower cap, heading for the gold-nozzled shower. Possibly it's their usual bathing and TV hour. I wouldn't know.

But then rounding the front outside corner of the house in pajamas, slippers, a black ski parka and a knit cap, Nick Feenster appears, talking animatedly into a cell phone. One hand holds the instrument to his ear like a conch shell, the other a retractable leash attached to Bimbo, their pug. A big man with a tiny dog could signal a complex and giving heart, if not straight-out homosexuality, but not in Nick's case. (Bimbo is the "pit bull" referred to on the sign.) Nick's gesturing with the hand holding Bimbo's leash, so that each time he gestures, Bimbo's yanked off his little front paws.

Nick's voice is loud but muffled. "Frankly, I don't get it," he seems to be saying, with gestures accompanying and Bimbo bouncing and looking up at him as if each jerk was a signal. "Frankly, I think you're making a *biiiig* mistake. A *biiiig* mistake. Frankly, this is getting way out of control."

Frankly. Frankly. Frank-ee. Frank-ee. There's so little that's truly inexplicable in the world. Why should it be such a difficult place to live?

The lighted bathroom square goes unexpectedly black—a purpose possibly interrupted. Nick, who's a husky, heavy-legged, former power lifter and has toted prostrated victims out of smoke-filled tenement stairwells, goes on talking in the cold, fog-misted yard (to whom, I don't even wonder). A yellow second-floor light square pops on. This in the cypress kitchen-cum-vu room— Mexican tile fireplace, facing Sonoran-style, silver-inlaid, hand-carved one-of-a-kind couches, Sub-Zero, commercial Viking, built-in Cuisinart and a Swiss wine cellar at cabinet level. Almost too fast, the first-floor window brightens. A sound, a seismic disturbance up through the earth's crust, permeating Nick's bedroom slippers—an intimation only misbehaving husbands can hear—causes Nick abruptly to snap his cell phone closed, frown a suspicious frown upwards (at me! He can't see me but senses surveillance). Then, in a strange, bumpy, big man's slightly balletic movement, reflecting the fact he's freezing his nuts off, Nick, with Bimbo struggling to keep up, beats it back around the house, past the topiary monkey and out of sight. Whatever he intends to say he's been up to outside—to Drilla, who's noted his absence and thought, *What the fuck?*—is just now larruping around in his brain like an electron.

I stare down into the sandy, weedy non-space Nick has vacated in guilty haste. Something's intensely satisfying about his absence, as if I'll never have to see him again. I think I hear, but probably don't hear, voices far away, buffered by interior walls, a door slammed hard. A shout. A breakage. The odd socketed pleasure of someone else's argument—not *your* night shot to hell, not *your* heart crashing in your chest, not *your* head exploding in anger and hot frustration, as when Sally left. Someone else's riot and bad luck. It's enough to send anyone off to bed happy and relieved, which is where, after a pit stop, I return.

*U*ntil . . . music awakens me. *Dum-dee-dum-dee-dum, dum-dee-dum-dee-dum.*

My bedroom's lit through with steely wintry luminance. I'm shocked to have slept till now—7:45—with light banging in, the day underway and noise downstairs. Rich coffee and bacon-fat aromas mix with sea smells. I hear a voice particle. Clarissa. Hushed. "We have to be . . . He's still . . . not usually so . . ." Mutter, mutter. A clink of cup and saucer. Knife to plate. A kitchen chair scrapes. A car murmurs past on Poincinet Road. The sounds now of the ball getting rolling. I've clenched my teeth all night. Small wonder.

The music's from the Feensters'. Show tunes at high volume out the vu-room sliding door, past the owl decoy that keeps sea-gulls at bay. *My Fair Lady.* ". . . And *oooohhh*, the towering fee-ling, just to *kn-o-o-o-w* somehow you are *ne-ah*." The Feensters often sit out on their deck in their hot tub during winter, drink Irish coffee and read the *Post*, wearing ski parkas, all as a way of smelling the roses. This morning, though, music's needed to put some distance between now and last night, when Nick was "walking the dog" at 3:00 a.m.

I lie abed and stare bemused at the stack of books on my bedside table, most read to page thirty, then abandoned, except for *The Road to the Open Heart*, which I've read a good deal of.

Much of it's, of course, personally impractical, though you'd have to be a deranged serial killer not to agree with most of what it says. "On the one hand make concessions, on the other take the problem seriously." It's no wonder Mike does so well selling houses. Buddhism wrote the book on selling houses.

Recently I've also dipped into *The Fireside Book of Great Speeches*, a leftover from Paul's HHS Oratory Club. I've sought good quotable passages in case a moment arises for valedictory words this Thursday. The speeches, however, are all as boring as Quaker sermons, except for Pericles' funeral oration, and even *he's* a little heavy-handed and patented: "Great will be your glory if you do not lower the nature that is within you." When is that not ever true? Pericles and the Dalai Lama are naturals for each other. Convalescence is supposed to be a perfect time for reading, like a long stint in prison. But I assure you it isn't, since you have too much on your mind to concentrate.

The sky I can see from bed is monochrome, high and lighted from a sun deep within cottony depths—not a disk, but a spirit. It is a cold, stingy sky that makes a seamless plain with the sea— decidedly not a "realty sky" to make ocean-front seem worth the money. I'm scheduled for a showing at 10:15; but the sky's effect— I already know it—will not be to inspire and thrill, but to calm and console. For that reason I'm expecting little from my effort.

The exact status of my marriage to Sally Caldwell requires, I believe, some amplification. It is still a marriage that's officially going on, yet by any accounting has become strange—

in fact, the strangest I know, and within whose unusual circumstances I myself have acted very strangely.

Last April, I took a journey down memory lane to an old cadets'
reunion at the brown-stucco, pantile-roof campus of my old military school—Gulf Pines on the Mississippi coast. "Lonesome
Pines," we all called it. The campus and its shabby buildings, like
apparently everything else in that world, had devolved over time
to become an all-white Christian Identity school, which had itself,
by defaulting on its debts, been sold to a corporate entity—the
ancient palms, wooden goalposts; dusty parade grounds,
dormitories and classroom installments soon to be cleared as a
parking structure for a floating casino across Route 90.

During this visit, I happened to hear from Dudley Phelps,
who's retired out of the laminated-door business up in Little Rock,
that Wally Caldwell, once our Lonesome Pines classmate, but
more significantly once my wife's husband, until he got himself
shell-shocked in Vietnam and wandered off seemingly forever,
causing Sally to have him declared dead (no easy trick without a
body or other evidence of death's likelihood)—*this* Wally Caldwell
was reported by people in the know to have appeared again. Alive.
Upon the earth and—I was sure when I heard it—eager to stir
up emotional dust none of us had seen the likes of.

Nobody knew much. We all stood around the breezy, hot
parade ground in short-sleeve pastel shirts and chinos, talking
committedly, chins tucked into our necks, the pale, wispy grass
smelling of shrimp, ammonia and diesel, trying to unearth good
concrete memories—the deaf-school team we played in football
that hilariously beat the shit out of us—anything we could feel

positive about and that could make adolescence seem to have been worthwhile, though agreeing darkly we were all of us pretty hard cases when we'd arrived. (Actually, I was not a hard case at all. My father had died, my mother'd remarried a man I pretty much liked and moved to Illinois, only I simply couldn't imagine going to high school with a bunch of Yankees—though, of course, I would someday become one of them and think it was great.)

The casino's big building-razing, turf-ripping machinery was already standing ranked along the highway like a small mean army. Work was due to commence the next morning, following this last muster on the plain. We had a keg of beer somebody'd brought. The Gulf was just as the Atlantic is in summer: brownish, sluggish, a dingy aqueous apron stretching to nowhere—though warm as bathwater instead of dick-shrinkingly cold. We all solemnly stood and drank the warm beer, ate weenies in stale buns and did our best not to feel dispirited and on-in-years (this was before my medical surprises). We chatted disapprovingly about how the Coast had changed, how the South had traded its tarnished soul for an even more debased graven image of gambling loot, how the current election would probably be won by the wrong dope. Surprisingly, many of my old classmates had gone to Nam like Wally and come back Democrats.

And then around 2:00 p.m., when the sun sat straight over our sweating heads like a dentist's lamp and we'd all begun to laugh about what a shithole this place had really been, how we didn't mind seeing it disappear, how we'd all cried ourselves to sleep in our metal bunks on so many breathless, mosquito-tortured nights on account of cruel loneliness and youth and deep hatred for the other cadets, we all, by no signal given, just began to stray away back toward our rental cars, or across the highway to the casino for some stolen fun, or back to motels or SUVs or the airport in New Orleans or Mobile, or just back— as if we could go back far enough to where it would all be forgotten and gone forever, the way it already should've been. Why were we there? By the end, none of us could've said.

How, though, do you contemplate such news as this possible Wally sighting? I had no personal memories of Cadet W. Caldwell, only pictures Sally kept (and kept hidden): on the beach with their kids in Saugatuck; a color snapshot showing a shirtless, dog-tagged Wally squinting into the summer sun like JFK, holding a copy of *Origin of Species* with a look of mock puzzlement on his young face; a few tuxedoed wedding photos from 1969, where Wally looked lumpy and wise and scared to death of what lay before him; a yearbook portrait from Illinois State, showing Walter "The Wall," class of '67, *plant biology*, and where he was deemed (sadly, I felt) to be "Trustworthy, a friend to all." "Solid where it counts" (which he wasn't). "Call me Mr. Wall."

These ancient, moistened relics did not, to me, a real husband make. Though once they had to Sally—a tall, blond, blue-eyed beauty with small breasts, thin fingers, smooth-legged, with her tiny limp from a tennis mishap—a college cheerleader who fell for the shy, heavy-legged, curiously gazing rich boy in her genetics class, and who smiled when she talked because so much made her happy, who didn't have problems about physical things and so introduced the trusting "Wall" to bed and to cheap motels out Highway 9, so captivating him that by spring break, "they were pregnant." And pregnant again and married by the time Wally got called to the Army and joined the Navy instead, in 1969, and went off to a war.

From which, in a sense, he never returned. Though he tried for a couple of weeks in 1971, but then one day just walked off from their little apartment in the Chicago suburb of Hoffman Estates, never to return with a sound or a glimpse. Kids, wife, parents, a few friends. A future. Boop. Over.

This was the extent of my knowledge of Wally the uxorious. He was already legally "dead" when I came on the scene in '87 and tried to rent Sally some expandable office space in Manasquan. She'd identified me from a bogus reminiscence I wrote for the Gulf Pines "Pine Boughs" newsletter, though I had no actual memory of Wally and was merely on the Casualties Committee, responsible for "personal" anecdotes about classmates nobody remembered, but whose loved ones didn't want them seeming like complete ciphers or lost souls, even if they were.

The thought that mystery-man Walter B. Caldwell might still be alive was, as you can imagine, unwieldy personal cargo to be carrying home, Mississippi to New Jersey. There could probably be stranger turns of events. But if so, I'd like you to name one. And while you're at it, name one you'd find easy to keep as your little secret, something you'd rather not have spread around. No more details were available.

On arriving back to Sea-Clift (we're only talking about last April here!), I decided that rogue rumors were always shooting around like paper airplanes in everybody's life, and that this was likely just one more. Some old Lonesome Pines alum, deep in his cups and reeling through the red-light district of Amsterdam or Bangkok, suddenly spies a pathetic homeless man weaving on a street corner, a large, fleshy, unshaven "American-looking" clod, filthy in a tattered, greasy overcoat and duct-taped shoes, yet who has a particularly arresting, sweet smile animating tiny haunted eyes and who seems to stare back knowingly. After a pause, there's a second cadged look, then a long unformed thought about it afterward, followed by a decision to leave well enough alone (where well enough's always happiest). But then, in memory's narrow eye comes a fixifying certainty, an absolute recognition—a sighting. And ker-plunk: Wally *lives*! (and will be in your house eating dinner by next Tuesday).

In eight years of what I thought were much more than satis-fying-fulfilling marriage, not to mention almost thirty since Wally walked away and didn't come back, Sally had made positive adjust-ments to what might've driven most people bat-shit crazy with anger and not-knowing, and with anxiety over the anger and not-knowing. Therefore, to drop this little hand grenade of uncertainty into her life, I concluded, would actually be unfriendly (I'd decided by then it wasn't true, so it really wasn't a hand grenade in *my* life). But what was either of us supposed to do with the news, short of a full-bore "Have You Seen This Man?" campaign (I didn't *want* to see him), "aged" photos of Wally put up on Web sites, stapled to bulletin boards and splintery tele-phone poles beside aroma-therapy flyers and lost-cat posters, with appeals made to "Live at 5"?

After which he still wouldn't show up. Because—of course—he'd long ago climbed over a bridge rail or slipped off a boat transom or rock face in the remotest Arizona canyon and said good-bye to this world of woes. Someday, I fantasized, I would sit with Sally on a warm, sun-smacked porch by a lake in Manitoba—this being once our days had dwindled down to a precious few. I'd be pensive for a time, staring out at the water's onyx sheen, then quietly confide to her my long-ago gesture of devotion and love, which had been to shield her from faithlessly rumored sightings of Wally that I knew weren't a bit true (everyone embroiders fantasies to please themselves), and that would only have kept her from what rewarding life she and I could cobble together, knowing what we knew and feeling what we felt. In this fantasy, Sally for a while becomes agitated by my deception and presumption. She stands and walks up and back along the long knotty-pine porch, arms tightly folded, her mouth official and cross, her fingers twitching as the sun burns the surface of Lake Winnipegosis, canoes set forth for sunset journeys, kids' voices waft in from shadowy cottage porches deeper in the great woods. Finally, she sits back into her big green wicker rocker and says nothing for a long time, until the air's gone cooler than we'd like, and as that old lost life still clicks past her inner gaze. Eventually, her heart gives a worrisome flutter, she swallows down hard, feels the back of her hand going even colder (in this fantasy, we have become Canadians). She sighs a deep sigh, reaches chair-arm to chair-arm, finds my hand, knows again its warmth, and then without comment or query suggests we go inside for cocktails, an early dinner and to bed.

Case closed. RIP, Mr. Wall. My dream, instead of my nightmare, come true.

To which fickle fate says: Dream on, dream on, dream on.

Because sometime in early May—it was the balmy, sun-kissed week between Mother's Day and Buddha's birthday (observed with dignified calm and no fanfare by Mike) and not long after my own fifty-fifth (observed with wonderment by me)—Sally caught the United Shuttle out to Chicago to visit the former in-laws in Lake Forest. I'm always officially invited to these events, but have never gone, for obvious reasons—although this might've been the time. The occasion was the aged Caldwells' (Warner and Constance) sixtieth wedding anniversary. A party was planned at the formerly no-Jews-or-blacks-allowed Wik-O-Mek Country Club. Sally's two grim, grown but disenchanted children, Shelby and Chloë, were supposedly coming from northern Idaho. They'd long ago fallen out with their mom over having their dad declared a croaker—prematurely, they felt. You can only imagine how they loathe me. Both kids are neck-high in charismatic Mormon doings (likewise, whites only) out in Spirit Lake, where for all I know they practice cannibalism. They never send a Christmas card, though they plan to be in the "Where's mine?" line when the grandparents shuffle off. When I first met Sally, she was still making piteous efforts to include them in her new life in New Jersey—all of which they rebuffed like cruel suitors—until she was compelled to close the door on both of them, which thrilled me. Too much unredeemed loss can be fatal, which is one of the early glittering tenets of the Permanent Period, one I firmly believe in and was fast to tell her about. At some point—and its arrival may not be obvious, so you have to be on the lookout for it—you have to let life please you if it will, and consign the past to its midden (easier said than done, of course, as we all know).

When she drove her renter from O'Hare up to Lake Forest and up to the winding-drive, many-winged, moss-and-ivy–fronted fieldstone Caldwell manse that sits on a bluff of the lake, she entered the long, drafty, monarchical drawing room with her folding suitcase—she was considered a beloved family member and didn't need to knock. And there seated on the rolled and pleated, overstuffed Victorian leather settee, looking for all the world like the Caldwells' gardener asked in to review next season's perennial-planning strategies ("Did we do the jonquils right? Is there reason to keep the wisteria, since it's really not their climate?"), there was a man she'd never seen before but queerly felt she knew (it was the beady, piggy eyes). There was "The Wall." Wally Caldwell. Her husband. Back from oblivion, at home in Lake Forest.

In time, Sally told me all the useless details, which, once the trap was sprung, took on a routinized predictability—though not to her. One detail that stays in my mind to this steely-sky morning all these months later is Sally standing, suitcase in hand, in the long, lofty drawing room of her in-laws' castle, the must of age and plunder tangy in the motionless air, the leaded-window light shadowy but barred, the house silent behind her, the door just drifting closed by an unseen hand, the old fatigue of loss and heavy familiarity permeating her bones again, and then seeing this lumpy, bearded, balding gardener type, and beaming out a big welcome smile at him and saying, "Hi. I'm Sally." To which he—this not-at-all, no-way-in-hell Wally, with a frown of inner accusing and insecurity, and in a vaguely Scottish accent—says, "I'm Wally. Remember me? I'm not entirely dead."

It is proof that I love Sally that when I replay this moment in my brain, as I have many times, I always wince, so close do I feel to her—what? Shock? Shocked by her shock. Celestially reluctant to have happen next what happened next. The only thing worse would've been if *I*'d been there, although a murderous thrashing could've turned the tables in my favor, instead of how they did turn.

I don't know what went on that weekend. Pensive, hands-behind-the-back walks along the palliative Lake Michigan beach. Angry recrimination sessions out of earshot of the old folks (her kids, blessedly, didn't show). Moaning-crying jags, shouting, nights spent sweating, heart-battering, fists balled in fury, frustration, denial and crass inability to take all in, to believe, to stare truth in the beezer. (Think how *you'd* feel!) And no doubt then the rueful, poisoned thoughts of *why*? And why *now*? Why not just last on to the end on Mull? (The craggy, wind-swept isle off Scotland's coast where Wally'd moled away for decades.) Mull life over till nothing's left of it, soldier the remaining yards alone instead of fucking everything up for everybody—again. TV's much better at these kinds of stories, since the imponderableness of it all conveniently is swept away when the commercials for drain openers, stool softeners and talking potato chips pop on, and all's electronically "forgotten," during which time the aggrieved principals can make adjustments to life's weird wreckage, get ready to come back and sort things out for the better, so that after many tears are shed, fists clenched, hearts broken but declared mendable, everyone's again declared "All set," as they say in New Jersey. All set? Ha! I say. Ha-ha, ha! Ha, ha-ha-ha! All set, my ass.

Sally flew home on Monday, having said nothing of johnny-jump-up Wally during our weekend phone calls. I drove to Newark to get her, and on the ride back could tell she was plainly altered—by something—but said nothing. It is a well-learned lesson of second marriages never to insist on what you absolutely don't have to insist on, since your feelings are probably about nothing but yourself and your own pitiable needs and are not appropriately sympathetic to the needs of the insistee in question. Second marriages, especially good ones like ours seemed, could fill three door-stop-size reference books with black-letter do's and don'ts. And you'd have to be studious if you hoped to get past Volume One.

I, of course, assumed Sally's strange state had to do with her kids, the little devil Christians out in Idaho—that one of them was in detox, or jail, or was a fugitive or self-medicating or in the nut house, or the other was planning a lawsuit to attach my assets now that therapy had unearthed some pretty horrendous buried episodes of abuse in which I was somehow involved and that explained everything about why his life had gone to shit-in-a-bucket, but not before some hefty blame could be spread around. My fear, of course, is every second husband's fear: that somebody from out of the blue, somebody you won't like and who has no sense of anything but his or her own entitlement to suffering—in other words, children—will move in and ruin your life. Sally and I had agreed this would not be our fate, that her two and my two needed to think about life being "based" else-where. Our life was ours and only ours. Their room was the guest room. Of course all that's changed now.

When we reached #7 Poincinet Road, the sky was already resolving upon sunset. The western heavens were their brightest-possible faultless blue. Pre-Memorial Day beach enthusiasts were packing up books and blankets and transistors and sun reflectors, and heading off for a cocktail or a shrimp plate at the Surfcaster or a snuggle at the Conquistador Suites as the air cooled and softened ahead of night's fall.

I put on my favorite Ben Webster, made a pair of Salty Dogs, thought about a drive later on up to Ortley for a grilled bluefish at Neptune's Daily Catch Bistro and conceivably a snuggle of our own to the accompaniment of nature's sift and sigh and the muttered voices of the striper fishermen who haunt our beach after the tide's turn.

And then she simply told me, just as I was walking into the living room, ready for a full debriefing.

Something there is in humans that wants to make sure you're doing something busying at the exact instant of hearing unwel-come news—as though, if your hands are full, you'll just rumble right on through the whole thing, unfazed. "Wally? Alive? Really? Here, try a sip of this, see if I put in too much Donald Duck. Happy to add more Gilbey's. Well, ole Wall—whadda ya know? How'd The Wall seem? Don't you just love how Ben gets that breathy tremolo into 'Georgia on My Mind.' Hoagy'd love it. Give Wally my best. How was it to be dead?"

I should say straight out: Never tell anyone you know how

she or he feels unless you happen to be, just at that second, stabbing yourself with the very same knife in the very same place in the very same heart she or he is stabbing. Because if you're not, then you don't know how anybody feels. I can barely tell you how *I* felt when Sally said, "Frank, when I got to Lake Forest, Wally was there." (Use of my name, "Frank," as always, a harbinger of things unpopular. I should change my name to Al.)

I know for a fact that I said nothing when I heard these words. I managed to put my Salty Dog down on the glass coffee-table top and lower myself onto the brown suede couch beside her, to put both my hands on top of my knees and gaze out at the darkening Atlantic, where the ghostly figures of the high-booted fishermen faced the surf and, far out to sea, the sky still showed a brilliant reflected sliver of azure. Sally sat as I did and may have felt as I did—*surprised*.

Sometimes simple words are the best, and better than violent images of the world cracking open; or about how much everything's like a sitcom and what a pity William Bendix isn't still around to play Wally—or me; or better than the ethical-culture response, that catastrophe's "a good thing for everybody," since it dramatizes life's great mystery and reveals how much all is artifice—connected boxes, world-within-worlds—the trap Clarissa's trying to break free of. How we express our response to things is just made-up stuff anyway—unless we tip over dead— and is meant to make the listener think he's getting his money's worth, while feeling relief that none of this shit is happening to him personally. *Surprised* is good enough. When I heard Wally Caldwell, age fifty-five, missing for thirty years, during which time many things had happened and substantial adjustments were made about the nature of existence on earth—when I heard Wally was alive in Lake Forest and had spent the weekend doing God knows what with my wife, I was surprised.

Sally knew I might be surprised (and again, I *was* surprised), and she wanted to make this news *not* cause the world to crack open, for me to go hysterical, etc. She'd had three days with Wally already. She had gotten over the shock of an older, bearded, avuncular and strange Wally hiding out in his parents' house like some scary older brother with a terrible wound, whom you only see fleetingly behind shadowy chintz curtains in an upstairs dormer window, but who may be heard at night to moan. Her attitude was—and I liked it, since it was typical of her get-up-and-fix-things attitude—that while, yes, Wally's reappearance *had* caused some tricky issues to pop up, needing to be resolved, and that while she understood how "this whole business" maybe put me in an awkward position (vis-à-vis, say, the past, the present and the future), this was still a "human situation," that no one was a culprit (of course not), no one had bad will (except me) and we would all address this as a threesome, so that as little damage as possible would be done to as few a number of innocent souls and lives (I might've known who the left-unprotected innocent soul would turn out to be, but I didn't).

Wally's story, she told me, sitting on the suede couch that faced out to the darkened springtime Atlantic, as our Salty Dogs turned watery and dark descended, was "one of those stories" fashioned by war and trauma, sadness, fear and resentment, and by the chaotic urge to escape all the other causes, aided by (what else?) "some kind of schizoid detachment" that induced amnesia, so that for years Wally wouldn't remember big portions of his prior life, although certain portions were crystal clear.

Wally, it seems, couldn't put everything all together, though he admitted he hadn't just gone out to pick up the *Trib* thirty years ago, bumped his head getting into his Beetle and suffered a curtain to close. It had to have been—this, he no doubt admitted on one of their cozy Lake Michigan beach tête-à-têtes—that "something unconscious was working on him," some failure to face the world he confronted as a Viet vet with a (minor) head wound, and a family, and a future as a horticulturist looming, the whole undifferentiated world just flooding in on him like a dam bursting, with cows and trees and cars and church steeples swirling away in the gully-wash, and him in with it. (There are good strategies for coping with this, of course, but you have to want to.)

Cutting (blessedly) to the chase, Wally's trauma, fear, resentment and elective amnesia had carried him as far away from the Chicago suburbs, from wife and two kids, as Glasgow, in Scotland, where for a time he became "caught up" in "the subculture" that lived communally, practiced good feeling for everything, experimented with cannabis and other mind-rousing drugs, fucked like bunny rabbits, made jewelry by hand and sold it on damp streets, practiced subsistence farming techniques, made their own clothes and set their communal sights on spiritual-but-not-mainstream-religious revelation. In other words, the Manson Family, led by Ozzie and Harriet.

Eventually, Wally said, the "petrol" had run out of the communal subculture, and with a satellite woman—a professor of English, naturally—he had migrated up to the wilds of Scotland, first to the Isle of Skye, then to Harris, then to Muck, and finally to Mull, where he found employment in the Scottish Blackface industry (sheep) and finally—more to his talents and likings—as a gardener on the laird's estate and, as time went on, as head gardener and arborist (the laird was wild for planting spruce trees), and eventually as the estate manager for the entire shitaree. A complete existence was there, Wally said, a long way from Lake Forest "and that whole life" (again meaning wife and kids), from the Cubs, the Wrigley Building, the Sears Tower, the river dyed green—*again*, the whole deluging, undifferentiated crash-in of modern existence American-style, whose sudsy, brown tree-trunk-littered surface most of us somehow manage to keep our heads above so we can see our duty and do it. I'm not impartial in these matters. Why should I be?

In due time, the lady friend—"a completely good and decent woman"—got tired of life on Mull as a crofter's companion and returned to her job and husband—likewise a professor, in Ohio. A couple of local lassies moved in and, in time, out again. Wally got used to living semi-officially in the manager's stone cottage, scrubbing the loo, restocking the fridge with haggis, smoking fish, burning peat, reading *The Herald*, listening to Radio 4, snapping on the telly, sipping his cuppa, keeping his Wellies dry and his Barbour waxed during the long Mull winters. This was the wee life, the one he was suited for and entitled to and where he expected his days to end amongst the cold stones and rills and crags and moors and cairns and gorse and wind-blown cedars of his own dull nature—here in his half-chosen, half-fated, half-fucked-up-and-escaped-to destination resort from life gone kaflooey.

Enter then the Internet—in the form of the old laird's young son, Morgil, who'd taken the reins of the property (having been to college at Florida State) and who'd begun to suspect that this lumpy American in the manager's accommodation was probably other than he'd declared himself, was possibly an old draft dodger or a fugitive from some abysmal crime in his own country, from which he'd exiled himself, some guy who dressed up in clown suits and ate little boys for lunch. The standard idea of America, viewed from abroad.

What young Morgil found when he checked—and who'd be shocked?—was a "Wally Caldwell" Web site the old Lake Forest parents had erected as a long last hope, or whatever inspires Web sites (I don't maintain one at Realty-Wise, though Mike does, www.RealtyTibet.com, which is how Tommy Benivalle found him). No outstanding warrants, Interpol alerts or Scotland Yard red flags were attached to the site, only several sequentially aged photos of Wally (one actually in a Barbour) that looked exactly like the Wally out planting spruce sprigs and pruning other ones like a character out of D. H. Lawrence. "Please contact the Caldwell Family if you know this man, or see him, or hear of him. Amnesia may be involved. He's not dangerous. His family misses him greatly and we are now in our eighties. Not much time is left."

Young Morgil didn't feel it would be right to send a blind message out of the blue—that a cove of Wally Caldwell's general description was working right on old Cullonden, on the Isle of

Mull, under the name of Wally Caldwell. It'd be better, he gauged, to tell Wally, even at the risk of its being sensitive news that might wake him up from a long dream of life and dash him into a world he had no tolerance for, send him screaming and gibbering off onto the heath, his frail vessel cracked, so that all his ancient parents would have to show for their Web site was a pale, broken, silent man in green pajamas, who seemed sometimes to smile and recognize you but mostly just sat and stared at Lake Michigan.

Morgil tacked a note to Wally's door the next morning—a color printout of the Caldwell home page—the computerized middle-aged face side-by-side with a yearbook photo from Illinois State ("Call me Mr. Wall"). No mention was made of Sally, Shelby and Chloë, or that he'd been declared *expired*. The only words it contained were his parents' tender entreaties: "Come home, Wally, wherever you are, *if* you are. We're not mad at you. We're still here in Lake Forest, Mom and Dad. We can't last forever."

And so he did. Wally crossed the sea to home and the welcome arms of his mom and dad. A changed bloke, but nonetheless their moody, slow-thinking son, all things suddenly glittering and promise-laden, whereas before all had been a closed door, a blank wall, an empty night where no one calls your name. I know plenty about this.

Which was the strange tableau my unsuspecting wife walked in upon, carrying her suitcase and lost memories, expecting only a "drinks evening" with the in-laws, followed by some whitefish au gratin, then early to bed between cold, stiff sheets and the next day making nice with elderly strangers at the Wik-O-Mek, trying patiently, pleasantly to re-explain to them exactly who she was (a former daughter-in-law?). But instead, she found Wally, bearded, older, fattish, balded, gray-toothed, though still innocent and vague the way she'd once liked, only dressed like a Scottish gamekeeper with an idiotic accent.

She was surprised. We were both surprised.

When she'd told me this whole preposterous story, it'd long gone dark in the house. Chill had filtered indoors off the surface of the moonlit sea. She sat perfectly still, peering out at the high tide, the fishermen vanished to home, a red phosphorescence seeding the water's swell. I left and came back with a sweater I'd bought years before in France, when I'd been in love in a haywire way (my then-beloved is now a thoracic surgeon at Brigham and Women's), though my love story, then, had an all-round satisfactory end that left life open for new investigations and not obstructed by problematical, profoundly worrisome insolubles.

Sally put on the sweater Catherine Flaherty had settled into on cold French spring nights facing the Channel. She hugged her arms the way Catherine had, burying her cold chin into the crusted, musty-smelling nap, giving herself time to think a clear thought, since Wally was in Lake Forest and I was here. All the safety netting of *our* little life was still up to catch her, and she could—as it seemed to me she should—just forget the whole commotion, writing it all off as a dream that would go away if you let it. My heart went out to her, I'll admit. But I also understood there could be no tweezing and tracing of slender filaments back through the knot to make loose ends become continuous and smooth. They weren't loose ends. These were what I called *my life*. And even though they were short, blunt and more frayed than what I'd rather, they were still what I had. If I'd known what awaited me, I might've phoned up some boys in Bergen County who owed me a favor and had 'em fly out and perform a penitential errand on Wally's noggin.

There are many different kinds of people on the planet— people who never let you forget a mistake, people who're happy to. People who almost drown as children and never swim again, and people who jump right back in and paddle off like ducks. There are people who marry the same woman over and over, while others have no scheme in their amours (I'm this man. It's not so bad). And there are definitely people who, when faced with misfeasance of a large and historical nature, even one that needn't cloud the present and forbid the future, just can't rest until the misfeasance is put right, redressed, battered to dust with study and attention so they can feel just fine about things and go forward with a clear heart—whatever that might be. (The opposite of this is what the Permanent Period teaches us: If you can't truly forget something, you can at least ignore it and try to make your dinner plans on time.)

In Sally's behalf, she was dazed. She'd gone to Illinois and seen a ghost. Everything in life suddenly felt like a cold higgle-piggle. It's the kind of shock that makes you realize that life only happens to you and to you alone, and that any concept of togeth-erness, intimacy, union, abiding this and abiding that is a hoot and a holler into darkness. My idea, of course, would've been to wait a week or two, go about my business selling houses, book a Carnival Cruise vacation to St. Kitts, then in a while nose back in to see how the land lay and the citizenry had re-deployed. My guess was that with time to reflect, Wally would've disappeared quietly back to Mull, to his spruce and cairns and anonymity. We could exchange Christmas cards and get on with life to its foreshortened ending. After all, how likely are any of us ever to change—given that we're all in control of most things?

Again, of course, I was wrong. Wrong, wrongety, wrong, wrong, wrong.

At the conclusion of Sally's long recitation of the lost-Wally saga, a chronicle I wasn't that riveted by, since I didn't think it could foretell any good for me (I was right), she announced she needed to take a nap. Events had pretty well wrung her out. She knew I was not exactly a grinning cheerleader to these matters, that I was possibly as "mixed-up" as she was (not true), and she needed just to lie in the dark alone for a while and let things— her word—"settle." She smiled at me, went around the room turning on lamps, suffusing the dark space she was then abandoning me to with a bronze funeral-parlor light. She came around to me where I'd stood up in front of the couch, and kissed me on my cheek (oh Lord) in a pall-bearerish, buck-up-bud sort of way, then ceremoniously mounted the stairs, not to *our room*, not to the marriage bower, the conjugal refuge of sweet intimacies and blissful nod, but to the *guest room*!—where my daughter now sleeps and also "sleeps" with new Mr. Right Who Drives A Fucking Healey.

I might've gone crazy right then. I should've let her mount the stairs (I heard the guest room floorboards squeezing), waited for her to get her shoes shucked and herself plopped wearily onto the cold counterpane, then roared upstairs, proclaiming and defaming, vilifying and contumelating, snatching knobs off doors, kicking table legs to splinters, cracking mirrors with my voice— laying down the law as I saw it and as it should be and as it served and protected. Let everybody on Poincinet Road and up the seaboard and all the ships at sea know that I'd sniffed out what was being served and wasn't having it and neither was anybody else inside my walls. One party left alone to his heartless devices, in his own heartless living room, while another heartless party skulks away to dreamland to revise fate and providence, ought to produce some ornate effects. No fucking way, José. This shit doesn't wash. My way or the highway. Irish (or Scots) need not apply. Members only. Don't even think of parking here.

But I didn't. And why I didn't was: I felt secure. Even though I could feel something approaching, like those elephants who feel the stealthy footfalls of those Pygmy spear toters far across savannas and flooded rivers. I felt at liberty to take an interest, to put on the white labcoat of objective investigator, be Sally's partner with a magnifying glass, curious to find out what these old bones, relics and potsherds of lost love had to tell. These are the very moments, of course, when large decisions get decided. Great literature routinely skips them in favor of seismic shifts, hysterical laughter and worlds cracking open, and in that way does us all a grave disservice.

What I did while Sally slept in the guest room was make myself a fresh Salty Dog, open a can of cocktail peanuts and eat half of them, since bluefish at Neptune's Daily Catch had become a dead letter. I switched off the lights, sat a while in the leather director's chair, hunkered forward over my knees in the chilly living room and watched phosphorescent water lap the moonlit alabaster beach till way past high tide. Then I went upstairs to my home office and read the *Asbury Press*—stories about Elián González being pre-enrolled at Yale, a plan to make postmodern sculpture out of Y_2K preventative gear and place it on the statehouse lawn in Trenton, a CIA warning about a planned attack on our shores by Iran, and a lawsuit over a Circuit City in Bradley Beach being turned down by the local planning board—with the headline reading HOW'S THE DOWNTICK AFFECTING HOLIDAY SHOPPING?

I rechecked my rental inventory (Memorial Day was three weeks away). I took note that the NJ Real Estate *Cold Call* reported four million of our citizens were working, while only 4.1 percent of our population was not—the longest economic boom in our history (now giving hissing sounds around the edges). Finally, I went back down, turned on the TV, watched the Nets lose to the Pistons and went to sleep on the couch in my clothes.

This isn't to suggest that Wally's re-emergence hadn't caught my notice and didn't burn my ass and cause me to think that discomforting, messy, troublesome readjustments wouldn't need to take place, and soon. Readjustments requiring Wally being declared un-dead, requiring divorcing, estate re-planning and updated survivorship provisos, all while recriminations cut the air like steak knives, and all lasting a long time and raking everybody's patience, politeness and complex sense of themselves over the hot coals like spare ribs. That was going to happen. I may also have felt vulnerable to the accusation of marital johnny-come-lately-ism. Though I'd have never met Sally Caldwell, never married her (I might still have romanced her), had it not been that Wally was gone—we all thought—for good.

What I, in fact, felt was: on my guard—but safe. The way you'd feel if crime statistics spiked in your neighborhood but you'd just rescued a two-hundred-pound Rottweiler from the shelter, who saw you as his only friend, whereas the wide world was his enemy.

Sally's and my marriage seemed as contingency-proof as we could construct it, using the human materials we're all equipped with. The other thing about second marriages—unlike first ones, which require only hot impulse and drag-strip hormones—is that they need good reasons to exist, reasons you're smart to pore over and get straight well beforehand. Sally and I both conducted independent self-inquiries back when I was still in Haddam, and each made a clear decision that marriage—to each other— promised more than anything else we could think of that would probably make us both happy, and that neither of us harbored a single misgiving that wasn't appropriate to life anyway (illnesses—we'd share; death—we'd expect; depression—we'd treat), and that any more time spent in deciding was time we could spend having the time of our lives. Which as far as I'm concerned—and in fact I know that Sally felt the same—we did.

Which is to say we practiced the sweet legerdemain of adulthood shared. We formally renounced our unmarried personalities. We generalized the past in behalf of a sleek second-act mentality that stressed the leading edge of life to be all life was. We acknowledged that strong feelings were superior to original happiness, and promised never to ask the other if she or he really, really, really loved him or her, in the faith that affinity was love, and we had affinity. We stressed nuance and advocated that however we seemed was how we were. We declared we were good in bed, and that lack of intimacy was usually self-imposed. We kept our kids at a wary but (at least in my case) positive distance. We de-emphasized becoming in behalf of being. We permanently renounced melancholy and nostalgia. We performed intentionally pointless acts like flying to Moline or Flint and back the same day because we were "archaeologists." We ate Thanksgiving and Xmas dinners at named rest stops on the Turn-pike. We considered buying a pet refuge in Nyack, a B&B in New Hampshire.

In other words, we put in practice what the great novelist said about marriage (though he never quite had the genome for it himself). "If I should ever marry," he wrote, "I should pretend to think just a little better of life than I do." In Sally's case and mine, we thought a *lot* better of life than we ever imagined we could. In the simplest terms, we really, really loved each other and didn't do a lot of looking right or left—which, of course, is the first principle of the Permanent Period.

Because today is November 22nd and not last May, and I have cancer and Sally is this morning far away on the Isle of Mull, I am able to telescope events to make our decade-long happy union seem all a matter of clammy reasons and practical-ities, as though a life lived with another was just a matter of twin isolation booths in an old fifties quiz show; and also to make everything that happened seem inevitable and to have come about because Sally was unhappy with me and with us. But not one ounce of that would be true, as gloomy as events became, and as given as I am to self-pity and to doubting I was *ever* more than semi-adequate in bed, and that by selling houses I never lived up to my potential (I might've been a lawyer).

No, no, no, no and no again.

We *were* happy. There was enough complex warp and woof in life to make a sweater as big as the fucking ocean. We lived. Together.

"But she couldn't have been *so* happy if she left, could she?" said the little pointy-nose, squirrel-tooth, bubble-coifed grief counselor I sadly visited up in Long Branch just because I happened to drive by and saw her shingle one early June afternoon. She was used to advising the tearful, bewildered, abandoned wives of Fort Dix combat noncoms who'd married Thai bar girls and never come home. She wanted to offer easy solutions that led to feelings of self-affirmation and quick divorces. Sugar. Dr. Sugar. She was divorced herself.

But that's not true, I told her. People don't always leave because they're unhappy, like they do in shitty romance novels written by lonely New England housewives or in supermarket tabloids or on TV. You could say it's my fatal flaw to believe this, and to believe that Wally's return to life, and Sally leaving with him, wasn't the craziest, worst goddamn thing in the fucking world and didn't spell the end of love forever. Yet that's what I believed and still do. Sally could decide *later* that she'd been unhappy. But since she left, the two polite postcards I've received have made no mention of divorce or of not loving me, and that's what I'm choosing to understand.

When Sally came down later that night and found me asleep on the couch beside the can of Planters with the TV playing *The Third Man* (the scene where Joseph Cotten gets bitten by the parrot), she wasn't unhappy with me—though she certainly wasn't happy. I understood she'd just come unexpectedly face-to-face with *big contingency*—the thing we'd schemed against and almost beaten, and probably the only contingency that could've risen to eye level and stared us down: the re-enlivening of Wally. And she didn't know what to do about it—though I did.

All marriages—all everythings—tote around contingencies whether we acknowledge them or don't. In all things good and giddy, there's always one measly eventuality no one's thought about, or hasn't thought about in so long it almost doesn't exist. Only it does. Which is the one potentially fatal chink in the body armor of intimacy, to the unconditional this 'n that, to the sacred vows, the pledging of troths, to the forever *anythings*. And that is: There's a back door *somewhere* to every deal, and there a draft can enter. All promises to be in love and "true to you forever" are premised on the iron contingency (unlikely or otherwise) that says, Unless, of course, I fall in love "forever" with someone else. This is true even if we don't like it, which means it isn't cynical to think, but also means that someone else—someone we love and who we'd rather have *not* know it—is as likely to know it as we are. Which acknowledgment may finally be as close to absolute intimacy as any of us can stand. Anything closer to the absolute than this is either death or as good as death. And death's where I draw the line. Realtors, of course, know all this better than anyone, since there's a silent Wally Caldwell in every deal, right down to the act of sale (which is like death) and sometimes even beyond it. In every agreement to buy or sell, there's also the proviso, acknowledged or not, that says "unless, of course, I don't want to anymore," or "that is, unless I change my mind," or "assuming my yoga instructor doesn't advise against it." Again, the hallowed concept of character was invented to seal off these contingencies. But in this wan Millennial election year, are we really going to say that this concept is worth a nickel or a nacho? Or, for that matter, ever was?

Sally stood at the darkened thermal glass window that gave upon the lightless Atlantic. She'd slept in her clothes, too, and was barefoot and had a green L.L. Bean blanket around her shoulders in addition to the French sweater. I'd opened the door to the deck, and inside was fifty degrees. She'd turned off *The Third Man*. I came awake studying her inky back without realizing it was her inky back, or that it was even her—wondering if I was hallucinating or was it an optical trick of waking in darkness, or had a stranger or a ghost (I actually thought of my son Ralph) entered my house for shelter and hadn't noticed me snoozing.

I realized it was Sally only when I thought of Wally and of the despondency his renewed life might promise me.

"Do you feel a little better?" I wanted to let her know I was here still among the living and we'd been having a conversation earlier that I considered to be still going on.

"No." Hers was a mournful, husky, elderly-seeming voice. She pinched her Bean's blanket around her shoulders and coughed. "I feel terrible. But I feel exhilarated, too. My stomach's got butterflies and knots at the same time. Isn't that peculiar?"

"No, I wouldn't say that was necessarily so peculiar." I was trying my white investigator's labcoat on for size.

"A part of me wants to feel like my life's a total ruin and a fuck-up, that there's a right way to do things and I've made a disaster out of it. That's how it feels." She wasn't facing me. I didn't really feel like I was talking to *her*. But if not to her, then to who?

"That's not true," I said. I could understand, of course, why she might feel that way. "You didn't do anything wrong. You just flew to Chicago."

"There's no sense to spool everything back to sources, but I might've been a better wife to Wally."

"You're a good wife. You're a good wife to *me*." And then I didn't say this, but thought it: And fuck Wally. He's an asshole. I'll gladly have him big-K killed and his body Hoffa'd out for birdseed. "What do you feel exhilarated about?" I said instead. Mr. Empathy.

"I'm not sure." She flashed a look around, her blond hair catching light from somewhere, her face appearing tired and marked with shadowy lines from too-sound sleep and the fatigue of travel.

"Well," I said, "exhilaration doesn't hurt anything. Maybe you were glad to see him. You always wondered where he went." I put a single cocktail peanut into my dry mouth and crunched it down. She turned back to the cold window, which was probably making her cold. "What's he going to do now," I said, "have himself re-incarnated, or whatever you do?"

"It's pretty simple."

"I'll keep that in mind. What about the being-married-to-you part? Does he get to do that again? Or do I get you as salvage?"

"You get me as salvage." She turned and walked slowly toward me where I sat staring up at her, slightly dazzled, as if she *was* the ghost I'd mistook her for. Her little limp was pronounced because she was beat. She sat on the couch and leaned into me so I could smell the sweated, unwashed dankness of her hair. She put her hand limply on my knee and sighed as if she'd been holding her breath and didn't realize it till now. Her coarse blanket prickled through my shirt. "He'd like to meet you," she said. "Or maybe I want him to meet you."

"Absolutely," I said, and could identify a privileged sarcasm. "We'll invite some people over. Maybe I'll interest him in a summer rental."

"That's not really necessary, is it?"

"Yes. I'm in command of my necessaries. You be in command of yours."

"Don't be bad to me about this. It flabbergasts me as much as it does you."

"That isn't true. I'm not exhilarated. Why are *you* exhilarated? I answered that *for* you, but I don't like my answer."

"*Mmmmmm.* I think it's just so strange, and so familiar. I'm not mad at him anymore. I was for years. I was when I first saw him. It was like meeting the President or some famous person. I know him so well and then there he is and of course I don't know him. There was something exciting about that." She looked at me, put her hands atop each other on my cold knee and smiled a sweet, tired, imploring, mercy-hoping smile. It would've been wonderful if we hadn't been talking about her ex-dead husband and the disaster he was casting our way, but instead about how good something was, how welcome, how much we missed something we both loved and now here it was.

"I don't feel that way," I said. I was on solid ground not feeling what she felt. It occurred to me that how she felt toward Wally was a version of being married to him, which was a version of the truth I mentioned before and couldn't argue with. But I didn't have to like it.

"You're right," she said patiently.

And then we didn't speak for a little while, just sat breathing in the cold air, each of us fancifully, forcefully seeking a context into which our separate views—of Wally, and disaster—could join forces and fashion an acceptable and unified response. I was further from the middle of events and had some perspective, so that the heavier burden fell on me. I'd already started suiting up in the raiments of patient understander. Oh woe. Oh why?

"Something has to happen," Sally said with unwanted certainty. "Something had to happen when Wally left. Something has to happen now that he's back. *Nothing* can't happen. That's my feeling."

"Who says?"

"Me," she said sadly. "I do."

"*What* has to happen?"

"I have to spend some time with him." Sally spoke reluctantly. "You'd want to do the same thing, Frank." She wrinkled her chin and slightly puffed her compressed lips. She often took on this look when she was sitting at her desk composing a letter.

"No, I wouldn't. I'd buy him a first-class ticket to anyplace he wanted to go in Micronesia and never think about him again. Where're you planning to spend time with him? The Catskills? The Lower Atlas? Am I supposed to be there, too, so I can get closer to *my* needs? I'm close enough to them now. I'm sitting beside you. I'm married to you."

"You *are* married to me." She actually gasped then and sobbed, then gasped again and squeezed my hand harder than anybody'd ever squeezed it, and shook her head from side to side, so tears dashed onto my cheek. It was as if we were both crying. Though why I would've been crying, I don't know, since I should've been howling again, shouting, waving my bloody fists in the air as the earth split open. Inasmuch as, with her certainty dawning like a new alien sun, split it did, where it stays split to this day.

I'll make the rest short, though it's not sweet.

I buttoned the buttons on my moral investigator's labcoat and got busy with the program. Sally said she'd be willing to invite Wally down to Sea-Clift—either to a rental she would arrange for him (using who as agent?), or to our house, where he could put up in one of the two guest rooms for the short time he'd be here. The oddest things can be made to seem plausible by insisting they are. Remember Huxley on Einstein. Remember the Trojan Horse. Or else, Sally said, she and he could "go away somewhere" (the Rif, the Pampas, the Silk Road to Cathay). They wouldn't be "together," of course, more like brother and sister having a *wander*, during which crucial period they'd perform what few in their situation (how many are in that situation?) could hope to perform: a putting to rest, an airing, a re-examination of old love allowed to wither and die, saying the unsayable, feeling the unpermitted, reconciling paths not taken and those taken. Cleanse and heal, come back stronger. Come back to me. Yes, there might be some crying, some shouting, some laughter, some hugging, some crisp slappings across the face. But it would be "within a context," and in "real time," or some such nonsense, and all those decades would be drained of their sour water, rolled up and put away like a late-autumn garden hose, never to leave the garage again. In other words, it *was* a "good thing" (if not for everybody)—life's mystery dramatized, all is artifice, connected boxes, etc., etc., etc.

Interesting. I thought it was all pretty interesting. A true experiment in knowing another person—me knowing her, *not* her knowing Wally, who I didn't give a shit about. A revealing frame to put on Sally's life and into which I could see, since this was between Sally and me—which I still think is true. Can you always tell a snake from a garden hose?

The Silk Road strategy didn't appeal to me, for obvious reasons. I suggested (these things *do* happen) that we invite The

Wall down for a week (or less). He could bivouac upstairs, set out all his toilet articles in the guest's bath. We could meet the way I used to meet Ann's previous, now dead, architect husband, Charley O'Dell—with stiffened civility, frozen-smile, hands-in-pockets mildness that only now and then sprang into psychotic dislike, with biting words that wounded and the threat of physical violence.

I could do better. I had nothing to fear from an *ex*-dead man. I'd tin his ears about the real estate business, let him experience Mike Mahoney, talk over the election, the Cubs, the polar ice cap, the Middle East. Though mostly I'd just stay the hell away from him, fish the Hendrickson hatch at the Red Man Club, spend a day with Clarissa and Cookie in Gotham, test-drive new Lexuses, sell a house or two—whatever it took, while the two of them did what they needed to do to get that moldy old hose put away on the garage nail of the past tense.

On the twenty-ninth of May, Wally "the Weasel," as he was known in military school, my wife's quasi-husband, father of her two maniac children, Viet vet, combat casualty, free-lance amnesiac, cut-and-run artist *par excellence*, heir to a sizable North Shore fortune, meek arborist, unmourned former dead man and big-time agent of misrule—my enemy—*this* Wally Caldwell entered my peaceful house on the Jersey Shore to work his particular dark magic on us all.

Clarissa and Cookie came down for the arrival to give moral support. Clarissa, who was still wearing a tiny diamond nostril stud (since jettisoned), felt it was an "interesting" experiment in the extended-family concept, but basically nonsensical, that something was "wrong" with Sally and that I needed to keep my "boundaries" clear and that they (being Harvard lesbians) knew all about boundaries—or something to that effect.

Sally became convulsively nervous, oversensitive and irritable as the hour of Wally's arrival neared (I affected calm to show I didn't care). She snapped at Clarissa, snapped at me, had to be talked to by Cookie. She smoked several cigarettes (the first time in twenty years), drank a double martini at ten o'clock in the morning, changed her clothes three times, then stood out on the deck, sporting stiff white sailcloth trousers, new French espadrilles, a blue-and-white middy blouse and extremely dark sunglasses. All was a calculated livery betokening casual, welcoming resolution and sunny invulnerability, depicting a life so happy, invested, entitled, entrenched, comprehended, spiritual and history-laden that Wally would take a quick peek at the whole polished array—house, beach, lesbian kids, damnable husband, unreachable lemony ex-wife, then hop back in his cab and start the long journey back to Mull.

I will concede that the real Wally, the portly, thin-lipped, timidly smiling, gray-toothed, small-eyed, suitcase-carrying, thick-fingered bullock who struggled out of the Newark Yellow Cab, didn't seem a vast challenge to my or anyone's sense of permanence. I had perfect no-recollection of him from forty years ago and felt strangely, warmly (wrongly) welcoming toward him, the way you'd feel about a big, soft-hearted PFC in a fifties war movie, who you know is going to be picked off by a Kraut sniper in the first thirty minutes. Wally had on his green worn-smooth corduroys—though it was already summery and he was sweltering—a faded, earthy-smelling purple cardy over a green-and-ginger rugger shirt, under which his hod-carrier belly tussled for freedom. He wore heavy gray woolen socks, no hat and the previously mentioned smelly but not mud-spackled Barbour from his days nerdling about the gorse and rank topsoil of his adopted island paradise.

He brought with him a bottle of twenty-year-old Glen Matoon and a box of Cohiba *Robustos*—for me. I still have the cigars at the office and occasionally consider smoking one as a joke, though it'd probably explode. He also brought—for Sally—a strange assortment of Scottish cooking herbs he'd obviously gotten for his parents at the Glasgow airport plus a tin of shortcakes for "the house." He was at least six feet two, newly beardless and nearly bald, weighed a fair seventeen stone and spoke English in a halting, swallowing, slightly high-pitched semi-brogue with a vocabulary straight out of the seventies U.S. He said Chicago Land, as in "We left Chicago Land at the crack of dawn." And he said "super," as in "We had some super tickets to Wrigley." And he said "z's," as in "I copped some righteous z's on the plane." And he said "GB," as in "I banged down a GB" (a gut bomb) "before we left Chicago Land, and it tasted super."

He was, this once-dead Wally, not the strangest concoction of *Homo sapiens* genetic material ever presented to me (Mike Mahoney has retired that jersey number), but he was certainly the most complexly pathetic and ill-starred—a strangely wide-eyed, positive-outlook type, ill at ease and conspicuous in his lumpy flesh, but also strangely serene and on occasion pompous and ribald, like the down-state SAE he was back when life was simpler. How he made it in Mull is a mystery.

Needless to say, I loathed him (warm feelings aside), couldn't comprehend how anybody who could love me could ever have loved Wally, and wanted him out of the house the second he was in it. We shook hands limply, in the manner of a cold prisoner exchange on the Potsdam bridge. I stared. He averted his small eyes, so I couldn't feel good about being insincerely nice to him and show Sally this was worthy of my patience—which I know she hoped.

I spoke tersely, idiotically. "Welcome to Sea-Clift, and to our home," which I didn't mean. He said something about "whole layout's . . . super," and that he was "chuffed" to be here. Clarissa instantly took me by the crook of my elbow and led me out to the road in front of the house, where we stood without speaking for a while in the thick spring breeze that stirred the vivid shore-line vegetation toward Asbury Park and points north. Dust from the town front-loader far up the beach, its yellow lights flashing, indicated civic efforts to relocate mounds of sand that had drifted over the promenade during the winter. We were making ready for Memorial Day.

Arthur Glück's dog, Poot, part Beagle, part Spitz, that looks like a dog from ancient Egypt and scavenges everyone's house (except the Feensters'), waited in the middle of Poincinet Road, staring at Clarissa and me as though it was clear even to him that something very wrong was underway, since events had driven all the humans out to the road in the morning, where it was his turf, his time, and where he knew how things worked.

Clarissa let go of my arm and just sat down in the middle of the sandy roadway—her gesture for separating us two from Sally and Wally, who'd already by fits and starts disappeared inside the house, though the door was left open. No one would've been driving down the road. Still, her gesture was a stagy, unplanned one I appreciated, even though it made me nervous and I wished she'd get up. Cookie, wise girl, had decided on a walk up the beach. I should have gone with her.

"You're a *way* too tolerant dude," Clarissa said casually, keeping her seat in the road, leaning back on one elbow and shielding her eyes from the noon-time sun. I felt even more awkward because of where she was and what she wasn't feeling. "Which isn't to say Mr. Wally isn't pretty much a *Wind in the Willows* kind of character in need of a good ass-kicking. It's pretty zen of you. In the girl community, this wouldn't stand up." Clarissa's nose stud sparkled in the brassy light, and made me touch my nose, as though I had one in mine. She was wearing tissue-thin Italian sandals that exhibited her long tanned feet and ankles, and a pair of cream-colored Italian harem pants with a matching tank top that showed her shoulders. She was like a mirage, languorous but animated.

"I'm not zen at all." Mike's hooded-eye, scrunched face appeared in my mind like one of the Pep Boys. He knew nothing of this day's events, but definitely would've approved of what I was doing.

"Don't you feel strange? It's pretty strange to have old Wally down here for a visit." Clarissa wrinkled her nose and squinted up at me as if I was the rarest of vanishing species.

"I had a good picture in my mind of how this would all happen," I said. "But now that he's here, I can't remember it." I looked at the house, my house, felt stupid being out in my road. "I think that's very human, though, to expect something and then have the expected event supplant the expectation. That's interesting."

"Yep," Clarissa said.

What I didn't say was even odder. That while I felt officially pissed off and deeply offended, I was not feeling that this fiasco was a real fiasco, or that my life was fucked up, or that any of the important things I hoped to do before I was sixty were going to be impossible to do. In other words, I felt tumult, but I also felt calm, and that I'd probably feel different again in another thirty minutes—which is why I don't pay fullest attention to how I feel at any given moment. If I'd told this to Clarissa, she would've thought I was suffering from stress-induced aphasia, or maybe having a stroke. Maybe I was. But what I knew was that you're stuck with yourself most of the time. Best make the most of it.

Clarissa struggled onto her feet like a kid at school after recess. She dusted off the seat of her pants and gave her hair a shake. It would've been a perfect day for a flight to Flint. Maybe by cocktail hour all would be settled, Wally packed off in another yellow taxi and happy to be, life resumable back at the Salty Dog stage, where I'd departed it a few days before.

"Is Sally a second child?" We were still standing in the middle of the road, as though expecting something. I was taking pleasure in the flashing yellow light of the town's front-loader, a half mile up the beach.

"She had a brother who died."

"I'm trying to be sympathetic to her. Second children have a hard time getting what they need. I'm a second child."

"You're a third child. You had a brother who died when you were little." Clarissa has scant memory of her dead brother and no patience with trying to feel what she doesn't really feel. Me, I feel like I'm Ralph's earthly ombudsman and facilitator to the living. It is my secret self. I give (mostly) silent witness.

"That's right." She was briefly pensive then, in deference to "my loss," which was her loss but different. "If Mom came back from the dead, would you invite her over for a visit?"

"Your mother's not dead," I said irritably. "She's living in Haddam."

"Divorce is kind of like death, though, isn't it? Three moves equal a death. A divorce equals probably three-quarters of a death."

"In some ways. It never ends." And how would this day rate, I wondered. Six-sixteenths of a death? About the same for Sally. And who cared about The Wall? Morbid dimness had always complicated his life, landing him over and over in strange situations, and not knowing what to do about it.

"I'm just trying to distract you," Clarissa said. "And humor you." She rehooked her arm through mine and bumped me with her girl-athlete's shoulder. She smelled of shampoo and clean sweat. The way you'd want your daughter to smell. "Maybe you should keep a diary."

"I'll commit suicide before I keep a fucking diary. Diaries are for weaklings and old queer professors. Which I'm not."

"Okay," she said. She was never sensitive to insensitive language. We were starting to stroll up Poincinet Road, past the fronts of my neighbors' houses—all similarly handsome board-and-batten edifices with green hydrangeas ready to sprout their showy blooms. Ahead, where our newer settlement stopped and where the old mansions had been blown away, there was open, sparsely populated beach and grass and sea. I could see a tiny ant in the hazy distance. It was Cookie. Poot, the Egyptian dog, had found her and was trotting along.

"I thought life isn't supposed to be like this when you love someone and they love you," I said to Clarissa, more speculative than I felt. "That intelligence won't get you very far. That's your father's perspective."

"I knew that." She kicked road sand with her rubied toenail. Already things with her and Cookie were wearing through. I couldn't have known, but she could. "What do you think's gonna happen?"

"With Sally and Wally?" I gave myself a moment to wonder, letting sea breeze make my ears feel wiggly, my view of the beach grown purposefully wide and generous. Such views are supposedly good for the optic muscle, and the soul. Something seemed to be riding on what I said, as if I was the cause of whatever happened to us all. "I can guess," I said breezily, "but I tend to guess bad outcomes. Most horses don't win races. Most dogs finally bite you." I smiled. I felt foolish in the situation I was in.

"Let's hear it anyway," Clarissa said. "It's good to pre-vision things."

"Well. I think Wally'll stay around a few days. I'll forget exactly why I don't like him. We'll talk a lot about real estate and spruce trees. We'll be like conventioneers in town from Iowa. Men always do that. Sally'll get sick of us. But then by accident, I'll walk into a room where they are, and they'll immediately shut up some highly personal conversation. Maybe I'll catch them kissing and order Wally out of the house. After which, Sally'll be miserable and tell me she has to go live with him."

Cookie was waving to us from out on the beach, waving a stick that Poot expected her to throw. I waved back.

Clarissa shook her head, scratched into her thick hair and looked at me with annoyance, her pretty mouth-corners fattened in disapproval. "Do you really believe that?"

"It's what anybody'd think. It's what Ann Landers would tell you—if she isn't dead."

"You're crazy-hazy," she said and punched me too hard on the shoulder, as if a slug in the arm would cure me. "You don't know women very well, which isn't news, I guess."

Cookie's clear, happy voice was already talking over the distance, telling something she'd seen out in the ocean—a shark's fin, a dolphin's tail, a whale's geyser—something the dog had gone after, trusting his Egyptian ancestry against impossible odds. "I don't believe it," Cookie said gaily. "You guys. You should've seen it. I wish you could've seen."

I wouldn't have been wrong about Sally, even not knowing women very well, and never having said I did. I'd always been happy to know and like them one at a time. But about some things, even men can't be wrong.

Wally was in my house in Sea-Clift for five uncomfortable days. I tried to go about my diurnal duties, spending time early-to-late in the office where I had summer renters arriving, plumbers and carpenters and cleaning crews and yard-maintenance personnel to dispatch and lightly supervise. I sold a house on the bay side of Sea-Clift, took a bid on but failed to sell another. Mike sold two rental houses. He and I drove to Bay Head to inspect an old rococo movie house, the Rivoli Shore—where Houdini had made himself disappear in 1910. Maybe we wanted to buy it, find somebody to run it, go into limited partnership with a local Amvets group, using state preservation money and turn it into a World War II museum. We passed.

Normally, I'd have been home for lunch, but in grudging deference to what was going on in my house, I ate glutinous woodsman's casserole one day, Welsh rarebit another, ham and green beans a third at the Commodore's table at the Yacht Club, where I'm a non-boating member. Two times, I ate at Neptune's Daily Catch, where I had the calzone, flirted with the waitress, then spent the afternoon at my desk, burping and thinking philosophically about acid reflux and how it eats potholes in your throat. I explained to Mike that Sally was having an "old relative" to visit, though another time I said an "old friend," which he noticed, so he knew something was weird.

Each evening I went home, tired and ready for a renewing cocktail, supper and an early-to-bed. Wally was most times in the living room reading *Newsweek*, or on the deck with my binoculars, or in the kitchen loading up a dagwood or outside having a disapproving look at the arborvitae and hydrangeas or staring out at the shorebirds. Sally was almost never in sight when Wally was, leaving the impression that whatever they were carrying on between them during the day and my absence—hugging, face slapping, laughing that ended in tears—was all pretty trying, and

I wouldn't like seeing her face then, and in any case she needed to recover from it.

Toward Wally—who'd taken to wearing gray leisure-attire leather shorts that exposed his pasty bulldog calves above thick black ankle brogues and another rugby shirt, this time with *Mackays* printed on front—toward Wally, I dealt entirely in "So, okay, howzit goin'?" "Did you get to do some walking?" "Are they feeding you enough in here?" "Thought of going for a swim?" And to me, Wally—large, sour earth-smelling, full-cheeked, with a tired, timid smile I disliked—toward me, Wally dealt in "Yep." "Super." "Oh yeah, hiked up to the burger palace." "Great spread here, looverly, looverly."

I certainly didn't know what the hell any of us were doing—though who would? If you'd told me the two of them never so much as spoke, or went for polka lessons, or read the *I Ching* together, or shot heroin, I'd have had to believe it. Was it, I wondered, that everything was just too awkward, too revealing, too anxious-making, too upsetting, too embarrassing, too intim-idating, too intrusive or just too private to exhibit in front of me—the husband, the patient householder, the rate-payer, the sandwich-bread buyer? And also now a stranger?

Sally made dinner for us all three on night two. A favorite—lamb chops, Cajun tomatoes and creamed pearl onions. This was not the worst dinner I ever attended, although conceivably it was the worst in my own house. Sally was nervous and too smiley, her limp worsening notably. She cooked the lamb chops too long, which made her mad at me. Wally said his was "astounding" and ate like a horse. I had three stout martinis and observed the dinner was "perfect, if not astounding." And, as I'd predicted, I forgot more or less who Wally was, let myself act like he was one or the other of Sally's cousins, talked at length about the history of Sea-Clift, how it had been founded in the twenties by upstart Philadelphia real estate profiteers as a summer resort for middle-middle citizens from the City of Brotherly Love, how its basic populace and value system—Italians with moderate Democratic leanings—hadn't changed since the early days, except in the nineties, when well-heeled Gothamites with Republican preferences who couldn't afford Bridgehampton or Spring Lake started buying up land from the first settler's ancestors, who pretty quick wised up and started holding on to things. "Okay. Sure, sure," Wally said, mouth full of whatever, though he also said "thas brillian" a few times when nothing was brilliant, which made me hate him worse and made Sally get up and go to bed without saying good night.

In bed each night with Sally returned—though asleep when her head hit the pillow—I lay awake and listened to Wally's human noises across in "his" room. He played the radio—not loud—tuned to an all-news station that occasionally made him chuckle. He took long, forceful pisses into his toilet to let off the lager he drank at dinner. He produced a cannonade of burps, followed by a word of demure apology to no one: "Oh, goodness, who let that go?" He walked around heavily in his sock feet, yawned in a high-pitched keening sound that only a man used to living alone ever makes. He did some sort of brief grunting calisthenics, presumably on the floor, then plopped into bed and set up an amazing lion's den of snarfling-snoring that forced me to flatten my head between pillows, so that I woke up in the morning with my eyes smarting, my neck sore and both hands numb as death.

During the five days of Wally's visit, I twice asked Sally how things were going. The first time—this was two seconds before she fell into sleep, leaving me in bed listening to stertorous Wally—she said, "Fine. I'm glad I'm doing this. You're magnificent to put up with it. I'm sorry I'm cranky. . . ." Zzzzzzz. Magnificent. She had never before referred to me as magnificent, even in my best early days.

The other time I asked, we were seated across the circular glass-topped breakfast table. Wally was still upstairs sawing logs. I was heading off to the Realty-Wise office. It was day three. We hadn't said much about anything in the daylight. To freshen the air, I said, "You're not going to leave me for Wally, are you?" I gave her a big smirking grin and stood up, napkin in hand. To which she answered, looking up, plainly dismayed, "I don't think so." Then she stared out at the ocean, on which a white boat full of day-fishermen sat anchored a quarter mile offshore, their short poles bristling off one side, their boat tipped, all happy anglers, hearts set on a flounder or a shark. They were probably Japanese. Something she noticed when she saw them may have offered solace.

But "I don't think so"? No grateful smile, no wink, no rum mouth pulled to signal no worries, no way, no dice. "I don't think so" was not an answer Ann Landers would've considered insignificant. "Dear Franky in the Garden State, I'd lock up the silverware if I were you, boy-o. You've got a rough intruder in your midst. You need to do some night-time sentry duty on your marriage bed. Condition red, Fred."

Wally gave no evidence of thinking himself a rough intruder or a devious conniver after my happiness. In spite of his strange splintered, half North-Shore-fatty, half earnest-blinking-Scots-gardener persona (a veteran stage actor playing Falstaff with an Alabama accent), Wally did his seeming best to spend his days in a manner that did least harm. He always smiled when he saw me. He occasionally wanted to talk about beach erosion. He advised me to put more aluminum sulfate on my hydrangeas to make the color last. Otherwise he stayed out of sight much of the time. And I now believe, though no one's told me, that Sally had actually forced him to come: to suffer penance, to show him that abandonment had worked out well for her, to embarrass the shit out of him, to confuse him, to make him miss her miserably and make me seem his superior—plus darker reasons I assume are involved in everything most of us do and that there's no use thinking about.

But what else was she supposed to do? How else to address past and loss? Was there an approved mechanism for redressing such an affront besides blunt instinct? What other kind of synergy reconciles a loss so great—and so weird? It's true I might've approached it differently. But sometimes you just have to wing it.

Which explains my own odd conduct, my fatal empathy (I guess), and even Wally's attempts to be stolidly, unpretentiously present, subjecting himself to whatever penitent paces Sally put him through in the daylight, essaying to be cordial, taking interest in the flora and fauna and in me at cocktail hour, eating and drinking his scuppers over, burping and snorting like a draft horse in his room at night, then making an effort to get his sleep in anticipation of the next day's trials.

He and I never talked about "the absence" (which Sally said was his name for being gone for nearly thirty years) or anything related to their kids, his parents, his other life and lives (though of course he and Sally might've). We never talked about when he might be leaving or how he was experiencing life in my house. Never talked about the future—his or Sally's or mine. We never talked about the presidential election, since that had a root system that could lead to sensitive subjects—morality, dubious ethics, uncertain outcomes and also plainly bad outcomes. I wanted to keep it clear that he was never for one instant welcome in my house, and that I pervasively did not like him. I don't know what he thought or how he truly felt, only how he *was* in his conduct, which wasn't that bad and, in fact, evidenced a small, unformed nobility, although heavy-bellied and gooberish. I did my best. And maybe he did his. I picked up some interesting tips about soil salinity and its effect on the flowering properties of seashore flora, learned some naturopathic strategies for combating the Asian Long-Horned Beetle. Wally heard my theories for combating sticker shock and enhancing curb appeal, got some insider dope about the second-home market and how it's always wedded to Wall Street. There was a moment when I even thought I *did* remember him from eons ago. But that moment vanished when I thought of him together with Sally on the beach while

I was alone eating tough, frozen woodsman's casserole at the Yacht Club. In the truest sense, we didn't get anywhere with each other because we didn't want to. Men generally are better at this kind of edgy, pointless armistice than women. It's genetic and relates to our hoary history of mortal combat, and to knowing that most of life doesn't usually rise to that level of gravity but still is important. I'm not sure it's to our credit.

*W*ally eventually departed on the morning of day five. Sally said he was going, and I made it my business to get the hell out of the house at daybreak and ended up snoozing at my desk until Mike arrived at eight and acted worried about me. I hung around the office the rest of the morning, catching cold calls, running credit checks on new rental clients and talking to Clarissa in Gotham. She'd called every day and tried to liven things up by referring to Wally as "Dildo" and "Wal-Fart" and "Mr. Wall Socket," and saying he reminded her of her brother (which is both true and not true) and that maybe the two of them could be friends because they're "both so fucking weird."

Then I drove home, where Sally kissed me and hugged me when I walked in the door, as if I'd been away on a long journey. She looked pale and drained—not like somebody who'd been crying, but like somebody who might've been on a roadside when two speeding cars or two train engines or two jet airplanes collided in front of her. She said she was sorry about the whole week, knew it had taken a toll on all of us, but probably mostly me (which wasn't true), that Wally would never again come into the house, even though he'd asked her to thank me for letting him "visit," and even though having him here, as awful as it was, had served some "very positive purposes" that would never have gotten served any other way. She said she loved me and that she wanted to make love right then, in the living room on the suede couch, where this had all started. But because the meter reader knocked at the front door and Poot started barking at him out in the road, we moved—naked as two Bushmen—up to the bedroom.

Next day I assumed—believed—matters would begin shifting back toward normal. I wanted us to drive over to the Red Man Club for an outing of fishing, fiddlehead hunting and a trek along the Pequest to seek out Sampson's Warbler pairs that nest in our woods and nowhere else in New Jersey. I intended to put in an order for a new Lexus at Sea Girt Imports—a surprise for Sally's birthday in three weeks. I'd already made a trip up there to consult color charts and take a test drive.

Sally, though, seemed still pale and drained on Saturday, so that I canceled the Red Man Club and (thank goodness) didn't get around to the Lexus.

She stayed in bed all day, as if she herself had been on a long and arduous journey. Though the journey that had left her depleted had left me exhilarated and abuzz, my head full of plans and vivid imaginings, the way somebody'd feel who'd gotten happy news from the lab, a shadow on an X ray that proved to be nothing, bone marrow that "took." While she rested, I drove myself over to the movies at the Ocean County Mall and saw *Charlie's Angels*, then bought lobsters on the way home and cooked them for dinner—though Sally barely rallied to work on hers, while I demolished mine.

She went to bed early again—after I asked if maybe she should call Blumberg on Monday and schedule a work-up. Maybe she was anemic. She said she would, then went to sleep at nine and slept twelve hours, emerging downstairs into the kitchen Sunday morning, weak-eyed, sallow and sunk-shouldered—where I was sitting, eating a pink grapefruit and reading about the Lakers in the *Times*—to tell me she was leaving me to live with Wally in Mull, and that she'd decided it was worse to let someone you love be alone forever than to be with someone (me!) who didn't need her all that much, even though she knew I loved her and she loved me. This is when she said things about the "circumstances" and about importance. But to this day, I don't understand the calculus, though it has a lot in common with other things people do.

She was wearing an old-fashioned lilac sateen peignoir set with pink ribbonry stitched around the jacket collar. She was thin-armed, bare-legged, her skin wan and blotchy from sleep, her eyes colorless in their glacial blue. She was barefoot, a sign of primal resolution. She blinked at me as if sending me a message in Morse code: Good-bye, good-bye, good-bye.

Oh, I protested. May it not be said I failed of ardor at that crucial moment (the past, critics have attested, seems settled and melancholy, but I was boisterous in that present). I was, by turns, disbelieving, shocked, angry, tricked-feeling, humiliated, gullible and stupid. I became analytical, accusatory, revisionist, self-justifying, self-abnegating and inventive of better scenarios than being abandoned. Patiently (I wasn't truly patient; I wanted to slit Wally open like a lumpy feed sack) and lovingly (which I surely was), I testified that I needed her the way hydrogen needs oxygen—she should know that, had known it for years. If *she* needed time—with Wally, in Mull—I could understand. I lied that I found it all "interesting," although I admitted it didn't make me happy—which wasn't a lie. She should go there and do that. Hang out. Plant little trees in little holes. Go native. Act married. Talk, slap, hug, giggle, groan, cry.

But come home!

I'd tear down conventional boundaries if we could just keep an understanding alive. Did I say beg? I begged. I already said I cried (something Clarissa chided me for). To which Sally said, shoulders slack, eyes lowered, slender hands clasped on the table top, her little finger lightly touching the covered Quimper butter dish she at one time had felt great affection for, and that I subsequently winged across the room and to death by smithereens, "I think I have to make this permanent, sweetheart. Even if I regret it and later come crying to you, and you're with some other woman, and won't talk to me, and my life is lost. I have to."

Strange grasp on "permanent," I thought, though my eyes burbled with tears. "It's not like we're dealing with hard kernels of truth here," I said pitiably. "This is all pretty discretionary, if you ask me."

"No," she said, which is when she took her wedding ring off and laid it on the glass pane of the table top, causing a hard little *tap* I'll never, ever, forget, even if she comes back.

"This is so terrible," I said in full cry. I wanted to howl like a dog.

"I know."

"Do you love Wally more than you love me?"

She shook her head in a way that made her face appear famished and exhausted, though she couldn't look at me, just at the ring she'd a moment before relinquished. "I don't know that I love him at all."

"Then what the fuck!" I shouted. "Can you just *do* this?"

"I don't think I can't do it," Sally—my wife—said. And essentially that was that. Double negative makes a positive.

She was gone by cocktail hour, which I observed alone.

Somewhere once I read that harsh words are all alike. You can make them up and be right. The same is true of explanations. I never caught them smooching. Probably they didn't smooch. Neither did they stop mid-sentence in an intimate moment just when I strode through a door (I never strode through any without whistling a happy tune first). Sally and I never visited a counselor to hash out problems, or ever endured any serious arguments. There wasn't time before she left. Apart from when I first knew Sally, Wally had never been a feature of our daily converse. Everybody has their casualties; we get used to them like old photographs we glance at but keep in a trunk. To understand it all in the way we understand other things, I would have to make an explanation up. The facts, as I knew them, didn't say enough.

For the first week after Sally left, I cried (for myself) and brooded (about myself) as one would cry and brood upon realizing that marriage to oneself probably hadn't been so great; that I maybe wasn't *so* good in bed—or anywhere—or wasn't good at intimacy or sharing or listening. My *completelys*, my *I love yous*, my *my darlings*, my *forevers* weighed less than standard issue, and I wasn't such an interesting husband, in spite of believing I was a very good and interesting husband. Sally, possibly, was unhappy when I thought she was ecstatic. Any person—especially a realtor—would wonder about these post-no-sale issues just as a means of determining what new home-work he was now required to do.

What I decided was that I may never have seemed to Sally to be "all in," but that "all in" is what I goddamn was. Always. No matter how I felt or described my feelings. Anything more "all in" than me was just a fantasy of the perfidious sort manufactured by the American Psychiatrists Association, that Sisyphus of trade groups, to keep the customers coming back.

Bullshit, in other words.

I *was* intimate. I *was* as amorous and passionate as the traffic would bear. I *was* interesting. I *was* kind. I *was* generous. I *was* forbearing. I *was* funny (since that's so goddamned important). I shared whatever could stand to be shared (and not everything can). Women both hate and love weakness in men, and I'd had positive feedback to think I was weak in the right ways and not in the wrong. Of course, I wasn't perfect at any of these human skills, having never thought I *had* to be. In the fine print on the boilerplate second-marriage license, it should read:

"Signatories consent neither has to be perfect." I did fine as a husband. Fine.

Which didn't mean Sally had to be big-H happy or do anything except what she wanted to do. We're only talking about explanations here, and whether anything's my fault. It was. And it wasn't.

My personal view is that Sally got caught unawares in the great, deep and confusing eddy of contingency, which has other contingency streams running into it, some visible, some too deep-coursing below the surface to know about. One stream was: That just as I was enjoying the rich benefits of the Permanent Period—no fear of future, life not ruinable, the past generalized to a pleasant pinkish blur—*she* began, in spite of what she might've said, to fear permanence, to fear no longer *becoming*, to dread a life that couldn't be trashed and squandered. Put simply, she wasn't prepared to be like me—a natural state that marriage ought to accommodate and make survivable, as one partner lives the Permanent Period like a communicant lives in a state of grace, while the other does whatever the hell she wants.

Only along galumphs Wally, turf-stained, resolutely unhandsome, vaguely clueless from his years in the grave (i.e., Scotland). And suddenly one of the prime selling points of second marriage—minimalization of the past—becomes not such a selling point. First marriages have too much past clanking along behind; but second ones may have too little, and so lack ballast.

Heavy-footed, un-nuanced, burping, yerping Wally may have reminded Sally there was a past that couldn't be generalized, and that she had unfinished business in the last century and couldn't reason it away in the jolly manner that I'd reasoned myself into a late-in-life marriage and lived happily by its easy-does-it house rules. (Millennium angst, if it's anything, is fear of the past, not the future.) In fact, with Wally both behind and also suddenly lumped in front, it's good odds Sally never experienced the Permanent Period, and so had no choice but to hand me her wedding ring like I was a layaway clerk at Zales and push herself out of the eddy of our life and take the current wherever it flowed.

Though I'll admit that even on this day, the eve of Turkey Day, I'm no longer so blue about Sally's absence, as once I was. I don't feature myself living alone forever, just as I wouldn't concede to staying a realtor forever and mostly tend to think of life itself as a made-up thing composed of today, maybe tomorrow and probably not the next day, with as little of the past added in as possible. I feel, in fact, a goodly tincture of regret for Sally. Because, even though I believe her sojourn on Mull will not last so long, by re-choosing Wally she has embraced the impossible, inaccessible past, and by doing so has risked or even exhausted an extremely useful longing—possibly her most important one, the one she's made good use of these years to fuel her present, where I have found a place. This is why the dead should stay dead and why in time the land lies smooth all around them.

8

This morning, I've scheduled the 10:15 showing at my listing at 61 Surf Road, and following that, at 12:30, a weeks-planned meet-up in Asbury Park with Wade Arsenault, my friend from years back, to attend a hotel implosion—the hotel in question being the elegant old Queen Regent Arms, remnant of the stately elephants from the twenties, surrendering at last to the forces of progress (a high-end condo development). Wade and I have been to two other implosions this fall, in Ventnor and Camden, and each of us finds them enjoyable, although for different reasons. Wade, I think, just likes big explosions and the controlled devastation that follows. In his young life, he was an engineer, and watching things blow up is his way of coping with being now in his eighties, and of fortifying his belief that the past crumbles and that staring loss in the face is the main requirement for living out our allotment (this is as spiritual as engineers get). On the other hand, I'm gratified by the idea of an orderly succession manifesting our universal need to remain adaptable through time, a lesson for which cancer is the teacher, though my reason may not finally be any different from Wade's. In any case, going along with Wade injects an interesting and unusual centerpiece activity into the course of my day, one that gives it shape and content but won't wear me out, since at the end I'll have Paul to contend with. (Business itself, of course, is the very best at offering solid, life-structuring agendas, and business days are always better than wan weekends, and are hands-down better than gaping, ghostly holidays that Americans all claim to love—but I don't, since these days can turn long, dread-prone and worse.)

This morning, however, has already turned at least semi-eventful. Up and dressed by 8:30, I spent a useful half hour in my home office going over listing sheets for the Surf Road property, followed by a browse through the *Asbury Press*, surveying the "By Owner" offerings, estate auctions, "New Arrivals" and "Deaths," all of which can be fruitful, if sometimes disheartening. The *Press* reported on the Peter Pan tour-bus accident Mike and I saw yesterday—three lives "eclipsed," all Chinese-American females on an Atlantic City gaming holiday from their restaurant jobs on Canal Street, Gotham. Others were injured but lived.

The *Press* also reported that the presumptive (and devious) Vice-President-in-waiting for the Republicans has suffered a mild heart trembler, and farther down the page that the device that exploded at Haddam Doctors took the life of a security guard named Natherial Lewis, forty-eight—which startled me. Natherial is/was the uncle of young Scooter Lewis, who chauffeured Ernie McAuliffe to his resting ground yesterday, and so must have known nothing of his own loss at the time, although today he's thinking on death with new realities installed. I knew Natherial when he himself was a young man. Several times when I was at Lauren-Schwindell, I employed him to retrieve wayward FOR SALE signs after Halloween pranksters had swiped them from front yards and set them up in front of area churches or their divorced parents' condos. Nate always thought it was funny. I'll phone in flowers through Lloyd Mangum, who'll be overseeing. New Jersey is a small place, finally.

When I looked up from my paper, though, and out the window—my home office gives onto the front, and down Poincinet Road toward the state park where Route 35 ends and a few old seasonal businesses are in sight (a chowder house, the Sinker Swim Doughnut)—I couldn't stop remembering something Clarissa was talking about on our after-Halloween beach walk: That she felt strangely insulated from contemporary goings on. Which, as I've said before, is also true for me. I watch CNN every night, but never afterward think much about anything I see—even the election, as stupid as it is. I've come to loathe most sports, which I used to love—a loss I attribute to having seen the same things over and over again too many times. Only death-row stories and sumo wrestling (narrated in Japanese) can keep me at the TV longer than ten minutes. My bedside table, as I've said, has novels and biographies I've read thirty pages into but can't tell you much about. A couple of weeks ago, I decided I'd write a letter to President Clinton—the opposite of Marguerite's letter—detailing the sorry state of national affairs (much of it his fault), suggesting he'd be wise to nationalize the Guard and protect the future of the Republic with regard to the "rogue state of Florida." But I didn't finish it and put it in a drawer, since it seemed to me the work of a crank that would've earned me a visit from the FBI.

But what I wondered, at my desk with a copy of the *Asbury Press*, gazing out my window, was—it was a kind of minor revelation: Am I not just feeling what plenty of other humans feel all the time but don't pay any attention to? People with no worrisome follow-up tests next Wednesday, civically alert citizens, members of PACs, schmoes who haven't lost their spouses to a memory of love lost? And if so, do I even have any excuse to feel insulated? At the end of this reverie, I took out my half-written letter to the President and threw it in the trash and promised myself to write a better one, posing more constructive questions I can work on in the meantime—all in an effort to seem less like a nutter and a complainer, and to do whatever the hell we're all supposed to do to display we're responsible and doing our best to make life better.

I had several calls waiting before setting off for Surf Road. One from the Eat No Evil people in Mantoloking, wanting to know if gluten-free, no-salt bread in the organic turkey stuffing would be desired, or if the standard organic Saskatchewan spelt was okay. And could they come at 1:45 instead of 2:00? Another was from Wade, a nervous-nelly call to be sure we're meeting at the Fuddruckers at Exit 102 on the Parkway at 12:30, and to say that he was bringing his own sandwich which he can eat while the Queen Regent comes down (this needed no answer). Another, which I also didn't answer, was from Mike, apologizing for engaging in the "non-virtuous action of senseless speech" last night—which he certainly did—and accusing himself of covetousness, which I take as a sign that he's maybe saying no to the Montmorency spaghetti and that I can keep him as a trusted employee and house-selling house-a-fire.

The fourth call, however, was from Ann, and strummed an ominous minor bass chord in my chest as it bespoke fresh assumptions I don't share but may have seemed to share at the end of a long and wearisome day.

"It's easier to leave this as a message than to say it to you, Frank." My name again. Years ago, when we were married, Ann used to call me "Tootsie," which embarrassed me in front of people, and then for a while she called me "Satch"—for private personal reasons—this being before "shit-heel" finally won the day. "I didn't really think ahead much about what I said tonight. I just blurted it. But it still seems right to me. You acted completely stunned. I'm sure I scared you, which I'm sorry about. I certainly don't have to come to Thanksgiving dinner. You were just sweet to ask. You were very good tonight, by the way, the best I can remember you—to me, anyway." Cancer obviously agrees with me. "Charley knew what a good man you were, and said so, though probably not to you." Definitely not. "He always thought I'd have been happier married to you than to him. But you can't re-calculate, I guess. We act on so many things we don't know very much about, don't you think? It's no wonder we're all a little fucked up—as they say in Grosse Pointe. Anyway, the idea of underlying causes to things has started to oppress me. I didn't tell you, did I, that I considered attending the seminary after Charley died. It was probably why I came back here. Then I decided religion was just about underlying causes, things that are hidden and have to be treated like secrets all the time. And I—" *Click.* Time was up.

I sat at my desk, deciding if I wanted to hear the rest, which waited in message five. Humans generally get out the gist of what they need to say right at the beginning, then spend forever qualifying, contradicting, burnishing or taking important things back. You rarely miss anything by cutting most people off after two sentences. Ann's spiel about how much we all don't know about everything we do is linked thematically to Mike Mahoney's fourth-grade perception on the Barnegat bridge last night that we all live in houses we didn't choose and that choose us because they were built to somebody else's specifications, which we're happy to adopt, and that that says something about the price of baloney. Each has the specific gravity of a rice-paper airplane tossed from the top of the Empire State Building that soars prettily before it's lost to oblivion. Another example of non-virtuous speech. Maybe Ann's now dabbling in Eastern religions, since her old-line Reform Lutheranism stopped packing a wallop.

Except. Our ex-wives always harbor secrets about us that make them irresistible. Until, of course, we remember who we are and what we did and why we're not married anymore.

Message five. "Okay, sweetie, I'll get this over with. Sorry for the long message. I've had a glass of New Zealand sauvignon blanc." Long messages ask for but don't allow answers, which is why they're inexcusable. "I just want to say that I can't get over the long transit we all make in our lives. The strangest thing we'll ever know is just life itself, isn't it?" No. "Not science or technology or mysticism or religion. I'm not looking for under-lying causes anymore. I want things to be evident now. When I saw you tonight, at first it was like being in a jet airplane and looking out the window and seeing another jet airplane. You see it, but you really can't appreciate the distance it is from you, except it's really far. But by the end, you'd gotten much closer. For the first time in a very long time you were good, like I said in my last message, or maybe I said it at school. Any-hoo, I just thought of one last thing, then I'm going to bed. Do you remember once when you took the little kids to see a baseball game? In Philadelphia, I guess. Charley and I were somewhere on his boat, and you had them down there. And some player, I guess, hit a ball that came right at you. Of course you remember all this, sweetheart. And Paul said you just reached up with one hand and caught it. He said everybody around you stood up and applauded you, and your hand swelled up huge. But he said you were so happy. You smiled and smiled, he said. And I thought when he told me: That's the man I thought I married. Not because you could catch an old ball, but because that's all I thought it took to make you happy. I realized that when I married you I thought I could make you happy just like that. I really did think that. Things made you happy then. I think you gave that ball to Paul. I have it somewhere. So okay. Life's an odd transit. I already said that. It'll be nice to see Paul tomorrow—at least I hope it will. Good night." *Click*.

"It's also true . . ." I said these words right into the receiver, with no one on the other end, my fingers touching my Realtor of the Year crystal paperweight from my early selling days in Haddam. It was holding down some unopened mail beside the phone. ". . . It's also true"—and here I quit speaking to no one—"that we conjure up underlying causes and effects based on what we want the underlying causes to be. And *that's* how we get things *all fucked up.*" But in any case, Ann would've done better marrying me *precisely* because I could catch a line drive with my bare hand, and then letting that handsome, manly, uncomplicated facility be the theme of life—one I might've lived up to—rather than thinking she could ever make me *happy*! The kind of happy I was that day at the Vet when "Hawk" Dawson actually doffed his red "C" cap to me, and everyone cheered and I practically convulsed into tears—you can't patent that. It was one shining moment of glory that was instantly gone. Whereas life, real life, is different and can't even be appraised as simply "happy," but only in terms of "Yes, I'll take it all, thanks," or "No, I believe I won't." Happy, as my poor father used to say, is a lot of hooey. Happy is a circus clown, a sitcom, a greeting card. Life, though, life's about something sterner. But also something better. A lot better. Believe me.

There was a sixth call. From my son Paul Bascombe, on the road, telling me he and "Jill" wouldn't make it in tonight—last night, now—due to "hitting the edge of some lake-effect snow" that "has Buffalo paralyzed clear down into western PA." They were "hoping to push on past Valley Forge." Weighty pauses were left between phrases—"has Buffalo paralyzed," "lake-effect snow," "western PA"—to denote how hysterical these all are, requiring extra time for savoring. The two of them, he said, "almost picked up a flop in Hershey." I've invited them to stay here, but Paul doesn't like my house and I'm happy for them not to. I have a sense, of course, that Paul has surprises for us. Something's in his flat, no-affect, Kanzcity-middlewestern, put-on phone voice that I don't like, since he seems to strive too hard to become that strange overconfident, businessy main-streamer with a mainstreamer's sealed-off certainty riven right into the lingo. I haven't given up on the notion of things generally "working out," or with either of my children "fitting in," but I'd also be pleased if they both thought these things had happened. I halfway expected Paul to say he'd "rest in the City of Brotherly Love," but he couldn't have suppressed a shout of hilarity, which would've ruined it.

Nine years ago, when he was an unusual and uninspired senior at Haddam HS—it was during the two years when Ann's husband, Charley, had his first cruel brush with colon cancer and Ann simply couldn't deal with Paul *and* Clarissa—Paul lived with me in the very house on Cleveland Street where he'd lived as a little boy, the house I bought from Ann when she moved away from Haddam and married Charley, and of course the very house she lives in this morning. It was the time when Ann—for some good reasons—thought Paul might have Asperger's and was forcing me, at great expense, to drive him down to Hopkins to be neurologically evaluated. He *was* evaluated and *didn't* have Asperger's or anything else. The Hopkins doctor said Paul was "unsystematically oppositional" by nature and probably would be all his life, that there was nothing wrong with that, nor anything I could do or should want to, since plenty of interesting, self-directed, even famous people were also that. He named Winston Churchill, Bing Crosby, Gertrude Stein and Thomas

Carlyle, which seemed a grouping that didn't bode well. Though it was amusing to think of all four of them writing greeting cards out in K.C.

The day from that relatively halcyon time which I remember most feelingly was a sunny Saturday morning in spring. Forsythias and azaleas were out in Haddam. I had been outside bundling the wet leaves I'd missed the fall before. Paul had few friends and stayed home on weekends, working on ventriloquism and learning to make his dummy—Otto—talk, roll his bulging eyes, mug, agitate his acrylic eyebrows over something Paul, his straight man, said and needed to be made a fool of for. When I came in the living room from the yard, Paul was seated on the old hard-seated Windsor chair he practiced on. He looked dreadful, as he usually looked— baggy jeans, torn sweatshirt, long ratty hair dyed blue. Otto was perched on his knee, Paul's left hand buried in his complicated innards. Otto's unalterably startled, perpetually apple-cheeked oaken face was turned so that he and Paul were staring out the window at my neighbor Skip McPherson's Dodge Alero, which McPherson was washing in front of his house across the street.

I was always trying to say things to Paul that were friendly and provoking and that made it seem I was an engaged father who knew things about his son that only the two of us *could* know—which maybe I was. These were sometimes dummy jokes: "Feeling a little wooden today?" "Not as chipper as usual?" "Time to branch out." It was one reliable strategy I'd found that offered us at least a chance at rudimentary communication. There weren't many others.

Otto's idiot head swiveled around to peer at me when I came

through the front door, though Paul maintained an intense, focused stare out at Skip McPherson. Otto's get-up was a blue-and-white-plaid hacking jacket, a yellow foulard, floppy brown trousers, and a frizz of bright yellow "hair," on top of which teetered a green derby hat. He looked like a drunk bet-placer at a second-rate dog track. Paul had bought him at a going-out-of-business magic shop in Gotham.

"I've decided what I want to be," Paul said, staring away purposefully. Otto regarded Paul, batted his eyebrows up and down, then looked back at me. "The invisible man. You know? He unwinds his bandages and he's gone. That'd be great." Paul often said distressing things just to be, in fact, oppositional and usually didn't really know or care what they meant or portended.

"Sounds pretty permanent." I sat on the edge of the overstuffed chair I usually read my paper in at night. Otto stared at me, as if listening. "You're only seventeen. Somebody might say you just got here." Otto spun his head round full circle and blinked his bright-blue bulbous eyes, as if I'd said something outrageous.

"I can act through Otto," Paul said. "It'll be perfect. Ventriloquism makes the best sense if the ventriloquist's invisible. You know?" He kept his stare fixed out at Skip, who was working over his hubcaps.

"Okay," I said. Somebody might've interpreted this as a silent "cry for help," an early warning sign of depression, some antisocial eruption in the offing. But I didn't. Adolescent jabber designed to drive me crazy, is what I thought. Paul has put this instinct to work in the greeting-card industry. "Sounds great," I said.

"It's great and it's also true." He turned and frowned at me.

"True. Okay. True."

"Greet 'n true," Otto said in a scratchy falsetto that sounded like Paul, though I couldn't see his whispering lips or his suppressed pleasure. "Greet 'n true, greet 'n true, greet 'n true."

That's all I remember about this—though I didn't think about it at the time in 1991. But it's probably not something a father could forget and might even experience guilt about, which I may have done for a while, but stopped. I also remember because it reminds me of Paul in the most vivid of ways, of what he was like as a boy, and makes me think, as only a parent would, of the progress that lurks unbeknownst in even our apparent failures. By his own controlling hand, Paul may now be said to have gotten what he wanted, willed invisibility, and may already be far down the road to happiness.

Clarissa's beau, the New Hampshire Healey 1000 guy, I'm grievously forced to meet as I make my hurried trip through the kitchen, wanting to catch a bite and beat it. I intentionally stayed in my office, hoping the lovebirds would get bored waiting for Clarissa's "Dad" and head out for a beach ramble or a cold Healey ride for a shiatsu massage up in Mantoloking. I could meet him later. But when I head through, my Surf Road listing papers in hand, aiming for a fast cup of coffee and a sinker, I find Clarissa. And Thom. (As in "Hi, Frank, this is my friend Thom"—I'm guessing the spelling—"who I woogled the bee-jesus out of all night long in your guest room, whether you approve or don't." This last part she doesn't say.)

The two of them are arranged languidly, side-by-side, yet somehow theatrically *intent* at the glass-topped breakfast table, precisely where Sally gave me my bad news last May. Clarissa's wearing a pair of man's red-and-green-plaid boxer shorts and a frayed blue Brooks Brothers pajama shirt—mine. Her short hair's mussed, her cheeks pale, her contacts are out, and she has her long-toed bare feet across the space of chairs in Thom's lap and is studying an Orvis catalog. (All evidence of a "committed relationship" with another female *gone*. Poof. Things happen too fast for me—which, I guess, is a given.)

Thom's frowning hard over an open copy of what looks like *Foreign Affairs* (thick, creamy, deckled pages, etc.) and looks up to smile weakly as my fatherly identity is expressed (in my own kitchen). I mean to proffer only the most carefully crafted, disinterested and hermetically banal sentiments and damn few of them, for fear I'll say extremely wrong things, after which terrible words from my daughter's razor tongue will lacerate my head and heart.

Only, Thom's *old*—at least *forty-six*! And even bumbling through my kitchen like a renter and barely daring a look or to meet his dark eyes—my listing papers being my something to hold on to—I know this character's rap sheet. And it has DANGER stamped on it in big red block letters. Clarissa has carefully mentioned noth-ing about him in the last days, only that he "teaches" equestrian therapy to Down's syndrome kids at a "pretty famous holistic center" over in Manchester, where she volunteers a day a week when she isn't working in my office. She's intended him to attract absolutely no vetting commentary from me. Apparently the "whole thing"—the connected boxes versus the complex, well-differentiated big swim I was unarguably in—was still pretty precarious, and she didn't need other people's (mine, her mother's) views making her difficult life harder to navigate. This is all re-conveyed to me now in my kitchen with one look of post-coital lassitude and menace.

Thom, however—Thom is no mystery. Thom is known to me and to all men—fathers, especially—and loathed.

Tall, rangy, long-muscled, large-eyed, smooth-olive-skinned Amherst or Wesleyan grad—read Sanskrit, history of science and genocide studies, swam or rowed till books got in the way; born "abroad" of mixed parentage (Jewish-Navajo, French, Berber— whatever gives you charcoal gray eyes, silky black hair on the back of your hands and forearms); deep honeyed voice that seems made of expensive felt; intensely "serious" yet surprisingly funny, also touchingly awkward at the most unexpected moments (not during intercourse); plays a medieval stringed instrument, of which there are only ten in existence; has mastered *Go*, was once married to a Chilean woman and has a teenage child in Montreal he's deeply committed to but rarely sees. Worked in Ghana for the Friends Service, taught in experimental schools (not Montessori), built his own ketch and sailed it to Brittany, wears one-of-a-kind Persian sandals, a copper anklet, black silk singlets suggesting a full-body tan, sage-colored desert shorts revealing a shark bite on his inner thigh from who-knows-what ocean, and always smells like a fine wood-working shop. He's only at the Equestrian Center now because of an "awakening" on the Going to the Sun Highway, which indicated he had yet to fully deliver on his "promise." And since he'd grown up with horses in North Florida or Buenos Aires or Vienna, and since his little sister had Down's, maybe there was still time to "make good" if he could just find the right place: Manchester, New Jersey.

And oh, yes, along the course, he also wanted to make good on some men's daughters and wives. On Clarissa. My Clarissa. My prize. My lifesaver. My un-innocent innocent. She was number 1001.

If I had a pistol instead of a handful of house-for-sale sheets, I'd shoot Thom right in the chest in the midst of their cheery bagel 'n cream cheese, eggs 'n bacon ambience, let him slump onto his *Foreign Affairs* and drag him out to the beach for the gulls. (Since I've had cancer, I've compiled an impressive list of people to "take with me" when things get governmentally irreversible—as they soon will. If I survive the hail of bullets, I'll happily spend my last days in a federal lockup with books to read, three squares, and limited TV in the senior block. You can imagine who I'll be seeking out. Thom is my new entry.)

". . . This is my dad, Frank Bascombe," Clarissa mutters, head down over her Orvis catalog. She casually retracts her shoe-less foot out of Thom's lap, gives her big toe a good scratching, then absently, lightly fingers the tiny red whelp where her diamond nose stud used to be. Breakfast dishes are disposed in front of them—bagel crescents, melted butter globs, a bowl of cereal bits afloat on a gray skim of milk product.

I proffer a hand insincerely across Clarissa. "Hi there," I say. Big smile.

"Thom van Ronk, sir." Thom looks up suddenly from *Foreign Affairs*, now smiling intensely. He shakes my hand without standing. Van Ronk. Not a Berber, but a treacherous Walloon. Clarissa could've been smarter than this.

"What's shakin' in *Foreign Affairs*, Thom?" I say. "Brits still won't go for the Euro? Ruskies struggling with a market economy? The odd massacre needing interpreting?" I smile so he knows I hate him. Every person he's ever known hates him—except my daughter, who doesn't like *my* tone of voice and glares up from her page of Gore-Tex trekking mocs to burn a dead-eyed frown into me promising complex punishments later. They'd be worth it.

"Your son, aka my brother, paid us a visit already this morning," Clarissa says, nestling her heel back comfy into Thom's penile package, while he re-finds his place in his important reading material. They seem to have known each other for a year. Possibly they're already on the brink of the kind of familiarity that leads to boredom—like a ball bearing seeking the ocean bottom. I hope so. Though neither of my wives ever stuck her heel into my package while fingering up breakfast crumbs. At Harvard, there's probably a course for this in the mental-health extension program: Morning-After Etiquette: Do's, Don'ts, Better Nots. "He seemed—surprise, surprise—extremely weird." She casts a bored look out at the beach to where the Shore Police are grilling some local teens freed from school for the holiday. "He's not as weird, though, as his girlfriend. Miss Jill." She frowns at the boys, four in all, with shaved heads, butt-crack jeans, long Jets and Redskins jerseys. Two enormous, hulking, hatless policemen in shorts are making the boys form a line and turn their pockets out alongside the black-and-white Isuzu 4 × 4. All of them are laughing.

Clarissa, I understand to be musing over the fact that mere mention of her brother makes her revert to teen vocabulary ten years out-of-date, when Paul was "weird beyond pathetic, entirely out of it, deeply disgusting and queer," etc. She's sophisticated enough not to care, only to notice. She and her strange brother maintain an ingrown, not overtly unfriendly détente she doesn't talk about. Paul admires and is deeply in love with her for being glamorous and a (former) lesbian and for stealing a march on transgressive behavior, which had always been his speciality. (I'm sure he was pleased to meet Thom.) Clarissa recognizes his right to be an insignificant little midwestern putzburger, card writer and Chiefs fan, someone she'd never have one thing to do with if he wasn't her brother. It's possible they're in contact about their mother and me by e-mail, though I'm not sure when they last saw each other in the flesh, or if Clarissa could even be nice to him in person. Parents are supposed to know these things. I just don't.

Though there's also an old, murky shadow over their brother-sister bond. When Paul was seventeen and Clarissa fifteen, Paul in a fit of confusion apparently "suggested"—I'm not sure how—that he and Clarissa engage in a "see-what-it's-like" roll in the hay, which pretty much KO'd further sibling rapport. It's always possible he was joking. However, three years ago—he told his mother this—Paul was summoned to Maine by Clarissa and Cookie, given a ticket to Bangor, brought down to Pretty Marsh by bus, then forced to sleep in a cold cabin and endure an inquisition for misfeasances he wouldn't go into detail about (reportedly "the usual brother-sister crap"), though clearly for trying to make Clarissa do woo-woo with him when she was underage and his sister. Paul said the two women were savage. They said he should be ashamed of himself, should seek counseling, was probably gay, wasn't manly, had self-esteem issues, was likely an addicted onanist and premature ejaculator— the usual things sisters think about brothers. He told Ann he finally just gave in (without specifically admitting to what) when they said none of it was his fault, but was actually Ann's and mine, and that they felt sorry for him. Then they each gave him a hug that he said made him feel crazy. They ended the afternoon with Paul showing them some of his sidesplitting "Smart Aleck" cards—the Hallmark line he writes for out in K.C.—and throwing his voice into the bedroom, and laughing themselves silly before sitting down to a big lobster dinner. He went home the next day.

"What's wrong with Jill?" I say.

"Way-ell." Clarissa casts an eyebrows-raised look of appraisal up at me. She can't see well without her contacts.

Thom suddenly snaps to, grins, showing huge incisors, blinks his eyes and says, "What? Sorry. I wasn't listening."

"Did he tell you she only has one hand? I mean she's perfectly okay. They probably love each other. But yeah. It's fine, of course. It's not a problem."

"One hand?" I say.

"The left one." Clarissa bites the corner of her mouth. "I mean she's right-handed, so to speak."

"Where'd it go?" I have both of mine. Everybody I know has both of theirs. I of course know people suffer such things—all the time. It shouldn't be a shock that Paul romances a girl with only one arm. But it is. (Never wonder what else can happen next. Much can.)

"We didn't get into it." Clarissa shakes her head, her foot still tucked away in plain sight into Thom's man department. "I guess they met on-line. But she actually works where he works, whatever that's called. The card company." (She knows what it's called.)

I say, "Maybe she works in the sympathy-card department."

Clarissa smiles an unfriendly smile and gives me one of her long looks that means everything I say is wrong. "A lot of people who write sympathy cards have disabilities themselves. She did tell us that—apropos of nothing. They didn't stick around that long. I think he wants to surprise you." She prisses her lips and goes back to her Orvis catalog.

Clarissa, who's my only earthly ally, if provoked in front of Thom, will jump to Paul's and one-arm Jill's defense for anything inappropriate in my body language, facial expression, much less my word-of-mouth. Never mind that she thinks it's all the strangest of strange. Paul may have hired an actor to bring home just to drive us all crazy. It's in his realm. Otto in a skirt.

"They said they were going to 'pick up a motel room.'" Clarissa's very businessy-sarcastic now because she wants to be—but I can't be. "They're going to Ann's for dinner." (First names only here.) I don't want to tell her I've invited Ann for Thanksgiving and hear from her what an insanely bad idea it is. "Surprises all around. She'll flip." Clarissa executes a perfectly glorious smile that says, I wish I could be there.

Words, I find, are not in full abundance. "Okay," I say.

"*We're* going to Atlantic City, by the way." She extends a hand over onto velvety Thom's singleted shoulder and rolls her eyes upward (in mockery). Thom seems confused—that so much could go on in one family in so short a period of time without any of it being about him. "We'll be back in the morning." More woogling, this time at Trump's. "I'm going to try my luck at roulette." She pats Thom's tawny, muscular thigh right where the shark took its nip or where he rappelled down the face of Mount whatever. Maybe they'll see the Calderons at the free high-roller buffet.

"Then I think I'll just go off and try to sell a house." I grin insincerely.

"Okay now, is that what you do?" Thom blinks at me. The widely separated corners of his mouth flicker with a smile that may be amused or may be amazed but is not interested.

"Pretty much."

"Great. Do you do commercial or just houses?" His smile's tending toward being amused. I'm sure his father did commercial in Rio and printed his own currency.

"Mostly residential," I say. "I can always use a mid-career salesman, if you're interested. I have a Tibetan monk working for me right now who's maybe going to leave. You'd have to take the state test, and I get half of everything. I'd put you on salary for six months. You'd probably do great."

Amazement. His teeth are truly enormous and white and unafflicted by worry. He likes flashing them as proof of invulnerability.

"I've got my hands pretty full at the Down's center," he says, smiling self-beknightedly.

"Do those little devils really stay on a horse without being wired on?"

"You bet they do," Thom says.

"Does riding horses cure Down's syndrome?"

"There isn't any *cure*." Clarissa smacks shut her Orvis catalog and retracts her heels from Thom's scrotal zone. It's time to go. This is her house, too, she wants me to understand—though it isn't. It's mine. "You know it doesn't cure Down's syndrome, you cluck." She starts gathering dishes and ferrying them noisily to the sink. "You should come over and volunteer, Frank. They'll let you ride a pony if you want to. No wires." Her back is to me. Thom's gazing at me wondrously, as if to say, Yep, you're getting a good scolding now, I'm sorry it has to happen, but it does.

"Great," I say jovially, and give Thom a chummy grin that says we men are always in the line of female fire. I pop the spindled listing sheets in my palm—three times for emphasis. "You kids have yourselves some fun pissing Thom's money away."

"Yeah, we will," Clarissa says from the sink. "We'll think of you. Paul has a time capsule with him. I almost forgot. He wants us to put something in it and bury it someplace." She's smirking as she rinses cups and doesn't turn around. Though this occasions a troubled look from Thom, as if Paul's a sad soul who's made all our lives one endless hell on earth.

"That'll be great," I say.

Clarissa says, "What're you going to put in it?"

"I'll have to think. Maybe I'll put in my Michigan diploma, with a listing sheet. 'Once there was a time when people lived in things called houses—or in their parents' houses.' You can put your old—"

"I'll think about me," Clarissa says. She knows what I was about to suggest. Her nose stud.

I consider confessing that I've invited her mother for Thanksgiving—just to discourage Thom from coming. But I'm late and don't have time for an argument. "Don't forget you're the acting lady of the house tomorrow. I'm depending on you to be a gracious hostess."

"Who's the husband?"

"I hope you sell a house," Thom says. "Is that what you want to do? My dad was in real estate. He sold big office buildings. He—" I'm on my way to the front door and miss the rest.

9

Up again, old heart. Everything good is on the highway. In this
instance, New Jersey Route 35, the wide mercantile pike up
Barnegat Neck, whose distinct little beach municipalities—Sea-
Clift, Seaside Park, Seaside Heights, Ortley Beach—pass my
window, indistinguishable. For practical-legal reasons, each boro
has its separate tax collector, deeds registry, zoning board, police,
fire, etc., and local patriots defend the separate characters as if
Bay Head was Norway and Lavallette was France. Though I, a
relative newcomer (eight years), experience these beach townlettes
as one long, good place-by-an-ocean and sell houses gainfully in
each. And particularly on this cold, clearing morning when it's
reassuring as a fifties memory all up the Shore, I thank my lucky
stars for landing me where they did.

Christmas decorations are going up in the morning sunshine.
The streets crew is stringing red-and-green plastic bunting to
the intersection wires, and swagging the firemen's memorial at
Boro Hall. Candy-cane soldiers have appeared on the median
strip, and a crèche with bearded, more authentic burnoose-clad
Semites is now up on the lawn of Our Lady of Effectual Mercy.
No revolving lights are in place. A banner announcing a Cadillac
raffle and a Las Vegas Night stands on the lawn by the announcements case offering CONFESSIONS ANYTIME.

In Frederick Schruer's *History of Garden State Development: A Portrait in Contrasts, Conflicts and Chaos* (Rutgers, 1984), Sea-Clift is favorably referred to as the "Classic New Jersey Shore Town-lette." Which means that owing to the beach and the crowds, we're not a true suburb, though there're plenty of pastel split-levels on streets named Poseidon, Oceania and Pelagic. Neither are we exactly a fishing village, though flounder fishermen and day charters leave from the bayside wharf. We're also not exactly a resort town, since most of the year tourists are gone and the steel Fun Pier's ancient and the rides closed for being life-threatening. There's not even that much to do in summer except float along in the crowds, hang out in the motel or on the beach, eat, drink, rent a boogie board or stare off.

There *is* a mix, which has encouraged a positivist small-businessman spirit that's good for real estate. The 2,263 year-rounders (many are south Italians with enormous families) run things, own most of the businesses, staff the traffic court, police and fire—which makes Sea-Clift more like Secaucus than the ritzier enclaves north of us. Our town fathers long ago understood that xenophobia, while natural to the species, will get you broke quick in a beach town, and so have fostered a not so much *"Mia casa é tua casa"* spirit as a more level-headed "Your vacation is my financial viability" expedience, which draws eight jillion tourists to our summer streets, plus a stream of new semi-affluent buy-ins from Perth Amboy and Metuchen, all of it spiced with Filipinos, Somalians and hard-working Hondurans (who come for the schools) to brew up a tranquil towny heterogeneity that looks modern on paper without feeling much different from the way things have always felt.

For me, transacting the business of getting people situated under roofs and into bearable mortgages and out again, Sea-Clift couldn't be a better place—real estate being one of our few year-round business incubators. People are happy to see my face, know that I'm thriving and will be there when the time comes, but still don't have to have me to dinner. In that way, I'm a lot like a funeral home.

Very little's abuzz and about today in spite of Thanksgiving being tomorrow. A few home owners down the residential streets are employed in pre-holiday cleanup, getting on ladders, opening the crawl space for termite checks, putting up storms, spooling hoses, closing off spigots, winterizing the furnace. In a town where everybody comes in the summer, now's when many year-rounders take their three-day trips—to Niagara and the Vietnam Memorial—since the town's theirs and empty and can be abandoned without a worry. Which doesn't make *now* a bad selling season, since niche buyers come down when the throngs are gone, armed with intent and real money to spend.

Of course, now's when any prudent newcomer—a software kingpin with new development dollars—would notice all that we *don't* offer: any buildings of historical significance (there are no large buildings at all); no birthplaces of famous inventors, astronauts or crooners. No Olmsted parks. No fall foliage season, no sister city in Italy or even Germany. No bookstores except one dirty one. Mark Twain, Helen Keller or Edmund Wilson never said or did anything memorable here. There's no Martin Luther

King Boulevard, no stations on the Underground Railroad (or any railroad) and no golden era anyone can recollect. This must be true for plenty of towns.

There is, however, little teen life, so car thefts and break-ins are rare. You can smoke in our restaurants (when they're open). The Gulf Stream moderates our climate. Our drinking water's vaguely salty, but you get used to it. We were never a temperance town, so you can always find a cocktail. College Board scores match the state average. Two Miss Teenage New Jerseys ('41 and '75) hail from here. We stage an interesting Frank Sinatra impersonator contest in the spring. Our town boundary abuts a state park. Cable's good. And for better or worse, the hermit crab is our official town crustacean—though there's disagreement over how large the proposed statue should be. You could also say that for a town founded by enterprising Main Line land speculators on the bedrock principles of buy low/sell high, we've exceeded our municipal mission with relatively few downsides. Since we're bounded by ocean and bay, there're few places where planning problems could ever arise. Water is our de facto open space plus a good population stabilizer. For a time, I sat on the Dollars For Doers Strike Council, but we never did much besides lower parking fines, pass a good-neighbor ordinance so tourists could reach the beach via private property, and give the Fun Pier a rehabilitation abatement the owners never used. Our development committee extended feelers to a culinary arts academy seeking growing room—though we didn't have any. There was a citizen's initiative for a new all-cement promenade, but it failed, and for establishing a dinosaur park, though we hadn't had any dinosaurs and couldn't legally claim one. Still, as old-timey, low-ceiling and down-market as Sea-Clift is, most people who live here like it that way, like it that we're not a destination resort but are faithful to our original charter as a place an ordinary wage earner comes for three days, then beats it home again—a town with just a life, not a lifestyle.

I make a stop by my office to pick up the Surf Road keys. Inside, it's shadowy and dank, my and Mike's desktops empty of important documents. Mike's computer (I don't own one) beams out his smiling picture of himself and the Dalai Lama, which coldly illuminates his Gipper portrait and his prayer flags on the wall. The office has a stinging balsam scent (mingled with a pizza odor through the wall) from the one time Mike burned incense in the john—which I put a stop to. The house keys, with white tags, are on the key rack. I have a quick piss in our bare-bones bathroom. Though when I come out, I see through the window that a car's stopped out front by my Suburban, a tan Lincoln Town Car with garish gold trim and New York plates. Since it's too early for a Chicago-style pizza, these are doubtless showcase shoppers eye-balling the house snapshots in the window. They'll be scared off when they see me, sensing I might drag them in and bore them to death. But not today. I frown out at the car—I can't see who's inside, but no one climbs out—then I go back in the bathroom, close the door, stand and wait thirty seconds. And when I come out, as if by magic the space is empty, the Lincoln gone, the morning, or what's left of it, returned to my uses.

The client for my Surf Road showing is a welding contractor down from Parsippany, Mr. Clare Suddruth, with whom I've already done critical real estate spadework the past three weeks, which means I've driven him around Sea-Clift, Ortley Beach, Seaside Heights, etc., on what I think of as a lay-of-the-land tour, during which the client gets to see everything for sale in his price range, endures no pressure from me, begins to think of me as his friend, since I'm spending all this time with nothing promised, comes after a while to gab about his life—his failures, treacheries, joys—lets me stand him some lunches, senses we're cut out of the same rough fustian and share many core values (the economy, Vietnam, the need to buy American though the Japs build a better product, the Millennium non-event and how much we'd hate to be young now). We probably *don't* agree about the current election hijacking, but probably *do* see eye-to-eye about what constitutes a good house and how most buyers are better off setting aside their original price targets in favor of stretching their pocketbooks, getting beyond the next dollar threshold—where the houses you *really* want are as plentiful as hoe handles—and doing a little temporary belt-tightening while the economy's ebb and flow keeps your boat on course and steaming ahead.

If this seems like bait-and-switch hucksterism, or just old-fashioned grinning, bamboozling faithlessness, let me assure you it's not. All any client ever has to say is, "All right, Bascombe, how you see this really isn't how I see it. I want to stay *inside*, not outside, my price window, exactly like I said when I sat down at your desk." If that's your story, I'm ready to sell you what you want—if I have it. All the rest—the considered, heartfelt exchange of views, the finding of common ground, the beginning of true (if ephemeral) comradeship based on time spent inside a stuffy automobile—all *that* I'd do with the Terminix guy. A person has only to know his mind about things, which isn't as usual as it seems. I view my role as residential agent as having a lay therapist's fiduciary responsibility (not so different from being a Sponsor). And that responsibility is to leave the client better than I found him—or her. Many citizens set out to buy a house because of an indistinct yearning, for which an actual house was never the right solution to begin with and may only be a quick (and expensive) fix that briefly anchors and stabilizes them, never touches their deeper need, but puts them in the poorhouse anyway. Most client contacts never even eventuate in a sale and, like most human exposures, end in one encounter. Which isn't to say that the road *toward* a house sale is a road without benefit or issue. A couple of the best friends I've made in the real estate business are people I never sold a house to and who, by the end of our time together, I didn't *want* to sell a house to (though I still would've). It is another, if unheralded, version of the perfect real estate experience: Everyone does his part, but no house changes hands. If there weren't, now and then, such positive outside-the-envelope transactions, I'd be the first to say the business wouldn't be worth the time of day.

I swing off Ocean Avenue at the closed-for-the-season Custom Condom Shoppe ("We build 'em to your specs") and motor down toward the beach along the narrow gravel lane of facing, identical white and pastel summer "chalets," of which there must be twenty in this row, with ten identical parallel lanes stacked neighborhood-like to the north and south, each named for a New Jersey shorebird—Sandpiper, Common Tern, Plover (I'm driving down Cormorant Court). Here is where most of our weekly renters—Memorial Day to Columbus Day—spend their happy family vacations, cheek-to-cheek with hundreds of other souls opting for the same little vernal joys. At several of these (all empty now), more pre-winter fix-up is humming along—hip roofs being patched, swollen screen doors planed, brick foundation piers regrouted after years of salt air. Three of these chalet developments lie in the Boro of Sea-Clift, where I own ten units and, with Mike's help, manage thirty more. These summer chalets and their more primitive ancestors have been an attractive, affordable feature of beach life on south Barnegat Neck since the thirties. Five-hundred-square-foot interiors, two tiny bedrooms, a simple bath, beaverboard walls, a Pullman kitchen, no yard, grass, shrubbery, no AC or TV, electric wall heaters and stove, yard-sale decor, no parking except in front, no privacy from the next chalet ten feet away, crude plumbing, tinted, iron-rich water, occasional gas and sulfur fumes from an unspecified source—and you can't drive vacationers away. A certain precinct in the

American soul will put up with anything—other people's screaming kids, exotic smells, unsavory neighbors, unsocialized pets, high rents (I get $750 a week), car traffic, foot traffic, unsound construction, yard seepage—just to *be* and be able to brag to the in-laws back in Parma that they were "a three-minute walk to the beach." Which every unit is.

Of course, another civic point of view—the Dollars For Doers Strike Council—would love to see every chalet bulldozed and the three ten-acre parcels turned into an outlet mall or a parking structure. But complicated, restrictive covenants unique to Sea-Clift require every chalet owner to agree before the whole acreage can be transferred. And many owners are among our oldest Sea-Clift pioneers, who came as children and never forgot the fun they had and couldn't wait to own a chalet, or six, themselves and start making their retirement nut off the renters—the people they had once been. Most of the people I manage for are absentees, the sons and daughters of those pioneers, and now live in Connecticut and Michigan and would pawn their MBA's before they'd sign away "Dad's cottage." (None of them, of course, would spend two minutes inside any of these sad little shanties themselves, which is when I get in the picture, and am happy to be.)

These days, I do my best to upgrade the ten chalets I own, plus all the ones I can talk my owners into sprucing up. Occasionally I let a struggling writer in need of quiet space to finish his *Moby-Dick*, or some poor frail in retirement from love, stay through the winter in return for indoor repairs (these guests never stay long due to the very seclusion they think they want).

Looked at differently, these chalets would be a perfect place for a homicide.

Three Honduran fix-up crews (all legal, all my employees) are at work as I drive down Cormorant Court. From the roof of #11, one of these men (José, Pepe, Esteban—I'm not sure which), suited up in knee pads and roped to a standpipe, replacing shingles, rises to his feet on the steep green asphalt roof-pitch and into the clean, cold November sky, leans crazily against his restraint line and performs a sweeping hats-off Walter Raleigh-type bow right out into space, a big *amigo* grin on his wispy-mustachioed face. I give back an embarrassed wave, since I'm not comfortable being *Don Francisco* to my employees. The other workers break into laughing and jeering calls that he (or I) is a *puta* and beneath contempt.

Clare Suddruth is already out front of the fancy beach house he thinks he might like to buy. Surf Road is a sandy lane starting at the ocean end of Cormorant Court and running south a quarter-mile. If it were extended, which it never will be due to the same shoreline ordinances that infuriate the Feensters, it would run into and become Poincinet Road a mile farther on.

Clare stands hands-in-pockets in the brisk autumn breeze. He's dressed in a short zippered khaki work jacket and khaki trousers that announce his station as a working stiff who's made good in a rough-and-tumble world. The house Clare's interested in is—in design and residential spirit—not so different from my own and was built during the blue-sky development era of the late seventies, before laws got serious and curtailed construction, driving prices into deep space. In my personal view, 61 Surf Road is not the house a man like Clare should think of, so of course he *is* thinking of it—a lesson we realtors ignore at our peril. Number 61 is a mostly-vertical, isosceles-angled, many-windowed, many sky-lighted, grayed redwood post-and-beam, with older solar panels and inside an open plan of not two, not three, but six separate "living levels," representing the architect's concern for interior diversity and cheap spatial mystery. More than it's right for Clare, it's perfect for a young sitcom writer with discretionary scratch and who wants to work from home. Asking's a million nine.

How the house "shows," and what the client sees from the curb—if there was a curb—are only two mute, segmented, retractable brown garage doors facing the road, two skimpy windows on the "back," and an unlocatable front door, through which you go right up to a "great room" where the good life commences. I don't much like the place since it broadcasts bland domiciliary arrogance, typical of the period. The house either has no front because no one's welcome; or else because everything important faces the sea and it's not your house anyway, why should you be interested?

Clare's a tall, bony, loose-kneed sixty-five-year-old, a bristle-haired Gyrine Viet vet with a thin, tanned jawline, creased Clint Eastwood features and the seductive voice of a late-night jazz DJ. In my view, he'd be more at home in a built-out Greek revival or a rambling California split-level. "Thornton Wilders," we call these in our trade, and we don't have any down here. Spring Lake and Brielle are your tickets for that dream.

But Clare's recent life's saga—I've heard all about it—has led him down new paths in search of new objectives. In that way, he is much like me.

Clare's standing beside my Realty-Wise sign—red block letters on a white field plus the phone number, no www, no virtual tours, no talking houses, just reliable people leading other people toward a feeling of finality and ultimate rightness. Clare turns and faces the house as I drive up, as if to allow that he's been waiting but time doesn't mean much to him. He's driven down in one of his company's silver panel trucks, which sits in the driveway, ONLY CONNECT WELDING painted in flowing blue script. His schoolteacher wife dreamed it up, Clare told me. "Something out of a book." Though Clare's no mutton-fisted underachiever who married up. He won a Silver Star with a gallantry garnish in Nam, came out a major and did the EE route at Stevens Tech. He and Estelle bought a house and had two quick kids in the seventies, while Clare was on the upward track with Raytheon. But then out of the blue, he decided the laddered life was a rat-race and took over his dad's welding business in Troy Hills and changed its name to something he and Estelle liked. Clare's what we call a "senior boomer," someone who's done the course creditably, set aside substantial savings, gotten his kids set up at a safe distance, experienced appreciation in the dollar value of his family home (mortgage retired), and now wants a nicer life before he gets too decrepit to take out the garbage. What these clients generally decide to buy varies from a freestanding condo (we have few in Sea-Clift), to a weekend home near the water (these we have aplenty), to a "houseboat on the

Seine"—aka something you park at a marina. Or else they choose a real honest-to-God house like this one Clare's staring up at: Turn the key, dial up the Jacuzzi. The owners, the Doolittles— currently in Boca Grande—detected the tech-market slowdown in September, were ready to shift assets into municipals and conceivably gold and are just waiting to back their money out. So far, no takers.

The other characteristic on Clare's buyer's profile is that three years ago—by his own candid recounting (as usual)—he fell in love with somebody who wasn't exactly his wife, but was, in fact, a fresh hire at the welding company—someone named Bitsy or Betsy or Bootsy. Not surprisingly, big domestic disruptions followed. The kids chose sides. Several loyal employees quit in disgust when "things" came out in the open. Welding damn near ceased. Clare and Estelle acted civilly ("She was the easy part"). A sad divorce ensued. A marriage to the younger Bitsy, Betsy, Bootsy hastily followed—a new life that never felt right from the instant they got to St. Lucia. A semi-turbulent year passed. A young wife grew restive—"Just like the goddamn *Eagles* song," Clare said. Betsy/Bitsy cut off all her hair, threw her nice new clothes away, decided to go back to school, figured out she wanted to become an archaeologist and study Meso-American something or other. Somehow she'd discovered she was brilliant, got herself admitted to the University of Chicago and left New Jersey with the intention of morphing her and Clare's spring- fall union into something rare, adaptable, unusual and modern— that he could pay for.

Only, at the end of year one, Estelle learned she had multiple sclerosis (she'd moved to Port Jervis to her sister's), news that galvanized Clare into seeing the fog lift, regaining his senses, divorcing his young student wife. ("A big check gets written, but who cares?") He moved Estelle back down to Parsippany and began devoting every resource and minute to her and her happiness, stunned that he'd never fully realized how lucky he was just to know someone like her. And with time now precious, there was none of it he cared to dick around with. (As heartening and *sui generis* as Clare's story sounds, in the real estate profession it's not that unusual.)

Which is when Sea-Clift came into play, since Estelle had vacationed here as a child and always adored it and hoped. . . . Nothing now was too good for her. Plus, in Clare's estimation our little townlette was probably a place the two of them would die in before the world fucked it up. (He may be wrong.) I've driven him past thirty houses in three weeks. Many seemed "interesting and possible." Most didn't. Number 61 was the only one that halfway caught his fancy, since the inside was already fitted with a nursing home's worth of shiny disabled apparatus, including—despite all the levels—a mahogany side-stair elevator for the coming dark days of disambulation. Clare told me that if he likes it when he sees it, he'll buy it as is and give it to Estelle—who's currently holding her own, with intermittent symptoms—as a one-year re-wedding/Thanksgiving present. It makes a pretty story.

"Dry as my Uncle Chester's bones out here, Frank," Clare says in his parched but sonorous voice, extending me a leathery hand. Clare has the odd habit of giving me his left hand to shake. Something about severed tendons from a "helo" crash causing acute pain, etc., etc. I always feel awkward about which hand to extend, but it's over fast. Though he has a vise grip even with his "off" hand, which fires up my own Bob Butts injuries from last night.

Clare produces his steady, eyes-creased smile that projects impersonal pleasure, then crosses his arms and turns to look again at 61 Surf Road. I'm about to say—but don't—that the worst droughts are the ones where we occasionally get a little rain, like yesterday, so that nobody really takes the whole drought idea seriously, then you end up ignoring the aquifer until disaster looms. But Clare's thinking about this house, which is a good sign. The color listing brochure I'm holding is ready to be proffered before we go in.

Down Surf Road (like my road, there are only five houses), a bearded young man in yellow rubber coveralls is scrubbing the sides of a white fiberglass fishing boat that's up on a trailer, using an extended aluminum hose brush—a blue BUSH-CHENEY sign stuck up in his weedy little yard. From back up Cormorant Court I hear the sharp *shree-scree* of a saber saw whanging through board filaments, followed by the satisfying bops of hammers hitting nails in rapid succession. My unexpected *jefe* presence has set my Hondurans into motion. Though it's only a game. Soon they'll be climbing down for their pre-lunch marijuana break, after which the day will go quickly.

The cold seaside air out here has a fishy and piney sniff to it, which feels hopeful in spite of the unpredictable November sky. My Thanksgiving worries have now scattered like seabirds. A squad of pigeons wheels above, as far beyond a jet contrail—high, high, high—heads out to sea toward Europe. I am rightly placed here, doing the thing I apparently do best—grounded, my duties conferring a pleasant, self-actualizing invisibility—the self as perfect *instrument*.

"Frank, tell me what this house'll bring in a summer?" Clare's mind is clicking merits-demerits.

I assume he's talking about rent and not a quick flip. "Three thousand a week. Maybe more."

He furrows his brow, puts a hand to his chin and rests it there—the standard gesture of contemplation, familiar to General MacArthur and Jack Benny. It is both grave and comical. Clearly it is Clare's practiced look of public seriousness. My instant guess is we'll never see inside #61. When clients are motivated, they don't stand out in the road talking about the house as if it'd be a good idea to tear it down. When clients are motivated, they can't wait to get in the door and start liking everything. I'm, of course, often wrong.

"Boy, oh boy." Clare shakes his head over modernity. "Three G's."

"Pays your taxes and then some," I say, breeze waffling my listing brochure and stiffening my digits.

"So who all's moving down to Sea-Clift now, Frank?" More standing, more staring. This is not a new question.

"Pretty much it's a mix, Clare," I say. "People driven out of the Hamptons. And there's some straight-out investment beginning. Our floor hasn't risen as fast as the rest of the Shore. No big springboard sales yet. Topping wars haven't gotten this far down. It's still a one-dimensional market. That'll change, even with rates starting to creep. A really good eight-hundred-thousand-dollar house is already hard to find." I take a glance at my sheet, as if all this crucial data's printed there and he should read it. I'm guessing coded chalk talk will appeal to Clare-the-small-businessman, make him think I'm not trying very hard to sell him the Doolittles' house, but am just his reliable resource for relevant factual info to make the world seem less a sinking miasma. Which isn't wrong.

"I guess they're not making any more ocean-front, are they?"

"If they could, they would." In fact, I know people who'd love to try: interests who'd like to "reclaim" Barnegat Bay and turn it into a Miracle Mile or a racino. "Fifty percent of us already live within fifty miles of the ocean, Clare. Ocean County's the St. Petersburg of the East."

"How's *your* business, Frank?" We're side-by-side—me a half step behind—staring at silent multi-this, multi-that #61.

"Good, Clare. It's good. Real estate's always good by the ocean. Inventory's my problem. If I had a house like this every day, I'd be richer than I am."

Clare at this instant lets go a small, barely audible (but audible) fart, the sound of a strangled birdcall from offstage. It startles me, and I can't help staring at its apparent point of departure, the seat of Clare's khakis, as if blue smoke might appear. It's the ex-Marine in Clare that makes such nonchalant emissions unre-markable (to him), while letting others know how intransigent a man he is and would be—in a love affair, in a business deal, in a divorce or a war. Possibly my reference to being rich forced an involuntary disparaging gesture from his insides.

"Tell me this now, Frank." Clare's stuffed both hands in his khaki side pockets. He's wearing brown-and-beige tu-tone suede leisure sneakers of the sort you buy at shoe outlets or off the sale rack at big-box stores and that look comfortable as all get out, though I'd never buy a pair, because they're what *doozies* wear (our old term from Lonesome Pines), or else men who don't care if they look like doozies. The Clint Eastwood look has a bit of doozie in it. Old Clint might wear a pair himself, so uncaring would he be of the world's opinion. "What kind of climate have we got, I mean for buying a house?"

I hear my workers up Cormorant Court begin laughing and their hammering come to a halt. "*¡Hom-bre!*" I hear a falsetto voice shout. "*Qué flaco y feo.*" One needn't wonder. Something involving somebody's "chilé."

"I'd say that's a mixed picture, too, Clare." He already knows everything I know, because I've told him, but he wants me to think he takes what we're doing seriously—which means to me this is a waste of my time, which I in fact *do* take seriously. Clare came into the picture saying he was ready to buy a house sight unseen, maximize the quality-of-life remaining for his dear-stricken-betrayed-but-timeless love Estelle. Only, like most humans, when it gets down to the cold nut cutting, it's do-re-mi his heart breaks over.

"Money's cheap down here, Clare," I say, "and the mortgage people have got some interesting product enhancements to shift weight toward the back end—for a price, of course. Like I said, our inventory's down, which tends to firm up values. Most sales go for asking. You read the technology sector's ready to cycle down. Rates'll probably squirt up after Christmas. You'd hate to buy at the top with no short-term resale potential, but you can't take your cue from the wind, I guess. We saw a forty percent price increase in two years. I don't tell clients to go with their hearts, Clare. I don't know much about hearts."

Clare gazes at me, brown eyes squinted near-to-closing. I've probably said too much and strayed over into sensitive territory by referring to the heart. This sleepy-eyed look is a recognition and a warning. Though I've found that in business, a quick veer into the soft tissue of the personal can confuse things in a good way. Clare, after all, has given me a giant earful—probably he does everyone. He's just suddenly gotten leery about forging an unwanted connection with me. But ditto. I like Clare, but I want him to spend his money and feel good about giving part of it to me.

"Can I show you something, Frank?" Clare peers down at his doozie tu-tones as if they were doing his thinking for him.

"Absolutely."

"It won't take a minute." He's already moving—in a bit of a slinking, pelvis-forward gait—along the driveway toward the back of the Doolittles', between it and the next-door neighbor's, a dull two-storey A-frame that's boarded for the winter and has a dead look: basement windows blocked with pink Styrofoam, plants covered with miniature wooden A-frames of their own, the basement door masked with plyboard screwed into the foundation. Winter gales are expected.

"I took a walk around here while I was waiting," Clare's saying as he walks, but in a more intimate voice, as if he doesn't want the wrong people hearing this. I'm following, my listing materials stuffed in my windbreaker pocket. The Doolittles' house, I can see, is in need of upkeep. The side basement door is weathered and grayed, the veneer shredded at the bottom. A scimitar of glass has dropped out of a basement window and shattered on the concrete footing. Something metal is whapping in the wind above the soffits—a loose TV cable or a gutter strap—though I can't see anything. I wonder if the solar panels even work. The house could do with a new owner and some knowledgeable attention. The Doolittles, who're plastic surgeons in joint practice, have been spending their discretionary income elsewhere. Though they may soon have less of it.

Clare leads around to the "front" of the house, between the windowed concrete basement wall and the ten-foot sand dune that's covered with dry, sparse-sprouted sea rocket from the summer. The dune—which is natural and therefore inviolable—is what keeps the house from having a full ocean view from the living room, and probably what's retarded its sale since September. I've put into the brochure that "imagination" (money) could be dedicated to the living room level (moving it to the third floor) and "open up spectacular vistas."

"Okay, look at this down here." Clare, almost whispering, bends over, hands on his knees to designate what he means me to see. "See that?" His voice has grown grave.

I move in beside him, kneel by his knee on the gravelly foundation border and stare right where he's pointing at an outward-curving section of pale gray concrete that's visible beneath the sill and the footing. It is one of the deep-driven piers to which the well-named Doolittles' house is anchored and made fast so that at times of climatological stress the whole schmeer isn't washed or blown or seismically destabilized and propelled straight out to sea like an ark.

"See that?" Clare says, breathing out a captured breath. He gets down on both knees beside me like a scientist and brings his face right to the concrete pillar as if he means to smell it, then puts his index finger to the curved surface.

"What is it?" I say. I see nothing, though I'm assuming there *is* something and it can't be good.

"These piers are poured far away from here, Frank," Clare says as if in confidence. "Sometimes Canada. Sometimes upstate. The Binghamton area." He employs his finger to scratch at the transparent lacquer painted on the pier's exterior. "If you pour your forms too early in the spring, or if you pour them when the humidity's extremely high . . . well, you know what happens." Clare's creased face turns to me—we're very close here—and smiles a closed-mouth gotcha smile.

"What?"

"They crack. They crack right away," Clare says darkly. He has a pale sliver of pinkish scar right along the border of his

Brillo-pad hairline. A vicious war wound, possibly, or else something discretionary from his second marriage. "If your manufacturer isn't too scrupulous he doesn't notice," Clare says. "And if he's unscrupulous he notices but then has this silicone sealer painted on and sells it to you anyway. And if your home builder or your GC isn't paying attention, or if he's been paid not to pay attention or if his foreman happens to be of a certain nationality, then these piers get installed without anybody saying anything. And when the work gets inspected, this kind of defect— and it *is* a serious defect and oughta show up—it might be possible for it not to get noticed, if you get my drift. Then your house gets built, and it stands up real well for about fifteen years. But because it's on the ocean, salt and moisture go to work on it. And suddenly—though it isn't sudden, of course—Hurricane Frank blows up, a high tide comes in, the force of the water turns savage and Bob's your uncle." Clare turns his gaze back to the pier, where we're crouched like cavemen behind the musty quicklime–smelling Doolittle house, which is built, I see, on much worse than shifting sand. It's built on shitty pilings. "These piers, Frank. I mean"—Clare pinches his nose with distaste and home-owner pity, pressing his lips together—"I can see cracks here, and this is just the four to five inches showing. These people have real problems, unless you know a sucker who'll buy it sight unseen or get an inspector who needs a seeing-eye dog."

Clare's breath in these close quarters is milky stale-coffee breath and makes me realize I'm freezing and wishing I was two hundred miles from here.

"It's a problem. Okay." I stare at the innocent-looking little curve of gray pier surface, seeing nothing amiss. The thought that Clare's full of shit and that this is a softening-up ploy for a low-ball offer naturally occurs to me, as does the idea that since I can't see the crack, I don't have to bear the guilty knowledge that adheres to it. A thin file of stalwart ants is scuttering around the dusty foundation, taking in the air before the long subterranean winter.

"A problem. *Definitely*," Clare says solemnly. "I was raised in a tract home, Frank. I've seen bad workmanship all my life." He and I are straggling to our feet. I hear youthful boy-and-girl voices from the beach, beyond the dune bunker.

"What can you do about a problem like that, Clare?" I dust off my knees, stuffing the listing sheet farther down in my pocket, since it won't be needed. I experienced a brief stab of panic when Clare revealed the cracked pier, as if this house is mine and I'm who's in deep shit. Only now, a little airy-headed from bending down, then standing up too fast, I feel pure exhilaration and a thrumming sense of well-being that this is not my house, that my builder was a board-certified UVa architect, not some shade-tree spec builder (like Tommy Benivalle, Mike's best friend) with a clipboard and some plan-book blueprints, and who's in cahoots with the cement trade, the Teamsters, the building inspectors and city hall. Your typical developer, Jersey to Oregon. "I'm fine." These murmured words for some reason escape my lips. "I'm just fine."

"Okay, there's things you can do," Clare's saying. "They're not cheap." He's looking closely at me, into my eyes, his fingers pinching up a welt of nylon on my windbreaker sleeve. "You all right, old boy?"

I hear this. I also hear again the sound of youthful boy-girl voices beyond the dune. They emerge from a single source, which is the cold wind. "You look a little green, my friend," Clare's friendly voice says. I'm experiencing another episode. Conceivably it's only a deferred result of my floor struggle with Bob Butts last night. Yet for a man who hates to hope, my state of health is not as reliable as I'd hoped.

"Stood up too fast," I say, my cheeks cold and rubbery, scalp crawly, my fingers tingling.

"Chemicals," Clare says. "No telling what the hell they spray back here. The same thing's in sarin gas is in d-Con, I hear."

"I guess." I'm fuzzy, just keeping myself upright.

"Let's grab some O_2," Clare says, and with his bony left fist begins hauling me roughly up the dune, my shoes sinking in sand, my balance a bit pitched forward, my neck breaking a sweat. "Maybe you got vertigo," Clare says as he guys me up toward the top, his long legs doing the work for my two. "Men our age get that. It goes away."

"How old are you?" I say, being dragged.

"Sixty-seven."

"I'm fifty-five." I feel ninety-five.

"Good grief."

"What's the matter?" Sand's in my shoes and feels cool. His doozie loafers must be loaded, too.

"I must look a lot younger than I am."

"I was thinking you did," I say.

"Who knows how old anybody is, Frank?" We're now at the top. Lavender flat-surfaced ocean stretches beyond the wide high-tide beach. A smudge of gray-brown crud hangs at the horizon. Breeze seems to stream straight through my ears and gives me a shiver. For late November, I'm again dressed way too lightly. (I believed I'd be inside.) "I look at twenty-five-year-olds and somebody tells me they're fifteen," Clare natters on. "I look at thirty-five-year-olds who look fifty. I give up."

"Me, too." I'm already feeling a bit replenished, my heart quivering from our quick ascent.

Thirty yards out onto the beach and taking no notice of our appearance—legionnaires topping a rise—a group of teens, eight or nine of them, is occupied by a spirited volleyball game, the white orb rising slowly into the sky, one side shouting, "Mine!" "Set, seeeet-it!" "Bridget-Bridget! *Yours!*" The boys are tall, swimmer-lanky and blond; the girls semi-beautiful, tanned, rugged, strong-thighed. All are in shorts, sweaters, sweatshirts and are barefoot. These are the local kids, gone away to Choate and Milton, who've left home behind as lowly townie-ville but are back now, dazzlingly, with their old friends—the privileged few, enjoying the holidays as Yale and Dartmouth early-admissions dates grow near. Too bad my kids aren't that age instead of "grown." Possibly I could do my part better now. Though possibly not.

"You back in working order?" Clare pretends to be observing the volleyballers, who go on paying us no attention. We are the invisibles—like their parents.

"Thanks," I say. "Sorry."

"Vertigo," Clare says again, and gives his long over-large ear a stiff grinding with the heel of his hand. Clare clearly likes the prospect from up here. It's the view one would get from a "reimagined" floor three of the big-but-compromised Doolittle house behind us. Maybe his mind will change. Maybe cracked piers aren't so troublesome. Things change with perspective.

"You're from California, you don't count," a girl volleyballer says breezily into the breeze.

"*I* count," a boy answers. "I absolutely count. *Ro*-tate, *ro*-tate."

"Could you entertain a quasi-philosophical question, Frank?" Clare's now squatted atop the dune and has scooped up a handful of sand, as though assaying it, sampling its texture.

"Well—"

"Pertains to real estate. Don't worry. It's not about my sex life. Or yours. That's not philosophical, is it? That's Greek tragedy."

"Not always." I am on the alert for some heart-to-heart I lack the stomach for.

Clare half closes his creased submariner's eye at the brown horizon murk then spits down into the sand he's just released. "Do you imagine, Frank, that anything could happen in this country to make *normal* just not be possible?" He continues facing away, facing east, as if addressing an analyst seated behind him. "*I* actually tend to think nothing of that nature can really happen. Too many cheeks and balances. We've all of us manufactured reality so well, we're so solid in our views, that nothing can really change. You know? Drop a bomb, we bounce back. What hurts us makes us stronger. D'you believe that?" Clare lowers his strong chin, then cranks his skeptical gaze up at me, wanting an answer in kind. His kind. His kind of stagy seriousness.

Semper Fi, Hué 'n Tet, the never-say-die Khe Sanh firebase of '67 seriousness. All the things I missed in my rather easy youth.

"I don't, Clare."

"No. Course not. Me, either," he says. "But I *want* to believe it. And *that's* what scares the shit right out of me. And don't think they're not sitting over there in those other countries that hate us licking their chops at what they see us doing over here, fucking around trying to decide which of these dopes to make President. You think these people here"—a toss of the Clare Suddruth head toward crumbling 61 Surf Road—"have foundation problems? *We've* got foundation problems. It's not that we can't see the woods for the trees, we can't see the woods *or* the fuckin' trees." Clare expels through his schnoz a breath heavy and poignant, something a Clydesdale might do.

"What does it have to do with real estate?"

"It's where I enter the picture, Frank," Clare says. "The circuit my mind runs on. I want to make Estelle's last years happy. I think a house on the ocean's the right thing. Then I start thinking about New Jersey being a prime target for some nut with a dirty bomb or whatever. And, of course, I know death's a pretty simple business. I've seen it. I don't fear it. And I know Estelle's gonna probably see it before I do. So I go on looking at these houses as if a catastrophe—or death—*can't* really happen, right up until, like now, I recognize it *can*. And it shocks me. Really. Makes me feel paralyzed."

"What is it that shocks you, Clare? You know everything there is to be afraid of. You seem way ahead of the game to me."

Clare shakes his head in self-wonder. "I'm sitting up in bed,

Frank—honest to God—up in Parsippany. Estelle's asleep beside me. And what I go cold thinking about is: If something happens—you know, a bomb—can I ever sell my fucking house? And if I buy a new one, *then* what? Will property values even mean anything anymore? Where the hell are we then? Are we supposed to escape to some other place? Death's a snap compared to that."

"I never thought about that, Clare." As a philosophical question, of course, it's a lot like "Why the solar system?" And it's just about as practical-minded. You couldn't put a contingency clause in a buy-sell agreement that says "Sale contingent on there being no disaster rendering all real estate worthless as tits on a rain barrel."

"I guess *you* wouldn't think about it. Why would you?" Clare says.

"You said it was pretty philosophical."

"I know perfectly well it all has to do with 'Stelle being sick and my other relationship ending. Plus my age. I'm just afraid of the circumstances of life going to hell. Boom-boom-boom." Clare's staring out to sea, above the heads of the lithe, untroubled young volley ballers—a grizzled old Magellan who doesn't like what he's discovered. Boom-boom-boom.

Clare's problem isn't really a philosophical problem. It just makes him feel better to think so. His problem with circumstances is itself circumstantial. He's suffered normal human setbacks, committed perfidies, taken some shots. He just doesn't want to fuck up in those ways again and is afraid he can't recognize them when they're staring him in the face. It's standard—a form of buyer's remorse experienced prior to the sale. If Clare would just take the plunge (always the realtor's warmest wish for mankind), banish fear, think that instead of having suffered error and loss, he's *survived* them (but won't survive them indefinitely), that today could be the first day of his new life, then he'd be fine. In other words, accept the Permanent Period as your personal savior and act not as though you're going to die tomorrow but—much scarier—as though you might *live*.

How, though, to explain this without arousing suspicion that I'm just a smarmy, eel-slippery, promise-'em-anything sharpster, hyperventilating to unload a dump that's already crumbling from the ground upward?

You can't. *I* can't. As muddled as I feel out here, I know the Doolittles' house has serious probs, may be heading toward tear-down in a year or two, and I would never sell this house to Clare and will, in fact, now have to be the bearer of somber financial news to the Doolittles in Boca. All's I can do is just show Clare more houses, till he either buys one or wanders off into the landscape. (I wonder if Clare's a blue state or a red state. Just as in Sponsoring, politics is a threshold you don't cross in my business, though most people who look at beach houses seem to be Republicans.)

Somewhere, out of the spheres, I hear what sounds like the Marine Corps Hymn played on a xylophone. *Dum-dee-dum-dum-dum-dum-dum-dee-dum, dum-dum-dum-dum-dum-dum-dum.* It's surprisingly loud, even on the dune top in the breeze. The volley-ball kids stop rotating, their heads turn toward us as if they've registered something weird, something from home or further back in the racial fog.

Clare goes fumbling under his jacket for a little black hand-tooled holster looped to his belt like a snub-nose. It's his cell phone, raising a sudden call to arms and valor—unmistakable as *his* ring and *only* his, in any airport, supermarket deli section or DMV line.

"Sud-druth." Clare speaks in an unexpected command voice—urgent message from the higher-ups to the troops in the thick of it down here. His snapped answer is aimed into an impossibly tiny (and idiotic) red Nokia exactly like every one of the prep school girls has in her Hilfiger beach bag. "Right," Clare snaps, jabbing a thumb in his other ear like a thirties crooner and lowering his chin in strict, regimental attention. He steps away a few yards along the dune, where we are trespassers. Every single particle of his bearing announces: All right. *This* is important. "Yep, yep, yep," he says.

For me, though, it's a welcome, freeing moment, unlike most cell-phone interruptions, when the bystander feels like a condemned man, trussed and harnessed, eyes clenched, waiting for the trap to drop. The worst thing about others blabbing on their cell phones—and the chief reason I don't own one—is the despairing recognition that everybody's doing, thinking, saying pretty much the same things you are, and none of it's too interesting.

This freed moment, however, strands me out of context and releases me to the good sensations we all wish were awaiting us "behind" every moment: That—despite my moment of syncope, my failed house-showing, my crumbling Thanksgiving plans, my condition, my underlying condition, my overarching condition—there is still a broad fertile plain where we can see across to a white farmhouse with willows and a pond the sky traffics over, where the sun is in its soft morning quadrant and there is peace upon the land. I suddenly can feel this. Even the prep school kids seem excellent, promising, doing what they should. I wish Clare could feel it. Since with just a glimpse—permitted by a kindly, impersonal life force—many things sit right down into their proper, proportionate places. "It's enough," I hear myself breathing to myself. "It's really enough."

"Yep, yep, yep." Clare's internalizing whatever's to be internalized. Get those fresh troopers up where they can see the back side of that hill and start raining hellfire down on the sorry bastards. And don't be back to me till that whole area's secured and you can give me a full report, complete with casualties. Theirs *and* ours. Got that? Yep, yep. "I'll get home around one, sweetheart. We'll have some lunch." It is a homelier communiqué than imagined.

Clare punches off his Nokia and returns it to its holster without turning around. He's facing north, up the shore toward Asbury Park, miles off, and where I'll soon be going. His posture of standing away gives him the aura of a man composing himself.

"Everything copacetic?" I smile, in case he should turn around and unexpectedly face me. A friendly visage is always welcome.

"Yes, sure." Clare does turn, *does* see my welcoming mug— a mug that says, We aren't looking at a house anymore; we're just men out here together, taking the air. The volleyballers have formed a caucus beside their net and are laughing. I hear one of *their* cell phones ringing—a gleeful little rilling that exults, *Yes, yes, yes!* "My wife, Estelle—well, you know her name." Clare glances toward the calm sea and its white filigree of sudsy surf, over which gulls are skimming for tiny fleeing mackerel. "When I'm gone for very long, it's like she thinks I'm not coming back." He dusts his big hands, cleaning off some residue of his call. "Of course, I did go away and didn't come back. You can't blame her."

"Sounds like it's all different now."

"Oh yeah." Clare runs his two clean hands back through his salt 'n pepper hair. He is a handsome man—even if part doozie, part fearful shrinker from the world's woe and clatter. We have things in common, though I'm not as handsome. "What were we gassing about?" His call has erased all. A positive sign. "I was bending your ear about some goddamn thing." He smiles, abashed but happy not to remember. A glimpse of my wide plain with the house, sun, pond and willows may, in fact, have been briefly his.

"We were talking about foundations, Clare."

"I thought we were talking about fears and commitments." He casts a wistful eye back at #61's troubled exterior—its weathered soffits, its gutter straps (defects I hadn't noticed). I say nothing. "Well," Clare says, "same difference."

"Okay."

"Somebody else'll want this place." He offers a relieved grin. Another bullet dodged.

"Somebody definitely will," I say. "You can bet on it. Not many things you can bet on, but on that, you can."

"Good deal," Clare says.

We find other things to talk about—he is a Giants fan, has

season tickets—as I walk him back down and out to his Only Connect truck. He's happy to be heading home empty-handed, happy to be going where someone loves him and not where somebody's studying archaeology. I'm satisfied with him and with my part in it all. He is a good man. The Doolittles, I'm sure, after a day of raging, then brooding, then grudging resolution, could easily decide to come down on their asking. Houses like theirs change hands every four to six years and are built for turnover. Not many people feel they were born to live in a house forever. I'll sell it by Christmas, or Mike will. Possibly to Clare. They truly aren't making any more of it here at the beach. And in fact, if the Republicans steal the show, they'll soon be trucking it away.

O n my way back out Cormorant Court, Clare blinks his lights, and I pull over in front of a chalet where my red-and-white REALTY-WISE sign stands out front. The Hondurans lounge on the little front steps, eating their lunches brought from home.

Clare idles alongside, his window already down so we can confer vehicle-to-vehicle in the cold air. Possibly he wants to set matters straight about my BUSH? WHY? bumper sticker, which I'm sure he doesn't approve of. I should probably peel it off now.

"What's the story with these?" he half shouts through his window (his passenger seat's been removed for insurance reasons). He's now wearing a pair of Foster Grants that make him look more like General MacArthur. He's talking about the chalet being spiffed up.

"Same old," I say. "I sell. You buy."

Clare's tough Marine Corps mouth, used to doing the talking, all the ordering, assumes a wrinkled, compromised expression of deliberate tolerance. He knows the opportunity to be taken seriously even by me is almost over. He gets most things—it's one of his virtues. But I'm as happy to sell him one of these as I am the Doolittles'. I've shown many a client a house they didn't want, then sold them a chalet as a consolation prize. Although blending business (potential rental income) with sentimental impulses (buying a house for the dying wife) can be troublesome for buyers. Internal messages can become seriously mixed, and bad results in the form of lost revenues ensue.

"What's the damage?" Clare says from the financial safety of his work truck.

"A buck seventy-five." Add twenty-five for wasting my time this morning, and since he's obviously got the scratch. "Walking distance to the beach."

"Rent 'em year-round?" Clare's smiling. He knows what a schmendrick he is.

"Make your nut in the summer. Seven-fifty a week last year. I take fifteen percent, get my crew in for upkeep. Capital improvement's yours. You probably clear seven per summer, before taxes and insurance. You really need to own three or four to make it happy." And you have to keep your heart out of your pocketbook. And this last summer wasn't that great. And Estelle won't like it. Clare's probably not ready for all this.

"That's assuming some miserable asshole doesn't sue you," he says out of the echo chamber of his truck. He may have heard me say something I didn't say. But he's refound his authority and begun frowning not at me but out his windshield toward NJ 35 at the end of Cormorant Court.

"There's always that." I smile a zany smile of *who cares.*

"Fuckin' ambulance chasers." Clare's two divorces could conceivably have left a bad taste in his mouth for the legal profession. He shakes his head at some unavenged bad memory. We've all been there. It's nothing to share the day before Thanksgiving. I try to think of a good lawyer joke, but there aren't any. "I see you voted for Gore. The patsy." He's acknowledging my BUSH? WHY? sticker.

"I did."

He stares stonily ahead at nothing. "I couldn't vote for Bush. I voted for his old man. Now we're in the soup. Wouldn't you say?"

"I think we are."

"God help us," Clare says, and looks puzzled for the first time.

"I doubt if he will, Clare," I say. "Are you staging a big Thanksgiving?" I'm ready to part company. But I want to celebrate Clare-the-redeemed-Republican with a warm holiday wish.

"Yeah. Kids. Estelle's sister. My mom. The clan."

It's nice to know Clare has a mom who comes for holidays. "That's great."

"You?" Clare shifts into gear, his truck bumping forward.

"Yep. The whole clan. We try to connect." I smile.

"Okay." Clare nods. He hasn't heard me right. He idles away up toward 35 and the long road back to Parsippany.

10

Since there's no direct-est route to Parkway Exit 102N, where Wade's already fuming at Fuddruckers, I take the scenic drive up 35, across the Metedeconk and the Manasquan to Point Pleasant, switch to NJ 34 through more interlocking towns, townships, townlettes—one rich, one not, one getting there, one hardly making its millage. I love this post-showing interlude in the car, especially after my syncope on the dune. It's the *moment d'or* which the Shore facilitates perfectly, offering exposure to the commercial-ethnic-residential zeitgeist of a complex republic, yet shelter from most of the ways the republic gives me the willies. "Culture comfort," I call this brand of specialized well-being. And along with its sister solace, "cultural literacy"—knowing by inner gyroscope where the next McDonald's or Borders, or the next old-fashioned Italian shoe repair or tuxedo rental or lobster dock is going to show up on the horizon—these together I consider a cornerstone of the small life lived acceptably. I count it a good day when I can keep *all* things that give me the willies out of my thinking, and in their places substitute vistas I can appreciate, even unwittingly. Which is why I take the scenic route now, and why when I get restless I fly out to Moline or Flint or Fort Wayne for just a few hours' visit—since there I can experience the new and the complex, coupled with the entirely benign and knowable.

Cancer, naturally, exerts extra stresses on life (if you don't instantly die). We all cringe with cancer *scares*: the mole that doesn't look right; the lump below our glutes where we can't monitor it, the positive chest X ray (why does *positive* always mean fatal?) resulting in CAT scans, blood profiles, records reviews from twenty years back, all of which scare the shit out of us, make us silent but wretched as we await the results, entertaining thoughts of apricot treatments in Guadalajara and inquiries about euthanasia for nonresidents in Holland (I did all these). And then it's nothing—a harmless fatty accumulation, a histoplasmosis scar from childhood—innocent abnormalities (there *are* such things). And you're off the hook—though you're not unfazed. You've been on a journey and it's not been a happy one. Even without a genuine humming tumor deep in your prostate, just this much is enough to kill you. The coroner's certificate could specify for any of us: "Death came to Mr. X or Ms. Y due to acute heebie-jeebies."

But then when the sorry news *does* come, you're perfectly calm. You've used up all your panic back when it *didn't* count. So what good is calm? "Well, I'm thinking we'd better do a little biopsy and see what we're dealing with. . . ." "Well, Mr. Bascombe, have a seat here. I've got some things I need to talk to you about. . . ." Be calm now? Calm's just another face of wretched.

And then what follows *that* is the whole dull clouding over of *all* good feeling, *all* that normally elevates days, moods, reveries, pretty vistas, *all* the minor uplifts known to be comforting . . . . Crash-bang! *Meaningless!* Not *real* reality anymore, since something bad had *always* been there, right? The days before my bad news, when I had cancer but didn't know I had it and felt pretty damn good—all of those days are not worth sneezing at. *Good* was a lie, inasmuch as my whole grasp on life required that nothing terrible happen to me, *ever*—which is nuts. It did.

So the on-going challenge becomes: How, post-op, to maintain a supportable existence that resembles actual life, instead of walking the windy, trash-strewn streets in a smudged sandwich board that shouts IMPAIRED! FEEL SORRY FOR ME! BUT DON'T BOTHER TAKING ME SERIOUSLY AS A WHOLE PERSON, BECAUSE (UNLIKE YOU) I WON'T BE AROUND FOREVER!

I wish I could tell you I had a formula for changing the character of big into small. Mike has suggested meditation and a trip to Tibet. (It may come to that.) Clarissa's been a help—though I'm ready for her life to re-commence. Selling houses is clearly useful for making me feel invisible (even better than "connected"). And Sally's absence has not been a total tragedy, since misery doesn't really want company, only cessation. Suffice it to say that I mostly do fine. I overlook more than I used to, and many things have just quit bothering me on their own. Which leads me to think that my "state" must not be such a thoroughly bad or altered one.

And I'll also admit that in the highly discretionary lives most of us lead, there *is* sweet satisfaction to this being *it*, and to not having *it* be always out there to dread: the whacker coronary; both feet amputated after paraskiing down K2 on your birthday; total macular degeneration, so you need a dog to help you find the can. This longing for satisfaction, I believe, is in the hearts of those strange Korea vets who admit to wartime atrocities they never committed and never would've; and may be the same for poor friendless Marguerite, back in Haddam, wondering what she has to confess. There *is* a desire to face some music, even if it's a tune played only in your head—a desire for the real, the permanent, for a break in the clouds that tells you, This is how you are and will always be. Great nature has another thing to do to you and me, so take the lively air, the poet said. And I do. I take the lively air whenever I can, as now. Though it's that *other thing* great nature promises that I rely on, the thing that quickens the step and the breath and so must not be thought of as the enemy.

11

I hatch a thought as I cross the Manasquan bridge and near the 34 cutoff: to stop at the Manasquan Bar for a beer and a piss in its nautical, red-lit cozy confines. Years ago, with a cohort of fellow divorcés, I would drive over from Haddam once a month, just to get out of town, seeking night-time companionship and large infusions of gin and scotch that always sent us back into the dark to Hightstown, Mercerville and home with a better grasp on our griefs and sorrows. A quick re-savoring of those old days—the rosy perpetual indoor bar light and beery bouquets—would, I'm sure, extend the good feeling I've concocted. But a piss is what I really need and a beer is not, since a beer would just require another piss sooner than I now consider normal (hourly). Plus, any venture into the swampy vapors of time lost—no matter how good I'd feel— could prove precarious, and make me late for Wade.

Instead then, I take 34 straight inland, north through suburban Wall Township, which is not truly municipal or even towny, but dense and un-centered, a linear boilerplate of old strip develop- ment, skeins of traffic lights and jug-handles with signage indicating Russians, Farsi speakers, Ethiopians and Koreans live nearby and do business. A cellular tower camouflaged to look like a Douglas fir looms up at an uncertain distance above roofs and fourth- growth woodlots. The Manasquan River winds past somewhere off to the left. But little is discernible or of interest. It is actually hard to tell what the natural landscape looks like here.

I pull in for my long piss at a Hess station across the avenue from Wall Township Engine Company No. 69, where a Thanksgiving CPR clinic's in progress on the station-house apron. Burly firefighters in black-and-yellow regalia are demonstrating modern resuscitative techniques on plastic mannequins and on citizens craving resuscitating firsthand. Cheerleaders from the Upper Squankum Middle School are running a five-dollar car wash at the curb. Inside the station house, so the sign-on-wheels says, selected items from the Hoboken Museum's traveling Frank Sinatra collection are on display, along with a DNR exhibit entitled "What to Do When Wild Animals Come to Call." A handful of citizens mills around on the asphalt—tall and skinny Ethiopians, with a few smaller Arabs in non-Arab sweaters—all having a perusal of the pumper rig and the hook 'n ladder, stealing nervous glances at the female dummy the firemen are working on and taking leaning peeks in at the Old Blue Eyes display. It is all a good civic pull-together, even if Thanksgiving's a quaint mystery to most of them and business is poor hereabouts. Rich soil is here for municipal virtues, though the philosopher would never have planted them in Wall Township.

At Garden State Exit 102N, it's half past noon, a cold November sun shining high. The Queen Regent implosion is scheduled for one, and since I haven't answered Wade's calls, he's likely to be fidgety and cross. In my view, oldsters with virtually zilch to do should squander their hours like sailors on shore leave, but instead end up hawking the clock and making everybody miserable, while us working clods would like to throw our watches in the ocean (I don't own one).

When I pull up, Wade is seated on the curb under the yellow awning of the Fuddruckers, which appears to be out of business, along with the empty sixties-era mall just behind it, whose long, vacant parking lot awaits reassignment. Wade starts theatrically tapping the face of his big silver and turquoise wristwatch and scowling when I wheel in beside his ancient tan Olds. I should've been here yesterday, or at least two hours ago, and now I've jeopardized his day.

"Did you get lost in Metedeconk?" he says, struggling up onto his tiny feet, getting his balance on the blue disabled sign. Metedeconk represents an insider joke I know nothing about.

"I did," I say through my window. "They all asked about you." I stay put behind the wheel. The warmer inland air carries a seam of dry cold as traffic swishes noisily on the Parkway.

"I know who asked about me, all right." He's shuffling— bow-legged, stiff-hipped, arms slightly held out like an outrigger. Wade says he's seventy-four, but is actually over eighty. And though he's dressed in youthful sporting attire—baggy pink jackass pants with a semaphore pattern, sockless white patent-leather slips-ons and a bright yellow V neck—he looks decrepit and shabby, as if he'd slept in this outfit for a week. "We're going in my vehicle," he growls, eyes fixed on the pavement in front of him as if its surface was tricking around.

"Not today," I say, cheerfully.

Wade is a menacing driver. He regularly runs stop signs, drives thirty-five on the Turnpike, barges through intersections, leans on his horn, has his turn signal constantly on, shouts religious and gender epithets at other drivers, and, because he's considerably shrunken, can barely see over his dashboard. He shouldn't be allowed near the driver's seat. Though when I've counseled him, during our monthly lunch at Bump's, that it's time to hang up his duster and ride, his blue eyes snap, his teeth clack, his foot and knee tremor starts whapping the table leg. "So are you volunteering to drive me? Good. I'll let you drive me—and wait for me everyplace I go until I'm ready to go home. Sounds perfect. Do you think I *like* to drive?" He has his point. Though I often think that death will come to me not naturally, but by being backed over by some stiff-necked old lunatic like Wade in front of the Marshalls in Toms River.

I sit my seat, shaking my head, which is certain to piss him off.

Wade pauses between our two vehicles and glowers at me. "Mine's all rigged up." Meaning his car seat's shoved up, his hemorrhoid donut's strapped to the extra cushion, the radio's tuned to a hillbilly station he likes in Long Branch, and the beaded back supporter that helps his arthritis is bungeed to the driver's side. For years, Wade worked as a toll taker at Exit 9 on the Turnpike and believes repetitive stress plus exhaust fumes degraded his skeleton and compromised his immune system, resulting in shrunkenness and unexplained night pains. I've explained to him he's just old.

"I've got a wife and children to think about, Wade." I'm waiting for him to get in.

"Hah! The missing wife. That's a good one." Wade knows all about my marital hiatus, as well as my prostate issues and most of the rest of my story, which he takes no interest in unless he can make a joke out of it (his own prostate is a memory). Due, I believe, to an occasional mini-stroke, Wade also sometimes confuses me with his son, Cade, a New Jersey State Trooper in Pohatcong, Troop W. And at other times, for reasons I don't understand, he calls me "Ned." This kind of impairment could pass for useful disinterest, I've thought. So that if Wade wasn't occasionally ga-ga and didn't yak your ear off, I'd get him certified to Sponsor fellow seniors out at the Grove, the staged senior community where he lives in Bamber Lake, where they hold weekly wine tastings, senior art openings and jigsaw puzzle contests, and boast gold-standard tertiary care, in-house cardiac catheterization, their own level-one trauma center, with six class-A hospitals a twenty-minute ambulance ride away, but where Wade says the oldsters are always looking for something extra.

Wade has given in to riding in my car and has crawled into his Olds to retrieve his brown-bag lunch and his video cam so he can eat while the Queen Regent falls in on herself and also get the whole thing on tape for public exhibit. At the Grove, he says, he's an A-list dinner guest and much sought after by the ladies as a raconteur.

"We're all better off to get over our pain," Wade says in a muffled voice inside his passenger's door. He's referring to my absent wife. He's on his hands and knees, fishing for something on the floorboard and making Frankenstein noises, his pink-pants ass in the air. I would help, but it's part of our compact that he never needs help. I stare glumly in at his inflatable hemorrhoid donut.

"I think you're a walking advertisement for a long life," I say, though he can't hear me. I could just as easily say, I'd like to string you up by your ankles and put a stopwatch on how long it takes your head to explode, and it would mean the same. Wade's not a proficient listener, which he credits to having had a full life and a reduced need to take anything in anymore.

"On the other hand." He's grunting, backing out, hauling his sack lunch and his Panasonic. "I'd kill myself if I wasn't afraid of the fucking pain." He stands up on the Fuddruckers' asphalt, facing inside his car as if I was there instead of behind him. He's become an odd-looking creature, after being pretty normal-looking when I first knew him. While his hands and arms and neck are dry and leathery as an alligator, his small head is round and pinkish-orange, as if he'd been boiled. He's fashioned his white hair into a Caesarian back-to-front comb-down that makes a bang, which—depending on barbershop visits—can be a simple-sad oldster fringe or else a Beatle-length mop that makes him appear seventy, which is how he more or less looks now. Add to this that when he takes off his glasses, his blue left eye wanders off cockeyed, that he wears a big globby hearing device in each ear, is an inexpert face shaver, plus always gets too close to you when he talks (spritzing you with Listerine spit), and you have a not always attractive human package.

When I first knew Wade, sixteen years ago, he lived in the suburb of Barnegat Pines, with his now-deceased second wife,

Lynette, and son, Cade. I was then lost in hapless but powerful love for his daughter, Vicki—an oncology nurse and major handful of daunting physical attainments. It was three years after my son died, and one after my divorce from Ann, a time when my existence seemed in jeopardy of fading into a pointless background of the onward rush of life. Wade was then a level-eyed, crew-cut engineer and truth seeker. He'd seen confusion in life, had looked the future in the eye and gotten down to being a solid citizen/provider who understood his limits, maintained codes and was glad to welcome me as a unique, slightly "older" son-in-law candidate. My present take on Wade comes mostly from those long-ago days. I didn't see him at all for sixteen years and only refound him four months back when Cade presented me with a speeding ticket on my way back late from the Red Man Club and I noticed the ARSENAULT on his brass name plate. Blah, blah, blah, blah, blah . . . I ended up calling Wade because as he wrote out the summons, Cade—thick-browed, fat-eared, wearing a black flak jacket and a flat-top—said that "Dad" had become "like a pretty sad case" and "maybe wouldn't last a lot longer" and that they (Cade and Mrs. Cade) had "pretty much our own lives up in Pohatcong, kids and whatever," and didn't make it down to visit the old man as often as they should. "Things like that are too bad in a way," he observed. And, oh, by the way, that'll be ninety clams, plus costs, plus two points, have a nice day and keep 'er under fifty-five.

I ended up rendezvous-ing with Wade at Bump's and reaffiliating. And in a short while, I managed to reconcile Wade *years back*—frontier Nebraskan with a trim physique and a

Texas Aggie engineering degree, with Wade *today*—orange-skinned, obstreperous bang-wearer and sour-smelling, weirdly dressed crank; and, by the force of my will, to make a whole person out of the evidence. Aging requires reconciliations, and nobody said getting old would be pretty or the alternative better.

What Wade and I actually do for each other in the present tense, and that makes putting up with each other worth the aggravation, is a fair question. But when he's in his right head—which is most of the time—Wade's as sharp as a Mensa member, still sees the world purely as it is and for this reason is not a bad older friend for me, just as I'm not a bad younger companion to keep him on his toes. We share, after all, a piece of each other's past, even if it's not a past we visit. We also like each other, as only truly consenting adults can.

*A*sbury Park, which we pass through and where I've done some bank work, has unhappily devolved over the years into a poverty pocket amidst the pricey, linked Shore communities, Deal to Allenhurst, Avon to Bay Head. Those monied towns all needed reliable servant reserves a bus ride away, and Asbury was ceded to the task. Hopeful Negroes from Bergen County and Crown Heights, Somalis and Sudanese fresh off the plane, plus a shop-keeper class of Iranis for whom Harlem was too tough, now populate the streets we drive down. Occasionally, a shady Linden Lane or a well-tended Walnut Court survives, with its elderly owner-occupant tending his patch while values sink to nothing and the element pinches in. But most of the streets are showing it—windows out, mansions boarded, grass gone weedy, sidewalks crumbling, informal automotive work conducted curbside, while black men wait on corners, kids ply the pavements on Big Wheels, and large African-looking ladies in bright scarves lean on porch rails, watching the world slide by. Asbury Park could be Memphis or Birmingham, and nothing or no one would seem out of place.

"One in five non-English speakers, right?" Wade's watching out his window, fingering his diabetic's Medi-Ident bracelet and looking abstracted. He's infected the interior of my car with his sour, citrusy elder-smell—mostly from his yellow sweater—that mingles with Mike's stale Marlboro residue from last night, making me have to crack open my window. He shoots me a fiery glance when I don't answer his non-English-speaker non-question, pink tongue working his dentures (his "falsies") as if he's warming up for verbal combat. Wade is of a generally conservative belief-base but wouldn't vote for dumb-ass Bush if the world was ablaze and Bush had the bucket. He grew up poor, lucked into A&M, worked two decades in the oil patch in Odessa and views Republicans as trustees for keeping government on the sidelines, out of his boudoir, the classroom and the Lord's house (where he's not a frequenter). Isolation's the way to go, keep the debt below zero, inflation nonexistent, blubbety-blubbety. Any kind of sanctimony's for scoundrels—hence the hatred of Bush. Smiling Rocky was Wade's hero, though he's voted Democrat since Watergate. "Housing's leveled off. D'you read that?" he says, just to make noise.

"Not where I live," I say.

"Oh, well of course," Wade says. "Being what you are, you'd know that. That's the kind of stuff you're the expert in. The rest of us have to read about it in the papers."

*A*t straight-up one o'clock, the day's turned warmer than in Sea-Clift. A pavement of gray clouds has streaked open up here to reveal febrile blue out over the ocean we're approaching. The day no longer feels like the day before Thanksgiving, but a late-arriving Indian summer afternoon or a morning in late March when spring's come in like a lamb. A perfect day for an implosion.

The Queen Regent sits opposite the boardwalk and the crumbling Art Deco convention hall—home to luckless club fights and poorly attended lite-rock record hops. Noisy gulls soar above and around the Queen's battlements, where she stands alone on a plain against the sky, as if the old buff-colored hospital-looking pile of bricks was occupying space no longer hers. Though even from a distance she's hardly an edifice to rate a big send-off: Nine stories, all plain (and gutted), with two U-shaped empty-windowed wings and a pint-size crenellated tower like a supermarket cake. A previously-canopied but now trashy glassed-in veranda faces the boardwalk and the Atlantic, and a wooden water tower with a giant TV antenna attached bumps above the roofline. Once it was a place where felt-hatted drummers could take their girlfriends on the cheap. Families with too many kids could go and pretend it was nice. Young honeymooners came. Young suicides. Oldster couples lived out their days within sound of the sea and took their meals in the dim coffered dining room. Standing alone, the Queen Regent looks like one of those condemned men from a hundred revolutions who the camera catches standing in an empty field beside an open grave, looking placid, resigned, distracted—awaiting fate like a bus—when suddenly volleys from off-stage soundlessly pelt and spatter them, so they're changed in an instant from present to past.

All around the Queen Regent is a dry, treeless urban-renewal savanna stretching back to the leafless tree line of Asbury. Where we're currently driving were once sweller, taller hotels with glitzier names, stylish seafood joints with hot jazz clubs in the basement, and farther down the now-missing blocks, tourist courts and shingled flophouses for the barkers and rum-dums who ran the Tilt-A-Whirl on the pier or waltzed trays in the convention hall, which itself looks like it could fall in with a rising tide and a breeze. Today it is all a PROGRESS ZONE! a sign says, with LUXURY CONDO COMMUNITY COMING!

Wade has his silver Panasonic up and trained tight on the Queen Regent through the wide windshield glass. His is the awkward kind you peer *down* into like a reverse periscope, and operating it through his bifocals makes him crank his mouth open moronically and his old lips go slack. He seems to believe the Queen is about to go down any instant.

"Drive us around to the front, Franky. What're we doin' over here?" He flashes me a savage gaping grimace. The V of Wade's yellow velour sweater, under which is only bare skin, shows his chicken chest with sparse white pinfeathers sprouting. I've seen

Wade naked once, in his "flat" in Bamber Lake, when I arrived early for dinner. I haven't gone back.

A tall cyclone fence, however, has been stretched around the Queen Regent, razor wire on top to discourage souvenir seekers and preservationist saboteurs who're always around looking to monkey-wrench a decent implosion. We the public can't go where Wade wants us to, or, in fact, get within three football fields of the site, since Asbury Park police and a cadre of blue-tunicked State Troopers have rigged a traffic diversion using cones and Jersey barriers and are forcing us off onto (another) Ocean Avenue and away from the hotel entirely. We can both see where a crowd of implosion spectators has been marshaled into a temporary grandstand the imploding company, the Martello Brothers—FIREWORKS, DETONATING, RAZING FOR PASSAIC AND CENTRAL JERSEY—has put up behind another cyclone fence at the remote south end of the Progress Zone, across from another big sign that says THIS STREET ADOPTED BY ASBURY PK CUB PACK 31. Some land—I'm thinking, as we follow Ocean Avenue toward the Temporary Parking—is better off with a few good condos.

"You can't see a fucking thing from over here." Wade's twisted in his seat, straining to see back to the Queen Regent, his throat constricted, his voice raised a quarter octave while he forces his Panasonic up to his bifocals in case the whole shebang goes down while I'm parking. "It might as well be the White Sands Proving Ground out here. What're they afraid of, the goddamn pecker-woods?" Wade never cursed when I first knew him and was wooing his daughter like Romeo.

"I'm sure insurance stipulates—"

"Don't get me going on those shitheads," he says. "When Lynette died, I didn't get a cryin' nickel." Lynette was Wade's wife number two, a tiny Texas termagant and Catholic crackpot who left him to enter a Maryknoll residence in Bucks County, where she became a Christian analyst auditing the troubled life stories of others like herself, until she had an embolism, assigned her benefits to the nuns and croaked. I've heard quite a bit about all that since the summer, and I consider it one of the fringe benefits of not marrying Wade's daughter, Vicki, that I missed having Lynette as my mother-in-law. Wade doesn't always perfectly remember I was ever in love with Vicki, or why he and I know each other. Vicki, however—he told me—has now changed her name to Ricki and lives a widow's life in Reno, where she works as an ER nurse and never ventures back to New Jersey. God works in sundry ways.

I've driven us around to the temporary parking remuda behind the Martello Brothers' bleachers. Back here are two trucked-in Throne Room portable toilets—always good to find—and several land yachts and fifth-wheel camper rigs, indicating that other implosion enthusiasts have spent the night to get the best seats. I've barely stopped and Wade is already quick out and stumping around toward the side of the bleachers, Panasonic in one hand, greasy sandwich bag in the other, not wanting to miss anything, since we're five minutes late.

The whole setup's like an athletic event, a Friday pigskin tilt between Belvedere and Hackettstown in the brittle late-autumn sunshine—only this tilt's between man's hold on permanence and the Reaper (most contests come down to that). The crowd around the front of the bleachers is exerting a continuous anticipatory hum as I approach. A raucous male voice shouts, "Not yet, not yet. Please, not yet!" An African-looking woman in a flowered daishiki has set up a makeshift table-stand, selling *I Went Down with the Queen* and *The Queen Regent Had My Child* tee-shirts. A large black man has secured the "Chicago Jew Dog" concession and is cooking franks on a black fifty-gallon drum. I'm famished and buy one of these in a paper napkin. Bush and Gore placards are leaned against the fence in case anyone wants to recant his vote. The Salvation Army has a tripod and kettle off to the side, with a tall blue-suited matron clanging a big bell and smiling. There are lots of Asbury Park cops. Everything is here but someone singing karaoke.

When I get near the edge of the grandstand (Wade has disappeared), I can see that the crowd's being addressed by a small stout man in a yellow jumpsuit and gold hard hat, who's talking through a yellow electric bullhorn. He's in the middle of declaring that thousands of man-hours, four million sticks of dynamite, nine zillion feet of wire, brain-scrambling computer circuitry, the services of two Rutgers Ph.D.'s, plus the generous cooperation of the Monmouth County Board of Supervisors and the Asbury Park city council, plus the cops, have made *here* be the safest place to be in New Jersey, which makes the crowd snicker. This man I recognize as "Big Frank" Martello of the fabled brothers. Big Frank is a homegrown Jersey product who, after mastering percussive skills blowing up VC caves in the sixties, came home to Passaic, turned away from the family's business of loan-sharking and knee-restructuring, took a marketing degree at

Drew and went into the legit business of blowing things to smithereens for profit (the fireworks came along later). Being the oldest, Frank sent his six siblings to college (one is a dentist in Middlebush), and little by little absorbed the ones who were inclined into the business, which was in fact, booming. There they thrived and became a famed family phenomenon the world over—a sort of black-powder Wallendas—capable of astounding destructive dexterities, pinpoint precision and smokeless, dustless, barely noticeable obliterations in which buildings safely vanished, sites were cleaned and the craters filled so that the concrete trucks could be all lined up for work the following day.

I'm acquainted with Big Frank "the legend" because his brother Nunzio, the dentist, made inquiries about a snug-away for one of his girlfriends in Seaside Heights. While we cruised the streets, one thing led to another and the family saga got unspooled. Nunzio finally bought a lanai apartment for his honey down in Ship Bottom, and I'm sure is happy there.

Big Frank's riling up the crowd—about two hundred of us—to a modest pitch, cracking dumb New Jersey Turnpike and Turkey Day jokes, taking off his yellow hard hat and dipping his dome to show us how few hairs his dangerous job has left him, then strutting around arms-crossed in front of the bleachers, like Mussolini. The crowd includes plenty of young parents with their kids in crash helmets, off for school holidays, plus a good number of older couples representing the land yachts and fifth-wheelers, who conceivably honeymooned in the Queen Regent, skating nights on the hardwood floors of the convention hall way back when. There's also, of course, the inevitable collection of singleton strangees like Wade and me, who just like a good explosion and don't need to talk about it. All are seated in rows, knees together, sunglasses and headgear in place, staring more or less raptly at a red plunger box Big Frank has stationed on a red milk crate in front of the temporary fence on which is attached a sign inscribed with his well-known motto, WE TAKE IT DOWN.

From where I'm standing to the side of the bleachers, eating my Jew Dog, I can see the red plunger is ominously *up*. Though no wires are connected. The whole plunger business, I suspect, is a fake, the critical signal likely to be beamed in from Martello Command Central in Passaic, using computer modeling, high-tolerance telemetry, fiber optics, GPS, etc. Nobody there will hear or see a thing but what's on a screen.

I cast up into the bleachers, half-wolfed hot dog in hand, seeking Wade's orange face, and find it instantly, sunk in the crowd at the top row. He's glowering down at me for not being up where he is, with a good view across the Progress Zone to the far away Queen Regent. Wade makes an awkward, spasmic hand gesture for me to get my ass up there. It's a movement a person having a heart attack would make, and people on either side of him give him a fishy eye and inch away. ("Some smelly old nut sat beside us at the implosion. You can't go anywhere—")

But I'm in no mood for climbing over strangers to achieve closer bodily contact with Wade—plus, I have my dog, and am as happy here as I'm likely to get today. The sun at the crowd's edge feels good, the air rinsed clean like a state fair on the first afternoon before the rides are up. No matter that we're in a no-man's-land in a dispirited seaside town, waiting to watch an

abandoned building get turned to rubble—the second explosion
I've been close to in two days.

I wave enigmatically up to Wade, raise my hot dog bun, point
to my wrist as if it had a watch on it that said zero hour. Wade
mouths back grudging words no one can hear. Then I turn my
attention back to Big Frank, who's standing beside his red plunger
box while a skinny white kid with technical know-how, wearing
a plain white jumpsuit, screws wires to terminals on top, looking
questioningly up at Big Frank as if he doesn't think any of this
is going quite right. In the distance, through the fence and across
the three football fields, I can make out small human figures
moving hastily inside the Queen Regent's secure perimeter
toward what must be the exit gates. Many more blue-and-white
Asbury PD cruisers are now apparent, all with their blue flashers
going. Yellow traffic lights I also hadn't noticed are blinking
along the emptied streets. A police helicopter, an orange-striped
Coast Guard chopper and a "News at Noon" trafficopter are
hovering just off the boardwalk in anticipation of a big bang
soon to come. The Salvation Army bell is clanging, and for the
first time I hear hearty, sing-song human voices chanting from
somewhere "Save the cream, save the cream," which, of course,
is "Save the Queen, save the Queen." The chanters are nicely
dressed (but unavailing) landmark loonies who've been forced
into a spot outside some white police sawhorses, where they can
make their voices heard but be ignored.

Big Frank, through his electric megaphone, which makes his
strong New Jersey basso seem to come out of a cardboard box,
is spieling about how the "seismic effects" of what we're about

to witness will be detectable in China, yet the charges have been so ingeniously calculated by his family that the Queen Regent will fall straight down in exactly eighteen seconds, every loving brick coming to rest in arithmetically predetermined spots. "Nat-ur-al-ly" there'll be some dust (none of it asbestos), but not even as much, he's saying, as a stolen garbage truck would kick up in Newark—this is also due to climatological gauging, humidity indexing, plus fiber optics, lasers, etc. The sound will be surprisingly modest, "so you might want to hire us to renovate your mother-in-law's house in Trenton, hawr, hawr, hawr." A Coast Guard cutter is stationed just off the boardwalk ("In case one of my brothers gets blown out there"). Scuba divers are in the water. Fish and geese migration patterns won't be disrupted, nor will air quality or land values in Asbury Park—a murmur of general amusement. Likewise hospital services. "All efforts, in other words," he concludes, "have been expended to make the demolition nuttin' more than a fart in a paint bucket."

Big Frank stumps heavily off his central master of cere-monies spot to confer, head-down, with the skinny technician kid, plus two other swart-haired parties in red jumpsuits, who look like they might be filling station employees, though for all I know are the Rutgers Ph.D.'s. One of these red-suits hands Big Frank a set of old-fashioned calipered earphones with a mouthpiece attached. Big Frank, hard hat in hand, holds one phone to his ear, seems to listen intently to something—a voice?—coming through, then begins barking orders back, his meathead's big mouth cut into a downward swoop of anger, his head nodding.

Conceivably something's amiss, something that might postpone the big mushroom cloud and send us all cruising back down the streets of Asbury Park seeking substitute excitements. A hush of waiting has fallen over the hurly-burly, and a low hum of individual voices and single laughters and beer-can pops arises. A rich fishy smell drifts in off the sea—contributor, no doubt, to the Queen Regent's run of bad luck, since it comes from discharge practices long banned, though the pollutants are still in the soil and the atmosphere. From some undetermined place, there's a high-pitched mechanized *whee-wheeing* in the air, like the ghost of an empty ferris wheel at the boardwalk Fun Zone, where millions idled and thrilled and smooched away summer evenings without a care for what came before or next. To me, there's good to be found in these random sensations. I've made it my business at this odd time of life, when the future seems interesting but not necessarily "fun," to permit no time to be a dead time, since you wouldn't want to forget at a later, direr moment what that earlier, possibly better, day or hour or era was "like"; how the afternoon felt when the implosion got canceled, what specific life got lived as you awaited the Queen Regent's decline to rubble. You definitely would want to know that, to have that on your mind's record instead of say, like poor Ernie, hearing the thanatologist droning, "Frankee, Frankee? Can you hear me? Can you hear any-ting? Is you all de vay dead?"

Then . . . *boom, boom, boom, boom. Boomety-boom. Boom, boom. Boomety-boomety!* The Queen Regent is going. Right now. I'm happy I didn't duck out to the Throne Room.

Innocent puffs of gray-white smoke, small but specific and unquestionably consequential, go *poof-poof-poof* all up and down the Queen's nine-storey height, as if someone, some authority inside, was letting air out of old pillows, sweeping her clean, putting her in top form for the big reopening. Birds—the gulls I'd seen before, diving, swooping and wheeling—are suddenly flying away. No one warned them.

Our entire crowd—many are standing—exhales or gasps or sighs a spoon-moon-Juning "ahhhh" as if this is the thing now, finally, what we've come for, what nothing else can ever get better than.

Big Frank's staring, startled, right along with us, his big baldy head still calipered, his mouth gapped open, though he quickly closes it hard as an anvil, nostrils flaring. The two swarthy red-suited assistants have backed away as if he might start wind-milling punches. The skinny kid who'd wired the plunger box is blabbing into Big Frank's sizable ear, though Big Frank's staring out at the building being consumed in smoke, the plunger still stagily *up* at his feet.

Boom. Boom. Boomety-boom. Again, puffs of now grayer smoke squirt out all around the Queen Regent's foundation skirting, and another big one at the top, from the crenellated crown. And now commences a set of larger sounds. These things never go off with one bang, but more like a percussive chess game—the pawns first, then the bishops, then the knights. Whatever's left stands and fights but can't do either. At least that's how it happened down in Ventnor.

Now another series of *boom-booms*, bigger towering ones erupt from the Queen Regent's core. The old dowager has yet to shudder, lean or sway. Possibly she won't go down at all and the crowd will be the winner. Some yokel up in the stands laughs and yaps, "She ain't fallin'. They fucked this all up." Spectators have begun smiling, looking side to side. Wade, I can see, is getting all on tape. The Grove ladies will love him even more if the Queen survives. Big Frank's now glaring. I can read his lips, and they say, Fuck you. It'll fuckin' fall, you pieces of shit.

Just then, as the Queen Regent is holding firm and the copters are darting in closer from over the water, and some of the Asbury cops with flashers are moving along Ocean Avenue in front of the convention hall, and our crowd has started clapping, whooping and even stomping on the risers (Big Frank looks disgusted in his caliper headgear, and no doubt's begun calculating who's gonna catch shit)—just then, as the demolition turns to undemolition—a scrawny, dark-skinned black kid of approximately twelve, wearing a hooded black sweatshirt, baggy dungarees down over big silver basketball sneaks and carrying a plastic Grand Union bag containing a visible half gallon of milk, a kid who's been standing beside me, letting his milk carton bap against my leg for five minutes as if I wasn't there, *this* kid suddenly makes a springing, headlong dash from beside me, out across the front of the crowd, and with one insolent stomp of his silver foot whams down the red plunger of the phony detonator box, then goes whirling back past me around the end of the grandstand, darting and dodging through the standees toward the parking lot, where he disappears around a big Pace Arrow and is gone. "Motherfuckin' *boool*shit" is all I'm certain he says in departure, though he may have said something more.

And now the Queen Regent is headed down. Maybe the plunger did it. Black smoke gushes from what must be the hotel's deepest subterranean underpinnings, her staunchest supports (this will be what the Chinese seismographers detect). Her longitude lines, rows of square windows in previously perfect vertical alignment, all go wrinkled, as if the whole idea of the building had sustained, then sought to shrug off a profound insult, a killer wind off the ocean. And then rather simply, all the way down she comes, more like a brick curtain being lowered than like a proud old building being killed. Eighteen seconds is about it.

A clean vista briefly comes open behind the former Queen—toward Allenhurst and Deal—leafless trees, a few flecks of white house sidings, a glint of a car bumper. Then that is gone and a great fluff of cluttered gray smoke and dust whooshes upward and outward. We spectators are treated to a long, many-sectioned, more muffled than sharp progression of rumblings and crumblings and earth-delving noises that for a long moment strike us all silent (it must be the same at a public hanging or a head lopping).

Someone, another male, with a Maryland Tidewater accent, shouts, "*Awww*-raaiight. Yoooooo-hoo." (Who are the people who do this?) Then someone else shouts, "Aww-right," and people begin clapping in the tentative way people clap in movies. Big Frank, who's stood glaring across the empty Progress Zone, turns to the crowd with a smirk that combines disdain with derision. Someone yells, "Go get 'em, Frank!" And for an instant, I think he's shouting encouragement to me. But it's to the other Frank, who just waves a sausage hand dismissively—

know-nothings, jerkimos, putzes—and with his two red-suited lieutenants, stalks away around the far side of the bleachers and out of sight. One could hope, forever.

Wade's gone pensive as we walk back across the grass lot to my Suburban, a mood that's infected other spectators retreating to their campers and SUVs and vintage Volvos. Most conduct intimate hushed-voice exchanges. A few laugh quietly. Some brand of impersonal closure has been sought and gained at no one's expense. It's been a good outing. All seem to respect it.

Wade, however, is struggling some with his motor skills. How he climbed the bleachers, I don't know, though he seems a man at peace. He's told me that after Lynette retreated to the Bucks County nunnery and he'd retired from the Turnpike, he decided to put his Aggie engineering degree to use for the public's benefit. This involved trying out some invention ideas he'd logged in a secret file cabinet down in his Barnegat Pines basement (plenty of time to dream things up in the tollbooth). These were good ideas he'd never had time for while raising a family, moving up to New Jersey from the Dallas area and working a regular shift at Exit 9 for fifteen-plus years. His ideas were the usual Gyro Gearloose brainstorms: a lobster trap that floated to the surface when a lobster was inside; a device to desalinate seawater one glassful at a time—an obvious hit, he felt, with lifeboat manufacturers; a universal license plate that would save millions and make crime detection a cinch. If he could dream it up, it could work, was his reasoning. And there were plenty of millionaires to prove him right. You just had to choose one good idea, then concentrate resources and energies there. Wade chose as his idea the manufacture of mobile homes no tornado could sweep away in a path of destruction. It would revolutionize lower-middle-class life, Florida to Kansas, he felt certain. He took half his lump-payment Turnpike pension and sank it in a prototype and some expensive wind-tunnel testings at a private lab in Michigan. Naturally, none of it worked. The coefficients to wind resistance proved 100 percent relatable to mass, he said. To make a mobile home not blow away—and he knew this outcome was a possibility—you had to make it really heavy, which made it not a mobile home but just a house you wouldn't think to put up on wheels and move to Weeki Wachee. And apart from not working, his prototype was also far too expensive for the average mobile-home resident who works at the NAPA store.

Wade lost his money. His patent application was turned down. He damn near lost his house. And it was at that point, twelve or so years ago (he told me this), that he began taking an interest in demolitions and in the terminus-tending aspects of things found in everyday life. It's hard to argue with him, and I don't. Though selling real estate, I don't need to say, is dedicated to the very opposite proposition.

A small plane pulls a banner across the blue-streaked November sky above us, heading north into the no-fly zone now abandoned by the Coast Guard and the "News at Noon" copters. BLACK FRIDAY AT FOSDICKS? the trailing sign says. No one in the departing crowd pays it any attention. Up ahead, a black man is helping the Salvation Army woman lift her red kettle into a white panel truck. Several landmark protestors are trailing their signs behind them as·they seek their vehicles, satisfied they've again done their best. No one's much talking about the Queen Regent, now a rock pile awaiting bulldozers and fresh plans. Many seem to be chatting about tomorrow's turkey and the advent of guests.

"What do you hope for, Franky?" Wade has taken a grip of my left bicep and given me his Panasonic, which is surprisingly light. He's eaten his sandwiches and left the sack behind. My Suburban's at the far·end of the parked cars. Wade intends, I know, to leap-frog on to weightier matters. The reminder of his own end, concurrent with the Queen Regent's demise, fastens him down even more firmly to the here and now.

"I'm not a great hoper, Wade, I guess." We're not walking fast. Others pass us. "I just go in for generic hopes. That good comes to me, that I do little harm and die in my sleep."

"That's a lot to hope for." His grip is pinching the shit out of me right through my windbreaker. Then he unaccountably loosens up. Vehicles are starting around us, back-up lights and taillights snapping on. "I'm not alive from the waist down anymore. How 'bout you?" Wade isn't looking at me, but staring toward what's ahead—my Suburban, which has an altered look about it.

"I'm shipshape, Wade. Fire in the hole." I'm reliant on Dr. Psimos's assessment, and on how things seem most mornings. You could say I have high hopes for life below the waist.

"I've plateaued," Wade says irritably. "Left it all in the last century." He's frowning, as if he, too, has spied something wrong up ahead of us. The Millennium clearly has different resonances for different age brackets.

"Maybe enough's enough, Wade. You know?"

"So other people tell me."

What Wade and I have seen altered about my car is that the driver's-side backseat window's been smashed and glass particles scattered on the sparse grass. Below the door, on top of the glittering glass, is a flesh-colored Grand Union plastic bag with the milk carton inside. Though when I pick it up, it's as heavy as a brick, and on closer notice I discover that the Sealtest carton inside—a pink-toned photograph of a missing teen on the label—actually contains a brick. The carton's mission hasn't been what it seemed when I felt it bumping my leg, its little brigand owner awaiting his chance at mischief. Did he sense I was a Suburban owner? Was I under surveillance from the beginning? This is why I never hope: Hoping is not a practical mechanism for events that actually happen.

"Little pissmires nailed you," Wade snarls, taking in the damage, completely clear-brained, bifocals flashing at the chance to be permissibly pissed off, instantly intuiting the whole criminal scenario. "Too bad Cade's not here," he says, "though they probably didn't leave any prints." He hasn't seen the actual culprit, only the virtual one (the real one's spitting image). "Shouldn't of stuck that stupid sticker on your bumper." He scowls, walking around behind my car, assessing things like a cop, his little bandy-legged self full-up with race bile, which makes me angrier than the busted window—and fingers me as a typical liberal. "They probably hate fat-ass Gore worse than they hate shit-for-brains," he says. (His only name for Bush.) Wade's mouth wrinkles into a twisted, unhumorous smile of seen-it-all pleasure. "What'd they get? Did you leave your billfold in there?"

"No." I touch my lumpy back pocket, then peer inside the mostly glassless window hole, trying not to touch a sharp edge. Glass kernels carpet the backseat and floor. Sunlight on the roof has turned it hot and boggy inside. The deed can't be more than five minutes old. I stand up and look longingly around, as if I could rerun things, set a guiding, weighted hand onto little Shaquille's or little Jamal's sun-warmed head, walk with him over to the boardwalk for a funnel cake and some unangrified, nonjudgmental, free-form man-to-man about where one goes wrong in these matters. Possibly he's a member of Cub Pack 31 and is at work on his larceny merit badge.

Nothing's present in the backseat but a torn-out *Asbury Park Press* real estate page, a couple of red-and-white bent-legged Realty-Wise signs and the pink Post-it with Mike's directions to Mullica Road. That seems long ago. Though yesterday wasn't better than today. If anything, it was worse. I haven't been in a fistfight today or had my neck twisted (yet). I haven't been vilified, haven't gotten in deep with my ex-wife, haven't gone to a funeral. It may not be the right moment to count my blessings, but I do.

An enormous Invector RV as big as a team bus, with Indian arrow markings on its side, comes rumbling past us, its owner-operator a tiny balding figure with sunglasses inside the slide-back captain's window. He frowns down at me with empathy and stops. He's a "Good Sam" and has the smiling, stupid mouthy-guy-with-the-halo decal on one of his back windows. These birds are always Nazis. The captain's sweet-faced wife's behind him in the copilot's space, craning past to see down to me and my lower-case woes. I know she feels empathy for me, too. But being peered down at, shattered glass around my feet, my car busted and an orange-skinned old loony as my teammate, makes me feel a wind-whistling loss far beyond empathy's reach.

"Vehicle crime's up twenty percent due to the Internet," the Invector captain says from behind his sunglasses, surveying the scene from above. He's weasly, with a puny little mustache that he may have just started. His wife's saying something I can't hear. Another man and woman, their lifelong friends, plus the square head of a Great Dane, appear in the back living-quarters window. All stare at me gravely, the dog included.

"What'd he say?" Wade says from behind my car.

I can't repeat it. A saving force in the universe forbids me. Something tells me these travelers are from central Florida, possibly the Lakeland area, which makes me hate them. I shrug and look back at my window hole. I'm still holding Wade's Panasonic, as if I was taping everything.

"No use callin' the cops," the land-yacht driver says, down from his little window. His wife nods. Their passengers have pulled the café curtains farther apart and are rubber-necking me and Wade and my broken vehicle. Both are holding tall-boys of Schlitz. I am another feature of the interesting New Jersey landscape, a textbook case of worsening crime statistics. Eighty percent of murders are committed by people who know their victims, which means many murders are probably not as senseless as they seem.

"I guess," I say, and fake a grateful smile upward.

"Oh yeah!" From somewhere, a hidey-hole the police wouldn't find—in a safe box, a glove compartment, under the sun visor—the land-yacht guy produces a nickel-plated revolver as big as Wade's video cam, from whose barrel end he coolly blows invisible smoke like an old-west gunfighter who is also a good samaritan. "They don't fuck with me," he smirks. His wife gives him a halfhearted whap on the shoulder for language reasons. Their friends in the back laugh soundlessly. I'm sure they're all Church of Christers.

"That oughta do it," I say.

"That already *has* done it," he says. "I'm ex-peace officer." He lowers his big Ruger, S&W, Colt, whatever, smiles a goofy sinister smile, then revs his Invector into new life, issuing an order over his shoulder to his passengers, who disappear from the window. He sets some kind of blue ball-cap with U.S. Navy braiding onto his skint head. "Buckle up. We're casting off," a man's voice says inside. The captain's wife mouths something to me as her window of opportunity closes, but I can't hear for the motor noise. "Okay," I say. "Thanks." But it's the wrong thing to say as they sway away over the dry grass toward new marvels awaiting them.

Cold pre-Thanksgiving winds whistle through my broken back window, stiffening my neck and making me feel like I'm catching something, even though I had a flu shot and am probably not. The advance weather of tropical depression Wayne is moving up the seaboard, and the once-nice sky has quilted into dense cotton batting, the cold sun that warmed us in the bleachers now retired. It's November. Nothing more nor less.

The Queen Regent's big finish has contributed little to Wade and me, only a bleak and barren humility, suggesting closure's easier to wish for than locate. Driving back out Lake Avenue toward the Fud druckers—through a precinct of crumbling mansions, a Dominican "hair station," the Cobra motorcycle club and the Nubian Nudee Revue, all bordering a pretty green lake with low Parisian bridges crossing to a more prosperous town to the south (Ocean Grove)—I spy my little culprit window smasher, tootling along down the crumbling sidewalk in his big silver shoes and hooded sweatshirt, under the heavy hand of the Chicago Jew-Dog purveyor, a giant coffee-black Negro with woolly hair and big inner-tube biceps. Wade's mooning out the window, sees these citizens and makes a satisfied grunt of approval, as if to say, See, now. More of this kind of parental oversight will get you less of that other stuff . . . pass on the vital gnosis of the civilization . . . a sense of what's right . . . intact units, yadda, yadda, yadda. Better than a perp walk into social services in plastic bracelets, I'll concede, and drive us on.

Wade is exhausted. His rucked hands, in the skinny lap of his jackass pants, have begun just noticeably to tremble, and his old white-fringed head won't exactly be still and is ducked, anticipating sleep—which he complains he does little of. He smells possibly more sour, and one of his scuffed patent-leather slip-ons taps the floor mat softly. Old people, no matter what anyone says, do not make the best company when spirits flag. They tend to sink toward private thoughts or embarrassed, uncomprehending silence, from whose depths they don't give much of a shit about anybody else's private thoughts—all the "great experience" they carry become essentially useless. Not that I blame him. Seeing an implosion has given him the peek into oblivion he wanted. It simply hasn't changed anything.

I remember, years ago, after my father died and my mother and I were living in a sandy, ant-infested asbestos-sided house near Keesler, my mother one morning backed our big green Mercury right over my little black-and-white kitten, Mittens. Apparently nothing caught her notice, because she continued out onto the street and drove away to her job. It was not the best time in her life. But Mittens made a terrible squawling scream I heard inside the house. And when I raced out in a panic of knowledge and cold helplessness, there was the sad, mangled little cat, not long for the planet, flopping and wriggling, making awful strangling noises out of his crushed little gullet and turning me crazed, since my mother was gone and no one was there to help.

Next door, on our neighbor's front porch, was the neighbor lady's—Mrs. Mockbee's—antique old daddy, a dapper turkey-necked fossil who told my mother he'd fought in the Civil War but of course hadn't. Still, he called himself Major Mockbee and sat long days on his daughter's concrete porch in a straw boater, red bow tie, suspenders, spats and seersucker suit, chewing, spitting and talking to himself while Keesler Saber jets flew over.

He alone was there when Mittens got flattened by my mother's Merc. The only adult. And it was to him I fled, my mind a fevered chaos, across the driveway in the sweltering Mississippi morning, across the damp St. Augustine and up the three steps onto the porch. The poor little cat had already grown quiet, breathing his troubled last. But I pushed his smushed limp body straight into Major Mockbee's field of vision—he knew me, we'd spoken before. And I said, tears squirting, my heart pounding, my limbs aching with fear (I shouted, really), "My mother ran over my cat. I don't know what to do!"

To which Major Mockbee, after spitting a glob over the porch rail into the camellias, clearing his acrid old throat and putting on a pair of wire spectacles to have a better look, said, "I believe you've got yourself a Persian. It looks like a Persian. I'd say something's wrong with it, though. It looks sick."

Unfair, I know. But truth is truth. I sometimes think of old people as being *like* pets. You love them, amuse yourself *with* them, tease and humor them, feed them and make them happy, then take solace that you're probably going to live longer than they will.

Back in the Barnegat Pines days of '84—when Wade took life more as it tumbled, projected a seamless, amiable surface, kept his garage neat, his tools stowed, his oil changed, tires rotated, went to church most Sundays, watched the Giants not the Jets, prayed for both the Democrats *and* the Republicans, favored a humane, Vatican II approach to the world's woes, inasmuch as we live amid surfaces, etc.—back then I just assumed he, like the rest of us (prospective son-in-laws think such things), would wake up one morning at four, feel queasy, a little light-headed, achy from that leaf raking he'd done the evening before and decide not to get up quite yet. Then he'd put his head back to the pillow for an extra snooze and somewhere around six and without a whimper, he'd soundlessly buy the farm. "He usually didn't sleep that late, but I thought, well, he's been under a strain at work, so I just let him—" Gone. Cold as a pike.

Only, age plays by strange rules. Wade's now survived happiness to discover decrepitude. To be alive at eighty-four, he's had to become someone entirely other than the smooth-jawed ex-Nebraska engineer who was cheered to see the sun rise, cheered to see it set. He's had to *adapt* (Paul would say "develop")—to shrink around his bones like a Chinaman, grow stringy, volatile, as self-interested as a pawnbroker, unable to see his fellowmen except as blunt instruments of his demon designs. Apart from merely liking him, and liking to match Wade-remembered to Wade-present tense, I'm also interested for personal reasons in observing if any demonstrable good's to be had from getting as old as Methuselah, other than that the organism keeps functioning like a refrigerator. We assume persistence to be a net gain, but it still needs to be proved.

"Why don't you come down to my place for dinner?" Wade says gruffly out of the blue, more energetic than I expected.

"Thanks, but I've got some duties." Not true. We're re-crossing 35, the route I'll take home. Some commercial establishment—I don't know where, but cultural literacy tells me it's there—will be eager to fix my back window, if only in a temporary way until after the holiday. Busted Back Windows R-Us.

"What the hell duties have *you* got?" Wade cuts his jagged eyes at me, working his tongue tip along his lower lip. He gives one bulky beige hearing device a jab with his thumb. "You don't have a new girlfriend, do you?"

"I have a wife. I have *two* wives. At least I—"

"Hah!" Wade makes a strangled noise that could be a cough or a last gasp of life. "You know the penalty for bigamy? Two wives! I had two. I'm single now. Never had so much fun." Wade's forgotten we're acquainted. He'll be calling me Ned next. Ned might be better than Frank now, since Frank's not feeling so enthusiastic.

Evenings down at the Grove are not for everybody. Dinner's at 6:00 and over by 6:25. Then the inmates (the ones that can) scuttle out to the common room for rapt-silence CNN viewing and alarming postprandial personal odors. Meals are color-coded—something brown, something red, something that once was green, with tapioca or syrupy no-sugar fruit to follow. If I went with Wade, we'd arrive early, have to wait in his two-room "en suite," full of his bric-a-brac, his bathroom full of medicines, his framed Turnpike battle insignias and vestigial home furnishings from Barnegat Pines. We'd watch a *Jeopardy* rerun, then get in an argument, like we did the one time I was a guest and unexpectedly saw him naked. It's no wonder Cade and family stay up in Pohatcong and don't much look in. What can you do? Things are what they are. If we hang on too long, we reach the back side of the Permanent Period, where life doesn't grow different, there's just more of it until the lights go dim.

"I've got a surprise for you." Wade's white slip-on's still tapping the floor mat, but his hand-trembling and neck-ducking have ceased. I've turned up the heater due to the back window draft. Suburbans have world-beating comfort systems, which is a reason to own one.

Wade claims he indulges in unbridled semi-sexual liaisons with several of the grannies at the Grove—in spite of being dead below the belt line. He charms them with his implosion videos and spicy narratives about things he's seen in the backseats of stretch limos passing through his tollbooth. During my one visit, he had a tiny powdery-cheeked, pink-haired lawyer's widow in her seventies as his squeeze. They smirked and winked, and Wade made lewd innuendos about night-time feats he was still capable of after two vodka gimlets and a Viagra chaser.

"I'd love to, but I've got a house-full back home," I say, easing into the Fuddruckers' lot across from the streaming Parkway. Wade's Olds sits nosed under the faded yellow awning. A blue-and-white Asbury Park PD cruiser with a Bush sticker is parked across the lot, its hatless occupant observing traffic through the intersection. Technically, I have *no one* waiting at home. Paul and the unusual Jill have checked into the Beachcomber and are dining at Ann's. Clarissa's off on her heterosex escapade with honey-voiced Thom. My house is ringingly empty on Thanks-giving eve. How does that happen?

"But how 'bout I mention there's somebody back at my place who'd love to lay eyes on you?" Wade's damp mouth wallops shut, suppressing a smile. He's up to mischief, stroking his Caesarish comb-down like an old Arab. One of his wrinkle-cheeked old squeezes no doubt has a freshly widowed sister from the Wildwoods who's a "young sixty-eight" and on the hunt.

"I need to get this window fixed, Wade."

"It's what?" Wade looks affronted. His tongue darts in and out like a viper's.

"My window." I motion backward with my thumb. "It's trying to rain."

"You're cracked! You need a new connection, mister. There's something hollow under you, you know that?" Wade's suddenly talking way too loud and vehement for our close quarters. He's been sneaking up on this with his questions about hoping and my sexual problems and barbs about my absent wife.

We're stopped alongside his Olds. I check in the rearview to see if the cop's surveilling us, which of course he is. Possibly the empty Fuddruckers' lot is a rendezvous point in the white-slave market.

Wade's eyes fix on me accusingly, making me feel accused. "I don't think that's true, Wade."

"You're a goddamn house peddler. You hang around with strangers all the time. You're gonna be poopin' in a bag one of these days—if you live long enough. Which you may not." His old mouth does something between a terrible grin and a furious frown. It's close to the look my son Paul turned on me last spring in K.C. Only Wade's upper falsie set sinks a millimeter, so he has to clack it back up with his lowers. I'm happy Wade's still in touch with who I am.

"Well." I glance again at the Asbury cop.

"Well what?" Wade dips his head like a goose, snorts, then suddenly stares down at his big watchband as if he was on a tight schedule.

Cold air is still drawing in on my neck. "It may not seem like it, Wade," I say softly, "but I'm connected enough. Real estate's a good connecter."

"Bullshit. It's putting stitches in a dead man's arm." He blinks, ducks, saws his wrist—the one with his Medi-Ident—across his red nose, then grabs his Panasonic off the seat. "You're an asshole."

"I just told you how I feel about things, Wade. I wasn't trying to piss you off. My belief is we all have an empty spot underneath us. It doesn't hurt anything." I tap my foot on the brake. This needs to end now.

"You're in a dangerous spot, Franky." Wade pops open his big door. "However old you are. Fifty-what?"

"Two." Which feels better than fifty-five. I gently bite down on a welt of my left cheek—a bad sign. I'm not going to the Grove with Wade and make woo-woo with some retired reference librarian from Brigantine. I'd end up driving home to Sea-Clift with black vanquishment filling my car like cyanide.

"Fifty-two doesn't mean *anything*!" Wade croaks. "You're *between* everything good when you're fifty-two. You need to get hooked up or you're screwed. I married Lynette when I was fifty-two. Saved my ass."

Wade of course has told me *never* to get married again, and Lynette, after all, left him for the Lord. Plus, I believe I'm still married. "You were lucky."

"I was *smart*. I wasn't lucky." Wade levers one trembling sockless white-shoed foot out and down onto the pavement, then the other, then cautiously scoots his scrawny ass off the seat, holding the door handle for support, emitting a tiny effortful grunt.

"I guess we might as well think our life's the way it is 'cause that's how we want it, Wade."

"Haw!" He's studying down at his feet as if to be sure they know their assignments. "That's in your brain."

"That's where a lot of stuff goes on."

"Think, think, thinky, think. In *your* life it does. Not mine." Wade gives my car door a fearsome, dismissive bang shut.

I power down the passenger window so he's not shut out. "Don't think I don't appreciate your thinking about me." Think, think, thinky, think.

"I'll tell my daughter you gotta think about gettin' your window fixed instead of seein' her." Wade's mouth wrinkles up bitterly as he starts his staggering departure.

Daughter?

"Which daughter?" I say through the window.

"Which daughter?" Wade's red-rimmed eyes glare in at me, as if I knew we'd been talking about his daughter this whole time, and why was I being such a stupe? Stupe, stupe, stupey, stupe. "I only have one, you nunce. Your girlfriend. You farted around with her till you ran her off right in my front yard. You're a nunce, you know that? You like being a nunce. You get to do a lot of good thinking that way." Wade starts struggling toward the front of my car, heading toward his Olds, his Panasonic bumping my fender panels he's holding onto for balance. I can only see the upper half of him, but he's not looking at me, as if I'd stopped existing in here.

But. Daughter!

For these weeks, traveling to the odd implosion here, another there, a cup of chowder or a piece of icebox pie in a Greek diner, I've all but expunged from my thoughts the truth that Wade is father to Vicki (now Ricki), my long-gone dream of a lifetime from when I, as a divorced man, wrote for a glossy New York sports magazine, horsed around with women, suffered dreaminess both night and day and had yet to list my first house. I rashly, wrongly loved nurse Arsenault with my whole heart and libido, was ready to tie the knot, move to Lake Havasu and live in an Airstream off savings (I had none). Only she lacked the necessary whatever (love for me) and sent me packing. So Wade's wrong about who heave-ho'd who. Vicki shortly afterward married a handsome, clean-cut Braniff pilot, moved to Reno, became a trauma nurse at St. Crimonies, eventually was widowed when Darryl Lee crashed his spotter plane in Kuwait under the command of Bush #1.

I haven't seen, spoken to or thought much about Vicki/Ricki, who I guarantee was a yeasty package, since '84, and wouldn't recognize her if she shot out of Fuddruckers on a pair of roller skates. Although *daughter* sets loose deep space-clearing stirrings. Not that I want to see her any more than I want to see the reference librarian from Brigantine. But the thought of Vicki/Ricki— once a bounteous, boisterous, fine-thighed and raven-haired dreamboat—sets my ribs atremble, I'm not ashamed to say it. On the other hand, driving to the Grove on the night before Thanksgiving for a surprise face-to-face, followed by an unwieldy *intime* in some ennui-drenched south Jersey "steak place," at the conclusion of which she and I disappear in opposite directions into the teeming night, is far from anything I want to happen to me. Even though I have nothing else to do: early to bed amid sea breezes after maybe getting my window fixed.

"Maybe Ricki and I can have lunch once the holiday's over," I say insincerely out the window to where Wade has navigated around the front of my car. I don't want him to feel condescended to on the topic of his marriageable daughter. I have some experience there.

"What?" he snaps. He's putting his video cam down on the passenger's side seat as if it was his honored guest.

"Tell Ricki I said howdy."

"Yeah, I'll do that."

"When am I likely to see you again? When's our next blow-up?" Wade has forgotten I've invited him for Thanksgiving, an offer I now silently retract in self-defense.

"I dunno." He's begun crawling into his car from the wrong side.

"Wade, are you okay in there?" My smile dwindles to a half smile of concern.

"How do I look?" His baggy ass and the scuffed soles of his slip-ons face me out of his open car door.

I could get the Asbury cop to come confiscate Wade's car keys if I thought he'd lost his marbles and presented a threat to the public. Except I'd have to drive him home. "You got your keys?" I sing out hopefully.

"Kiss my ass." He's struggling down onto his donut, his feet to the floor, back to his cushion. I hear him breathe sternly. "Goddamn piece of shit."

"What's happening in there, Wade? You need some help?"

Wade burns a scowl back at me, then looks at his instruments. "Goddamn door's busted. Some idiot woman backed into me at CVS. Now get your silly ass out and close my door. You nunce." He's got his little biscuit hands fastened to the wheel at ten and two, like Mike Mahoney. His keys dangle from the ignition, where they've been the whole time. He gets her cranked as I get out into the cold. It's sizing up to rain more. Yesterday's weather is hanging over the seaboard like a bad memory. Plus there's tropical disturbance Wayne.

"I wanted you to get to see Vicki," Wade says. "She wants to see you." He can't remember her new name and won't look at me, only out at the Fuddruckers' chained and locked front door. He's resigned more than mad and, like all good fathers, ineptly keeping vigil for his offspring's improvement. "We'll have lunch" is not what he wants to hear. Wade wants me in the steak place with his honey bunch, ordering our third martini, with love—belated, grateful, willing, candid, budding and, above all, permanent—saturating the dark, rich airs like gardenias. It's his last try to set things right before his hour's called.

Though based on history, there's nothing I can do. The last thing Vicki Arsenault ever said to me sixteen years ago, from her bachelorette apartment in Pheasant Run on the Hightstown Pike, by phone to my former, since-demolished family home in Haddam, was, "Woo, boy-hidee, you like to of fooled me." She talked in a wide, east Dallas, barrel-racer lingo, just right for barrooms, bronco-buster sex and no bullshit but hers. I loved it.

"How did I fool you, sweetheart? I love you so much," I said. It was spring. The copper beech was in abundance. The wisteria and lilacs in bloom. The dreamy time of love's labors lost.

"'Sweetheart'?" she pooh-poohed. "Love *me*? Opposites cain't love. Opposites just attract. And we're done through with that. Least I am. But I almost took a tumble. I'll give you that." I remember her wonderful tongue-cluck, like a jockey signaling giddy-up.

"I still want you to marry me," I said. And I dearly did— would've in a minute and been happy. Although it would've been the lamp business more than the realty business, the unexamined life more than the life steeped in reflection and contingency. Win-win.

"Yeah, but first we'd get married"—I knew she was beaming her big Miss Cotton Bowl smile—"and then we'd have to get divorced. And I need somebody who'll get me all the way to death. And that id'n you."

Death. Even then!

"I'll give a call in the next couple days, Wade." I'm leaning into his open door, radiating bad faith. "Maybe Ricki'll have time to grab lunch. It'd be good to catch up." The prospect makes my brain swell.

Wade carefully uncouples his spectacles from his crusted ears and gives his old eyes a good knuckle-kneading that's probably painful. He turns toward me, sockets hollowed, pale and knobby, his left pupil orbited out to left field. Age is not gentle or amusing.

"I can't talk you into it?" he says, insulted.

"I guess not, Wade." I smile the way you would into the upside-down mirror of an iron-lung patient. "I'll call. We'll stage a lunch."

"You're not vital anymore. You know that?" He sniffs as if my words carried a bad odor, then looks disgusted and shakes his head. His Olds is idling. The Asbury cop, his gray exhaust visible in falling temps, eases out into traffic and slowly motors

away. The wind has a bite that stings my butt. Across the access
road, the Parkway groans with the *hum-bum-bum* sounds of pre-
Thanksgiving hurry-up.

"I'm working on vital," I say. "It's on my short list." I try a
smile.

"Hunh," Wade grumps. He doesn't know what I'm talking
about. "You're a nunce. I already said that."

"Could be true." I'm holding his car door open.

"Remember the three boats, Franky?" The three boats parable
is Wade's favorite. He's told me the three boats story six times
in support of six different points of reference—most recently the
presidential race and the American people's blindness to the
obvious.

"I do, Wade. I only get three boats."

"What?" He can't hear me. "You only get three, and you
already had two." He gives me a mean threat-look across the
seat, where his silver Panasonic lies full of new implosion footage.
"This is your last one." My first pair of boats, I take it, symbolizes
my two marriages, though they could also reference my prostate
condition.

"Okay, I'll give it some serious thought. Maybe it'll make me
more vital. I hope so."

"How long has it been for you?" Wade drops the Olds into
gear, causing a sinister metal-on-metal *ker-klunk*.

"How long's what been? There's been a lot of 'it's' this year.
Hard to keep 'em straight."

"Since you were with anybody?" His scraggly old brows dart
up lewdly.

"Since I was *with* anybody?" Wade's lips tremble with a hint of below-the-belt seaminess. "What do you mean?" I'm still holding open the passenger door, but I must be squeezing it, because my thumb's gotten numb. What's the matter with the world all of a sudden?

"Ah, forget it. The hell with you." He's scowling up into his rearview. Conversation over. He's ready to make a move.

"I don't want to think about the implications of what you're saying, Wade." Why does this sound so pompous and stupid?

"Yeah, yeah," Wade growls. "Think, think, thinky, think. Where do you think you're gonna end up?"

"Go fuck yourself. Okay?" I stand back and give his car door a powerful slam closed. I can just hear him say, "Yeah, maybe I will."

Wade's begun backing up, using his mirror in the tried-and-true manner of the old and joint-frozen. I have to step lively since he hauls on the wheel like a stevedore, swerves and nearly swipes my foot. I can see his mouth working, in furious converse with the face in the rearview.

"Be careful, Wade," I call out. He's glued to his mirror and can't see the fat red postpole holding aloft the gold sunburst Fuddruckers' WORLD'S GREATEST HAMBURGERS sign, plus a smaller white one that says EAT HEALTHY! TRY AN OSTRICH BURGER!

The old Eighty Eight crunches straight into the postpole with a hollow metallic *bung* noise, the whole vehicle caroming back and jangling to a stop, giving Wade a jolt inside. He glowers up at the mirror, half-cocks his head around as three black letters off the Ostrich Burger sign spiral down—the *O*, the *N* and the *H*—and clatter onto his rusted-through vinyl roof.

Wade's twisted around, facing back, able now to see the pipe he's smacked. Without looking, he sends the Olds lurching forward in "D," burns rubber, then stabs the brakes and stops again, the motor racing to indicate he's somehow gotten into "N."

"Wade!" I shout. "Hold it. Hold it." I'm coming to give assistance, in spite of Wade being the shameless procurer for his own daughter. I'll have to take charge of him now, transport him home in *my* vehicle, meet Vicki/Ricki, go to dinner, etc., etc., none of which I want to do. Too bad the Asbury cop's left already. He could arrest Wade, call the EMS and Ricki could claim him in the Monmouth County ER, where she'd know all the procedures.

Wade's mouth's still working vigorously. He fires a look of betrayal out at me, seeing I'm coming to help him. I'm to blame for all of this. If I'd gone down to the Grove and made everybody happy, none of this horseshit would be happening. I don't know what made me think I could befriend the father of a former love interest who spurned me. These conjunctions aren't meant to happen except among the primitive Yanomami. Not in New Jersey.

Wade's staring down at his dashboard. Rust and road crap have dislodged from the Olds' chassis, though nothing seems broken or hanging. One of the Ostrich Burger letters has slid off his roof and lodged under the passenger-side wiper blade. It is an *H*. The sign now reads EAT EALTHY.

I step out in front of Wade's car and raise my hand like an Indian. I see he's furious. He could easily run me over. You read about these deaths in the paper every day. Wade grimaces at me through the windshield. His engine suddenly kicks up a mighty *whaaaa*, and I start back-pedaling, my hand still up in the original peace sign, and almost stumble back on my ass as he socks it into "D" again and the Olds springs ahead with a screech, headed toward the EXIT and the traffic-clogged business street leading to the Parkway. I'm all out of the way but can feel the Olds' side panel whip past me. It's as if I'm not here, not even a holiday statistic. Wade's fighting the wheel to get himself into the EXIT side of the curb-cut. His shoulder dips left, his hands still at ten and two. *Brack, brack, brack.* The old Eighty Eight judders, bucks, then judders again—probably the parking brake's on—heading across the empty lot into the ENTRANCE side, not the EXIT. "Wade!" I shout again, and start walking toward his car, its brake lights glowing, exhaust shooting out. I'll help him. I'll drive him. The Olds dips stopped, then noses out toward the traffic that's backed up at the red light. Though the red immediately goes to green, and the cars commence smoothly forward. Wade's head is oscillating back and forth, hawking a place in the line, his mouth still going. I'm moving toward him. I haven't helped him. I'm very aware of that, but I will—for all the difference it'll make. A young woman in a blue Horizon full of kids smiles at Wade, waves a hand, motions his beater out into the flow. And in just that number of precious seconds and before I can get there to give help, Wade smoothly becomes traffic, his taillights blending into the flux of the street and on under the Parkway overpass. And gone.

12

Eyes peeled, I cruise busy 35 South—Bradley Beach, Neptune, Belmar. I'm expecting a storefront to be open at 3:30 on Thanksgiving eve, with GLASS on the menu. These places thrive on every street corner in America, though they vanish when you want one. Cultural literacy's never perfect.

Wintry effluvium has turned my vehicle into an icebox, and I've cranked the heat up on my feet, my belly already sensing a mixed signal from my hot dog. The three boats parable is, in fact, a useful moral directive, and though Wade would sneer at me, in my own view I've heeded it by giving a wide berth to the Grove and Vicki/Ricki, or whatever her name is. Of course, my more natural habit would be to consider most all things as mutable, and to resist obstinance in human affairs, an attitude which has helped me to think more positively about Sally's return and not to be flattened like roadkill by her abandoning me (I think of myself as a variablist). The realty profession itself thrives on the perpetual expectation of changes for the better, and is permanently resistant to the concept of either the rock or the hard place. Ann, however, once pointed out to me that a variablist can be a frog who sits in a pan of water, looking all around and feeling pretty good about things, while the heat's gradually turned up, until cozy, happy pond life becomes frog soup.

In the three boats story, a man is floating alone in an ocean without a life jacket when a boat passes by. "Get in. I'll save you," the boatman says. "Oh, no, it's fine," the floating man answers, "I'm putting my faith in the Lord." In time, two more boats come along, and to each rescuer the man—usually me, in Wade's telling—says, "No, no, I'm putting my faith in the Lord." Eventually, and it isn't very long in coming, the man drowns. Yet when he stands up to meet his Maker at the fated spot where some rejoice but many more cower, his Maker looks sternly down and says, "You're a fool. You're assigned to hell forever. Go there now." To which the drowned man says, "But your honor, I put my faith in you. You promised to save me." "Save you!?" fearsome God shouts from misty marmoreal heights (and this is the moment the old liver-lipped procurer of his own daughter likes most, when his scaly eyelids blink down hard and his tongue darts like a grinning Beelzebub). "Save you? *Save* you?" God thunders. "I sent you three boats!" And off goes Frank forever.

The last time Wade told this story—in reference to who the American people should've chosen but probably didn't in this doomed election now awaiting God's wrath—God supposedly said, "Three *fucking* boats! I already sent you three *fucking* boats, you morons. Now go to hell." God, Wade believes, sees most things as they are and has no trouble telling it.

But the point's plain. Drowning men save themselves, no matter how it looks from the shore and even though it's not always easy to assess your own situation. Vicki/Ricki's my last boat, Wade believes. Though in my view (and what could she look like after sixteen years), she's only a ghost ship out of the mists. To drive to the Grove and re-connect with that old life would be treacherous even for a variablist—as asinine as Sally heading off to Mull or Ann wanting to forge a new union with me. In the modern idiom, that boat won't float. And I'm resolved to stay here even in the deep water, waiting for the next one, even if it's the boat to you-know-where.

*T*he first glass place I see—Glass, Glass, & More Glass— is closed, closed, & more closed. The second, Want a Pane in the Glass? in the 35 U-Need-It Strip Mall, has its metal grate chained to the sidewalk and everything dark within. The third, in Manasquan—forthrightly called Glass?—appears open, though when I walk inside the dingy, echoing, oily-lit front show-room with its big sheets of plate glass leaned against the walls, there's not a soul in evidence. I step through a door to a long, cold, shadowy room with empty wide-topped tables where glass could be cut. But no one's around—no sounds of skilled labor in progress, or the after-work noises of back-room pre-holiday whiskey cheer. Which suddenly turns me spooky, as if a storage bin of cooling corpses awaits beyond the next door, a preholiday revenge-hit by elements from north of here.

"Hello," I timidly call out—but only once—then, quick as a flash, beat it back to my freezing car.

It has somehow become four o'clock. Daylight's sunk out of the invisible east. Sunset's at a daunting 4:36. Brash wind and slashing rain sheets have begun whacking my windshield and beading moisture on the backseat. Headlights are now in use.

It's drive-time, the race home, the time no one but the doomed want to be on our nation's roadways—including me, with nobody waiting at the doorway, no plans to make the hours resemble the true joy of living.

A drink's what I require. I usually hold the line till six, a discipline well known to weary corporate accountants, single-handed sailors and hard-luck novelists in need of cheering. But six is a state of mind, and my state of mind says it's six, which even out front of the spooky Glass? confers a jollying self-confirming certainty that positive elections can still be mine—not just refusals to drive Wade to the Grove or to romance the unspecified Ricki. I can have a drink. *Some* good things, warm sensations, await me.

I'm once again only a stone's short throw from the old Manasquan Bar, below the river bridge, where I took the 34 cutoff earlier. There I can certainly have a drink (and a piss) in familiar, congenial surroundings. Save an Hour, Save an Evening—the late-occurring motto for the day.

The Manasquan, which I head straight toward, would ordinarily—as I said before—be off-limits to me due to its anchorage in the past and prone-ness to fumy nostalgias. In the middle eighties, it had its scheduled and amiable purpose. After a night's chartered fishing excursion on the *Mantoloking Belle*, the Manasquan was the Divorced Men's special venue for demonstrating residual rudimentary social, communicative and empathy skills (we actually weren't very good at any of these things and not good at fishing, either), and we all fled to it the instant we stepped off our boat—our legs rubbery, arms weak from manning our rods, thirsts worked up. The charter captain's mustachioed brother-in-law owned the place—an extended family of crafty Greeks. And it sat where it sat—hard by the dock—to make sure the Mouzakis family got all our money before sending us home happier but wiser. Which, as if by magic, is what happened— until it didn't, at which point and by no agreed-upon signal, we all quit going and consigned it to the past and oblivion, where we wished our old marriages would go.

Though I sense I have nothing to fear now from the Manasquan, for reason of its prosaic, standard-dockside, snug-away character—the red BAR sign on its shingled roof, muted rose-blue accent lights, tar-ry nautical smells, plenty of cork buoys and shellacked swordfish husks on the walls alongside decades of dusty fishermen photos. It will be as it was years back: detoxified and inoculated by inauthenticity, with no negative juju powers to give me the creeps about not throwing my life over to become a second mate on a halibut hauler off the Grand Banks, and instead being a realtor—or a State Farm agent in Hightstown, or a garden supply owner-operator in Haddam, or a podiatrist in Rocky Hill—all those things we were back in '83. Of course, I anticipated the same at the Johnny Appleseed last night, with sorry results.

I take the Manasquan jug-handle and loop down around to the small embarcadero fronting the River Marina, where banners are still up from the annual striper derby in September, an antique fair and last summer's Big Sea Day on the beach. All is familiar— the Mouzakis Paramount Show Boat Dock and the lowly Manasquan itself, red BAR warmly glowing through the early-evening rain.

Although names have changed. The Paramount Dock is now Uncle Ben's Excursions. The old *Belle*, with a fresh pink paint job, is dimly visible at the dock's end, bearing the name *Pink Lady.* The shingled, barn-roofed Manasquan, once in neon above the portholed entry, has become Old Squatters, with a plain black-letter sign hung to the door itself.

And by a good stroke, across the puddled lot from the dock and bar, there's now, outside the old Quonset shed where nautical gear was once stored for the charter business, a shingle that says BOAT, CARS, TRAILER REPAIRS. NO JOB TOO ABSURD. Lights are on in the garage and the tiny office. I swing around, stop in front and walk up to ask about a back-window repair.

Inside, a small black-haired man in need of a shave is seated behind the counter, close to a gas space heater, listening to a Greek radio station playing twiny bouzouki music while he eats an enormous sandwich. A long-legged, peroxided, pimpled kid with tattoos on his arms, possibly the son, sits in a tipped-back dinette chair across the tiny overheated office, bent over a foxed copy of *The Great Gatsby*—the old green-gray-and-white Scribner Library edition I read in "American Existentialism and Beyond" in Ann Arbor in 1964. For decades, I reread it every year, exactly the way we're all supposed to, then got sick of its lapidary certainties disguised as spoiled innocence—something I don't believe in—and gave my last copy to the Toms River Shriners' Xmas Benefit. Garage mechanics, of course, play a pivotal role in Fitzgerald's denouement, transacted scarcely a hundred miles from here as the gull flies. It is this boy, I'm certain, who's authored the sign outside, and he I address about my window.

His eyes raise above his book top and he smiles a perfectly receptive smile, though the older attendant never looks at me. He may only wait on other Greeks.

"Okay," the boy says before I can explain the whole situation and how little I'll be satisfied with. "I'll do it. Duct tape okay?" He looks back with interest to his page. He's near the end, where Meyer Wolfsheim says, "When a man gets killed I never like to get mixed up in it in any way. I keep out." Sound advice.

"Great," I say. "I'll head over to the Manasquan and try the cocktails." I offer a nod of trust that promises a big tip.

"Leave me them keys." He's wearing a blue mechanic's shirt with a white patch that says *Chris* in red cursives. Likely he's a Monmouth College student on Thanksgiving break, the first of his immigrant family to blub, blub, blub.. I'm tempted to poll his views about Jay Gatz. Victim? Ill-starred innocent? Gray-tinged antihero? Or all three at once, vividly registering Fitzgerald's glum assessment of our century's plight—now blessedly at an end. The "boats against the current, borne back ceaselessly into the past" imagery is at odds with the three boats imagery of the old Nick Carraway doppelganger, Wade. It's possible of course that as a modern student, Chris doesn't subscribe to the author concept *per se*. I, however, still do.

Keys handed off, I head across the drizzly gravel lot to the Old Squatters né Manasquan, heartened that the time-honored shade-tree way of doing business "While-U-Wait" is still a tradition in this part of our state—among immigrants anyway—and hasn't caved in to the franchise volume-purchasing-power mentality that only knows "that's on back order" or "the manufacturer stopped making those"—the millennial free-enterprise canon in which the customer's a bit-part player to the larger drama of gross accumulation (what the Republicans want for us, though the liars say they don't).

Dense, good bar smell meets me when I step inside, surprising for being the exact aroma I remember—stale beer, cigarette smoke, boat tar, urinal soap, popcorn, wax for the leather banquettes, and floor-sweep granules—a positive, good-prospects smell, though probably best appreciated by men my age.

The dark-cornered, barny old room looks the same as when Ernie McAuliffe pounded his fists on the table and racketed on about Ruskies—the long-raftered ceiling, the long bar down the right side, back-lit with fuzzed red and blue low-lights and ranked rows of every kind of cheap hooch you'd dream of, all reflected in a smoky mirror on which the management has taped a smiling cartoon turkey with a cartoon Pilgrim pointing a musket at it. Two patrons sit at a table at the booth-lined rear wall. There's a tiny square linoleum dance floor, where no one ever danced in my day, and hung above it a mirror-faceted disco ball useful when things are jumping, which I don't remember ever being the case. Once the Manasquan served a decent broasted-chicken basket and a popcorn-shrimp platter. But no one's eating, and no food smell's in the atmosphere. The swinging chrome doors to the kitchen are barred and padlocked.

I am, though, happy to arrive, and to take a stool at the near end of the bar, with a view toward the other patrons—two women drinking and talking to the bartender.

*A*s I left Asbury Park, with Wade careering off toward what destiny I don't know, and an empty nest awaiting me and the weather swarming into my car, I tried—just as I did the day I returned from Mayo last August, radiating anti-cancer contamination like Morse code—to imagine what a really good day might be. And in each instance I thought of the same thing (this strategy, as childlike as it seems, ought not be scoffed at).

Two years ago, Sally and I set off on one of our cut-rate one-day flying adventures—this time to Moline—with the intention of taking an historic boat trip down the Mississippi, visiting some interesting Algonquian earthworks, seeing a Civil War ironclad that had been hauled out of the muck and given its own museum, and maybe stopping off at the Golden Nugget casino, which the same Algonquians had built to recoup their dignity. We planned to finish the day with an early dinner in the rotating tenth-floor River Room of the Holiday Inn-Moline, then get back on the plane in time to be home by 3 a.m.

But when we got to the departure dock of the romantic old paddlewheeler, the S.S. *Chief Illini*, a storm began dumping every manner of precip on us—snow, rain, sleet, hail, arriving by turns with a coarse wind at their backs. We'd bought our tickets off the Internet ahead of time, but neither Sally nor I wanted any part of a river cruise, wanted only to head back up the old cobbled streets of the historic district in search of a nice place to have lunch and to hatch a new plan for the hours that remained—

possibly a leisurely trip through the John Deere Museum, since we had time to kill. I went aboard and told the boat captain, who was also the concessionaire and proprietor of the cruise business and owner of the *Chief Illini*, that we were sacrificing our tickets due to weather skittishness but wanted him to know (since he seemed personable and accommodating) that we'd be back another time and buy more tickets. To which the captain, a big happy-faced galoot dressed in his river pilot's blue serge uniform with gold epaulettes and a captain's cap, said, "Look here, you folks, we don't want anybody not to have a good time in Moline. I know this weather's the pits and all. I'll just return your money, and don't you sweat it. We're not in the business here in River City to take anybody's dough without rendering a first-class service. In fact, since you've come all this way"—he didn't know we'd flown from Newark but recognized we probably weren't locals—"maybe you'll be my guest at the Miss Moline diner my sister runs, where she makes authentic Belgian waffles with farm-fresh eggs and homemade sticky buns. How 'bout I just give her a call and say you're on your way up there? And here're some tickets to the John Deere Museum, the best one you'll find from here to South Dakota."

We didn't end up eating at the Miss Moline. But we did take in the museum, which was well-curated, with interesting displays about glaciation, wind erosion and soil content that explained why in that part of America you could grow anything you wanted pretty much anytime—forget about the growing season.

When I think about it now, here in the Manasquan—or the Old Squatters—with my window being fixed while I take my ease in these familiar detoxified surrounds, I can almost believe I made it up, so perfect a day did it produce for Sally and me, and so enduring has it been as illustration of how things can work out better than you thought—like now—even when all points of the spiritual weather vane forecast dark skies.

"Okay, I could aks you again, but it ain't good to wake up de dead." A small mouse-faced woman with a silver flat-top and two good-sized ears full of tiny regimented gold loops stacked lobe to helix, faces me across the empty bar surface. A look of wry, not hostile, amusement sits on her lips, though her lips also have a permanent wrinkle to their contours, as if harsh words had once passed through but things had gotten better now.

I don't know what she's been saying, but assume it's to do with my drink preference. I've decided on the time-honored highball, the all-around drinker's drink, to commemorate the old divorced men, many of whom have now died. It's perfect for me in my state. "I'd like a tall bourbon and soda on ice, please."

"Dat ain't what I sed. But whatever."

I smile pointlessly. "Sorry."

"I aksed wuz you sure you wuz meetin' your friends in de right place here." The bartender casts a look around down the bar toward her customers, two large older women elbowed in over birdbath-size cocktails, covertly eyeing me but clearly amused.

"I think so." Her accent is pure swamp-water coon-ass,

straight from St. Boudreau Parish, far beyond the Atchafalaya. She's trying to be nice, making me know as gently as possible that the atmospheric old Manasquan has become a watering hole for late-middle-passage dykes and possibly I might be happier elsewhere, but I don't have to leave if I don't want to.

Except I couldn't be happier than to be here amidst these fellow refugees. The nautical motif's intact. The framed greasy-glass heroic fish photos still cover the walls with coded significance. The light's murky, the smells are congenial, the world's held at bay, as in the storied Manasquan days. Probably the drinks are just as good. I couldn't care less whose orientation's bending its big elbow beside mine. In fact, I feel a strong Darwinian rightness about what was once a hard-nuts old men's hidey-hole transitioning into a safe house for tolerant, wry, full-figured, thick-armed goddesses in deep mufti (one's wearing a Yankees cap, another a pair of bulgy housepainter's dungarees over a Vassar sweatshirt). My own daughter used to be one of their number, I could tell them—but possibly won't.

"I used to come in here when Evangelis owned it," I say gratefully, referring to old Ben Mouzakis's sister's husband.

"Fo' my time, dahlin'," the bartender croons, organizing my highball. I see she has a vivid green tattoo on her skinny neck, inches below her ear. Gothic letters spell out TERMITE, which I guess could be her name, though I'm not about to call her that.

"How's ole Ben doing?"

"He's okay. He in the whale-watch bidnus anymore." My drink set down in front of me, Termite (I'm only calling her that privately) begins giving a sink full of dirty glasses the three-tub, suds-rinse-rinse treatment, her little hands nimble as a card sharp's. "Dat ole charter boat bidnus played out. He got into burials-at-sea for a while. Den dat crapped. Annend dis whale thing jumped up."

"Sounds great." I take a first restorative sip. Termite has poured me a double dose of Old Woodweevil, meaning it's happy hour. Soon the bar will be filling up with big women fresh from jobs as stevedores, hod carriers and diesel mechanics—happy warriors happy to have a place of their own. I wonder if Clarissa has a tattoo someplace I don't know about, and if so, what does it say? Not Dad, we're sure of that.

The two shadowy women from the rear booth, one in a floral print muumuu her belly doesn't fit into too well, the other in a bulky red turtleneck, stand up and walk arms around each other to the antique jukebox. One puts in a quarter and cues up Ole Perry singing "I'll Be Home for Christmas," then they begin slowly to dance to the sweet-sad melody underneath the unmoving disco globe.

"She'd fuck a bullet wound, *that* skanky bitch," I hear one of the two full-figured gals at the bar—the one in the Yankees cap—saying to Termite, who's back down where they are, conniving about one of their friends.

"Well, guess what?" Termite is brazenly smirking, rising up onto her toes on the duckboards better to get into the faces of the two women patrons. "Ah ain't no fuckin' bullet wound. I heeerd dat. You know what ahm sayin'?" She shoots a sudden feral look my way, then lowers her voice to a big stage whisper. "Ahmo be dat bitch's worst nightmare." Termite, I see, wears

THE LAY OF THE LAND 493

an enormous Jim Bowie sheath knife on her oversized silver-studded black bruiser-belt that's drawn up so tight she must have trouble breathing. She herself is entirely in black—jeans, boots, tee-shirt, eyeshadow—everything but her silver flat-top, ear decor and TERMITE tattoo. I imagine she's already been a lot of people's nightmare, though she's been completely welcoming to me and could bring me another highball and I wouldn't mind it. My car window's not fixed yet, and the roof's drumming with sheets of merciless rain I'm happy to be out of.

Termite sees me angling for her eye and leaves the disputers and saunters down to me, still carrying most of her fuck-you attitude with her. She's skinny-bowlegged in her jeans, with excessive space between her taut little spavined thighs, so that she swaggers like the long-departed Charlie Starkweather, no small-change nightmare himself.

"How *you* doin'? You still thirsty?" She rests her little hands on the bar rail and tap-taps an oversized silver thumb ring against the wood. "You suck dat one down like you needed it."

"It was good," I say. "I'll have another one just like it." I have to take my piss now. My eye wanders to where the gents used to be.

"Oh yeah, dey good." Termite's filling my glass where it sits, using the old ice, lots of whiskey and a quick squirt from the soda gun. "It's over in dat corner," she says, seeing where I'm looking without looking there. "Light's burnt out. It don't get the use it used to."

"Great." I slide off my stool and test my walking stability, which is solid.

Termite flashes a nasty smile down at her two friends as I
go, and in the same stagy voice says, "It might be a ole alligator
in dere, so you better be careful."

"Or worse," one of the girls cracks back, and snorts.

"Okay," I say. "Will do."

Inside the GENTLEMEN door, nothing's forbidding. The ceiling
bulb actually works, though the grimy porcelain fixtures are
decrepit fifties-era Kohler, the hand-dryer fan's hanging on a
screw, and the woolly old window vent whose outside cover bangs
in the wind lets cold mist in onto the layer of brown that gunks
up everything. Still, the pissing facility's perfectly usable. No
alligators.

Plenty of messages have been left on the wall for future users
to ponder, all illustrated with neatly-penciled, magic-markered
or rudely carved depictions of the engorged male equipment,
plus a variety of women with miraculous breasts, several demonstrating uncanny coupling postures. Appeals are made for the
"Able-bodied Semen," the "Lonely Hards Club" and "Fearless
Fast-Dick Dick-tective Agency." One, to the side of the urinal,
has the nostalgic old 609 area code, with a request for "Discreet
Callers Only." Several messages propose reckless sexual chicanery
with members of the Mouzakis family, including Grandma
Mouzak and the Mouzakis pet sheep, Mouzy, who's shown scaling
a fence. The only items of unusual note as I complete a long,
knee-weakening piss—other than the BUSH-GORE BOTH
SUCK, lipsticked onto the scaly old mirror—is a chartreuse cell
phone, a little Nokia that's been tossed in the urinal as a gesture,
I suppose, of dissatisfaction with its service. And beside it on the

rubber grate is a half-eaten lunch-meat sandwich on white bread. It feels odd to piss on a sandwich and simultaneously into the ear hole of the miniature green telephone. But I'm past having a choice. My time in unlikely men's rooms has tripled since my Mayo insertions, and I tend not to be as finicky as I once was.

When I re-take my place at the bar, feeling immensely better, my fresh highball's waiting along with a new twin. Ms. Termite has stayed at my end and wants to be friendly, which makes me even happier to be here.

"So whadda you do? You some kinda salesman?" She hauls a soft pack of Camels out of her jeans, retrieves one with pinched lips and lights it with a silver Zippo as big as a Frigidaire. *Click-crack-tink-snap*. She exhales a gray smoke trickle out the corner of her mouth, skewing her lips like a convict. "Mind if I smoke? Ain't spose to, but fuck it."

"You bet," I say, grateful for the forbidden aroma in my nostrils. When Mike fired up last night, I realized you don't smell it as much as you used to. I'm tempted to bum one, though I haven't smoked since military school and would probably suffocate. "I *am* a salesman," I answer. "I sell houses."

"Where at? Florida? One-a dem?"

"Right down in Sea-Clift. A ways south of here. Not far, really."

"Oh yeah? Well ain't dat sump'n." Eyes squinted, her smoke in the corner of her mouth, Termite goes searching under the bar and produces a copy of the *Shore Home Buyer's Guide*. The East Jersey Real Estate Board publishes this guide, and if Mike Mahoney's done his homework, there's a boxed Realty-Wise ad in the south Barnegat section showing 61 Surf Road, which the storm outside—vanguard of tropical depression Wayne—may now be washing out to sea.

"I been lookin'," Termite says.

"What kind of place you lookin' for?" I drop my *g*'s as a gesture of camaraderie. Termite would be a challenging client, though possibly I could let Mike do the honors. He'd think it was great—and it would be.

"Oh. You know." She plucks a fleck of tobacco off her tongue tip and in doing so gives me a glimpse of a silver stud punched through her tongue skin like a piece of horse tack. I want it to be still so I can get a better look, but in an instant it's flickered and gone. "Just sump'n grand, overlookin' de ocean and dat don't cost nothin'. Maybe sump'n somebody died in, like what used to be about the Corvette dat girl died in in Laplace and dey couldn't get the smell out, so they had to junk it. I could live with it. You got sump'n like dat? Where was it you live?"

"Sea-Clift."

"Okay." She sucks a molar and rolls her punctured tongue around her cheek at the concept of a town by that name. "Course, I got my momma. She in the wheelchair since I don't know when."

"That's nice," I say. "I mean it's nice she can live with you. It's not nice she's in a wheelchair. That's not nice."

"Yeah. Diabetes amputated her leg off." Termite frowns as if this was, for her, personally painful.

"I see."

The two big ladies down the bar are re-animating their

conversation at higher decibels. "Every time I get on a fuckin' plane, I think, This sumbitch is gonna blow up. Makes me sleep better if I just accept it." The couple from the back booth are still dancing, though Perry has long ago finished his Christmas song.

"Look. Lemme aks you somethin'." Termite hikes her booted foot onto the lip of the rinse sink and holds her smoke like a pencil between her thumb and index finger. In spite of her tough-as-rivets, knife-wielding personal demeanor—little biceps veined and sculpted, brown eyes slightly, skeptically bulged, ringed fingers raw and probably callused from pumping iron—she is not the least bit masculine. In fact, she's as feminine as Ava Gardner—just not in the same way as Ava Gardner. Her waist, with her big silver and black belt pulled tight, is as tiny as a dragonfly's. And her breasts, possibly encased in something metal under her black muscle shirt, are sizable breasts no man would sniff at. I'd like to know what her mother calls her at home. Susan or Sandra or Amanda-Jean. Though she'd pop you in the kisser if you breathed it. "Where you come from originally?"

"I'm pure cracker," I say. "Mississippi."

"I heeerd dat," Termite sneers. A lineage check means we're aiming toward subject matter her customers down the bar wouldn't tolerate, something, in her experience, only another southerner could possibly comprehend: exactly why your colored races are constitutionally unsuited to work a forty-hour week; the consequences of their possessing statistically proven smaller brains; why they can't swim or leave white women alone. It's too bad there can't be something good to come from being a southerner. However, I'm getting happily drunk on my second highball and these are subjects easily skirted.

"Okay. See. I read this." Termite inches in close to the bar, drops her voice. "Your brain don't have no manager, see. Not really. It's just like a plant. It go dis way, den it go dat way. Dey ain't no *self* ever runnin' it. It just like adapts. We all just like accidents dat we got minds at all." Her little rodent's face grows solemn with the dark implications of this news. I know something about this matter from my bathroom study of the Mayo newsletter, where such matters are regularly reported on. The mind *is* a metaphor. Consciousness *is* cellular adaptation, intelligence *is* as fortuitous as pick-up sticks. All true. I only hope Termite's not vectoring us toward adumbrations about The Lord and His Overall Design. If she is, I'll run right out into the storm. "You know what ahm sayin'?" She's whispering in a secret-keeping voice the other bar patrons aren't supposed to hear. "You know what ahm sayin'?" she says again.

"I do."

"Millennium! What fuckin' Millennium?" The big boisterous girls are getting drunker, too, and have decided they've got the place to themselves, which they nearly do. No one's come in since I did. "I musta been in the crapper when that happened!"

Termite gives them a disgusted look and begins spindling the *Shore Home Buyer's Guide* into a tight tube, scrolling it smaller and smaller into itself until it looks solid. "So, see," she says, still confidentially. "Like I'm fifty-one"—I'd have said forty—"and I try to like test ma mind sometimes. Okay?" I smile as if I know, and simultaneously try to know. "I try to think of a specific thing.

I try to remember somethin'. To see if I *can*. Like—and it's usually a name—de name of dem flowers with red berries on 'em we useta always have at Christmas. Or maybe something'll come up when ahm talking, and I wanta say, 'Oh, yeah, that's like . . .' Den I can't think of it. You know? They's just a hole there where what I want to say ought to be. It ain't never nuttin important, like what's Jack Daniel's or how you make a whiskey sour. It's like ahm sayin', '. . . and den we all drove over to Freehold.' But den I can't say Freehold. Dat ain't the best example. 'Cause I can say Freehold, whatever. But if I give you a good example, den I won't think of it. I can't even think of a good example. You know what I'm talkin' about with dis thing?"

Termite takes a long consternated drag on her Camel, then douses it in the rinse sink and tosses the butt into a black plastic garbage can behind the bar, blowing smoke straight down without lowering her head.

"I've had that happen to me plenty of times," I say. Who hasn't? This is the kind of pseudo-problem that would easily succumb to a Sponsor call. And as always, my solution would be: Forget the hell about it. Think about something better—a new apartment with a wheelchair ramp and maybe a Jenn-Air and lots of phone jacks. Your mind's not the fucking Yellow Pages. You've got no business asking it to perform tasks it's not interested in just so you can show off. To me, it's a worse signal that anybody would ever worry about these things than that he/she can't remember every little bit of nibshit minutiae you can dream up but that maybe doesn't even exist.

"Pyracantha?"

"Say what?" Termite blinks at me.

"That Christmas flower with the red berries."

"Dere it is, okay. But dat ain't all. 'Cause the real baddest thing is that when I can't get what you just said into my mind, den I worry about dat, and den dat like opens the floodgates for stuff you wouldn't believe."

"What stuff?"

"Stuff I don't wanna talk about." Termite guardedly eyes the two large-bodies down the bar again, as if they might be snickering at her. They are, in fact, pulled in close together, whispering, but holding hands like married bears.

"But I mean, true stuff?" I'm wondering but not wondering very hard.

"Yeah, true stuff. Stuff I don't like to think about. Okay?"

"You bet." I take a subject-changing sip of my—now—third happy-hour highball. I may have had enough. I don't have the stamina I used to. I'm also on the brink of a discussion that threatens to tumble into seriousness—the last thing I want. I'd rather talk about beach erosion or golf or the Eagles' season or the election, since I'm sure these girls have to be Democrats.

"You think ahm losing my mind?" Termite asks accusingly.

"Absolutely not. I *don't* think that. Like I said. I've had that happen to me. Your mind's just got a lot in it." Tattoo and piercing decisions, who's a good knife sharpener, her invalid mom.

"'Cause Mamma thinks mebbe I'm losing it. Ya know what ahm sayin'? And sometimes *I* think I am, too. When I want de name of some got-damn red flower, or whatever dat woman's name is who's the Astronaut—whatever—then I can't think of it." Her lips curl in a smile of disgust with herself—a look she's used to.

And then, in by-the-book bartender protocol, she turns and walks away, resuming something with the lovebirds who've been smooch-dancing to Perry. I hear her say, " . . . they just treat Thanksgiving like it really meant somethin'. What I want to know is, what *is* it?"

"Me, too," one of the slow dancers speaks, with an echo that registers sadly in the bar.

Termite's left me the spindled *Home Buyer's Guide*. I intend to show her my ad and leave my card. Sometimes a new vista, a new house number, a new place of employ, a new set of streets to navigate and master are all you need to simplify life and take a new lease out on it. Real estate might seem to be all about moving and picking up stakes and disruption and three-moves-equals-a-death, but it's really about arriving and destinations, and all the prospects that await you or might await you in some place you never thought about. I had a drunk old prof at Michigan who taught us that all of America's literature, Cotton Mather to Steinbeck—this was the same class where I read *The Great Gatsby*—was forged by one positivist principle: to leave, and then to arrive in a better state.

I take this opportunity to climb off my stool and walk to the porthole door and have a check across the lot to find out if my car window's ready. It isn't. Chris, the Fitzgerald scholar, has pulled it into the fluorescent-lit garage bay and is moving around the murky shop interior, seeming to be in search of the right materials for the job. The other man, small and raffish and unshaven, stands at the office door, looking up at the rain-torn skies as if into a cloud of sorry thoughts. Edward Hopper in New Jersey.

I reclaim my bar stool and remind myself to grab another piss or be faced with again relieving myself in the rain, behind some darkened Pathmark, where I've already been caught more than once by security patrols, resulting in a lot of unwieldy explanation. In each instance, however, the officers were moonlighting middle-age cops and completely sympathized.

Termite's staying down with the girls at the end of the bar. No one else has shown up for happy hour (weather and the holiday are always negatives). I leaf through the *Buyer's Guide*, perusing the broker-associate faces in their winning, confidence-pledging smiley cameos. The glam Debs, Lindas and Margies with their golden silky hair, big earrings, plenty of lens gauze to disguise what they really look like, and the men all blow-dried Woodys and mustachioed Maxes in hunky poses—blue jeans, open-collar plaids, tasteful silver accessories and gold throat jewelry. Most of what's for sale are "houses," our term of art for cookie-cutter ranches and undersized split-levels— nothing different from our basic inventory in Sea-Clift. Every few pages, there's a grandiose one-of-a-kind "palatial beach estate" that doesn't list the price but everyone knows is seizure-inducing.

My 61 Surf Road listing is back on page ninety-six, a boiler-plate box with the Doolittles' house in washed-out color, a shot captured by Mike using our old Polaroid. It strikes me again, even knowing what I now know, that it's as good as there is at this location, at this time, at this price. There are nicer listings in Brielle, but at twice the ticket. Monday morning, I'll call Boca and discuss options regarding foundation issues and amending the disclosure statement. "Foundation needs attention" is naturally a death knell in a saturated market unless the buyer sees the whole thing as a tear-down. My bet is the Doolittles jerk the listing and hand it to a competitor who knows nothing about the foundation. I'm not sure I'd blame them.

"Hey! You!" the big Yanks-cap mama bear down the bar (she's shitfaced) is addressing me. I smile as if I'm eager to be spoken to. "You wouldn't happen to be named Armand, would you? And you wouldn't happen to be from Neptune, I guess?"

"Or Ur-a-nus." Her can't-bust-'em friend bursts out a guffaw.

"Nope. Afraid not." Smiling back winningly. "Sea-Clift."

"Told ya," the overall woman gloats.

"Big deal. Well then, do you wanna dance? I promise I'm a woman."

"He doesn't give a shit," her companion stage-whispers, leaning in front of her to grin down at me. "Look at him." More laughing.

"That's really nice. But no thanks," I say. "I'm taking off pretty soon."

"Who isn't?" she growls. "Tough luck for you. I'm a good dancer."

"On her feet and yours, too," her friend mocks.

"You two should dance," I say.

"There you go," the second woman agrees.

"*Where* I go?" the first woman grumbles, and they immediately forget about me.

It is a fine and fortunate feeling to be beached here—stranger and welcomed onlooker. I could've easily gotten mired into nowhere-no-time, with only the night's dark cave in front of me. But I'm not. I'm found, though I'm not sure anyone but me would see it like that.

Still, my day has accomplished much of what I wanted when I set forth—which is full immersion in events. Three occurrences have been of a positive nature: a good if unproductive house showing, a successful implosion and a salubrious interlude here. Versus only two and a half of a low-quality: a not-good kitchen encounter with my daughter and her beau; my car busted into; Wade blowing a gasket and ending up—where? (Home, I hope.)

Any of the latter events would be enough to set a man driving to North Dakota, ending up at a stranger's farmhouse east of Minot, pleading amnesia and letting himself be sheltered for the day—Turkey Day—before regaining his senses and heading home. Suffice it to say, then, that when you see a man bending an elbow, head down, shoulders hunched before a dark brown drink, chatting elliptically, *sotto voce* with the barkeep, looking tired-eyed, boozy, but apparently happy, you should think that what's being transacted is the self giving the self a much-needed reprieve. The brain may not have a true manager, but it's got a boss. And it's you.

Several pairs of fresh patrons have rumbled in out of the rain, which turns the bar more festive. All the ladies—a couple being 200-plus-pounders—are in some species of loose-fitting work clothes with durable footwear, as if they were members of the pipe fitters' union. Some have donned amusing headgear (a pink beret, a zebra-striped hard hat, a backwards Caterpillar cap), and they're all in cracking good spirits, know everyone else's name and are joking and ribbing one another just like a bunch of men—though these women are younger than men would be, and more amiable and tolerant, and would undoubtedly make better friends.

They each give me a surreptitious appraising eye upon entering and share a quick naughty remark, as if I was actually a woman. One or two of them smile at me in a haughty way that means, we're happy you're here, we're on our best behavior, so you better be on yours (which I intend to be). Termite, they all treat like a beloved little sister, but a scandalous little sister with a vicious mouth any parent would have trouble with. She stalks the duckboards with their drink orders, calling everyone "gents" and "goyls" and "douchebags," occasionally wisecracking something down to me that I'm not supposed to answer. She drifts my way, eyes snapping, offers me something known as an "Irish Napalm" that the "goyls" all like, and that's served on fire. "They'll all be wanting 'em in a minute," she says in a tough, loud voice over the enlarged noise, "after which all shit'll break loose in here. Anyway, an-y-way." She's forgotten about having talked to me twenty minutes ago about being afraid she's going crazy.

"De thing I want to know," she says, leaning in again, tiny eyes slitted, as if this is definitely not for general consumption, her right hand resting on her bowie knife handle, "is—when did everything get to be about bidnus? You know what ahm sayin'? Bidnus this, bidnus that."

One thing I hadn't noticed, now that Termite's moved in close to me again, is that she's wearing silvery orthodontic appliances on her lower incisors, in addition to her silver tongue rivet—which makes her look even stranger.

"The business of business is business," I say with a frank expression to suggest I know what that means.

"Okay." She nods, then glances over her shoulder at her bar full of business, as if the new raucousness in here gives us some privacy we hadn't had. "You a good listener. Did ma old husband, Reynard, hear one thing I ever said, ah mighta been stayed married to dat knucklehead. You know what ahm sayin'? But no way. Uh-uh. Wudn' no listenin' involved. Just him talkin' and me jump'n round like a old hop-frog."

"That's too bad. Some men aren't good listeners, I guess."

"Oh yeah." She sucks a tooth and looks down. "You a good-lookin' man, too. You got you a good young hotsy down-ere where you livin' at Sea-what's-it-called?" Termite suddenly smiles at me both directly and sweetly, a smile that features her lower line of silver braces, and tentatively advances a thought that a better, stronger bond might form between us, with other things possibly permissible.

"I do," I cheerfully lie. I'm picturing my daughter with polyethnic Thom, who I hope never to see again.

Termite's sweet smile turns instantly professional-impersonal. "Yeah. Well. Das good. Yep," she says crisply. "Happy hour almost over wid. You need anything?"

"I'm already happy," I say, wanting to sound affirming about all her life's prospects but one.

"Dere you go," she says, and turns straight away again and saunters down the duckboards, proclaiming, "Now ya'll fatsos try to control ya'll selves."

"Fuck you and that goat you rode in on, you skinny little bitch," one of the women shouts in merry mirth, and they all convulse full-throated.

I browse back through the curled pages of the *Buyer's Guide*, wanting to give mechanic Chris another ten minutes. These publications can actually be the most helpful and news-packed that any citizen could hope for when entering a community or region where he knows no one and might grow dispirited and feel tempted just to head home to Waukegan. In the interest of plain and simple commerce, but for the price of nothing, the *Guide* provides a well-researched list of "essential services," crisis numbers, "Best Bet" Italian, Filipino and Thai cuisines, walk-in wellness clinics, an e-mail address for a mortgage-consultant clearing house, emergency dental care and pet health hot-line numbers, oxygen tank delivery, bump shops and bail bondsmen. And, of course, bi-weekly training classes in the real estate profession. There's even a list of local numbers for Monmouth and Ocean County Sponsors Anonymous. Plus, many small-business opportunities are advertised, situations where you can walk in and take over like I did. I always find one or two new summer rental properties every year by leafing through these pages on slow Saturday afternoons in January—often chalets I could buy myself if they're in presentable shape, or manage for a good fee if they're not. I also read through these crowded pages just to acquire (by osmosis) some sense of how we're all basically doing, what we need to be wary of, look forward to or look back on with pride or relief. These spiritual sign-pointers are revealed to me in old fire stations, rectories or Chrysler agencies that are for sale, or once-thriving businesses in turnaround, or the number of old homes versus new ones on the sale block, or the addresses and plat maps of new constructions, the ethnicity (gauged by the names) of who's selling what, who's doing the cooking or who's going out of business. And finally, of course, what costs what, versus what used to cost what. There's in fact a listing in the middle Green Pages of every property sold in Monmouth and Ocean counties and how much was paid and by whom—sure signs of the time. Little of this will be anything I make a note about or mention to Mike in our Monday strategy breakfasts at the Earl of Sandwich. It's just the soft susurrus, the hick and tick of the engine that warms us when it's cold, soothes us when it's beastly, and that we all hear and feel on our arms, necks and faces like atmosphere, whether we know it or whether we never do.

On page sixty-four, however, amidst all that's familiar, a new *Guide* feature attracts my eye, part of a double-truck layout for the Mengelt Agency in Vanhiseville. Mengelt offerings are generally small, characterless scrub lots in old interior suburbs on their way to extinction, exactly like the ones Mike and I rode past on our trip to Haddam. The Mengelt motto, in hopeful serifs, is, "We find your home. You find the happiness." There's the usual row of tiny page-bottom snapshots showing the mostly unsmiling, mostly female Mengelt agents—a new batch of Carols, Jennifers and a Blanche—contributing to the impression that the institution of marriage may be losing some traction in Vanhiseville.

But in a larger framed box, under the title "Profiles in Real Estate Courage," is a sharp color photo of "Associate of the Month" Fred Frantal, smiling and cherub-cheeked, a sausage of a fellow with a round weak chin, crinkly hair, a fuzzy mustache and two happy, saucerish eyes. Fred's wearing a red-and-green lumberjack shirt that hints of a decent-size personal sculpture below the frame. And under his picture there's printed a lengthy story apparently pertaining to Fred, which the Mengelt associates want the world to know about. I'd probably be smart to plaster Mike's squinting, beaming mug onto our ad, with a boiled-down account of his improbable but inspirational life's journey from Tibet to the Jersey Shore. It would attract the curious, which is often where commerce begins.

" 'Frog' Frantal," the Mengelt story goes, "is not just our *Associate of the Month* but our *Associate of the Millennium*. A two-year Vanhiseville resident and graduate associate from Middlesex Community College, Fred got gold-plated lucky when he married Carla Boykin back in '82 and moved to Holmeson to be an EMS technician for the H'son Rescue Unit, where he saved many lives and made a big impression on many others. Fred and Carla raised two great kids, Chick and Bev, and have always trained Rottweilers. The Frantals moved to Vanhiseville in 1998, when Fred retired from the FD, having earned his real estate license at night. He joined the Mengelt family last year and made an instant impact here, too, on our residential sales, due to his EMS contacts and generally positive outlook (he loves cold calls). Fred's a Navy vet, a brown belt in tae kwon do, an avid surfcaster and snowmobiler, a Regular Baptist Church member and these days is in demand as a motivational speaker on youth and grieving issues. Sadly, last winter tragedy struck the Frantals, when their son Chick, 20, was killed by a drunken snowmobiler in eastern PA. We all mourned Fred and Carla's loss. But with support of friends, loved ones and the Mengelt crew, Fred's back and ready to list your house and sell you another one. Frog has topped our leaders board eight of the last ten months, and deserves the distinction of *Associate of the Millennium*. He believes that whatever doesn't kill you makes you stronger, and that you meet triumph and disaster and make friends with both. If either of these describes your current real estate situation, give Fred a call at (732) 555-2202, or e-mail him at frog@mengelt.com. Happy Thanksgiving from all of us!"

Voices in the bar. Laughter. The tinkle-clinkle of glasses. Shuffle of booted feet, squeezing bar-stool leather, heavy coats rustling, exhale of heavy breaths. Outside, there's the hiss of wind, the spatter splat of rain on the metal roof. A sigh of a door closing. These sounds of mutuality and arrival recede down a hallway, yet grow more distinct, as though I viewed the livening bar on a screen, with the sound track elsewhere.

Down the bar, little silver-haired Termite frowns toward me, narrows her eyes suspiciously, then turns back to the bar full of women, all laughing at something. Someone says, pretty loud, "So it turns out, see, that China's *really fucking BIG*." "Whoa," someone else says.

I am, I now perceive, immobilized on my stool, though in no danger of toppling off. I don't feel drunk, though I could be. My head isn't swimming. My extremities aren't dulled or immobilized. I'd recognize all the money denominations in my pocket if I had to, could pay my tab and walk right out into the stormy parking lot and take command of my vehicle (which must be fixed by now). Yet I'm heavy-armed and moored to the bar rail, my heels stuck to the brass footrest. My empty highball glass seems small and distant—once again, as when I was a feverish kid and the contents of my room got pleasantly distant, and the sound of my mother's footsteps in another room were all I experienced of ambient sound.

I've said it before. I do not credit the epiphanic, the seeing-through that reveals all, triggered by a mastering detail. These are lies of the liberal arts to distract us from the more precious here and now. Life's moments truly come at us heedless, not at the bidding of a gilded fragrance. The Permanent Period is specifically commissioned to combat these indulgences into the pseudo-significant. We're all separate agents, each underlain by an infinite remoteness; and to the extent we're not and require to be *significant*, we're not so interesting.

And yet. In this strange, changed state I for this moment find myself, and for reasons both trivial and circumstantial (the bar, the booze, the day, even Fred Frantal), my son Ralph Bascombe, age twenty-nine (or for accuracy's sake, age nine), comes seeking audience in my brain.

And I am then truly immobilized. And with what? Fear? Love? Regret? Shame? Lethargy? Bewilderment? Heartsickness?

Whimsy? Wonder? You never know for sure, no matter what the great novels tell you.

It may go without saying, but when you have a child die—as I did nineteen years ago—you carry him with you forever and ever after. Of course you should. And not that I "talk" to him (though some might) or obsess endlessly (as his brother, Paul, did for years until it made him loony), or that I expect Ralph to turn up at my door, like Wally, with a wondrous story of return or of long, shadowy passageways with luminous light awaiting, from which he bolted at the last second (I've fantasized that could happen, though it was just a way to stay interested as years went by). For me, left back, there's been no dead-zone sensation of life suspended, hollowed, wind-raddled, no sense of not leading my *real* life but only some consolation-prize life nobody would want—I'm sure that can happen, too.

Though what *has* developed is that my life's become alloyed with loss. Ralph, and then Ralph being dead, long ago became embedded in all my doings and behaviors. And not like a disease you carry that never gets better, but more the way being left-handed is ever your companion, or that you don't like parsnips and never eat them, or that once there was a girl you loved for the very first time and you can't help thinking of her—nonspecifi-cally—every single day. And while this may seem profane or untrue to say, the life it's made has been and goes on being a much more than merely livable life. It's made a good life, this loss, one I don't at all regret. (The Frantals couldn't be expected to believe this, but maybe can in time.)

Of course, Ralph's death was why Ann and I couldn't stay

married another day seventeen years back. We were always thinking the same things, occupying and dividing up the same tiny piece of salted turf, couldn't surprise and please each other the way marrieds need to. Death became all we had in common, a common jail. And who wanted that till our own deaths did us part? There would be a forever, we knew, and we had to live on into it, divided and joined by death. And not that it was harder on us than it was on Ralph, who died, after all, and not willingly. But it was hard enough.

Out of the rosy bar-light distance, as though emerging from a long passageway, so long she'll never reach me in my state—I'm drunk, okay—is Termite, thumbs provocatively in her black denim pockets, inquisitive grin on her mousy mouth, eyes shining, fixed on me. We are like lovers who've become friends late in life: She knows my hilarious eccentricities and failures and only takes me half seriously. I love her to bits but no longer feel the old giddy-up. We could spend hours now just talking.

"You know all what I was yakkin' about back den? I'm probably gon' forget about it tomorrow. It ain't permanent—goin' crazy. You know whut ahm sayin'?" She sweeps away my empty highball glass, drops it *plunk* into the sudsy sink. "Do you say *drought* or *drouth*?" She stares across at me, though her face has turned suspicious in a hurry, as though I'd offered her a counterfeit tenner. She takes a step back, cocks her flat-topped head, her mouth curls cruelly the way I knew it could. "Whut's wrong witch you?"

Unexpectedly, my eyes flood with tears, my hot cheeks taking the runoff. I've known about them for the better part of a minute but have been stuck here, unable to blink or wipe my nose with my sleeve or to think about a trip to the gents or about seeking a breath of rescue in the out-of-doors. I don't know what to say about *drought* or *drouth*. *Dry* comes into my mind, as does *I'm in a terrible state*. Though like a lot of terrible states, it doesn't feel so bad.

"I-I—" My old stammer, not heard from in years but always lurking were I to laugh inconsiderately at another stammerer—which I never do—now revisits my glottus. "I-I-I don't know." I want to smile but don't quite make it.

Termite's hard little ferret's eyes fix on me. She performs one of her flash glances back down the bar, as if my predicament needs to be kept under wraps. "Wadn't nuthin *I* said," she announces, but not loud.

"N-n-n-o." My hands clutch the *Buyer's Guide* and give it another fierce re-spindling. *N* is a hard one for stutterers. My chest empties as if somebody has just stamped on it. Then it heaves a big sigh-sounding noise, which I manage not to let out as a groan, though stifling it hurts like hell. I have to get out of here now. I could die here.

"You piss drunk is all," Termite snarls. This is not old-lovers-become-friends. This is, "I've seen the likes of you all my life, been married to it, fucked it, wallowed in it, but I'm well out of it as you see me now." That's what this is.

"Ahhh, yeah." This time an actual groan issues forth. Then more tears. Then a shudder. What's going on? What's going on? What's going on?

"Jew drive here?"

"Yeah." I reach my nose with my jacket sleeve and saw back and forth.

"You drive off and git in a wreck and kill some kid, you ain't sayin' you been in here. You got dat? I'm spose to take dem keys"—She regards me with revulsion, right hand on her silver bowie knife hilt. How can things change so fast? I haven't done anything—"but I don't wanna touch you." She snorts back a stiff breath, as if I smell bad.

I am climbing off my bar stool, feeling light-headed but terribly heavy, like a sandbag puppet.

"Y'hearin' what ahm sayin'?" Her eyes narrow to a threat. Termite might be her real name.

"Okay. Sure." From my pocket I produce a piece of U.S. paper currency along with my Realty-Wise card. It could be a million-dollar bill. These I place on the bar. "Thanks," I say, my mouth chromy. My hands are cold, my feet thick.

Termite doesn't regard my pay-up. I've become her problem now, something else to lose sleep over. Will there be repercussions? Her job in jeopardy? Jail time? One more thing not to be thankful for.

But I'm already away, heading for the door, my gait surprisingly steady, as if the way out was downhill. I am, in fact, not drunk. Though what I am is a different matter.

*R*ain needles sting my cheeks, nose, brow, chin, neck when I make it out into the dark parking lot—painful but alerting. It was burning up in there, though I was frozen. Again, I may be catching something.

Cars with cadaverous colored headlights pass over the Route

35 bridge, motoring home to relatives, a quiet night before the holiday tangle, a long weekend of parades, floating balloon animals, football and extra plate-fulls. I have no idea what time it is. Since Spring Ahead gave way to Fall Back, I've been uncertain. It could be six or nine or two a.m. Though I'm clear-headed. My heart's beating at a good pace. I even give a sudden optimistic thought to Ann and Paul (and Jill) in Haddam, enjoying each other's company, reacclimating, forging new bonds. I don't feel panicky (though that could be a sure sign of panic). It is merely odd to be here now—the opposite of where the evening seemed to be heading, though, again, I had no plans.

But bad luck, bad luck heaped on bad luck! The Quonset across the lot looms dark and silent, from all appearances closed up forever, the big metal door rolled down, the office—I can see from here—wearing a fat bulletproof padlock that catches a glint off the sulfur lights from the boatyard next door. Cut-out turkeys and Pilgrims in happy holiday symbiosis are taped to the window there, too. NO JOB TOO ABSURD.

I am incensed—and breathless. If I could just get out of here, I'd gladly hunt down the faithless Chris asleep somewhere, and strangle him in front of his father, uncle, whatever, then smoke a cigarette before attacking the old man with a pair of needle-nose pliers. Except I spy a rear bumper's shine, a BUSH? WHY? sticker and a pale-blue-and-cream AWK 486, *Garden State* plate—mine. My Suburban's parked in the oily shadows between the Quonset and a pile of tire discards. *Left out*, where I'm supposed to find it. I'll send young Chris a whopper check that'll pay his way through Monmouth and pave the path to dental school. If he'd hung around,

I'd have bought him a shore dinner and told him about the things in life he needs to beware of—starting with lesbian bars and the false bonhomie of treacherous little coon-ass bartenders.

I hustle through the remnant mist, avoiding the lakes and flooded tire tracks. Most of the women in Squatters seem to have arrived in pickups with chrome toolboxes or else junker Road-masters with rusted rocker panels. Despite the shadows, Chris, I can see, has performed a creditable repair, including sweeping out the broken glass. My window's masked by multiple layers of gray duct tape backed by a slat of jigsawed plywood fitted to the hole. I could drive it this way for weeks and be fine.

The driver door's unlocked and the interior I crawl into stiff and cold and dank. My eyes are still flooding with unavailing tears. But I am eager to get going.

Only where are the keys? The ones with the fake Indian arrow-head and miniature beaded warrior-shield fob made by the retarded son of Louis the Dry Cleaner and for sale on a card for three dollars (and you'd better buy one or your shirts come back with their buttons crunched). I handed them to Chris just before the "boats against the current, borne back ceaselessly" part. He had them, or the car wouldn't be here and fixed. I saw it half-in the lighted garage bay when I checked—how long ago? Twenty minutes. How can a place of business go dark and its employees vamoose like ghosts all in twenty minutes? Why wouldn't he just skip across and give me the high sign, a hand signal, a raised eyebrow, two monosyllables—"Yer done." Cultural literacy should make this kind of masculine transaction a no-brainer— even in Greece. But not in Manasquan.

I go rifling through all the places keys can hide. The visor. The side map pocket. The glove box—full of extra chalet keys. The ashtray. Under the rubber floor mat. In the fucking cup holder. Tears are flowing, my fingers clammy, stinging when I scrape them on every sharp or rough surface. I've given my extra set to Clarissa in case I fall over dead and there're complications with the authorities about getting my valuables sacked up and returned in a timely fashion. These things happen. How mindless would it have been to have Assif Chevrolet-GMC requisition twenty extras to distribute in every corner of my existence. I swear that on Monday, when I take my window hole for proper fixing (assuming I make it to then), I'll issue the order no matter the cost, even though computer chips aren't cheap. I consider getting out in the cold and crawling underneath, probing my bunged fingers under the gritty bumpers, into the wheel wells, inside the grille face. Though I'd only soak myself and compromise my flu-shot immunity. In any case, I know the sons of bitches aren't there. They're hanging "safely" on a fucking nail in the office, attached to a paper tag that says "Older dude. Red Sub keys. Payment due," meaning the little Greek cocksuckers didn't trust me to pay the twenty-five bucks the moment the sun comes up tomorrow; were happier to let me do whatever in hell a human being does in asshole Manasquan outside a dyke bar, the night before Thanksgiving, when you're too crocked to call the police. While-U-Wait, my ass.

I pound my fists on the steering wheel until they ache and it's ready to crack. "Why, why, why?" These actual words come with an all-new freshet of frustrated tears. Why did I do what's so ill-advised? Why did I risk the Manasquan, knowing what might lurk here? Why did I, a nunce, trust a Greek? One who reads Fitzgerald? Faithless Chris, himself a callow young Nick. Why, oh why did I rashly count my blessings and leave myself at risk? *Thanksgiving?* Thanksgiving's bullshit.

I should've driven down to the Grove with Wade, hied off with a mid-forties-body-style Ricki, downed the martinis, eaten the hanger steak, skived away in the night, right to the blind golfers Quality Court to test the lead left in the ole pencil. What higher ground am I occupying? For what greater purpose am I preserved? Do I have anything to accomplish before I'm sixty that makes an unserious boinking a bad idea when it never was before? Am I preserving clarity? Am I too good, too intent, too loyal, too cautious, too free to grab a little woogle when it's offered and otherwise in short supply?

Tears and more tears come fairly flooding. Rage, frustration, sorrow, remorse, fatigue, self-reproach—a whole new list. Name it, I've suddenly got it. I gawk around through the fogged windows at the Squatters' lot. A low-rider Chevette idles through and noses into the handicapped space. Two women in big coats climb out, one on crutches, and move slowly through the doors, which when open cast a blue-red blur into the night, where I'm trapped, wanting, needing someone to help me. No one inside would even remember me, though probably plenty possess automotive skills.

It's another moment for cell-phone service. A chance to use the Triple-A I never bought. The ideal dilemma for an in-car computerized hot-line-to-Detroit for dispatched emergency assistance—though my Suburban's a '96. Too old. Of course, there aren't pay phones anymore.

And for God's sake and beyond all: What *else* is happening to me out here? I'm not about to *die* (I don't think). ".Bascombe was discovered deceased in his car outside a Manasquan bump shop, across from an alternative night spot on Thanksgiving morning. No further details are available." No, no, no. Except this feeling I'm having *reminds* me of death and presents itself as pain right where my heart ought to be; only nothing's spazzing down my arm, no light-headed, gasping or blue-faced constriction. It's as if I'd done death *already*. Though I'd give anything, promise any promise, admit anything just to not feel this way, to see instead a hopeful, trusting Sponsoree materialize out of the misty night, seeking good counsel for his or her issues and shifting the focus away from mine. Since mine seem to be not that I'm dying, but that I just have to *be* here in some fearsome way—and me the last person on earth to truckle with stagy ideas of *be*-ness. *Be*-ness means business to me. (What is it about being trapped in your cold vehicle with no help coming and the promise of the night spent curled up like a snake in the luggage compartment that gives rise to the somberest of thoughts: the finality of one's *self*, in defeat of all distractions put in the way? Possibly it's cloying Thanksgiving *it*self—the recapitulative, Puritan and thus most treacherous of holidays—that clears away the ordinary pluses and leaves only the big minuses to be totaled.)

Of course, anyone could tell, even me, that it's the Frantals' sad family mini-saga that's whop-sided me into painful, tearful grieving (if you've lost a child, other people's child-loss stories magnetize around you like iron filings). And what else would you call my symptoms but grieving? Inasmuch as tucked away in the *Home Buyer's Guide*, where I'd least expect it, is the jugger-naut of *acceptance*—grief's running mate. *Their* acceptance—of life's bounty and its loss—which the world can honor, in the Frantals' case, by plunking down some earnest money on a cunning Cape on Crab Apple Court.

But what the hell more do *I* need to accept that I haven't already, and confessed as the core of my *be*-ness? That I have cancer and my days are numbered in smaller denominations than most everyone else's? (Check.) That my wife's left me and probably won't come back? (Check.) That my fathering and husbanding skills have been unexemplary and at best only serviceable? (Check.) That I've chosen a life smaller than my "talents" because a smaller life made me happier? (Check, check, double check.)

More tears are falling. I could laugh through them if I didn't have a potentially self-erasing pain in my chest. What is it I'm supposed to accept? That I'm an asshole? (I confess.) That I have no heart? (I don't confess.) But what would be the hardest thing to say and mean it? What would be the hardest for others? The Frantals? For Sally? For Mike Mahoney? For Ann? For anybody I know? All good souls to God?

And of course the answer's plain, unless we're actors or bad-check artists or spies, when it's still probably plain but more tolerable: that your life is founded on a lie, and you know what the lie is and won't admit it, maybe can't. Yes, yes, yes, yes.

Deep in my heart space a breaking is. And as in our private moments of sexual longing, when the touch we want is far away, a groan comes out of me. "Oh-uhhh." The sour tidal whoosh the dead man exhales. "Oh-uhhh. Oh-uhhh." So long have I *not* accepted, by practicing the quaintness of acceptance by. . . . "Oh-uhhh. Oh-uhhh." Breath-loss clenches my belly into a rope knot, clenching, clenching in. "Oh, oh, ohhhhhpp." Yes, yes and yes. No more no's. No more no's. No more no's.

*A*single rain spatter strikes the hood of my cold vehicle. I'm roused and gaunt, mouth open. Ears stinging. Fists balled. My feet ache. My neck's stiff. My interior parts feel wounded, as if I'd been sealed in a barrel, tupped off a cliff, then rolled and rolled and rolled, bracing myself inside until stopped, upon a dark terrain I can't see but only dream of.

"What now?" These are spoken words I manage. In the rearview, through the fogged back glass, there's still the red smear of BAR across the lot. Two cars are left—the low-rider and a big Ram club cab. It feels late. Traffic on the 35 bridge has thinned to a trickle. "What now?" I offer again to the fates. I breathe a testing breath (no heart pain), then a deeper, colder one I fill my chest with and hold for my inner parts to register back. My temples go bump-bump-bump-bump behind my eyes, which feel tight. It's better to close them, hands in my lap, cold knees together, elbows in, cranium on the headrest, chest expanded with held-in air. Dampness sits in the cockpit. I breathe out my deep inhale. And though it's said (by ninnies) that we can never experience the exact moment of sleep's arrival, still— and in a speed that amazes me—I do. "So it turns out, see, that China's *really fucking BIG*" are the words I'm thinking, and they are like velvet with their comfort.

ap, tap, tap. Tap, tap, tap. A pale moon's face, young, mostly nose and chin and eyebrows, hangs outside my window glass—apprehensive, puzzled, a slight uncertain smile of wonder.

Is he dead? Is it too late?

At first it doesn't scare me. And then, when I realize how deep in sleep I've been, I'm startled. My eyes blink and blink again. My heart goes from imperceptible to perceptible. Robbed, bludgeoned, dragged, heels in the muck, to the cold Manasquan and schlumped onto the tide like a rolled-up rug. I shrink from the glass to escape. I utter a small frightened sound. "Aaaaaaaaaa."

The moon's mouth is moving. Its muffled voice says, "I went to a club over in . . ." *Static, static, static . . .* "I seen your vehicle from the bridge . . . like . . ." *Static, static.*

I gawk through the glass, unable to fix on the face. My cheeks are cobwebby, my mouth bitter and dry. I'm frozen in my jacket and thin pants, but I'm willing to go back to sleep and be murdered that way.

". . . So, are you, like, okay?" the pimpled young moon mouth says.

"Yep," I say, not knowing who to.

But criminals don't wonder if you're okay. Or they shouldn't.

The muffled voice outside says, "Did you find your keys?" An agreeable grin says, You're a poor dope, aren't you? You don't know a goddamn thing. You'll always have to be helped.

I push at the window button. Nothing happens. I struggle at the ignition, where there's no key inserted. Things fall into place.

Chris speaks something else, something I can't make out. I push open the heavy-weight door right into his chest and forehead as I hear him say "... under the mat."

I stare up. He is no longer in his blue mechanic's shirt that shows off his tattoos, but in a Jersey long-coat of inexpensive green vinyl manufacture, which makes him look like a seedy punk and is meant to. He's cold, too, his hands stuffed in his shallow pockets. He's rocking foot to foot. His nose is running, his forehead reddened, his hair a yellow tangle. But he is in positive spirits, possibly a little wine-drunk or stoned.

Cold air smacks my cheeks. "What time is it?"

Chris breathes out a congested nasal snurf. "Prolly. I don't know. Midnight." He looks over to Squatters. The BAR sign's dark, but visible. No cars sit outside. Route 35's a ghost highway, the bridge empty and palely lit. A garbage truck with a cop car leading it, blue flasher turning, moves slowly south toward Point Pleasant. "I seen your rig still here. I go, 'Uh-oh, what the fuck is this?' " Chris shudders, tucks his chin into his lapel and breathes inside for warmth.

"I looked under the goddamn mat," I say. I'm feeling extremely rough, as if I'd been manhandled for the second night in a row. I'm grinding my molars and must look deranged.

"That mat out front of the office," Chris says, fidgety, chin down, pointing around toward the front door at a mat that's invisible from my car. "We leave 'em there. That way, the car looks like it's just sitting."

"How the hell am I supposed to know that?"

"I don't know," says Chris. "It's how everybody does it. How'd you get in?"

"It was unlocked." I am slightly dazed.

"Oh. Man. I messed that up. I shoulda locked it. Lemme get them keys."

Chris doesn't act like a struggling American Existentialist scholarship boy at Monmouth, but a sweet, knuckleheaded grease monkey weighing a stint in trade school or the Navy. He is who he ought to be. It is a lesson I could apply to my son Paul if I chose to, and should.

Chris hustles back with my arrowhead fob, but grinning. "Didn't you get cold in 'ere?" He swabs his nose, sucks back, hocks one on the gravel. He is someone's son, capable of a good deed performed without undue gravity. He has saved me tonight, after nearly killing me. I now see he has SATAN inked into the flesh of his left metacarpals and JESUS worked into the right ones. Both inexpertly done. Chris is on a quest, his soul in the balance.

"Yeah, but it was fine," I say. "I went to sleep. How much for the window?" I straighten my left leg, where I'm sitting half out the door, so I can reach my billfold. I'm tempted to ask who's winning his soul. Old number 666 rarely has a chance anymore except in politics.

"Thirty," he says. "But you can mail it to him. It's all shut up. I gotta get home. Tomorrow's a holiday. My wife'll kill me."

Wife! Chris has one of those *already*? Possibly he's older than he looks. Possibly he's not even Greek. Possibly he's a father himself. Why do we think we know anything?

"Me, too." A marital lie to make me feel better. "Thanks." I effect a sore-necked look back at the duct-taped window, seemingly as impregnable as a bank.

"No problem," Chris says. His skin-pink Camaro with a bright green replacement passenger door sits idling behind us, headlights shining, interior light on, its door standing open. "You'd be surprised how many of them babies I fix a month." He grins again, a boyish grin, his teeth straight, strong and white. He's leaving, rescue complete, heading home to his Maria or his Silvie, who won't be mad, and will thrill to his return (after modest resistance).

"How old are you?" It seems the essential question to ask of the young.

"Thirty-one." A surprise. "How 'bout you?"

"Fifty-five."

"That ain't so old." His breath is thin smoke. His vinyl coat affords little warmth. "My dad's, like, fifty-six. He does these tough-guy competitions for his age group, up at the convention hall in Asbury. He's on his fourth wife. Nobody fucks with him."

"I bet not."

"Bet they don't fuck with you," Chris says to be generous.

"Not anymore they don't."

"There you go." He breathes down into his lapel again. "That's all you gotta worry about."

"Happy Thanksgiving," I say. "Early." We are beating on, Chris and me, against the current.

"Oh yeah." He looks embarrassed. "Happy Thanksgiving to you, too."

*C*onceivably it's two. I've avoided clocks on my drive home, likewise during the passage through my empty house. Knowledge of the hour, especially if it's later than I think, will guarantee me no sleep, promising that tomorrow's celebration of munificence and bounty will degrade into demoralized fatigue before the food arrives.

Clarissa's bedroom window's been left open, and I crank it closed, intentionally noticing nothing. I listen to none of my day's messages. I've shown one house to one serious client on the day before Thanksgiving, a day when most toilers in my business are headed off to convivial tables elsewhere. For that reason I'm ahead of the game—which is generally my tack: With few obligations, turn freedom into enterprise. Thoreau said a writer was a man with nothing to do who finds something to do. He would've made the realty Platinum Circle. His heirs would own Maine.

But passing by my darkened home office a second time, I'm unable to resist my messages. After all, Clarissa herself might've called with a plea that I shoot down and collect her at the elephant gate at the Taj Mahal. In my unwieldy state of acceptance, I concede that something once unpromising could show improvement.

Clare Suddruth has, not surprisingly, called at six—a crucial interval, and at the vulnerable cocktail hour. He says he definitely wants to "re-view" the Doolittle house on Friday, if possible.

"At least let's get through the damn front door this time." He's bringing "the boss." "At my age, Frank, there's no use worrying about the long run in anything." He says this as if I hadn't spoon-fed him those very words. Estelle, the MS survivor, has been counseling with Clare about matters eschatological. I'm just relieved not to have to call the Drs. Doolittle with unhappy news that would cost me the listing. Though Clare's the type to come in with a low-ball offer, consume weeks with back-and-forth and then get pissed off and walk away. My best strategy is to say I'm tied up until next week (when I'll be at Mayo) and hope he gets desperate.

Call #2 is from Ann Dykstra, more cut-and-dried-businessy than last night's sauvignon blanc ramble about what a good man I am, what a long transit life is, me snagging the Hawk's liner at the Vet in '87. "Frank, I think we need to talk about tomorrow. I'm thinking maybe I shouldn't come. Paul and Jill just left, which was very strange. Did you know she only has one hand? Some awful accident. Maybe I'm just saving myself." What's wrong with that? "Anyway, maybe I'm getting ahead of myself on several fronts. I sort of sense you may feel the same. Call me before you go to bed. I'll be up."

Too late.

Call #3 listens to my Realty-Wise recording, waits, breathes, then says "Shit" in a man's voice I don't recognize and hangs up. This is normal.

Call #4 is from the Haddam Boro Police—putting me on the alert. A Detective Marinara. The room where he's speaking is crowded with voices and phones ringing and paper rattling. "Mr.

Bascombe, I wonder if I could talk to you. We're investigating an incident at Haddam Doctors on eleven twenty-one. Your name came up in a couple of different contexts." A tired sigh. "Nothing to be alarmed about, Mr. Bascombe. We're just establishing some investigative parameters here. My number's (908) 555-1352. That's Detective Mar-i-nar-a, like the sauce. I'll be working late. Thanks for your help." *Click.*

What investigatory parameters? Though I know. The boys at Boro Hall are hard at it, connecting dots, leveling the playing field. My license number was mentally logged by Officer Bohmer. Dot one. My years-old connection with the grievously unlucky Natherial (who couldn't have been the target) has been cross-referenced from his list of life acquaintances. Dot two. Possibly my passing association with Tommy Benivalle (who's conceivably under indictment somewhere) has hit pay dirt via the FBI computer. Dot three. My fistfight with Bob Butts at the August has disclosed an unstable, potentially dangerous personality. Dot four. Who of us could stand inspection and not come out looking like we did it—or at least feeling that way? I am again a person of interest and my best bet is to call and admit everything.

Call #5 is, also predictably, from Mike, at ten, and sounds as if he may have been into the sauce (he's a Grand Marnier man). Mike hopes that I've enjoyed an excellent day with my family around me (I haven't); he also notes that Buddha permits individuals to make decisions without giving offense because "the nature of existence is permanent, which can include temporarily taking up a quest to free oneself from the cycle of time." There's more, but I don't intend to hear it at what is probably two-something. He'll be naming streets in Lotus Estates by Monday. His arc is shorter than most.

I'm relieved there's no call-out-of-the-weirdness from Paul, and half-relieved/half not that there's nothing from Wade. Nothing's from Clarissa. And I'll be honest and admit, in the new spirit of millennial necessity, that not a night begins and ends without a thought that Sally Caldwell might call me. I've played such a call through my brain cells a hundred times and taken pleasure in each and every one. I don't know where she is. Mull or not Mull. She could be in Dar es Salaam, and I'd welcome a call gratefully. A lot of things seem one way but are another. And how a thing *seems* is often just the game we play to save ourselves from great, panicking pain. The true truth is, I wish Sally would come home to me, that we could be we again, and Wally could wear a tartan, hybridize many trees and be satisfied with his hermit's lot—which he chose and, for all I know, may long for, given the kind of lumpy-mumpy bloke he was in this house. Possibly I will call her on Thanksgiving, use the emergency-only number. Nothing has qualified as an emergency—but may.

The sea and air outside my window are of a single petroleum density, with no hint of the tide stage. One socketed nautical light drifts southward at an incalculable distance. I've always attributed such lights to commercial craft, dragging for flounder, or a captaincy like the *Mantoloking Belle*, commandeered by divorced men or suicide survivors or blind golfers out on the waves for a respite before resuming brow-furrowing daylight roles. Though I know now, and am struck, that these can be missions of another character—grieving families scattering loved ones' ashes, tossing wreaths upon the ocean's mantle, popping a cork in remembrance. Giving rather than taking.

When our sweet young son Ralph breathed his last troubled breath in the now-bomb-shattered Haddam Doctors, in time-dimmed '81 (Reagan was President, the Dodgers won the Pennant), Ann and I, in one of our last free-wheeling marital strategizings—we were deranged—sought to plot an "adventurous but appropriate" surrender of our witty, excitable, tenderhearted boy to time's embrace. A journey to Nepal, a visit to the Lake District, a bush-pilot adventure to the Talkeetnas—destinations he'd never seen but would've relished (not without irony) as his last residence. But I was squeamish and still am about cremation. Something's more terrifying than death itself about the awful, greedy flames, the sheer canceling. Whereas death seems a regular thing, a familiar, in no need of fiery dramatizing, orderly to the point of stateliness, just as Mike says. I couldn't cremate my son! Only to have him come back in powdered form, in a handy box, with a terrifying new name I'd never forget in four hundred years: *Cremains!* I've scattered the ashes of two Red Man Clubmen, and these residues turn out not to be powdered nearly *enough*, but are ridden through with bits of bone—odorless gray grit—like the cinders we Sigma Chi pledges used to shovel onto the front walk of the chapter house in Ann Arbor.

Ann felt exactly the same. We had two other children to think about; Paul was seven, Clarissa five. Plus, there was no way to transport a whole embalmed body on an around-the-world victory lap. It would've cost a fortune.

For a few brief hours, we actually thought about, and twice talked of donating Ralph's physical leavings to science, or of possibly going the organ donor route. Though we pretty quickly realized we could never bear the particulars or face the documents or stand to have strangers thank us for our "gift," and would never forgive ourselves once the deeds were done.

So finally, with Lloyd Mangum's help, we simply and solemnly buried Ralph in a secular ceremony in the "new part" of the cemetery directly behind our house on Hoving Road, where he rests now near the founder of Tulane University, east of the world's greatest expert on Dutch elm disease, a stone's throw away from the inventor of the two-level driving range and, as of yesterday, in sight of Watcha McAuliffe. Interment at sea—a shrouded bundle sluiced off the aft end of a sport-fishing craft with a fighting seat and a flying deck, performed under cover of darkness and far enough out so the Coast Guard wouldn't come snooping—wasn't an option we knew about. But it's on my list for when my own time arrives and final thoughts are in the ballpark.

But. Acceptance, again. What have I now accepted that visits me in my stale bedroom, where I'm warm and dank beneath the covers, my stack of unread books beside me, and at an unknown but indecent hour? What is it that rocked me like an ague, turned me loose like a flimsy ribbon on a zephyr? All these years and modes of accommodation, of coping, of living with, of negotiating the world in order to fit into it—my post-divorce dreaminess, the long period of existence in the early middle passage, the states of acceptable longing, of being a variablist, even the Perma-nent Period itself—these now seem *not* to be forms of acceptance the way I thought, but forms of fearful nonacceptance, the laughing/grimacing masks of denial turned to the fact that, like the luckless snowmobiler Chick Frantal, my son, too, would never *be* again in this life we all come to know too well.

It's *this* late-arriving acknowledgment that's unearthed me like a boulder tumbled down a mountain. *That* was my lie, my big fear, the great pain I couldn't fathom even the thought of surviving, and so didn't fathom it; fathomed instead life as a series of lives, variations on a theme that sheltered me. The lie being: It's not Ralph's death that's woven into everything like a secret key, it's his *not death*, the *not* permanence—the extra beat awaited, the mutability of every fact, the grinning, eyebrows-raised chance that something's waiting even if it's not. These were my sly ruses and slick tricks, my surface intrigues and wire-pulls, all played *against* permanence, not *to* it.

Hard to think, though, that the Frantals alone could've sprung me this far loose with their sad acceptance *qua* sales pitch. Chances are, with the year I've had, I was headed there anyway, preparing to meet my Maker. When I asked what it was I had to do before I was sixty, maybe it's just to accept my whole life and my whole self in it—to have that chance before it's too late: to try again to achieve what athletes achieve when their minds are clear, their parts in concert, when they're "feeling it," when the ball's as big as the moon and they hit it a mile because that's all they can do. When nothing else is left. The Next Level.

A cooling tear exits my eye crease where I'm turned on the pillow to face the inky sea. The single-lighted ship is nearly past the window's frame. Possibly they do more than one cremains box per night if no mourners are along. This could be what the funeral business means when it says "We're trustworthy." No tricks. No shameless practices. No doubling up. No tossing Grandma Beulah in the dumpster behind Eckerd's. We do what we say we'll do whether you're along or not. A rarity.

Somewhere below the ocean's hiss I hear Bimbo's doggy voice, musical within the Feensters' walls, yap-yap-yap, yap-yap-yap. Then a muffled man's voice—Nick—not decipherable, then silence. I detect the murmur of the Sumitomo banker's limo as it motors down Poincinet Road past my house for his early morning pickup, hear two car doors close, then the murmured passage back. No Thanksgiving for the Nikkei.

My last tear, after this many, and many more not shed, is a tear of relief. Acceptable life frees you to embrace the next thing. Though who's to say it all wouldn't have worked fine anyway—those familiar old rejections and denials performing their venerable tasks. Years ago, I knew that mourning could be long. But *this* long? Easy to argue some things might be better left alone, since permanence, real permanence, not the soft blandishments of the period I invented, can be scary as shit, since it rids you of your old, safe context. With whom, for instance, am I supposed to "share" that I've accepted Ralph's death? What's it supposed to *mean*? How will it register and signify? Will it be hard to survive? Can I still sell a house? Will I want to? And how would it have been different if I'd accepted everything right from the first, like the CEO of GE or General Schwarzkopf would've? Would I be living in Tokyo now? Would I have died of acceptance? Or be in Haddam still? God only knows. Maybe all would've been about the same; maybe acceptance is over-rated—though the shrinks all tell you different, which just means they don't know. After all, we each carry around with us plenty of "things" that're unsatisfactory, "things" we're wanting to undo or ignore so other "things" can be happier, so the heart can open wider. Ask Marguerite Purcell. As I said, acceptance is goddamned scary. I feel its very fearsomeness here in my bed, in my empty house with the storm past and Thanksgiving waiting with the dawn in the east. Be careful what you accept, is my warning—to me. I will if I can.

Out in the dark, I hear a motorcycle, nazzing, gunning, high-pitched, somewhere out on Ocean Avenue, though it fades. Then I think I hear another car, a smaller foreign one with narrow-gauge tires and a cheap muffler, slowing at my driveway. For a moment, I think it's Clarissa, home now, with Thom in the Healey, or alone in a rented Daewoo—safe. I'll hear the front door softly open and softly click closed. But that's not it. It's only the *Asbury Press*. I hear music from the carrier's AM as his window lowers and the folded paper whaps the gravel. Then the window closes and the song fades—"Gotta take that sentimental journey, sen-ti-men-tal jour-ur-ney home." I hear it down the street and down into my sleep. And then I hear nothing more.

Part 3

13

Brrrp-brrrrp! Brrrp-brrrrp! Brrrp-brrrrp! Brrrp-brrrrp!

My Swiss telephone, stylish, metal, minuscule (a present from Clarissa on my return to the land of the living), sings its distressing Swiss wake-up song: "Bad news, bad news for you (and it ain't in Switzerland, either)."

I clutch for the receiver, so flat and sleek I can't find it. My room's full of morning light and cottony, humid, warmer air. What hour is it? I knock over my pile of books, detonating a loud and heavy clatter.

"Bascombe," I say, breathless, into the tiny voice slit. This is never how I answer the phone. But my heart's pounding with expectancy and a hint of dread. It's Thanksgiving morning. Do I know where my daughter is?

"Okay, it's Mike." This is not how he talks, either. My answer-voice has startled him. He says nothing, as if someone's holding a loaded gun on him.

"What time is it?" I say. I'm confused from too deep sleep, where I believe I was having a pleasant dream about eating.

"Eight forty-five. Did you hear my message last night?"

"No." Half true. I didn't listen past the Buddhist flounces and flourishes.

"Okay—" He's about to tell me it's been one heckuva hard

decision, but the world's a changing place and, even for Buddhists, is entirely created by our aspirations and actions, and suffering doesn't happen without a cause and effort is the precondition of positive actions—the very reason I didn't listen last night. I'm in bed, fully clothed, with my shoes still on, the counterpane wrapped around me like a tortilla. "Could you drive over to 118 Timbuktu at eleven and meet me?"

"What the hell for?"

"I sold it." Mike's accentless voice is fruity with exuberance. "Cash deal."

"One eighteen Timbuktu's *already* sold." I'm about to be aggravated. Acceptance is right away posing a challenge. I'm relieved, of course, it's not Clarissa telling me she and lizard Thom are married, that I somehow missed all the big clues yesterday. "It's up on trucks," I say. "I'm moving it over to 629 Whitman." Our Little Manila section, which has begun gentrifying at an encouraging rate. He knows all this.

"My people want the house right now, as is." It's as though the whole idea tickles him silly and has elevated his voice half an octave. "They want to take over the moving and put it on a lot on Terpsichore that I'm ready to sell them."

"Why can't this wait till Monday?" I'm about to doze off, though I have to piss (the third time since 2 a.m.). Outside my open window, up in the scrubbed azure firmament, white terns tilt and noiselessly wheel. The air around my covers feels soft and cushiony-springlike, though it's late November. Laughter filters up from the beach—laughter that's familiar.

"You hold the deed on that, Frank." Mike uses my name only

at moments of all else failing. Usually, he calls me nothing at all, as if my name was an impersonal pronoun. "They have to buy it direct from you. And they're ready right now. I thought you might just drive over."

He, of course, is right. I sold 118 Timbuktu in September to a couple from Lebanon (Morris County), the Stevicks, who planned to demolish it first thing next spring and bring in a new manufactured dwelling from Indiana that had a lifetime guarantee and all the best built-ins. I stepped back in and offered to take the house in lieu of commission, since it's a perfectly good building. They agreed and I've been arranging to move it to a lot I own on Whitman, where it'll fit in and bring a good price because the inventory's low over there. At 1,300 sq. ft., it'll be bigger than most of its Whitman Street neighbors and be exactly the kind of small American ranch any Filipino who used to be a judge in Luzon, but who over here finds himself running a lawn-care business, would see as a dream come true. Arriba House Recyclers (Bolivians) from Keansburg have been doing the work on a time-permits basis, and throwing me a break. I'm looking at a good profit slice by the time the whole deal's over. Except, if I sell it off the truck like a consignment of hot Sonys, get a good price (less Mike's 2 percent), dispense with the rigamarole of moving a house up Route 35, getting a foundation dug and poured and utilities run, paying for all the permits and line-clearance fees, I'd need to have my head examined not to do Mike's deal on the spot. It's true that as deeded owner, only I can convey it if we're conveying this morning. (We call deals like this WACs, for "write a check.") Only I'm not certain I have the heart for real estate on Thanksgiving morning, even if all I have to do is say yes, sign a bill of sale and shake a stranger's hand. The Next Level and universal acceptance may be closing the shutters on the realtor in me.

I haven't spoken for several moments, and may have gone to sleep on the phone. I hear laughing again, laughing that's definitely known to me but unplaceable. Then a voice talking loudly, then more laughter.

"Can we do it?" Mike's voice is forceful, anxious, fervent—odd for a Tibetan who'd rather cut a fart in public than seem agitated. Possibly I've discouraged him. What about Tommy Benivalle?

"Will I come where?"

"To Timbuktu." A pause. "One eighteen. Eleven o'clock."

"Oh," I say, pushing my head—still sore from Bob Butts' wrenching it—deep into the yielding pillow, letting air exit my lungs slowly, then breathing in body odor in my winding-sheet, loving being where I am, but where I cannot stay much longer. "Sure," I say. "Sure, sure."

"Terrific!" Mike says. "That's terrific." He says "terrific" in his old Calcutta telemarketer style, as when a housewife in Pennsauken tumbled to a set of plastic-wicker outdoor chairs and a secret bond was forged because she thought he was white: "Terrific. That's terrific. I know you're going to enjoy that, ma'am. Expect delivery in six to ten weeks."

The laughing voice, the laughing man I see when I stand to the window for the day's first gaze at the beach, the sky, the waves is my son Paul, hard at work with a shovel, digging a hole the size of a small grave in the rain-caked sand between the beach and the ocean-facing foundation wall of my house, where some rhododendrons were planted by Sally but never thrived. The hole must be for his time capsule, which Clarissa told me about but which doesn't seem present now. What would a time capsule look like? How deep would you need to bury one for it to "work"? What haywire impulse would make anyone think this is a proper idea for Thanksgiving? And why do I not know the answer to these questions?

Paul is not alone. He's spiritedly shoveling while talking animatedly from three feet down in his hole to the tiny Sumitomo banker, Mr. Oshi, who's surprisingly back from work and standing motionless beside Paul's hole, dressed in a dark business suit as shovel-fulls of sand fly past onto a widening pile. Paul's hair looks thinner than when I saw him last spring, and he's heavier and is wearing what look like cargo shorts and a tee-shirt that shows his belly. He has the same goatee that connects to his mustache and surrounds his mouth like a golf hole. Though his haircut, I can see, is new—a style that I believe is called the "mullet," and that many New Jersey young adults wear, and also professional hockey players, but that on Paul looks like a Prince Galahad. Mr. Oshi appears to be listening as Paul yaks away from his hole, haw-hawing and occasionally gesturing out toward the ocean with his shovel (from my utility room, no doubt), nodding theatrically, then going on digging. Mr. Oshi may also be trying to speak, but Paul has him trapped—which is his usual conversational strategy. Two dachshunds are rocketing around off the leash through the dune grass (where they're forbidden) and out onto the beach, then back round the house and the hole and out of sight. These must be Mr. Oshi's wiener dogs, since he's holding in each hand what looks like a sandwich bag of dog crap that I'm sure he'd like to get rid of. Such is the private nature of neighborly life on Poincinet Road, that I've never seen these dogs before.

As the first thing one sees on Thanksgiving morning, it's an unexpected sight—my son and Mr. Oshi in converse. Though I'm sure it's what the higher-ups in Sumitomo hope for when they dispatch a Mr. Oshi to the Shore: chance encounters with the natives, cultural incumbency taking root, exchange of ground-level demographic and financial data, gradual acceptance of *differences*, leading quickly to social invisibility. Then *bingo!* The buggers own the beach, the ocean, your house, your memories, and your kids are on a boat to Kyoto for immersion language training.

Still, it's saving that I've seen Paul before he sees me, since I'd begun—terrible to admit this—to dread our moment of meeting following last spring's miscommunication. I've pictured myself standing in the middle of some indistinct room (my living room); I'm smiling, waiting—like a prisoner who hears the foot-falls of the warden, the priest and the last-mile crew thudding the concrete floor—anticipating my son to come down a flight of stairs, open a closed door, emerge from a bathroom, fly unzipped, and me just being there, grinningly *in loco parentis*, unable to utter intelligible sounds, all possible good embargoed, nothing promising ahead. No wonder fathers and sons is the subject of enigmatic and ponderous literatures. What the hell's it all about? Why even go near each other if we're going to feel such aversion? Only the imagination has a prayer here, since all logic fails.

What I desire, of course, is that the freshening spirit of acceptance render today free of significant pretexts, contexts, subtexts—texts of any kind; be just a day when I'm not the theme, the constant, not expected to make things better, having now, with an optimistic outlook, put holiday events into motion. (I'm by nature a better guest than a host anyway.) But isn't that how we all want Thanksgiving to be? Perfectly generic—the state of mind we enjoy best. In contrast to Xmas, New Year's, Easter, Independence Day and even Halloween—the fraught, load-bearing holidays? We all project ourselves, just the way I do, as regular humans capable of experiencing a regular human holiday with selected others. And so we should. It was what I intended: Acceptance—a spirit to be thankful for.

Only easier said than done.

The beach beyond the grassy furze—where my son's digging away and lecturing poor captive Mr. Oshi—is nonetheless a good beach for a holiday morning. After last night's drought-ending rain, the air has softened and become salt-fragrant and lush, tropical depression Wayne having missed its chance with us. Light is moist and sun-shot. A tide is changing, so that fishermen, their bait pails left back on the sand, have edged out into the tame surf to cast their mackerel chunks almost to where a pair of wet-suited kayakers is plying a course up the coast. Tire tracks dent the beach where the Shore Police have passed. A few straggler tourists have returned with the good weather to stroll, throw Frisbees, shout gaily, let their kids collect seashells above the waves' extent. Mr. Oshi's dachshunds skirmish about like water sprites. Surely here in the late-autumnal tableau one can feel the holiday's sweetness, the chance that normal things can happen to normal folk, that the sun will tour the sky and all find easy rest at day's end, full of gratitude on gratitude's holy day.

Though my son's vocalizing and excavating make me know that for normal things to happen to normal folk, some selected normal folk in a frame of mind of acceptance, prudence and gratitude need to get kick-started and off the dime. Since the day is full, and it is here.

I've awakened to several new certainties, which make themselves known, as certainties often do, when I'm in the shower—the first pertaining to the day's clothing commitments. As I've already said, I prefer mostly standard-issue "clothes." Medium-weight chinos I buy from a New Hampshire mail-order firm where they keep my size, cuffing preferences, inseam—even which side I "dress" on—stored in a computer. I generally wear canvas or rawhide belts, tabbed to the season; white or pale oxford-cloth shirts, or knitted pullovers in a variety of shades—

both long sleeve and short—along with deck shoes, penny loafers or bluchers all from the same catalog, where they showcase everything on unmemorably attractive human mannequins, pictured beside roaring fireplaces, out training their Labradors or on the banks of rilling trout streams. I hardly have to say that such clothing identifies me as the southern-raised frat boy I am (or was), since it's a style ideal for warm spring days, perched on the balcony at Sigma Chi, cracking wise at passing Chi O's, books to bosoms, headed to class. These preferences work very well in the house-selling business, where what I wear (like what I drive) is intended to make as little statement as possible, letting me portray myself to clients as the non-risk-taking everyman with a voice of reason, who only wants the best for all, same as they want for themselves. Which happens to be true.

However, for today I've decided to switch away from regular clothes, based on the first perceived certainty: that something different is needed. My new attire is *not* to dress up like a Pilgrim, ready to deliver an oration like the kids over in the Haddam Interpretive Center. I merely mean to wear blue relaxed-fit 501s— I had them already, just never thought to put them on—white Nikes from a brief try at tennis two years back, a yellow polo and a blue Michigan sweatshirt with a maize block-M, which the alumni association sent me for becoming a lifetime member (there was other stuff—a substandard-size football, a Wolverine bed toy, a leather-bound volume of robust imbibing songs—all of which I threw in the trash). I'm dressing this way strictly for Paul's benefit, since it will conceivably present me as less obviously myself—less a "father," with less a shared and problematic history, even less a real estate agent, which I know he thinks is an unfunny joke (a greeting-card writer being a giant step up). Dressing like an orthodontist from Bay City down for the Wisconsin game will also portray me as a willing figure of fun and slightly stupid in a self-mortifying way Paul generally appreciates, permitting us both (I hope) to make wry, get-the-ball-rolling jokes at my expense.

My father always wore the same significant blue gabardine suit, with a button-hole poppy in his wide lapel, for Thanksgiving dinner, while my mother always wore a pretty one-piece flowered rayon dress—pink azaleas or purple zinnias—with sling-back heels and blazing stockings I hated to touch. Their attire lives in my mind as the good touchstone for what Thanksgiving symbolized of material and spiritual life—steadiness. I had a blue Fauntleroy outfit given to me by Iowa grandparents, although I hated every minute I had it on and couldn't wait to wad it in the back corner of my closet in our house in Biloxi. But my parents didn't experience the same challenges with me that I face with Paul—resentment, zany oppositional behavior, too-abundant access to language, eccentric every-day appearance—jeopardy, in other words. Plus, at the Next Level, all things count more and can be ruined. So you could say that I'm building a firewall, allowing myself to become an accepting new citizen of the new century, walling myself off from being an asshole by dressing exactly like one in hopes everybody will get my well-intended message.

The second batch of certainties I've awakened clear-headed about and mean to put into motion even before heading to

Timbuktu are: (1) call Ann to make sure she doesn't show up today (there is acceptance here, but it's of rejectionist character); (2) call the Haddam PD to be certain Detective Marinara understands I'm not a hospital bomber, but a citizen ready to help in any way I can; (3) send the thirty dollars plus a tip to the car repair, though I lack the address, so will have to deliver it in person; (4) call Clarissa's cell phone to find out her arrival time to start hostessing Thanksgiving—and to make certain she's not married; (5) call Wade in Bamber Lake; (6) put in an overseas call to Sally to inform her that after careful thought I officially accept the logic that it's worse to let a person you love be alone forever when you don't have to—and I'm that person.

Actually, I *have* done some homework on this last topic and now believe that "Sally-Wally"—I think of them in the same spirit as "priced to sell," "just needs love," "move in today"— makes about as much sense as wanting your dead son to come back to life, or wanting to marry your long-divorced former wife, and has the same success potential: Zero. And therefore *something* different and *better* has to goddamn happen *now*—and will—just like when Wally showed up at my doorstep as empty-headed as a rutabaga, and *something* had to happen then. And did.

I definitely, however, am not going to tell Sally I have, or did or still do have a touch of cancer, since that could be viewed as a cheap late-inning win strategy—and might even be—and therefore prove unsuccessful. One of the hidden downsides of being a cancer victim/survivor is that telling people you've got it rarely comes out how you want it to, and often makes you feel sorry for the people you tell—just because they have to hear it—and spoils a day both of you would like to stay a happy day. It's why most people clam up about having it—not because it scares them shitless. That only happens the first instant the doctor tells you and doesn't really last that long, or didn't in my case. But mostly you don't tell people you've got cancer because you don't want the aggravation—the same reason you don't do most things.

*F*rom my desk upstairs, where I go to make my calls, I detect unfamiliar noises downstairs. It's too bad the prior owners never carried out their retrofitting plans for a maid's quarters/back staircase, so I could see what's what down there now. Paul, I believe, is still outside digging and lecturing Mr. Oshi, since his voice is still audible, laughing and yorking like a used-car salesman. This noise downstairs, then—morning TV noise, plates rattling, strangely heavy footfalls, a feminine cough—can only be Jill, the one-handed girl (which I'll believe when I see).

Call one I decide to make to the Haddam PD. Detective Marinara won't be there anyway and I can just leave my cooperative citizen's message. Only he *is* there, picks up on the first half ring with the standard indifferent-aggressive TV cop greeting, full of dislike and spiritual exhaustion. "*Mar*-i-nara. Hate Crimes."

"Hi, it's Frank Bascombe over in Sea-Clift, Mr. Marinara. I'm sorry, I didn't get your call till late." I must be lying and am instantly nervous.

"Okay. Mr. Bascombe? Let me see." Pages shuffling. *Clickety-click, click-click.* My name's on a list, my number traced automatically. "Okay. Okay." *Clickety-click-clickety*. I imagine the youthful bland face of a small-college dean of students. "Looks like—" A heavy sigh. Words come slowly. "We got a match. On your VIN at the crime scene yesterday. This is about the explosion here in Haddam, at Doctors Hospital. You might've read about it."

"I was *there*!" I blurt this. Producing instant galactic silence on the line. Detective Marinara may be flagging to other cops at other desks, silently mouthing, "I got the guy. I'll keep him on the line. Get the Sea-Clift police to pick him up. The fuck."

"Okay," he says. More silence. He is trained to be as emotionless as a museum guard. *These people always call. They can't stand not to be noticed. Actually, they want to be caught, can't bear freedom; you just have to not get in their way. They'll put the noose around their own necks.* I'm sure he's right.

More *clickety-clicking*.

"I mean, I was there because I came over to eat lunch at the hospital." I'm fidgety, self-resentful, breathless. Paul's voice is still audible through the bedroom window, in through my office door. Distant children's voices are behind his. Out of the empty blue empyrean, I hear the calliope sounds of a Good Humor truck patrolling the beach, appealing to the hold-out holiday visitors, people not talking to the police on Thanksgiving Day about bloody murder.

"I see." *Click, click, click.*

"I used to live in Haddam," I say. *Clickety-click.* "I sold houses there for seven years. For Lauren-Schwindell. I actually knew Natherial. Mr. Lewis. I mean, I knew him fifteen years ago. I haven't seen him in blows. I'm sorry he's deceased." Am I not supposed to know it was Natherial, and that he's dead? I read it in the newspaper.

Silence. Then, "Okay."

I hear more kitchen noises downstairs. Something made of glass or china has shattered on the floor, something a girl with only one hand might easily do. The TV volume jumps up, a man's voice shouts, "Ter-*rif*-ic! And what part of Southern California do you hail from, Belinda?" Then it's squelched to a mumble. "You say you knew Mr. Lewis?" Detective Marinara speaks in a monotone, very cop-like. He's typing what I'm saying. My worries are his interests.

"I did. Fifteen years ago."

"And, uh, under what circumstances were those?"

"I hired him to go find For Sale signs that had gotten stolen from properties we had listed. He was real good at it, too."

"He was real good at it?" More typing.

"Yeah. But I haven't seen him since." *Which is no reason to kill him* is what I'd like to imply. My innocence seems bland and inevitable, a burden to us both. The HPD apparently hasn't yet linked me to the August Inn dust-up with Bob Butts. I must seem exactly the harmless, civic-minded cancer victim I am. Of course this is the plodding police work—the investigative parameters, the mountain of papers, the maze of empty hunches, dismal dead ends and brain-suffocating phone conversations—that will relentlessly lead to the killer or killers, like the key to Pharaoh's tomb. But for a moment, on Thanksgiving morning, it has led to Sea-Clift and to me.

"And you live where?" Detective Marinara says. Possibly he yawns.

"Number seven Poincinet Road. Sea-Clift. On the Shore." I smile, with no one to see me.

"My sister lives up in Barnegat Acres," he says. "It's on the bay."

"A stone's throw. It's nice over there." Though it isn't so nice. The water has a sulfurous bite and a cheesy smell. Quirky bay breezes hold acrid fog too close to shore. And it's not far from the shut-down nuke facility in Silverton, which depresses house sales to flat-line.

"So." More typing, a squeak of Detective M's metal chair, then an amiable sniff of the constabulary nose. "Would you be willing, Mr. Bascombe, to drive over tomorrow and take part in an identification protocol?"

"What's that? Mine or somebody else's?"

"Just a lineup, Mr. Bascombe. It's not very likely we'll even do it. But we're trying to enlist some community cooperation here, do some eliminating. We've got witnesses we need to double-check. It'd be a help to us if you'd agree. Mr. Lewis has a son in the department here." (A cousin to young Lawrence, the hearse driver.)

"Okay. You bet." If I don't agree, my name goes into another pile, and the next person I'm interviewed by won't be yakking about his sister Babs in Barnegat Acres but will be one of the neatnik, black-belt karate guys with Arctic blue eyes in an FBI windbreaker. It lances into my brain that I haven't called Clare Suddruth back yet but am supposed to show him

61 Surf Road tomorrow. Then I remember I intend not to be available.

"Okay, then, that's all set," Detective Marinara says, more clicking. "Will. Participate. In. IDP. And . . . that's great."

"I'm happy to. Well. I'm—"

"Yep," Marinara says. "Ya still in the realty business over there?"

"Sure am. Realty-Wise. You want to buy a house on the ocean? I'll sell you one."

"Oh yeah, I just gotta get these citizens over here to quit killing each other, then I'll be over with you."

"That's a tall order but a noble quest, Detective."

"It's changed, Mr. Bascombe. It's a big difference than when you lived over here."

Just as I thought! He knows all about me. My life's displayed on his green screen. My mother's maiden name, my freshman GPA, my blood pressure, my tire pressure, my Visa balance and sexual preference. Probably he can see when I'm scheduled to die.

"People get rich, they get upset a lot easier. They keep me hoppin', I'll tell you that. Homicide rate's inchin' up in Delaware County. You don't hear about it. But I hear about it."

"Is your family together for Thanksgiving?"

"Oh, well. I'm workin', ain't I? Let's don't go down that road. You just have a good one."

"It's always complex."

"Whew. You got that right. Thanks for your cooperation, Mr. Bascombe. We'll be contacting you about tomorrow." And *click*, Marinara's gone, sucked into a computer dot just as I hear my son outside shout out, "He who smelt it, dealt it. That's all I know." It's hard to know what he's talking about, but my guess is the election.

I called last night," Ann Dykstra-Bascombe-Dykstra-O'Dell-Dykstra says before I can say it's me. I've called her cell. Where is she? In an underwear boutique at the Quaker Bridge Mall? On the 18th at HCC? In the can? You have no control over where your personal private voice is being heard, what audience it's being piped into, who's lying about who's where. It's an intrusion but isn't quite. I was ordering two cubic yards of pea gravel at the Garden Emporium in Toms River last week, and the customer beside me at the register was blabbing away, "Listen, sweetheart, I've never been so in love with anybody in my whole fucking life. So just say yes, okay? Tell that imbecile to go fuck himself. We can be on Air Mexico to Puerto Vallarta at ten o'clock tonight—"

"We need to talk about some things, Frank," Ann says in a disciplined voice. "Did you just elect to *not* call me last night?"

"This *is* calling you. I wasn't home last night. I was busy." Sleeping in my car. I've now showered and shaved and positioned myself, in my plaid terry-cloth robe and fleece mukluks, in as steadfast a sitting position as possible at my desk, coccyx flush to the chair back, feet flat to the floor, knees apart but nervous, breath regulated. It is the posture for hearing disappointing biopsy reports, offer turn-downs and "Someone's been badly injured" calls. It's also the posture for *delivering* bad news.

Yet I'm already on the defensive. My toes curl in my mukluks; my sphincter reefs in. And I'm the *delivering* party: Don't come here today. Or ever. My heart thumps as if I'd sprinted up a fire escape to get here. Ann has perfected the skill of making me feel this way. It's her golfer's inner meritoriousness. I'm forever the hunch-shouldered, grinning census taker at the door; she, the one living the genuine life. I have my questionnaire and my stubby pencil but will never know what reality—the one behind her, within the complex rooms—is all about. Hers is the voice of reasoned experience, sturdy values, good instincts and correct outlook (no matter how conventional); I am outside the threshold, the regretted one in need of sobering lessons. It's why she could turn away from me seventeen years ago and never (until now) look back. Because she was right, right, right. It's amazing I don't hate her guts.

"I think Gore should concede, don't you?"

"No."

"Well. He should. He's a sap. The market'll go crazy if he wins." Sap. The all-around Michigan term of disparagement. Her father characterized me as a sap when Ann and I were dating. "Where'd you find that sap?" Its sound twists a tighter knot in my gut. No one ever gets called a sap without feeling he probably is one.

"He may be a sap, but the other guy's unmentionably stupid." I can't actually mention the other guy's name.

"What did John Stuart Mill say?"

"I don't know. He didn't say it was better to have a stupid President."

"Better to have a happy, unmentionable pig than a something, something something."

"That's not what he said." And it's not what I want to talk about. Mill would've supported Gore and the whole ticket and feel betrayed just like I do.

"Have you talked to Paul?" She is progressing down a checklist.

"No. He's out on the beach right now, digging a grave for his time capsule. I haven't talked to Jill, either."

"Well, she's interesting. She's different." I hear Paul laugh again, then shout, "G'day, mate." Possibly Mr. Oshi has freed himself.

"Listen," I say. "About today. I mean this afternoon."

Dense silence. Different from the galactic dead space Detective Marinara receded into. This silence of Ann's is the silence known only to divorced people—the silence of making familiar but unwelcome adjustments to evidence of continued bad character, of second-tier betrayals, unreasonable requests, late excuses, heart stabbings that must be withstood but are better defeated in advance. It's what communication becomes between the insufficiently loved. "I'm not coming," Ann says, seemingly without emotion. It's the same voice she'd use to cancel a hair appointment. "I think we are who we are, Frank."

"Yeah. I sure am."

"Since Charley died, I've had this feeling of something about to happen. I was waiting for something. Moving down from

Connecticut seemed to be getting close to it. But I don't think I thought it was you." I am entombed in the silence she was just entombed in. Now comes revised testimony (including Charley's) of my foul, corrupt and unacceptable nature. I wonder if she's pacing her living room like an executive or sitting on a bench with her clubs, awaiting her tee time, while she dispenses with me again. "But then you got sick."

"I wasn't sick. Not *sick* sick. I had prostate cancer. Have. That's not sick." It's just fatal. SBD. I'm still the census taker, weakened by illness but still in need of reproval and some lessons.

"I know," Ann says officiously. I hear her footsteps on a hard floor surface. "Anyway, I didn't *really* think it was you."

"I get it." A stack of mail's on my desktop under my Realtor of the Year paperweight. It's unopened since Tuesday—a measure of my distraction, since I'm usually eager to read the mail, even if it's steak-knife catalogs or a pre-approved platinum-club membership. I don't think I'm going to be allowed to say what I want to say, which is all right. "What do you think it was? Or who?" I'm staring at the cover of the AARP magazine—a full-color (staged) photograph showing a silver-haired gent lying on a city street looking dead, but being worked on by heavy-suited firemen in fireman hats, equipped with oxygen cylinders, defibrillator paddles, with intubation paraphernalia standing at the ready. A silver-haired old lady in an electric blue pantsuit looks on, horrified. The headline reads RISK. WILL THERE BE TIME?

"Gee, I don't know," Ann says. "It's strange."

"Maybe you missed Charley. Didn't you meet him at Haddam

CC? Maybe you thought you'd find him again." No use mentioning her thoughts of the seminary.

"You didn't like Charley. I understand that. But *I* did. You were jealous of him. But he was a fine man."—In death, and when he thought my name was Mert. "He was the love of my life. You don't like hearing that. You're not a very good judge of people." Whip. Crack. *Pow!* But I'm ready for it. The slow-rhythm meticulousness of Ann's rhetorical style is always an indicator that I'm coming in for a direct hit. All bad roads lead to Frank. We have, of course, never talked about Sally—my wife—in the entire eight years I've been married to her. Now might be the optimum moment to set me straight about that misstep, since it's led me where it's led me: to this conversation. I'm not surprised to learn that I don't win the "love of my life" gold medal. Except in rogue bands of lower primates, you don't abandon the love of your life. Death has to intervene.

Out my front window, beyond the low hedgement of arborvitae, I spy Mr. Oshi moving in quickened, mechanized Japanese banker steps along Poincinet Road, hustling back to his own house to bolt the door. His business suit still looks neat, though he's holding one Dachshund under his arm like a newspaper and he still has both plastic bags of dog shit. His other wiener's prancing at his feet. Mr. Oshi takes a quick, haunted look toward my front door, as if something might rush out at him, then hastens his steps on to home.

I have not spoken into the receiver since Ann fingered me as a bad judge of human flesh, in preparation for apprising me that my marriage to Sally was a lot of foolishness that led to no good, whereas hers to architect Charley was the stuff myth and legend are made of.

"I have something I want to say to you," Ann says, then sighs heavily through her nose. I believe she's stopped pacing. "It's about what I said when you were at De Tocqueville on Tuesday."

"What part?"

"About wanting to live with you again. And then when I left a message that night."

"Okay."

"I'm sorry. I don't think I really meant all that."

"That's okay." An unexpected wrench in my heart, with no pain associated.

"I think I just wanted to come to a moment, after all these years, when I could say that to you."

"Okay." Three okays in a row. The gold standard of genuine acceptance.

"But I think I just wanted to say it for my own purposes. Not because I really needed to. Or need to."

"I understand. I'm married anyway."

"I know," Ann says. Once again, it's good there're telephones for conversations like this. None of us could stand it face-to-face. Hats off to Alexander Graham Bell—great American—who foresaw how human we are and how much protection we need from others. "I'm sorry if this is confusing."

"It's not. I guessed if I wasn't a good choice once, I'm probably not now, either." For every different person, love means something different.

"Well, I don't know," she says disapprovingly but not sadly. A last disapproval of me as I genially disapprove of myself.

It's tempting to wonder if a new goodly swain's now in her picture, with a more attractive lunch invitation. That's usually what these recitations mean but don't get around to admitting. Teddy Fuchs, maybe. Or a friendly, widowed Mr. Patch Pockets, a gray-maned De Tocqueville Colonial history teacher, someone "youthful" (doesn't need Viagra), coaches lacrosse and feels simpatico with her golfing interests. Amherst grad, Tufts M.A., a summer retreat in Watch Hill and whose grown kids are less enigmatic than our two. It would be a good end to things. They can be "life companions" and never marry except when one of them gets brain cancer, and then only as encouragement for life's final lap. I approve.

"Is that all right?" Ann says, self-consciously sorrowful.

"It *is* all right." I could let her know I'd already figured out that getting divorced after Ralph died just deprived the two of us of the chance to get properly divorced later on, and for simpler reasons: that we weren't really made for each other, didn't even love each other all that much, that the only lasting thing we did love about each other was that we each had a child who died (forgetting the two who didn't die), which admittedly is a strange love and, in any case, wasn't enough. Better, though, just to let her believe she's the one who knows mystical truths, even if she doesn't really know them, just feels them all these years later. Ann may be many good and admirable things, but a mystic is not one of them.

In the stack of unopened letter-mail, beneath the Mayo

newsletter, a Thank You from the DNC, circulars for a 5-K race and the Pow-R-Brush Holiday promotion in Toms River, I spy a square blue onionskin envelope—not the self-contained kind I always open wrong because it can't be opened right, and end up tearing and reading in three damaged pieces, but a fuller, sturdier one—on whose pale tissue-y surface is writing I recognize, the writer's firm hand flowing with small peaked majuscules and even smaller perfectly formed, peaked and leaning minuscules: Frank Bascombe, 7 Poincinet Road, Sea-Clift, New Jersey 08753. USA.

"We just have to be who we are, Frank," Ann is saying for the second time.

"You bet." I separate the letter from its cohort and stare at it.

"You sound strange, sweetheart. Is this upsetting you? Are you crying?"

"No." I almost miss the "sweetheart." But how did I miss this letter—of all letters? "I'm not crying, I don't think."

"Well. I haven't told you Irma's ready to die. Poor old sweetie. She spent her life believing my father should've moved out with her from Detroit to Mission Viejo thirty years ago, which of course he never would've, because he was tired of her. She has Alzheimer's. She thinks he's arriving next week, which is nice for her. I wish she and the children could've been closer. They're like you are about personal connections."

"Really?" The salmon-colored stamp bears a stern-looking profile of the Queen of England in regnal alabaster, framed in fluted molding. It's the most exciting stamp I've ever seen.

"They're mostly okay without them, of course. At least not strong ones anyway." Cookie never counted to her.

"I understand."

"I'm sorry if all this is distressing you. I made a mistake and I regret it."

"Well—" Fingering the letter's heft upon my fingertips, I raise it to my nostrils and breathe in, hoping for a telltale scent of its far-off sender. Though it bears only a starchy stationery odor and the unsweet aroma of stamp glue. I hold it to the window light—there's no return address—and turn it front to back, bring it instinctively to my nose again, touch my tongue tip to its sealed flap, put its smooth blue finish to my chin, then my cheek and hold it there while Ann continues blabbing at me.

"Paul said last night Clary has a new beau."

"I—" Thom. The multicultural cipher.

"Has Paul told you yet that he wants to leave K.C. and come work in the realty office with you? He's—"

Whip. Crack. *Pow!* Again. I am *not* ready. My swelling heart as much as founders. I don't hear the next thing she says, though my mind offers up "You know a heart's not judged by how much you love, but by how much you're loved by others." I don't know why.

But. The *mullet*? My son? A promising second career after greeting cards? Chauffeuring clients around Sea-Clift? Holding court in the office? Farming listings? Catching cold calls? Wandering through other people's precious houses, stressing the distance to the beach, the age of the roof, the lot-line dimensions, the diverse mix here in New Jersey's Best Kept Secret? He could bring Otto out and sing a chorus of "Shine on, Harvest Moon," like he used to do when he lived with me. "Realty-Wise. This is Paul. Our motto is, He Who Smelt It, Dealt It."

"I haven't heard about that," I say. Whip-sawed.

"Well, you will. I assumed you'd asked him, since your surgery last summer and all of that. We talked a bit about that. I'm surprised you two hadn't—"

"I didn't have surgery. I had a procedure. They're different." I was going to tell him about my condition. And I didn't ask him to "join the firm," *because I'm not crazy.* I realize what an ideal job writing greeting cards is for my son.

"Women know about things like procedures, Frank."

"Good for women. I'm not a woman yet."

"I know you're angry. I'm sorry again. I used to wonder if you ever *got* angry. You never seemed to. I always understood why you didn't make it in the Marines."

"I *was* sick in the Marines. I had pancreatitis. You didn't even know me then. I almost died."

"We don't have to be angry at each other, do we? You may not realize it, but you don't want to go any further with this, either."

"I realize it." Sally's blue letter is pinched between my thumb and forefinger as though it might float upward and I need to cling to it for my life's sake. "That's what I called to say. You just beat me to it."

"Oh," Ann says. Ann my wife. Ann my not wife. Ann my never-to-be. The things you'll never do don't get decided at the end of life, but somewhere in the long gray middle, where you can't see the dim light at either end. The Permanent Period tries to protect us from hazardous moments like this, makes pseudo-acceptance only a matter of a passing moment. A whim. Nothing that'll last too long. Which is why the Permanent Period doesn't work. Acceptance means that things, both good and sour, have to be accounted for. Relations, as the great man said, end nowhere.

"I encouraged Paul to come work with you. I think that would be good."

I'm stunned silent by this preposterous prospect. Anger? If I spoke, I would possibly start cursing in an alien tongue. This is the stress Dr. Psimos advised me to avoid. The kind that burns out my soldier isotopes like they were Christmas lights and sends PSA numbers out of the ballpark. I'd like to say something apparently polite and platitudinous yet also shrewdly scathing. But for the moment, I can't speak. It is entirely possible I *do* hate Ann's guts. Odd to know that so late along. Life *is* a long transit when you measure how long it takes you to learn to hate your ex-wife.

"Maybe we just don't need to say anything else, Frank."

Mump-mump, mump. Mump. Silence.

I hear her chair squeak, her footsteps sounding against hardwood flooring. I picture Ann walking to the window of 116 Cleveland, a house where I once abided and before that where she abided, following our divorce, when our children were children. She is once again its proprietor, fee simple absolute. The big eighty-year-old tupelo out front is now spectral but lordly in its leaflessness, its rugged bark softened by the damp balmy air of false spring. I've stood at that window, my breathing shallowed, my feet heavy, my hands cold and hardened. I've calculated my fate on the slates of the neighbors' roofs, their mirroring windowpanes, roof copings and short jaunty front walks. This can be both consoling (You're here, you're not dead), and unconsoling (You're here, you're not dead. Why not?). The past just may not be the best place to cast your glance when words fail.

Mump-mump.

My silence speaks volumes. I hear it. My voice is trapped within.

Mumpety-mump. Mump. Mump.

"Well," I hear Ann say. More steps across the hardwood. Fatigue shadows her voice. "I don't know," I hear her say. Then *ping-ping.* I hear a truck in the street, outside her window—in Haddam (this I can picture)—backing up. Miles from where I stand. *Ping! Ping! Ping! If you can't see me, I can't see you.* I wait, breathe, say nothing. "Well," Ann says again. Then I believe she puts the phone down, for the line goes empty and our call in that way ends.

M y darling Frank,
      I would like to write you something truly from my heart that would reveal me, good and bad, and make you feel better about things. But I'm not sure I am capable. I'm not sure I know my truest feelings, even though I have some. I don't have any idea what you could be thinking. I guess I have Thanksgiving envy, since I've been thinking about you, and about that nice Lake Laconic we went to before. I bet you're doing something really interesting and good for T'giving. I

hope you're not alone. I bet you're not, you rascal.
Maybe you've connected with some snappy realtor type
and are headed somewhere out of town (I hope not to
Moline). What I'm feeling now, true feelings or not, is
that everything in my life is just all about me, and I can't
find a way to change the pronouns. I'm aware of myself,
without being very self-aware. My kids would agree—if
they spoke to me, which they don't. But does that make
any sense? (Possibly I won't send this letter.) I think I
should apologize for all that happened last June—and
May. I am sorry for the difficulty it caused you. It's
probably hard to understand that someone can love you
and feel great about everything, and then leave with her
ex. I always thought people decided they were unhappy
first, and then left. But maybe things in life are just fine
and then you do some crazy thing, and decide later if
you were. Unhappy, that is. What's that the evidence of?
But I can't really be sorry for doing it, so why apologize
only for half? This sounds like something you would say
maybe about selling a house to somebody, some house
you didn't approve of, except you knew the people
needed a home. If I'm right (about you), you'll think this
is funny and not very interesting—something a person
from south-central Ohio would do. You are like that.

When I left with Wally last June, I just wasn't feeling
enough. I couldn't take others in. You, for instance—
hardly at all. It was so shocking to experience Wally. I
made him come, by the way. He didn't want to and was

pretty embarrassed, you might've noticed. I think I just
left on an idea—to go back and experience something I
never got to experience before. (That word's coming up
a lot.) I've never even been stupid enough to think
anyone can do that. You really ought to leave some
things where they lay, whether you got to feel them or
not. I think that now. I don't think I'm sounding breezy
here, do you? I don't want to. I'm not breezy at all.
Coming to the end of the millennium year, I wonder if
I've been affected by it at all? Or if all this tumult and
upset is the effect of it. Has it affected you yet? It hadn't
last spring, I don't think. We're both "only children."
Maybe I just fear death. Maybe I feared that you and I
weren't going anywhere and never realized it before. I
am not very reflective. You know that. Or at least I
wasn't before. I ask questions but don't always answer
them or think about the answers.

I don't want to go into too much detail here. I know
I went away with Wally for my own reasons, probably
selfish. And by August, I knew I wouldn't stay much
longer. He was a strange man. I loved him once, but I
think I may have driven him crazy at least twice. Because
the whole thing thirty years ago was that he was just
very unhappy living with me, and couldn't tell me. So he
left. It's so simple. I can't say what we both knew back
then. Probably very little. We did try to enlist the
children's sympathies this time. But they are both crazy
as bats and treated us as though <u>we</u> were lunatics and

wouldn't talk to us and receded into their nutty beliefs, even though we said to them, "But we're your parents." "Who says?" they said. I guess I think they're lost to me.

I would've left then (late August), but I got concerned about Wally. He began eating very little and lost <u>a lot</u> of weight. He would sit in the bathtub until the water was freezing (we lived in his cottage, which was okay, if small). I would see him standing out in his little row of apple trees he loved, just talking and talking, to no one— though I guess it was to me. I would catch him looking strangely at me. And then he began going for swims in the ocean. He was a very large white figure out there, even with his lost weight. I think, as I said, I drove him crazy. Poor man.

I don't want to tell all the rest of it. Sooner or later you'll find out. The best way out may not be through, though. Whoever said that?

But I am not in Mull anymore. (Isn't that a funny name? Mull.) I am in a place called Maidenhead, which is funny, too, and is in J.O.E. (Jolly Old England). Talk about wanting to go back in time! I've come all the way back to Maidenhead. From Mull to Maidenhead. That's a hoot. It is just a suburb here, not very nice or very different than any other one. I am doing temporary work in a sweet little arts centre (their spelling), where they need my skills for organizing older citizens' happiness. It is like Sponsoring, although old English people are easier than our old people by a lot. England is not a bad place to be alone (I was here twice before). People are nice. Everyone gives solid evidence of feeling alone a lot, but seems to think that's natural, so that they don't get terribly, terribly invested in it. Unlike America where it's just one mad fascination after another one, but no one's any more invested—or so it seems to me. I did <u>not</u> vote, by the way, and now things are in this terrible twist with Bush. Can you believe it? Can that numbskull actually win? Or steal it? I guess he can. I'm sure you voted, of course, and I'm sure I know who you voted for.

How are your kids? Are you and Paul still feuding? Is Clarissa still being a big lesbian? (I bet not.) Who else do you see? Are you selling a lot of houses? I bet you are. (You can tell I'm fishing.) I am fifty-four this year, which of course you know. And I am not a grandparent, which is very odd, even though my children dislike me so much—for what, I don't know exactly. I am thinking of going to a retreat in Wales—something Druidic— since I feel I'm heading someplace but don't feel too confident about it. Though I am pretty comfortable in my skin. Being fifty-four (almost) is also odd. It kind of doesn't have an era, and I know you believe in all human ages having a spiritual era. This one I don't know. I think everybody needs a definition of spirituality, Frank (you have one, I believe). You wouldn't want to go on a quiz show, would you, and be asked your definition of spirituality and not know one. (Apropos this retreat.) June doesn't seem that far back to me. Does it to you? I can't say that how things are now is how I thought they would end up. Though maybe I did.

But I do want to say something to you (a good sign, maybe). I want to tell you one reason why I'm sure I love you. There are people we can be around, and we take them for granted sometimes, and who make us feel generous and kind and even smarter and more clever than we probably are—and successful in our own terms <u>and</u> the world's. They are the ideal people, sweetheart. And that's who you are for me. I'm sure I'm not that way for you, which bothers me, because I think I'm kind of a roadblock for you now. No one else is like that for me, and I don't know why you are that way, but you are. So just in case you were wondering.

(The reason I'm writing this is to see how it comes out. If it seems okay, then you're reading it "now.") Finally (thank God, huh?), I don't know if I want to be married to you anymore. But I don't know if I want a divorce, or if I can't live without you. Is there a precise word for that human state? Maybe you can make something up. Maybe New Jersey is it. Though here in Maidenhead (what a name!), where for some reason tourists come, I hear Americans saying they're from all over. Iowa and Oregon and Florida. And I think—that doesn't matter anymore. Maybe it would be good to move away from New Jersey. Maybe all we need is a change. Like the hippies used to say when there were so many of them, and they were begging quarters back in

the Loop in Chicago: "Change is good." I thought that
was a riot. At least we don't have cancer, Frank. So
maybe we have some choices to make together still. I
also want you to know—and this is important—that you
were not boring in bed, if you ever worried about that.
I'll call you on Thanksgiving, which is not a holiday in
Maidenhead so I can probably use the trunk line at the
arts centre. Love with a kiss. Sally (your lost wife).

I'm shocked. Humbled. Emptied. Amazed. Provoked.
Delighted. Thrilled to be all. If man be a golden impossibility,
his life's line a hair's breadth across, what is woman? A golden
possibility? Her life's line a lifeline thrown to save me from
drowning.

I'm ready to wire greenbacks—except it's Thanksgiving. Mr.
Oshi could be of service, though he's probably huddled in his
house. I'll send solicitors out to Maidenhead in a black saloon
car to spirit Sally down to Heathrow, provide a change of clothes,
get her into the VIP lounge at BA and right into a first-class
seat—on the Concorde, except it crashed. I'll be waiting at Newark
Terminal 3 with a dinner-plate smile, all slates cleaned, agendas
changed for the future, bygones trooping off to being bygones.
Cancer's a dot we'll connect in due time. Since she doesn't know
I have/had it, it's almost as if I don't/didn't—so powerful is her
belief, so unreal is cancer to begin with.

Except there's no call-back number here. No 44+ bippety,
bippety, bippety, bip. When I come back from Timbuktu, I'll

coax the Maidenhead Arts Centre number out of *inquiries*, where they're always helpful (our *information* won't give you the time of day). Or else I'll declare an emergency.

I go to the window again in my terry-cloth robe, my heart pumping, a zizzy bee-sting quiver down my arms and legs, my bare feet cold on the floor planks. "Is this really happening?" I say to the window and the beach beyond, in a voice someone could hear in the room with me. Is this happening? Is there a celestial balance to *things*? A yin/yang? Do people come back once they've gone away to Mull? Life is full of surprises, a wise man said, and would not be worth having if it were not. My choice then, since I have a choice, is to believe they do come back.

Out upon the dun Atlantic, a Coast Guard buoy tender sits bestilled on the water's roll, its orange sash promoting bright, far-flung hope—the same it gives to all sailors adrift and imperiled. I train my powerful U-boat-quality binoculars, given to me by Sally, on its decks, its steepled conning bridge, its single gray gunnery box, its spinning radar dish, the heavy red nun already winched aboard. Fast-moving miniature sailors are in evidence. A davit's employed, a dory's lowering off the landward side. Sailors are there, too. No doubt this is a drill, a dry run to pass the time on Thanksgiving, when all would be elsewhere if only our shores were safe. I pan across the swells (how do they ever find anything?), but there is nothing visibly afloat. I put the lens bottles to the window glass and lean into the ferrules, as if finding a foreign object was essential to a need of mine. Only nothing's foreign. A second red buoy, whose bell I sometimes hear in the fog or when the wind blows in, rocks in the slow swell, its red profile low, its clapping now inaudible. I, of course, can't find what they're after. And maybe it's nothing, a coordinate on a chart, a signal down deep they must track to be accomplished sailors. Nothing more.

I sweep down the beach and find the surfcasters—close-up—in their neoprenes and watch caps, their backs to the shore, up to their nuts in frigid, languid ocean, their shoulders intent and hunched, their long poles working. A blue Frisbee floats through my circled view. A white retriever ascends to snare it. I find the Sea-Clift Shore Police's white Isuzu trolling back along its own tracks, the uniformed driver, as I am, glassing the water's surface. For a shark fin. A body (these things happen when you live by the sea). A periscope. Icarus just entering the sea, wings molten, eyes astonished, feet spraddling down.

And then I see my son Paul again, wading out of the surf in his soaked cargo shorts, his pasty belly slack for age twenty-seven. He is shoeless, shirtless, his skull—visible through his mullet—rounder than I remember, his beard-stached mouth distorted in a smile, hands dangling, palms turned back like a percy man, his feet splayed and awkward as when he was a kid. He does not look the way you'd like your son to look. Plus, he must be frozen.

I track down to the hole he's dug beyond the hydrangeas, and it's there, "finished," coffin-shaped, not large, ready for its casket to be borne down. My shovel stands in the sandpile to the side.

When I find Paul again, he's seen me glassing him like a sub-captain and has fixed his gaze back on me, his red-lipped smile distorted, his feet caked with sand, pale legs wide apart like a pirate's. He flags his bare arm like one of those drowners out of reach—lips moving, words of some sentiment, something possibly that any father would like to hear but I can't at this distance. Paul cocks his fists up in a Charlie Atlas muscle man's pose, jumps sideways and bears down stupidly and shows his soft abs and lats. The young Frisbee spinners, the elderly walkers in bright sweats, the metal-detector cornballs, a late-arriving fisherman just wading into the sea—all these see my son and smile an indulgent smile. I wave back. It's not bad to wave at this remove as our first contact. On an impulse, I put down my binocs and give my own Charlie Atlas double-bicep flexer, still in my tartan robe. And then Paul does his again. And we are fixed this way for a moment. Why couldn't we just stop here, not go on to what's next—be two tough boys who've fought a draw, stayed unvanquished, each to leave the field a victor? Fat Chance.

In front of my closet mirror, I get into my 501s, my Nikes and my block-M sweatshirt with the yellow polo underneath. I am Mr. Casual Back to Campus, booster dude and figure of wholesome ridicule. I have called Clarissa and left a message: "Come home." I have called Wade and left a message: "Where are you?" Clearly, I'm fated to wait for Sally's call, at least until I'm back from Timbuktu and can make calls of my own. I have another full-out yearning for a cell phone, which would render me available (at all times) to hear her voice, answer a summons and go directly to Maidenhead if necessary—though she would need to know *my* number. I'd gladly forget Thanksgiving (like any other American). Most of my guests have been decommissioned anyway. I'd take the organic turkey, the tofu stuffing, the spelt, the whatever else, straight down to Our Lady of Effectual Mercy, where the K of C ministers to Sea-Clift's neediest and thankfulest. Or else I'd put it in Paul's time capsule and bury it for later generations to puzzle over.

I am, however, exhilarated, and take a last scrutinizing look at myself. I look the way I want to—dopey but defended—the genial Tri-cities orthodontist. Though as usual, exhilaration doesn't feel as good as I want it to—as it used to—since all sensation, good or bad, now passes through the damping circuitry of the cancer patient, victim or survivor. The tiramisu never tastes as sweet. The new paint job doesn't shine as bright. Miss America's glossy life-to-come wears a shadow of lurking despair, her smile a smile of struggling on in a dark forest. That's what we survivors get as our good luck. Though think about the other poor bastards, the ones who get the real black spot—not just my gray one—and who're flying home to Omaha this morning, urged to put their affairs in order.

I've, however, learned to let exhilaration be exhilaration, even if it only lasts a minute, and to fight the shadows like a boxer. Staring at the mirror, I give myself a slap, then the other side, then again, and once more, until my cheeks sting and are rosy, and a smile appears on my reflection's face. I blink. I sniff. I throw two quick lefts at my block-M but hold back on the convincer right. I'm ready to step into the arena and meet the day. Once again, it's Thanksgiving.

I'm taking this bad-boy outside to see how it fits," Paul's saying energetically. I've come down munching a piece of bacon, following voices to the daylight basement, chilly mausoleum of old Haddam furniture—my cracked hatch-cover table, my nubbly red hide-a-bed, my worn-through purple Persian rug, several non-working brass lamps bundled in the corner and a framed map of Block Island, where Ann and I once sailed when we were kids and thought we loved each other. I've thought of opening things up down here as a rumpus room.

I'm already smiling as I come to the bottom of the stairs, very conscious of my booster-club get-up, though Paul is just exiting the sliding glass door to the beach, toting his time capsule, which is a chrome bomb-shaped cylinder as long as two toasters. A tall young blond woman he's been talking to is in the middle of the room and she looks at me. She's beside the defunct old rabbit-eared DuMont that was my mother's and that I've kept as a memento, and she unexpectedly smiles back widely to broadcast her surprise and enthusiasm—for me, for Paul, for the overall good direction things are taking down here. This is Jill, dressed—I don't know why I'd expect any different—in bright red coveralls with a white long-john shirt underneath and some kind of green wooden clog footwear that makes her look six foot seven, when she may only be six three. Her long yellow hair hangs straight past her shoulders and is parted in the middle Rhine maiden–style, exposing a wide Teutonic forehead. Her generous mouth is unquestionably libidinous, though her sparkling dark eyes are welcoming—to me, in my own basement. A great relief. And as advertised, at the bottom of her left sleeve is the alarming hand absence, though there's good evidence of a wrist. Here, I realize, is the girl who may become mother of my grandchildren, mourner when my obsequies are read out, will tell vivid rambling tales of my exploits once I'm gone. It'd be good to get off on the right foot with her. Though in a day's time, I've met two of my children's chosen ones. What's gone wrong?

"Hi, I'm Frank," I say. "You must be Jill."

"Listen, Frank," Paul's saying, just leaving through the door. "You wanna come out and attend the trial internment?" He may mean *interment*, but possibly not—though he's talking too loudly for indoors. He pauses, grinning from behind his smudged specs (we're all grinning down here), his capsule clasped to his wet tee-shirt, which bears an Indian-warrior profile in full eagle-feather war bonnet—the Kansas City Chief. Paul's still barefoot, still has his gold stud in his left ear. He looks like the guy who delivers the *Asbury Press* before dawn out of his backseat-less '71 Cutlass and, I suspect, lives in his car.

"You bet I want to." I make a step forward. "Let's do it." But he's already out the sliding door, heading toward his site. My positive response hasn't registered. I look to Jill and shake my head. "We don't communicate perfectly all the time."

"He'd really like you to approve of him," Jill says in a slightly nasal midwestern voice. Though startlingly and with an even bigger, eager-er smile, she strides across the linoleum and with her right hand extended gives mine a painful squeeze, the kind lady shot-putters give each other outside the ring. Her smile makes me look straight at her nose, which is noble and makes her wide eyes want to draw in, in concentration, toward the middle. One central incisor has shouldered a half-millimeter over onto its partner, but not to a bad effect. In someone less imposing, this could be a signal to exercise caution (turbulent brooding over life's helpless imperfections, etc.), but in Junoesque Jill, it is clearly trifling, possibly a giggle, in contrast to her injury and to how monstrously beautiful she otherwise is. I like her completely and wish I wasn't wearing this preposterous get-up. She looks admiringly out the glass door at Paul, who's already down inside his hole, bent over, apparently testing the dimensions of things. "He's really a big fan of yours," she says.

"I'm a big fan of his," I say. Jill exudes a faint lilac sweetness, though the air's gone musty as a ship's hold down here. Jill lets her friendly dark eyes roam all around the low-ceilinged basement and sniffs. She smells it, too. I amiably swallow my last bit of bacon—left in plain sight (by who?) on a paper towel in the kitchen. I want to say something forward-thinking about my son, but being up close to his sweet-smelling, pulchritudinous squeeze is far from what I thought would be happening, and I'm not exactly sure what's appropriate to say. Physical closeness to an abject (and smaller) stranger, however, doesn't seem to faze her one bit. Clarissa's the same—relaxed, defensible boundaries— something my age group didn't understand. I could ask Jill how she likes New Jersey so far or how everything went with Ann last night (though I don't want to mention Ann's name), or what's a bounteous beauty like her doing with an oddment like my son.

But what I do say, for some reason, is, "What happened to your hand?"

Which doesn't faze her one bit more. She looks down at the vacant sleeve end, then raises it to eye level. She is still very close to me. A pink stump becomes visible, starting (or ending) where her carpal bone would be, the flesh finely stitched to make a smooth flap. Jill's happy demeanor seems undiminished by a hand being conspicuously not there. "If everybody would just *ask* like that," she says happily, "my life'd be easier." We both look straight at the stump like surgeons. "I was in the Army, in Texas," she says, "training for land mine work. And I guess I got the worst-possible grade. I shouldn't have been doing it, as big as I am. It's better if you're small." She moves the appendage around in a tight little orbit to exhibit its general worthiness and I suppose to permit me to touch it, which I don't think I'll do. I've never knowingly been this close to or conversant with an amputee. Doctors get used to these things. But no one much gets anything cut off in normal real estate goings-on. Without meaning to, I inch back and give her what I hope is an affirming nod. "So when I got to Hallmark," she goes on chattily, "they thought, Well, here's a natural for the sympathy-card department." I knew it. "Which I was, but not because of my hand, but because I'm really sympathetic." She rolls her eyes and shakes her head as though getting rid of that ole hand was the best-possible luck.

"So, is that where you two met, then?" I say. Out the corner of my eye, I uncomfortably spy Paul crawling back out of his hole, dusting off his knees, looking as if he'd just invented fluid mechanics.

His silver capsule lies in the beach grass. He begins speaking toward the hole as if someone, a member of his crew, was still down there doing last-minute deepening and manicuring.

"We really met on the Internet," Jill says, "though I'd already seen him at a film series and knew he'd be interesting. Which he is." She stows her stump in her red coveralls pocket and warmly regards my son, who's still outside talking away. I should go out there. Though my instinct is to stay where I am and chat up the big blondie, even if the big blondie belongs to my son and only has one hand. "We were really shocked when we finally met face-to-face at a bookstore"—conceivably the place where I got into hot water last spring—"and realized we were both writers at Hallmark." In a bikini, Jill probably looks like young Anita Ekberg (minus a hand). It's difficult to envision Paul, who's a lumpy five ten, raree-ing around with her in his little Charlotte Street billet. Though no doubt he does. "Odd couple's redundant is what we think," Jill says. I've begun to think about what Paul, in his rage last spring, told me about his job—that it was the same as what Dostoyevsky or Hemingway or Proust or Edna St. Vincent Millay did: supplied useful words to ordinary people who don't have enough of them. I, of course, thought he was nuts.

But suddenly, here is something crucial. I could spend the next six weeks locked in a room with these two, learn how Jill felt about boot camp, learn the mascot's name of her girls' basketball team, where she was the center, learn how she found her star-crossed way to K.C., how she came to write Ross Perot's name in on her presidential ballot; and possibly at the same time get to know Paul's closely guarded ideas about matrimony (coming as he does from a broken home), get his overview about parity in the NFL, hear his long-term thoughts for leaving Hallmark and joining Realty-Wise—things most fathers hear. But I still wouldn't know much more that's important about them as a couple than I do after these five perfectly good minutes. It's electrifying to think Jill's a lusty young Anita Ekberg, and interesting to know that Paul is interesting. But they are what they seem—which is enough to be. I don't want to change them. I'm willing and ready to jump right to the climax, confer fatherly blessings on their union (if that's what this is) before Paul makes it back inside. If they make each other happy for two seconds, then they can probably last decades—longer than I've lasted. I bless you—I say these words silently in anticipation of leaving. I bless you. I bless you. *Sum quod eris, fui quod sis.*

"Did you really go to Michigan?" Jill steps back and takes a look at my block-M, a studious cleft formed between her dark eyebrows. She leans forward and gives me the sensation of being loomed over. Obviously, she doesn't see my outfit as comical.

"Did I what?"

"My dad went to U of M," she says.

"Did he? Great."

"I'm from Cheboygan." She holds up her right hand to exhibit how much the state of Michigan—lower peninsula only—resembles a hand. With her stunted left arm, she taps the hand at about where the town of Cheboygan lies, near the top. "Right there on Lake Huron," she says, making Huron sound like *Hyurn.* I knew a boy from Cheboygan back in the icy mists. Harold

"Doodlebug" Bermeister, defenseman on our pledge hockey team, who longed to return to Cheboygan with his B.S. and buy a Chevy franchise. Doodlebug got blown to cinders in Vietnam the year he graduated and never saw Cheboygan again. No way this Jill is Doodlebug's daughter. She's twice as tall as he was. But if she *is* a wandering Bermeister and life's à long journey leading to my son, it doesn't need any explaining. I accept. Though you could work up a good greeting card out of the whole improbability, something on the order of "Happy Birthday, son of my third marriage to my foster sister of Native American descent."

"I never really got up there," I say in re Cheboygan.

"It's where they have the snowmobile hall of fame," she says earnestly.

Paul's letting himself back in through the sliding glass door, his capsule wedged under his arm pigskin-style, wiping his bare feet on the rug and still talking away as if we'd all been outside doing things together. With his smudged glasses, mullet, his beard-stache and general unkempt belly-swell under his Chiefs shirt, Paul looks oddly elderly and therefore ageless—less like the *Asbury Press* guy and more like one of the beach loonies who occasionally walk into your house, sit down at your dinner table and start babbling about Jesus running for president, so you have to call the police to come haul them away. These people never harm anything, but it's hard to see them (or Paul) as mainstream.

"So. You got it all set?" I say and give him one of our sly-shrewd chivvying looks, meant to draw attention to my Bay City orthodontist outfit. Such greeting is our oldest workable code:

common phrasings invested with secret double, sometimes quadruple "meanings" that are by definition hilarious—but only to us. As a troubled boy of tender years, Paul was forever anticipating, keeping steps ahead, as if the left-behind brother of a dead boy had to be two boys, doubly, even triply aware of everything, could not just be a single yearning heart. Other priorities tended to get overlooked, and our code became our only way to converse, to keep love fitfully in sight and the world beneath us. In adulthood, of course, this fades, leaving just a vapor of lost never would-bes.

"Sherwood B. Nice," Paul says—not really an answer—though he elevates his chin in a victorious way, possibly having to do with Jill. In the corner of his right eye, a small dent retains an apple redness from the terrible beaning at age fifteen, which he claims not to remember. I've never been sure how well he sees, though the doctors back then said he'd have vitreous swimmers, shortened depth perception, and in later life could face problems. Elevating his chin to see out the bottom of his eyes is compensatory. None of this, naturally, is ever discussed. "So. Aaaallll at once," Paul immediately starts in, bringing his time capsule over to the hatch-cover table. It is his patented Tricky Dick voice. "Just out of nowhere, out of the clear blue." He hoods his eyes and extends his schnoz like Nixon. "I realized. That what I really needed to do, you understand, was to help others. It was just *that* simple." He gives his jowly face a solemn pseudo-Nixon head shake. "I hope you all can understand what I'm getting at here." This may be his reaction to my get-up. I'm satisfied, though as always to me he is a borderless uncertainty. I don't even feel like his father—more like his uncle or his former parole officer. It's good if Jill, queen of Cheboygan, can try to admire, understand and please him, and he her. I bless you. I don't know what we're supposed to do now. "How's your mom?"

"She's not coming over today," Paul says. He's monkeying with his time capsule while I'm standing here. It has a little silver side door that slides open to permit installation of sacred artifacts. Where do you get one of these things? Is there a Web site? Why are we even down here where I never come? "She said you had cancer. How's that going?" He frowns at me, then down again, as though this was another encoded joke of ours.

"Oh, it's great," I say. "I have a prostate full of radioactive BBs I didn't have when I saw you last."

"Cooo-ul. Do they hurt?"

"It—"

"My stepfather had that," Jill says, the cleft reappearing between her wide-set eyes. A show of sympathy.

"How'd *he* do?"

"He died. But not from that."

"I see. Well, this is all pretty new to me." I say this as if we were talking about changing car-repair affiliations. I smile and look around my shadowy basement. In addition to the Block Island map, there's a large hanging framed reproduction left by the prior owners, depicting the *Lord Barnegat*, famed two-masted whaling schooner that plied the ocean right outside in the 1870s and is currently in a museum in Navesink. I should toss out all this shit and turn the space into a screening room for resale to TV people. "I don't see life as a perfect mold broken," I say uncomfortably when neither of them says anything more about my having cancer. Possibly Jill and I share this point of view. What else has Ann blabbed to them?

The cancer topic has struck them both mute, the way it does most people, and I feel suddenly stupid standing here dressed like a nitwit, as if none of us has anything to say to the other on any subject but my "illness." Aren't they in the greeting-card business? Though probably we're all three waiting for one of us to do something unforgivable so we can convulse into a throat-slashing argument and Paul can grab Jill and clear out back to K.C. I think again of him whonking away with this bounteous, one-handed Michigan armful and I admit I'm happy for him.

"The caterers'll be here at one-forty-five," I say to have something to say so I can leave. "Did your sister say when she might be back?"

Mention of Clarissa instantly inscribes a displeased/pleased smile on Paul's beard-encircled lips. His sister is, of course, his eternal subject, though she has always treated him like a dangerous mutant, which he relishes. By taking possession of the most-unsettling-life-course trophy, she has further put him off his game. Jill could be his attempt to wrest back the trophy.

"So did you meet Gandhi's grandson?" Paul smirks while he goes on fiddling with his time capsule, though he's nervous, his eyes snapping at Jill, who regards him encouragingly. His mouth breaks into a derisive grin. "He's into fucking equitation therapy. Whatever that is. He's probably writing a semi-autobiographical novel, too." Paul combs one hand back through his mullet and frowns with what I'm supposed to know is dismayed belief. "I like asked him, 'What's the most misunderstood airline?' And he goes, 'I don't know. Royal Air Maroc?' I go, 'Fucking bullshit. It's Northwest. It flies to the Twin Cities of Minneapolis and Saint Paul. No contest.' " Paul's lip curls in its right corner. Something's setting him off.

"Maybe he didn't understand what you were getting at," I say to be fatherly. "I'm guessing she's not too serious about him anyway."

"Oh, what a *giant* relief *that* is." Paul's odd round face assumes an expression of profoundest disdain.

"I thought he seemed pretty interesting," Jill says—her first semi-familial utterance and the first uncoded words anybody's spoken since Paul came back inside. Although, of course, she's wrong.

"He's a butthole. Case closed," Paul snarls. " 'Are you all right? Are *you* all right?' He's like a fucking nurse. He's one of those dipshits who's always asking people if they're all right. 'Are you all right? How 'bout you? Are *you* all right, too? Do you want a fucking foot massage? How 'bout a back rub? Or a blow job? Maybe a high colonic?' " In this frame of mind, as a junior at Haddam High, Paul used to get so angry at his teachers, he'd beat his temples with his palms—the universal SOS for teen troubles ahead. It's hard to imagine him selling residential real estate.

"I think you should let this go, okee, honey?" Jill says and smiles at him.

Paul glowers at Jill, then at me, as if he's just exited a trance—blinking, then smiling. "Issat it?" he says. "You done? That be all? You want cheese on that?" It's possible he might bark, which is also something he did as a teen.

Someplace, from some sound source I can't locate, as if it came out of the drywall, I hear music. Orchestral. Ravel's *Bolero*—the military snares and the twiny oboes, played at high volume. No doubt it's the Feensters. What more perfect Thanksgiving air? Possibly they're in the hot tub, staging a musicale for the beach visitors and, of course, to aggravate the shit out of me. At Easter, they played "The March of the Siamese Children" all day long. Last 4th of July, it was "Lisbon Antigua" by Pérez Prado, until the Sea-Clift Police (summoned by me) paid them a courtesy call, which started a row. It's conceivable that in the cathode-ray tube business, Nick got too close to some bad-actor chemicals that are just now being registered in his behavior. To ask them to turn it down would invite a fistfight, which I don't feel like. Though I'm happy to call the police again. Then, just as suddenly, *Bolero* stops and I hear voices raised next door and a door slam.

"Look here, you two." I'm tempted to say *lovebirds*, but don't. "I've got some bees wax of my own to take care of before the food gets here. I want you to treat the place like you own it."

"Okay. That's great." Jill puts her arms behind her and nods enthusiastically.

"No, but wait!" Paul says, and suddenly abandoning his time capsule, he essentially rushes me across the basement. I manage to take one unwieldy backward-sideways step, since he seems maybe to want to go right by me and head up the stairs—to where, I haven't the foggiest. But instead, he lurches straight into me, thudding me in the chest, expunging my breath and clamping his terrible grip on me. "I haven't given you a hug yet, *Dad*," he howls, his whiskery jaw broxed against my shaved face, his belly to my belly. He's got me grappled around my shoulders, his bare knee, for some reason, wedging between mine the way a high school gorilla would body-press his high school honey. My shocked eyes have popped open wider, so that I see right down into his humid manly ear canal and across the red bumpy landscape of his awful mullet. "Oh, I've been *so* bad," he wails in deepest, crassest sarcasm, clutching me, his head grinding my chest. I want to flee or yell or start punching. "Oh, *Christ*, I've just been so terrible." He's taken me prisoner—though I mean to get away. I'm backed into the narrow stairwell and manage to anchor one Nike against the bottom riser. Except with Paul grasping and rooting at me, I miss my balance and start listing backward, with him still attached, his glasses frame gouging my cheek. "Ooooh, ooooh," he boo-hoos in mock contrition. We're both going over now, except I catch a grip, hand-rasping and painful, on the banister pole, which stops us, saving me from knocking the crap out of myself—snapping a vertebra, breaking my leg, finishing the job Bob Butts started. What's wrong with life?

"What the fuck, you idiot," I say, clung to the sloping banister like a gunshot victim. "Are you losing your fucking mind?"

"Bonding." Paul expels a not-wholesome breath into the front of my block-M sweatshirt. "We're bonding."

"Sweetie?" Jill's beseeching voice. At the angle I'm suspended, and from behind the top of Paul's head, Jill's wide, disconcerted face comes into view, looking troubled, as she's trying to gain a one-handed grip on Paul's back to pry him off me before I lose my own hand-hold and brain myself on the riser edge. "Sweetie, let your dad up now. He's gonna hurt himself."

"It's *so* important," Paul murples.

"I know. But—" Jill begins raising him like a child.

"Get off me." I'm struggling, trying to shout but breathless. "Jesus Christ." What I'd like to do is wham a fist right in his ear, knock him into a stupor, only I can't turn loose of the banister without falling. But I would if I could.

"Come on, Sweetie." Jill has both her milky arms—hand and handless—about Paul's sides. My nose is against her shoulder— the sweet smell of lilacs possibly associated with her Ekberg bosoms. Though it's still an awful moment.

And then I'm loose and able to pull myself up. Paul is six inches in front of me, his bleared right orb glowing behind his spectacles, his mouth gaping, heaving for air, his gray pupils fixed on me.

"What's wrong with you?" I let myself sit down onto the third stair leading up to the kitchen. I'm still breathless. Jill still has a wrestler's grip around the middle of Paul's red Chiefs shirt. He looks dazed, surprised but pleased. He may feel things couldn't have turned out better.

"Are you one of those people who shies away from physical intimacy with loved ones?" He's now speaking in a deep AM dee-jay voice, dead-eyed.

"Why are you such an asshole, is what I want to know."

"It's easier," he snaps.

"Than what, for Christ's sake? Than to act like a human being?"

Paul's round face inches closer. Jill's still got him. His body smells metallic—from his time capsule—his breathing stertorous as a smoker's (which I hope he isn't). "Than being like you." He shouts this. He is furious. At me.

Except I haven't done anything. Meant no harm or injury—other than to love him, which might be enough. This is all loss. "What's so terrible about me? I'm just your old man. It's Thanksgiving Day. I have cancer. I love you. Why is that so bad?"

"Because you hold everything fucking *down*," Paul shouts, and he accidentally spits in my face, catching my eyelid. "You smother it."

"Oh bullshit." I'm shouting back now. "I don't smother *enough*. How the hell would you know? What have you ever restrained?" I almost blurt out that someone ought to smother *him*, though that would send the wrong message. I begin hoisting my aching self off the stair, using the banister. "I've got things to do now. Okay?" My hand burns, my knees are quaky, my heart's doing a little periwinkle in its cavity. Outside the sliding glass door, where the light's diaphanous, the late-morning beach—what I can see of it—stretches pristine, sprigged up with airy yellow beach grass and dry stems. I wipe my son's cool saliva off my eyelid and address Jill, who's peering at me as if I might expire like her stepfather in Cheboygan. I wonder if I'd get used to her having only one hand. Yes.

I try to smile at her over my son's shoulder, as if he wasn't there anymore. "Maybe you two just oughta take a long walk down the beach."

"Okee," Jill says—good, staunch Michigan beauty who sees her job.

"You need to take the hostility quiz." Paul's eyes dance behind their specs. "It was on a napkin in a diner down in Valley Forge."

"Maybe I'll do that later." I am defeated.

" 'How many times a week do you give the finger? Do you ever wake up with your fists clenched?' Let's see—" He's forgotten how I smother things and make his difficult life unlivable. I'm sure he meant it when he said it. His mind is cavorting now, his way of letting the past go glimmering. " 'Do you think people are talking about you all the time? Do you think a lot about revenge?' I forget the rest." He stares expectantly, blinking, as if he needs re-acclimating—to me, to being here, to his niche in the world. There is nothing wrong with my son. It's us. *We're* not normal. No wonder life seems better in Kansas City.

I have nothing available to say to him. He has placed himself outside my language base, to the side of my smothering fatherly syntax and diction, complimentary closes, humorous restrictive clauses and subordinating conjunctions. We have our cocked-up coded lingo—winks, brow-archings, sly-boots double, triple, quadruple entendres that work for us—but that's all. And now they're gone, lost to silence and anger, into the hole that is our "relationship." I bless you. I bless you. I bless you. In spite of all.

14

Hurriedly now, or I'll have nothing to show for the day. It's past 10:30. I head up Ocean Ave, my duct-taped window holding fast. I check the news-only station from Long Branch for something on the Haddam hospital explosion that might keep me out of the lineup tomorrow. But there's only holiday traffic updates, a brewing controversy over the new 34-cent stamp, last night's Flyers' stats and Cheney doing swell in the Georgetown Hospital.

I'm certain I've missed Mike's house prospects, though I may not now be in the best realty fettle—after my "conflict" with my son—and am just as likely to scare clients away. Plus, I'm missing my call from Sally and, at the very least, depriving myself of an easeful morning in bed following last night's ordeal. I'd like to settle my blood pressure and stopper the seep of oily stress into my bloodstream before I show up in the phlebotomy line at Mayo on Wednesday. Even in stolid Lutheran Rochester, where sheikhs, pashas and South American genocidists go for tune-ups, and where they've seen everything, I still want to make as good a biomedical impression as possible, as if I was selling myself as a patient. If Paul's right that I hold everything down, my wish would be that I could hold down more.

Sea-Clift, viewed out my Suburban window on late Thanksgiving morning, is as emptied, wide-streeted and spring-y as

Easter Sunday—despite the Yuletide trimmings. No cars are
parked along the boulevard shopfronts. Wreathed traffic lights
are flashing yellow. The regular speed trap—a black-and-white
Plymouth Fury "hidden" behind the fire station load lugger—is
in position and manned (we locals know) by a rubber blow-up
cop named "Officer Meadows" for a since-deceased chief fired
for sleeping on the job. My Realty-Wise office at 1606 looks
unpromising as I pass it. Only the crime-barred Hello Deli and
Tackle Shop is lighted inside and doing business—three cars
angled in, another Salvation Army red-kettle tender out front
chatting with a pair of joggers in running gear. The Coastal
Evacuation signs leading to the bay bridge and points inland
appear to have been heeded, leaving the rest of us to fend for
ourselves.

A beach town in off-season doldrum may seem to have bliss-
fully reclaimed its truest self, breathing out the long-awaited sigh
of winter. But in Sea-Clift, a nervous what-comes-next uneasiness
prickles down the necks of our town fathers due to last summer's
business slow-down. Growth, smart or maybe even stupid, is the
perceived problem here; how to grow an entrepreneurial culture
where our hands-on family-based service commitment could
survive till doomsday (because of the beach), but will never go
all the way to gangbusters without a tech sector, a labor-luring
signature industry, a process-driven mentality or a center of
gravity to see to it we get rich as shit off beaucoup private dollars.
In other words, we're just a place, much like another.

I, of course, moved here for these very reasons: because I
admired Sea-Clift's *face* to the interested stranger—seasonal,

insular, commuter-less, stable, aspirant within limits. There was no space to grow *out* to, so my business model pointed to in-fill and retrench, not so different from Haddam, but on a more human scale. My house-moving plan on Timbuktu is the perfect case in point. You could teach it over at Wharton. To me, commerce with no likelihood of significant growth or sky-rocketing appreciation seems like a precious bounty, and the opposite of my years in Haddam, when *gasping increase* was the sacred article of faith no one dared mention for fear of the truth breeding doubt like an odorless gas that suffocates everybody.

Mine, of course, is not the view of the Dollars For Doers Strike Council, who sit Monday mornings in the fire station bullpen and who've seen the figures and are charged to "transition" Sea-Clift into the "next phase," from under-used asset to vitality pocket and full-service lifestyle provider using grassroots support. This, even though we all like it fine here. Permanence has once again been perceived as death.

This fall, after the summer down-tick—fewer visitors, fewer smoothies and tomato pies, fewer boogie-board and chalet rentals (I credit the election and the tech-stock slide)—new plans went on the table for revitalizations. The Council floated a town naming-rights initiative to infuse capital ("BFI, New Jersey" was seriously suggested, but met with a cold shoulder from citizens). A proposal came up to abandon the "seasonal concept" and make Sea-Clift officially "year-round," only no one seemed to know how to do that, though all were for it until they figured out they'd have to work harder. There was support for dismantling a lighthouse in Maine and setting it on the beach, but regulations forbid new construction. The Sons of Italy offered to expand the Frank Sinatra contest to include a permanent "New Jersey Folk Traditions" exhibit to go on the Coastal Heritage Trail (no one's taken this seriously). The most ambitious idea—which *will* take place, though not in my lifetime—is to reclaim acres of Barnegat Bay itself for revenue-friendly use: a human tissue–generator lab or possibly just a golf course. But no one's identified partnering capital or imagined how to buy off wetlands interests. Though one day I'm sure a man will rollerblade from where the Yacht Club used to be across to the condom plant in Toms River without noticing that once a great bay was here. The only new idea that seems to be genuinely percolating is an Internet rental-booking software package (Weneedabreak.com) that's worked in towns farther north, and that Mike's all for. In all these visionings, however, my attitude's the same: Quit fretting, keep the current inventory in good working order, rely on your fifties-style beach life and let population growth do its job the way it always has. What's the hurry? We've already built it here, so we can be sure in time they'll come. This is why I'm not on the Dollars For Doers anymore.

*J*ust ahead, at the left turn onto Timbuktu Street, I see the scheduled Turkey Day 5-K Sea-Clift-to-Ortley-and-back road race nearing its start time in front of Our Lady of Effectual Mercy RC church. A crowd—a hundred or so singleted body types—mingles on the cold grassy median right where I have to turn. The runners—string-thin men and identical females in weightless shorts, expensive-as-hell running shoes, numbered Turkey Day racing bibs and plastic water bottles—are dedicatedly goading themselves into road race mentality, stretching and twisting, prancing and bending and ignoring one another, hands on hips, heads down, occasionally erupting into violent bursts of in-place jogging to fire their muscles into exertion mode. They are, I have to say, a handsome, healthy, sinewy, finely-limbed bunch of sociopathic greyhounds. Most are in middle years, all obviously scared silly of serenity and death, a fixation that makes them emaciate themselves, punish their bones and brains (many of the women quit menstruating or having the slightest interest in sex) and cut themselves off from friend, foe and family—everyone except their "running friends"—in order to pad out along the dark early-morning streets of America, demonstrating sentience. My time in the USMC, three decades back, and in spite of what Ann says about my suitability, made me promise myself that if I got out alive, I'd never hasten a step as long as I lived, unless real life or real death was chasing me. I pretty much haven't.

On the margins of the crowd are the usual wheelchair athletes—chesty, vaguely insane-looking, leather-gloved men and women strapped into aerodynamic chairs with big cambered wheels and abbreviated bodies like their owners. There are also spry oldsters—stiff, bent-over and balding octogenarians of both genders, ready to run the race with extinction. And set apart from these are the true runners, a cadre of regal, tar-black, starved-looking, genuine Africans—women and men both, a few actually barefoot—chatting and smiling calmly (two talk on cell phones) in anticipation of tearing all the neurotic white racers brand new Turkey Day assholes. For all the runners, it's hopeful, I know; but to me it's a dispiriting spectacle to witness on a morning when so much less should be strived for under a wide, pale-clouded and slightly pinkish sky. I feel the same way when I go in a hardware store to have a new tenant's key cut and smell the cardboard and corrugated-metal and feed-store aromas of all the dervish endeavors a human can be busily up to if he's worth a shit: recaulking that shower groin with space-age epoxies, insulating the weather-side spigot that always freezes, re-hanging the bathroom door that opens the wrong way and clutters the nice view down the hall that reveals a slice of ocean when the trees aren't in leaf. It gives me the grims to think of what we humans do that no one's life depends on, and always drives me right out the door into the street with my jagged new key and my head spinning. It's no different from Mike's idea of putting up magnum-size "homes" on two-acre lots with expectations of luring hard-charging young radiologists and probate lawyers who'd really be just as happy to go on living where they live and who need six thousand square feet like they need a bone in their nose. Neither am I sure that the second-home market, where I ply my skills, is immune from the same complaint.

Sea-Clift police are of course a presence, a pair of thick-necks in helmets and jodhpurs on giant white-and-black Kawasakis, waiting to be escorts. A green EMS meat wagon sits beyond the crowd at the curb, its attendants sharing a smoke and a smirk. The priest from Our Lady of Effectual Mercy, Father Ray, wearing his dress-down everyday white surplice, has mounted a metal stepladder at the curb and is using a bullhorn and an aspergill to bless the race and runners: May you not fall down and bust your ass; may you not tear your Achilles or blow out an ACL; may you not have an aneurysm in your aorta with no one to give you last rites; may you have a living will that leaves all to the RC Church; now run for your lives in the name of the Father, the Son, etc., etc., etc.

I need to make my turn here, cross the median cut and the white markings the race organizers have painted on the pavement. All the milling soon-to-be-racers give me and my Suburban the cloudy eye, as if I might be about to plow into them, cut a bloody swath right through. What's this Suburban all about, their hard looks say. Do you *need* a boat that big? There oughta be a special tax on those. What's with the window and the fucking tape? Is this guy local?

I'm grinning involuntarily as I make the turn, my head ducking, nodding unqualified 5-K approval along with my guilty admission that I'm not one of them, not brave enough, will have to try harder. I mustn't accidentally hit the horn, punch the accelerator, veer an inch off course, or risk setting them to yelling and contesting and reviewing their civil rights. But seeing them congregated and intent, so pre-preoccupied, so vulnerably clad and unprotected, so much one thing, makes me feel just how much I'm a realtor (in the bad sense); even more so now than in my last Haddam days, when I felt coldly extraneous and already irremediably what I was—a house flogger, cruising the periphery of all the real goings-on: the shoe-repair errands, the good-results doctor and dental visits, the 5-K races, the trips to the altar to kneel and accept the holy body and blood of kee-rist on a kee-rutch. I felt something akin to this somber sensation when I didn't give Bud Sloat a ride in Haddam on Tuesday.

But I'm sorry to be here feeling it now. Though it is but another in the young day's cavalcade of good-for-my-soul, Next Level acceptances for which I'll be thankful: I am this thing, seller of used and cast-off houses, and I am not other. It's shocking to note how close we play to unwelcome realizations, and yet how our ongoing ignorance makes so much of life possible. However, gone in a gulp are all the roles I might still inhabit but won't, all the new learning curves I'd be good at, all the women who might adore me, the phone calls bearing welcome news and foretelling unimagined happiness, my chance to be an FBI agent, ambassador to France, a case worker in Mozambique— the one they all look up to. The Permanent Period permitted all that, and the price was small enough—self-extinguishment, becoming an instrument, blah, blah, blah. And now it's different. The Next Level means me to say yes to myself just when it feels weirdest. Is this what it means to be mainstreamed like my son?

"I'm one of you," I want to say to these joggers out my window like a crowd in a jogger republic undergoing a coup. "The race is ahead of me, too. I'm not just this. I'm that. And that. And that. There's more to me than meets your gimlet eye." But it isn't so.

A bare coffee-colored arm flags out of the milling crowd, with a squat body attached and a face I know above the three blue stars 'n bars of the Honduran flag worn as a singlet. This is Esteban, from the Cormorant Court roofing crew, waving happily to me, *el jefe*, his gold restorations flashing in the hidden sun's glint. He's socked into the runner crowd, way more a part of things than I feel. My thumb juts to tap the horn, but I catch myself in time and wave instead. Though it's then I have to press across the opposing lane of Ocean Ave and onto Timbuktu. The electric carillon in Our Lady commences its pre-race clamor, startling the shit out of me. The runner crowd shifts as one toward the starting line and up goes the gun (Father Ray is the shooter). I carry through with my turn, extra careful, since the motorcycle cops are eyeing me. But in an instant, I'm across and anonymous again as the gun goes off and the beast crowd swells with a sigh, and then all of it's behind me.

*M*ike Mahoney—bony, businesslike, crisply turned-out realty go-getter—is the first human I see down Timbuktu. He's out in the street beside his Infiniti with its REALTORS ARE PEOPLE TOO sticker and Barnegat Lighthouse license tag, waving, a happy grin on his round flat face, as though I'd gotten lost and just happened down the right street by dumb luck. He's wearing his amber aviators and clutching a bouquet of white listing sheets. Twenty yards beyond him is a beige Lincoln Town Car, the exact model Newark Airport limo drivers drive. Outside the Lincoln waits a small, ovoid mustachioed personage in what looks like, through my windshield, a belted linen-looking suit that matches the Town Car's paint job, into which the man almost perfectly blends. This is the client Mike has somehow convinced to hang around. I'm a half hour late—for reasons of my difficult son—but frankly don't much care.

Timbuktu Street is a three-block residential, connecting Ocean Avenue to Barnegat Bay out ahead. The closed-for-the-season Yacht Club is at the end to the left, and across the gray water the low populous sprawl of Toms River is two-plus miles away. The bay bridge itself is visible, though at 11:30 on Thanksgiving morning, it is not much in use.

Houses on Timbuktu (Marrakesh Street is one street south, Bimini one street north) are all in the moderate bracket. The bay side is naturally cheaper than the ocean side, but prices go up close to the water, no matter what water it is. Most of these are frank plain-fronted ranches, some with camelbacks added, some with new wood-grained metal siding, all hip-roofed, three-window, door-in-the-middle, pastel frame constructions on small lots. Most were put up en masse, ten streets at a time, after Hurricane Cindy flattened all the aging cypress and fir bungalows the first Sea-Clift settlers built from Sears kits in the twenties. A few of those '59-vintage owners are still around, though most houses have changed hands ten times and are owned by year-rounders who're retired or commute to the mainland, or who keep their houses as rentals or a summer bolt-hole for the extended family. Several are owned and kept in mint condition by Gotham and Philadelphia policemen and firefighters who store their big trailered Lunds and refurbished Lymans, shrink-wrapped in blue plastic, on their pink-and-green crushed-marble "lawns." These small streets, with their clean-facade, well-barbered, moderately-priced dwellings (250–300 bills) are, in fact, the social backbone of Sea-Clift, and even though most newcomers are Republicans, it's they who oppose the Dollars For Doers schemes to grow out the economy like a mushroom.

It's also these same home owners who're made rueful by the sight of a neighbor house being torn off its foundation and trucked away, leaving behind scarred ground that once was a compatible vista, to be replaced by some frightening new construction. The worst is always assumed. And even though the identical houses along these identical, all but tree-less streets are simplicity and modesty's essence, and finally no great shakes, that's exactly how the owners want it, and know for certain a new house of unforeseeable design will rob their street of its *known* character and kick the crap out of values they're looking to cash in on. I've already received concerned calls from the Timbuktu Neighbors Coalition, advancing the idea that I "donate"(!) the emptied lot at 118 for a passive park. Though even if I wanted to (which I don't), no one in the Coalition would keep it up or pay the liability premiums, since many Coalition-owners are absentees and quite a few are elderly, on fixed whatevers. Eventually, the "park" would turn into a weedy eyesore everyone'd blame me for. Prices would then fall, and everyone would've forgotten that an attractive new house could've been there and made everything rosy. Better—as I told the Coalition lady—to sell the lot to some citizen who can afford it, then let the community do what communities do best: suppress diversity, discourage individuality, punish exuberance and find suitable language to make it seem good for everyone and what America's all about. Placards (like election placards) still stand in some yards, shouting SAVE TIMBUKTU FROM

EVIL DEVELOPERS!!! Though the house at 118 is already up on steel girders and in a week will be history.

Mike's heading toward my driver's window as I pull to the curb. He's smiling and glancing back, nodding assurances to his client and generally brimming with house-selling certainty.

"I got tied up," I say out the window, and look annoyed.

"It's better, it's better," Mike says in a whisper, then has another glance at the Town Car clients. He looks like a dashboard doll, since he's wearing a strange knee-length black knitted sweater with a mink-looking collar, a Black Watch plaid sports-car cap, green cords and green suede loafers with argyle socks. It would seem to be his Scottish ensemble. "It's good to make them wait." He has drawn close to my face, so that I'm almost nose-into the fur trim on his sweater. The breeze on the bay side of Barnegat Neck is stouter than I expected. Inland weather is bringing change. We'll have a proper blustery Thanksgiving cold snap before the day's done. I bend forward against my steering wheel and give a look through the windshield up at pleasant, leaf-green #118, hiked up on dull red girders that have several impressive-looking hydraulic jacks under them, so the entire house, sill and all, has been elevated five feet off its brick foundation, exposing light and air and affording a view to the back yard. Two sets of heavy-duty tires and axles await use in what was once the front yard, in preparation for actually moving the house—which, like its neighbors, is unornamented, aluminum-sided, with brighter, newer green roof shingles mixed with old. The Arriba house movers have put their enigmatic sign up in the yard: EL GATO DUERME MIENTRAS QUE TRABAJAMOS.

This is the first time I've seen 118 up on its sleds, and I frankly can't blame the neighbors for feeling "violated," which is what the Coalition lady said before she started to cry and told me I was a gangster. It's not a very good thing to do to a street's sense of integrity—prices or no prices—to start switching houses like Monopoly pieces. I'm actually sorry I've done it now. It would've been better if the new owners had torn 118 down as planned and put their new house up in its dust. Orderly residential succession would have been satisfied, although possibly nobody would've been any happier. All the more reason to let Mike sell it to his clients right off the sleds and shift the focus to them— who at least plan to live in it, albeit someplace else.

"I've been telling them inventory's down a third and demand's kicking up." Mike's whispered breath is warm and once again has tobacco on it. He practices all kinds of breath-purifying techniques, as if that's the thing buyers look for first. His Infiniti has a Dalai Lama-approved incense air-freshener strung to the rearview, and his car seats are always strewn with Clorets and Dentyne papers. But today's efforts are so far unavailing.

I stare curiously out at Mike's shiny round face—a face of high, far-away mountain crags, clouded pinnacles and thinnest airs, all forsaken for the chance to sell houses in the Garden State. And just for that instant, I cannot for the life of me think of his name—even though I just thought it. I'd like to say his name, frame a question in a confidential manner that lets him know I'm behind his deal 110 percent, and why doesn't he just take my thumbs-up from right here in the car. I'll wave a cheery welcome aboard to the fat little Hindu (or Mohammedan or

Buddhist or Jainist or whatever he is), then motor off to be home when Sally calls and Clarissa returns with tales. Possibly Jill will have given Paul a sedative and we can all watch the Patriots pregame on Fox before the food's festive arrival.

Only, my mind has problematically swallowed up this bright-eyed little brown man's name, even though I can tell you everything *else* there is to know about him. Gone from me like a leaf in the wind.

"Uhmmm," I say. Of course I don't need to know his name to carry on a conversation with him. Though not knowing it has had the added defect of sweeping clean the conversational path from in front of me, like the police sweeping pedestrians from in front of the 5-K to Ortley and back. I remember all *that* perfectly! What the hell's going on? Am I having a stroke? Or just bored to nullity by one more house going on the sale block? This may be how you know you've reached the finish line in real estate. I even remember *that*.

I smile out at this strangely dressed, burbling little man, hoping to neutralize alarm from my face. Though why should there be any? Whatever we're about to do—I assume sell a house—doesn't seem to require me. I peer out toward the small pear-shaped man in his wrong-season suit, beside his Lincoln, which wears what looks like blue-and-white Empire State plates and also, I see now, a blue BUSH sticker on its left bumper. He has his short fat-man's arms folded and is staring thoughtfully at 118 up on its girders, as if this is a marvelous project he's now in charge of but needs to study for a while. The Town Car appears packed with shadowy human cargo—three distinct heads in back, plus a dog staring through the back window, its tongue out in a happy-dog laugh.

I look back at this diminutive unnamed man at my window. It's possible I don't look normal. "So," I say, "are we all set, then?" I smile exuberantly, suddenly invigorated with what I'm here for and ready to do it—press the flesh, seal the deal, say howdy and make the outsider feel wanted—things I'm good at. "I'm ready to meet the pigeon," I say for some reason, which seems to distress and sink the grin on ———'s round mug. Bill, Bert, Baxter, Boris, Bently . . . I'll come to it.

"Mr. Bagosh, Frank," ——— says, *sotto voce* through my window. Frank. Me.

——— smiles in at me faintly. His thumb is, I can see, twisting his pinkie ring. Thank goodness he doesn't know I can't say his fucking name. He'd think I'm demented. Which I'm not. This kind of thing happens. Possibly vertigo again.

"How is it again?" I say.

"Bagosh," Carl, Carey, Chris, Court, Curt, Coop says, pushing his listing papers into his silly sweater's side pocket, then pulling down on his sports-car cap to look more official. He doesn't want me involved in this now. Something doesn't feel right. He sees his deal evaporating. But I'm doing it, if only because I don't know how to leave. He casts a guarded look at my block-M sweatshirt. Then behind his aviators, his eyes drift down to my jeans, as if I might not be wearing pants at all.

"Bagosh it *is*." I start out of the car, surprisingly feeling damn good about selling a house on Thanksgiving. Cash deal to sweeten the pot—if I remember right. I actually love this kind of shirtsleeve, write-a-check, hand-it-over deal. Real estate used to have plenty of them. Nowadays, parties are walled off from exposure, require exit strategies, escape hatches in case a sparrow flies against a screen on the third Tuesday and this is thought to be a bad omen. America is a country lost in its own escrow.

I don't know why I can't say Ed, Ewell, Ernie, Egbert, Escalante, Emerson, Everett's name, but I can't. He's Tibetan. He's my associate. I've known him for a year and a half. He and his wife are estranged, with genius-level kids. He's a Libertarian but a social moderate. A Buddhist. A tiger in our trade, a clotheshorse, a happy little business warrior. I just can't come up with his handle, even out on chilly Timbuktu, with a mind-clearing whistle-breeze gusting off the bay. Maybe I should ask to borrow his business card to make a note.

Mr. Bagosh is heading toward us with a big pleased grin on his plump lips. He has a toddling-sideways motoring gait you sometimes see experienced waiters use. What I couldn't see from the car is that he's wearing walking shorts with his belted Raj jacket, plus rattan loafers and socks of the thinnest white silk up to his knees. We are in Rangoon (when it was still Burma). I'm just out of the cockpit of my Flying Fortress, ready for a gin-rickey, a good soak, a new linen suit of my own and some social introductions. This man—Bagosh—coming across the lobby is just the fellow to make it all happen (in addition to being a spy for our side).

"Bagosh," this good man says into the Barnegat breezes, far from Rangoon, here now on Timbuktu. He must've thought it'd be warm here.

"Bascombe," I say in the same robust spirit.

"Yes. Wonderful." We clasp hands. He gives me his two-hander, which is okay this time. "Mr. Mahoney has told me superior things about you."

Bingo! But *Mahoney*? I wouldn't have guessed it. I extend to Mr. Mahoney an affirming business associate's smile. Mike. All is normal again. We at least know who we are.

"I love your house!" Mr. Bagosh nearly shouts with pleasure. In his toddling way, he half-turns and regards 118 up on its severe machinery, as if it was a piece of rare sculpture he was connoisseur to. "I want to buy it right now. Just as we see it here. Up on its big boats. Whatever they are." He leans back and beams, as if saying "its big boats" afforded him inexpressible pleasure.

"Well, that's what we're here for." I nod at Mr. Mahoney at my side. He's re-examining his listing sheets and looking more confident. I have the rich, ineradicable fetor of English Leather burning in my nostrils and also, I believe, on my hand. It's no doubt Mr. Bagosh's signature scent since his school days in Rajpur or some such outpost.

"We're down from the Buffalo area, Mr. Bascombe," Mr. Bagosh says pridefully. "I own an awards and trophies business, and my business has been good this year." He has twinkling black eyes, and his fine white hair has been choreographed into a swirling comb-down from the far reaches that complements a little goatee, which is not so different from my son Paul's beard-stache, only presentable. On anyone but an Indian—if that's what he is—this configuration would make him look like a masseur.

The three of us, me in my block-M and Nikes, Mike in his Scotch get-up, Bagosh in his tropical lounging-wear, are probably the strangest things anyone on Timbuktu—a street of cops, firemen, Kinko's managers and plumbers—has yet witnessed, and might make them all less sorry to see the house head down the road.

"I'm not sure what that is," meaning the "awards business," though I have an idea.

"Oh, well," Mr. Bagosh says expansively in a plummy accent. "If you become a salesman of the year in New Jersey. And you receive a wonderful awahd for this honor. We supply this awahd— in the Buffalo area. In Erie, as well. We're a chain of six. So." His mouse-brown face virtually glows. Possibly he's five eight and sixty, and obviously happy to see the complex world in terms of bestowing awards on inhabitants and to make a ton of money doing it. "We say ours is a rewarding business. But it has been very profitable." This is his standard joke and makes him lower his eyes to stifle a look of pleasure.

"That's great." I pass an eye over his Town Car, which has all gold accessories—gold door handles, gold side mirrors, gold and silver hubcaps and gold window frames. Even the famed Lincoln hood ornament is gold-encrusted. It is the car I saw at the office yesterday. In the passenger's seat, a swarthy Madonna-faced woman with dense black hair and a pastel scarf covering part of her head is talking non-stop into a cell phone and paying no attention to what we're doing. In the back I count possibly three sub-teen faces (there could be more). A large-eyed girl peers at me through the tinted window. The others—two slender boys with vulpine expressions—are fidgeting with hand-held video gizmos as though they don't know they're in a car in New Jersey. The dog is not to be seen.

But *ecce homo*—Bagosh. Family number two is my guess. The cell-phone Madonna looks not much older than Clarissa and is probably a mail-order delivery from the old country, where she may have been unmarriageable in ways Buffalo residents couldn't care less about. A young widow.

"I guess a lot more people are getting awards now," I say.

"Oh my, yes. It's very good today. Very positive. When my father started in the business in 1961, everyone said, 'Oh, Sura, my God. This doesn't make sense. There's no possible way for you. You're mad as a hatter.' But he was smart, you know? When I finished at Eastman and came into the firm, he had two stores. And now I have six. Two more next year, maybe." Mr. Bagosh links his manicured fingers across the belted front of his Raj cabana jacket and rests them on his prosperous little belly—one pinkie wears a raucous diamond Mike is probably envious of. He's a better candidate for one of the mansionettes Mike's planning in Montmorency County than for 118. Though he may already have one of those in Buffalo, and maybe in Cozumel. In any case, the first commandment of residential sales is never to question the buyer's motives. Leave that for the lawyers and the bankruptcy referees, who get paid to do it.

"Is there anything I can tell you about the house?" I have to say something to merit being here. I look down at my Nike toes and actually give the asphalt a tiny Gary Cooperish nudge.

"Oh no, my goodness," Mr. Bagosh exults. His teeth are

straight and white and uniform—top of the line, in dental terms. "Your Mike here has done his job splendidly. I could use twenty of him."

Stood off to the side so the two of us can talk, Mike, I see, is unsmiling. Being commodified in front of me is distasteful to him and will make skinning money off this gentleman less than a hardship. I'm certain he's reciting his Ahimsa, since he's begun gazing up into the sky as if a passing pelican was his soul dispersing to bliss. When reason ends, anger begins. Mike's little flat face, I think, looks weary.

"Have you even been *in* the house?" I say for no particular reason.

"No, no. But I really don't—"

"Let's just have a look," I say. "You don't want any surprises once it's yours."

"Well—" Bagosh shoots a dubious look at Mike and then over to the Lincoln, where his girlfriend, wife, daughter, grand-daughter is still yakking on the phone. A hurry-the-hell-up frown wrinkles her features, as if she's wanting lunch and to be rid of the kids. I see the dog now, a black Standard Poodle seated beside her in the driver's seat, staring out toward Barnegat Bay, a block and a half away, where a late-staying pair of Tundra swans browses on the weedy shore. In his doggy mind, they are his future. "It's conceivably not safe, I think," Bagosh says, his smile gone measly. In fact, both the house and the red girdering have PELIGRO! NO ENTRADA! painted on in big, crude, no-nonsense letters. Except I know the Bolivians crawl these houses like lemurs and the whole rigamarole's solid as a bank.

"*I'm* gonna have a look," I say. "I think you should, too. It's just good business." I'm only doing this to put chain-store, second-family Bagosh through some hands-on experience he won't enjoy—this, because he gloated over Mike's subaltern status (and voted for Bush). Though it's Mike's fault for thinking he can sell a house to an Indian and not feel cheated. Last year, he sold a condo to a Chinese family and accepted an invitation to dinner once they moved in. I asked him how it had gone, and he answered that the little man-god no longer opposes Chinese sovereignty and that Buddhists bear exile well.

Mike projects a beetled expression and definitely does not support a trip inside the house or hauling his customer up with me. He's worried what the place looks like—huge cracks in the ceilings, floor joists compromised by wet rot—the cold vastness of all that's unknown but not good and therefore *peligro*. Only a nitwit would expose a client to the unexpected when cash is smiling at you. Despite being a Buddhist—full of human compassion for all that lives, and who views real estate as a means of helping others—when it comes to clinching deals, Mike sees clients as rolls of cash that happen to be able to talk. He is no more bothered by Bagosh's undervaluing his essence than if Bagosh fell down and barked like a dog. To Mike—eyes blinking, hands thrust into his absurd sweater pockets—Bagosh is "Mr. Equity Takeover." "Mr. Increased Disposable Income." It wouldn't matter if he was a Navajo. I've never felt exactly that way in fifteen years of selling houses. But I'm not an immigrant, either.

Bagosh, against his will and judgment, but shamed, has begun clambering up onto the girder behind me, bumping the back of my Nikes with his noggin and making me breathe in big burning whiffs of his English Leather. He's taking deep grunting breaths as he ascends, and because he's a shrimp, has to struggle up on his bare knees to reach the red girder surface.

Once onto the flat I-beam, however, it's easy to step along past the front window, holding to the siding panels, and to walk straight to the front door opening that gives entry to the house. Bagosh keeps crowding me on the girder, breathing unevenly, a couple of times saying, "Yes, yes, all right, this is fine now," and smiling wretchedly when I look back at him. We're only eight feet off the ground here and wouldn't do any damage if we did a belly flop.

But there's a nice new view to take in from here, one I'm happy to have and that makes the whole climb-up worthwhile, no matter what we discover inside. Getting a new view—even of Timbuktu Street—is never a waste of time. From here the community is briefly re-visioned: Mike Mahoney down in the street, looking skeptically up at us; our three cars; Bagosh's little closeted brood, all now watching us—the wife at the window, smiling a smile of disapproval. The view stresses the good uniformity of the houses, with their little crushed-marble front yards of differing hues (grassy green, a pink, two or more oceany blues). Few have real trees, only miniature Scotch pines and skimpy oak saplings. None have political placards (meaning the Republicans have won), though several still have their SAVE TIMBUKTU FROM EVIL DEVELOPERS!!! protests. Some yards have boats stored and others feature white statuary of Ole Neptune leaning on his trident—purchasable off the back of trucks on Route 35. No house has nothing, though the effect is to re-enforce sameness: three windows (some with decorative crime bars), center door, no garage, fifty-by-a-hundred-foot lots the original way the (not yet evil) developer designed it. A housing concept which permits no one ever to feel he was *meant* to be here, and so is happy to be, and happier yet to pack up and go when the spirit moves him or her—unlike Haddam, which operates on the Forever Concept but is really no different.

Up the street toward Ocean Avenue, where the 5-K racers have disappeared and the carillon tower at the RC chapel is just visible, some owners are out busying. A man and his son are erecting an Xmas tree in a front yard, where the MIA flag flies on its pole below the Italian tricolor. A man and wife team is painting their front door red and green for Yuletide. Across at 117, in the skimpy back yard, a wrestling ring's been put up and two shirtless teens are throwing each other around, springing off the ropes, taking goofy falls, throwing mock punches, knee lifts and flying mares, laughing and growling and moaning in fun. Number 117, I see, is for sale with my competitor Domus Isle Realty and looks fixed up and spruced for purchase. To the west, the bay stretches out toward the scrim of Toms River far beyond the white Yacht Club mooring markers set in rows. A few late-season sailors are out on the water, seizing the holiday and the land breeze for a last go.

"Ahhhh, yes, now. This is very fine now, isn't it?" Bagosh is close to my shoulder, taking the view, and has actually fastened ahold of my arm. This may be as far above ground as he's been

without walls around him. His English Leather is happily beginning to dissipate in the breeze. His womanish knees have smudges
from clambering onto the girder. We're outside the vacant front
doorway, at a level where the sill comes to my waist. Mike, at
street level, is frowning at the bay. He is envisioning better events
than these.

"We have to go inside still," I say. "You have to inspect your
house." This is purely punitive. I've, of course, already been in
the house when it was attached to the ground and I was selling
it to the Morris County Stevicks following the departure of the
previous owners, the Hausmanns. Though climbing up and in
constitutes a pint-size good adventure I didn't expect and is much
more rewarding than fighting with my son.

"I'll certainly inspect it when these moving chaps finish,"
Bagosh says, and widens his onyx eyes in a gesture of objection
that seems to agree.

"You'll own it by then," I say, and start pulling myself over
the metal sill strip that's half-worked out of its screw holes and
a good place to get a nasty cut.

"Yes. Well—" Bagosh casts a fevered frown down at his luxury
barge, clearly wishing to be driving it away. He coughs, then
laughs a little squealy laugh as I reach down from the doorway
and haul him up into the house that will soon be his.

But if it's good to see the familiar world from a sudden new
elevation, it may not be to see inside a house on girders, detached
from the sacred ground that makes it what it is—a place of safety
and assurance. This is what Mike was trying to make me understand by saying nothing.

Down on the street, temps must be low forties, but inside here it's ten degrees colder, and still and dank as a coal scuttle and echoey and eerily lit. It's different from what I thought—without being sure what I thought. The soggy-floored living room–dining room combo (you enter directly—no foyer, no nothing) is tiny but cavernous. The stained pink walls, old green shag and picture-frame ghosts make it feel not like a room but a shell waiting for a tornado to sweep it into the past. Leaking gas and backed-up toilets stiffen the cold internal air. If I was Bagosh, I'd get in my Town Car and not stop till I saw the lights of snowy Buffalo. Good sense is its own reward. I may be losing my touch.

"O-kay! Well. Yes, yes yes. This is fine," Bagosh says jauntily. We're both too big for the cramped, emptied living room, our footfalls loud as thunder.

I walk through the kitchen door to a tiny room of brown-and-gold curling synthetic tiles, where there's no stove, no refrigerator, no dishwasher. All have been ripped out, leaving only their unpainted footprints, the rusted green sink and all the metal cabinets standing open and uncleaned inside. There's a strong cold scent in here of Pine-Sol, but nothing looks like it's been scrubbed in two hundred years. Police enter rooms like this every day and find cadavers liquefying into the linoleum. It didn't look like this when I showed it to the Stevicks.

Bagosh is heading down the murky hall that separates the two small bedrooms and ends in the bath—the classic American starter-home design. "Okay, this is fine," I hear him say. I'm sure he's frozen in his shorts. The Hausmanns lived in these rooms twenty years, raised two kids; Chet Hausmann worked for Ocean County Parks and Lou-Lou was an LPN in Forked River. Life worked fine. They were normal-size people, with normal-size longings. They bought, they saved, they accrued, they envied, they thrived and enjoyed life right through the Clinton administration. The kids left for other lives (though Chet "the Jet" Jr.'s currently in rehab #2). They grew restless for Dade County, where Lou-Lou's parents live. Things seemed to be changing here—though they weren't. So they left. Nothing out of the ordinary, except it's hard to see how it could've happened inside these four walls, or, if it did, how things could look like this four months later. Empty houses go downhill fast. I should have been more vigilant.

I have a look out the kitchen window into the ditched-up and vacant back yard, and the square, fenced back yards of Bimini Street. Several houses there are closed and boarded for the season, though some have dogs chained up and clothes on the line. Up on Ocean Avenue, the noon carillon at Our Lady has begun chiming "O come, all ye faithful, joyful and triumphant—" Then the wail of a farther-off siren signals the hour. Sirens are rare in Sea-Clift in the off-season, though routine in summer.

"O-kay!" I hear Bagosh say conclusively. It's time to leave. I've said not a word since forcing us to come in here.

And then there's a loud, violent, scrabbling, struggling commotion down the hall, where Bagosh is carrying out his unwilling presale inspection. "Oh my Gawd," I hear him shout in a horrified voice. Then *bangety, bangety, bang-bang.* The sound of a man falling. I'm moving, without bidding myself to move, across the mud-caked floor of the back family room, with its water-clouded picture window overlooking the wrecked back yard. It's less than twenty feet to the hallway entrance and another twelve down the passage. It's possible Bagosh has come upon the overdosed Chet, Jr., is all I can think. Then "Ahhhhh," I hear poor Bagosh shout again. "My Gawd, oh my Gawd." I still can't see him, though unexpectedly I'm faced with *me*, reflected in the mirror on the dark bathroom medicine chest at the end of the hallway. I look terrified.

"What's wrong? Are you all right?" I call out. Though why would he be all right and be howling?

Then out from the right bedroom, where I take it Bagosh is and has hit the floor, a good-size bushy-tailed red fox comes shooting into the hallway. "Ahhh," Bagosh is wailing, "my-Gawd, my-Gawd." The fox stops, paws splayed, and fixes its eyes on me, hugely blocking the path of escape. Its eyes are dark bullets aimed at my forehead. Though it doesn't pause long, but turns and re-enters the room where Bagosh is, provoking another death wail (possibly he's being ripped into now and will have to undergo painful rabies shots). Immediately, the fox comes rocketing back out the bedroom door, claws scrabbling powerfully to gain purchase. For an instant, its spectral, riotous eyes consider the other tiny bedroom—the kids' room. But without another moment's indecision, the fox fires off straight toward me, so that I stagger back and to the left and pitch through the arched doorway into the living room and right off my feet onto the filthy green shag, where I land just as the fox explodes after me through the door, claws out and scrabbling right across my block-M chest, so that I catch a gulp of its feral rank asshole as it springs off, straight across to the metal threshold and out into the clean cold air of Timbuktu, where, for all I know, Mike may believe the fox is me, translated by this house of spirits into my next incarnation on earth. Frank Fox.

15

When the Bagoshes' taillamps have made the turn up onto Ocean Avenue and disappeared ceremoniously into the post noon-time, holiday-emptied streets, Mike and I have ourselves a side-by-side amble down to the bay shore, malodorous and sudsed from last night's storm.

Sally will have called by now. Paul will have answered and could possibly have blurted things I don't want her to know (my illness, for one). Though Clarissa will be home, and the two of them can have a sister-brother parsing talk about my "condition," my upcoming Mayo trip, etc., etc. Possibly Clarissa could also talk to Sally, fill in some gaps, welcome her back on my behalf, no recriminations required. As is often the case, one view is that life is as fucked up as ground chuck and not worth fooling with. But there's another view available to most of us even without becoming a Buddhist: that with an adjustment or two (Sally moving home to me, for instance), life could perhaps be fine again. No need for a miracle cancer cure. No need for Ann Dykstra to vaporize off the earth. No need for Clarissa to marry a former-NFL-great-become-pediatric-oncologist. No need for Paul to dedicate himself to scaling corporate Hallmark (new wardrobe concepts, a computerized prosthesis for his sugar pie). I can't say if this view is the soul of acceptance. But i⁻ all important ways, it is the Next Level for me and I am in it and still taking breath regularly.

Mike and I trek stonily down toward the bay's ragged edge. He, it seems, has a proposition for me. The not-good outcome of the Bagosh deal, he believes, only underscores the wisdom and importance of his plan, as well as the "time being right" for me. There's a bravura opportunity for "everybody," should I take him seriously, which I do. I'm always more at home with chance and transition than with the steady course, since the steady course leads quickly, I've found, to the rim of the earth.

The Bagoshes, not surprisingly, couldn't get away from us fast enough. Bagosh emerged uninjured from his ordeal—a small tear in his linens, a scuffed wrist (no chance of a bite), his hair disfigured. But the sight of the fleeing fox incited the big poodle, Crackers, to a primordial in-car carnivore rage, so that the kids got deep scratches, broke their computer games and eventually had to pile out on the street, letting Crackers give pursuit out of sight. (He came back on his own.) Mrs. Bagosh, if that's who the Madonna-faced woman was, didn't leave the front seat, never lowered her window, did nothing more than say nothing to anyone, including her husband, a silence lasting up to Ocean Avenue, I suspected, but no longer.

Bagosh himself couldn't have been nicer to me or to Mike. Mike couldn't have been nicer. And neither could I, since I was responsible for everything. Bagosh said he would "definitely" buy the house on Monday. He and his family, however, had Thanksgiving reservations in Cape May that night, planned to travel up to Bivalve to see the snow geese wintering ground, then on to

Greenwich, Hancocks Bridge and around to the Walt Whitman house in Camden before driving home weary but happy on Sunday, back to Buffalo, where there's now ten feet of snow. He'd be calling. The story made him happy to tell. And even though Mike knew Bagosh had at that moment a choker wad of greenbacks in his shorts pocket and could've counted out big bills while I executed a quit-claim deed on my Suburban hood, he seemed jolly about money he would never see. He actually took off his sports-car cap, revealed his bristly dome, rubbed his scalp and joked with Bagosh about what a dog's breakfast the Bills were making of the regular season, but that with luck a new O.J. would come along in the draft—a possibility that made them both laugh like Polacks. They are both Americans and acted like nothing else.

When the Bagoshes were all loaded in and maneuvering the big Lincoln around on Timbuktu, Mike stood beside me, hands thrust in his sweater pockets. "Wrong views result in a lack of protection, with no place to take refuge," he announced solemnly. I took this to mean I'd fucked up, but it didn't matter, because he had more significant things in mind.

"I loused this up," I said. "I apologize."

"It's good to *almost* sell a house," he said, already upbeat. The Bagosh children were waving at us from inside their warm, plush car (unquestionably at the command of their father). The little girl—wispy, sloe-eyed, with a decorative red dot on her forehead—held up Crackers' paw so he could wave, too. Mike and I both waved and smiled our good-byes to dog, money and all as the Lincoln, its left taillight blinking at the intersection, rumbled out of sight forever.

"I'd rather have their money than their friendship," I said. I noticed that I'd ripped my 501s somewhere in the house. My second fall of the day, third in two days. A general slippage. "Did he say what he thought he wanted the house for?"

"He didn't know," Mike said. "The idea just appealed to him. It's why I didn't want him to go inside." He looked at me to say I should've known that, then smiled a thin, indicting smile meant not to be condescending.

"I'm an essentialist in things," I said. "I believe humans buy houses to live in them, or so other people will."

Mike didn't attempt a reply, just looked up at the frosted clouds quickly forming. I cast a speculative eye up at the unsold green house, raised and allowing the glimpse of fenced back yards on Bimini Street. Possibly Thanksgiving wasn't really a great day to sell a house. On a day to summon one's blessings and try to believe in them, it might be common sense not to risk what you're sure you have.

*L*ast night's storm has widened the bay's perimeter and shoved water up onto Bay Drive, where it exudes swampy-sweet odors of challenged septics. Yellow fluff rides in the weeds where the black-billed swans have foraged. This part of the bay shore has remained undeveloped due to seventies-era open-space ordinances mandating jungle gyms, slides and merry-go-rounds for younger, child-bearing families in the neighborhood. These apparatuses are here but now disused and grown dilapidated on the skimpy beach. A billboard announcing WE CAN DO IT IF WE

TRY has been erected on the bay's sandy-muddy shore. I'm not sure what this message means. Possibly save the bay. Or possibly that condos, apartments and shops will soon be here where there's now a pleasant vista across the water, and that the families with kids will have to do their own math or else take a flying fuck at a rolling doughnut.

The two swans have moved off among the Yacht Club buoys. Bits of white Styrofoam, yellow burger wrappers and a faded red beach ball have washed in among the weeds with last night's blow. A gentleman is working alone on his black-hulled thirty-footer, readying it for winter storage. His white-helmeted kid plays with a cat on the dock plankings. Thanksgiving now and here feels evasive, the day at pains to seem festive. It's cold and damp. The usual band of bad air along the far, cluttered Toms River horizon has been washed away in the night. I have noted in our walk down that I am not keen to walk as fast as Mike, whose little green loafers step out lively as he talks in his businessy voice. I'm hoping not to forget his name in mid-announcement of his developer plans. I want to be upbeat and comradely—even if I don't feel that way. We can, after all, always set aside our real feelings—which usually don't amount to a hill of beans anyway, and may not even be genuine—and let ourselves be spontaneous and bounteous with fast-flowing vigor, just as when we're at our certifiable best. This is the part of acceptance I welcome, since it has down-the-line consolations.

On our walk down, Mike has said matter-of-factly that the last two nights have been a "great sufferance" to him, that he dislikes dilemmas (the middle way should preclude them), hates causing me "uncertainty," is uncomfortable with ambition (though he's been practicing it for a coon's age), but has had to concede these "pressures" are a part of modern life (here in America, apparently not in Tibet) and there's no escaping them (unless of course you can get stinking rich, after which you have no real problems). I was curious if he was fingering a pack of Marlboros in his sweater pocket and would've preferred to be puffing away Dick Widmark-style as he spieled all this out to me.

I've begun to enjoy the lake-like bay, the clanking halyards of the remaining Yacht Club boats, the rain-cleared vista across to the populous mainland, even the distant sight of the newer homes down the shore, from the go-go nineties. There's nothing wrong with development if the right people do the developing. At the gritty water's edge, with the wind huskier, I can see that the WE CAN DO IT billboard has a tiny Domus Isle Realty logo at its bottom corner, an artist's conception of a distant desert atoll with a lone red palm silhouetted. Unfortunately, though maybe only in my view, the desert-island motif calls to mind Eniwetok, not some South Sea snug-away where you'd like to buy or build your dream house, but in any case has nothing at all to do with Sea-Clift, New Jersey. I've met the owners, two former sports-TV execs from Gotham, a husband and wife team, and by most accounts, they're perfectly nice and probably honest.

Farther down Bay Drive, where it approaches the first of the newer nineties homes, a two-person survey crew has set up—a man with a tall zebra stake and a girl bent over a svelte-looking digital transit on a tripod. Something's already afoot, out ahead of public approval and opinion. These two are working where a sign designates CABLE CROSSING. I can make out the tiny red digitalized numerals in the transit box, glowing at me each time the young surveyor girl stands up to take a sight line.

There's absolutely no reason to drag out Mike's epic new-vistas announcement and spend all day out here where it's cold and gusty. I'm ready to get on board, whatever it is. I regret our last collaboration hasn't been a money-maker. Averages of showings-to-sales run 12 percent, and we came close on an unpromising day. I want to get home in case Sally hasn't called. But because Mike's a Buddhist, he can only proceed the way he wants to proceed and not the way anybody else does, which means he often has to be humored.

In my rising spirit, I take a cold seat on the low barn-red kids' merry-go-round and give it a rounding push with my toe, so that Mike has to come where I am to speak his piece.

"So're we gonna jump into the McMansion business with our new pecorino *cumpari*?" I say, and give another spin around. The wrecked old contraption squalls with a metal-on-metal *skweeeee-er* that unfortunately nullifies my spirited opening. I'm succeeding in feeling munificent, but can't be sure how long it'll last.

"Tom's a real good guy," Mike says gravely.

I can't hear that well as the merry-go-round takes my gaze past the surveyors, across the bay, past the nineties housing, then back to Mike, who's stationed himself legs apart, arms folded like an umpire. His brow's furrowed and he looks frustrated that I won't be still.

"Yep, yep, yep," I say. "He seemed pretty solid—for a bozo

developer." Benivalle, however, also once knew my precious son Ralph—whose death I have now accepted—and thus occupies a special place in my heart's history book. But I don't want to piss Mike off after I've queered the Bagosh deal like an amateur, so I stop the merry-go-round in front of him and offer up a general smile of business forgiveness for quitting on me when I'm not feeling my best.

"I think now's the right time to make a change," Mike says, seeming to widen his eyes to indicate resolution, his pupils large behind his glasses. "I think it's time to get serious about real estate, Frank. Bush is going to win Florida, I'm sure. We'll see a turn-around by fiscal '01." I don't know why Mike has to sear his little self-important gaze into my brain just to tell me what he's going to do.

"You could be right." I try to look serious back. I'd like to take another spin on the old go-round, but my ass is frozen on the boards and what I need to do is stand up. Only then I'd tower over Mike and ruin his little valedictory. I just want him to get on with it. I've got places to go, telephone calls to answer, children to be driven crazy by.

"People need to stay the course, Frank," he says. "If it isn't broken, don't break it, you know. Stick with old-fashioned competence. Thanksgiving's a good time for this." Mike uncorks a giant happy-Asian smile, as if I'd just said something I haven't said. He's, of course, kidnapping Thanksgiving for his own selfish commercial lusts, the same as Filene's. "I've got a new person in my life," Mike says.

"A new what?" I suspected it.

"A new lady friend." He rises fractionally on the soles of his shoes. "You'll like her."

"What about your wife?" And your two kids at their laptops? Don't they get to make the transition, too? What about the soulful, clear-sighted immigrant life that delivered you to me? And old-fashioned competence not breaking what isn't broken? "I thought you two were reconciling."

"No." Mike tries to look tragic, but not too. He doesn't want to go where what he's said gets all blurred up with what he means. A true Republican.

But it's okay with me. I don't want to go there either.

"Love-based attachments," Mike says indistinctly enough that I don't hear the next thing he says—lost in the breeze—something about Sheela and the kids in the Amboys, the discarded part of his history the business biographers will gloss over in the cover stories once he and Benivalle break through to developer's paradise: "Little Big Man: Tiny Tibetan Talks Turkey to Tantalize Trenders, Trenton to Tenafly." But who could a new squeeze be—suitable for a forty-something Himalayan in the lower echelons of the realty trade? And in New Jersey? An arranged union, like Bagosh, with a Filipina daughter grown too long in the tooth for her own kind? A monied Paraguayan military widow seeking a young "protégé"? A Tibetan teen flown in like a pizza, on a pledge he'll care for her always? I wonder what the Dalai Lama says in *The Road to the Open Heart* about monogamy. Probably not much, given his own curriculum vitae.

"So, is that all the news that's fit to tell?" From my cold merry-go-round, I can address Mike at eye-level. His plaid cap has drifted down an inch and off to the side, so he looks once again like a pint-size mobster.

"No. I want to buy you out." His now invisible eyes go grim as death. Then again his mouth cracks a big smile, as if what he's just said was absolutely hilarious. Which it isn't.

My own mouth opens to speak, but no words are ready.

"I've tamed myself," Mike says, jubilant. A lone passing duck quacks one quack high in the misty sky, as if all the creatures agree, yes, he's tamed himself.

"From what?" I manage. "I didn't know you needed taming. I thought you were rounding up your courage."

"They're the same." He, as usual, gets instantly giddy at talk like this—word riddles. "There's some unhappiness never to be as rich as J. Paul Getty." Another of Mike's earthly deities. "Filthy rich," he adds buoyantly. "But I can make money, too. Helping people this way can make money."

He means helping them out of their cash. There's a reason these people don't get cancer in their countries. And there's a reason we do. We make things too complicated.

"I believe you want to think about this proposal," he says. His tough little hands are clasped priest-like. He likes being the presenter of a proposal. *Believe, want, think*—these are words used in new ways.

"I don't want to sell you my business," I say. "I like my business. You go develop McMansions for proctologists."

"Yes," he says, meaning no. "But if I make a good business proposal and pay you a lot of money, you can transfer ownership, and everything will stay the same."

"Everything's already the same. It ain't broke. Due to old-fashioned competence. Mine."

"I knew you'd say this," Mike says happily. For the first time since I've known him, he's talking like the departed Mr. Bagosh, with whom he shares, after all, a stronger regional bond than he shares with me. "I think we should agree, though. I've thought about this a great deal. It'll give you time to travel."

Travel is code for my compromised health status, which Mike is officially sensitive to, and means in Mike's enlightened view—Buddhist crappolio—that I "need" to ready myself for the final conjugation by taking a voyage on the *Queen Mary* or the *Love Boat*. He's "helping" me, in other words, by helping me out of business. "I've got time to travel," I say. "Why don't we not talk about this anymore. Okay?" I attempt a faint smile that feels unwelcome to my cold cheeks. Munificence is gone. I don't like being strong-armed or felt sorry for.

"Yes! Okay!" Mike exults. "This is just what I thought. I'm satisfied." It's all about him, his confidence level, his satisfaction. I'm as good as out of work, a cat in need of herding.

"Me, too. Good. But I'm not going to sell you Realty-Wise." I give my sore knees a try at prizing me up off the butt-froze planks. I hold onto the curved hang-on bar that wants to glide away and spill me over. Mike semi-casually secures a light grip on my sweat-shirt sleeve. But I'm up and feel fine. The bay breeze cools my neck. My eyes feel like they've both just freshly opened all the way. Down Bay Drive, the boy-girl surveyors are walking side-by-side toward a yellow pickup parked farther along the curve, where houses are. One holds the collapsed tripod, the other the striped pole.

"So, you're not going into business with what's his name?" I say gruffly.

Mike dusts his little hands together as if dirt was on them. He's pretending we didn't have the conversation we just had, and that he feels good about something else. It's possible he'll never bring this subject up again. Intention is the same as action to these guys. "No," he says, pseudo-sadly.

"That's probably smart. I didn't want to say that before."

"I think so." He gives his little Black Watch cap a straightening as we begin walking back to the cars.

Mike is pleased by my rebuff of his unfriendly takeover try. He knows I know it's nothing more than what I did with old man Barber Featherstone and how the world always works. Plus, he's smart. He knows he's succumbed to the little leap into the normal limbo of life. That he's facing down the big fear of "Is this it?" by agreeing "Yes, this *is*." He also knows I might sell him Realty-Wise after all, possibly even very soon, and that he can then start video-taping virtual tours, building Web-based rental connections, adding a new Arabic-speaking female associate, change the company name to Own It . . . TODAY!.com, subscribe to recondite business studies from Michigan State and concentrate more on lifestyle purchasing than essentialist residential clientele. In two to twelve years, when he'll be my age now, he'll be farting through silk. One hardly knows how or when or by what subtle mechanics the old values give way to new. It just happens.

*T*ommy Benivalle taught me some invaluable—" Mike's maundering on as we trudge at my slower pace back up Timbuktu. Ahead, his new-values silver Infiniti and my broke-window, old-values, essentialist Suburban sit end to end in front of 118, perched sturdily up on its girders. "Only a fool—" Mike rattles on. I'm not interested. I was his mentor and am now his adversary—which probably mean the same thing, too. I admire him but don't particularly like him today, or the fresh legions he commands. How much life do I have to accept? Does it all come in one day?

"So, are you putting on a big holiday feed bag with your new squeeze?" I say this just to be rude. We stand mid-street, looking exactly like what we are—a pair of realtors. Mike's eyes move toward my Suburban. The duct-taped back window may be a worrisome sign that he needs to hurry up with his business proposal, get the deal nailed down before the mental-health boys show up. There *was* the puzzling scene at the August on Tuesday. I could be discovered tomorrow sitting silently in the office, "just thinking." He could be forced to negotiate with Paul.

"She's got her big place up in Spring Lake. The kids come. They're Jewish. It's a big scene." Mike nods a sage "not my kind of thing" nod. He's gone back to talking like a Jerseyite.

But I knew it! A dowager, a late-model divorcée like Marguerite. She's adopted "little Mike-a-la," who's giving her "investment counsel" over and above his unspecified services of a consensual nature. The kids, Jake, a Columbia professor, Ben, a fabric artist on Vinalhaven, and one daughter, Rachel, who lives alone in Montecito and can't seem to get started. They all keep the zany parent on a frugal budget so she can't ruin their retirements with her funny enthusiasms. Mike's "interesting," a minority, resembles the Dalai Lama—plus, who cares, if he makes "Gram" happy and keeps her away from ballroom dancing. At least he's not a Mexican.

"Do they let you carve the turkey and serve?" I don't try to suppress a smirk, which he hates but won't show. He knows what he's up to and doesn't care if I know. It's business, not a love-based attachment.

"I'll just drop by late," he says, and frowns, not at me, but at how he'll pass the night. He is, as we all are, taking his solaces as they come. "I have the business proposal already written up." He produces a white Realty-Wise business envelope from his sweater pocket, rolled up with the listing sheets for 118. This he proffers like a summons, bowing slightly. I'm not sure Tibetans even bow. It may be something he picked up. Though I, the defendant, accept it and bow back (which I can't seem to prevent myself from doing) before folding it and stuffing it in my Levi's back pocket like junk mail.

"I'll read this someday. Not today."

"That's splendid." He is elated again. It pleases him to conduct business in the street, in the elements, far from the ancestral cradle. To Mike, this is a sign of progress: the old lessons from the life left behind still viable here in New Jersey.

"Am I going to see you again?" My hand's on my cold door

handle. "I don't know what you're doing. I thought you were moving your base of operations over to Mullica Road. You're a mystery wrapped in a small enigma."

"Oh, no." His smile—all intersecting angles—radiates behind his specs. He's risen onto his little toes again, Horatio Alger-style. "I work for you. Until you work for me. Everything's the same. I love you. I keep you in my prayers."

I'm fearful he may hug, kiss, high-five or double-hander me. Two male hugs in one morning is a lot. Men don't have to do that all the time, even though it doesn't mean we're not sensitive. I open the car door and stiffly get myself inside before the inescapable happens. I shut the door and lock it. Mike's left standing out on Timbuktu in his black sweater with its fake-fur collar and his little Black Watch cap. He's speaking something. I can hear the buzz of his voice, but not the sense, through the window. I don't care what he's saying. It's not about me. I get the motor started and begin to mouth words he'll "understand" through the window glass. "Abba-dabba, dabba-dabba, dabba-dabba-dabba, dabba-dabba," I say, then smile, wave, bow in my car seat. He says something back and looks triumphant. He gives me the thumbs-up sign and nods his head proudly. "Abba dabba, dabba, dabba-dabba," I say back and smile. He nods his head again, then steps back, effects a small wave, laughs heartily. And that is it. I'm off.

16

A dual sensation—pleasure and enthusiasm—unexpectedly skirls through my middle by the time I reach Ocean Avenue; and alloyed with it is another bracing sensation, from my arms down to my fists, of complete readiness to "take hold." I actually envision these words—*take hold*—in watery letters like an old eight-ball fortune. And there's also, simultaneously, a seemingly opposite feeling of *release*—from something. Sometimes we know complex pressures are building and roiling, and can finger exactly what they're about—a gloomy doctor visit, a big court case before a mean-spirited judge, an IRS audit we wish to God wasn't happening. And other times, we have to plumb the depths, like seeking a warm seam in a cold pond. Only, this time it's easy. Full, pleasurable release and bold, invigorating authority both exude from the sudden, simple prospect of handing over the Realty-Wise reins to Mike Mahoney.

At first blush, of course, it's a heresy. Except, life on the Next Level is only what you invent. And as Mike pointed out two days ago (and I scoffed at), residential real estate's all about what somebody invented. I could sign the papers right now and be on top of the world. Even if it's the worst idea in the world and leaves me rudderless, with yawning angst-filled days during which I never get out of my pj's, it still feels like the right invention now. And now is where I am. (This feels, of course, like a Permanent Period resurrection. But if it is, I don't care.)

There's no sign of returning 5-K runners here at the corner, or much mid-day traffic, not even post-race street litter—only the starting line, whitewashed across the north-bound side of the avenue. A black man—the docent at Our Lady—is just now carting Father Ray's aluminum blessing ladder across the lawn to an arched side doorway. He leans the ladder against the stucco exterior, steps in the door, closes it behind him and does not come out again.

My instinct now is to turn right and get myself home—a better second act with my son, the hoped-for return of my daughter, the crucial call from Sally. The resumption of the day's best, if unlikely, hopes for itself.

Only another powerful urging directs me not to turn right, but to cross the median and go left, and north, up the peninsula toward Ortley Beach. I know what I'm up to here. I'm empowered by the dual sense of release and take hold, which don't come often and almost never together, and so must be heeded as if ordained by God.

There are—I admit this at risk to myself, though all men know it's true and all women know men think it—there *are* ideal women in the world. Sally said it about me in her letter—which means the same is true for how women calculate men. In my view, there's at least one ideal person for all of us, and probably several. For men, these are the women who make you feel especially smart, that you're uniquely handsome in a way you yourself always believed you were, who bring out the best in you and, by some generosity or need in themselves, cause *you* to feel generous, clever, intuitive as hell about all sorts of things and successful in the world exactly the way you'd like to be. Pity the man who marries such a woman, since she'll eventually drive him crazy with undeserved approval and excessive, unwanted validations. Not that I'd know, having married two "challenger" types, who may have loved me but never looked upon me with less than a seasoned eye, and whose basic watchwords to friend and foe alike were, "Well, let's just see about that. I'm not so sure." In any case, they both left me flat as a flounder—though Sally may be coming back at this moment.

These ideal women can actually *make* you be smarter than you are, but are finally only suitable for fleeting escapades, for profound and long-running flirtations never acted on, for unexpected driving trips to Boston or after-hours cocktails at shadowy red-booth steak houses like the one Wade Arsenault tried to lure me to yesterday with his Texas-bred, ball-crusher, definitely *not* ideal daughter, Vicki/Ricki, who anybody'd be smart to steer wide of, but who I once unaccountably wanted to marry. These women are also meant for sweetly intended, affectionate one-nighters (two at the max), after which you both manage to stay friends, conduct yourselves even better than before, possibly even "enjoy" each other a time or two every six months or six years, but never consider getting serious about, since everybody knows that serious ruins everything. Marguerite might've qualified, but wasn't truly ideal.

Perfect for *affairs* is what these women are. They almost always know it (even if they're married). They realize that given the kind of man they find attractive—usually ruminant loners with minimal but quite specific needs—to strive for anything more lasting would mean they'd soon be miserable and hoping to get things over with fast, and so are happy for the escapade and the cocktails and the rib-eye and the one-nighter where everything works out friendly, and then pretty quick to get back in their own beds again, which is where they (and many others) are happiest.

"Enlightened" thought by headshrinkers with their own rich broth of problems has twisted these normal human pleasures and delights into shabby, shameful perversions and boundary violations needing to be drummed out of the species because someone's always seen as the loser-victim and someone's definition of wholesome and nurturing doesn't always get validated. But we all know that's wrong, whether we have the spirit to admit it or don't. Women are usually full participants in everything they do (including heading off to Mull), and I'm ready to say that when it comes to wholesome, nurturing and long-lasting, a frank, good-hearted roll in the alfalfa, or something close to it, with an enthusiastic and willing female is about as nurturing and wholesome as I can imagine. And if it doesn't last a lifetime, what (pray tell me) does, except marriages where both parties are screaming inside to let light in but can't figure out how to.

The old release-and-take-hold has worked its quickening magic on me and routed me north toward Neptune's Daily Catch Bistro and (I hope) to Bernice Podmanicsky, who may be my savior for the day just when a savior's needed. Sally's call offers some things, but pointedly not others. And she herself authorized a female companion for the day. I'd be a fool to pass on the opportunity, should there be one.

Bernice Podmanicsky, who's one of the wait-staff at Neptune's, is my candidate for the aforementioned ideal woman. A lanky, full-lipped, wide-smiling brunette with big feet, a hint of dark facial hair, but oddly delicate hands with shiny pink nails, a proportionate bosom, solid posterior and runway-model ankles (always my weakness once the butt's accounted for), Bernice would be considered pretty by some standards, though not by all: mouth too big (fine with me); hair taking root a sixteenth of an inch too far down the forehead (ditto); augmented eyebrows (neutral); libidinous chin dimple when she smiles, which is often; fortyish age bracket (I prefer women with adult experience). Altogether, hard not to like. I've known Bernice three years, ever since her long-standing love relationship in Burlington, Vermont, blew a tire and she came down to live in Normandy Beach with her sister Myrna, who's a Mary Kay franchisee. Waitressing was what she'd always done since college at Stevens Point, where she took art (waitressing leaves time for drawing). She is a reader of serious novels and even abstruse philosophical texts, owing to her father, who was a high school guidance counselor in Fond du Lac, and her mother, who's in her seventies and a serious painter in the style of Georgia O'Keeffe.

I actually like Bernice immensely, though there hasn't been any but the most casual contact between us over the course of the three years. When Sally was my regular dinner companion, Bernice was gregarious and jokey and impudently friendly to both of us. "Oh, you two again. Somebody's gonna get the wrong

idea about you. . . . And I guess you'll have the bluefish rare."
But when Sally left, and I was often alone at a window table with
a gin drink, Bernice was more candid and curious and personal
and (on occasion) clearly flirtatious—which I was happy about.
But mostly she was interested and corroborative and even spontaneously complimentary. "I think it's odd but completely understandable that a man with your background—writing short stories
and writing sports and a good education—would be happy selling
houses in New Jersey. That just makes sense to me." Or "I like
it, Frank, that you always order bluefish and pretty much dress
the same way every time you come in here. It means you're sure
about the little things, so you can leave yourself open for the
big ones." She smiled so as to show her provocative dimple.

I told her about my Sponsoring activities and she said I
seemed, to her experience, unusually kind and sensitive to others'
needs. Once she even said, "I bet you've got a big lineup at your
door, handsome, now that you're single again." (I've heard her
call other men "handsome" and could care less.) I decided *not*
to tell her about the titanium BBs situation, for fear she'd feel
sorry for me—I couldn't see a use for pathos—but also because
talking about the BBs can convince me I've lost the wherewithal
even if I still have the wherefore.

Several times, I've stayed late at the Bistro, feeling better
about myself and also about Bernice. Sometimes her shift would
end and she'd come out from the kitchen in a pea jacket over
her pink waitress dress and walk over and say, "So, Franklin"—
not my name—"happy trails to you." But then she'd sit and
we'd talk, during which occasions I'd become the funniest,

cleverest, the wisest, the most instructive, the most complex, enigmatic and strangely attractive of all men, but also the best, most attentive listener-back that anybody on earth had ever heard of. I'd quote Emerson and Rochefoucauld and Eliot and Einstein, remember incisive, insightful but obscure historical facts that perfectly fitted into our discussions but that I never remembered talking about to anyone else, all the while dredging up show-tune lyrics and Bud & Lou gags and statistics about everything from housing starts in Bergen County to how many salmon pass through the fish ladder up at Bellows Falls in a typical twenty-four-hour period during the spring run. I became, in other words, an ideal man, a man I myself was crazy about and in love with and anybody else would be, too. All because— though I never specifically said so to her—Bernice was herself an ideal woman. Not ideal *per se*, but ideal *per diem*, the only place ideal really makes much difference. I realize as I say all this that my "Bernice experience" and my current willingness to rekindle it represents another small skirmish into the Permanent Period and away from the strict confines of the Next Level. Sometimes, though, you have to seek help where you know you can find it.

On late after-shift evenings, I sometimes would walk outside the Bistro with Bernice onto the warm beach-town sidewalk, when the air was cooling and things were buzzing last summer and, later on, after my procedure, and when most visitors had gone home in September. We'd stand at the curb or walk, not holding hands or anything like that, down to the beach and talk about global warming or Americans' inexplicable prejudice against the French or President Clinton's sadly missed opportunities and the losses that won't ever be recovered. I always had, when I was with Bernice, unusual takes on things, historical perspectives I didn't even know I possessed, bits of memorized speeches and testimony I'd heard on Public Radio that somehow came back to me in detail and that made me seem as savvy as a diplomat and wise as an oracle, with total recall and flawless sense of context, all of it with a winning ability to make fun of myself, not be stuffy or world-weary, but then at a moment's notice to be completely ready to change the subject to something she was interested in, or something else I knew more about than anybody in the world.

In all of this rather ordinary time together, Bernice had persistently positive things to say about me: that I was young for my age (without knowing my age, which I guessed she guessed was forty-five), that I led an interesting life now and had a damn good one in front of me, that I was "strangely intense" and intuitive and probably was a handful, but not really a type-A personality, which she knew she didn't like.

I said about her all the good things that I thought: that she was "a major looker," that her independent "Fighting Bob" La Follette instincts were precisely what this country needed, that I'd love to see her "work" and had a hunch it would wow me and I'd be drawn to it, implying but not actually saying that *she* wowed me and I was drawn to her (which was sort of true).

Once, Bernice asked me if I'd like to take a drive and smoke some reefer (I declined). And once she said she'd finished a "big nude" just that day and would be interested to know what a guy with my heightened sensibilities and intuition would think about it, since it was "pretty abstract" (I assumed it was a self-portrait and burned to see it). But I declined that, too. I understood that how we felt, standing out on the curb or at the edge of the beach, where the street came to an end and the twinkling shank of the warm evening opened out like a pathway of stars to where the old ferris wheel turned like a bracelet of jewels down at the Sea-Clift Fun Pier—I understood that how we felt was good and might conceivably get better if we had a Sambuca or two and a couple of bong hits at her place and took a look at her big nude. But then pretty quickly who we really were would assert itself, and it wouldn't feel good for long and we'd end up looking back at our moment on the curb, before anything happened, with slightly painful nostalgia—the way emigrants are said to feel when they leave home, thrilled to set sail for the new land, where life promises riches but where hardships await, and in the end old concerns are only transported to a new venue, where they (we) go back to worrying the same as before. When you're young, like my daughter, Clarissa, and maybe even my son, you don't think like that. You think that all it takes is to get free of one box and into a bigger one out in the mainstream. Change the water in your bowl and you become a different fish. But that's not so. No siree, Bob, not a bit. It's also true that because of the fiery BBs in my prostate, and despite early-morning and even occasionally late-night erectile events giving positive testimony, I wasn't sure of my performance ratings under new pressures and definitely didn't want to face another failure when so few things seemed to be going my way.

Now, though, I believe is the time—if ever one was ordained—for Bernice and me to lash our tiny boats together, at least for the day, and set sail a ways toward sunset. Nothing permanent, nothing that even needs to last past dark, nothing specifically venereal or proto-conjugal (unless that just happens), but still an occasion, an eleventh-hour turn toward the unexpected—the very thing that can happen in life to let us know we're human, and that could even prove I'm the handful Bernice always knew I'd be and perhaps still am. All this, of course, if it seems like a good idea to her.

Neptune's Daily Catch Bistro, I already know from our local Shore weekly, is serving its twenty-dollar turkey 'n trimmings buffet to all Ortley Beach seniors, eleven to two. Bernice—because she casually told me—is without companionship today and only working to give herself something to do, then heading home with a jug of Chablis to "watch the Vikes and Dallas at 4:05," before turning in early. My guess is if I cruise in right at one, almost now, and tell her I'm taking her away for a holiday feast, she'll beg off with the boss, leave her apron on the doorknob, see the whole idea as a complete blast that I've had planned for weeks, feel secretly flattered and relieved and sure she's had me pegged right and that I'm fuller of surprises than she imagined and that all her appreciation of me these years wasn't wrong or wasted. In other words, she'll recognize that I recognize *her* as the ideal woman, and that even if she's home in time for the nightly news, she'll have gotten more than she bargained for—which is all that usually counts with humans.

And as an added inducement, bringing Bernice Podmanicsky

for Thanksgiving dinner will drive my kids crazy. Worse than if I'd brought home a Finnish midget from the circus, a six-foot-eight fag comb-out assistant from Kurl Up 'n Dye in Lavallette, or a truckload of talking parrots that sing Christmas carols *a cappella*. It'll drive them—Paul especially—into paralyzed, abashed and scalding, renunciating silence, which is what I may now require of my Thanksgiving festivity. Loathing will run at warp speed. Sinister "What's happened to *him*?" grimaces will radar between siblings who already don't like each other. Your kids may be the hapless victims of divorce and spend their lives "working out" their "issues" on everybody in sight, but they damn straight don't want you to have any issues, or for *their* boats to get rocked while they're doing their sanctified "work." They want instead for you to provide them a stable environment for their miseries (they might as well *be* adopted). Except my view is that if kids are happy to present us aging parents with their own improbabilities, why not return the favor? A diverse table of Paul, Jill, Clarissa, Thom, Bernice and myself seems more or less perfect. As is often the case, given time, "things" come into better focus.

And yet. Best case? It could bring out the unforeseeable best in everybody and cause Thanksgiving to blossom into the extended-family, come-one-come-all good fellowship the Pilgrims might (for a millisecond) have thought they were ringing in by inviting the baffled, mostly starved Indians to their table. Paul's time capsule could turn out to be the rallying projectile he may—or may not—want it to be. Clarissa could send Thom away two-thirds through the bulgur course, and we could all laugh like chimps at what a sorry sack he was. Bernice could do her full repertoire of America's Dairyland imitations. We might even ask the Feensters in and watch them combust. I could be made happy by any or all or none of these, and the day could end no worse than it began. Though I'd still like Bernice Podmanicsky with me, just as my personal *friend* against the difficulties that are likely waiting. She would think it was all—whatever it was—a riot or a trip or awesome, and be agreeable when we excused ourselves from the table to take a sunset stroll on the beach, where we could both make ourselves feel ideal all over again, after which I could take her home for the second half of the Vikes' game—which I might stay for. I'd tell Sally all about it later and be certain she wouldn't care.

C'entral Boulevard enters Ortley Beach from Seaside Heights without fanfare—both being Route 35—the same no-skyline weather-beaten townscape of closed sub shops, blue Slurpee stands, tropical fish outlets and metal-detector rentals, where I'm thinking the 5-K runners must have now come and gone, since I see none of them. In the election three weeks ago— the life-threatening part of which is still unsettled in the Florida court—Ortley Beach gave its own voters their chance to ratify a non-binding "opinion" by the Boro attorney that the town could secede from New Jersey and join a new entity called "South Jersey." But like our naming-rights initiative, this was hooted down by Republicans as being fiscal suicide, not to mention civically odd and bad for business. Sea-Clift—nearer the end of

Barnegat Neck, and farther south—would've ended up marooned in "Old Jersey," tolls could've been exacted just for the privilege of leaving town, while Ortley would have had a different governor and a state bird. Municipal conflict would've erupted, had cooler heads not prevailed. Though even now I see a few inflaming SECESSION OR DIE stickers still plastered on stop signs and a few juice-shop windows. It's always been a strange place here, though you can't tell by looking.

What I see as I approach the Neptune's Daily Catch doesn't make my heart hopeful. No cars are parked in front. The blue neon FISH sign is turned off. As I pull to the curb, inside appears empty. Grainy daylight falls in through the big windows, turning the interior dishwater gray. Chairs are upside down on tabletops. Next door, the Women of Substance second-hand shop is closed. The Parallel Universe video arcade is open three doors down, but only a thin bald man's standing in the door alone, reading a magazine. Four men in khaki clothing and heavy corduroy jackets wait at the corner under the Garden State Parkway sign, smoking cigarettes and drinking coffee from the Wawa across Central. Mexicans, these are. Illegals—unlike my Hondurans—hoping to be picked up for a job across the bridge, unaware today's a holiday. They eye me and laugh as if I'm the cops and they're invisible.

The thought, however, that I may be wrong and Bernice is inside at a back table having an Irish coffee alone, awaiting opening time, makes me get out and peer through the plate-glass window. Arnie Sikma, the owner, is an old Reed College SDSer who's evolved into a community-activist, small-business booster, and has stuck various groups' advertising stickers on his front window beside the door. ORTLEY, AN UNUSUAL NAME FOR THE USUAL PLACE. WE ROOT FOR THE PHILLIES. SUPPORT OUR TROOPS (from Gulf War days). PROTECT RAPTORS, NOT RAPISTS. THIS, TOO, SHALL PASS—JERSEY SHORE NEPHROLOGY CLINIC. PEOPLE HAVE TO DIE . . . SOMEWHERE (a hospice in Point Pleasant).

But no Bernice when I peer in between my cupped hands. Or anyone. Arnie's left the Christmas Muzak on outside—"Good King Wenceslas" sung by a choir. "Yon-der pea-sant, who is he, where and what his dwel-ling—" No one out in the cold hears it but me and the Mexicans.

Though a hand-written note scotch-taped to the door announces that, "We will be closed Thanksgiving Day due to a loss in our family. God Bless You All. The Mgt."—naturally a sign that alarms me. Since does it mean *family* family (Arnie's of Dutch extraction in Hudson, New York, up-river—a distant relation of the original patroons)? Or does it mean extended family? The Neptune's Daily Catch Bistro "family" of trusted employees. Does it mean Bernice, heretofore scheduled to work the buffet? Though wouldn't it mention her name—like the Van Tuyll daughter Ann told me about two nights ago? "Our trusted and beloved Miss B—"

A hot sizzling sensation spreads up my cold neck, then spreads down again. How can I find out? I once called *information* to learn if Bernice was listed, in case I someday decided to call her and needed to be made to feel like my best self in return for a movie ticket to the Toms River Multiplex and a late dinner at Bump's. I found out she possessed a phone but didn't choose to list its number. Waitresses rarely do. I couldn't very well tell the operator, "Yeah, but she thinks I'm great. It's fine. I won't give the number to anybody or do anything weird." Those innocent days are behind us now.

Gusty ocean air with a strong grease smell in it pushes a white Styrofoam container along the sidewalk—the kind of container you'd carry your unfinished fried calamari home in. One of the khaki-suited Mexicans gives the container a soccer kick out into the boulevard, which inspires another, smaller Mexican to address the box with a complex series of side kicks and heel kicks that finally send it flying in the air. His associates all laugh and sing out "Ronal*dito*," which amuses the kicker, who sashays back up onto the curb and makes them all howl.

A skinny, elderly bald man in red running shorts and a blue singlet with a 5-K card on his chest—#174—glides past us up Central on bulky in-lines, arm swings propelling him like a speed skater, one hand tucked behind, his old eagle's face as serene as the breeze. He is heading home. The Mexicans all eye him with amusement.

I gaze up to the woolen sky and think of good-soul Bernice, her sweet breath, full smiling lips, dainty ankles, dense virile hair not everyone would go for and that possibly I didn't go for or else I'd know her phone number. Where is she today? Safe? Sound? Not so good? How would I find out? Call Arnie Sikma at home the minute I arrive. Ask for her number as a special favor. High up and to the north, a pale blue and optimistic fissure has opened in the undercloud. Two jet contrails, one southerly, one headed east and out to sea, have crossed there, leaving a giant and, for an instant, perfect X at 39,000 feet above where I am, in Ortley, outside a good fish place, contemplating the life of a friend. X marks my spot (and every place else that can see it). "Begin here. This is where I left it. This is where the gold is. This is—" what?

Only the most dry-mouthed Cartesian wouldn't see this as a patent signal, a communiqué from the spheres, an important box on an important form with my name on top—X'd in or X'd out, counted present or absent. You'd just need to know what the fucker means, wouldn't you? There may have been others. Two swans on the bay shore. A quick red fox in the bedroom. A letter. A call. Three boats. All can be signage. I'd thought Ralph's finality, my acceptance and succession to the Next Level and general fittedness to meet my Maker were my story, what the audience would know once my curtain closed—my, so-to-speak, character. "He made peace with things, finally, old Frank." "He was kind of a shit-bird, but he got it sorted out pretty good just before—" "He actually seemed clear-sighted, damn near saint-like toward the end there—" This happens when you have cancer, though it's not a fun happening.

Except now there's *more*? Just when you think you've been admitted to the boy-king's burial chamber and can breathe the rich, ancient captured air with somber satisfaction, you find out it's just another anteroom? That there's more that bears watching, more signs requiring interpretation, that what you thought was all, isn't? That this isn't *it*? That there's no *it*, only *is*. Hard to know if this is heartening or disheartening news to a man who, as my son says, believes in development.

The cloud fissure has now closed primly, and what was a sign—like a rainbow—is no more. Somehow I know that Bernice Podmanicsky is not the family member lost. She'd laugh to know I even worried about her. "Oh, handsome"—she'd beam at me—"I didn't know you cared. You're just such an unusual man, aren't ya? A real handful. Some lucky girl—" It's odd how our fears, the ones we didn't know we had, alter our sight line and make us see things that never were.

The Mexicans are all looking at me as if I've been carrying on a boisterous conversation with myself. Possibly it's my block-M. I should take it off and give it to them. Their faces are serious, their small grabby hands jammed in their tattered jacket pockets. Their expectancy of work is being clouded over by my suspicious starings into the Bistro and the firmament. They are religious men and on the lookout for signs of their own, one of which I may have become. Possibly I'm "touched" and am about to be drawn up into heaven by a lustrous beam of light and they (in the good version) will find true vocations at last: to tell the thing they saw and of its wonders. Is that not the final wish of all of us on earth? To testify of our witness to wonders?

But as an assurance, since I cannot ascend to heaven in front of them today, I'd still like to speak something typically First World and welcoming, put them off their guard. We are together, after all. Simple me. Simple them.

Only when I turn their way, a welcome grin gladdening my cheeks, my eyes crinkling up happy, my mind concocting a formulation in their mother tongue—"*Hola. ¿Cómo están? ¿Pasando un buen día?*"—they stiffen, set their narrow shoulders and lock their knees inside their khakis, their faces organized to say they want *nada* of me, seek no assurance, offer none. So that all I can do is freeze my grin like a crazy man caught in his craziness. They look away at the empty boulevard to search for the truck that isn't coming. For all five of us, together and apart, the moment for signs goes past.

*H*eaded home now, fully contextualized, vacant of useful longing. Bernice could've conferred a sporty insularity, made me feel my own weight less. Even un-ideal women can do this. But help's not available, which is a legitimate mode of acceptance. It just doesn't feel good.

Traffic lights are working again, candy-cane ornaments weakly lit. Commerce is flickering to life as I drive out of Seaside Park and re-enter Sea-Clift. LIQUOR has illuminated its big yellow letters at noon, and cars are flocking. The drive-thru ATM at South Shore Savings is doing a smart business, as is the adult books, Guppies to Puppies and the bottle redemption center— the former Ford dealership. The Wiggle Room has opened up, and a hefty blue New Jersey Waste snail-back is swaying into its back alley. There are even tourists outside the mini-golf/batting cage, their nonchalant gestures betraying seasonal uncertainty, their gazes skyward. The green EMS wagon rests back in its Fire Department bay, the same crew as earlier out front under the waving American flag, sharing a smoke and a joke with the two jodhpured motorcycle cops who guarded the race. The Tru-Value is holding its "Last Chance Y-2K Special" on plastic containers and gas masks. THE FUTURE WAS A BOMB, their hand-lettered sign says.

Many of the 5-K runners are here straggling home along the sidewalks and down the residential side streets, their race run, their faces relaxed, limbs loosened by honest non-cutthroat competition, their water bottles empty, their gazes turned toward what's next in the way of healthy, wholesome Thanksgiving partaking. (There's no sign of the Africans.) I still wouldn't want to be any of them. Though one scrawny red-shoed runner waves at my car as I pass—I have no idea who—someone I sold a house to or busted my ass trying, but left a good impression of the kinda guy I am. I give a honk but head on.

When I cruise past my Realty-Wise office, Mike's Infiniti sits by itself in front. The pizza place is lighted and going, though no one seems to want a pizza for Thanksgiving. Doubtless, Mike's at his desk tweaking his business plan, re-conferring with his new friend, the money bags. He may be trying the Bagosh family on his cell before they hit the Parkway after lunch. I lack the usual gusto to go have a look-see at what he's up to—which makes business itself seem far away and its hand-over a sounder idea. How, though, will I feel to "have sold" real estate and sell it no more? The romance of it could fade once the past tense takes over. Different from, "Well, yeah, I usta fly 16's up in that Bacca Valley. Pretty hairy up there." Or, "Our whole lab shared credit on the malaria cure." The only way to keep the glamour lights on in the real-estate commitment is to keep doing it. Do it till you drop dead, so you never have to look back and see the shadows. Most of the old-timers know that, which is why so many go feet first. This won't please Mike, but fuck Mike. It's my business, not his.

Ahead, beyond the old shuttered Dad 'n Lad, where the Boro of Sea-Clift originally ended because the topsoil ran out and the primeval white sand beach took up, the old Ocean Vista Cemetery, where Sea-Clift's citizens were buried back in the twenties, lies shabbily ignored and gone to weeds. The Boro officially maintains it, keeps up its New Orleans-style wrought iron fence and little arched filigree gate that opens pleasantly down a slender *allée* three-quarters of a city block toward the sea, where the ocean vista's long been blocked by grandfathered frame residences that have gone to seed themselves but can't be replaced. No one is currently at rest in Ocean Vista, not even gravestones remain. The ground—alongside the Dad 'n Lad—looks like nothing but a small-size shard of excess urban landscape awaiting assignment by developers who'll tear down the whole block of elderly structures and put up a Red Roof Inn or a UPS store—the same as happened on a grand scale in Atlantic City.

The particular reason our only town cemetery no longer has residents is that the great-great-grandchildren of Sea-Clift's first Negro pioneer, a freed slave known only as "Jonah," somehow discovered him interred plumb in the middle of the otherwise-white cemetery, and began agitating at the state level for a monument solemnizing his life and toilsome times as a "black trailblazer" back when being a trailblazer wasn't cool. Jonah's progeny turned out to be noisy, well-heeled Philadelphia and D.C. plutocrat lawyers and M.D.'s, who wanted to have their ancestor memorialized as another stop on the Coastal Heritage

Trail, with an interactive display about his life and the lives of
folk like him who valiantly diversified the Shore—a story that
was possibly not going to be all that flattering to his white
contemporaries.

Whereupon all hell broke loose. The town elders, who'd
always known about Jonah's resting place and felt fine about him
sharing it with their ancestors, did not, however, want him
"stealing" the cemetery and posthumously militating for importance he apparently hadn't claimed in life. Jonah had his rightful
place, it was felt, among other Sea-Clifters, and that was enough.
The grandchildren, however, sniffing prejudice, commenced
court proceedings and EEOC actions to have the Boro Council
sued in federal court. Everything got instantly blown out of
proportion, at which point an opportunistic burial-vault company
with European Alliance affiliations in Brick Township offered
free of charge to dig up and re-inter anybody whose family wanted
its loved one to enjoy better facilities in a new and treeless memory
park they had land for out Highway 88. Everyone—there were
only fifteen families—said sure. The town issued permits. All the
graves—except Jonah's—were lovingly opened, their sacred
contents hearsed away, until in a month's time poor old Jonah
had the cemetery all to his lonesome. Whereupon, the litigious
Philadelphians decided Jonah and his significance had been
municipally disrespected and so applied for a permit themselves
and moved him to Cherry Hill, where people apparently know
better how to treat a hero.

The town is still proprietor of the cemetery and awaits the
happy day when the Red Roof site-evaluation crew shows up

seeking a variance and a deconsecration order. For a time—two winters ago—I proposed buying the ground myself and turning it into a vernal park as a gesture of civic giving, while retaining development rights should the moment ever come. I even considered not deconsecrating it and having myself buried there—a kingdom of one. This was, of course, before my prostate issues. I'd always pondered—without a smidge of trepidation—where I'd "end up," since once you wander far from your own soil, you never know where your final resting place might be. Which is why many people don't stray off their porch or far from familiar sights and sounds. Because if you're from Hog Dooky, Alabama, you don't want to wind up dead and anonymously buried in Metuchen, New Jersey. In my case, I thought it would've saved my children the trouble of knowing what in the hell to do with "me," and just deciding to entrust my remains to some broken-down old Cap'n Mouzakis who'd "return" me to the sea from whence as a frog I came. You could say it's a general problem, however—uncertainty over where and how you want to be eternally stowed. Either it represents your last clinging to life, or else it's the final muddled equivocation about the life you've actually lived.

Not surprisingly, insider development interests on the Dollars For Doers Council saw disguised dreams of empire behind my petition and declined my cash offer for the cemetery. The "civic giving" part put them on their guard. Which was and is fine with me. Money not spent is money saved, in my economy. Though it has left as an open subject the awkward issue of my ending-up formalities. I have a will which leaves the house and

Realty-Wise to Sally and all remaining assets to the kids—not much, though they'll get plenty from their mom, including a membership in the Huron Mountain Club. But that picture's different since Sally left for Mull, and could shift again, since she could come back and Mike now wants the business. I'd even thought the three of us nuclear-family components might sit around a congenial breakfast table during the coming days and talk these sensitive matters into commonsense resolution. But that was prior to re-exposure to Paul (and Jill), and hearing of his secret dreams to be my business partner. And before Clarissa hied off to Atlantic City, leaving me with the uneasy sensation she'll return changed. In other words, events have left life and my grasp on the future in as fucked-up a shape as I can imagine them. Life alters when you get sick, no matter what I told Ann. Don't let any of these Sunny Jims tell you different.

What I don't expect to find in my driveway is activity. But activity is what I find. Next door at the Feensters', as well. Thanksgiving, in my playbook, is an indoor event acted out between kitchen and table, table and TV, TV and couch (and later bed). Outdoor activity, particularly driveway activity, foreshadows problems and events unwanted: genies exiting bottles, dikes bursting, de-stability at the top—anti-Thanksgiving gremlins sending celebrants scattering for their cars. The outcome I didn't want.

The Feensters appear unimplicated. Nick has set up shop in his driveway and is giving his twin '56 vintage Vettes the careful hand-waxing they deserve and frequently get (cold-weather bonding issues, what the hell). Drilla, in a skirt and sweater, is seated on the front step, hugging her knees and petting Bimbo in her lap as if now was July. Nick is, as usual, luridly turned out in one of his metallic Lycra bodysuits—electric blue, showing off his muscles and plenty of bulgy dick—the same outfit the neighborhood is used to seeing during his and Drilla's stern-miened beach constitutionals, when they each listen to separate Walkmen. Though because it's wintry, Nick has added some kind of space-age silver-aluminum anorak you'd buy in catalogs only lottery winners from Bridgeport get sent for free. Seen through his derelict topiary, he is a strange metallic sight on Thanksgiving. Though if Nick wasn't such an asshole, there'd be something touching about the two of them, since clearly they don't know what to do with themselves today, and could easily end up gloomy and alone at the Ruby Tuesday's in Belmar. Likewise, if Nick weren't such an asshole, I'd walk over and ask them to come join our family sociality, since there's too much food anyway. Possibly next year. I give him a noncommittal wave as I pass and turn in my own drive. Nick repays it with a black stare of what looks like disgust, though Drilla, clutching the dog, waves back smally and smiles in the invisible sunshine—her smile indicating that if a man like Nick is your husband, nothing's easy in life.

However, it's my own driveway that's cause for concern. If I'd noticed in time, I might've driven back to the office, listened to Mike's business proposal, sold the whole shitaree, then come home a half hour later in a changed frame of mind.

Paul and his lofty Jill are out on the pea-gravel drive in holiday attire and absorbed in an arms-folded, head-nodding confab with a man I don't know but whose chocolate brown Crown Vic sits on the road by the arborvitae and Paul's ramshackle gray Saab. Possibly this is a client prospect who's tracked me down, holiday or no, in hopes I'll have the key to the beach house he's noticed in the *Buyer's Guide* and can't wait to see. Paul may be dry-running his new agent's persona, gassing about time capsules, greeting-card pros and cons, the Chiefs' chances for the Super Bowl and how special it is being a New Jersey native.

Only this guy's no realty walk-up, nor is his car a usual car. His body language lacks the tense but casual hands-in-pockets, feet-apart posture of protective customer indecision. This man is dapper and small, with both hands free at his sides like a cop, with thick blunt-cut Neapolitan hair, a long brown leather jacket over a brown wool polo and heavy black brogues with telltale crepe soles. He looks like a cop because he is a cop. Plenty of ordinary Americans living ordinary citizen lives dress exactly this way, but nobody looks this way dressed this way but cops. It's no wonder crime's on the uptick. They've given away the element of surprise to the element—to the window bashers, hospital bombers and sign stealers of the world.

But why is a cop in my driveway? Why is his brown cop car with MUNICIPAL license plates conspicuously parked in front of my house on Thanksgiving, dragging my family outside when law-abiding citizens should be inside stuffing their faces and arguing?

Clarissa. A heart flutter, a new burning up my back. He is an emissary of doleful news. Like in *The Fighting Sullivans*, when the grief squad marches up the steps. Her re-entry to conventionality has already come to ruin. Not thinkable.

All three turn as I climb out, leaving Mike's business plan on the seat, my gait hitched again and slowed. I'm smiling—but only out of habit. The Feensters—I couldn't hear it from my car—have their boom box at its usual high decibels, apparently to aid in waxing. "Lisbon Antigua" again—their way of getting their Thanksgiving message out: Fuck you.

"Hi," I say. "What's the trouble here, Officer?" I intend this to be funny, but it isn't. There can't be bad news.

"This is Detective Marinara, Frank," Paul says in the most normal of imaginable voices, tuned to the exquisite pleasure of saying "Detective Marinara." I can smell cops. Though this, thanks to the signs above, will not be about Clarissa, but me.

Paul and Jill—she's looking at me sorrowfully, as though I'm Paul's crippled parent—have transubstantiated themselves since our basement get-together. Jill has severely pulled much of her long, dense yellow hair "back," but left skimpy fringe bangs, plus a thick, concupiscent braid that swags down behind her like a rope. From her travel wardrobe, she's chosen a green flare-bottomed pantsuit with some sort of shiny golden underhue and a pair of clunky black shoes that show off the length of her feet and that, as an ensemble, renders her basically gender-neutral. She's also attached a flesh-tinted holiday hand prosthesis, barely detectable as not the real thing, though not flexible like a hand you'd want. Paul, from somewhere, has found a strange suit—a too-large summer-weight blue-gray-and-pink plaid with landing-strip lapels, gutter-deep cuffs and English vents—a style popular ten years before he was born and that everyone joked about even then. With his mullet, his uncouth beard-stache and ear stud, his suit makes him look like a burlesque comedian. He looks as if he could break out a ukelele and start crooning in an Al Jolson voice. Just seeing him makes me long for sweet and affirming Bernice. She could set things right in a heartbeat, though I don't really know her.

"I'm impressed with your place here, Mr. Bascombe." Detective Marinara scans around and grins at the way some people can live, but not him: ocean-front contemporary, lots of glass and light, high ceilings—the works. He's a small, handsome, feline-looking man with long, spidery fingers, dark worried eyes and a small shapely nose. He could've been a sixth-man guard in Division III, maybe for Muhlenberg, who only heeded the call to police work because of his "soshe" degree and a desire to stay close to his folks in Dutch Neck. These guys make detective in a hurry and aren't adept at cracking skulls.

"I'd be happy to sell it to you," I say, and try to look happy. "I'll move out today." I'm not comfortable standing in front of my house with a cop, as if I'm soon to be leaving in handcuffs. Though it could happen to any of us.

"I was down at my sister's," Detective Marinara says. "I told you she lives in Barnegat Acres." His interested eyes survey around professionally. They pass my busted duct-taped window, Sally's LeBaron, pass the Feensters, my son, Jill. "They do the whole Italian spread," he says. "You need to take a breather though. So I wandered down here. Your son happened to be outside."

"We asked Detective Marinara to have Thanksgiving with us," Paul says with barely suppressible glee at the discomfort this will cause me (it does). His fingers, I can see, are working. When he was a boy, he "counted" with his fingers—cars on the highway, birds on wires, individual seconds during our lengthy disciplinary discussions, breaths during his therapy sessions at Yale and Hopkins. He eventually quit. But now he's counting again in his weird suit, his warty fingers jittering, jittering. Something's wound him up again—a cop, of course. Jill is aware and smiles at him supportively. They are an even stranger pair all dressed up.

"That'd be great," I say. "We've got plenty of free-range organic turkey."

"Oh, no. I'm all set there. Thanks." Marinara continues panning around. This is not a social visit. He pauses to give a lengthy disapproving stare at Nick Feenster, buffing his Vettes in his Lycra space suit, Pérez Prado banging up into the atmosphere, where a whoosh of blackbirds goes over in an undulant cloud. "That's a plate-full over there, I guess."

"It is," I admit. Though the old sympathy again filters up for the poor all-wrong Feensters, who, I'm sure, suffer great needless misery and loneliness here in New Jersey with their Bridgeport social skills. My heart goes out to them, which is better than hoping they'll die.

Nick has seen Detective Marinara and me observing him across the property line. He stands up from buffing, his Lycra further stressing his smushed genitals, and gives us back a malignant "Yeah? What?" stare, framed by topiary. He doesn't know

Marinara's the heat. His lips move, but "Lisbon Antigua" blots out his voice. He jerks his head around to fire words off to Drilla—to crank up the volume, probably. She says something back, possibly "don't be such an asshole," and he waves his buffing pad at us in disgust and resumes rubbing. Drilla looks wistfully out toward where Poincinet curves to meet 35. She'd be a better neighbor married to someone else.

"I could flash my gold on that clown, tune him down a notch." Marinara shoots his sweater cuffs out of his jacket sleeves. An encounter would feel good to him about now. Conflict, I'm sure, calms him. He's a divorcé, under forty. He's full of fires.

"He'll quit," I say. "He has to listen to it, too."

Marinara shakes his head at how the world acts. "Whatever." It is the policeman's *weltanschauung*.

Exactly then, as if on cue, the music stops and airy silence opens. Drilla—Bimbo under one arm—stands and walks inside, carrying the boom box. Nick, his voice softened to indecipherability, speaks something appeasing to her. But she goes inside and closes the front door, leaving him alone with his buffing implements. It's the way I knew it would happen.

I am thinking for this instant, and longingly, about Sally, whose call I've now missed. And about Clarissa. It's 1:30 already. She should be home. The Eat No Evil people will be here soon. All this brings with itself a sinking sensation. I don't feel thankful for anything. What I'd like to do is get in bed with my book of Great Speeches, read the Gettysburg Address out loud to no one and invite Jill and Paul to go find dinner at a Holiday Inn.

The mixed rich fragrance of salt breeze, Detective Marinara's professional-grade leather coat and no doubt his well-oiled weapon tucked on his hip, all now enter my nostrils and make me realize once again that this is not a social call. Nothing can make a day go flat like a police presence.

Paul and Jill stand silent, side-by-side in their holiday get-ups. They say nothing, intend nothing. They are as I am—in the thrall of the day and the law's arrival.

"This is not a social call, I don't think."

"Not entirely." Detective Marinara adjusts his cop's brogues in the driveway gravel. His precise, intent features have rendered him an appealing though slightly sorrowing customer—like a young Bobby Kennedy, without the big teeth. I have the keenest feeling, against all reason, that he could arrest me. He's sensed "something" in my carriage, in my house's too rich *affect* (the redwood, the copper weather vane), my car, my strange children, my white Nikes, something that makes him wonder if I'm not at least complicitous *somewhere*. Surely not in setting a bomb at Haddam Doctors and heedlessly taking the life of Natherial Lewis, but in *something* that still requires looking at. And maybe he's exactly right. Who can say with certainty that he/she did or didn't do anything? Why should I be exempted? Lord knows, I'm guilty (of something). I should go quietly. I don't say these words, but I think them. This may be what Marguerite Purcell experienced, though I'll never know.

What I do say apprehensively is, "What gives, then?" The corners of Paul's mouth and also his bad eye twitch toward me. "What gives, then?" is gangster talk he naturally relishes.

"Just standard cop work, Mr. Bascombe." Marinara produces

a square packet of QUIT SMOKING, NOW gum from his jacket pocket, unsheathes a piece, sticks it in his mouth and thoughtlessly pockets the wrapper. Possibly he wears a nicotine "patch" below his BORN TO RUN tattoo. "We're pretty sure we got this thing tied up. We know who did it. But we just like to throw all our answers out the window and open it up and look one last time. You were on our list. You were there, you knew the victim. Not that we suspect you." He is chewing mildly. "You know?"

"I tell people the same thing when they buy a house." I do not feel less guilty.

"I'm sure." Detective Marinara, chewing, looks appraisingly up at my house again, taking in its modern vertical lines, its flashings, copings, soffit vents, its board-and-batten plausibility, its road-facing modesty and affinity for the sea. My house may be an attractive mystery he feels excluded from, which silences him and makes him feel out of place now that he's decided murderers don't live here. Belonging is no more his metier than mine.

"Must be okay to wake up here every day," he says. Paul and Jill have no clue what we're talking about—my car window, an outstanding warrant, an ax murder. Children always hear things when they don't expect it.

"It's just nice to wake up at all," I say, to be self-deprecating about living well.

"You got that right," Marinara says. "I wake up dreading all the things I have to do, and every one of them's completely do-able. What's that about? I oughta be grateful, maybe." He gazes up Poincinet Road, along the line of my neighbors' large house fronts to where only empty beach stretches far out of sight. A few seaside walkers animate the vista but don't really change its mood of exclusivity. The air is grainy and neutral-toned with moisture. You can see a long way. On the horizon, where the land meets the sea, small shore-side bumps identify the Ferris wheel Bernice and I admired on our evenings together months ago. I wonder again where and how my daughter is, whether I've missed Sally's call. Important events seem to be escaping me.

"Detective Marinara was considerate enough to give me his business card to put in the time capsule." Paul speaks these words abruptly and, as always, too loud, like someone introducing quiz-show contestants. Jill inches in closer, as if he might lift off like a bottle rocket. She touches her prosthesis to his hand for reassurance. "I gave him one of my Smart Aleck cards." Paul, my son, mulleted, goateed, softish and strange-suited, again could be any age at this moment—eleven, sixteen, twenty-six, thirty-five, sixty-one.

"Okay, yeah. Okay." Marinara jabs a hand (his wristwatch is on a gold chain bracelet) into his leather jacket pocket, where his QUIT SMOKING packet went, and fishes out a square card, which he looks at without smiling, then hands to me. I have, of course, seen Paul's work before. My impolitic response to it was the flash point in last spring's fulminant visit. I have to be cautious now. The card Marinara hands me seems to be a photograph, a black and white, showing a great sea of Asians—Koreans, Chinese, I don't know which—women and men all dressed in white Western wedding garb, fluffy dresses and regulation tuxes, all beaming together up into an elevated camera's eye. There must be no fewer than twenty thousand of them, since they fill the picture so you can't see the edge or make out where the photograph's taken—the Gobi Desert, a soccer stadium, Tiananmen Square. But it's definitely the happiest day of their lives, since they seem about to be married or to have just gotten that way in one big bunch. Paul's side-splitting caption below, in red block letters, says "GUESS WHAT????" And when opened, the card, in bigger red Chinese-looking English letters, shouts "WE'RE PREGNANT!!!"

Paul is staring machine-gun holes into me. I can feel it. The card I stupidly didn't respond to properly last spring featured a chrome-breasted, horse-faced blonde in a fifties one-piece bathing suit and stiletto heels, grinning lasciviously while lining up a bunch of white mice dressed in tiny racing silks along a tiny starting stripe. It was clearly a *still* from an old porn movie devoted to all the interesting things one can do with rodents. The tall blonde had dollar bills sprouting out her cleavage and her grin contained a look of knowing lewdness that unquestionably implicated the mice. Paul's caption (sad and heart-wrenching for his father) was "Put Your Money Where Your Mouse Is." I didn't think it was very funny but should've faked it, given the fury I unleashed.

But this time, I'm ready—though the cold driveway setting isn't ideal. I've slowly creased my lips to form two thick mouth-corners of insider irony. I narrow my eyes, turn and regard Paul with a special Chill Wills satchel-faced mawp he'll identify as my instant triple-entendre tumbling to all tie-ins, hilarious special nuances and resonances only the truly demented and ingeniously witty could appreciate and that no one should even be able to think of, much less write, without having gone to Harvard and edited the *Lampoon*. Except *he* has and can, even though he's in love with a big disabled person, is twenty pounds too pudgy and has mainstreamed himself damn near to flat line out in K.C. You can hang too much importance on a smile of fatherly approval. But I'm not risking it.

"Okay, okay, okay," I say in dismissal that means approval. Standard words of approval would be much riskier. I do my creased-mouth Chill Wills mawp again for purposes of Paul's re-assessment and so we can travel on a while longer functioning as father and son. Parenthood, once commenced, finds its opportunities where it can. "Okay. That's funny," I say.

"I'm willing to admit"—Paul is officiously brimming with pleasure, while smoothing his beard-stache around his mouth like a seamy librarian—"that they rejected that one as too sensitive, ethnically. It was one of my favorites, though."

I'm tempted to comment that it pushes the envelope, but don't want to encourage him. His plaid joker's jacket is probably stuffed with other riotous rejects. "Grape Vines Think Alike." "The Elephant of Surprise." "The Margarine of Error." "Preston de Service"—all our old yuks and sweet guyings from his lost childhood now destined for the time capsule, since Hallmark can't use them. Too sensitive.

And then for the second time in ten minutes we are struck dumb out here, all four of us—me, Marinara, Paul and Jill—aware of something of small consequence that doesn't have a name, as though a new sound was in the air and each thinks the others can't hear it.

Loogah-loogah-loogah, blat-blat-blat-a-blat—a sound from down Poincinet Road. Terry Farlow, my neighbor, the Kazakhstan engineer, has fired up his big Fat Boy Harley in the echo chamber of his garage. We all four turn, as if in fear, as the big CIA Oklahoman rolls magisterially out onto his driveway launching pad, black-suited, black-helmeted as an evil knight, an identically dressed Harley babe on the bitch seat, regal and helmeted as a black queen. *Loogah, loogah, loogah.* He pauses, turns, activates the automatic garage-door closer, gives his babe a pat to the knee, settles back, gears down, tweaks the engine—*blat-a-blat-BLAT-blat-blat-blat*—then eases off, boots up, out and down Poincinet, idling past the neighbors' houses and mine with nary a nod (though we're all four watching with gaunt admiration). He slowly rounds the corner past the Feensters'—Nick ignores him—accelerates throatily out onto 35, and begins throttling up, catches a more commanding gear, then rumbles on up the highway toward his Thanksgiving plans, whatever they might offer.

To my shock, I can't suppress the aching suspicion that the helmeted, steel-thighed honey, high on the passenger perch, gloved hands clutching Terry's lats, knees pincering his buns, inner-thigh hot place pressed thrillingly to his coccyx, was Bernice Podmanicsky, my almost-savior from the day's woolly woes, and who I was just thinking might still be reachable. Wouldn't she know I'd sooner or later be calling? The Harley, already a memory up Route 35, stays audible a good long time, passing through its gears until it attains its last.

I've handed back Detective Marinara's "We're Pregnant" card. He studies it a moment, as though he'd never really looked before, then effects a mirthless, comprehending smile at all the grinning brides and beaming grooms. This is not what Paul had in mind: vague amusement. I'm close enough to smell Marinara's QUIT SMOKING gum, his breath, cigarette-warm and medicine-sweet. He dyes his hair its shiny shade of too-black black, and down in his bristly chest hair, tufted out of his brown polo, he wears a gold chain—finer than his watchband—with a gold heart and tiny gold cross strung together. My original guess was Dutch Neck, but now I think Marinara hails from the once all-Italian President streets of Haddam—Jefferson, Madison, Monroe, Cleveland, etc.—a neighborhood where I once resided, where Ann resides today and where once Paul and Clarissa were sweet children.

"Maybe you want to come in and try that organic turkey," I say. "And some organic dressing and mock pumpkin pie with plain yogurt for whipped cream." Paul and Jill grin warm encouragement for this idea, as if Detective Marinara was a homeless man we'd discovered to have been a first violinist with the London Symphony and can nurse back to health by adopting him into our lives and paying for his rehab.

"Yeah. No," Marinara says—proper Jersey syntax for refusal. He cranes his fine-featured head all around and winces, as if his neck's stiff. "I gotta get back to my sister's to get in on the fighting. This is just, you know—" He smiles a professional, closed-mouth smile and plunges both hands in his brown jacket pockets, giving Paul's "We're Pregnant" card a good crunching.

"You'll still come over and do our show-and-tell for us, will you?" He now reminds me of a young Bob Cousy in his Celtic heyday, all purpose and scrap, maximizing his God-givens but strangely sad behind his regular-Joe features.

"Absolutely. Just tell me when. I'm always happy to come to Haddam." (Not at all true.)

"Like I said. We think we got him. But you never know."

"No, you don't." I'm not asking who's the culprit, in case I sold him a house or he was once a fellow member in the Divorced Men's Club.

"You go to Michigan?" Marinara side-eyes my maize-and-blue block-M as if it was worthy of esteem.

"I did."

He sniffs and looks around as Nick Feenster's entering his house, carrying his buffing supplies clutched to his electric blue chest. At the door, he turns and gives us all a look of warning, as if we were gossiping about him, then regards his twin Corvettes the same way. It's cold as steel out here. I'm ready to get inside.

"I wanted to go there," Marinara says, wagging his shoulders an inch back and forth with the thought of Michigan.

"What stopped you?"

"I was a Freehold kid, you know?" Wrong again. "I got all intoxicated with the band and the neat football helmets and the fight song. Saturday afternoons, leaves turning. All that. I thought, Man, I could go to Michigan, I'd be, you know. All set forever."

"But you didn't go?"

"Naaaa." Marinara's bottom lip laps over the top one and presses in. It is a face of resignation, which no doubt strengthens his aptitude for police work. "I was the wrong color. Scuse my French."

"I see," I say. I'm of course the wrong color, too.

"I did my course over at Rutgers-Camden. Prolly was better, given, you know. Everything. It isn't so bad."

"Seems great to me." I shiver through my thighs and knees from the accumulating cold. It's just as well, I think, that Detective Marinara has his family to go back to. Police, by definition, make incongruous guests and he could turn unwieldy with a glass of merlot, once he got talking. Though he doesn't seem to want to leave, and I don't want to abandon him out here.

"Okay. So. Good to meet you. I'll be in touch tomorrow." He smiles, proffers a hand to me, a hand as soft as calfskin and delicate—not large enough to palm a basketball. I have yet to hear his first name. Possibly it's Vincent. He extends his smile to Paul and Jill, but not a hand. "Thanks for the card," he says, and seems pleased. Detective Marinara is, in fact, a regular Joe, could've been my little brother in Sigma Chi, done well in management or marketing, settled in Owosso, become a Michiganian. He might never have given the first thought to carrying a shield or a gun. It's often the case that I don't know whether I like fate or hate it.

"Great to meet you," I say. "Have a happy Thanksgiving."

"Yeah. That'd be different." He shrugs, his smile become sun-less but mirthful. Then he's on his way, back to his cruiser, his radio (hidden somewhere on his person) crackling unexpectedly with cop voices. He doesn't look back at us.

17

Inside, behind the coffered front door of the steam bath that's become my residence, in the candle-lit dining room that's too small and boxy and windowless (a design flaw fatal to resale), arrayed on the Danish table accoutred with bone china, English cutlery, Belgian crystal, Irish napkins as wide as Rhode Island, two opened bottles of Old Vine Healdsburg merlot, all courtesy of Eat No Evil, who've arrived early and paved every available table inch with pricey ethical food, including an actual, enormous, glistening turkey, is: Thanksgiving, broadcasting its message through the house with a lacquered richness that instantly makes my throat constrict, my cheeks thicken, my saliva go ropy and my belly turn bilgy. It's exactly the way I ordered it. But just for the moment, I can't go in the room where it is. No doubt my condition's asserting itself through the belly and up the gorge.

"Isn't it great?" Jill's ahead, beaming, peeking in at the flickering festive room, not wanting to enter before I do, eyes wide back to Paul and me like a daughter-in-law, her prosthesis tucked behind her.

"Yeah," I say, though the whole spread looks like a wax feast in a furniture store showroom. If you put a knife to the turkey or a spoon to the yellow squash or a fork to the blamelessly white spuds, it would all be as hard as a transistor radio. And at the last second before entering, I swerve right, and into the kitchen, where there are windows, big ones, and a door out, giving air, which is what I need before I chuck up. "Yeah, it is," I say as I push open the sliding door and struggle onto the deck for the ocean's chill that'll save a big mess (I'm also dying to grab a leak). You can say yours is a "nontraditional" Thanksgiving when you have cancer and the sight of food makes you sick and you nearly piss your pants and the police check in and your wife's split to England—which isn't counting your kids. From out here, Drilla Feenster's in view, deck to deck, alone in her hot tub— naked, it would seem—listening to "The March of the Siamese Children" (clearly her favorite) on the boom box, drinking some kind of milky white drink from a tall glass and staring out past the owl decoy to the sea. Bimbo sits on the hot tub ledge beside her, staring in the same direction. I must be invisible to her.

"Who turned the fucking heat up to bake?" I say back through the open doorway into the kiln of a kitchen, where Jill and Paul have stopped, looking concerned by the fact that I am (I can feel it) pale as a sheet. "Where's Clarissa?"

The beach and ocean are oily-smelling, the sand stained lifeless brown and packed by the tide. Long yellow seaweed garlands are strewn from the turbulence at sea (these are what stink). Two hundred yards out, a black-suited surfer sits his board, prow-up, on the barely rising sheen of ocean. Nothing's happening. Paul's time-capsule hole and pile of sand are the only things of note close by.

"There's a kind of story involved in that," Paul says from the kitchen, through the door out to the deck. A small bird-like female is visible behind the stove island in the kitchen, holding a dish towel, insubstantial through the mirroring glass. She's got up in a floppy white chef's toque and a square-front tunic that engulfs her.

"Who's that?" I say. The sight of this tiny woman makes me unexpectedly agitated—and also enervated. I'm sure this is the way the dying man feels as his final breaths hurry away and word goes through the house: "It's time, it's time, he's going, better come now." The room fills with faces he can't recognize, all the fucking air he'd hoped to salvage is quickly sucked up. It's the feeling of responsibility colluding with pointlessness, and it isn't good.

"That's Gretchen," Paul says. I feel like I've entered a house not my own and encountered circus performers—the one-handed mountain woman, the midget chef, the wise-cracking pitchman in the horse-blanket suit. Everything's gone queer. It wasn't supposed to.

"What's *she* here for?" I'm now burning to piss. Were it not daylight and Drilla not in her hot tub in full view, I'd lariat out right here, the way I do all the time behind Kmart.

"She's part of the food," Paul says, and looks uncomfortably at Jill, who's beside him. "She's nice. She's from Cassville. She and Jill both do yoga."

"Where's your sister?" I snap. "Did Sally call me?"

"She did," Paul says. "I told her that you were doing fine, that your prostate stuff was a lot better and probably in remission, and that you and I had—"

"Did you say that to her?" My lips stiffen to a grimace. This was *my* news. My story to spin, to bill me as more than a penile has-been. Guilt, shame, regret will now cloud all Sally's intentions toward me. Love will never have its second chance. She'll be on a plane to Bhutan by sundown. I'll become a pitiful thing in her horoscope ("Better watch your p's and q's on this one, hon"). I could strangle my son and never think of him again.

"I just thought she prolly knew about it." Paul elevates his chin semi-defiantly, thumbs over his belt cow-puncher-style. This is his new take-charge posture—somewhat compromised by his suit. Tiny Gretchen stares out at me apprehensively, as if I was being talked off a high ledge. She doesn't know who I am. Introductions were neglected. "She said she'd be here tomorrow. She seemed a little distressed, I guess."

I, of course, was too busy *not* selling a cracker box on wheels to awards-store Bagosh and hunting for—and not finding—Bernice Podmanicsky. At the Next Level, the old standards vanish. You don't know where your interests lie or how to contact them. "Where's your sister. Did she call?"

"Okay." Paul casts a fugitive look around the kitchen. Jill is nowhere in sight now. Probably she's snuffing the dining room candles so the smoke alarm doesn't go off.

"Okay? Okay what?" Paul stands his ground, separated by the open sliding doorway, his brow heavy, his damaged eye twitching but focused. What's wrong here? What's the story? *Is* she hurt, after all? Maimed? Dead? And everyone's too embarrassed to tell me? Me, me, me, me. Why does so much have to be about me? That's the part of life that makes you want to end it.

"She, like, called right after you left and talked to Jill and said she'd be late because there were some issues with dumb-fuck whatever. Thom."

"Tell me what issues." Atlantic City's eighty miles south. I can be there in a twinkling (and be glad to go).

"She didn't say. Then half an hour later she called back and asked to talk to you, and you were gone, I guess."

"Yeah. So? What'd she say? What's this about?"

"I didn't know then. She asked for Mom's cell and I gave it to her." Paul isn't used to being the bearer of important news that doesn't seek its source from his everlasting strangeness. For that reason, he's reverted to talking like a halting seventeen-year-old.

"Is that it?" It. It. It. And why am I hearing about *it* on the deck and not twenty minutes ago instead of "We're Pregnant"? My fists ball up hard as cue balls. I've gratefully lost the urge to piss, though I might've pissed and not noticed. That's happened. Little Gretchen's still staring at me, dish towel in hand, as if I'm an intruder wandered in off the beach. "Is that *it*? Is there anything *else* to the fucking story? About *your sister*?"

"Okay." Paul blinks hard, as if he's recognized I might do something he might not like. I may look frightening. But what I am is scared—that my son is about to calmly mention, "Well, like, um, I guess Clarissa got decapitated. It was pretty weird." Or "Um . . . some guys wearing hoods sort of kidnapped her. One guy, I guess, saw her get shot. We aren't too sure—" Or "She was, I guess, trying to fly off the thirty-first floor. But she didn't really get too far. Except like down." This is how real news is imparted now. Like reading ingredients off the fucking oatmeal box.

"Would *that* 'okay' be the same 'okay' as the first 'okay' that meant *not* okay?" I say. I'm staring a hole in him. "What the fuck's the matter with you, Paul? What's happened to your sister?"

"She's in Absecon." His gray eyes behind his lenses roll almost out of sight in their sockets, as if under slightly different circumstances this information could be hilarious. Paul sways back on his heels and drops his hands to his sides.

"Why?" My heart's going thumpa-thumpa.

"She and Thom got into some kind of fight. I don't know. Clary took his keys and went and got his car"—the Healey—"and started driving back up here. But then shit-for-brains called the police and said it was stolen. And the police in Absecon, I guess, tried to pull her over. And she panicked and drove into one of those lighted merge-lane arrows on a trailer at Exit Forty, and knocked it into a highway guy and broke his leg." Paul runs his left hand back through his mullet, and for an instant closes his eyes, then opens them as if I might be gone, suddenly, blessedly.

"How do you know this?" My chest is twittering.

"Mom told me." His hands slip nervously down into his baggy plaid suit-pants pockets.

"Is she in Absecon, too?" Where the fuck *is* Absecon?

"I guess. Yeah."

"Is your sister hurt?" Thumpa-thumpa-thump, thump.

"No, but she's in jail."

"She's in *jail*?"

"Well. Yeah. She hit that guy." Paul's gray eyes fix on me as though to render me immobile. They blink. He coughs a tiny unwarranted cough and begins to say something else, his hands in his pockets.

But I'm already moving. "Well, Jesus Christ—"

I shoulder past him into the kitchen, past Gretchen and go for the stairs, skinning off my block-M, already contemplating how I will portray myself as a good, solid, not-insane-but-still-distressed father to all of ranked Absecon officialdom justifiably angry about one of their own being mowed down by my daughter. Ann, I absolutely know, will bring a lawyer. It's in her DNA. My job will be simply to get there—down there, over there, wherever.

Standing shirtless in my closet, I immediately understand that regulation realtor clothing's what's called for—attire that causes the wearer to look positive-but-not-over-confident, plausible, capable but mostly bland on first notice; suitable for meeting a client from Clifton, or the FBI. In the real estate business, an agent's first impression is as an attitude, not a living being. And for that, I'm well provided. Chinos (again), pale blue oxford button-down, brown loafers, nondescript gray socks, brown belt, navy cotton V neck. My uniform.

From inside my closet, I can hear the high-pitched nazzing, ratcheting, gunning, insect-engine noise of a dirt bike out on the beach. Local ball-cap hooligans, younger siblings of the prep school kids from yesterday, freed up—due to relaxed holiday police staffing—to go rip shit over our fragile shore fauna and pristine house-protecting dunes. If I weren't on a dire mission,

I'd call the cops or go put a stop to things myself. Possibly they'll drive into Paul's time-capsule bunker.

As I tie my shoes, I meditate darkly (and again) upon the very model of young manhood I once had in mind for my daughter—not to *marry* necessarily, or run away with, but to seek out as a good starter boyfriend. There was just such a staunch fellow when she was at Miss Trustworthy's. A small, wiry, bespectacled, slate blue–eyed, blinking Edgar-of-Choate, who went on to read diplomatic history at Williams and Oxford but chose the family maritime law practice on Cape Ann, who coxed the heavyweight eight, could do thousands of knuckle push-ups, had an intense, scratchy, yearning voice, dressed more or less like me, and who I liked and encouraged (and who Clarissa humored and also liked), even though we all knew she was destined for a sage older man (who also remarkably resembled me), a fact that young Edgar didn't seem to mind the hopelessness of, since a chassis like Clarissa Bascombe was way beyond the planet Pluto in terms of his life's hopes. All seemed safe and ideal. Clarissa would begin adult life believing men were strange, harmless beings who couldn't always be taken completely for granted, needed to be addressed seriously (now and then), but ultimately were hers for the taking—low-hanging fruit for a girl who'd seen some things. Edgar is now a hang 'em high prosecutor out in Essex County in Mass.—and a Republican, natch. I hardly have to say that a perilously bogus over-oiled character like van Ronk-the-equestrian is not the safe finish line for which good, solid Edgar was ever the starting gate. Beware when you have children that your heart not be broken.

Outside, the bracking, whining dirt-bike racket hasn't stopped, has, in fact, seemed to migrate down through the space between my and the Feensters' houses (where I observed Nick having his secret phone rendezvous two nights ago). The ruckus carries out to the front, where the vandals, I'm sure, are whipping out toward 35 before the police can trap them. "The March of the Siamese Children" is still blaring off the Feensters' deck. As I finally take my long, jaw-clenching piss, I'm able to think that Absecon and whatever yet transpires there may offer the only relief and achievement the holiday will deliver to me. Although, did I not hear my son say that Sally would arrive? Tomorrow? A good sign.

Jill, large and green-suited, Paul, fidgety and zoot-suited, loiter in the front foyer, waiting on me like scolded servants. Jill's hands are clasped behind her, schoolmarm-style—a habit. Both are grave but seem confident there's nothing they can do. Our decommissioned and paralytically expensive Thanksgiving feast lies cooling, inedible and uncelebrated on the dining room table. The Men's Ministry at Our Lady can come for it in a panel truck—and throw it in the ocean if they want to. Minuscule white-suited Gretchen is nowhere in sight. She may have been smart enough to leave.

My furniture, when I stop to put on my barracuda jacket, all seems bland and too familiar, but also strange and unpossessed— the couches, tables, chairs, bookcases, rugs, pictures, lamps—not mine. More like the decor of a Hampton Inn in Paducah. How does this happen? Does this mean my time here is nearing its end?

"I'm heading to Absecon, okay?" I have seen an Absecon exit on the Garden State but never gotten off.

"I'm going with you," Paul announces commandingly.

"No way. You almost fucked this all up." It's still a furnace in here. Sweat sprouts in my hairline. My jacket—slightly grimed from my Bob Butts one-rounder—is the finishing touch of persuasive but distressed fatherdom.

"That's really not fair." Paul blinks behind his glasses. I didn't notice before, but Otto, Paul's dummy—his stupid blue eyes popped open, lurid orange hair, hacking jacket, fingerless wooden mitts, black patent-leather pumps with white socks, plus his green derby all making him appear perfectly at home in my house—is seated at the table-full of food like a stunned guest. Thanksgiving is all his now.

"I can't explain it to you right now, Paul. But I will. I love you." I'm moving out the front door. Outside, the dirt-bike noise is intense, as if whoever it is, is running a gymkhana around my or the Feensters' front yard. Nick will be out if he isn't already, primed to deal cruelly, etc., etc. It could be a chance for us to act in concert, only I have to leave. My daughter's in jail.

"I think you need me with you. I think—" Paul's saying.

"We'll talk about it later."

Then abruptly all is silenced outside—*no-noise* as palpable as noise.

And I feel just as suddenly a sensation of *beforeness*, which I've of course felt on many, many days since my cancer was unearthed, the sensation of when there was no cancer, and oh, how good that was—*before*—what a rare gift, only I was careless and didn't notice and have kicked myself ever since for missing it.

But I feel that same *beforeness* now. Though nothing's happened that a *before* should be expected. Unless I've missed something—more than usual. The Next Level wouldn't seem to be in the business of letting us miss important moments. Still, why does *now*—this moment, standing in my own house—feel like *before*?

"What's going on out there?" Paul says in a superior-sounding voice. His gray eyes bat at me. These words come from some old movie he's seen and I have, too. Only he means them now, looks stern and suspicious, moves toward the doorknob, intent on turning it—to get to the bottom of, shed some light on, put paid to. . . .

"No! Don't do that, Paul," I say. We all three look to one another—wondrous looks, different looks, because we are all different, yet are joined in our *beforeness*. It's quiet outside now—we all say this with our silence. But it's just the usual. The holiday calm. The peace of the harvest. The good soft exhale along this stretch of nice beach, the last sigh and surrender the season is famous for.

"Let me look," I say, and go forward. "I'm leaving anyway."

Paul's brow furrows. Even in his horse-blanket suit, he is imploring. He heard what I said. "I'm going with you," he says.

It's hard to say no. But I manage. "No."

I grasp the warm knob, give it a turn and pull open my front door.

And, just as it's supposed to, everything changes. *Before* is everlastingly gone. There is only everlastingly *after*.

At first, I see nothing strange from my doorway, into which a cold gasp floods by my damp hairline. Only my hemispheric driveway. The high seaboard sky. My Suburban, its window duct-taped. Paul's junker Saab behind the arborvitae. Sally's LeBaron. Sandy Poincinet Road, empty and mistily serene toward the beach. And to the left, the Feensters' yard with its sad topiary (the monkey, the giraffe, the hippo all neglected). Nick's aqua Corvettes, enviably buffed, the upbraiding signs—DON'T EVEN THINK OF TURNING AROUND. BEWARE OF PIT BULL. DANGEROUS RIPTIDES. Nothing out of the ordinary. William Graymont, who's caught something—possibly a bird—stands under the monkey, calmly staring down at his kill.

I begin walking toward my vehicle. Paul and Jill stand in the doorway behind me.

Where's the clamorous, peace-destroying dirt bike, I wonder. Can it have simply vanished? I open the driver's door, thoughts of Absecon re-encroaching with unhappy imagery—Clarissa in a room wearing beltless jailhouse garb; a two-way mirror with smirking men in suits behind it; an Oriental detective—a female—with small clean hands and a chignon; loathsome Thom at a desk, filling out forms. Then Clarissa remote from everything and everyone, forever. I test the gray duct tape across my broken window with an estimating poke—it gives but holds. Then Sally re-enters—on a Virgin flight from Maidenhead. How am I to re-establish myself as a vigorous, hearty, restless, randy Sea Biscuit, who's also ready to forgive, forget, bygones staying bygones? I give Paul and Jill a fraught frown back where they stand in the doorway, followed by a bogus Teddy Roosevelt thumbs-up like Mike's. A flight of geese, audible but invisible, passes over—honk-honk-honk-honk-honk in the misted air. I raise my eyes to them. "What the hell happened to your window?" Paul in his silly suit says, starting heavily out the door.

"Nothing," I say. "It's fine. It'll be fine."

"I should go with you." He's crossing the driveway, for some reason putting his hands on his hips like a majorette.

And that is when all hell breaks loose at the Feensters'.

From inside their big white modernistic residential edifice— the teak front door, I can see, is left open—comes the blaring, grinding, reckless start-up whang of a dirt bike. Possibly it's sound effects, something Nick's ordered from an 800 number on late-night TV, delivered in time for the holidays. *The Sounds of Super-X.* Give those neighbors something to be thankful for— when it's turned off.

Paul and I stare in wonder—me across my Suburban hood, he mid-driveway. Inside the Feensters', the dirt-bike racket winds up scaldingly, very authentic if it's a recording—*raaa-raaa-raaa-raaa-raaaaaaaaaaa-er-raaaaaaa.* I hear, but am not sure I hear, Drilla Feenster in a shrill operatic voice say, "No, no, no, no, no. You *will* not—" Her voice gets husky, insisting "no" to be the only acceptable thing about something. And then, through the Feensters' open front door, wheeled up and rared back on its thick, black, cleated, high-fendered rear tire, a monstrous, gaudy, electric-purple Yamaha Z-71 "Turf Torturer" screams straight out onto the front drive, where the Corvettes are and the cat was. Astride the bike, captaining it, is a small-featured miniature white kid wearing green-and-black blotch camo, paratrooper boots, a black battle beret and a webbed belt full of what look to me like big copper-jacketed live rounds. (There is no way to make this seem normal.) The instant the bike touches front wheel down in the Feensters' driveway, the kid snaps the handlebars into a gravel-gashing, throttle-up one-eighty that spins him around to face the house, at the same time giving the Yamaha more *raaaa-raaaa-raaaa-rer-raaaas*—popping the clutch out, in, out, spewing gravel against the Corvettes and looking neither left (at Paul and me, astonished across the yards) nor right, but back into the house, his face concentrated, luminous.

It's not possible to know what's happening here, only that it is happening and its consequences may not be good. I look at Paul, who looks at me. He seems perplexed. He is a visitor here. Jill steps out into the driveway to view things better. Gretchen has come to the door still in her chef's hat and carrying a large metal kitchen spoon.

"Go back inside." I say this loudly to Jill over the bike whine. The kid rider now takes note of me, fastens his eyes on me (he could be fourteen), then looks intently back through the Feensters' open door, where someone he's communicating with must be. He's wearing an earpiece in the ear I can see, and his lips are moving. The kid rider points over to me and wags his gloved finger for emphasis. "You go back inside, too," I say to Paul and turn to go in myself—just for the moment, lock the door, wait this one out. These sorts of things usually pass if you let 'em.

Then I hear Drilla inside saying over again, "No-no-no-no-no-no." And then very sharply, possibly from the Great Room— where there are Jerusalem marble countertops, copper fixtures, mortised bamboo floors, no expense spared top to bottom—there come two short metallic *brrrrp-brrrrp!* noises. And Drilla stops saying "No-no-no-no."

"Oh, *man*," Paul says mid-driveway.

Almost in the same instant as the *brrrrp-brrrrp* sounds, Nick Feenster appears, marching out the door, bulky and muscular in his electric-blue Lycra get-up—no anorak. He is barefoot, being led like a prisoner by another undersized white kid, the match of the first one, camo'd, booted, beret'd and web-belted, but who is holding pressed to Nick's jawbone an oddly shaped, black boxy contraption with a stubby barrel that looks like a kid's gun and is—unless someone else is still in the Feensters' house—what I just heard go *brrrrp-brrrrp*. Nick's eyes cut over to me across the yards through his topiary as he's being shoved ahead. His walking style is bumpy, a bulky man's gait. His jowly face is stony, full of hatred, as if he'd like to get his hands on the parties responsible, just have five minutes alone with one or all of them.

I have no idea what this is that's happening in the yard. I look at Paul, who's motionless, hands riding his hips in his plaid suit, staring across the yard as I've been. He is transfixed. Jill is a few steps behind and motionless, her generous mouth opened but silent, hands (real and inauthentic) clasped at her waist. Little Gretchen has disappeared from the doorway.

"Go inside. Call somebody," I say—to Paul, to Jill, to both of them. "Call 911. This is something. This isn't good."

And as if her switch has been thrown, Jill turns and walks directly back inside the front door without a word.

"You go inside, I said," I say to Paul. I have to have them inside, so I can know what to do. But Paul doesn't budge.

Nick Feenster, when I look again, is exactly where he was in his driveway. But the kid from the fiery purple Yamaha is just getting in the driver's seat of one of the Corvettes—becoming instantly invisible behind the wheel. The big bike has been allowed to fall on its side in the gravel but is running. The other boy's still holding the black machine pistol under Nick's chin. They're stealing his cars. That's all this is. This is about stealing cars. They get the keys and then they shoot him. He knows this.

The Corvette rumbles to life. Its headlights flick on, then off, its fiberglass body trembling. Then the kid is quick out of it, hurries around, jumps in the other Corvette. He has both sets of keys. The second aqua-and-white Corvette cranks and shimmies and vibrates. Smoke puffs out of its dual pipes. The kid revs and revs the big mill, just like he did the Yamaha, but then drops it in reverse, sends it springing backward, spewing gravel underneath, then (I can see him looking down at the gear shifter) he yanks it down into first, rips a buffeting, wheel-tearing power left in the gravel and, in a clamor of smoke and engine racket and muffler blare, gurgle and clatter, spins out of the Feensters' driveway, bouncing out onto Poincinet Road and straight away toward Route 35.

"They're going to shoot Nick," I say—I suppose—to Paul, who hasn't gone inside the way I told him to. The boy with the machine pistol is talking to Nick, and Nick, at the point of the stubby barrel, is talking to the boy, his lips moving stiffly, as if they were discussing something difficult. I hear a siren not so far away. A silent alarm has gone off. The police will have stopped the first boy already, and none of this will go much further. I begin walking toward Nick and the boy, who're still talking. I lack a plan. I'm merely impelled to walk across the driveway and the tiny-bit of scratchy lawn separating our two houses to do something productive. You're not supposed to think thoughts in these moments, only to see things distinctly for the telling later: the remaining vibrating aqua-and-white Corvette; the topiary monkey and the hippo; the cottony sky; Nick's house; the kid with the machine pistol; Nick, muscular and stern-jawed in his blue Lycras and big bare feet. Though I do think of the boy, this lethal boy with his gun, threatening Nick. But as if he was a mouse. A tiny mouse. A creature I can corner and trap and hold in my two hands and feel the insubstantial weight of and keep captured until he's calm. They're still talking, this boy and Nick. Behind me, I hear Paul say, "Frank." Then I say, "Could I just. . . . Could I just . . . get a little involved here in this?" And then the boy shoots Nick, shoots him straight up under the jaw. One *brrrrp!* I am beside the measly topiary giraffe and say, "Oh, gee." And almost as an afterthought, more a choice of activities he didn't know he'd have to make, the boy shoots me. In the chest. And that, of course, is the truest beginning to the next level of life.

18

I wonder at what Ms. McCurdy saw as she fell. What were her last recorded visual inputs before she closed her amazed eyes upon this toilsome, maybe not entirely bad life forever? Did she get to see the crack-brained Clevinger squeeze the final round into his melon? Did she see her astonished nursing students get the education of their lives? Did she see, for one last eye flutter, the sands of Paloma Playa or glimpse an oil derrick out at sea? A bather? A man standing in a tepid surf, looking back at her curiously, waving good-bye? I have the hope of a man who never hopes.

You're told about the long, shimmering corridor with the spooky light at the end and the New Age music piped in (from where?). Or of the chapter-by-chapter performance review of your muddled life, scrolling past like microfiche while you pause at death's stony door for some needed extra suffering. Or of the foggy, gilded, curving steps leading to the busy bearded old man at the white marmoreal desk with the book, who scolds you about the boats he's already sent, then sends you below.

Maybe for some it happens.

But what I tried very, very hard to do, there on Nick Feenster's lawn, was keep my eyes open, stay alert, maintain visual contact with as much as possible, keep the dots connected. Shooting three living humans apparently does not make a big impression on a fourteen-year-old, because even before I let myself kneel on the lawn and take notice of the two holes in my barracuda jacket high up in my left pectoral region, then look up at the boy with an odd sensation of gratitude, he'd already climbed into Nick's Corvette and put it into clunking gear, after which he wheeled around in the driveway and roared off, narrowly missing Nick and geysering gravel in my whitening face, turning onto Route 35, where possibly the Sea-Clift police were already waiting to catch him as he headed onto the Toms River bridge.

My son Paul appeared at once to aid me where I lay on the lawn, as did Jill. Oddly enough, Paul kept asking me—I was awake for all of this—if I felt I was going to be all right, was I going to be all right, was I going to be all right. I said I didn't know, that being shot in the chest was often pretty serious. And then Detective Marinara arrived—I may have dreamed this— having decided to celebrate Thanksgiving with us after all. He said—I may have dreamed this, too—that he knew quite a lot about bullet wounds to the chest, and mine might be all right. He called an ambulance from the radio in his jacket pocket.

And it came. I was lying on the cold ground, breathing shallow but religiously regular breaths, staring up glass-eyes into the misty sky, where I again could hear the geese winging through the smoky air, even see their spectral bodies, wings set, barely agitating. A stocky red-haired man with a red beard and a purple birthmark on his lower lip arrived and looked down at me. He had a hypodermic syringe in his mouth and a pink-tubed stethoscope around his rucked neck. "So, how's it going there, Frank?" he said. "You gonna die?" He had one of the clotted Shore accents and grinned at me as if my dying was the furthest thing from his mind. "You ain't gonna gork off on us, are you? Right here on your own lawn, in front of God and everybody. And on Thanksgiving? Are you, huh? That wouldn't be too cool, big ole boy. Ruin everybody's day. Specially mine." He was giving it to me in the arm. The ground was very cold and hard. I wondered if the bullets (I didn't know how many, then) had entered my chest and gone out the other side. I wanted to ask that and to explain that it wasn't my lawn. But I must've lost consciousness, because I don't even remember the needle being taken out, only that I hadn't been called "big ole boy" in a long time. Not since my father called me that on our golfing days on the sun-baked Keesler course, when he would smack the living shit out of the ball, then look down at me, with my little junior clubs, and say, "Can you hit it that far, big ole boy? Let's see if you can, big ole boy. Give her a mighty ride." It's worth saying that it doesn't hurt *that* much to be shot in the chest. It was something I always wondered about as far back as my Marine Corps days, when people talked a lot about it. There's the hit and then it's hot and hurts some, then it's numb. You definitely hear it. *Brrrrp!* You instantly feel strange, surprised (I was already cold, but I felt much colder) and then you—I, anyway—just kneel down to try to get some rest, and there's the feeling then that everything's going on without you. Which it pretty much is.

Of course—anyone would expect the rest to happen—I wake up in the Sea-Clift EMS truck, strapped to a yellow Stryker stretcher, shirtless and jacketless, covered with a thin pink blanket, my feet toward the back door. It is just like all the movies portray it—a fish-eye view, a jouncing, swerving ride under an elevated railroad in the Bronx, siren *whoop-whooping*, diesel motor growling, lights flashing. The fluorescent light inside is lime green, barely sufficient for decent patient care. The turns and roaring motorized dips make me roll against my nylon belt restraints. There's the smell of rubbing alcohol and other disinfectants and aluminum. And I believe I've died and this is what death is—not the "distinguished thing," but a swervy, bumpy ride with a lot of blinking lights all around you that never ends, a constant state of being in between departure and arrival, though that might be just for some. I'm bandaged and strung up to a collapsing clear plastic drip bag, and wearing a mask to aid my breathing. I can see the scruffy, heavy-set, red-bearded guy in a white shirt with his stethoscope, sitting beside me, talking to someone else in the compartment who I can't see, talking in the calmest of voices, as if they're on break from the produce department at Kroger's and taking their time about clocking back in. They talk about the 5-K race and some guy they thought had "stroked out" but, it turns out, hadn't. And some woman with a prosthetic leg whom they admired but couldn't see having decent sex with. And about how no one would catch them out running in the street on Thanksgiving when they could be home watching the Sixers, and then something about the police saying the boys who'd shot me and Nick (and possibly Drilla) being Russians: "Go figure." I am gripping. My hand can touch something cold and tubular, and I would like very much to sit up and see out the little louvered side windows to find out where we are. The clock on the wall here says it's 2:33. But when I stir toward rising, the red-bearded EMS guy with the purple birthmark says, "Well, our friend's come alive, looks like," and puts a big freckled hand heavily on my good shoulder so that I can see he's wearing a milky blue plastic glove. I'm aware that I say from under my mask, "It's all right, I don't have AIDS." And that he says, "Sure, we know. Nobody does. These gloves are just my fashion statement." And I may say, "I do have cancer, though." And he may say, "In-te-*rest*-ing. Four inches lower and this would be a more leisurely trip." Then I relax and stare at the dim, rocking, metallic-gray ceiling as the boxy crate roars on.

The ceiling has a color snapshot of a thinner version of the red-haired paramedic in an Army desert uniform, kneeling, smiling down at me from a far-away land, and above his head a thought-balloon says "Oxygen In Use. Ha-ha-ha-ha-ha." I may dream then that we're passing onto the long bridge to Toms River, across Barnegat Bay, and that these two men are talking and talking and talking about the election and what a joke it is: "suspended agitation," "diddling while home burns," how no one has loyalty to our sacred institutions anymore, which is a national disgrace, since institutions and professions have always carried us along. In their view, it is a nature-nurture issue, and they agree that nurture is, while not everything, still very important (which I don't feel so sure about). And then I think someone, I'm not sure who, is flossing his teeth and smiling at me at the same time.

And at this point it becomes clear to me (how does one know such things?) that I'm not going to die from merely being shot in the chest by some little miscreant mouse who needs to spend some concentrated time alone thinking about things, particularly about his effect on others. Now, today, may be an end—time will tell what of—but it is not *the* end the way Ernie McAuliffe's and Natheriel Lewis's ends were unarguably *the* end for those good and passionate souls. And Nick, too, who can't have survived his wounds. To know such a thing so clearly is a true mystery, but one does, which puts an interesting spin on the rest of life and how people pretend to live it, as well as on medical care and on religion and on business and the pharmaceutical industry, real estate—most everything, when you get right down to it.

I could, of course, die in the hospital. Thousands do, victims of lawless pathogens that make their home there, felled by an otherwise-non-fatal wound; or I could suffer my titanium BBs to turn traitor to my tissues and become my worst enemy. These things are statistically possible and happen. Listen to *Live at Five* or read the *Asbury Press*. Nature doesn't like to be observed, but can be.

Whoop-whoop, whoop-whoop! Blaaaant, blaaaant! Vroom, vroom. "That's right, that's it. Just sit there. You mother*fucker*! I gotta dead guy in he-ah, or soon will. Ya silly son of a bitch."

It's good to know they actually care—that it's not like driving a beer truck or delivering uniforms to Mr. Goodwrench. What is their average time in traffic, one wonders.

BANG! BANG! Bangety-ruuuump-crack. We've hit something now. "That's right, asshole. That's why I got this cowcatcher on this baby, for assholes like you!" *Vroom, vroom, vroom-vroom.* We're off again. It can't be far now.

When I'm turned loose from this current challenge, I am going to sit down and write another letter to the President, which will be a response to his yearly Thanksgiving proclamation—generally full of platitudes and horseshit, and no better than poems written for ceremonial occasions by the Poet Laureate. This will be the first such letter I've actually sent, and though I know he will not have long to read it and gets letters from lots of people who feel they need to get their views aired, still, by some chance, he *might* read it and pass along its basic points to his successor, whoever that is (though of course I know—we all do). It will not be a letter about the need for more gun control or the need for supporting the family unit so fourteen-year-olds don't steal cars, own machine pistols and shoot people, or about ending pregnancies, or the need to shore up our borders and tighten immigration laws, or the institution of English as a national language (which I support), but will simply say that I am a citizen of New Jersey, in middle age, with wives and children to my credit, a non-drug user, a non-jogger, without cell-phone service or caller ID, a vertically integrated non-Christian who has sponsored the hopes and contexts and dreams of others with no wish for credit or personal gain or transcendence, a citizen with a niche, who has his own context, who does not fear permanence and is not in despair, who is in fact a realtor and a pilgrim as much as any. (I will not mention cancer survivor, in case I'm finally not one.) I'll write that these demographics confer on me not one shred of wisdom but still a strong personal sense of having both less to lose and curiously more at stake. I will say to the President that it's one thing for me, Frank Bascombe, to give up the Forever Concept and take on myself the responsibilities of the Next Level—that life can't be escaped and must be faced entire. But it's quite another thing for him to, or his successor. For them, in fact, it is very unwise and even dangerous. Indeed, it seems to me that these very positions, positions of public trust they've worked hard to get, require that insofar as they have our interests at heart, they must graduate to the Next Level but never give up the Forever Concept. I have lately, in fact, been seeing some troubling signs, so that I will say there is an important difference worth considering between the life span of an individual and the life span of a whole republic, and that. . . .

"Absecon," I hear someone say. "That's Ab-*see*-con." That's not how I've been pronouncing it, but I will forever. Surely we're not going to a hospital there. "When I was a kid, in Ab-see-con—" It's the big red-headed Army medic, blabbing on in his south Jersey brogue. "My old man useta go to Atlantic City. They still had real bums over there then. Not these current fucks. This was the seventies, before all this new horseshit. He'd go get one a these bums and bring him home for Thanksgiving. You know? Clean him up. Give him some clothes. Useta look for bums about his own size. My mom useta hate it. I'll tell ya. We'd—"

We are slowing up. The siren's gone silent. The two men inside with me are moving, legs partly bent, stooping. A two-way radio crackles and sputters from someone's belt beside my face. The clock says it's 3:04. "Could be you'll want some backup," a woman's metallic voice says from a place where it sounds like the wind's blowing. "Oh boy. Ooooohh boy. Oh man," the woman's faraway voice says. "This is somethin'. I promised you fireworks." Sputter and fuzz. And we are, because I can feel it, backing up and turning at once. I strain against my webbed restraints to see something. My hands are cold. I feel my upper chest to be cold, too, and numb. A randy taste has dislodged from somewhere in my mouth. My chest actually hurts now, I have to admit. I'm not breathing all that well even with oxygen in use, though I'm glad to have it. "Delivery for occupant," I hear a man's voice say. "He had a big heart, my old man." The medic is speaking again, "For all the good it did 'im." The red-bearded face is peering down into mine out of the minty fluorescence. "How ya doin', big ole boy? You holdin' up?" the red mouth with the birthmark says. His blue eyes fix on me suspiciously. I wonder what my own eyes say back. "How'd you like your ambulance ride? Just like TV, wasn't it?"

"Life's interesting," I say from under my mask.

"*Oh* yeah."

Suddenly, there's lots of outside light and a burst of cold air. The door, which I can see, has opened, and my stretcher is moving. The face of a bright-eyed, smiling young nurse, a black woman in a long white labcoat, and corn-rows with gold beads intertwined and tortoiseshell glasses, is staring into my face. She's saying, "Mr. Bascombe? Mr. Bascombe? Can you tell me how you feel?"

I say, "Yes. I don't feel like a big ole boy, that's one thing."

"Well then, why don't you tell me how you are," she says. "I'd like to know."

"Okay," I say. And as we move along, that is what I begin to do—with all my best concentration, I begin to try to tell her how I am.

Thanksgiving

Violence, that imposter, foreshortens our expectancies, our logics, our next days, our afternoons, our sweet evenings, our whole story.

At 23,000 feet, the land lies north and east to the purple horizon. Terminal moraine, which in summer nurtures alfalfa fields, golf courses, sod farms, stands of yellow corn, is now masked and frozen white, fading into dusk. Wintry hills pass below, some with frail red Christmas lights aglitter on tiny porches, then a gleaming silver-blue river and the tower trail of our great midwestern power grid. It is all likable to me. Minnesota.

My fellow passengers on Northwest Flight 1724 (world's most misunderstood airline), all thirty of us, are Mayo bound. O'Hare straight up to Rochester. The blond, heavy-boned, duck-tailed flight attendant—a big Swede—knows who her passengers are. She acts jokey-light-hearted if you're just flying up for a colonoscopy—"the routine lube job"—but is chin-set, hard-mouth serious if your concerns are more of an "impactful," exploratory nature. As usual, I fall into the mid-range of patient-passenger profiles—those who're undergoing successful treatment and on our way to Rochester to hear encouraging news. At 23,000 feet, no one is the least bit reluctant to discuss personal medical problems with whoever fate has seated next to them. Above the engines' hum, you hear earnest, droning heartland voices dilating on what an aneurysm *actually* is, what it feels like to undergo an endoscopy or a heart catheterization ("The initial incision in your leg's the goddamn worst part") or a vertebra fusion ("They go in through the front, but of course you don't feel it, you're asleep"). Others, less care-laden, discuss how "the Cities" have changed—for the better, for the worse—in the years they've been coming up here; where's the best muskie fishing to be found (Lake Glorvigen); whether it was King Hussein or Saddam Hussein who was a Mayo patient once upon a time (AIDS and "the syph" are rumored); and what a good newspaper *USA Today* has turned out to be, "especially the sports." Many tote thick manila envelopes containing crucial evidentiary X rays from elsewhere. BRAIN, SPINE, NECK, KNEE are stamped in red. I have only myself—and Sally Caldwell—plus a prostate full of played-out BBs destined to be with me forever. And I have my thoughts for a sunny prognosis and a good start to year two of the young Millennium, which includes a new direction in the Presidency—one it's hard to see how we'll survive—though the enfeebled new man's little worse than his clownish former opponent, both being smirking cornpones unfit to govern a ladies' flower show, much less our frail, unruly union.

Sally, beside me on the aisle of our regional Saab 340 turboprop, is reading a book encased in one of the crocheted book cozies women years ago employed to sneak *Peyton Place* or *Bonjour Tristesse* into the beauty parlor (my mother did it with *Lady Chatterley's Lover*), books requiring privacy for full enjoyment.

Sally's reading a thick paperback called *Tantrism and Your Prostate*, by a Dr. White. She's assured me there're strategies woven into his recommendations that are part of our (my) natural maturing process and pretty much common sense anyway, and will clear out a lot of underbrush and open up some new paths we'll both soon be breathless to enter. The sex part is still a source of concern—for me but not, apparently, for Sally—since we've yet to fully reconvene since she returned from Blighty and I cleared customs at Ocean County Hospital from my successful gunshot surgery, which left amazingly small scars and wasn't nearly as bad as you'd imagine (pretty much the way it happens on *Gunsmoke* or *Bonanza*). I *did* wake up on the operating table, though the Pakistani surgeon, Dr. Iqbal, just started laughing at my shocked, popped-opened peepers and said, "Oh, well, my goodness, look who can't stand to miss anything." They put me out again in two seconds, and I have no memory of pain or fear, only of Dr. Iqbal laughing. The two .32 slugs are at home on my bedside table, where I have in the past two weeks studied them for signs of significance and found none. Sally believes there's nothing to worry about on the sexual front and that she knows everything'll kick into gear once I regain full strength and get some good news in Rochester.

Sally's hand, her right hand, grazes mine when we encounter turbulence and go buffeting along over the oceany chop, while our fellow passengers—all regional flying veterans and all fatalists—start laughing and making *woo-hoo*-ing noises. Someone, a woman with a nasal Michigan voice, says, "Up-see-daisee. Ain't this fun now?" None of us would mind that much if our ship went down or was hijacked to Cuba or just landed someplace other than our destination—some fresh territory where new and unexpected adventures could blossom, back-burnering our inevitables till later.

Since she's been back from her own *Wanderjahr*, Sally has seemed unaccountably happy and hasn't wanted to sit down for a full and frank debriefing, which is understandable and can wait forever if need be. I was in the hospital some of the time, anyway, and since then there's been plenty to do—police visits and sit-down interviews with prosecutors, an actual lineup at the Ocean County Court House, where I identified the perpetrators, all this along with Clarissa's difficulties in Absecon. (The pint-size accomplices were twins *and* Russians, boy-friends of the faithless Gretchen. It turns out there's a story there. I, however, am not going to tell it.)

Paul and Jill, it should be said, proved to be much better than average ground support in all our difficulties, although they've now driven back to K.C. to celebrate the Yule season "as a couple." Paul and I were never precisely able to get onto the precise same page because I was in the hospital, but we now seem at least imprecisely to be reading the same book, and since I was shot, he has seemed not as furious as he was before, which may be as good as these things get. I don't know to this moment if he and Jill are married or even intend to be. When I asked him, he only smoothed his beard-stache and smiled a crafty, uxorious smile, so that my working belief has become that it doesn't matter as long as they're "happy." And also, of course, I could be wrong. He did, as an afterthought, tell me Jill's last name—which is Stockslager and not Bermeister—and I'll admit the news made me relieved. But again, as to Sally's and my true reconciliation (in both the historical and marital senses), it will come in time, or never will, if there's a difference. In her letter, she said she didn't know if there was a word that describes the natural human state for how we exist toward each other. And if that's so, it's fine with me. *Ideal* probably wouldn't be the right word; sympathy and necessity might be important components. Though truthfully, love seems to cover the ground best of all.

When she arrived the day after Thanksgiving, Sally carried with her a wooden box containing Wally's cremains. (I was zonked in the Ocean County ICU and she didn't actually bring the box up there.) Wally, it seems, had just been a man who no matter how hard he tried could never find full satisfaction with life, but who actually came as close to happiness as he ever would by living alone, or as good as alone, as a bemused and trusted arborist on a remittance man's estate (there are words for these people, but they don't explain enough well enough). His nearly happy existence all went directly tits-up when Sally forcibly re-inserted herself into his life for reasons that were her own and were never intended to last forever—though poor Wally didn't know that. After a few weeks together on Mull, Wally grew as grave as a monk, then gradually morose, apparently feared his paradise on earth would now not be sustainable, but could not (as he couldn't from the start) explain to Sally that marriage was just a bad idea for a man of his solitary habits. She said she would've welcomed hearing that, had tried lovingly to make him discuss it and put some fresh words in place, but hadn't succeeded and saw she was spoiling his life and was already planning to leave. But with no place else to run away to, and not realizing he could just stay in Mull, and thus in a fit of despair and incommunicable fearfulness and sorrow, Wally took a swim with a granite paving stone tied to his ankle and set his terrible fears and unsuitedness for earth adrift with the outward tide. She said when he was found he had a big smile on his round and innocent face.

Sally has admitted—seated at the same glass-topped breakfast table overlooking the ocean where she'd told me she was leaving and gave me her wedding ring only a short, eventful six months ago—that she simply never made Wally happy enough, though she loved him, and it was too bad they couldn't have gotten a divorce like Ann and I did and freed each other from the past. In time, I will find words to explain to her that none of this is as simple as she thinks, and in doing so possibly help explain herself *to* herself, and let her and Wally off some hooks—one of which is grief—hooks they couldn't get off on their own. It's my solemn second-husbandly duty to do such things. In these small ways, there's been appreciable progress made in life in just the twelve days since I got out of Ocean County. We both feel time is precious, for obvious reasons, and don't want to waste any of it with too much brow beetling.

In any case, I rescheduled my Mayo post-procedure checkup, which will be tomorrow at nine with blunt-fingered Dr. Psimos. And since Chicago was, in a sense, on the way, Sally asked me to go with her to Lake Forest to present a solid-front *fait accompli* when she delivered Wally's ashes to the aged parents. It is an unimpartably bad experience to have your son die *once* in a life-time, as my son Ralph did. And even though I have officially accepted it, I will never truly get over it if I live to be a hundred—which I won't. But it is unimpartably worse and in no small measure strange to have your son die *twice*. And even though I knew nothing to say to his parents and didn't really want to go, I felt that to meet someone who knew Wally as an adult, as I did in a way, and who knew his odd circumstances and could vouch for them, and who was at the same time a total stranger they'd never see again, might prove consoling. Not so different from a Sponsor visit, when you settle it all out.

The elderly Caldwells were rosy-cheeked, white-haired, small and trim Americans, who welcomed Sally and me into their great field-stone manse that backs up on the lake and is probably worth eight million and will one day be turned into a research institute run by Northwestern to study (and interpret) whatever syndrome Wally suffered from that made everybody's life a monkey house. I couldn't help thinking it could also be turned into four luxury condos, since it had superb grounds, mature plantings and drop-dead views all the way to Saugatuck. A big conical blue spruce was already up and elaborately lighted in the long drawing room with the stone fireplace, where Sally (I guessed) first re-encountered Wally last May. The Caldwells were soon to be off to a *do* at the Wik-O-Mek that evening and wanted us to come along and stay over, since there would be dancing. I'd have died before doing anything like that and, in fact, managed to work into the conversation that unfortunately I'd recently been shot in the chest (which seemed not to surprise them all that much) and had trouble sleeping, which isn't true, and Sally said we were really just stopping by on our way up to Mayo for my checkup and needed to get going—as if we were driving all the way. They both acted cheerful as could be, fixed us each an old-fashioned, talked dishearteningly about the election (Warner described all their neighbors as decent Chuck Percy Republicans) and how they felt the economy was headed for recession, witness the tech sector and capital-spending cuts. Constance took grateful but unceremonious possession of Wally's ashes—a small box upholstered in black velvet. They both guardedly mentioned Sally's two children in a way that made me sure they sent them regular whopper checks. Then they talked about what an exotic life Wally had chosen to live—"Strange and in some ways exciting," Constance said. We all sat around the huge but cozy spruce-and-apple-wood-scented room and drank our cocktails and thought about Wally as if he was both with us and as if he had never lived, but definitely not as though he'd sharked my wife away from me—even if unwillingly. At some point all four of us started to get not-surprisingly antsy and probably fearful of our words beginning to take on meanings we might regret. Sally and Constance excused themselves, in a southern way, to go upstairs together with the cremains box. Warner took me out the French doors to the low-walled patio, which was snowy and already iced in. He wanted me to see the lake, frozen and blue, and also where he'd put up his fancy covered and heated one-man practice tee he could use all winter. He wondered if I played golf—as though he was sizing me up as a son-in-law. I said no, but that my former wife was a golf coach and played for the

Lady Wolverines in the sixties. With a pixyish grin—he looked nothing like Wally, which leads to speculation—he said he'd played for the purple and white when he came back from the Marianas. We had nothing else to say after that, and he walked me around the outside of the big rambling house through the gleaming crust of snow to where the ladies were just then exiting the front door (it was their standard way to hustle you out). And in no more than three minutes, after we'd all uncomfortably hugged one another and said we'd definitely visit somewhere, someday on the planet, Sally and I headed out the drive, out of Lake Forest, back toward the Edens and toward O'Hare.

But since there was still plenty of light left and I had my old orienteering feel for streets and cardinal points—realtors all think we have this, but can be calamitously wrong—I said I wanted to drive past my mother's last address in Skokie, where she'd lived while I was in college, with Jake Ornstein, her good husband, and where she'd died in 1965. We got off at Dempster Avenue and drove east to where I thought it would intersect, via a tricky set of small-street maneuverings, with Skokie Boulevard. Everything felt familiar to me, equipped as I was with the sense of near-belonging I'd had from thirty-five years ago, when I used to ride over from Ann Arbor on the old New York Central and be picked up at the LaSalle Street Station by my mother. But when I got to where I thought Skokie Boulevard should've been (possibly my old-fashioned was working on me), there was a big but past-its-prime shopping mall, with an Office Depot and a poorly patronized Sears as its anchors and a lot of vacant store spaces in between. I realized then that somewhere toward the back of the employee-parking section of the Sears was where my mother and Jake's house had been—a blue-roofed, single-dormer, center-stoop, quasi-Colonial Cape where my mother had lived out her last days, and where I'd gone to see her before being officially rendered an orphan at age nineteen.

"Do you know where your mom's buried?" Sally was driving our renter Impala and wasn't in a hurry, since her duties toward Wally and herself were now forever discharged. She'd happily have driven around all day.

I said, "It's one of those places where you just see miles of granite headstones and freeways go by on three sides. I could probably find it from the air. She's buried beside Jake."

"We can look for it," she said, widening her eyes like a challenge. "I think it'd be nice if you went there once before you died. Not that you're in jeopardy of dying. At least you better not be. I have plans for you." That was our sexual code in prior days. "I've got plans for *you*, buster." An eyebrow cocked. I'd certainly like those plans to see good results again soon.

"I hope you do," I said. We were again headed back toward the Edens and the route to the airport. "It's enough that I tried to find it. She'd think that was good. It's one of the ways life's like horseshoes."

"There're more than you know, you know." She smiled broadly at me, her eyes shiny in a way I hadn't seen them shine in a while. This also clearly meant something amorous and made me happy, though also apprehensive that something close to amorous was all I was expected to manage. We got to the airport with two hours to spare.

I will say that in the days since Sally's return, some of which time I was in the hospital in Toms River, before I walked out as a convalescing man, holey-chested as a minor-league saint, she has treated me—as I feared she might—with kid gloves, almost as if in some karmic way she believes she caused what happened to me. I probably have not objected enough, though Mike Mahoney says karma doesn't work like that. Still, Sally often seems to be "attending" to me, and sometimes addresses me in an over-animated third-person manner—spirited attendant to fractious attendee: "So what does Frank have on his mind today?" "So is Frank going to clamber out of bed today?" I've heard this is what people do in therapy sessions when straight talk hits the wall. "Frank believes, or at least is willing to speculate, that Sally is overcompensating for prior behavior that requires no compensation, and Frank is wishing it would stop." I actually said this to her. And for a day she turned silent and evasive, even a little testy. But by the second day, she was cheerful again, though still more solicitous than makes me happy.

I'm actually ready to believe that what any marriage might need is a good whacking abandonment or betrayal to test its tensile strength (most of them survive that and worse). In any case, I'm pretty well over being angry and feel an exhilarated sense of necessity just to be alive still and have her back. Marriage, in fact, does not even feel much like marriage anymore, even though Sally has asked for her wedding ring back (but has yet to put it on). Possibly it never really felt like marriage, and that in spite of two efforts I don't know what marriage is. Maybe it's not our natural human state, which is why Paul only smiled when I asked him about it.

But in these days since being shot in the chest, as this Millennial plague year ends and the confounding election's finally resigned to, what I've begun to feel is a growing sense of enlightenment, even though I have plenty of pain from my bullet holes. Enlightenment often gets lost in intimate life with another person: the positive conviction, for instance, that the person *you are now* would make precisely the same choices you're living with and that your life is actually the way you want it. That enlightened understanding can get lost. Life with Sally returned to Sea-Clift feels, in fact, less like a choice I made long ago, and more like the feeling of meeting someone you instantaneously like while on a walking trip along the Great Wall, and who seems sort of familiar and who by the end of the day you decide to share your pup tent with.

Not that I'm totally in the clear. If I intend to be healed and be a full participant more than an attendee, I believe I will have to become more interesting *per se*. Although being shot with a machine pistol by a fourteen-year-old assassin and living to tell about it gives me a good, unconventional story that most people probably won't have. I may also need to become more intuitive, which I would've said I was anyway, until cancer got in the picture. And possibly I could stand an improved sense of spirituality—which Sally seems to have come home with, and Mike Mahoney sells like popsicles. "Faith is the evidence of things unseen" always seemed a reasonably reliable spiritual credo to have, and evoked me to myself in a secular sense—though you could also say it gave rise to problems. Or: "In an age of disbelief . . . it is for the poet to supply the satisfactions of belief in his measure and his style"—except of course I am not a poet, though I've read plenty of them and find their books easy to finish. But in the most purely personal-spiritual vein—since I took two slugs four inches above my own—the best motivational question in the spirituality catechism, and one seeking an answer worth remembering, may *not* be "Am I good?" (which is what my rich Sponsorees often want to know and base life on), but "Do I have a heart at all?" Do I see good as even a possibility? The Dalai Lama in *The Road to the Open Heart* argues I definitely do. And I can say I think I do, too. But anymore—as they say back down in New Jersey—anymore than that is more spiritual than I can get.

How any of this jibes with acceptance and the Next Level, I'm not sure. Self-improvement as a concept already smacks of the Permanent Period, of life you *can* live over again, which is a thought I've put behind me now but may be harder to outlive than it seems. Truly, at a certain point around the course, can you do much to change your chances? Isn't it really more a matter of readying? Of life as prelude?

*I*n a purely itemized way, then, these things are now of record at the end.

I've always liked the joke about the doctor coming into the examining room, holding a clipboard, wearing his stethoscope and mirrored visor, and saying, "I've got good news and bad news. The bad news is you have cancer and you'll be dead in a week. The good news is I fucked my nurse last night."

My good news is I have cancer, but I sleep better than ever since being shot and nearly offed. The Ocean County Hospital doctors said this is not unusual. Death can take on a more contextualized importance relative to our nearness to it. And truthfully, I do not fear death even as much as I used to, which wasn't much, although these things can get hidden. I did not, for example, get on the plane today and feel as I once felt—that I recognized the flight attendant from other flights (they never recognize me) and that therefore my odds of averting disaster were shortened. Neither today did I feel the urge I've felt for years—even on my happy, worry-erasing trips to Moline and Flint—to repeat my traveler's mantra upon taking my seat: "An airplane is forty tons of aluminum culvert, pressure-packed with highly volatile and unstable accelerants, entering a sky chockfull of other similar contraptions, piloted by guys with C averages from Purdue and carrying God only knows what other carnage-producing incendiary materials, so it's stupid not to think it will seek its rightful home on earth at the first opportunity. Therefore today must be a good day to die." I used to take strength from those words, spoken silently as I watched my luggage ride the conveyor and the baggage handlers secretly stealing glances up at my face in the window and mouthing words I couldn't lip-read but that seemed to be directed to me, smirking and laughing while they sent on board whatever fearsome cargo the other people were carrying (these baggage people rarely fly themselves).

For item number two, my strange syncopes have quit occurring since I was wounded. Why, I can't say, but it may be that I meditate now without really realizing it.

On other fronts, the mystery of Natherial Lewis's death was brought to a sad but sure solution—one that seems unrelated to a hate crime. A simpler matter than guessed was at its heart, as is often true in these cases. A man of the Muslim faith desired to "send a message" to a medical doctor of the same persuasion who, this first man believed, lived too much in the world of infidels and needed reminding. The medical doctor, of course, had already left to spend Thanksgiving in Vieques on the day the reminder was delivered—which must have proved to the bomb maker he was right. Only Natherial was there in the cafeteria, in the early a.m., listening to his transistor radio, looking out the window, watching dawn come up on the hospital grounds, waiting to go home and to bed—which he never did. No one was supposed to be hurt, the guilty man said. It was just a message.

Meanwhile our long drought is officially declared ended in New Jersey on the strength of tropical depression Wayne, which never became a hurricane but brought a change for all. Some people associate the dry season's ending with the election being settled and a hoped-for upturn in the economy. But these people are Republicans who'll do fine no matter who's elected. They are the ones who sell you water in a desert.

On a less optimistic note, Wade Arsenault has, unhappily, died. Of a stroke. A general system failure. "Eighty-four," as Paul Harvey would say, on the Sunday after Thanksgiving. No surprise to him and probably not disappointing, either, if he knew anything about it. I did not go to the funeral because I was in the hospital and didn't hear until later. Though I wouldn't have gone. Wade and I were not the kind of friends who need to attend each other's funerals. In any case, his daughter, Ricki, and his thick-necked policeman son, Cade, were there to send him on to glory. Ricki called me in the hospital and sounded much the same as when I last saw her sixteen years ago, her voice a bit deepened and made less confident by time. I pictured her with a mall haircut, an extra thirty pounds strapped to her once-wonderful hips and a look of non-acceptance camouflaged behind a big Texas smile. "Deddy liked you s'much, Frank. Like me, I guess—hint, hint. It made a big difference to him havin' you be his big buddy. Life's peculiar, idn't it?" "It is," I said, staring apprehensively out my hospital window down onto Hooper Avenue choked with Christmas shoppers and misted with tiny snowflakes. I hoped she wasn't calling from downstairs or out in her car, and wasn't about to come check me out, being a nurse and all. But she didn't. She was always a smarter cookie than I was a cookie. She told me that she'd discovered the Church of Scientology and was a better person for that, though at her age she doubted anybody would ever love her for what she was—which I said was dead wrong (I couldn't remember what her exact age was). Our conversation did not range far after that. I think she would've liked to see me, and some parts of me would've liked to see her. But we were not moved enough to do that, and in a while we said good-bye and she was gone forever.

On the nearer-to-home front, Clarissa Bascombe's scrape with local law in Absecon was indeed serious, but ended not nearly as badly as it might've. Her mother *did* bring down a lawyer from Haddam, a big, blond, handsome Nordic-looking palooka with eyes on both sides of his head—who I'd seen a hundred times and never paid any attention to, and who, I believe, is Ann's new goodly swain—not the patch-pockets history teacher I previously imagined. She told me this lawyer, Otis—I don't know if that's his last name or his first—had "good connections," which meant either the mob or the statehouse, whatever the difference might be. But by six p.m. Thanksgiving Day, this Otis had Clarissa sprung from the Absecon lockup and had made allegations that the police applied reckless and undue force by running her off the road and into the blinking lane-change arrow and on into the NJDOT employee, whose foot was only sprained and may have been sprained a week before. Otis also claimed Clarissa had possibly been the victim of date rape, or at the very least of a pretty scary dating experience that amounted to assault, leaving her traumatized—as good as innocent. She was actually fleeing for her safety, he said, when she made contact with the Absecon police. Thom may pay the freight for this or he may not, since he naturally turns out to have a past no one knew about but, also naturally, has mouthpieces of his own. It's enough that Clarissa was unharmed and will eventually look less like a fool than she felt at the time. When she arrived at the hospital late on Thanksgiving night, when I'd been in surgery and was just waking up, feeling surprisingly not so bad but out of my head, she stood close by my bed, gave me her serious stare, put her two hands on my wrist below where they had me strung up to fluids and infusions and heartbeat monitors, then smiled gamely and said in what I remember as an extremely softened, chastened, worn-out, had-it-with-life voice, "I guess I've become number one in number two." This was our joke of possibly longest standing and refers to a sign we once saw on a septic-service truck on the back roads of Connecticut, when she was just a girly girl and I was an insufficient father trying to find sufficiency. There were, or seemed to be, others in the room with her— Ann, possibly Paul, possibly Jill, possibly Detective Marinara. I may have dreamed this. Along the top of the green wall, where it corniced with the white ceiling, was a frieze bearing important phrases that the hospital authorities wanted us patients to see as soon as we opened our eyes (if we did). What I read said, "When patients feel better about their comfort level they heal faster and their length of stay is shortened."

I looked at my sweet daughter, into her fatigue-lined, handsome face, at her thick honeyed hair, strong jaw, her mouth turned down at the corners when her smile was gone. I could see then, and for the first time, what she would look like when she was much older—the opposite of what a father usually sees. Fathers usually think they see the child in the adult's face. But Clarissa would look, I thought, just like her mother. Not like me, which was acceptable along with the rest. I thought as I lay there, how few jokes we'd shared and how rarely I had seen her laugh since she'd become a grown-up. And while you could say the fault for that belonged to her mother and me, that fault in truth was mostly mine.

I said something then, in my daze. I believe I said, "I should've spent more time with you when you were young."

She said, "That's not true, Frank. I didn't want to spend more time with you then. Now's better." That's all I remember from those early hours in the hospital and from my daughter, who's now back "camping out" with Cookie in Gotham, which pleases me, since she may have decided that "the big swim," the "out in the all of it" were just mirages to keep her from accepting who she is, and that the smooth, gliding life of linked boxes may not be the avoidance of pain but just a way of accepting what you can't really change. It's possible she's come to feel fortunate.

The passengers across the aisle from Sally have turned out to be Kansas Citians, a jolly, rotund couple named the Palfreymans. Burt Palfreyman is hairless as a cue ball, from chemo, and as blind as Milton from retinal cancer, but full of vim and vigor about a whole new round at "the clinic." He's had many others and tells Sally his hair's getting tired of growing in and has just decided to stay gone. They don't say what's ailing Burt this time, though Natalie mentions something about "the whole lymph system," which can't be good. Sally remarks that my son lives in Kansas City, too, and works for Hallmark, news that turns them reverent, provoking approving nods, though Burt's nod is more toward the seat-back in front of him. "First-class outfit," Burt says soberly, and Natalie, who's pleasingly rounded, with frizzed salmon-colored hair and puffy cheeks gone venous with worry and long life, stares over at me, around Sally, as if I might not know what a first-class outfit Hallmark really is and that that's a serious lapse of info, needing correction. I smile back as if I cannot speak but can nod. "It's all family-owned," she says. "And they do absolutely everything for Kanzcity." Burt grins at nothing. He's wearing a blue velour lounging outfit with purple piping down the legs and looks as comfortable as a blind man can look in an airplane. "They're right up there with UPS," Burt says (which he calls "ups"), "or any of those big outfits when it comes to employee benefits, compassionate leave, that kind of thing. Oh yeah. You bet." He might've worked for them in the Braille card department.

Sally touches my left hand as if to say, Don't let these nice souls give you the blues. We'll be landing soon.

Natalie goes on to say that Burt has just retired after thirty-five years working for a company that makes laundry starch—another solid family-owned outfit in K.C.—which made a place for him in the accounting department once his eyes got to be a problem. They have kids "out west," which Sally admits she does, too, allowing Natalie to know we're second-timers. Natalie says the two of them are thinking of going ahead and moving up to Rochester after selling their family home in Olathe. "At least get a condo," she says, since they're up and back so much now. They like Burt's cancer doctor, who's had them to dinner once, and feel they could fit well into the Rochester community, which is not so different from K.C. "A good deal less crime." They'll just need to get used to the winter, which seems a fun idea to her. They've made some "relator" appointments to see some places in between Burt's tests. "Health's the last frontier, isn't it?" Natalie hoods her eyes and looks straight to me, as if this is a fact men need to be aware of. I smile back a smile of false approval, though my mind runs to the idea of a barium enema self-administered on a cold bathroom floor, which is what I always think of when I envision my "health"—either something not good or else something that was good but will soon be no more. A permanent past tense. A *lost* frontier, not just the last one. *Health*'s a word I never use.

Getting on to the end, then.

Paul, as I said, along with Jill, has returned to K.C. and to the sweet feasible life of greeting cards and giving words to feelings others lack their own words for. On the day I left the hospital, we buried Paul's time capsule behind the house in a quiet ceremony that was very much like burying a dog or a goldfish. Paul put in some of his riotous rejects, Jill put in a lock of her yellow hair for purposes of DNA, later on. Detective Marinara (whose name turns out to be Lou) put in a broken pair of handcuffs Paul had wangled out of him, in addition to his police business card. Sally put in a smooth granite pebble off the beach at Mull and another off our beach in Sea-Clift. Clarissa, with Cookie present, put in the mahogany gearshift knob off Thom's Healey. Mike put in his signed Gipper photo and a green prayer flag. Ann did not attend, although she was invited and may now have made some positive strides with her daughter. I, as a joke, put in one of the spent titanium BBs (packaged in a plastic baggie), which I apparently "passed" on the operating table in Toms River, no doubt when I woke up in mid-surgery and everyone had a good laugh at my expense. Paul was pleased, made a couple of corny wisecracks about the Millennium, and then we covered the little missile up with sand. (I'm sure in the next big blow it'll be unearthed and washed away and turn up in Africa or Scotland, which will work out just as well.) For whatever Paul may have said to Ann or Ann to him about wanting to break into the real estate industry, this never came up between us—a relief, since his style of everyday mainstream life would never adapt well to the need to coax and coddle and be confessor, therapist, business adviser and risk assessor to the variety of citizen pilgrims who cross my threshold most days. He would like them, do his level best for them, but ultimately think everything they said was a riot and wouldn't understand the heart from which their words drew strength—much as he doesn't understand mine. He is a different kind of good man from most. And though I love him and expect him to live long and thrive, I don't truly understand him much, cannot do much for him except be happy he's where he is and with his love, and that he will know increase in his days. Perhaps over time, if I have time, I will even come to know them better than I do.

As to Mike and the sale of Realty-Wise, I have elected to take a Tibetan partner. In the time that I was laid up, he not only sold the Timbuktu house-on-wheels to a wholly different Indian client—they apparently come in droves when they come— but also sold 61 Shore Road, cracked piers and all, plus four chalets, to Clare Suddruth, who showed up Friday morning after Thanksgiving with Estelle, having called the emergency number when I didn't answer, and was so eager to get his money out of his pocket and into somebody else's that Mike feared he might be "losing an inner struggle" (experiencing a psychotic detach- ment) and possibly wasn't responsible for his acts. A call to the bank settled that. Mike also turned down a listing on the Feen- sters' beach house when he was approached by poor dead Drilla's sister, and discreetly passed the business along to Sea-Vu

Associates. Nick, it turns out, had many more enemies than the two Russian kids, and had not been as fastidious in his personal affairs as would've been needed to keep him above ground.

At first, Mike didn't see how partnership would suit his ambitions or his arrangements with his Spring Lake dowager. But I convinced him that in the long run, which might not be such a long run, all will be his to buy out. I said I was not ready for *éminence grise* status or to retire to an island, and that in the coming housing climate with a big shiny bubble around it, he'd be smarter to be half-in instead of all the way, to retain some liquidity, keep a diverse portfolio and his options open for the deal you can't see coming until it's suddenly there. He has his children to think about, I reminded him, and a soon-to-be former wife he may someday feel differently about. We're not having a new shingle made or opening a bigger office, though we've subscribed to the Michigan State *Newsletter* and to "Weneedabreak.com." On his business card it will soon say "Mike Mahoney, Co-Broker," and he is thinking of enrolling in an executive boot camp in the Poconos, which I approve of. On the scale of human events and on the great ladder that's ever upward-tending, this has left him satisfied. At least for now.

Winds buffet us. Our flying culvert makes a sudden shimmying *eee-nyaw-eee* noise, and a tiny red seat belt emblem illuminates above me. The big brassy stewardess, whose name tag says Birgit, stands up like a friendly stalag matron and begins talking into a telephone receiver turned upside down, working her dark mannish eyebrows at the comedy of knowing none of us can understand anything she says. Though we're all veterans of this life. We know where we're descending to. No one's surprised or applauding. "Here goes nuttin'," someone says behind me and guffaws. Sally Caldwell, sweet wife of my middle season, squeezes my hand, smiles a falsely gay smile, rolls her eyes dreamily and leans to give me a "be brave" kiss on my oddly cold cheek.

Below us I see the whited landscape stamped out in squares despite the early snow and failing light. It is nearly four. We pass, lowering, lowering over farms and farmettes and farm-equipment corrals, single stores with gas pumps along the ribbon of Route 14, where Clarissa and I walked and talked and sweated last August. Settlement's thickening and widening to include vacant baseball diamonds, a Guard armory with starred tanks and trucks out back (in case the fuckers make it this far inland, and they might), the Applebee's, the red blinking tower of an old AM transmitter morphed now into all new radiography—cell phone, cable, radar, NORAD, government surveillance. I don't yet see the great Mayo citadel with its own antennas and helipads, ICBM launchers and surface-to-air missiles to shoot down marauding microbes, but it's there. It's what we've come for. I press my cheek to the cold window, try to see the airport out ahead, establish the world on a more human scale. But I see only another jet, tiny and at an incalculable distance, its own red beacons winking, vectored for some different landing.

It is, of course, only on the human scale, with the great world laid flat about you, that the Next Level of life offers its rewards and good considerations. And then only if you let it. A working sense of spirituality can certainly help. But a practical acceptance of what's what, in real time and down-to-earth, is as good as spiritual if you can finagle it. I thought for a time that practical acceptance, the final, certifying "event" and extra beat for me had been my breathless "yes, yes," to my son Ralph Bascombe's death, and that I would never again have to wonder if how I feel now would be how I'd feel later on. I felt sure it would be. *Here* was necessity.

But get shot in the heart and live, and you'll learn some things about necessity—and quick. Lying in my ultramodern hospital bed in Toms River, looped to this machine and that fluid, with winter's woolen days coming on, I determined to be buried in powdered form somewhere at sea off Point Pleasant (it seemed simplest), and set about the solemn details that only a cold hospital room in New Jersey can make seem congenial: compiled my list of pallbearers, jotted down some basic obituary thoughts, concluded how I wanted my assignables assigned, to whom and with what provisos; who to take the business (Mike. Who else?). Happily, there wasn't so much. For a day or two afterward, I lay there and it all made me glad, and I thought I'd feel glad that way forever. Only by day three, I'd started to feel differently about everything— saw that what I'd decided was a mistake, probably a vanity—I'm not sure why. But right then and there, in that motorized bed with a hospital priest shanghaied from his everyday death duties and not at all sure if what he was doing was right, I fired all my pallbearers, forgot about a sea-burial, tore my organ-donor card in half and executed a document provided in the "welcome kit" by the hospital ethicist, consigning all my mortal leavings to science—the option I and Ann had failed for lack of courage to choose for our first son years ago. The medical kids, I felt, would treat me with all the dignity and compassion I'm due and no doubt with a measure of irreverence and amusement, which seemed right and a better way to turn a small event—my death and life—into a slightly less small one, while keeping things simple and still making a contribution. Not a contribution you can see from a satellite, like Mount St. Helens or the Great Wall, but one that puts its money where its mouth is.

On the day I got home from the hospital, the weather turned ice-cream nice, and the low noon sun made the Atlantic purple and flat, then suddenly glow as the tide withdrew. And once again I was lured out, my pants legs rolled and in an old green sweatshirt, barefoot, to where the soaked and glistening sand seized my soft feet bottoms and the frothing water raced to close around my ankles like a grasp. And I thought to myself, standing there: *Here* is necessity. *Here* is the extra beat—to live, to live, to live it out.

We are going down fast now. Sally clutches my fingers hard, smiles an encouragement. The big engines hum. Our craft dips, shudders hard, and I feel myself afloat as the white earth rises to meet us—square buildings, moving cars, bundled figures of the other humans coming into clear focus as we descend. Some are watching, gaping up. Some are waving. Some turn their backs to us. Some do not notice us as we touch the ground. A bump, a roar, a heavy thrust forward into life again, and we resume our human scale upon the land.

Acknowledgments

An unusual and embarrassing number of people made significant contributions to the writing of this book, none as illuminating, as consequential and as sweetly given as those made by Kristina Ford. My dear friends Gary Fisketjon, Amanda Urban, Gill Coleridge and Gabrielle Brooks have again given me the benefit of their judgment and encouragement, which have been indispensable. I wish also to thank Liz Van Hoose, Jennifer Smith, Amy Loyd, Field Maloney and Richard Brody for their kindness in extending the range of my notice. I'm grateful to Alexandra Pringle and Nigel Newton, to Olivier Cohen, to Elisabeth Ruge and Arnulf Conradi, to Claus Clausen, Jorge Herralde and to Inge and Carlo Feltrinelli for their trust in me. I'm also indebted to Katherine Hourigan, to Lydia Buechler, Carol Edwards and Margaret Halton for their generosity. I wish to thank Helen Schwartz for her essential writing on New Jersey houses, Deborah Treisman for her editorial counsel, Rachel Bolton for her trust, Tom Campbell for his saving advice and Debra Allen for her friendship for this work and for me. It is also true that I would not have written this book had I not met Mike Featherston, and would not have felt I could write it had I not met Dennis Iannaccone and Paul Principe, the kings of the New Jersey Shore. Finally, I wish to express my lifetime's gratitude and affection to Christopher and to Koukla MacLehose, for expanding the horizon I see, and for their enduring friendship. RF

A NOTE ON THE TYPE

This book was set in Janson, a typeface long thought to have been made by the Dutchman Anton Janson, who was a practicing typefounder in Leipzig during the years 1668–1687. However, it has been conclusively demonstrated that these types are actually the work of Nicholas Kis (1650–1702), a Hungarian, who most probably learned his trade from the master Dutch typefounder Dirk Voskens. The type is an excellent example of the influential and sturdy Dutch types that prevailed in England up to the time William Caslon (1692–1766) developed his own incomparable designs from them.